THE TALE OF ELSKE

Also by CYNTHIA VOIGT

The Tale of Gwyn
The Tale of Birle
The Tale of Oriel

THE TILLERMAN CYCLE

Homecoming
Dicey's Song
A Solitary Blue
The Runner
Come a Stranger
Sons from Afar
Seventeen Against the Dealer

TALES OF THE KINGDOM

THE TALE OF ELSKE

CYNTHIA VOIGT

atheneum

Atheneum Books for Young Readers

New York London Toronto Sydney New Delhi

atheneum

ATHENEUM BOOKS FOR YOUNG READERS

An imprint of Simon & Schuster Children's Publishing Division

1230 Avenue of the Americas, New York, New York 10020

Text copyright © 1999 by Cynthia Voigt

Cover illustrations copyright © 2015 by Adam S. Doyle

For information about special discounts for bulk purchases, please contact Simon & Schuster Special Sales at 1-866-506-1949 or business@simonandschuster.com.

The Simon & Schuster Speakers Bureau can bring authors to your live event. For more information or to book an event, contact the Simon & Schuster Speakers Bureau at 1-866-248-3049 or visit our website at www.simonspeakers.com.

Also available in an Atheneum Books for Young Readers hardcover edition

Book design by Debra Sfetsios-Conover

The text for this book is set in Dolly.

Manufactured in the United States of America

This Atheneum Books for Young Readers paperback edition May 2015

2 4 6 8 10 9 7 5 3 1

The Library of Congress has cataloged the hardcover editions as follows:

Voigt, Cynthia, author.

[Elske]

Tale of Elske / Cynthia Voigt.

pages cm. — (Tales of the kingdom ; 4)

Originally published under the title Elske. New York : Atheneum, 1999.

ISBN 978-1-4814-2189-8 (hc)

ISBN 978-1-4814-2190-4 (pbk)

ISBN 978-1-4814-4570-2 (eBook)

1. Princesses—Juvenile fiction. 2. Queens—Juvenile fiction. 3. Brothers and sisters—Juvenile fiction. 4. Friendship—Juvenile fiction. [1. Princesses—Fiction. 2. Kings, queens, rulers, etc.—Fiction. 3. Friendship—Fiction. 4. Fantasy.] I. Title.

PZ7.V874Tak 2015

813.54—dc23

[Fic]

2014044091

*For Bob Fraser, in fond memory, and
for his beloved wife, Penny—
two halves of one*

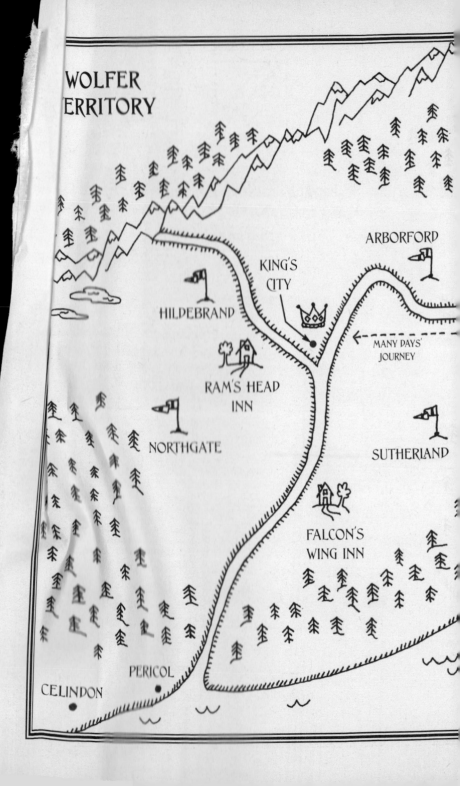

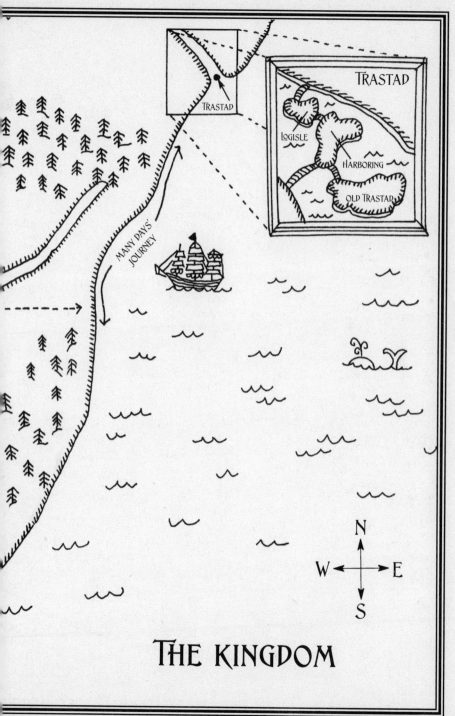

TRASTAD

LOGISLE

HARBORING

OLD TRASTAD

TRASTAD

MANY DAYS' JOURNEY

N
W — E
S

THE KINGDOM

THE TALE OF ELSKE

CHAPTER 1

THE VOLKKING STRUGGLED, BUT HIS sickness attacked him both day and night, a war band giving the enemy no respite of sleep. From the longest day until harvesttime, the Volkking sickened, and as it was with the King, so was it with his land. Crops grew unnourished, unrained on, sickly. Streams sank back into their stony beds and fish died in the shallow water. Game was scarce and scrawny, the pelts thin. The people of the Volkaric, too, across that wasting summer, fell into a sickness of lethargy.

The days grew shorter, and still at each sunrise the Volkking came out to sit on his carved wooden throne. Each morning the wounds of the night's battle were visible on his whited face, and in his shaking hands—but still the Volkking kept his treasure under his eye. He counted the chests his warriors had filled for him with coins, golden jewelry, silver plates and goblets pillaged from the rich southern lands; he measured the piles of furs his hunters had gathered, wolf, bear and beaver, ermine; he counted his women and his sons. The Volkking kept his treasure close. His people he also kept close, as if he believed that all standing together might withstand Death's attack, or at least conceal their King from Death's cold eye.

The people of the Volkaric did not question him.

All the long days of his slow dying, the Volkking sat enthroned, and his eye measured his treasure and measured his people, and then he turned his face to the western distances, waiting to glimpse Death's approach.

His captains, too, awaited Death and the Strydd that came after. That captain who rose victor from the Strydd— dead comrades at his feet, vanquished comrades on their knees—became Volkking.

His women, too, awaited Death. They would then wash the Volkking's body one last time, dress him in the richest of his woven robes, and cover his face with pale, fine hair cut from their own heads. They knew that after the death feast and the death fire and the Strydd, some among them would be taken to give sons to the new Volkking.

The Death Maiden, chosen for her honey skin and dark grey eyes, picked out by the Volkking himself from among the girlchildren, when his previous choice started her moonly bleeding—the Death Maiden, too, awaited her day.

Elske was the chosen Death Maiden.

Even the ironhearted women of the Volkaric, who bore their children soundlessly and lost their men without an eyeblink for grief, would have wished some other girlchild for Death Maiden, even if this did make a good vengeance on Mirkele, that man-snarer, that schemer. Mirkele had never had a captive's proper shame, not when she was a plump young woman proud of her dark hair and dark eyes, and not now either. She had grown old and thin as a wolf in winter, but still proud, now of this granddaughter. The women would have hated Elske if they could, but not being able to do that, they hated Mirkele the more.

The vengeance on grey-haired Mirkele was good, better even than when the last of her sons was slain in far-off battle. But an unaccustomed lightness would be taken from the Volkaric when Elske entered into the Death House so that she might follow the Volkking into Death's great halls and serve him there until the sun burned out. For Elske had been fed of the honey which Mirkele received from the Volkking whenever a boychild was born, and the sweetness of honey cake was on Elske's breath and her skin was the color of pale new honey, and her greeting glance sweetened the day around her as honey sweetens water. Elske was different from the Volkaric, as small and dark and different as her grandmother, but no schemer, no deceiver, and even the jealous women named neither of them coward. Elske was like the flowers that suddenly swept across the meadows in

3

the spring, appearing without warning, gone almost before they could be seen, delicious in color and scent, a brief gladness. But unlike the flowers, smoke-eyed, bright-hearted Elske had lingered among the Volkaric season after season, until now, when Death would lead her away from them all and the women would have their revenge.

At last, with the harvest sun high in the sky over him, the Volkking rose up before his throne, and would not move or speak or hear, all the long afternoon. The Volkking stood stiff before his throne, a dead man, yet living, and his silent people watched. Seated on the hard ground around him, as numerous as the grasses in the lands he ruled over, they waited with the Volkking until—long into the star-pricked night—Death felled him.

Then the captains dug out the shallow lake for his Death House, and covered its dirt floor with straw, and wove together dried reeds for its walls, and made its low roof out of straw and branches. That done, they carried the Volkking within, and set the torch into its stand by his head, that he might have a light beside his eyes. All around his bed they spread full half of his treasure. At last they came out again, to drink the King's mead and eat the festal meat.

Then the women sent for the Death Maiden. Small in the silver wolf cloak, she walked through the moving shadows of the fires, her bright face hidden in the darkness of her hair. She turned neither to right nor to left as her bare feet took her up to the doorway of the Death House.

The people of the Volkaric watched, silent, as she approached her fate. At the low entrance, she halted—her back to her watchers—and dropped the cloak around her feet, for the Death Maiden must enter to the Volkking clothed only in her nakedness. The people saw a glimpse of white skin, and the tumbling fall of long dark hair, and she was gone.

Now the greatest among the Volkking's captains emptied their drinking horns, set aside their robes and weapons and followed the Death Maiden, themselves naked. The people of the Volkaric, listening, heard what they could not see. They heard the Maiden's cries as the Volkking's captains held her down and raped her—as cruelly as they could, in a fury of grief and mead. Listening, the Volkaric beat on their thighs with their hands, to carry her shrieks of fear and pain into the Halls of Death to honor the Volkking. The Volkaric drank deep of the honey mead, beat their thighs, listened to the terror from within and sometimes themselves howled like wolves, the war cry of the Volkaric. When the captains were done, they would leave Maiden and Volkking together, and the last captain would turn at the doorway to lay the torch on the straw floor. Then the Death House and all within it would burn to dust.

But on this night, for this Volkking's death, when the Death Maiden no longer cried out, and the beating hands had tired, and throats were too raw to howl again, and silence flowed like night out of the low doorway of the Death House, flames erupted—

The captains had not emerged.

Great flames roared forth, driving the people of the Volkaric back with their heat. The flames seized the Death House in their red-fingered grasp and tossed it up into the empty sky as King and Maiden and treasure, and captains, too, in a burial fit for the greatest of Volkkings, all were at once devoured.

CHAPTER 2

ELSKE WAS AWAY TO THE east when the sky behind her began to glow on the horizon, as if a small sun—perhaps a child sun taking his first clumsy, confused steps—had lost his way and was trying to rise in the west, at night. Elske had often looked behind her, anxious to see that light. Only then could she know that Mirkele had finished the death meant for Elske. When Elske at last saw the western sky stained with fire, she turned back onto her own way with a lighter step.

There was no path, but Mirkele had instructed Elske carefully: Go to the east, up into the hills. Elske moved quickly over the rough land. Having seen the fire behind her, she had no further need to look back. The wolf cloak she wore was too warm for the mild night, and the sack she carried on her back was heavy with baked wheat breads and smoked meat strips, and her winter boots, too; so Elske was bathed in a cool, cleansing sweat. Her grandmother said she must travel to the east and the north, away from the gentle southern lands where the Volkaric war bands marauded. If the men of the Volkaric ever found Elske—

Mirkele had told her: She must go to the eastern hills and not stop to rest until she was the night and a day distant from the Volkking's stronghold.

Darkness wrapped itself around Elske like friendly arms, concealing her soft footsteps in its own noises. Elske slid through the night like a boat through water.

She had never seen a boat, of course. But her grandmother—

Elske could feel the emptiness beside her, where Mirkele had once stood. All the twelve winters of her life had been lived in Mirkele's company, in the Birth House where the Volkking had placed the little, dark southern captive. In the Birth House, Mirkele lived apart from the others, whose houses crowded together against the King's walls. Mirkele was midwife, and she also kept those unwanted female children who survived their births, until the spring when she must take those unnecessary babes out into the northern wildness, and leave them there to feed the wolves. That had become Mirkele's work, after she had been captured and set aside for the Volkking, that he might admire her dark southern beauty and be the first to rape her.

But her grandmother—

Elske now told herself the story she had often been told, but told it silently, her voice kept inside of her head, as she traveled east. Her grandmother had been no maiden. Mirkele had deceived the Volkaric war party with her slight girl's body, and her silence. Mirkele was clever, and she had kept silent until she could understand the language of her captors, and learn what they had planned for her. She kept silent, and never said that she had been a wife and borne children, until she spoke it into the Volkking's ear.

The Volkking's wrath at learning this had fallen not on Mirkele, who deserved it, but on his own men, whom he shamed with beating, and shamed by keeping their sons for his own, and shamed by mocking their ignorance of women. Mirkele he set apart, to midwife the women of the Volkaric and to bear whatever children were got upon her; for the Volkking wished her to live and not—as the women hoped—die.

The streams Elske splashed through now were cold on her bare feet and ankles, and that refreshed her, helping her along her way, just as the sharp stones and bristling undergrowth pricked, to speed her on. All of that night's journey Elske remembered her grandmother, filling the empty place beside her with memories.

She remembered Mirkele when her grandmother's hair

was dark and her voice sweet as she sang the babes to sleep; she remembered how Mirkele would look up from where a root stew bubbled, or glance over at Elske as she showed the steps of a dance; and she remembered Mirkele's gladness, as if her life among the Volkaric were no more trouble than a moth, fluttering at her face. But when the Volkking chose Elske Death Maiden, something changed in Mirkele, as if this last was the smithy's anvil blow that hardened her to steel; and Mirkele's hair began to turn grey.

Elske remembered Mirkele in their own language, the language of the southern cities. This was one of their secrets, that Elske could speak Souther. Another was that Mirkele had taught Elske to read letters, and to scratch words into the dirt, as she herself had been taught, when she was a girl, in her father's many-roomed house. In their secret language, Elske gave her grandmother her true name, Tamara, and she called the Volkaric as Tamara had, Wolfers.

"Wolfers know only fear and greed," Tamara said. "They cannot taste the sweetness of honey."

Tamara had instructed Elske: She must travel to the east until she came to a path made by merchants carrying goods northwards from the wealthy cities of the south. Years ago, Tamara had been seized from her home and husband, and then falsely bartered for gold by the Wolfer captain to merchants who spoke of that path, leading eventually to a great city in the north. The foolish merchants were stripped of life and goods by that same captain before the day's end, and Tamara was taken to her life among the Volkaric. "Well," Tamara always ended the story, "and so I have you, my Elskeling."

Two times earlier in her life, Tamara had escaped the Wolfers, but not the third. She instructed Elske: "Travel northwards. Listen to me, and haven't you always had goodness happen for you? Maybe you will reach some place to winter over, but if winter does come down before you reach safety, that will be a gentle death."

Elske knew that Tamara's end in the Death House had not been gentle. She also knew, however, that in her death Tamara had taken revenge on those who had seized her from husband and children, from her birthright, too, and she had taken revenge for the two young men who once gave their lives for hers, in the first Wolfer raid she survived. So Tamara had a good death.

Night's darkness cloaked Elske, covering her as the winter snows cover mountains, from peak to foot. Elske moved with the weight of darkness on her shoulders, on her head; and she tasted it in her mouth like the flavorless rills that ran so fast in spring melts. Now there were trees around her, tall, thick, dark shapes, rooted, and the spaces between them—into which she moved—blocked sight with their dense blackness. She heard the rustling of leaves at her feet, and a sighing wind, and occasionally the owl's questioning cry. It was the harvest season. Wolves would not yet be on the hunt and bears would be fatted for winter, slow and sleepy. The darkness smelled empty, clean, safe. Elske felt herself part of the darkness, moving steadily through it, as invisible as the night air.

Because she could not tire, Elske did not tire. It would be a day, or maybe two, before any of the women went out to Mirkele's hut, so much did the Volkaric fear her. The women would draw close to the hut, and hear nothing. They would enter to find—if animals hadn't carried them all away—the bodies of the babes in Mirkele's care. "I *am* caring for them," Tamara always said before she and Elske snapped the necks of those girl babies, giving the wolves bodies as flesh to be eaten, not living babes as prey. In this, too, Tamara defied the Volkking; had it been known that the babes had been killed before being fed to the wolves, it would have meant Tamara's death, and Elske's, too. But she always said, "I set these children free from life before they know any greater harm than hunger." On that final night she sent Elske away before the slaughter. "You go off now, Elskeling, Elskele. I do not fear my death when it makes your life." And Elske obeyed.

So the women, when they dared to approach the Birth House, would find the babes dead, the larder empty and the fire cold. They would think they saw Mirkele's revenge for the loss of her granddaughter.

In part, they would have seen truly. Tamara's hope, and Elske's, too, was that they would not see completely. Tamara's hope, and Elske's, too, was that the women of the Volkaric would think that such a girl as Elske would go gladly into the Death House. So foolish and fearless a girl would want no more for herself than to satisfy those around her. Tamara's hope, and Elske's, too, was that the two sharpened knives the old woman had strapped to her own feet, invisible in the night, would lie undisturbed in the ashes of the Death House, as unrecognizable as the grey hair Tamara had stained dark with the blood of the slain babes.

As to the captains, their hope lay in the nature of drunken men—drunk on their desires for the Kingship to come, drunk on the heavy mead and the pride of their importance to the King, drunk with rape. Even if they are warriors tried and trained, drunken men cannot defend themselves against a sharp knife, and well-honed hatred.

Tamara's and Elske's best hope was that the Wolfers would believe that these captains had chosen to follow the Volkking into deathlong service. "After that," Tamara said, "the new Volkking will be busy enough, finding some harvest in his fields, sending out swift raiding parties to fill his storerooms and build his treasure troves, filling women's bellies with his sons. Why would he chase down an old woman, crazed with age and grief? With his people to keep under his hand and winter to survive." And so they hoped Elske would be spared her life.

Day came greyling first, and then golden shafts of light greeted Elske from among trees, and she walked towards them. She stumbled, with the weight of sack and memories, and with the uneven ground underfoot where undergrowth tangled around her legs. But the warmth of sunlight tasted sweet on her tongue, and brought her fresh sweat.

Deep in forest now, she let the eastern hills pull her to them. She could see but a little distance ahead, into thickly grown trunks and fading leaves on low branches. She could hear birds, and a chuckling of water.

Elske followed that watery sound to a brook that tumbled across her way. Without dropping the sack, she knelt to drink. She had carried in her hand the small loaf that would make her day's dinner, and when her thirst was refreshed with icy water, she walked on—pulling off little bites of tough, nutty, dry bread, chewing them slowly. With food, more of her strength returned.

The sun moved across its arched sky path, as slowly as Elske moved up steep hillsides. When at last the sun lowered at her back, Elske halted at a stream. She dropped the sack from her back and put her face into the water. She finished her small loaf and took out a piece of meat to chew.

There need be no fire that night. The air was warm

enough and she could do without the light. When darkness closed around her, she wrapped herself in the wolf cloak, even knowing that this sleep made the last ending of Tamara. For Elske, now, everything must be unknown and companionless.

CHAPTER 3

WAKING, ELSKE SATISFIED HER THIRST and set off into the rising light. Damp air rode a lively breeze and she lifted her face to it, in welcome. All across the grey morning, Elske kept her own silence in order to hear the day's voices, the whispering wind, the hum of insects and, starting at midday, rain thrumming through the trees with a noise like the beating of tiny drums. No sunset troubled the end of the watery day. No stars troubled the sky as Elske lay down to sleep in the company of trees and stones, inhaling the dark, rich smell of wet earth.

During the night the sky emptied itself of rain and the sun rose up into a blue field across which clouds ran like wolves, hunting, or like a herd of deer, fleeing the wolf pack. By full sunlight, the earth and stones were warm against the soles of Elske's feet. This untraveled wildness was crowded with undergrowth and thick with trunks of trees, a place where boulders hunched up out of the ground. After that day's rough travel, Elske lay down under her cloak and her tiredness opened its arms in welcome as if sleep was a lost child come safely home at last.

The fourth morning's air hung quiet and moist over steep hills. There were pine trees here and their fallen needles made a soft carpet under Elske's feet. Instead of growing warmer as the day wore on, the air grew cooler. It was the afternoon of this day's travel when Elske came at last to the merchant's path of which her grandmother had spoken.

The path was broad enough for two men to walk abreast; it was worn down to dirt and scarred with the tracks of boots and what Elske guessed might be hooves. Tamara had told her about horses, four-legged and tireless, large enough to carry a grown man on their backs, strong enough to bear a barrowload of goods. Under Elske's eager questioning, as they sat alone with the babies in the Birth House, Tamara told her about the sea and the boats that rode on it, and about cities, cones of salt, beds that were feather mattresses set on boxes to raise them above the floor, pearls, like river-polished pebbles but white, and round, hung in strings around a woman's bare neck, and dolls, miniature lifeless people for little girls to play with. The more Tamara told, the more Elske asked, until Tamara's tales made that other world so real Elske could recognize the tracks the round hooves of horses made in the dirt path. Elske placed her feet carefully on the dirt and turned to the north, as Tamara had instructed.

That night Elske built a fire and sat by its warmth, chewing on bread and dried meat strips, feeling how the empty spaces around her guarded her solitude. She slept deep and awoke at first light.

The merchant's path made easy walking. Elske moved on into winter and the north, through air the sun could not warm. She walked, and listened, and when she heard thudding sounds behind her, she knew she was being overtaken.

But no human foot stepped so.

Then, straining to hear, she heard voices, so it was human; and more than one.

They were men's deep voices, and one lighter that might be a boy's or a woman's, and although many of the particular words were strange to Elske, it was the familiar language of the Volkaric they spoke. The voices drove away the forest silence as they argued about the speed of their travel and the sharpness of their hungers. The thudding steps accompanied the voices and Elske hoped that she might soon see a horse, and touch its long velvety nose with her own hand. She was listening so hard behind her that she stumbled.

Stumbling upright, she heard the voices see her.

First, the footsteps ceased, human and animal, then

"Hunh?" she heard, and "Father?" and "Look!" "Who's—"

A conversation was held in lowered voices.

Elske did not turn around; she started walking again.

"Hoy!" a man's voice called. "Hoy, you! Stranger!"

Elske stopped. The forest kept close around her, trees hovering nearby.

"Friend?" the voice asked. "Or foe?"

Elske waited four heartbeats before she turned to begin what would be next in her life.

"It's a girl," the lighter voice said. "What's she doing alone? What's she wearing?"

There were three of them, one a boy, and behind the three, two beasts which she guessed to be horses. The horses' gentle-eyed heads were level with the men's broad, bearded faces.

The men of the Volkaric had their women pluck out the hairs on their cheeks, to leave long, thin beards growing from their chins, but these men had such thick beards that only their mouths showed, as if they went bearded for warmth, as an animal wears its fur. All three wore short cloaks over trousers stained with travel. The two younger had yellow hair but the older had hair the color of dried grass, and grey streaked both his head and beard. Two sons with their father, Elske guessed. Merchants, from the packs on their own and their horses' backs.

"Friend or foe?" the father asked again.

How could Elske know? She only knew the word *foe*.

"Maybe she doesn't speak Norther," the older son suggested.

"She's small and dark-haired, so she could be from the south," the younger agreed.

Elske guessed now at the meaning of the father's question but before she could speak her answer, he asked, with his finger pointing at her, "You good me?" in Souther so awkward that it took Elske a moment to understand that this was the same question.

Before she could answer him, he stepped closer. Behind him, the horses stamped. He pointed to his own chest with a finger. "Tavyan," he said. He pointed at the young man. "Taddus," he said, and then named the boy, "Nido."

The boy pointed to the older man's chest and said, "Father." Then he bowed at Elske, grinning widely. "May we be well met," he added in Norther.

"My name," Elske said then in the Norther they had first used to her, "is Elske." She might have added, like the boy, *May we be well met*, but she didn't know what this would mean.

"You speak our language?" Taddus asked, surprised.

Elske answered him carefully. "There are—different words." Then she addressed herself to the man, the father. "I can hear you, almost, what you say. Not every word."

The path on which they stood threaded through this deep

forest like a well-hidden secret, so there were both time and safety for all the questions the men had.

By careful attention Elske understood that Tavyan, the father, wondered where she was going, and she answered that she was traveling to the north. He asked about her parents and she could say she had none, only a grandmother newly dead.

Tavyan asked her what country she came from, and that meaning she couldn't guess. He asked her again, and again she couldn't answer, until Nido interrupted impatiently to say, "What land, what people?" and Elske could tell the father, "The people of the Volkaric."

They looked to one another, wary, and said nothing, all three ranged against Elske.

"The Volkaric are yellow-haired," Tavyan said to her, "blue-eyed. Like us."

"My grandmother was taken captive from the south. They say, I am like her."

"But why have you left your people?" Tavyan asked.

Elske told him nothing false. "My grandmother sent me away."

"Well," Tavyan said. "Well, then. How far—?"

"Father." This time it was Taddus interrupting impatiently and Tavyan gave way, making his decision, asking her, "Shall we four travel on together? We also go to the north." He explained, "The city, Trastad, is our home."

"Trastad." This could be the northern city Tamara's merchants had hoped to reach, as if Elske might complete the journey Tamara had begun, as if their lives were still connected. She answered Tavyan with a smile, "Where else should I go, and who else travel with?"

So they set off, with Elske in the lead. She had answered their questions and any she had for them could wait until they halted at nightfall. Tamara had always told Elske stories, tales of foreign people and their foreign ways, tales of watery oceans stretching out as far as the eye could see, tales of a Kingdom hidden away safe from the rest of the world, where the King looked on his subjects as a gardener looks on the plants whose well-being makes his own. In her stories, Tamara had spoken of men like these three, whose work was carrying goods from one place to another, for buying and selling. Merchants traded goods for gold, as if each merchant were a Volkking, to have his own treasure-house.

Elske listened carefully to her traveling companions. In their talk, his father and brother scolded Nido for speaking foolishly, and teased him for his laziness, and for wandering off the path. Nido pestered them to tell him how many more days it would be before they were home at last, until they told him sharply not to be so impatient. They talked about men they had done business with in the southern cities, and whether the cloth Taddus had insisted they purchase would please the women of Trastad or if, as Tavyan predicted, it would prove profitless.

Elske liked the sound of that word, *profitless*; it was narrow and tidy, like the Birth House in Tamara's care.

The men spoke quickly and with much argument, although they often laughed. Elske wished she could walk backwards, to see their faces. The Volkaric laughed at another's pain, or shame; their laughter was as sharp as their swords; like swords, laughter was used to wound. The Volkaric argued over things that could be taken, a bowl of stew, a pelt, a woman, and they talked only to give orders. These three used talk differently.

Nido talked the most. He thought they had been ten days and nights on the path, for he had been counting carefully. He thought the mother would be watching for them over the sea, and asked could he be the one to go up behind her and put his hands over her eyes to surprise her, and her new baby, too. For weren't babies born in summer?

Taddus scolded his brother for talking as if they had arrived safely home already, tempting fortune to do ill by them, and said something about Elske that she didn't understand.

"She wouldn't harm us," Nido argued.

"Don't go ——ing her," Taddus warned. "She's Volkaric."

Elske turned the sound into letters in her head, as Tamara had taught her. T-r-u-s-t-ing.

"She's trusting us enough to travel with us," Nido argued. "That's evens up."

They spoke in Norther, but with a difference. Elske's accustomed language was like the broth made from gnawed bones, but this language of theirs had meat in it, too, and onions, and other unknown foods, even pinches of salt.

"How do we know she's not leading us into an ambush?" Taddus asked his father.

"How does she know we won't rape her or sell her as a slave?" Tavyan answered. "I've decided that she'll travel with us, and that settles that."

Taddus ignored his father's last words. "You know what they call them, in the south. Wolfers. You know that, and do you know why?"

"She's not like a wolf," Nido said. "Anybody can see that."

"Wolves," Taddus continued, "will smell out a pregnant doe, and they'll trail after her until she gives birth. Then the wolves take the helpless newborn, and the mother too weak to escape. That's what Wolfers are. They know nothing of mercy or law, government or trade."

Elske said nothing, and asked nothing, not when they spoke of things she knew, not when she wondered at the meaning of their words. She walked and listened.

When they halted at sunset, with four it took almost no time to gather wood and start a fire. Elske had her own loaf and scraps of dried flesh, which she offered around to the others. They turned away from her food. In turn, they offered her a round, speckled-red object. "Apple," they called it.

Elske took it into her hand. The apple was hard, not as heavy as a rock, palm-sized. A short twig rose out of its top, like the cut cord on a newborn. She looked across the fire to Nido's face, shadowy in the firelight, then to Taddus, and Tavyan.

Tavyan held one of these apples in his own hand and said, "Eat." He bit into it.

Elske tried to tell them. "My grandmother spoke of apples, and trees with white blossoms in the spring." Tamara had also told of little cakes, like bread only so light and so sweet with honey and something called raisins that, speaking of them, Tamara smiled to remember what it was to have such a cake in her mouth, and taste it. Elske held out her hand, the apple in her palm. "I never thought I would eat an apple."

"— it," Nido urged. "There's nothing to be afraid of."

T-r-y. Elske put the new word away in her head and promised him, "I'm not afraid." She opened her mouth and bit into the apple. Her teeth cut through its tight skin and she heard a sound—like frosty grasses underfoot just before the snows begin—as her teeth closed around the flesh and a bite fell off it, into her mouth. She chewed it. The taste was like—clear as water, and sweet, like Tamara's winter medicine of water with three drops of honey stirred into it. But this apple was dense as a turnip, this apple was food. Elske opened her eyes to smile. Two of the watching faces smiled back at her, but Taddus asked his father, "Do they know the value of the skins they wear? Do you think she knows how much her cloak is worth?"

"You don't think to take it from her, do you?" His father laughed.

Then Taddus, too, smiled at Elske. "We won't harm you."

"Why should you harm me?" Elske asked, and took another bite of the apple. When these Trastaders smiled, their teeth gleamed white, especially when the smiling man was bearded; these Trastaders smiled freely.

"And you won't harm us," Nido announced.

"Why should I harm you?" she asked, her smile broadening.

Nido added, "You couldn't, anyway, you're only a girl," at which both Taddus and Tavyan laughed, and warned Nido that he was too young to understand what harm girls could do to a man. Then Nido became angry, and asked why, if Taddus felt that way, he was in such a hurry to get home and get married?

Like Nido, when Elske finished the apple she tossed the core into the fire, where it sizzled and steamed and sweetened the rising smoke. A white crescent of new moon hung in a black, star-speckled sky above them, the fire had burned down to bright warm coals, and they were all tired; so they lay down and slept.

In the morning Tavyan showed Elske what their journey would be. "The mountains lie between us and Trastad," he said. "We are heading for the pass," he said, and took a stick to draw in the dirt. Elske crouched beside him. "This line is our path, running north." Then he drew uneven lines, approaching the path and forcing it to turn west, "Mountains," showing how the path turned back towards the north and east, between the jagged lines. After the mountains, the path he drew became a river, he said, as he ended it with the letter T.

"Trastad?" Elske guessed, and he said, "Beyond Trastad is only the open sea. At this time of year, most of our merchants return to Trastad by sea."

Elske was studying the lines in the dirt.

"You can drown in the sea," Nido told her, but she couldn't understand what was so important in that. "Men do, sailors, all the time."

"That's nothing to do with us," Taddus pointed out to his brother, and Tavyan, too, ignored his younger son, saying to Elske, "It's only a roughly drawn map."

"Map," Elske said, shaping the word in her mind. Now that she had seen a map, she could travel on her own—if she wished—to Trastad. Now that she had seen a map, she couldn't lose her way. Without thinking, she wrote the word with her finger in the dirt. Then she stood, and picked up her sack.

The others were staring at her. At last, "You know letters," Nido said.

Elske sensed some danger. "My grandmother taught me."

"Do all the Volkaric know letters?" Taddus asked.

To think of that made Elske laugh, and when she laughed the danger was gone. "The Volkaric didn't care to know, and what need did they have? They had no parchment, or"—she remembered the odd little word, a Souther word—"ink."

"Father," Taddus said again, reminding them that the morning was going rapidly by.

"My brother's bride awaits him," Nido explained to Elske.

"And we all have winter moving towards us," Taddus said.

"Two good reasons for haste," Tavyan said, and they set off.

For that day and the next the path took them west, until on the third morning they came to a broad, shallow stream, its stones gleaming in the water. This stream led them back to the north and east. Then, every day the mountains came closer, taking up more of the sky with their white peaks, and the stream the travelers climbed beside ran away behind them, down rocky hillsides. Rain fell, so cold that Elske wore her wolfskin boots, which kept her legs and feet as warm as summer.

Taddus wished he could have such boots. "Not for myself, for Idelle. My wife, as she soon will be, when we return. At the Longest Night, Idelle and I will become a husband and his wife," Taddus told Elske, proud to say it, and eager.

By the full moon they had entered a high valley, its narrow meadows and steep hillsides dusted with frosts. There another stream tumbled down into the valley bottom and this new stream followed the valley to the east, curling and coiling between mountain steeps.

These mountains were so high that the travelers fell asleep before they could see the moon risen into the night sky, and awoke after she had once again slipped behind the mountains. They were accustomed to traveling together, now, and Elske knew much that she had not known before. She knew that a wife was the woman a man of Trastad had chosen to be his lifelong companion, promising never to move another woman into his house; marrying his wife, a man became a husband. She knew that Nido had three sisters waiting at home, two of them older than he but the last younger, and his mother expected another child, which Nido eagerly hoped would be a boy. The reason for this was the Trastader customs of inheritance, and Elske needed many questions to understand these. By Trastader custom, when he married, Taddus would live with his wife's family, where he would become the inheritor of her father's wealth, all other children of the father having died. But Tavyan, too, must have an heir, which Nido would be, as a son. But if the expected baby was a boy, then there would be another heir for Tavyan's property, to feed the family and give dowries to the daughters. So Nido would be able to apprentice himself to a ship's carpenter, which was his desire. And if the boy did not live? But Nido would be already apprenticed, contracts signed, fees paid; so then one of his sisters' husbands must inherit the business. It was all arranged by law. "Law?" Elske asked.

Elske learned that Tavyan was bringing back from the south not only rich fabrics and colorful threads to stitch them, but also two barrels of a drink called wine, for which the richest merchants of Trastad would pay many coins. "Wine is cheap in the south, where grapes are plentiful," Tavyan explained to Elske, "but comes very dear in Trastad." The horses also carried many cones of the finest salt. Because this would be a Courting Winter, Tavyan told Elske, there would be much call for salt.

Elske asked what a Courting Winter was. They told her that every second year great and rich families from many distant lands sent their sons and daughters to Trastad, where they were welcomed, for a price, into the best houses of the city. These Adeliers, as the foreigners were called, were offered various entertainments, dances, feasts and Assemblies, during the course of which many of the sons chose wives, many of the daughters husbands. Whatever the Adeliers made of the opportunities Trastad offered, Tavyan said, the Trastaders made profits.

Before they left the shelter of the high valley, snow had caught them twice. Then the stream they followed led them out of the mountains and through steep hills, growing deeper, its banks becoming steeper as other streams ran down from the north and west to join it. By the time the land became rolling hills, their stream had become a river, and they were drawing close to Trastad. "How will you live," the three asked her now, "in Trastad, in the winter?" Elske had no answer; how could she know how to get food and shelter in Trastad? "We'll help you," they promised her. "Don't worry."

Elske had never thought to worry.

The river looped through gentle country, close to the city; here the land was cleared and farmed. On the last night they slept in the stable yards of an inn. Just as Tamara had told, the inn bustled with activity of hosts and guests and animals; it offered foods richer than Elske had even imagined, and rooms with beds. But Tavyan preferred to dine on bread and onions, and to sleep the four together, close to their horses and goods, discouraging thieves.

When they asked her what the Volkaric did with someone who stole, Elske couldn't make them understand that only the Volkking owned treasure, so that a man could steal only from the Volkking, which was treason. For treason, a man's feet were cut off and they drove him away, crawling, to feed the wolves. "I never saw this, but my grandmother remembered," Elske told them. "We had no thieves," she told them, and she thought that the Trastaders must honor this in the Volkaric.

But "Brutish," Tavyan said and "Cruel," Nido said, shaking their heads. Taddus said nothing, but only because they were so close to Trastad that he could think only of his Idelle.

They met no other travelers. "At this time of year, merchants choose to travel by sea," Tavyan told Elske. "So would we have, except there was a storm from the northeast and I have no wish to die by drowning. We found horses to carry our goods, and set off, leaving the sea captains in the port awaiting fair weather. Also, one of us was impatient to be home."

"We risked the Wolfers," Nido interrupted, proudly.

"We'll be home before we are expected," Taddus said.

"They'll be expecting us to come by sea," Tavyan said.

"I think Mother must have had a boy. There have already been three girls and only two boys," Nido said. "It wouldn't be fair if it wasn't a boy."

"You must wait and see," his father reminded him. "Like Elske," Tavyan said, "you must wait and see what chance will be offered you."

CHAPTER 4

TAVYAN HAD DRAWN ANOTHER OF his rough maps, showing Trastad. Although it was a single city, Trastad included three islands, lying in the sheltering arms of land where the broad river spread out into the sea, and hamlets and farmlands on the mainland. The island at the river's mouth, the largest, was Old Trastad, "where the first traders settled. Old Trastad is where the most important business of the city is conducted, by merchant houses and merchant banks, in the great marketplace. Also there are taverns and inns, as well as the Council meeting hall and of course the docks, warehouses and shipyards."

"Council?" Elske asked.

"The men who rule Trastad."

"The Council is your Volkking," Elske said.

"We want no King when we have our Council," Tavyan said, and Elske asked, "Where is your own house?"

On the middle island, Tavyan explained, called Harboring, where most of the lesser merchants lived, behind and above their shops, and the craftspeople, too, and manufacturers. Harboring had its own taverns and livery stables, although not so large or many as were to be found in Old Trastad. The last island, most inland and thus most protected from the sea, had used to be farmland but now the wealthiest merchants—the great Vars—built their magnificent villas there. Logisle, this innermost island was named, for the lumber it had supplied to build the great docks of the city, and the bridges that joined the three islands to one another, and to both banks of the river, also.

The Trastaders were famous builders of bridges, Tavyan told her proudly, drawing quick lines in the dirt to join the three islands to each other and to the mainland.

"Then will I be close to the saltwater sea?" Elske asked.

"Close enough to touch, if you wish. Ours is a seafaring city. Can't you smell it?"

"But you don't see the ocean from Harboring," Nido said. This last path on this last day of journey was a roadway broad enough for six men to walk abreast. On this road they saw some other men, fishers and farmers Elske was told; some of the men were accompanied by women whose hair was wrapped around with colored cloths. These men and women stared at Elske, in her fur boots and wolfskin cloak, but when she stared back at them they looked away.

The bridge, when they came to it, stood as tall as a house above the river's watery surface. Elske crossed over to the island on planks of wood, with the water visible between them, looking down on the river as a bird might, from above. On the island the dirt road had been covered by stones, some small and sharp, some as large as a fist—to make walking less dusty in dry weather and less muddy in wet, they explained to her. Just beyond the bridge, a man hailed them from his small, steep-roofed house.

The man spoke to Tavyan. After some talk, Tavyan took out a purse of coins and gave some to the man. When he rejoined his three companions, Tavyan said, "The taxer reports a storm, not four nights past, lasting from afternoon on through the night, and all the next day and night as well. There was tidal flooding on Trastad, but no loss of merchandise. Some boats may well have been lost to the storm, those carrying Adeliers, but most merchants have returned."

"No other urgent news in the city?" Taddus asked.

This new street was crowded with people moving in both directions. Between tall, close-built buildings the stony road climbed and dipped, and they followed it.

"No news," Tavyan said. "So, no fires, no fever epidemics over the summer. No sudden deaths. We may well find all as we left it."

"Except there will be the baby. You hope for a boy, don't you?" Nido demanded.

"I have only a small store of hope," Tavyan answered his

son with a smile. "So when I expend any of it, I think not of more sons but of lower taxes. Tell me, Elske, must the Volkaric pay tax moneys to their King?"

Elske told him, "The Volkaric have no money."

"They are a fortunate people," Tavyan laughed.

Nido asked, "Then who pays to keep the streets cleaned of garbage and offal? Who hires justices to say when a law has been broken, and name the punishment, and who sets guards over the cells? Who gathers together the tribute money, for the Emperor?"

"The Volkking pays tribute to no one," Elske said. "And if his people please him, then he will give them all they need."

"What if they displease him?" Taddus asked.

"None wish to."

"Are his people slaves?" Nido asked, but Elske didn't know that word.

"What do you think of Harboring?" Tavyan asked Elske. His hand waved about him, indicating people and doorways, houses crowded together until their roofs made a single line, and he told her, "All the storehouses will be filled by now, and wood chopped and stacked, with winter coming down on us. Attic spaces will be piled high with round cheeses, and barrels of salted fish, and boxes of smoked fish. The cellars will be crowded with sacks of ground wheat and stacked onions, turnips—"

"Ugh, turnips," Nido said.

"Come spring, you're glad enough of anything not salted, even turnips," Taddus reminded his brother.

"You're just acting—" Nido started to answer, but his father cut him off, explaining to Elske, "Trastaders lay in great stores, before winter comes. Our lives depend on being ready for the worst. Should things fall out other than we expect, well, then, we will feast in spring, but we are like bears, fattened for winter."

"Especially the Courting Winters," Taddus said, "when there is so much profit to be made from the Adeliers. This winter, Father's house should make—"

"Let's add up our profits in the spring, when they fill our pockets not our dreams," Tavyan warned his son. "What is it, Nido? Have you fleas in your trousers?"

"May I go ahead, Father? May I surprise them? They'll expect us by sea, and I can surprise them. Elske can lead my horse. She's strong enough and she's not afraid of horses. Are you, Elske?"

Elske took the rein without a thought, and Nido dashed off. Her eyes were full of the faces and dress of the people around her. Smells crowded the air as closely as houses crowded the sides of the streets. Was the entire island of Harboring filled with houses, tumbled upon one another like onions in a basket?

They came at last to an open gate beside a narrow timber house in a row of narrow timber houses, where Nido stood watching for them. "It *is* a boy!" he called. A plump woman watched with him, and two younger women stepped out of the doorway. All three wore dark dresses, protected by aprons; all three had their heads wrapped around with colored scarves. A little girl, her hair also covered, hid behind the opened door. The older woman—the mother, Elske guessed—greeted Tavyan with pink-faced surprise. "I thought, if you lived, you'd be another sennight at least," she said. "I am glad to greet you safely home, my husband."

"You have another son to learn your trade, Father!" Nido cried, and his mother asked him to hush, now, if he'd be so good.

Tavyan moved all of them through the gate and into a small open yard beside the house, with two outbuildings against its far wall. He and Taddus took apart the packs the horses carried, and instructed the others where to carry each item. The mother bustled about, promising a hot meaty stew for everyone, repeating again and again how Nido surprised her, knocking on the shop door as if he were a customer, and how she was wiping her hands dry on her apron when she saw who it was. "Didn't I scream?" she asked her older daughters, who agreed that their mother had frightened them out of two years' growth with her screams.

Nobody remarked Elske, who stood silent and aside, although the two older sisters looked as if they might have, if their father hadn't had them hurrying about so.

Finally, Nido and Taddus were sent off to take the horses to the livery, and then run back so that their mother could serve up the meal, if they wanted food in their bellies this day; because Tavyan had much to do arranging his goods, and taking his inventory after the summer shopkeeping. And this was a baking day, especially now that there were so many to feed. Now that they were safely returned, more bread would be needed. And who was this person?

"This person is Elske," Tavyan said, waving her forward. "Bertilde, I present Elske, who joined us on our journey. Daughters? Dagma, Karleen, Sussi, I present Elske to you. Don't be shy, my little Sussi, she's very friendly. We'll be glad of another hand, with so many in the house, and Elske is both strong and willing."

"I never asked for a servant," Bertilde humphed. "Nor a pretty one, neither. And what is she wearing under that barbaric cloak? It looks like animal. What kind of creature have you brought to my house, Husband? Look at her hair!"

Elske did not know *servant* or *pretty*, but she had heard Tamara spoken of in just that way, all her life. The girls— as thickbodied, short, round-faced and blue-eyed as their brothers and parents—ignored their mother and urged Elske inside, and so she did not know how Tavyan answered his wife. The girls were proud of their cook room, warmed by a fire in the hearth, over which a cauldron bubbled, proud of the long table at its center now displaying a line

of shallow wooden troughs in which bread dough was rising, proud of what they called glass in the window. They
knocked on it with their hands, and suggested Elske do the
same, but she did not wish to. She watched through it, to
the yard, where Tavyan had an arm around his wife's waist
as he spoke to her, and two cats strolled out of the shed, one
with a bellyful of kittens.

The sisters called her into the shop at the front of the
house, to admire its windows and its empty shelves. At the
back of this room, a narrow staircase climbed up.

Elske had heard from Tamara that there were such dwell-
ing places, one level resting on top of the other; so she was
not surprised. Each of the three rooms above held a bed,
with a mattress as deep and puffy as a summer cloud, and
each had a small window under the low roof. Elske could
not take it all in at first sight, the wooden floorboards, the
whited walls; and the sisters enjoyed her amazement.

Back in the cook room, she stood to the side while the
mother ladled out wooden bowls of stew and Dagma set
them around the table, and Karleen sliced off chunks of pale
bread and set out metal spoons. By the stone hearth, Tavyan
crouched low and looked into a little box where a baby slept.
A cradle, they called it, used only for a baby to sleep in.

They ate seated on benches facing one another across the
wooden tabletop. Elske ignored the talk and ate until she
could eat no more, however much her mouth still longed to

taste the tastes of meat and broth and onion, carrot, turnip and other flavors she had no names for. "Ouff," she said, at the fullness of her belly, and looked up when the others laughed.

She had forgotten they were present. Her bowl was empty and theirs were still almost full. "Oh," she said, and put down a half-eaten chunk of bread.

Bertilde now seemed pleased with her. "We Trastaders have forgotten the taste of hunger. I think we do not enjoy our food as much as Elske does."

"I do," Nido asserted, and dipped bread into his bowl, and they all laughed again.

The baby fussed then and Elske went to quiet it. This was an easy task, with only one baby, and he well-fed and warm, his swaddlings dry, and with a lap to himself. Tavyan, his wife and children talked among themselves and she could listen unobserved as she gently rocked the baby back to sleep. "I've not coins to spare for a servant," Bertilde said, so now Elske knew that a servant belonged to a wife. "And it will be many years before we have no daughter's hands to work beside mine," she said, so Elske knew what work a servant would do. "We'll give her one of Sussi's worn dresses. She looks little more than Sussi in age, just a child, but she can't stay. However good-tempered she might be. However skilled a nursemaid, if you look at her now."

"Where would we keep her, besides?" Dagma asked. "On the floor in here?"

Elske felt as fat and contented as the baby on her lap, and thought the cook room floor would make a fine bed.

Nido couldn't be long distracted from his own interests, and announced, "Tomorrow, at first light, I will apprentice myself to the ship carpenter. You'll give me the coins, Father? Elske," he called to her, "I am going to become a builder of ships. And now, when my father and my new brother, Keir, who will inherit my father's trade, wish to have ships of their own, I will be a partner in their growing riches. Until we will be so wealthy, father and brothers, such great Vars of Trastad, that Taddus will be chosen one of the Councillors—won't you, Taddus?"

"It's not impossible," Taddus said, "when I represent two such merchant families."

"When do you go to Idelle, Taddus?" Dagma asked. "She has been waiting all these long days, sending her aunt to ask at the docks what ships have come to port, carrying what traders safely home."

"I'll see a barber first—"

"Yes, or your beard will frighten her off forever, and you'll never get sons to inherit the property she brings you," Karleen said.

"You go with him, Husband," Bertilde said. "You also need barbering, and you can bring back news about the losses from the storm. I've heard two ships were seen to go down."

"Drowned men sink under the waves. It's from filling their bellies with water, when they try to breathe water," Nido told Elske, with the same pleasure the war bands took in telling of their battles. He told her, "When they rise up again they are black and swollen with death, and the soft parts of their faces and flesh are eaten—"

"We don't need to be reminded," his mother said.

Tavyan said, "There is nothing anyone can do now, to make or mar those fortunes. So let us consider a fortune we have at our disposal. What shall we do with Elske?"

Elske hoped they would let her sit by the fire with the sleeping baby on her lap, and feed her again when she was next hungry.

Bertilde asked, "Can't she hire herself out elsewhere as a servant?" and Elske understood that in other houses a servant might be wanted.

"I could marry her," Nido said.

"You're still a boy," Karleen said, then asked, "How old are you, Elske?"

The warmth of the stones against her back had made Elske drowsy, so it took her a moment to answer. "This will be my thirteenth winter."

"You look younger, but that's still too young to marry," Dagma decided.

"What do we know about her?" Bertilde asked.

"She's strong," Taddus said. "She's clever."

"She knows letters," Tavyan said. "Reading and writing."

"She kept us from fighting," Nido said, but "How would a girl do that?" his father demanded, and Nido answered, "Well, we didn't, did we? Also, Elske never once complained."

"She seems to know about babies," Bertilde said. "If she kept her cleverness to herself—for who wants a servant who can read?—she might find a place in one of the great houses, in a Courting Winter."

That night, Elske slept beside the warmth of coals, and woke early. She had the fire built up before anybody else stirred in the house; although, having done that, she could only sit beside it and wait for what the morning would bring.

After their morning meal, the two men left the house for Old Trastad, leaving the women in charge of the shop and the home. Bertilde kept Nido back, to accompany her to the marketplace on Old Trastad, where she hoped to find a good fowl for the pot, and cabbage, and a fat, sweet onion, too. Elske, clothed now in a dress that rested light as a summer wind on her flesh, despite its long arms and tangling skirts, asked if she might go with the mother, but Bertilde told her that Nido couldn't be expected to be protection for two women. So Elske stayed with the baby in the cook room, and when Karleen came running in with the troublesome news of eight kittens born, with none needed or wanted,

Elske snapped their delicate damp necks while the sisters watched horrified through the window. She placed the bodies in a sack, which she left beside the shed.

"She could have spared one!" Karleen cried, when her mother returned.

"Taddus will remove the remains," Bertilde answered. "None of us enjoy getting rid of kittens, so stop your sniveling, Karleen, and you, Dagma, spare us your outrage. You're not children. You should be glad Elske was here, or you might have had to drown them yourselves."

"But why drown them when by snapping their necks they die quickly?" Elske asked.

No one had an answer for her, and when Karleen reported Elske's heartlessness to her father, at their meal, Tavyan told his family, "We've determined today what to do about Elske, at least until the Longest Night. Elske? Tomorrow, Taddus and Nido will take you to the house of Var Kenric, who is Idelle's father. You will serve Idelle, until she marries."

Nido was holding his hands in front of him and twisting them, saying, "Snap! Snap!" until Sussi wept again and Dagma said, "That's not funny, Nido," and his father told him to behave himself, when he was at table.

Elske asked, "And after she marries?"

Taddus explained it. "I will be the husband. You can't be my servant when we have traveled as equals."

Elske didn't argue although she didn't understand.

45

After all, the Trastaders had their own ways as much as the Volkaric, and like the Volkaric, the Trastaders preferred their own ways. Who a servant was, for what work and uses, that she could guess at; and it was no more than who and what every woman of the Volkaric was.

"By Longest Night we'll have found you another place, for many houses take on extra servants in a Courting Winter. That's my decision," Tavyan told her, as if Elske had argued. But Elske had no such wish.

Then the men told the gossip and news they had brought home from the city. Two ships had come into harbor, both with sails ripped out and one half-masted, reporting what they knew about the wrecks of the storm. It had not been as bad as it might have been, and none of the Adeliers had been lost. "Which is a piece of luck," Taddus said, "although—" and then his shorn face lit up with laughter.

There was one Princess, he reported, laughing with Tavyan at the story, one Adelinne who had refused to be sent belowdecks with the rest of her kind during the storm. The waves were tossing the ship about, as if it were no more than a leaf falling, and all the other Adeliers on board were weeping and vomiting below, making a great moan. This was trouble enough for the captain, who cared only about keeping his ship afloat, but here was this girl—no more than a girl, young for an Adelinne—stamping her foot at him, while the gale grabbed at her cloak. No, she would not go below, she told him. She didn't have to obey him, or anyone, because she was a Queen and obeyed none but herself.

Tavyan took up the tale. She was a brat, the captain had told her bluntly, a misbehaved and misguided brat, and if she was his own daughter she'd have the flat of his hand across her backside. But if she wouldn't be sent below, he couldn't waste the time worrying about the waves washing her overboard, so he turned his back on her.

When the captain next thought of her, Taddus continued, there she was hauling down a sail, a sailor at work on either side of her, her hair hanging down wet, and her cloak soaked and dragging. She wasn't afraid, not of waves, wind, water or drowning. She'd been as good as a sailor in the storm, the captain admitted, even though he'd have liked to throw her overboard with a stone tied to her ankles, for the trouble she'd have caused him had harm come to her.

"Well, it's a good profit we make from the Adeliers, so let them be a trouble," Bertilde said, but nobody answered her because Dagma was exclaiming, "Who would want to marry such a girl?" and Nido said he wouldn't, and Tavyan said he hoped this Princess had a rich dowry, because she would need it to overcome the reputation this story would earn her, growing fatter as it was told throughout the city until they would say she was sailing the boat alone, the captain clouted across the ears and sent about his business. Taddus wondered how she could have not been afraid, for the one storm he'd been caught in had been enough to overfill his stomach for sailing adventures.

Elske asked, "A Queen? What is it, if she is a Queen?"

"The Queen is the wife of a King," Dagma told her.

"As a Varinne is the wife of a Var," Taddus explained. "Idelle's father is Var Kenric and her mother thus becomes Varinne Kenric."

"But this girl—this Adelinne who claims to be a Queen— isn't married, so no King has given her the title. So she's a liar, as well," Dagma laughed. "I pity the family that has her for guest, this winter."

"They'll be given recompense," Bertilde said. "I wouldn't mind giving up a bedroom to have some Adelier filling my purse with coins."

"Just wait until I'm a shipbuilder, trained and proven," Nido told her. "After Taddus and his sons have multiplied Var Kenric's fortune, we'll build you a villa on Logisle, and you can fill it to the roof beams with Adeliers."

"By that time, I'll be too old for such things," Bertilde said.

"She must be swollen with pride," Dagma said, "this Adelinne. And ignorant, to think she can fool us as to her station."

"She can't be too proud," her mother answered, "if she is sent to Trastad to catch herself a husband. Don't waste jealousy on her, Dagma."

"I have no jealousy," Dagma answered, but Karleen said to Elske, "My sister wishes her Henders were not a farmer. She will miss the easy life of the city."

"I am perfectly content with my choice of husband," Dagma said.

"As you should be," her father told her. "You'll be wife of a goodly house, and the flocks that feed around it."

"You're the one jealous, for any husband," Dagma said sharply to Karleen, who answered, "I need no lout of a husband, thank you, Sister," and Elske wondered why, with stores against winter, warm fires and soft dresses, these girls should still speak as bitterly as the women of the Volkaric, who were the first to go hungry, and kept farthest from the fire. Her own belly was too full for bitterness.

CHAPTER 5

TADDUS AND NIDO DELIVERED ELSKE the next day to Var Kenric's house and service. As they crossed the center market of Harboring, Nido pointed down an alley. "See that sign? With a ship's wheel painted on it? My master's workshop is there." In only seven years, Nido told her, he would be a journeyman carpenter, sailing on merchant vessels as a skilled craftsman.

The street they walked along branched down towards the riverside now, and there were no more taverns or market squares; the houses rose three stories tall and their shops were kept in separate buildings, beside. Taddus knocked on one of the wooden doors, then told Elske, "The Varinne hasn't left her bed since winter. They say she is ill with the death of her sons."

Before he could tell her more, a grey-haired woman, pale as a parsnip, her grey dress covered by an apron, opened the door and asked them to step inside. "Idelle sits with the Varinne at this hour," the woman said to Taddus, who answered that he only wished to introduce Elske. "Elske, this is Ula, Idelle's aunt. I will return this evening," he said to the woman, who answered, "I should hope so, young master. May we be well met," the woman said to Elske, who responded in echo, "May we be well met," and the woman said, "Aunt, not servant. My husband was Var Kenric's brother. When his ship went down, so many summers ago that I can no longer remember his face, I came here to live, to be of what use I can. So you are to be our young lady's maidservant. It's true enough that the Var is a busy man," Ula told Elske, "and with no one to share his burdens—until our young mistress weds this handsome fellow, of course. But you go off now, young men. I have affairs to manage."

Tavyan's sons left Elske to make her own way among these strangers and Ula hurried her upstairs to show her the chamber where she would sleep on the floor beside Idelle's bed. "You'll be comfortable," Ula told her. "Now we'll fit you out with a dress proper for Var Kenric's servant, and shifts as well, I expect. I'll teach you how to scarf your hair, first thing; you'll not want it hanging loose. And stockings, I wager you have no stockings. Luckily I've stockings to spare, for you can't go about bare-legged and be dead by midwinter. So we've undertaken to clothe you as well as house you, and feed you, and I hope you prove worth the trouble you're causing. Put your cloak in here," Ula told Elske, opening a chest at the foot of the bed. "I hope you're strong," Ula said, lowering the top of the chest. "I've been needing a kitchen girl for years, and it's worse now with the Varinne useless. There's only the two of us to get everything ready for the marriage day and the marriage feasts, since the Varinne has taken to her bed with grief and is determined to die there."

Elske followed Ula back down the stairs, and drew the high stockings she was given up over her knees, put on the light shift and the grey long-sleeved dress Ula found for her, and protected her skirts with an apron. Ula wrapped her head around with a soft white scarf, to cover all of her hair. She was told to knead bread dough while Ula watched, "for cooking's a burden I'll gladly share, now there's a servant for the house. The sons died of fever, one after the other; it was the spotted fever and it broke their mother's heart. Aye and mine, too, truth be told. They were lovely boys, a great loss to their father," Ula said. "The sooner Idelle gives us her own sons, the better off we'll all be."

Elske looked around her. This cook room was furnished like Tavyan's, but it was larger, with more cupboards, more plates and mugs on shelves, and a bigger hob. A fish lay waiting on the table, and when Ula had shaped four round loaves, and covered them with a cloth, she turned a knife to it. As she slit open the fish's belly, a young woman came into the room. She was thick of body, like her aunt, and had a broad, Trastader face, with freckles spread across it as plentifully as stars across a night sky. Her eyes were pale blue, her dress a dark blue, and her head scarf a duplicate of Elske's. She was taller than Elske, and older; when she spoke her voice was soft. "Is this the girl, Aunt?"

"This is Elske," Ula said. "I've shown her her place in your chamber."

"And Taddus?" the young woman asked eagerly.

"He's a man, with a man's day's work to get done. He'll come calling tonight, he said."

There was a disappointed pause, then Idelle greeted Elske. "May we be well met. Taddus said you've no experience serving in one of the better homes, but can you cook? Launder? Sew?"

Elske shook her head, three times.

"I've never trained a servant," Idelle said, worried, and "I can learn," Elske offered.

"You can hem the bed linens, which is an easy, if time-consuming, task. That will help."

Ula reminded her niece, "Don't forget the work of the marriage feast. Even an inexperienced pair of hands can clean pots, scrub floors—"

"When I've no need for her," Idelle reminded her aunt. "She is first for me. There are not many weeks left before I marry."

Elske thought that she was learning if not what a servant

was, at least what a servant did. As she came to know, a servant did what she was told, from first light to late into the night. The preparations for a wedding and the celebration feast—the cleaning and polishing, the ordering of game and fish from butcher and fishmonger, of sweet rolls from the baker and barrels of ale from the brewer, so that all might be ready on the day—those preparations, added to helping Idelle at her dress and wrapping her hair with scarves, accompanying her to the market, hemming the bridal bed linens—all of this kept Elske fully occupied.

Most evenings saw Taddus come to the house, to dine with Idelle and her father. Elske did not serve them, not being skilled in waiting on table, but when the plates and pots were put away, when the floor was scoured clean and Ula was satisfied that all was ready for the morrow, Elske was sent to sit by the fire in the front room, with its table and candlesticks and whitewashed walls, to join the three who had pulled their chairs up close to the fire, on these cold nights. When Var Kenric had talked with Taddus about stores and sales, profits and investments, he went up to make his nightly visit to his wife and Elske remained, turning the hem on the bridal bed linens. It was necessary for a servant to attend a courting couple. This made no sense to her, but a servant asked no questions, as Elske learned.

One of the first nights by the fire, while Elske sewed, Taddus and Idelle sat at the table to compose the announcement which made public offer of Elske's services as maidservant.

When Idelle saw what Taddus wrote, "You can read? And write?" she asked in surprise. "But our merchants and bankers wouldn't want maidservants who know such things. It's not as if you were a manservant," Idelle said to Elske, and Elske agreed that she was not a man.

"Still, it might prove desirable," Taddus disagreed, and wrote, adding, *She is experienced with babies.* "Is there any other use you have, Elske?"

Elske, a stranger in Trastad, could not tell him.

"She can sew a good hem," Idelle said, and her cheeks turned pink, as if that were a blushing matter. "She is always willing, and she doesn't tire."

"Father said that the men who seek to hire you should come first to our house, Elske," Taddus told her, as he wrote down Tavyan's name at the bottom of the paper. "He wishes to see you well-protected."

"Thank you," Elske said. "My thanks to Tavyan, as well." Her stomach was full with the fish soup she had helped to prepare, served with slices of thick bread; her stockinged legs were warmed by the fire while thick snow fell silently outside; a winter night covered the city but she would sleep on soft furs beside Idelle's high bed. What more could she ask for?

She had never had anyone near her own age to talk with

before, not any sister or even a brother, only Tamara, who was a grandmother and wise. Idelle was four winters older than Elske and soon to be a married woman, but the two lived companionably, walking out to the marketplace together, talking about the gown Idelle would be married in and the nightdress in which she would present herself to her new husband. "I had no fortune when he chose me, so he chose me, not my fortune," Idelle announced, so vehemently that Elske knew she doubted it.

Elske could tell her young mistress, "He was impatient to be back in Trastad."

Idelle blushed. "Young men are always eager when a marriage bed awaits them. Should my nightgown have lace at the neck?" she asked Elske. "Would a man desire such finery?"

Elske could not say. It seemed to her that, except to marry, the women of Trastad feared men, except for their fathers, and brothers; and the fathers, brothers and husbands mistrusted all other men. The women of Trastad could not go out of doors alone, lest they be set on, and ruined. Ruined, Elske deduced, meant raped, although Idelle seemed to anticipate having Taddus in her bed. "So it is good to be raped by a husband?" Elske inquired, and Idelle covered her face with her hands before she said, "When it's your husband it isn't rape. Rape is when the woman is unwilling. When the man forces her."

Among the Volkaric, the women were neither willing nor

unwilling. They had no will in the matter, just as they had no marriages.

Seeing that Elske did not understand, Idelle explained, "If a woman is ruined, no man will have her to wed."

"What if," Elske asked, "a woman is willing?"

"A woman *must* be willing for her husband, or how will she get her children?"

"What if," Elske asked, "a woman is willing for a man not her husband?" If a woman bore the Volkking a son she got honor and importance, and other men then wished to rape her, this woman who had produced a son for the Volkking.

"No woman would wish such a thing," Idelle told her. "Or else why would any man look for a wife?"

Elske did not know and could not have said. All she could do was accompany Idelle to the great marketplace, and to the shops that crowded around the Council Hall, whenever the needs of house or wedding sent the young woman out of doors. In Trastad, if a female servant was the only companion a woman's house could afford her, then the female servant made her company, to keep her safe. A Trastader woman did need her safety guarded, Elske learned. The young men of Trastad made a game of teasing women, especially young women. Elske walked at Idelle's shoulder through crowds and when someone approached her mistress too close, or too roughly, or with words that were too bold, Elske stepped forward. Seeing Elske there, "We only jest," they might say, turning to find another woman to trail, adding as a parting unpleasantness to Idelle, "If you were prettier, Varele, I'd take more trouble over you."

The days went slowly by. When Taddus came in the evenings, he sometimes brought men of the city whose houses needed a maidservant. Often, the man would be pleased with Elske and then Taddus would come the next afternoon to take Elske to meet the mistress of the house. But always the Varinne would say, "She will not do." Even though Elske looked like any other Trastader serving woman, with her hair scarfed, under a man's protection, still "She will not do," the Varinne would report to her Var. Elske was found too young, too inexperienced, too old to train, too ignorant of the ways of Trastad or too clever.

The Longest Night drew closer and still Elske had been offered no place. Var Kenric's house was hung with greens, to celebrate the season and the marriage. The bed linens were hemmed and folded up into the chest at the foot of Idelle's bed, ready for the wedding night. Snow piled high in the courtyard behind the house, where evergreens showed black against the whiteness of the snow. It was full winter, almost the Longest Night. "A place will be found for you, Elske," Idelle assured her, uneasily. "Somewhere. Soon. Maybe tomorrow."

They were returning through the empty streets of Old Trastad from the bakeshop where Idelle's marriage cake would be made. There would be bad fortune on the marriage if the guests were offered no marriage cake of dense, heavy sweetness, rich in honey and nuts and ale-soaked raisins, so they had stayed on, discussing ingredients with the baker. They walked back in the long darkness that devoured winter's brief day. At one corner they almost ran into a group of young men, Adeliers accompanied by two servants. The Princes held their heavy cloaks close around them, and were wrapped also in the perfume of ale. They leaned into one another, joking and cursing in Souther. The servants followed behind, carrying jugs of drink.

Elske knew, immediately and without question, that Idelle was in danger. She smelled danger as strongly as might one of the wolves whose skins made the cloak she wore.

The darkening air was thick around them. The snow-covered street was empty of people, the shop-fronts shuttered at day's end. Sounds were muffled, in these twisting streets.

The young men stumbled by, laughing. Then Elske heard them halt, turn, and come to walk only a few paces behind Idelle, boasting to one another about their knowledge of women, speaking about Idelle in her heavy woollen cloak, "one of these precious virgins of Trastad. Plump as a honey cake, isn't she? Would she be sweet in the taking?" they asked, and answered themselves, "Who's to stop us finding out?"

Although she didn't know Souther, Idelle seemed to understand her danger. She began to walk more quickly, concentrating on the snowy ground ahead of her feet.

"And a maidservant, too. Two's double one, and always will be," one voice said and another answered, "She's a child, too young to be worth the trouble," but he was hooted down. "Where are your eyes, fool?"

Elske pretended to trip in her haste to get away, and she fell forward. She used her hands to break her fall, and heard laughter from the young men behind. The snow stung her skin as she reached beneath it; and when she scrambled back to her feet, she held one fist-sized rock in each hand.

Now the Adeliers made their move, and rushed ahead to face the two women. Idelle started to cry out, a thin wailing cry, pleading for kindness.

Elske kept her hands under her cloak. She considered the seven laughing young men.

Two were so ale-sodden that they were obviously no danger. One, with full lips and a jewel in his ear, she counted their captain. All had eyes bright with eager cruelty, like a war band going together into battle. Two of the Adels held back the menservants, who now called out warnings in Norther. "Run, Varele. They'll ruin—"

Elske stepped between Idelle and the young captain. "Quietly now," she advised her trembling mistress. "Your fear will make them the more cruel."

Idelle raised her hands to her face, and whimpered into her fingers.

Two young men grabbed her from behind, and she screamed out.

Elske screamed, too. But when Elske screamed, it was the war cry of the Volkaric that came out of her mouth, a howling like the voice of a wolf. The cry wound around the narrow streets as if they were in the wild and merciless northlands. She howled again and the Adels loosened their hold on Idelle. They turned to their captain.

This young man paused where he stood, his jewel glinting in the lantern light. Elske saw in his eyes a tingle of fear and his own pleasure at the fear. Quick, she swung her fist at him, and hit him on the side of the head.

He fell sideways onto his knees in the snow.

The other Adeliers stood wordless. And watched. Idelle, too, had fallen silent.

Elske howled once more as she bent over the young man and lifted his head by the thick, dark hair. She smiled down at this drunken Adel Prince with the rich jewel in his ear, knowing what revenge she would take on him.

Holding the second stone like a fist, Elske raised her arm and smashed it into his lip and nose. Then she let his head fall back.

Now it was the captain who whimpered, and his hands covered his face, and he curled up on the ground. "Help me!" he cried.

The snow beside his hidden face stained out a bright red.

The servants, now free, called to Idelle and Elske. "Run! Run! We have no weapons! We can't help you! Run!"

Idelle sobbed, asking Elske, "What have you done? What have you done?" But Elske turned to the Adeliers, three now lifting their fallen captain, and spoke to them in Souther. "If you had succeeded, you would all have been dead men."

They stared at her.

"*Fruhckmen*," she named them, the Volkaric word. They didn't know the language but they understood her meaning.

Now Idelle was running awkwardly home, her feet tripping on her own cloak in her haste and fear, but Elske knew they had no more to fear from these Adeliers, these cowards. And their captain would be marked for life for what he was. She'd seen his bloody teeth in the snow. She'd split his lip like a nutshell.

WHEN IDELLE TOLD HER STORY to Ula, and then again to her father after he had returned in the evening, there was a great commotion. Var Kenric pressed Elske over and over, "And she was never touched? Never harmed?" When Taddus came to call, Var Kenric pulled him aside and spoke to him in a low voice, in the corner of the front room.

Idelle sat wrapped in a blanket in her chair by the fire, sometimes weeping in remembered fear. They gave her wine to soothe and strengthen her. "If it hadn't been for Elske," she kept saying, and Ula stroked her hair and spoke to her as softly as if she were a little child.

After a time, Var Kenric said quietly, "I thank you, Elske." He had started to add, in warning, "But you—" when he was interrupted by a pounding on his door.

He opened it to four men accompanied by servants carrying lanterns. The men stamped their feet in the snow and asked to enter the house.

"Certainly," Var Kenric said. "May we be well met, gentlemen." He offered to take their cloaks and he offered tankards of ale. They shook their heads, declining to give up their cloaks, declining refreshment, and to persuade them he said, "It's a cold night."

"Colder for some than others. You must know, we've a gravely wounded princeling on our hands."

At that, Var Kenric called for Elske to join them around the table, leaving Ula, Idelle and Taddus near the fire.

The four visitors were thickset Trastaders and one stood taller than the others, a bearlike man with heavy-lidded eyes and a thin mouth. Elske didn't know how they would deal with her. Among the Volkaric, reward for courage was given as swiftly as death for cowardice—but she was among Trastaders.

One of the shorter men spoke. "You have attacked and injured an Adel."

"Yes," Elske agreed.

"Why would you do such a thing?"

Elske found herself talking to the bearlike man even though he was not one of her questioners. "That one was the captain, and the others only followed him. They hoped to ruin Idelle," she said. Then, seeing by their faces that she had not answered them, she explained, "If a wolf pack is after you and you can chase off the leader, the others will not stay to fight."

She thought it was the tall man's judgement that would rule the others.

"They meant rape," Var Kenric said. "I don't understand why you are here, Vars, and under the darkness of night as if in secrecy," he said, although Elske guessed he well knew. Idelle's father was trying to help her, she could see. And thus she saw that she needed help.

The big man answered Var Kenric. "They say they were only teasing, only flirting, they had drunk too much and were stupid with ale. They say, these guests of Trastad, these Adels who have come here for the Courting Winter which puts them under the Council's protection, they say that the attack was unprovoked."

"But that is not so," Elske said.

"We wonder, how you could know they intended harm to your mistress, when they speak Souther," he answered, and watched her face carefully.

"Ask the two servants," Elske suggested.

"The servants have been sent out of the city, and so cannot be questioned. The young men deny everything. They demand that we punish you." He kept his eyes on her face.

Her death, then. Elske didn't know what else there was for her to say, so she said nothing. These men had come to take her to her death and only waited for the tall man to speak the order. She would give Idelle her wolfskin boots, for the young woman had admired them.

"Are you not afraid?" the tall man asked her.

Elske shook her head.

"And were you not afraid when there were seven of these Adeliers ready to attack and rape you both?" he asked.

She corrected his mistake. "There were only three, for two held the two servants back, and two more were soft-legged with drink, not dangerous. There was only the one who was truly a danger to Idelle."

"No reason for fear, then," he said, with what might have been a smile. "And if the princeling dies?"

"Why should he die?" Elske asked. "I gave him a scarring blow, not a killing."

"But how could you be so certain they planned ill?" one of the others asked. "I want to be merciful, but I don't see how you could be so certain they planned ill."

Elske tried to explain. "When men take too much mead, and they are together, and each wants the others to know his manhood—such men are as dangerous as a pack of wolves at the hungry end of winter. They smelled dangerous, and they said Idelle was a precious virgin of Trastad, and they asked one another, 'Who's to stop us?'"

"But how do we know—?" one of the shorter ones started to ask, before another cried him down, demanding, "Do you care more for the profits of these Courting Winters than for the safety of our women?" but "Will you have it known abroad that such an attack went unpunished?" the first countered.

The tall man gave his orders. "Speak no more of it. Let the servants carry tales, as they will, being servants, and all the Adeliers will hear soon enough from their own servants, and from Prince Garolo's face when he reappears in their midst. The story will be told, and it will grow, and if we neither punish nor praise this girl—if we say nothing, as I advise—then the story will act as a deterrent for years to come. It will be known that the Adeliers may not with impunity act like beasts in Trastad," he concluded, with another small smile that was not a smile.

"But I think the girl had better come with me. I am in need of a nursemaid for my three daughters. I would like my daughters," he said, unsmiling now, "to be in the care of someone who can defend them."

"What will your wife say, Var Jerrol, to such a choice?"

"My wife will say what I say," the man answered. "Come now, what is your name?"

"Elske," she told him as Var Kenric called across the room, "Daughter? Make your farewells to Elske."

"But who will be my servant?" Idelle asked. "Elske was to stay with me until I marry."

"You'll be safer apart, now," Var Kenric told his daughter. "I'm sorry you leave us, Elske, but this is the better way. When my daughter has no maidservant, then she could not have been the Trastader maiden who was attacked in the street. When you have been hidden away in Var Jerrol's house, nursemaid to his daughters, you could not have been that half-wild servant from off island, for if you were, who could trust you with his own helpless children?"

Elske knew Var Kenric meant to remind her of how great her strangeness was, how perilous her position in Trastad, as a warning not to protest. She needed neither reminder nor warning. And she would move warily in her new position, for this big Trastader was as dangerous as any man of the Volkaric. She bade farewell to Taddus, and to Var Kenric and Ula, and sorrowfully to Idelle, whom she wished joy on her wedding day. Then she followed the four men back out into a night filled with dark falling snow.

CHAPTER 6

T HE PARTY MOVED SILENT AS a Volkaric war band through the night. Snow muffled the sounds of their footsteps and the only light came from the lanterns carried by the servants.

Elske moved in their midst like some captive of great worth being taken to the Volkking.

After they had crossed the snow-covered bridge to the old city of Trastad, the party divided. Elske was to go on with the tall man, Var Jerrol, and his two servants. Parting, Var Jerrol said to his companions, "One of you will take the notice down from the door of the Council Hall," and "We'll see to that," they promised him. "Good sleep, Var," they bid farewell to one another, adding that this was a good night's work. "These foreign Adels need to be ridden with a short rein," they said. "Good sleep, Var."

The icy air was thick with falling snow. The four made

their way, turning now left, now right, past ship chandleries and livery stables, warehouses and taverns. Then they were walking between the flat faces of tall houses, their ground-floor windows shuttered but the upper ones showing cracks of light that lit the snow as it fell.

At one of these tall houses the party halted. The door opened as if they had been watched for, and they entered into a small room. The tall Var told Elske, "The wolf cloak must be burned," taking it from her. And those were all the words he spoke.

A maidservant gave Elske a candle, and led her up three flights of stairs. She opened a door into a dark, cold chamber that contained a bed, a chest and a short-legged box made out of flat tiles. As Elske watched, the servant struck a tinderbox to light a fire in the box, blew on it until the flames burned eagerly, then took three pieces of wood from a basket and fed them to the fire. She half-closed a metal door at the front of the box. "Once your room warms, you should close and latch the door of the stove," she told Elske, and left the room.

Stove, Elske thought; and she thought she understood; she had already learned *latch*. It was wonderful, Elske thought, to keep fire tamed in a box that took its smoke away with pipes and chimneys. Winter in the one-roomed houses of the Volkaric was a choking season, unless you opened the shutters and let clean icy air blow through.

Elske looked about her to see what the candlelight

revealed. The bed had fat covers lying on it, and pillows, too. Two small windows were tucked under the low ceiling, and they showed a black curtain of night, with little white flakes blowing up against the outside of the glass. She set the candleholder down on the wooden chest, hung her dress on a peg beside the door and latched the door of the stove, closing in its fire. Then she climbed up on the bed. She slipped down under the coverlet, as if all her life she had been used to such a bed. But she did not sleep. She remembered.

She remembered the orderly quiet of Var Kenric's house, and the days as Idelle's maidservant, days as like one another as one onion to the next; and she remembered the young men's threats, in the lonely street. She remembered the strength of her arm against their captain; remembering, she noticed what she had not seen at the time, which was how easily cowed they all were—Idelle, the Adels, the servants.

What she would be now, Elske did not know. Nursemaid, if she could believe Var Jerrol, and she had no reason to disbelieve him. Had he not taken her under his protection? But Elske knew enough about Trastaders to know he would have his own uses for her, for his own profit.

Remembering, Elske noticed again Var Jerrol's eyes, how they had measured her, and then she noticed how he had—having taken her measure—given orders to arrange the outcome to his will. Among the Trastaders she had met, only Var Jerrol might be dangerous, Elske thought.

And then she noticed that she had taken her own measure of him.

Her legs and shoulders were already sleeping, but a newly born person behind her eyes struggled to stay awake, just a little longer, to ask if Elske had also noticed this: that she could change things. For had she not changed everything?

Almost, she reminded herself, changed everything to her death. And now Elske noticed that while, like any Volkaric man or woman, she did not fear death, she would, like any Trastader, prefer to live. Her further safety was up to her, Elske thought, as sleep finally overmastered her.

WAKENED BY THE DOOR—OPENING—and somebody entering the room, Elske sat up in a room filled with sunlight. She had slept well into the morning.

A red-faced Trastader girl, wearing an apron over her dark dress and a white kerchief around her hair, stood at the foot of the bed, her arms full of cloth. Elske waited for her to speak. The girl stared.

This went on until Elske moved to get out of bed, setting her feet on the floor.

"Odile says you're to dress and come down. Into the cook room." Her message delivered, the girl left the room.

Elske bent down to see out the windows.

Black bare-armed trees grew up out of the snow, and grey stones made a low wall at the end, and beyond that stretched a river so shoreless it had to be the sea, Tamara's sea.

"Oh," Elske said, aloud alone, and "Oh," again.

That morning the sky shone so clear and so blue that the sea sparkled deep and bright, blue as the tiny bellflowers that appeared in the brief Volkaric spring, and bluer. Blue as only itself, the sea shone back at the shining sky, outside her window.

Elske laughed out loud. But she could not linger. She dressed and followed the stairways down to the entrance hall and then followed her nose.

The large cook room was filled with the odor of bread and porridge. A thin woman stood at the long wooden table, her knife raised. The carcass of a rabbit lay before her, skinned, its guts removed, the head and paws chopped off. The woman had blood on her hands.

"You'll be the girl," she greeted Elske. She didn't wait for any response. "I'm to feed you and then take you to the master. That's Var Jerrol, in case nobody told you, and I'm Odile, housekeeper for the Var. His wife is so worn out by childbirth that she is dying of the coughing sickness, so there are the little girls to look after. Do you know anything of children?"

Elske said, "I only know about babies."

"What, how to get one?" Odile laughed, loud and short, like a dog's bark, and drove her knife into the shoulder of the rabbit. "How old are you? Are you bleeding yet?"

"This is my thirteenth winter and no, I am not."

"It'll be any day, from the look of you, and what's your name? Sit, I've porridge."

Elske sat on the bench and the woman dipped a bowl into a cauldron set on the hob, then set it steaming down on the table. Elske took the spoon the woman gave her, and ate.

After a bite, "Good," she said, and it was. Porridge was food to fill a belly, and keep it full. "Elske," she said, between mouthfuls. "That's my name."

Odile cut the rabbit into pieces which she dropped into a second, smaller cauldron, then swung it on a metal hook back over the open fire. "That's done," she said. "And you're fed. Now you go to Var Jerrol. I'll warn you, you'd better tell him whatever's true. He'll find you out easy as breathing if you lie to him, and that'll be the end of you."

So openness would be her safety, here in Var Jerrol's house, as much as it had been what kept her safe among the Volkaric. Elske followed Odile to a chamber off of the entrance hall. When she entered that room, she saw the Var sitting straight-backed in a chair, and he was busy with the many papers opened out in front of him. Shelves on the wall held leather boxes, and squares were on the walls, most colored, one blank. The man was writing.

Elske went up to one of the colored squares, to look at it more closely. This was not cloth, although when she touched it, it was as smooth as her skirt. This square showed a man's head, smaller than a real man's head. Although it was as flat as glass, it didn't look flat. The man stared off, as if he saw something over Elske's shoulder. But when she turned there was nothing to be seen.

Var Jerrol paid no attention to her.

Elske went to the blank square. Now a face filled it, dark-eyed, a girl's face, with dark thick eyebrows over eyes of so dark a grey they reminded her of rainclouds, and wolf pelts. The girl had a short nose and her hair was worn Trastader fashion, under a scarf. Except for the color of her eyes, the girl looked a great deal like Tamara when she was thinking out the day's work. The girl looked so much like her grandmother that Elske smiled.

The face smiled back at her, as if it were alive, and happy to see her.

She stepped back, and the girl stepped back. She reached a hand out, to touch the face, but the girl's hand reached towards hers, until their fingertips touched. But all Elske felt was flat and cold.

"Elske," the man spoke from behind her, and she whirled around. "It's all right, it's a beryl glass. Don't be afraid."

"I'm not afraid," Elske told him, and now Var Jerrol smiled at her, to say, "Of course. I'd forgotten."

"But who is she? And where?" Elske asked, turning back to the beryl glass.

"She's you. That's you." He rose to stand beside her, and

she saw him appear also beside the girl. The girl's face, her own, was not a broad Trastader face, although neither was it narow, like the Volkaric. "The back of the glass is painted silver, and that causes it to reflect what is before it, as the harbor on a windless day reflects the sky and masts, or the river water its banks. But come over to the window," Var Jerrol said. "Let me see you by daylight. You don't look strong enough to have smashed the Adel's mouth."

"And nose," Elske told him.

"And nose." He smiled again.

She explained it to him. "I had a stone. Actually," she added, for perfect openness, "I had two stones, from the street, because I smelled danger when they turned to follow us and I could hear what they said to one another. I needed to keep them from ruining Idelle."

"So you do speak Souther. Yet you are Volkaric."

What did he know of her, Elske wondered, and why would he know anything about her? But she had decided to keep no secrets and by the time he finished asking her, he knew about her warrior father, dead in some distant battle, her Volkaric mother and Tamara, who let her live, and raised her. What he did not ask, he did not know. "Why did you leave?" he asked and "My grandmother sent me away," she told him. He desired to know no more, but said then, "I am the eyes and ears of the Council. Do you know what that means?"

"You tell the Council the secrets you learn," she guessed.

"In part," he said. "Also, I hear their worries and their schemes, and I set my spies to gather information the Council needs, to settle their worries, to enact their schemes. I do not tell everything, Elske, just what they need to know. You will be safe in my house. If you are nursemaid to my daughters, and unseen, the misadventure will be forgotten." Then, in a different voice, he asked, "You can read? As the posted notice claims?"

"I know letters," Elske answered.

The Var rose and took down one of the leather boxes from his shelves. This turned out to be sheets of paper, sewn within a stiff leather cover—not a box at all. The cover was made so that it could be opened to display the pages one after another. She could see words on the open page and reached out a hand to touch them. The page was smooth, flat, and the letters lay smooth and flat upon it. "What do you call this?" she asked and "A book," he answered. "Can you read it?"

Elske studied the letters, making the sounds in her head, until she remembered them well enough to read him the tale of the eagle who was shot with an arrow fletched with his own feathers, a story Tamara, too, had known. When she was done, he returned the book to the shelf and said, "I've kept visitors waiting. Odile will take you to my daughters." He went to the door and opened it, that she might leave him. Following her out of the room, he reached out his hand to greet a cloaked man, who was just then crossing the hall in loud boots. "May we be well met," Var Jerrol said to this guest, and to the manservant he said, "Bring us hot drinks," and Elske was forgotten.

She went back into the cook room where Odile asked what she was to be paid for her labors and when Elske said she did not know, promised to settle it with the Var. "It's hard to put a price on the kind of work you'll be doing for him," she said. "And he'll work you without recompense if you let him." Then, "I don't know where you come from, to know so little of the world," Odile added, and laughed. She led Elske up two sets of stairs, to knock on a wooden door and open it without waiting for an answer.

This was a large room, where the serving girl who had awakened Elske sat sewing and two little girls, of one and two winters, whispered together on a bed. There was a cradle set near the warmth of a tile stove. Windows let in sunlight, and there were two beds with small chests at their feet, as well as a round table at the center of the room, with four chairs around it. When Odile led Elske in, the sleeping baby was the only one who didn't stare solemnly.

"Here's the new nursemaid," Odile announced. "Elske. And that means you"—she jabbed the girl with a finger—"will be back in the cook room—where I have need of you, what with the Courting Winter, and the master's meals, and the Varinne's dainty stomach. Your soft days are finished and I don't want to hear any snuffling on that account." The girl rose from her seat.

Odile spoke to the little girls with more courtesy, and in a gentler voice. "Our oldest—she's two. Can you give a curtsey, Mariel?" The child shook her head, No, and sucked on a finger. "And this is Miguette," Odile said, as the younger, just steady on her own legs, took her sister's hand and bobbed downwards. "The baby is Magan. The sewing is an old cloak of Mariel's we're taking up. You can sew, can't you?"

"Mine," Miguette said, pointing to the cloak.

"Little girls can't get sick," Mariel said. "Poor Maman is sick," she told Elske.

Odile and the serving girl left Elske with the two little girls and the sleeping baby. Without a word, Elske sat on the low seat beside the cradle, took up the cloak and continued the hem where it had been left off. She knew the sisters were watching her from the bed where they sat, each with a doll in her hands. When the baby woke, Elske could ask Mariel where the clean cloths were, and where the baby's soiled cloths were kept, and so they would grow comfortable with one another.

By the time bowls of fish soup were brought up for them, and chunks of bread, with honey to pour on them, the little girls had grown comfortable with this stranger. Elske noticed this, and noticed, too, that her spirits rose to have little children in her care, and for companions.

CB EO

78

THE LONGEST NIGHT ARRIVED AND passed by without Elske having time to do more than silently wish Idelle well. Not only were Var Jerrol's daughters in her care, but also Elske could be summoned to the cook room to assist Odile; for the cook was kept busy, as the Councillors met with Var Jerrol to plan and manage the Courting Winter. The men needed to govern the high spirits of the Adels, so these young men were taught sword-fighting by two masters of that art, and when the snow was packed solid in the streets they had permission to race their horses, and when weather kept them inside they were taught dances, and songs. The city feasted its guests frequently, and regular Assemblies, with hired entertainers, were held in the Council Hall. Still, the Adels had too much time for drinking and quarreling and making mischief, and that interfered with the Council's intention of bringing them to marriage by the end of winter. Luckily, the Adelinnes understood their purpose in Trastad and caused no trouble.

One day, as Odile unrolled a pastry crust over the top of the fish pie she was preparing for a tableful of Councillors, in satisfaction at her work she announced, "I may have been a bad woman, but none can say I'm a bad cook."

"Was it difficult to become bad?" Elske asked, hoping to cause Odile to laugh.

Odile obliged her, turning the bowl in her hands as she pinched the crust down into place. "The opposite of difficult,

Miss Curiosity. It's a short and easy road, but not—as some say—scattered over with flowers and pieces of gold. The law of the city had me bound for the cells, but Var Jerrol took me instead. All the servants of his house he's rescued from the cells, and that keeps us loyal. You, for example. If the Var hadn't fetched you home with him that night, where do you think you'd have lodged the next, and all the rest of your life? And that wouldn't have been long, down in the cells. You'd have not wished it to be long, either."

"But if the Adels threatened to rape Idelle, why is it I who would go to the cells?" Elske asked.

Odile shrugged. "The law places Adeliers under the Council's protection, so when you harm an Adel you have transgressed against the law. Justice does not always harness well with profit, as any of our merchants will tell you. So Var Jerrol brought you here, to keep you from the cells; and let the world think you in the cells—for there is no doubt the world has thought of you, and spoken of you. Let them think you if not dead in the cells, then dying there." Odile laughed again, "You're fat for a corpse," and Elske laughed with her. She placed the fish pie into the baking oven and asked Odile, "*Why* were you a bad woman?"

"Oh, well, I was young. I had a husband but his boat went down in a storm, driven onto sharp rocks, and I left child-less and penniless. A widow without property has nothing to attract a husband. So I stole what I could, usually from visitors to the city, and they found me out and set me before the Council. 'Why did you not go whoring, woman?' they asked me. With the cells awaiting me, I wished I had. But Var Jerrol claimed me for his cook. The Council didn't like to say him nay. None of them naysays any other, if they can help it, and no one wants to cross Var Jerrol. He's given orders to have you trained at waiting table."

"I think I will obey," Elske said, and earned another bark of laughter.

"The Council knows that without Var Jerrol, whose ships carry his spies as well as his goods, whose whores pick the heads but not the pockets of our visiting merchants and traders, their own profits might fall off. He keeps Trastaders, too, under his eye, for men who look to profit will often be tempted to take profit where the law forbids it. The city is full of thieves, Elske, and not all of them sleep rough in streets and stables." But Odile could not be long diverted from her instructions. "He has said you are to wait at table under Red Piet. When you do that, Saffie will watch over the little girls."

Elske, wondering if her safe place in the house would be at risk with this more public task, asked, "What if I prefer not?"

"I'd prefer so, if I were you, my Missy, unless you prefer the cells. They might send you there to serve this Fiendly Princess."

"An Adelinne has been sent to the cells?" Elske asked, then answered herself, "No, they would never; but she must trouble them severely. Is she the Adelinne who wouldn't go into safety in the storm?"

"The very same and a very devil, they say. Uncooperative, disobedient, proud, uncivil, she refuses to go to the Assemblies. She demands to be taught swordplay. She tries to take part in the street races—she doesn't know her purpose here, and doesn't wish to. No maidservant will stay long with her, for her temper and tongue, each as bad as the other, both sharp as a sword, hot as a firebrand. And she offers her servants no coins. Now, you do this second pie, fold the pastry over the top, as I did—yes, over, and pick it up from the two ends—yes, and lay it down. Pinch it tight, lest the good juices be lost. *And* she has run away so often they keep her in a locked room, they send her under guard, this Fiendly Princess, when she must be out in the city. But you'll make a good cook, Elske. You're a clever one, aren't you?"

Elske was more interested in the Adelinne. "She must have courage."

"And if she does, what good will that do her," Odile decided. "Obedience and beauty get more marriage proposals than courage, and wealth gets the most, and you are needed upstairs in the nursery now, unless my ears deceive me."

AS THE DARK WINTER DAYS went by, Elske was kept busy, with all she had to learn and all she had to do. Var Jerrol gave her a book of animal tales to read to his daughters, to begin the widening of their world. "With wealth, and knowledge gained from books, my daughters will make wives worthy of any man," he told Elske. "And why should my daughters not marry as well as any Adelinne?" He also had Elske taught to serve at table, having her practice by serving him whenever he dined alone on the golden plates he brought out only for those occasions. All that long winter, Elske stayed within Var Jerrol's property, but she was not restless. The little girls gave Elske wild nursery games and wild nursery laughter, and that lightened the long darkness. Var Jerrol explained his importance to the Council, how his ships brought not only information and goods, but also rarities from foreign lands to introduce the Trastaders to the newest luxuries, embroidered silks, silver filigree, peppercorns. Odile gave her the gossip of the house and the city—how the Varinne had brought a good fortune to her husband but failed to give him a son, how his own housekeeper had named High Councillor Vladislav, the wealthiest Var in Trastad, father of her child, how a clever thief had emptied a merchant's strongbox in broad daylight.

Elske only saw the Varinne when she took the daughters to her. The Varinne didn't have the strength to have the girls linger, but she was always glad to see them. Once or twice, when Elske had wrapped the two older girls up warm and taken them outside to fall down in the snow, and make snowballs to throw at her, she saw the pale face at the window, looking down at her lively, healthy daughters.

Eventually, winter loosened its grip on the land. Then it rained as often as it snowed, but when the sun shone out of a clear sky, the sea shone back blue. Some few boats ventured out, fishermen hungry to end the winter shortages and eager for profits. As soon as it was safe to travel, the Adeliers returned to their homelands and whatever futures they had made or found during the Courting Winter.

When she no longer risked recognition, Elske could carry the basket for Odile, with Red Piet and Piet the Brown accompanying them to the shops and markets. She grew accustomed to the city, the many faces and crowded streets, and to its smells—a combination of offal and salt air and bakehouses, with their roasting meats, and yeasty breads and honey-nut cakes. The sea was now a familiar sight, jigging at the edges of the land.

Elske was growing out of her girlhood, and she started her woman's bleeding that winter; the little girls were growing, too, and so were the days which stretched now into one another, with only a shadowy darkness to act as night. Elske could bake a meat pie, now, or a fish pie, or an apple pastry, and the daily porridge and loaves of bread. She could prepare a meal, if Odile was taken with her women's pains, and she could stand beside Red Piet to wait at table when the Var entertained guests.

The serving at table, she discovered, was one of Var Jerrol's uses for her; for some of his guests were merchants from the south, come to Trastad to buy lumber, furs and ores. These merchants were cautious when Var Jerrol sat with them, but if he was called away they would speak unguardedly in Souther. Afterwards, the Var called Elske into his chamber and asked her to recite what the merchants had said when they were alone and, as they thought, unheard. She reported to him their disgust at the delicate whitefish the Trastaders ate pickled in vinegar and onions, their hopes that the Council would approve their offering price for a hundredweight of ore and their calculations of how much their profits would increase at that price. She reported when they schemed to mix fine ground grain in with a shipment of spices, assuring themselves that the simple Trastaders would not know the difference between the pure and the diluted.

The merchants also spoke among themselves about wars and Wolfers, about the ambitious Counts who ruled over the cities of the south, about diseases and their cures, and about magic weaponry; there was always information they wished to keep to themselves, lest the Trastaders know and take advantage.

"I don't blame them," Var Jerrol remarked to Elske. "I am the eyes and ears of Trastad and much of my wealth comes from information which—when I know it—also protects the city and its people."

Elske never made the mistake of keeping anything back from Var Jerrol. She knew that Var Jerrol trusted her reports and noticed that he smiled, with a private pleasure, whenever he saw her. But she believed that information was her true work for his house, for some of the merchants were more than merely greedy. Some had secrets.

Once she reported to Var Jerrol what three merchants of Celindon had said to one another when he left them alone with glasses of wine, and Elske there to keep them filled. The merchants had spoken in lowered voices of something called black powder. When Elske repeated that name to the Var, he looked at her long and silent, dangerously, before asking, "What did they say about the black powder?"

"They said that you were ignorant," at which news Var Jerrol smiled, and she added, "Thus, they said, their supplies of lumber were assured."

"Did they say what lumber had to do with the black powder?" Var Jerrol asked, his eyes intent upon her face, as if he could read there more than the words she spoke, as if although she might not know more still he would find more there, in her face, in her eyes, and seize it to himself.

"No. They spoke as of something they all already knew. Although they did observe," Elske reported, remembering carefully, "that your stables were lined with saltpeter, and that in Trastad the waste from the copper smelters is dumped into the rivers."

Var Jerrol lowered his eyelids, to think about this. After a long time he looked at her again. "If you're as clever as I think, Elske, you are also a danger to me. Are you so clever?"

"Yes," she said.

"Well," he said; then, "Was there anything more these merchants said?"

"That was when you returned."

"Go back to my daughters now. But, Elske," he ordered her, "this is no matter you need to remember. Unless, of course, you hear anyone else speak of black powder, and that you must report immediately."

Elske almost laughed to hear him instruct her thus; and he almost smiled as he watched her face.

Var Jerrol smiled seldom now, for when the Varinne coughed, she coughed blood. The apothecary said she wouldn't live to see another spring, and so he allowed her to open her windows on fine days to taste the warm salty air, and hear the voices of her daughters while they played in the gardens.

On days when Elske accompanied Odile to the markets she saw more and more swollen bellies among the young wives of Trastad. Each market day she looked for Idelle. But when she found her—a manservant three paces behind—Idelle's belly was as flat and empty as Elske's. Idelle was glad at first to meet with Elske, but that gladness soon washed away and she said, "As you see, I will have no baby to welcome Taddus home."

"As I see," Elske answered.

Idelle sighed. "But it could happen that our second winter bears more fruit than our first. It often happens so, I've heard that. You've always been luck to me, Elske," Idelle said. "Maybe meeting you will bring good fortune."

Odile called Elske away then, for the Emperor's messengers had arrived to collect the tribute money and Odile was poaching a redfish whole, to be the centerpiece of their dinner. Var Jerrol would feast the messengers and then give to them the chest of tribute coins. It was to meet this expense that the grandfathers of the present Trastaders had first opened their houses and their city to those Adeliers; the profit from the Courting Winters made up most of the tribute. The tribute bought peace, safety in which they might continue their trading.

The long, sun-filled summer days ran on. Sometimes the sky was clear and the sea blue. Sometimes storms whipped up white-headed waves that roared against the stone seawall. Sometimes the water ran grey between the mainland and Trastad, and all of the sea beyond was grey, too. The summer air blew warm over three-islanded Trastad, and the Trastaders kept out in the air as much as they could, because summer's stay among them was only brief. As long as it wasn't raining, the little girls in their light summer dresses stayed outside in the warmth and light, until they were sent inside to sleep.

There came a day in full summer—but it was really a night; that was part of the wonder of this time, sunlight at night. In this golden evening the Var's older daughters ran about barefooted, laughing, singing, dancing, delighted with themselves, delighted to be themselves with the light washing around them like water, and the baby sat upright in the grass, clapping her fat hands in admiration of her sisters.

Elske and Odile sat beside the Var's two young apple trees, watching. The air hung so sweet neither of them wanted to gather the little girls together and end the day. Mariel's high laughter rolled along the grass behind the wooden ball she was chasing. Then Odile murmured something in her low woman's voice. Magan fell sideways, fussing now. And Elske had a sudden sharp memory of Tamara, standing in the doorway of the Birth House, speaking in just such a low, rough voice, with just such sounds of laughter and misery coming from the room behind her. The memory sliced into Elske.

"Whatever is it? Whyever are you weeping?"

Elske shook her head, and wiped her eyes on her apron, and wept more tears, and didn't answer. The babies and toddlers she and Tamara had left out for the wolves, after winter had drawn back, were just such children as these three. Those Volkaric girls would have grown fatter and more clever, just as Magan had over the spring and summer, and grown into small ladies like Mariel who danced like a flower in the wind. Miguette, not yet two winters, was already secretive and solemn like her father. To think what might happen to these three little girls in their helplessness, and to remember all those for whom the Volkaric had no use, and so she and Tamara had wheeled them by the cartload out to a stony place, and been able only to end their short lives quickly— Elske's heart felt as if it were being ripped apart by wolves.

She had not even noticed that great change in herself, to have a heart where before she had had none.

CHAPTER 7

NOT THAT ELSKE DECEIVED HERSELF into thinking she was a Trastader. She only knew what she no longer was.

Fall was a short, fat season in Trastad, busy with preparing vats of salted and smoked fish, pots of fruit and jars of honey; busy with filling the pantries of Var Jerrol's house for the long winter. Only those fish caught by ice fishermen, who spent winter mornings dangling baited hooks through holes they sawed in the ice, would be fresh food for Trastad in the winter; and it was the high price those fish brought that made the discomfort and danger a risk worth taking for the fishermen.

The fall was busy and brief in Var Jerrol's house, but it was not sweet, for the Varinne was dying. The household fell quiet around her, as she made her way into death. The air in every chamber was thick with sorrow, and the food they ate tasted bitter with loss, so that when the Varinne had at last breathed out the end of her life, even though it was the deep dark of winter something light came back into Var Jerrol's house.

Since it was not a Courting Winter, the Trastaders could go quietly about their own business. Elske went once to visit Idelle in Var Kenric's house, accompanied by Red Piet. On this occasion, she had a mission for Var Jerrol, but she hoped to hear also that Idelle was with child. This hope was disappointed and Idelle could speak only of the sadness that stained her life. So now Elske saw two grieving women, Var Kenric's wife and daughter, each inconsolable, gazing out from behind his windows. One wept for the past, one for the future, and when Elske found Taddus in the counting room she could see that he was eager for spring, to give him the reason to leave the gloom of his home.

Elske's mission for Var Jerrol was to ask Taddus about a rumor that had reached Trastad. In his travels of the summer, had Taddus heard of an exploding ship? Yes, he had, but he didn't credit the rumor. Could a ship, and its crew of eleven men, with its two tall masts and its long keel, simply fly apart up into the air? Taddus had heard tales but none of the tellers had been eyewitness to the event and when he asked in which city's harbor the event had happened, none of the tellers agreed. Each had heard it from a friend; each friend had heard it from the sole survivor of the catastrophe.

The tales told of the sky filled with charred pieces of

wood, and parts of bodies, and the water of the harbor clotted with debris. The tales had a ship riding peacefully at anchor and then—without warning, with no sound as of galloping hooves to herald danger—a roar filled the air. Everyone agreed about the sound; it was thunder trebled. But nobody could agree about what they had seen—an explosion of fire, a sun burning in the harbor, the air darkened with evil-smelling smoke. Taddus shrugged, telling Elske this. "So the rumors go. And the rumors go farther, too, with talk of demon warriors risen in the south, come to lay everything waste and barren. The Wolfers are their slaves, and run before them, rumors say. But we are distant enough, here in islanded Trastad, Elske. You needn't fear."

"I'm not afraid," Elske answered him. "I was sent to ask."

"If I had married you, we'd have a child by now—do you think?" Taddus asked her suddenly. "But I will be named Var this spring, or the next, and that will give Idelle a new place among the ladies of the city. Maybe that will console her."

Elske joined in that hope, and left him there with his coins and his dreams and his books of cost and profit. She bid farewell to Idelle and called Red Piet from Ula's kitchen to escort her back to Var Jerrol's home.

"I suspect this is no demon army, but some new weapon of war," Var Jerrol said, "and I would not wish Trastad to be surprised by such a weapon. Such weapons give too much power to those who wield them, and cause dangerous fears in those who know of them. You are a girl and you may wrap your ignorance around you, but I am the eyes and ears of the Council."

"You think this is the black powder," Elske decided.

He wore the mourning band for his wife across his chest, but now he smiled at Elske. "Perhaps I should marry you. Other men have clever wives to work beside them."

"Why should everyone suddenly think of marrying me?" Elske demanded, and he smiled more broadly but did not tell her, so she could only laugh. Then he dismissed her, to return to the little girls. "And why *should* I marry again?" he asked as she turned to leave him.

"You wish for a son," Elske told him.

"Go now," Var Jerrol ordered, "before I change my mind."

VAR JERROL SENT A PARTY into the south, men willing to risk the hazards of winter travel for the sums Var Jerrol offered. When the survivors of the party returned, marked by blackened, frostbitten toes, fingers and ears, they brought with them a captive, a nervous, quick-eyed man, who asked question after question. Elske translated between the man and Var Jerrol. "What is he going to do with me? Why was I taken?" the man asked. "I'm not a wealthy man. How can they hope for ransom from a simple apothecary? Have you no pity for me? Can you not pity my wife, who must wonder what has befallen me? I'll reward you, I promise, Elske, whatever you ask. A rich husband? If you'd just tell me what he wants. Jewels? In my own city, I have the ear of the Count. The Count will give you whatever I tell him, if you help me get away."

The apothecary grew bolder with food and drink and warmth and rest. Var Jerrol shared meals with his captive, but kept Elske always in the room, to translate. As the man looked around him more, he no longer asked Elske to help him escape. At last, one day, he inquired of Var Jerrol directly, "What do you desire of me?"

Var Jerrol, who like all of the merchants spoke some Souther, answered this question himself. "The formula for black powder."

The apothecary laughed, then. "I thought it was something like that. Well, it's simple enough—for a man who knows its secret." He watched Elske, as she translated. "But I need some incentive to persuade my secret from me. For I'll have broken faith with the Count, and his writ will be out on my life."

"I could make you glad to tell me anything I asked of you," Var Jerrol said, but the man only laughed again, and suggested, "You prefer to have me tell you willingly, and truthfully."

Var Jerrol didn't argue.

"If I'm to lose everything, I'd be a fool to ask nothing in return. I'd need a new home, and large wealth," the apothecary said. Var Jerrol nodded, eyelids lowered; he accepted the bargain. "I might want a new wife. Young, and unknown to any man, to get my sons upon. I might want Elske," the apothecary said.

"Elske doesn't wish to marry you," Var Jerrol said.

"What do her wishes matter?"

"In Trastad, no woman weds against her will," Var Jerrol said. "Not even a servant. Besides, she is Wolfer bred and raised. And who would take such a woman into his bed, where he must sometimes lie helpless in sleep, when he has taken her against her will? You're safer with the wife I find for you," Var Jerrol said. "Now, tell me what you know."

The apothecary sighed, and then announced cheerfully, "I know everything." As he spoke, Elske repeated the information to Var Jerrol.

Mixed in proper proportions, the ingredients for black powder responded to flame by bursting apart. Like a pig's bladder, when children fill it with air and then knot its neck; if the children drop it into a fire, it blows itself apart. Black powder explodes, the captive said.

The evil smell that accompanied the explosion was burned sulfur, familiar to those who lived near where iron and copper were extracted from their ores. It was charcoal, ground fine, that gave the powder its black color. Charcoal was in short supply in the south, where the forests had been cleared to farmlands to feed the growing citizenry, and there was little wood to burn down to charcoal. Thus, unless the apothecary was mistaken, Trastad would find more and more ships come into its harbor, to be filled with lumber, for use by the southern manufactures of black powder.

Yes, a city could easily be taken with the black powder, its walls breached by the explosion. There was even talk that some of the Emperor's armies had long tubes, out of the ends of which the black powder propelled sharp pellets, to kill a man before he could come close to you with his drawn sword. This was killing your enemy as soon as you could see him, and he could have no protection against you. But the apothecary doubted these stories, for why didn't the long stick blow up in a man's hands when the fire flashed through the black powder?

Oh, yes, there was a third ingredient, to be ground in with the others, and the joke was it could be found in any cellar, on the wet walls, and it could be found growing atop any manure heap of every farm. This third ingredient was the pale saltpeter that, added in proper proportion—things must always be in the right proportions or the powder wouldn't work, it was knowledge of proportion that made the apothecary's information so valuable—made the black powder. Now, if the distinguished gentleman would give his word to the bargain—?

Var Jerrol would, and offered his hand to seal it.

Then the apothecary could easily write the formula down, if Elske would bring him paper and pen.

She set them down before him, and watched as he wrote, and saw how simple it was.

At this point, Var Jerrol sent Elske from the room, and she never saw the apothecary again. She never asked about him, either, for she had seen Var Jerrol's eyes.

WINTER'S END FINALLY CAME NEAR, the ice melting out into the sea, first, and then separating into chunks on the rivers. When the grass grew green and the apple trees threw lacy shawls of blossoms over their shoulders, Var Jerrol began talking to Elske about the proper education of his daughters, that they might attract husbands worthy of their father's position. He wished them to learn not only letters and numbers, but also how to mount and ride a horse, and even sword skills, that they might defend themselves, and even to have some knowledge of trade, and banking.

The long, honey-colored summer days flowed over Trastad. Piet of the brown hair asked for Elske's hand in marriage and she declined him. Var Jerrol warned her that when he himself wed—for he had chosen his new wife—Elske must leave his house if she would not take Brown Piet. He warned her that she was approaching her fifteenth winter, entering her marrying years, so she should look about her for a man who pleased her most. He would give her a dowry, Var Jerrol said. But Elske had no desire to marry.

She had chosen her future, he said. The city would give her as maidservant to an Adelinne, to serve the young woman during the Courting Winter, to companion her to the Assemblies and other entertainments and probably, since most of the Adeliers spoke that language, speak her familiar Souther. Elske would be sent to Var Vladislav, High Councillor of Trastad, the wealthiest of its citizens, master of many vessels and a large banking house, possessor of vast forest estates on the mainland, and farms and copper mines as well. She would be just one among many maidservants in his great villa on Logisle. This must be her future if she would not marry, Var Jerrol told her and waited again for her answer.

Risking his displeasure—for she found herself unwilling to bend to his will—Elske again declined to take a husband. She had no desire for any man to husband her, she said, and while there would be an emptiness in her heart where the little girls had lived, still, her choice was to be sent away from them.

"Do you think to overmaster me so easily?" he asked, and she laughed, partly for the pleasure of seizing her will from him.

"I don't think to overmaster you at all," she said. "I'm not such a fool."

She accepted the purse of coins he gave her, and wished him well with his new wife, wished the daughters well with their new mother, and when the cool, brief days of autumn spilled over the three islands, Elske said her farewells to Var Jerrol's household, made her curtsey to the new Varinne—as round and rosy as the first had been slim and pale—and followed Red Piet for the last time through the stony streets of Trastad. They walked past docks and warehouses busy at the concluding days of the trading season, and over the bridge to Harboring where—as she knew—Idelle awaited Taddus's return with the sorrow of an empty cradle, and then across another bridge to Logisle. There, the stone villa of High Councillor Vladislav opened its heavy doors to Red Piet's pounding.

The manservant told Elske she must go around the side of the palace, as he called it, and reminded Red Piet, before he closed the door upon them, that he should know better than to come pounding at the front door of the High Councillor's palace.

"You could marry me and come back to Var Jerrol's," Red Piet said to Elske, then.

"Why does everyone wish to wed me?" Elske asked him and he told her, "To keep you safe among us, and have you in my bed. But you won't marry me?"

"I'm to serve the Adelinne."

"And after that?" he asked her.

"How can we know what comes after?" she asked him, bidding him farewell.

Alone now, she followed the sandy path around the villa, passing tall empty windows, passing through gardens where the last of the summer roses faded on their thorny branches, passing into the kitchen gardens—herbs, and the tall stalks of onions trampled down onto the dirt, the green fronds of carrots, waiting in the earth and apple trees behind all—passing on to a plain wooden doorway. The villa was like a bird, with its two wings spread out. The central section rose up four stories, its windows growing smaller with each ascent; it needed four great chimneys. Elske faced one of the wings, only two stories. She could look into the windows and see dried herbs hanging in bunches down from the rafters.

Then the door opened to her knock, and the same stern manservant urged her inside. "You've come from Var Jerrol. You're to be maidservant to our Adelinne. You're called Elske," he told her. "I am steward to the house of Var Vladislav, who is the High Councillor of Trastad." As he named his master, and gave him his title, the steward became even stiffer than before, and more dignified.

Elske said nothing, and this pleased him.

He led her down a narrow dark hallway, past a large cook room—where three open fires burned, and several young women were at work at a table, and cauldrons steamed on the great hob—into a moist, windowless washroom. There two vats of water boiled over open fires, and two women stirred them with thick poles while a third watched them at their work. The third woman introduced herself.

"I'm housekeeper to the High Councillor. Var Jerrol has sent you to us, and Var Vladislav takes his spy's word for you, so who am I to question? We are to have the Fiendly Princess for our Adelinne. For they've sent her back, to angle again for a husband, and you are to be her maidservant. Carry on here, girls," she said, and "Yes, Missus," they answered her.

They were stirring around among white cloths, sweat running down their red faces and chests heaving with the effort. The housekeeper took Elske by the arm and led her out of the washroom, then down a long hallway, lit by dim daylight.

There was first a room where servants dined but Elske would not, and then storerooms holding food and linens, pots, brooms, stacks of wood for the stoves, as well as eight large copper tubs for bathing. At the end, a door opened onto the entrance hall of the villa. There, the housekeeper allowed Elske to look into the two reception rooms, one for the Varinne when she had callers, the other for the Var to conduct his business. She pointed out the room in which the Var and his family dined, and the large dining room where the Var entertained. There was also a ballroom, the walls hung with beryl glass, which in daylight made it as bright as outdoors. At the foot of the broad staircase that rose up from the back of the great hall, the housekeeper told

Elske, "Under no circumstances will you ever go up into the family's private apartments."

"Yes, Missus," Elske said, having no desire to ascend. The housekeeper, satisfied, opened a door beside the staircase, to allow Elske a brief glance into a room smaller than any of the others she had been shown. This room had windows that opened onto the front gardens of the villa. There were maps spread out on a table at the center and books standing in rows on the shelves. "Sometimes the Adelinnes like to read," the housekeeper said, "although what care *she* might take of the Master's books, I don't like to think. That will be your responsibility, Elske. Also, her mischiefs and even crimes will be on your head." Then, giving Elske no chance to protest, she opened a door into the wing opposite the kitchen wing. "These are your apartments."

Here the hallway had broad wooden floors and polished wooden walls; it was lit by candles in wall sconces. One doorway, of dark carved wood, opened off to the left, and that was a small anteroom with the bedchamber beyond. The bedchamber had a waist-high row of windows, the sills deep enough to sit on, a stove with its bucket of wood beside it, a table, a cupboard fitted into the wall, a chest, a chair with arms and a small stool, as well as a high bed, the four posts of which were draped around with a heavy cloth. A beryl glass hung in a thick gold frame, and a bowl of flowers was set out on the table. All was in readiness.

The anteroom was where Elske would sleep, the house-keeper explained, on a pallet that was now rolled up, and Elske could just set her pack down here.

Across the hallway was a privy room, and at its end a reception room furnished for dining. "She, of course, does not bring her own servant, so you must also wait on her at table. The meals will be brought to you, and if she requests any particular delicacy, you may send word to me. Also, the Adelinne may take exercise on the villa grounds. Can you remember all that?"

"Yes, Missus," Elske said, keeping all expression from her voice and face. If she could not remember such simple instructions, she would be a sorry creature.

"The Adeliers will start arriving any day now, but until then—what use are you?" the housekeeper demanded and said, without waiting for Elske's answer, "The washroom always needs an extra hand. You can work there until your Fiendly Princess arrives. Well, she was little more than a child the last time they sent her here to find a husband, perhaps the years have improved her, although they say she was the demon imp himself."

"Yes, Missus." Almost, Elske was eager to meet this troublesome Adelinne.

ELSKE'S TWO COMPANIONS IN THE washroom were farmers' daughters, come to the city to try their chance at marriage and pleased to be servants in the High Councillor's villa, where any man who wished to court them would know their superior status. At first they mistrusted Elske. "You've the look of a house servant. Soft."

"But I'm not," Elske protested, and later they admitted, "You're stronger than you look." They became more at ease with her, and told her what they knew about service to the Adeliers. "You'll take meals with your Adelinne, unless you're accompanying her to an Assembly, or to a ball. Or a feast, sometimes there are feasts," they reminded each other, and advised Elske, "You'd better make good use of the winter because afterwards—everyone says, everybody knows—the girls who are maidservants for Adelinnes have been ruined."

"Raped?" Elske asked, and they covered their mouths, muffling their laughter.

"What do you think of Trastad, if you think that? Where did you come from to think such a thing? No, those who serve the Adelinnes are spoiled for other employments, because they have developed a taste for rich food and wines, and entertainments, for the company of people of higher station. No house will hire them, afterwards. They go to the inns and taverns, to work there, and that's the end of their hopes."

"Hopes for what?"

"For a husband, and children of their own. What else

should a girl hope for? Although, I've heard of maidservants going off with their mistresses, but I wouldn't want to do that. Who is anything other than a Trastader, I pity that man or woman."

"But even if he's a Trastader," the other said, "I'd never marry a herder, however great his flock."

"No, nor any man who goes off to work in the mines, and not a fisherman, neither—for those too often never come home again."

"And when they do, they smell of—"

"Oh, agreed, agreed. I'd never wish—"

"A clean, well-mannered house servant would do me very well."

"Nor a sailor, neither. Unless he already owned a house of his own where I might live should his ship be lost."

"A house servant looks to his wife's comforts."

Elske took her meals alone in the apartment her Fiendly Princess would occupy, and slept on her pallet in the ante-chamber. Often, she stood at the bedchamber window, leaning her elbows on the deep sill, looking out to where the river ran, silvery in a dawning light, black under the stars. As best she could, in her secluded position, she was considering how she might secure further choices, and what they might be—once this, her first free choice, had played itself out.

And then, one morning, she was summoned from the

washrooms and presented by the housekeeper with two new dresses, and new stockings also, and a pair of soft leather boots. "The ship's in port, and she's on it, and all the others are arriving, too. Well, if she wants a more richly dressed maidservant, she'll have to see to you herself. Don't fail us, Elske."

Elske spent that afternoon awaiting her mistress's arrival, but no one came. The next morning a small sea chest arrived, and a heavy trunk. Elske shook out the Adelinne's dresses, and hung them in the dry, clean air of the washroom to freshen them. She placed on the cupboard shelves the shifts and stockings, underskirts and the cloths for the Adelinne's monthly bleedings. This Princess had clothing that was no more plentiful than Var Jerrol's daughters, and no finer, either. This Princess also had hidden among her shifts a sharp dagger, its blade as long as Elske's hand and its hilt iron, worked into the forms of a bird and a bear—the bear on its hind legs, the bird with its wings outstretched— one on each side, and each rounded to make a firm grip easy. It was not a rich weapon, but it was well-made, and well-honed. Elske hid it away again, back among the folded shifts.

Elske waited alone in the apartments all that second day, too, and still no one came. Most of the time she watched out of the window. Only sheep moved about on the wide lawns. Little boats, some small enough to require only a pair of oars to move them, some with a single red sail raised on the short mast, moved along the river. She began to think that perhaps the Adelinne would never arrive, but deep in the second night there came a pounding at the chamber door. Elske leapt up out of her sleep.

The door opened and the housekeeper stood there, a candle in her hand, a scarf around her shoulders, her grey hair loose. "Well, they've found her," she said to Elske. "She thought she'd be able to have her own way loose in the city, but Trastaders have good noses to smell out foreigners." Then turning from Elske she said, "Come here, my fine Lady. Step forward. You'll have to sleep in your filth, for I'm not asking any of my girls to heat bathwater at this hour. Get"— with a shove against the back of the tall young woman—"in now. There. This is your maidservant."

The young woman walked into the room without a glance at Elske, as slow and unconcerned as if she was not the object of the housekeeper's scorn and irritation.

One of the servants gave his candle to Elske, who took it without a word. The door was shut, again.

Elske turned to greet her mistress.

Behind her, a key turned in the lock.

CHAPTER 8

THE YOUNG WOMAN GLARED AT the thick wooden door, as if she were devising suitable punishment for its misconduct. Her long, hooded cloak had a thick band of mud at its hem, and the boots that showed under the cloak were equally travel worn. She was tall, and seemed taller when she drew herself up and let the hood fall back. Her long brown hair hung tangled. She had a pale, oval face, with a long straight nose and wide mouth; her forehead wrinkled as she drew her dark eyebrows together in vexation. She was two or three winters the older, or so it seemed to Elske.

The Adelinne stood with her shoulders high, as if she faced an enemy, not a locked door. She unfastened the clasps at the neck of her cloak and let it fall to the floor behind her, as she turned to move through the narrow doorway from Elske's anteroom into her own unlit bedchamber.

Elske had seen Volkaric women in a fury of vengeance;

she had seen furies of fear and sorrow in the women of Trastad; but this Adelinne was not furious as a woman is. Hers was an imperious anger, firm, steady; you could warm your hands at it. Elske picked up the cloak and hung it on a peg—first it must dry out, and then she would brush it clean. The heavy woven wool, dyed dark blue, the smooth blue lining—these were rich cloths, although this was not a cloak made for harsh winter.

Elske heard the chest being opened, then its lid dropped down, impatiently. She heard the cupboard doors creak apart, and a rustle of fabric, and more rustling. Then the Adelinne spoke, her voice curling out of the doorway. "Enter to me," the voice said, in clumsy Norther.

Elske obeyed.

The Adelinne had lit the oil lamps and now she stood at the window, looking out at the darkness. She had changed into one of the heavy nightdresses Elske had folded away and she spoke without turning to look at her servant. "My travel dress—those—you must wash."

Elske gathered the dress, the underskirts and the shifts up in her arms. "Yes, Missus," she said.

At that, the Adelinne spun around, and Elske saw that her eyes were blue, the color of the sea under a clear sky, a deep, bright blue.

"Say me 'my Lady,'" the Adelinne said, pointing at her own chest whenever she said "my Lady." "Yes, my Lady. This you say to me. What I speak, do you hear it?" she asked.

"Yes, my Lady," Elske answered.

"There is—to eat?" She gestured at her mouth with her fingers.

"No, my Lady," Elske said.

"They"—her hand reached out and rotated—"keyed me."

This wasn't a question, and Elske didn't know if she was supposed to answer, or not.

"These dolts and dimwits. She doesn't wonder why we should be prisoners," the Adelinne muttered to herself in Souther, her voice quick in her own tongue, as quick as song. Then in Norther she said, "I am sleeping hungry. You not rest here." She pointed to the floor. "Not to sleep next me." She added in Souther, "So your spying will have to be confined to the daylight hours."

"I am not a spy," Elske answered in that same tongue.

The Adelinne stood absolutely still, her hands quiet in front of her. The blue eyes were fixed on Elske. "And a liar, too."

Elske's spirit rose to meet that scornful glance. If the Adelinne thought that Elske could be bullied by a false accusation then she had a surprise waiting for her, like those foolish Adels and their pretty-faced captain. Elske's eyes rose to meet the Adelinne's and she saw, with an unspoken breath of her own surprise—"Oh!"—that the young woman would welcome a battle. She explained, "If I were here for that use, my old master, Var Jerrol, would have told me what to listen for, and how I would report my information to him. Var Jerrol is the eyes and ears of the Council," she explained. "My Lady."

"Why should they have given you to me, when you know my language, unless to know my thoughts? But what should they hope a spy to tell them of me? They starve me into confusion," the Adelinne said, and ordered, "Take those dirty clothes out of this chamber, then return to me. I don't understand, and you will not sleep until I do."

Elske obeyed. She was not at all sleepy, and she was curious, too, to know how the Adelinne would seek out understanding. When she returned her mistress seated herself in the chair and challenged Elske to show her skills as a hairdresser by combing out the knots and tangles in her hair. "It's been more than a day since I've put food into my mouth," the Adelinne told her. "I've drunk from public fountains, but that's not like good bread and meat in the belly. Nor strong wine, either."

"No, my Lady," Elske agreed.

"You'll be useful to me, to teach me Norther," the Adelinne said, and admitted, "I think you know why they have locked me in." And Elske answered, "You are that same Adelinne who stayed out on the ship's deck during the great storm two years back. Disobedient, they said. They complained that you ran away. You are the Fiendly Princess."

The Adelinne answered her quickly. "Not a Princess, a Queen. I am the Queen that will be. Or ought to be, if I can keep them from exiling me, which is their plan. Marrying me off to some poltroon pip-squeak princeling from some distant land—that's their hope. They wish to be rid of me and they think that if I am out of the Kingdom they can crown my brother. And Guerric thinks he can rule. . . . So, I am called the Fiendly Princess?" the Adelinne asked, not displeased. "And what do they call you?"

"Elske."

"Elske. And you were a servant of this Var Jerrol? This eyes and ears of the Council, you were his spy?"

"Since I speak Souther," Elske explained. "I could tell him how the merchants hoped to cheat him, in trade, or what they said about the black powder. I knew what they spoke of when they thought they couldn't be understood, when I served his guests at table."

The Adelinne turned her head at this, to look up over her shoulder at her servant. "What do you know of this black powder?" but this question Elske chose not to answer. She met the blue eyes with her own grey glance.

The Adelinne looked long at her, then said, "I will ask again later. When you know me. When you know it is safe to answer me truthfully," she said.

Elske didn't doubt that time to come. There was in this Fiendly Princess something to which Elske's spirit answered.

The Adelinne went on. "The Kingdom lies so far from the world, news comes to us so slowly, we could be lost and taken before we even know that there are the weapons to destroy us." She turned around again and Elske went back to working the comb through the tangles. "I think any man might have this weapon in his hand, and why should not I, too, possess it? I don't wish to be ignorant on the subject of black powder. What were you in Var Jerrol's house, besides his spy?"

"I was nursery maid to his three daughters. After the Var remarried, it was better that I leave his house. Once the Var had a bride, his house had no need of me."

The Adelinne turned again to look at Elske full. "You shared his bed?"

"Why would I do that? The Trastaders protect women from ruin. Women are dear to the Trastaders."

"Not dear enough to be masters of merchant houses, Elske, not even the widows. Nor of inns, nor of ships, not even in the market stalls, and never dear enough to sit on the Council," the Adelinne answered. "And that's too dear a dear for my purse. You were not the Var's bedmate, then. Nor any other man's?"

"No, my Lady." Elske patiently worked the comb through and through the tangles, until her mistress's nut brown hair hung smooth down her back.

"A pity, that. But it can't be helped. What skills do you have? Besides a gentle hand on the comb."

Elske could only answer everything she knew, since she didn't know why the Council had placed her with this Adelinne. "I speak both Souther and Norther. I read and write in both tongues. I can figure with numbers. I know how to care for babies, and children, and something about cooking. I can snare small animals and skin prey of any size, dig over soil, plant it and harvest a crop. I can serve at table," she said. She thought of her most recent experiences. "I can launder clothing. I can mend with a needle and thread."

"And do you know the streets of the city?"

"Of the two other islands, yes, Old Trastad and Harboring. Logisle is not familiar, but I think I might be lost anywhere on three-islanded Trastad and find my way."

"I *will* know their use for you," her mistress warned her, but promised, "And so will you. Braid my hair. Maybe you will do well for me, as my maidservant. But tell your masters, I will look through you like glass and see their plans, let them imprison and starve me as much as they will. You will be a window for me to see through to their intentions."

"I am not glass," Elske said, "and I don't know how to be such, not even for you, my Lady. If that is what you require in your maidservant, perhaps you should ask for another. I can help you in other things, as in teaching you their language, or perhaps finding food, but—at most I can be your beryl glass, and that cannot be seen through."

Something in Elske's words caused the girl to smile, some secret mischief amused her, and she rose to look at herself in the room's beryl glass, as if that would hide her from Elske. Seeing herself, her mouth set firm. "I'll not be forced to any husband," she said, whether to herself or to Elske, Elske didn't know, although she spoke as if Elske had thought to contradict her. "Who thinks he can force me will pay with his own blood for that. Sooner or later, he'll pay. I can be patient," she said, thoughtfully. Then she demanded, "You said food? You've food hidden here? You have a friend to let us out?"

"If I go out the window—I was only outside the once, the day I was brought here, but I saw kitchen gardens, or I think they might have been."

"I want bread and meat, and wine."

"I saw trees, so perhaps there might be apples."

"Only apples? But I need sustenance," the Adelinne protested. Then she surrendered. "Bring me my cloak. I'm going with you."

"I think, better not, my Lady."

The Adelinne drew herself up, her shoulders high and proud. "You say no to me?"

Elske explained it. "If I can't climb back in, and they find me outside in the morning, then that is one kind of disobedience, which they may punish. But if you're out—and it's you they've locked into her room, for they never locked me in while I have been alone here—then they may take stronger measures against you. If you've already once been lost to them—"

At this, the Adelinne smiled again. "As I have." Then she frowned again. "You will do this," she determined. "You will go out the window and immediately climb back in. If you can do it then so can I. My cloak is clothing enough for night. Do it," the Adelinne ordered.

Elske obeyed, fetching in both cloaks, pulling on her fur boots.

The bedchamber's narrow windows opened outwards. Standing sideways, Elske could easily slip through. She opened a window and climbed up onto the deep sill, and looked out.

It was a lightless night, with the moon at half and behind clouds, the stars hidden, too. The dark air breathed a great silence, over all the grounds of the villa. Elske stood on the windowsill, listening to the darkness. On this windless night, the river greeted the land with little watery sounds.

"Go. Now, Elske."

Elske sat down on the broad stone sill. Her feet did not touch ground. She couldn't remember how high these windows were, so rather than jump, she rolled over onto her stomach and slowly lowered herself. Almost immediately she felt solid land underfoot. Her shoulders and head reached above the open window.

"Well? Can you get back in?"

Elske reached her arms up and over the sill, and pulled

her weight up. Her boots scratched at the wall for purchase and she found she could thus push her body up, to scramble back onto the sill, so she dropped back onto the ground.

With a grunt the Adelinne dropped down beside her, then said, "Wait for my eyes."

Elske waited. The air had an edge to it, a knife blade edge of cold.

"What's that?" the Adelinne demanded at her ear.

"What, my Lady?"

"That sound, like—is there a river here? Is it the sea?"

"The river. The High Councillor lives on Logisle, the inmost island, and his villa lies on the riverside. By daylight—"

"Are there boats? Does he keep boats here?"

"Yes, little—"

"Then I could go home," she said, her voice in the darkness filled with longing. "Oh, Elske—" the Adelinne said, and then her voice changed and she said, "A small boat would never survive the open waters, I know that as well as any other fool. When you report to them what I say, tell them I know that I can't run away by sea."

"Why would I tell them anything you say?" Elske asked.

"Why, indeed?"

"And why would the Council want to know what you say?"

"As to that, they're employed to keep me here by those who wish to keep my throne from me, and so they are my enemies."

"The Council employs me but they don't own my choices," Elske said, understanding now. "Might not they be so employed by your enemies?"

"I cannot think," the Adelinne said. "I must get food. Hunger and judgement don't harness well together."

"This way, my Lady," Elske said and moved off, but "Am I to follow you?" the Adelinne demanded. "When I know the way," Elske said, and the Adelinne announced, "I know my own way." But she let Elske lead.

The blank, dark face of the house showed no light other than their own windows. Elske moved swiftly back around to where she remembered the kitchen gardens. In the dark, the villa seemed longer, taller than she remembered, the kitchen wing farther from her own than she would have guessed. Beyond the kitchen entrance she came upon the low stone wall that edged the gardens. The Adelinne started to enter the garden but Elske held her back.

She pulled herself loose.

"Farthest in that direction," Elske pointed, "are trees. I think they may have apples on them. What lies in here, and where, I don't know." She kept her voice low, as muffled as the night sky.

The Adelinne answered at the same pitch, but angry. "Do you think I complain of hunger because I am soft with having been waited upon?"

"No, my Lady," Elske answered. "I don't think you are

119

soft. Nor do I think you have been much waited upon." She waited for an angry expostulation, but it did not come.

"Well?" the Adelinne asked.

"I will go down for apples if you gather what you can find here."

This they did. Elske went on to blindly reach fruit down from low branches, then she returned to where they had separated, to wait until the Adelinne found her. Night lay over them as undisturbed as a heavy robe as they crept back along the side of the villa until the light guided them back to the opened window. Her mistress stepped up on Elske's cupped hands to make an easy ascent back into the chamber. Elske clambered after her.

Her mistress had tied her cloak up around its burden of plump onions. She bent to untie it while Elske pulled the window closed.

"Were there apples?" The Adelinne held a hand out, and when Elske gave her one, she bit into it. With the apple held in her teeth, she shrugged off her cloak and went to the cupboard, from which she took the dagger Elske had hidden there. "I'll have two of the onions," she said. "And you? What do you want?"

Elske added one onion for herself, out of curiosity. With the onions, her mistress threaded two of the apples onto her dagger, which she held into the flames of the open stove. As they heated, their skin blistered and blackened, and then it split. A liquid, clear and sweet-smelling, like the blood of the apple, oozed through the split skins. The onions, too, bled so. The chamber air was perfumed with the smells of cooking onions and apples.

They ate gingerly, so as not to burn their fingers, and without speaking. The stove consumed whatever they did not—the thick papery outer layers of onions, the cores of the apples. "Better," the Adelinne said, and said no more. She merely went across to the privy and returned, to climb up onto her bed.

Elske picked up the cloak from the floor and placed the uneaten apples and onions into the cupboard. She had never expected to be locked in, and she couldn't guess how long it would be before they were released. Furthermore, she had never seen Var Vladislav, or spoken with him, so she had no idea how he planned to deal with this willful Adelinne. They two might well spend the whole Courting Winter locked into these rooms together.

Elske thought, she could be in worse company, for a winter's imprisonment. She blew out the flames of the oil lamps.

The Adelinne's voice spoke out of darkness. "I sleep behind closed doors."

Elske pulled the door closed behind her and returned to her own pallet for what was left of the night.

There were no windows in Elske's antechamber, and so

she did not know what hour of the night, or morning, it was when she was wakened by the sound of a key turning in the lock. No other sound followed, so she returned to her slumbers. How long after that it was that the door was opened and one of the kitchen maids set a tray on the floor, Elske couldn't say.

The tray was covered with a white cloth. Under the cloth were two bowls of porridge, with spoons, a platter of bread and cheese, and two cups of ale. Honey made a sweet pool at the center of each of the bowls of porridge.

Elske pulled on her dress and then looked out into the hall, where the light showed her that morning was well begun. When she returned from the privy, she saw that a jug of water and a bowl had been set down beside the tray. The water was warmed, for washing. There had been no summons nor sound from beyond the bedchamber door, but the wooden door was so heavy and the villa walls so thick that Elske was not sure she would have heard any sound her mistress might have made.

She pushed open the door. A still mound lay on the bed. The fire in the stove had burned out and an early morning chill lingered in the room. Elske slipped into the chamber and took chunks of wood from the basket, opened the door and laid them on the glowing ashes. She blew into the heart of the fire until smoke rose in thin wisps. She closed the stove again.

Turning, she saw that the still figure had not moved.

Outside, beyond the windows, beyond the grass on which sheep grazed, the river was flowing, and beyond that she saw the mainland shore, where forests stretched back endlessly.

"Leave me," ordered a voice behind her.

Before drawing the door closed behind her, Elske said, "There is a tray here, with food, when you wish it, my Lady."

It wasn't long before the door opened and the Adelinne stood in it, her wrapper tied at the waist, in stocking feet, her face expressionless. "The chamber pot is ready. You may bring in the tray," she said, and withdrew to sit at her table beneath the windows. Elske brought in the tray, and uncovered it. She removed the chamber pot and emptied it into the privy, then returned for whatever service might next be required.

Her mistress ate hungrily, spoonfuls of porridge. She drank at the cup of ale, took a chunk of bread and finally asked impatiently, "Do you expect to be asked to sit down with me?" She thrust the second bowl of porridge into Elske's hands. "Do you need to be *told* to eat? What do you expect?"

"I don't know what to expect, my Lady."

The dark blue eyes studied her suspiciously. "I can tell you to expect no coins of me. My purse is empty. Have you never served an Adelier before?"

"No, my Lady."

"Eat, then, Elske, and trust me to instruct you how to

serve me to my satisfaction. And I don't mind admitting that you have thus far proved satisfactory."

Elske smiled to hear that, for if she had a choice of masters this Adelinne would be the one she chose.

"Of course," her mistress went on, "good beginnings can lead to bad ends. But today, I will walk out and you will accompany me. While Adelinnes are usually taken out only for display, to flirt and attract, we *are* permitted exercise in good weather. When there are entertainments, Assemblies, and dances, you must accompany me." She watched Elske's face, as if it were a page of words she was puzzling out. "As my maidservant, you eat what I eat, and when we dine, we dine alone. At feasts, you serve me and do not eat. You may have the bathwater when I am done. Now, you may sit on the stool, and eat your porridge," her mistress told her, and Elske obeyed.

Her mistress remained lost in thought for some time.

Then, "When you return this tray to the kitchen, tell them: I will bathe this evening. Also tell them: I require wine with my midday meal, and tell them also that I have no coins in my purse."

"Why should they know anything of your purse?" Elske wondered.

"Because those who serve the Adeliers expect coins for every service. But my gold is already spent, and much besides, too."

Elske protested. "I don't wish to tell them that, my Lady, for your sake. These are proud servants, for this is the house of the High Councillor—"

"Servants too proud to take coins?" Her mistress was doubtful.

"Too proud to ask for coins," Elske said, "and also ashamed not to be given them. It is better to tell them nothing of your purse; they will assume that your purse is fat and it will be only a matter of time before you fill theirs, when we come to the end of the Courting Winter."

"You presume to advise me?"

"Why should you wish the house servants to neglect you?"

"You presume to know better than I how to deal with servants?"

"Yes, my Lady, since I know them a little and you know them not at all."

The Adelinne stood up then. "I think I know now why they chose you for me. They think your disobedience will be their revenge on me. But understand this, Elske: I will be obeyed. I will not keep my pennilessness a secret, as if I were ashamed. Any person who serves me, and any man who courts me—which is unlikely, since they send me dowerless to Trastad—will take me for myself alone. I offer nothing more."

"Yes, my Lady," Elske said. The Volkaric would not wear

their pride on that shoulder, but that didn't mean they went naked of pride. She picked up the tray.

"All the same," her mistress said, now, "I will ask you *not* to tell them in the kitchen that my purse is empty."

In the cook room, Elske delivered her Lady's instructions.

"She wants wine, is it? And a bath? She's realized how soft a bed she's sleeping in, and quickly, too, hasn't she? It didn't take long for her to show us her true colors, this Fiendly Princess. You'll soon be wishing yourself back in the peace and quiet of the laundry room, Elske."

Elske did not think so, but said nothing. "Will more Adelinnes come to this house?" she asked, and they told her that for the High Councillor to take in even one was unusual. So Elske asked when the Assemblies would begin, and was told, "All in good time, tell her. Tell Lady Impatience that."

"She will walk outside today."

"You must be with her at all times, especially such a one as she. If we were to send her back ruined to her home, other fathers might keep their daughters from us, and there would be no Courting Winters in Trastad, and then where would we find the gold to pay the Emperor's tribute? She is in your keeping, Elske, and if harm comes to her, you are for the cells."

"Why should harm come to her?" Elske asked, and the other servants exchanged knowing looks.

"She is the kind of Adelinne who puts herself in harm's way. She does not behave as a Princess ought."

"Because she is a Queen," Elske explained.

"And I am the Emperor's daughter," they laughed.

Elske returned to her mistress's bedchamber, where she was told, "Fetch my cloak. I am restless."

The proper way to the outside was through the dining chamber, a door that opened onto the lawns they saw from the windows. Outside, a wind blew, but not ungently, and her mistress instructed, "You will follow me."

"Yes, my Lady," Elske answered and fell into step behind her mistress, but the Adelinne said, "You must keep close enough that we can speak," and Elske stepped obediently up to her mistress's shoulder, remaining just a little behind.

They walked towards the river, where on this morning two boats were tied up at the dock. The Adelinne asked, "Where are you from, Elske? What people? What land? You must be a foreigner, because the Trastaders do not speak Souther."

"I am of the people of the Volkaric," Elske answered, but seeing that the Norther word meant nothing to her mistress, she risked saying, "I am Wolfer."

That halted the Adelinne. She turned to face Elske, placing them face-to-face where they stood between the villa and the river, and no one to overhear their words. The girl looked directly into Elske's face and her eyes shone with the blue of the sea.

"You're the one who split his face open, aren't you? Don't

deny it. Not if it's the truth. It was you, wasn't it? They hid him away, they told tales, but we all knew—and he deserved it, and he was not the only one who needed his vile heart showing on his handsome face. I was but a child two years ago, but if I'd had the chance—and my weapon— Is it true, what he boasted? That he'd had many virgins of Trastad?"

Elske could not answer what the Adel had done except for the time of their meeting, when he had done nothing, she having forestalled him.

"*Was* it you?" her mistress demanded. "Rumor said, it was a man disguised as a maidservant, a Trastader trick to protect their women from the Adels. Rumor said, a girl's brothers had ambushed the Prince, to revenge her ruin, and there was a great skirmish that left many Trastaders wounded. Rumor said, the girl was a Wolfer and she ripped his face in half with her teeth."

Elske could not still the laughter in her throat. "It was only a stone. He was only a coward."

"It *was* you."

"Yes, my Lady." Elske didn't think this Adelinne, this Fiendly Princess, would fear her, or condemn her; and she was right, for at the acknowledgement the Adelinne smiled, a smile like the warmth of a fire on an icy winter's night, as heady as the wine-rich autumn air they breathed. "It was *you*. I never thought I'd meet you, and now I have. You gave me courage, two years ago, Elske, and since then, too. I wished to be you, when I didn't even know your name."

The Adelinne reached her hands out from under the cloak she wore, and removed the gloves she wore. She held her right hand out to Elske, as if they were two merchants closing on a sale, and she bowed her head to Elske, as if they were two swordsmen ending a match, and she looked Elske in the eye, as if they were Wolfer captains, about to risk their lives in battle. The girl took Elske's naked hand in hers and said, "I give you greeting, Elske. I am Beriel, who will be Queen in the Kingdom."

CHAPTER 9

T HE TWO WALKED ON, DOWN to the river's edge, Elske once again at her mistress's shoulder, close enough for speech. In appearances, nothing had changed; but the Adelinne had given Elske her name, and so everything had changed.

"Beriel," Elske said, "the Queen that will be." There was no question about that. Every word the Lady Beriel uttered, and the manner of her speaking, every gesture of her hands and turning of her body, were those of a Queen. Elske knew this, although the Volkking like the rest of his people having no wife, the Volkaric had no Queen. In the Lady Beriel's high-shouldered way of standing and her refusal to give way, Elske could see what a Queen must be.

At the river's edge the soil was moist and the grass grew thick. A salty wind blew against their faces, from the south and the sea. These drew Beriel's thoughts in their direction, for next she said, "I *could* take one of these little boats, if I never ventured far from shore. Perhaps. If there were no storm. I'd know Pericol from the water and if I had coins in my purse, I could pay my way through Pericol. Although, it's never sure what gold will do, when you offer bribes to thieves and pirates," she said.

"I have coins," Elske offered, for she did. Var Kenric had given her some, in gratitude, and Var Jerrol had paid her a servant's wages; she kept them hidden in her Wolfer boots. "You might take them."

"I will not give over my land," Beriel said, not hearing Elske's words. "In the north of my Kingdom, the forests stretch up the mountainsides, like dark waves running up snowy sands. That country yields up not only timber but also iron, and there is silver, too, buried deep in the mountains. There are lakes in my northern lands, as full of fish as the sea. A great river runs through the Kingdom, with water as good as wine to drink, and to lie in that river, to swim through it, is as if sleeping through a dreamless night. Can you swim, Elske?"

"Swim?"

"I will show you. The fishermen taught me when I was a girl, before my nurse discovered us, and you also must know it. In the south, the soil is black and rich. In the south, all autumn long, apples sweeten on the trees—"

"I never had an apple until I left the Volkaric."

"I am afraid I will never see my land again, Elske."

"Why should you not? If you wed no Adel, and you are the Queen that will be?"

"You know nothing," Beriel said then, swinging around to face Elske in a Queen's quick fury. "But I promise you this, I would fight to the death to keep my throne."

Elske wondered, "Why should you not become Queen, if it is your throne?"

"Because they will bring me down, if they can. If they have not already. Speak no more of it," Beriel commanded.

Now they walked along the river's edge, far from the broad front of the villa. Beriel seemed lost in thought from which she would sometimes emerge to ask a question. She asked about the wealth of Trastad and Elske told what she knew. Beriel asked about the tribute paid by Trastad to the Emperor, but Elske knew little of this. "Who is this Emperor?" she asked in return, so Beriel told her, "He rules the east. They say he is as tall as three men, and he never sleeps. They say he makes caskets of the bones of those his armies have slain, to hold his riches. The story goes that he traded his daughter to an alchemist in exchange for the formula for black powder. But nobody has seen this Emperor, and his lands lie so far away even the great ships of Trastad have never crossed the distance, so I don't lose sleep over him," Beriel said.

"Could a man be as tall as three men together?" Elske

asked, for if this were false, then all the rest was doubtful.

"Are you a simple after all?" Beriel asked, but gave no time for an answer.

This young mistress was like none of the women of Trastad, nor of the Volkaric, either, for all that she was as protected as the one and as fierce as the other. Elske thought, walking at Beriel's shoulder, that if she were a man, and there were battle, she would rather ride to her death for this Lady than for the Volkking, whose terrible revenges earned him obedience. She would rather face danger for Beriel than for Trastader coins.

Elske also thought it strange that Beriel could be forced to the Courting Winter, and a second time, too; and she wondered by what means her mistress had been made obedient.

That question was answered in the quiet evening, when the maidservants had brought in the copper tub for a bath, and given Elske the jug of scented oil to sweeten the hot water they carried in, one following the other, steam rising out of the top of their buckets. When Beriel—her brown hair loose for washing—stepped out of her shift and lifted a foot to step up onto the footstool, Elske saw that the Adelinne was belly-swollen with child.

Beriel, naked and proud, glared at Elske.

As she soaped the long, thick hair, and poured jugs of rinsing water through it, Elske understood that Beriel must find a husband to marry, and before the Longest Night, too, for she must be near four moons from her time; if this was the first child she carried, when a woman showed latest and least, she might be nearer. So perhaps she was three moons from the birth?

Beriel leaned forward and Elske poured rinsing water, which fell over her head and down her slim shoulders.

But Elske had never heard of marriages performed among the Adeliers while they were still in Trastad.

"I will wash myself," Beriel said.

When Beriel sat in her chair by a stove so warm that the occasional drops of water sizzled on its tiles, she told Elske to bathe before calling the maidservants to empty and carry away the tub. Elske obeyed, slipping out of her dress and stockings and shift to climb into the tub, and sit there in its failing warmth before taking up the cloth and soap.

Beriel watched this, whether Elske permitted it or not.

"Is it a crime among the Wolfers when a girl has a child before she has a husband, then?" Beriel demanded. "Are such women punished?"

"No, for women—"

"Do they exile them? Execute them? In the Kingdom, a royal Princess is so punished. The people do not have so strict a law over them as do the Lords, and the Lords run with a lighter rein than do the members of the royal family. What are you going to do now, Elske?"

"Soap my hair, my Lady."

"No, about me. What will you do about me? My shame is yours, when you serve me and I carry shame with the child, for all that the real shame is someone else's."

When Elske had finished, she climbed out and dried herself on her underskirts. Beriel by then had covered herself with her night shift. "Then there must be no child," Elske said. It seemed simple enough.

"You know how to rid me of it?" Beriel's face was transformed by relief. "Have I wasted all of my coins, and two gold chains and a silver bracelet, too, and the medallion of my mother's house, given to me by my grandfather—? Have I gone skulking around this islanded city, looking to rid myself of this burden in my belly, have I slept cold and hungry and unguarded—? And all the time you were waiting here for me? What do I do? Drink something? Is it a potion? Is there danger it will kill me? Don't worry, I'll drink it, but I'd rather know those dangers I face. Or do you reach inside me, to—?"

Elske understood. "Ah, no, my Lady—"

"I should have guessed that the Wolfers—"

"My Lady, I mean when you have birthed it."

Beriel withdrew back into a cold pride. "You said, 'There must be no child.' And I believed you, and now I am betrayed."

"My Lady, I don't betray you. A woman can give birth and still have no child on her breast."

"Ah." Beriel nodded her head several times. "I see. But how will you do this, Elske?"

Elske had no answer ready. "Give me time to consider," she asked.

"Take all the time you like," Beriel granted it, almost gaily, "so long as you are ready when I need you." But then she covered her face with her hands, as if to hide from her own thoughts. "But if I must birth it, where will I go to hide until it comes? I think I *am* lost."

Elske asked, "Why should you hide yourself away? It is winter and your gowns are heavy. When I have altered the waists, the child will be hidden under the high, full skirts."

Beriel uncovered her face, to consider this. She looked down at her belly under the heavy nightgown, and nodded. "Perhaps. Perhaps I may go undiscovered. If I do, and if I live, I'll have revenge," she said then. "My brother, who led them to me, my cousins, who raped me, again and again, until they had filled my belly—"

"Why should they wish to ruin you?" Elske wondered.

If the sea could hold flame, that would have been the color of Beriel's eyes. "Because I am the Queen that will be. And my brother—he is the King that wishes to be, although I am the firstborn, and thus named royal heir, by law. But I am also the first female to claim my inheritance through this law. Years before, with my mother's birth, came a new law that a female might inherit her father's domain if she were first-born. But my mother gave up her own claim to her Earldom to marry my father, the King. Neither she nor my father now wish me crowned—despite the law, despite the word of the Priests and the will of my people, despite my own worth and my brother Guerric's base nature. If they have their way, I will be wed into another country; and now if I do not cooperate in that, then I will be driven from my rightful place by the shame my brother has placed on me. If I live, whatever else, I will return to take these cousins, and this brother, too, if I can lay hands on him, and I will feed them black powder until their bellies are swollen with it, and I will put their heads into the fire so they breathe in flame."

She stared at the dark window.

"I'll have them screaming, swearing they never meant me ill, begging for mercy. As I never did, when they came at me."

Beriel caught her breath and looked back at Elske, as much like a wolf as a woman. "If I do not die in childbirth." As she said that, Beriel's voice sank.

"Why should you die in childbirth?" Elske asked.

"That is the fortune of women," Beriel announced.

Elske was puzzled. "I have been at many births and but few deaths."

"You know midwifery?" Beriel stared at her, wordless, shook her head as if amazed, and then laughed, as if she were a girl again and not a ruined woman, her belly filled with the child her rapists left in her. Laughter flowed out of her, until she could ask, "Who are you, Elske? What were you, among the Wolfers?"

"I was the Death Maiden," Elske said.

"Which is?" Beriel asked, her voice now quiet, dangerous.

Elske explained how the Volkking journeyed into the land of the dead with his treasures around him and the Death Maiden to answer his needs. "That is a terrible custom," Beriel said, but Elske answered that it was the feeding of infant girls to the wolves that she had learned to think terrible. "The Death Maiden was given food when others went hungry. I was kept clothed and sheltered, for I was good fortune to the Volkking."

"You are ignorant," Beriel told her angrily. "These Wolfers are brutes—albeit straightforward brutes, unlike more civilized men. Oh, but Elske," Beriel said. "Where would I be if Tamara had not saved you?"

RAIN FELL HARD THE NEXT morning so they remained in Beriel's apartments, and Beriel called for needles and threads; for her gowns, she told the housekeeper, had been ill prepared. Elske worked at altering her mistress's clothing and this occupied them until the midday meal. After that, because the rains had stopped, they walked again, following the tall stone wall that hid the High Councillor's villa from the road. Eventually, this wall ran in among a woods and became no higher than Elske's knees. That was what Beriel had been looking for. "That is our way out," she said quietly. "A way out and back in, if we wish it. So we have the road, now, as well as the river, and the window always ready to be opened. Let them think they have me prisoner, when I am not."

That evening, Beriel turned to the matter of Elske's dress. "You must alter, I think, two of my gowns to fit yourself. I'm taller than you are, and you're rounder—except now, of course."

"But I have my own dresses and the Var supplies aprons."

"You don't understand," Beriel told her. "Don't be stupid, Elske, not now. The menservants and maidservants display the wealth of their Adeliers, so a poorly dressed servant bespeaks a poorly filled purse. If I wish to answer any doubts, then my servant must be richly outfitted."

So Elske and Beriel took out her several gowns, one after the other, and selected two for Elske to wear when she waited upon her mistress at the feasts and Assemblies. One of the dresses given to Elske was as red as groundberries, the other as green as the leaves of crawling ivy; the fabric cut off from the hems, to shorten them, would make scarves to wrap her hair. The gowns Beriel kept were blue and golden and wine red; some of them were sewn over with golden threads, so that they glittered in the lamplight. "You'll set me off well," Beriel told Elske, pleased. "My last maidservant was chap-faced and clumsy and I wished to murder her, at least once each day."

Elske was cutting out the stitches that held a skirt to a bodice.

"I have no use for a stupid servant," Beriel said. "Although if I had been more clever myself, I might not be in this pre-dicament. Elske, you must not tell anyone about the child," Beriel said, then. "Whatever I choose to do you must not speak of it. Although I can't even think about what to do. Other than find some boy stupid enough to take me for bride, and take him for my husband. And that will make him King, to gainsay my will, to share my high position, to keep me tamed. What other ways have you thought of, Elske? Have you thought of another way than marriage? Another way than death?"

"I can see two or three," Elske answered.

"You can see," Beriel echoed her. "You are one of those who can always see another way, aren't you? And that's a gift, Elske. Do you know what a great gift it is to see a way through, or past? Although, when it's not your belly or your crown, vision comes easier. But if I am ignorant, must I not also be innocent? Yes, I think I must, and if innocent then guiltless. So can I give the matter over into your hands, Elske?" Beriel asked.

"Yes, my Lady. Of course." Let Beriel choose which way and Elske would then work out a plan of events. "The ways are—"

"Tell me nothing. I wish to know nothing of it," Beriel said. "You must never tell me what you do, Elske. Give me your word on that."

"I give you my word," Elske said, surprised. She had never been asked for her word before. Before, she had not had a word of her own to give.

"No, Elske, this is not so light a thing, your word," Beriel said and stood before Elske, where she sat on the low stool, sewing. Beriel crouched down until their heads were level and reached to put her hand on Elske's shoulder.

"*Swear* to me that, no matter what, you never will reveal to me what has happened to this baby. Swear it," Beriel insisted.

"I swear," said Elske, who had sworn to nothing before in her life.

"Give me your hand on it," Beriel insisted, as she stood up again, and held out her right hand. Elske reached up to put her own hand into her mistress's. "For I know myself," Beriel said. "Whatever I feel now, I know that I will ask you. I will try to persuade you, order you to obey, force you. You must give me your word, for I trust you more than myself in this."

"I promise, my Lady," Elske said, the words rolling up from her heart and out of her throat as heavy as stones.

"THAT LAST COURTING WINTER, YOU would have been no older than I am now," Elske said, on one long evening. She was still at the work of sewing her mistress's gowns. "This is my fifteenth winter, and I am still young for marriage."

Beriel stood by the window, staring out into the darkness, and answered, "It has been days since I've seen boats on the river, and it feels cold enough for ice to form."

"But you had no choice but to return to Trastad, did you?" Elske asked.

"What else could I do? At least, I am far from where I am known, and watched, and hated, and now betrayed by a brother. He has no thought for the people, their labors and well-being. He cares nothing for law, or honor. How can I give my land and people to such a King?"

Elske could not answer this.

"My grandparents wished me Queen," Beriel said. "The Earl and his Lady, those two, and the people, my people: They have backed my claim. I know this, even though I was young when my grandmother died. That is when my grand-father gave me her golden medallion—"

She stopped speaking and turned back to the night.

Elske watched how the white needle slid into the heavy fabric, and came out again, joining skirt to bodice.

"When we are in the city," Beriel said, "as we go about in this Courting Winter, I promise you I'll be watching for a woman. I will know her when I see her, for she took the medallion from me, and promised me help, and although I waited where she told me—waited through the whole night and the next day—she never came back. If I see her, I'll have my medallion back—or she'll wish she'd never gulled me."

Elske stitched.

"The coins and the gold chains were nothing to lose," Beriel said. "But the medallion was put into my hands that I might remember, always, that I am the Queen. And I gave all to that woman. I've been a fool, Elske," Beriel said, turning around and in a fury.

Elske said nothing until she thought to offer again, "I have coins, my Lady, which are yours if you want them."

"You are a fool, too."

"Why should you not take them?" Elske asked.

"You are poor and a servant. It isn't fitting that I should take your coins."

"How can I be poor, when I have coins and no need of them?"

"It's of no matter, anyway," Beriel said. "No man will ask for me, and I wouldn't have any of them anyway. We are all of us here in Trastad because no one in our own lands will have us. So we hope to find marriages where we are not known, except for our faces and our purses." Beriel returned to the window, and said, "I have no purse and my face does not please." She stared back out into darkness.

Elske sewed, and thought about this baby Beriel would have, how it might be gotten rid of without discovery. Death was easiest, as is often the case, but with the river frozen over, the body presented difficulties. The land, too, would be frozen hard, and what did a people do with the bodies of its unwanted babies when there was no wolf pack to feed them to? A babe could be easily killed, by smothering, by a knife thrust, by drowning, strangling, exposure in a winter night, or its neck snapped like a kitten. If the baby must die, to save Beriel, the killing wasn't the problem; but the body presented difficulties.

Then Elske thought of the holes in the ice through which the fishermen pulled their catch, and her eyes filled with tears as she thought of thrusting a small body down into the icy black river.

Elske could begin to understand why the Trastaders cared so much about a woman's ruin; it had to do with these babies. For the Trastaders valued children. It was a deep grief when a child died, and a lasting sorrow when a woman proved barren, as Idelle feared.

Elske sewed on, blindly. In one house a child was desired, in another unwanted; the world worked backwards. But if that was the way of it—and that *was* the way of it—why not move the child from the one place to the other?

"When will your babe be born?" she asked Beriel.

"I don't wish to think of that," Beriel answered.

"Nay, but you must, my Lady. And you must think of bearing the pains silently. The women of the Volkaric give birth with no crying out," Elske told her mistress.

"What any woman can do, I can do," Beriel declared. "Don't doubt my courage. When the time comes—"

"When will that be?" Elske persisted.

"How should I know? I've never had a child before, and my mother would have no reason to tell me. I've heard the servants counting backwards say it takes ten moons to make a baby."

Elske sewed, the needle leading its trail of thread in and out, and the fabric lay heavy and warm as a cloak over her legs.

"It has been eight moons since I had my woman's bleeding," Beriel told her reluctantly. "Or perhaps it's only seven. How could I find time to count the moons, when— I will have those cousins under my heel," she promised Elske, with another swift change in spirits. "I will take my brother by the hair and cut his throat open. My cousins I will drop into the lake, with stones tied to their feet, let them stand beside one another there, and have the skin eaten off of their hands and faces, the eyes eaten out of their skulls. Let them stand together as they stood by my bed." Beriel overmastered her anger then, and rested in the law. "They plotted to bring me down, and that is treason."

Elske sewed, and made her own choice under her own law: The child who would be born she would choose not to kill unless she must.

CHAPTER 10

O N THE DAY OF THE first Assembly a fine, misty snow fell through grey air. Snow dusted the road, and the cloaked shoulders of the young men on horseback. The Adels rode to the Assembly, displaying their horsemanship and their fine trappings, as well as their high-stepping mounts. The Adelinnes rode in covered chairs, each chair carried by a pair of menservants, while the attendant maidservants walked alongside.

Elske wore her wolfskin boots for the long walk from Logisle to the Council Hall; once there she would change them for soft indoor slippers. She wore her second finest dress, the red one, and a head scarf made from the cloth cut off to raise the hem. At this first Assembly, and throughout the Courting Winter, Elske would take her place among the other servants at the back of the hall, to watch over her mistress while Beriel took her pleasure.

"Although what pleasure anyone could take in these . . . Assemblies," Beriel said, spitting the last word out of her mouth as if she had bitten into a wormy apple. "We parade around the great hall saying nothing, although many words are spoken and there is much laughter. Everyone looks everyone else over—it's a horse market, a pig fair, no different. And the Vars watch us, drinking their wine, their greedy eyes counting up all the profit we bring them."

Elske admitted, "I'm curious, to see everything."

"I've already seen everything and everybody—or no one and nothing very different—two years ago," Beriel grumbled. Then she had a cheering thought. "Later, when they think they've got our measure, we'll be allowed to visit the markets, and the shops—to look at furs and feathers, sweet cakes, anything that amuses us, anything they hope to sell to us. We'll be allowed to wander," Beriel remembered. "We'll make our freedom out of that, shall we?"

"If you wish it," Elske agreed. She took a careful look at Beriel. The babe did not reveal its presence, beneath the high waist and full, heavy skirt. Beriel looked in fine health, fat and ripe. Elske had noticed this among the women of the Volkaric, too, towards the end of their child-carrying months; they would bloom out, not like flowers but like ripening foods, plump onions, swollen grains of wheat, and—now that Elske had seen them—round and reddened apples.

Elske entered the hall four paces behind her mistress,

who looked neither to left nor to right, but stepped into the midst of those Adeliers who had already gathered. Elske joined the servants.

The wide hall was as tall as ten men standing on one another's shoulders, and there was a railed balcony to which Adeliers hoping for privacy in conversation could retire. This balcony rested on spiraled wooden pillars, and it was in the cloistered area behind these pillars that the servants gathered. Fir garlands hung around the windows and long tables covered by bright woven cloths were set out with platters of dainties, both sweet and meaty, as well as jugs of mulled apple cider, which mingled its spicy smell with the sharp odor of the greens.

The finely dressed Adeliers, smiling, looking about, talking, moved around the room in a promenade. From the balcony came the music of six lutes played by six men wearing the Council's livery. The Adeliers paraded, and watched themselves parade. The leading merchants of the city took part in this opening promenade, black-garbed figures with the bright ribbons of office across their chests.

A manservant standing close to Elske pointed out the wealthiest Adels and named the Trastader dignitaries; he instructed his fellow servants in their behavior. Servants kept to the background, but as long as they remained back they could move around freely, conversing with whomever they wished, and even—he said, and winked at Elske—make their own matches. He himself, he admitted with a smile for a yellow-haired maidservant standing at his elbow, had been married after the last Courting Winter.

In the hall, Adels and Adelinnes kept arriving and arriving, Princes and Princesses, Counts and Barons, the heirs and heiresses of large fortunes, the distant cousins of great men, until the room grew crowded with the sounds of their voices, and the colors of their clothing.

Elske saw that Beriel kept herself aloof. Sometimes, as they passed, an Adelier might speak to Beriel. She would answer, hold out a hand whether it was a young man or young woman who claimed her attention, then walk on. They would follow her with their eyes.

Beriel walked by putting one foot in front of the other, her hands at her sides. She drank by raising a goblet to her lips, and ate by taking bites. She did nothing extraordinary. Other Adelinnes were more richly clothed, their hair more beautifully dressed, their faces more lovely. Even the Adels wore more jewelry than Beriel, and many of them moved with a more graceful step. And yet, watching, Elske could see how unlike her mistress was to the other Adeliers.

When he spoke from behind her, Var Jerrol used a low voice to tell her, "Don't be alarmed." Then he drew her aside, so that it would be difficult for any of the other servants to hear what they said to one another.

"May we be well met," Var Jerrol said to her. Laughter

lay behind his eyes, although his face expressed boredom. "So the Fiendly Princess doesn't wear you down with her demands?"

Elske waited silently to hear his purpose. Var Jerrol was not a man to spend his attentions without making a profit from them.

"What does she tell you about her homeland?" he asked her. "Could you travel to it, and know how to make your way around in it? What are its riches, has she told you? Its weaknesses?"

Elske chose her answer carefully, to tell nothing false, and answered him, "I know only that her homeland is beautiful to her, and precious."

"She will be Queen there?"

"I think her parents wish her brother to be King," Elske reported, "and so they hope to marry my mistress into a foreign country, whence she can't claim the crown away from him."

"So her claim is good, and thus they fear her," Var Jerrol said. "As I think they might well, now I've seen her for myself. Tell me, Elske, if you know, what she names this land."

"The Kingdom," Elske said.

"And can you also tell me, in the Kingdom, if they have black powder for their wars?"

"She has told me of no wars," Elske answered.

Var Jerrol moved away then, motioning her to follow. He led her among servants and then among the overseeing Vars, keeping her beside him as if she were not a servant. "We'll take cider, shall we? You haven't answered me about the black powder."

They approached one of the food tables and Var Jerrol poured the drink from a jug into a silver goblet, which he gave to Elske, then took another goblet for himself. Elske again made her choice for plain truth. "She has heard talk of the black powder, rumors. She has no more experience of it than I do," she said, and filled her mouth with the flavor of liquid apples.

Var Jerrol's hooded eyes studied Elske. "Do you enjoy life in the High Councillor's villa?"

"How could I not?" Elske asked, wondering what he wished to learn now.

"The food, as I hear, is of rare delicacy."

This was nothing. "My mistress is locked into her chamber at night," Elske said. "There is no need," she said.

"No need," he agreed. "In exchange—for I think your Fiendly Princess will have seen us speaking. She doesn't miss much, I think," Var Jerrol said, as if he had not paraded Elske out for all to see. "If she asks, can you tell her we didn't speak of her?"

"Why should I lie to her?" Elske asked. She had Var Jerrol and he knew it. He opened his mouth as if to answer, then shut it. He looked out over the crowd of Adeliers in their brightly colored gowns and coats, their glittering rings and necklaces, the white arms and necks of the young women, the broad shoulders of the young men.

Elske, easily locating her mistress, saw an Adel approach Beriel to offer her a goblet and gesture with his hand towards a table spread with food. Her mistress took the drink with a sternness of expression that the young man— himself in a fine brocaded jacket, his chest crowded with heavy gold chains—smiled his way through. Seeing the Lady halted, two more young men approached, and she gave them no warmer welcome.

"No, you would not lie, not to your mistress, and not to me, either, would you?" Var Jerrol asked. He already knew the answer, so Elske did not need to say anything. "But I have something for your mistress," he said, his lowered lids hiding his thoughts. Unnoticed in the crowd of Vars, he put a purse into her hand. What it held was round, and flat, much larger than a coin, heavy. Elske could guess what it was.

Elske put the purse strings around one wrist. "The Lady will thank you." She added, then, because she liked the chance to use Var Jerrol for her own purpose, "There were also gold necklaces, and some coins."

"She scattered them around freely, as I hear. As I hear it," he warned Elske, "your mistress was on an urgent errand, her spirits as desperate as her need."

Elske understood him and chose to say, "All will be well."

"When she is in your care, I think it may," he answered carefully, and bowed to the two Adels who approached Elske as the Var moved away from her. The two were bright-eyed with wine, and said to Elske, "We are brothers-in-arms, or we would be, Lady, if there were any enemy you would ask us to defend you from. We come to ask your name, so that when you send for us—"

"Why would I send for you?" She thought they must know from her wrapped hair that she was no Lady. And Var Jerrol must have meant to discomfit her by leaving her with them.

"In your need," said the second merrily. They were both dark-haired, clean-shaven and richly attired. "We would be your knights, and slay your dragons. We would dance and duel for your amusement."

"We would, in short, know your name, Lady," the first spoke again.

"I am Elske, serving maid to the Lady Beriel," Elske told them.

Either the wine interfered with their ability to understand, or they were dumbfounded to hear her deny herself the higher birth. There was a silence, and then they laughed into one another's faces, clapped one another on the shoulder, and stepped back from Elske. "You should be the Lady," the second one said over his shoulder, "and she the serving maid."

Perhaps they didn't recognize a Queen when she walked

among them. Or perhaps they hoped that Elske might prove gullible and be lured by them into her own ruin. But Elske was in no danger from them. She moved back to the rear of the hall and stood among the servants again, her hands clasped behind her to hide the heavy purse.

Before her, the scene spread itself out. The colors of gowns, tights, tunics and coats moved and mixed, like a school of small fishes darting through the water. Oil lamps washed everything with warm light, and the air was filled with music. The high, hopeful voices of the young women melded into the bold and hopeful voices of the young men; and like riverbanks containing and guiding the flow of water, the deeper voices of the Vars could be heard, speaking in their more guttural northern tongue.

Elske stood back against the wall, watching. There was something of the beauty of spring wildflowers in the scene before her, as if the room were a meadow with winds blowing over it, and she followed her mistress's slow journey around and around, among all the Adeliers but never one of them. She saw Beriel turn her head to listen to what one of the Adeliers said to her, courteously attentive. The young man spoke with a graceful gesturing of his hand. He was a pretty fellow, Elske noticed, although he wore no golden chain, nor rings on his fingers, so he was not rich. His light brown hair curled, shining clean, and a smile rested comfortably on his face. He said something that caused Beriel to shake her head at him, although with a slight smile of her own. At that he backed away, bowing; he was not disappointed.

Too soon for Elske, the Assembly was over. Servants brought the cloaks to wrap around the shoulders of the milling Adeliers. The faces of their masters or mistresses— cheeks that were pink with excitement or pale with withheld tears or red with anger—told the servants how to greet them. Beriel's face had no expression, and Elske greeted her with equal dignity.

Outside, snow fell thick on the unswept stone steps, but Beriel didn't hesitate. The steps would be where she wished them to be. Her dainty boots would not slip from under her. Her servant would follow.

When they had returned to Beriel's chambers and a meal of stewed rabbit, Beriel sighed. "There are so many more such occasions to be got through," she said. "It seems forever before I will be done with them."

Then Elske asked, "The Adeliers, the young men especially, what did they say to you, and what did you answer?"

"It was nothing. There was nothing said."

"There were words spoken," Elske argued patiently. "I was watching."

Beriel told her, "They praised my beauty, as if I wished to hear my beauty praised, as if there were nothing but her beauty a woman might wish to speak of. Such words are nothing."

"And you responded . . . ?"

"Oh, I asked, If they thought beauty a thing of substance, If they thought men also had beauty, If they believed that beauty of face predicted beauty of character." Beriel smiled then, as she had not during the Assembly, with pleasure and mischief.

"And they said?" Elske smiled, also.

"They praised my skin, or my hands. My eyes," Beriel added, and then her smile faded. "I, too, was watching. I saw you in conversation with two Adels. This was after the tall Var brought you out among us, and gave you a silver cup. I saw everything," Beriel said, as if she was not pleased to have seen this.

Elske answered with her own mischief, "They might well praise your eyes."

"Yes," Beriel agreed impatiently. "But they might better speak of more germane matters, of their own lands, for example, and how they guard against droughts, famines, fierce winters. If my eyes are blue tonight, they were blue yesterday and it is an old story."

Beriel did not command, so Elske volunteered, "Var Jerrol, the tall Var—"

"He has a snake's eyes."

"He returns this to you, my Lady."

When Elske put the purse into Beriel's hands, her mistress breathed out a long, soft breath. Unaware or unconscious of

Elske, she opened the neck of the purse to slide out onto her palm a thick, golden disk, emblazoned with a wide-winged bird.

Beriel folded her two hands around the disk and brought it up to her heart. She closed her eyes. When she opened them, and looked at Elske, they were as bright and blue as if it were midday in summer, and the sun flecked the dancing sea with gold.

After a time, Beriel returned the disk to its purse. Then Elske told her mistress, "I asked about the chains, and mentioned the coins."

Beriel waved a hand in front of her face, as if waving away a cloud of gnats, to show how little the coins and chains mattered. "He is the eyes and ears of the Council," Beriel said. "What was it he wanted to know from you?"

"He asked if I knew the location of your Kingdom. He asked if you have the black powder there, or know of it."

"Did you tell him?"

"Why should I not tell him what I know?"

This was the same answer Elske had given to Var Jerrol, but Beriel heard it crossly, although, like him, she made no response. After a while, she asked Elske if Var Jerrol knew of her child that was to be born, and Elske answered, "I believe he does."

"Will I be punished? Can you guess his mind? Will he betray my secret to shame me?"

"I told him all would be well and he seemed satisfied," Elske reported. "The door will no longer be locked," she said, seeking to give her mistress some good news.

Beriel rose, then, and went to the window, and looked out. She stood there, with her back to Elske, as if listening to the snow falling; and when she spoke again her voice was low with anger. "I don't need your help. I don't want your help. All I ask from you is to be served as befits my station. Am I making myself clear?" she asked, in deliberate, slow Norther.

"No, my Lady," Elske protested, which displeased Beriel further.

"I don't know why I must put up with such a maidservant," Beriel remarked to the falling snow. "It must be that there are only stupid servants among the Wolfers."

"The Volkaric have no servants," Elske reminded her mistress, not hiding her own displeasure.

"Leave me now," Beriel said.

THEY HAD TO GO TOGETHER to the next evening's entertainment, a dance given by one of the Vars at his villa on Logisle. Before leaving her chambers, Beriel ordered Elske to remain that evening among the servants, and reminded her of the impropriety of any servant responding as an equal to any Adelier. "How these Vars of Trastad behave is up to them, but my maidservant must act as I would, and I do not engage servants in idle talk, as if we were equals."

"But you have no equal, even among the Adeliers," Elske said.

"I won't be flattered!" Beriel cried, openly angry now.

"It's not flattery but truth," Elske argued. "It was what all saw at the Assembly."

For the first time since the previous evening, Beriel looked at Elske with interest. She asked, "What is it that all saw?"

"A Queen," Elske said, "who must stand apart from all others. You might talk with servants, as you do with me—when it suits you—and remain a royal Queen. You might dine at your ease with the Emperor, because you are a Queen."

"Yet you don't fear me."

"Why should I fear you?" Elske asked. "Is it my fear that makes you Queen?"

And Beriel laughed then, but still she maintained, "As my maidservant, you must behave as would the highest servants in the greatest of palaces. Remember your place," she instructed Elske, and Elske agreed to do so. "And do not speak openly to your Var Jerrol," Beriel instructed, but Elske answered, "I like to know his purposes for you, my Lady," and Beriel agreed that she, too, would prefer knowledge to ignorance. "But if you would not discredit me, you *must* remember your place," she warned Elske.

Elske's place that evening was back against the wall that ran the length of a ballroom. She stood with the other servants while the Adeliers danced, in lines and circles, to the music of lutes. Hanging cloths covered the darkness beyond the long, frosty windows. Chandeliers dangled over the dancers, their many candles giving a warm light; candles also burned in their holders in the wall and in many-branched silver candelabra on tables. The polished wood floor gleamed, two large fires burned warmly, and the servants of the villa set out silver goblets of mulled wine and silver trays of sweet pastries for the refreshment of the Adeliers.

Elske spoke to those who stood near her, and watched the Adeliers turn in answer to the music's turns. Beriel never lacked for partners. Adels who joked with other Adelinnes became dignified for Beriel, stood straighter and performed the steps of the dance with more studied grace. Beriel looked about her and was looked at by those about her, unless what her partner said caught her attention; and then she looked into his face so closely that he stepped back, as if in alarm, although he was flushed, too, with the honor of her attention.

A message passed down the line of servants summoned Elske out to the villa's broad entry hall. There, Var Jerrol greeted her. "May we be well met," he said, and handed her a purse lighter than that which he'd brought the previous day. "And what more can you tell me of this Kingdom tonight?"

"Nothing," Elske said. "How should I tell you of the Kingdom, where I've never been?"

"You told her I inquired." He did not ask this but still waited for her answer.

"Of course."

"How did she respond?"

"She was angry."

Satisfied, Var Jerrol sent her back.

As Elske watched, Beriel moved through the measures of the dance, her hand held by her partner as she crossed places with him in the line. She did not dance like a girl with her shame bellied out in front of her. She danced in her pride like a boat under sail, straight-backed and stately.

A manservant moved along until he pushed between Elske and the maidservant standing next to her. He spoke softly into Elske's ear. "Which is your Adelinne?" he asked, and added, "That's mine." He pointed to a young man with dark, curly hair and bright brown eyes. "Var Jerrol," the manservant said, his voice like a breeze as it crossed her ear, "watches my Adel as he does your Adelinne. Mine he watches because of his father's armies, which have won him rule over five great cities in the south."

"The father is a King?" Elske asked. The Adel's face was delicately boned and he danced as if music came from within him to join the flowing sounds of the lutes.

"To be a King, a man must have royal blood in his veins, which is why the son comes to our Courting Winter. The father looks for a royal bride, that the son's sons may be royal, as their warrior grandfather can never be."

"Did not those five cities defend themselves?" Elske wondered.

"No army can win without the black powder," the man whispered into her ear. "No city can build walls thick enough to withstand that weapon."

"Where does the father get black powder?" Elske wondered.

"I wouldn't want to speak aloud my thoughts about that," the manservant answered. "But our Trastader merchants— Vars and Councillors, the banking houses, aye, and the shipbuilders, too—they're as eager as a man with a new wife. Lively as crickets. Your mistress is much improved since the last Courting Winter. Is it you who have taught her manners?"

Elske laughed then, and shook her head. She knew nothing of manners and, even if she did, she didn't imagine Beriel could be taught.

"What use has Var Jerrol for her?" the manservant asked. "What does he use you for?"

Elske shook her head again. Ignorance, she decided, was the wisest gown to dress herself in, when this fellow questioned her. She wondered what *his* uses for her were, and then wondered if he was in Var Jerrol's employ. That last thought she chose not to reveal.

"Unless it is your face," he suggested, looking at her with

a smile that hinted at some private understanding, and promised that she would enjoy it were he to share it with her. "With your eyes the color of a wolf's pelt. Do you know, it is not only the Adeliers who are betrothed at the end of a Courting Winter. And I might marry you myself, Var Jerrol permitting."

Elske laughed, as if this was all a mischief. And it was a mischief, or at least misprision, if he thought he would gain something by having her for wife. "I do not choose to marry," she answered him. "Not you, nor any other man."

"You will," he promised her.

Perhaps she would, but first must come the business of the babe. When that was accomplished, then everything might change, but until that was finished, Elske—like Beriel—could only wait.

CHAPTER 11

ELSKE THOUGHT THAT SHE HAD guarded against every danger the child presented, but Beriel had a more cunning and suspecting mind. One evening, she called Elske into the bedchamber and gave her servant the dagger. "I can't do this, so you must," she said, and held out her left hand, palm upwards. "Take the dagger and make a cut, here—where the blood flows freely. Along the soft pads of my fingers, Elske."

Elske took the weapon, willing to obey, but she first asked, "Why, my Lady?"

Beriel lifted a soft cloth from beside her. "Do you know nothing of how servants gossip? If I never once have my woman's bleedings, do you think they won't notice, those washerwomen? And haven't you sent in your bloody cloths, and haven't they been washed and folded and returned to you?"

So Elske held Beriel's hand firm in hers and sliced deep across the fingertips, ignoring her mistress's quick hissing intake of breath. Then she took up a cloth, to catch the bright blood. They both watched red drops soak into the white cloth.

Beriel voiced their opinion. "It's not enough, it's not—"

Elske agreed. "If we were to mix it with some wine?"

"Or snow, we can get snow by the window, and melt—?" Beriel suggested.

In the end they did both. Elske sent to the kitchen for a second goblet of wine, and Beriel set her first goblet on the stove to melt the snow she'd filled it with. Also, Beriel cut across the tips of Elske's fingers, and they gained more blood that way, and shared the same pain, and took the same comfort from thrusting their fingertips into the snow. And in the end the results were satisfactory. Melted snow thinned out the liquorish smell of the wine and blood brightened the color of the stain.

"Now we have a few more weeks," Beriel announced, satisfied.

"And there will be blood in plenty at the birth," Elske promised. But that did not cheer her mistress.

"It has been too long," Beriel spoke in a low voice, "since I knew how things are for my land. I remember this from the last Courting Winter, how I am imprisoned in ignorance. Northgate gives generously from the storerooms when his people need, and Arborford, too, cares for his, but there are royal lands that can be gripped hard by winter, and my father is too sick and greedy to remember how the people starve, and die of cold on their holdings."

"These Trastaders know how to prepare against winter's siege," Elske observed, but Beriel was lost in her own thoughts and memories: "The people of the Kingdom fear the royal house, and fear not our strengths but our weaknesses. But they do not fear me. They long to have me for their Queen," Beriel said, proud and sure. "If I claim my rightful place."

"And your brother?"

"Guerric is like my father, greedy, and his appetites will not learn patience. His advisors use him for their own gains—"

"These are they who raped you?"

"No, those were—"

Beriel ceased speaking, studied her hands where they were clasped together now to halt their bleeding. "I will not think of that," Beriel said. "When the time comes for my revenges, then I will think of those cousins. And that brother. Leave me now," she ordered.

Elske withdrew to the antechamber. There, she added the bloodied cloths to the accumulated shifts and nightdresses left for washing, and considered her own plans.

At the next Assembly, Elske left the hall while the Adeliers, the overseeing Vars, and all the servants watched the antics of little dolls on strings, who moved and spoke like people, quarreling, fighting, playing tricks upon one another, and stealing one another's prizes and women. She took her cloak and slipped out into the marketplace, where snowflakes floated down through the windless air.

She hurried down towards the docks and Var Kenric's storehouse, where she hoped to find Taddus, or at least leave word that she had need to meet with him. As it happened, Taddus was there that afternoon, walking about the shadowy warehouse with a long book in his hands as he counted up stacked bolts of cloth and recorded their number. He was surprised to see her. "Alone?" he asked, welcoming, but she answered him without pleasantries. "Is Idelle with child?" She could spare no time for niceties.

"No," Taddus said. "I've a barren wife. Barren, and grief-filled. If I'd known—"

Elske interrupted him. "If I were to bring you a babe?"

"Who has done this to you?" Taddus asked, and Elske shook her head, impatient.

"If I were to bring a babe, a newborn, would Idelle take it? Would you accept such a child, if I could give you my word that the blood in its veins was as good as yours?"

Now Taddus hesitated. This Elske gave time, however little time she had to spare here. Behind her, in the shopfront, people moved about and sometimes spoke, buying and selling.

"Yes," Taddus decided.

"Idelle will need to prepare for a babe, as if she approached its birthing," Elske told him. "It must seem to be your own child you raise. You will want a cow, for milk, or a goat."

"Not a wet nurse?"

"The fewer who suspect, the safer is your secret. If I can, I will bring the babe to you before the end of winter. I have heard," Elske told him now, "how a barren woman's womb may open up with the joy of a child to raise, not her own but as good as her own. I have seen her womb now welcoming to the man's seed where before it was stony ground."

That hope eased the last of Taddus's doubts. "My house will be ready," he told Elske. He asked, "And when—?"

"I can't be certain," she said. "I think between the next full moon and the moon after. I must return now, before I'm missed."

"Alone?" he asked again.

"I am safe, alone. For the brief distance, safe enough."

Elske had already decided to go out in man's clothing, when she went out alone, if she went out alone again, even in day-light. She would make herself a set of trousers, and that would be all the disguise she would need under her winter cloak, a shirt and trousers. She could tie back her hair, as many men did. Nobody would notice a solitary cloaked boy on the winter streets. But what if the child were wailing at the time?

How could she keep the child from wailing, when she carried it out of the villa on Logisle and across the bridge to Var Kenric's house on Harboring?

If it were night, Elske thought, there would be none to hear a wailing child, muffled as the cries would be beneath her cloak, against her breast. These winter days were mostly night, and that was in her favor. But if there were danger of discovery, then she must strangle or smother it. Lest Beriel be betrayed.

All of this went through her mind in a flash as brief as sunlight on water, as she wished Taddus farewell and he thanked her, and she returned to the Council Hall and the assembled Adeliers, and to her mistress's service.

DAY FOLLOWED DAY, EACH DAY growing longer in such small steps that it was impossible to be sure that there was any difference between them. Like them, Beriel's belly grew imperceptibly.

Beriel was impatient for the birth to be completed. Once the child was gone, done with, and the afterbirth burned away in the stove, "then I can think of my return," she said. "If I live." Anger burned in Beriel more brightly, and shone out of her eyes, too, the closer the babe came to its birth. The Adels stood back from her anger, asking her, "Why so imperious, Lady?" And their menservants sought out Elske to ask, "Little lovely, can't you sweeten your mistress's disposition?"

Neither Beriel nor Elske cared to answer such questions. The questions Elske did answer were those Beriel asked.

"How do I know when birth has begun?" and Elske explained about the waters, breaking and flowing. "And that is all? Why do women moan so about it?" Beriel asked, and Elske spoke of the slowly closing gap from one cramping pain to the next, through much of which a woman might continue at her daily life—until the end, when a woman could think only of pain, and the desire to push the child out into the world. "How do you know these things?" Beriel demanded.

"My grandmother—the women came to her for their births. Our house was the Birth House."

"Was your grandmother, like you, not so strengthless as she looked?"

"Do I look strengthless?" Elske asked.

"You look of such cheerful heart, people think you guileless, which they take for weak. You smile as if this was a world without cruelty, hunger, injustice, ill luck, a world with neither fear nor shame. You smile like someone who is not life's prisoner."

"When I can so easily die, how can I be thought a prisoner?"

"As the world sees things," Beriel began, and then stopped.

They had lingered at table after their meal. Beriel had eaten little and drunk two goblets of red wine. Outside, a thick snow fell steadily. There would be no Assembly that day.

"As the world sees things," Beriel began again, and again

didn't finish her sentence. She rose from the table and walked over to the door, opened it and for a long time stood with her back to Elske, looking out into the falling snow.

Elske sat still. She waited to hear her mistress speak the thought that had moved her to open the door.

When Beriel at last turned around, her blue eyes shone as if there were not a gathering darkness outside, and a confining snow. "It's starting. I think it is— Now it's gone again, but—You said, the pains would come wide apart at first, and these—but I am not at peace," Beriel said. "The King my father is an old man, ill, and if he should die while I'm sent away here into the exile of courtship—"

Beriel fell silent again. Elske could not know if it was a birth pain that silenced her, or her own thoughts.

"A dead woman is no danger to a living King," Beriel said. "I must be careful to live."

Elske gathered their plates onto the serving tray.

They returned to the bedchamber, but Beriel still did not sit. She paced slowly from door to window, and back again, and back again, as steady as the sea against its shores.

"The Wolfer women make no sound?" she asked once.

Elske nodded. If the labor had begun, then she needed to prepare for many hours of sleeplessness. The first child might curl up smallest against his mother, but he was also the most reluctant to leave her. The first labor was the hardest, longest; but not necessarily the most dangerous.

Unless, of course, the baby lay wrong in its mother, lay feet down and head up, for example, or crossways; those births were the most difficult. Whether first or not, such births were often the last.

"This Guerric, this brother, is only a year younger than I am. A year and a little less, my mother having been in a great hurry to produce a son. And heir, as if she did not wish me to inherit the throne. They make no sound at all?"

"Mewlings, sometimes, like a kitten," Elske said. "Later, all panted—" She tried to remember everything, and was about to mention groanings when Beriel announced, "What any other woman can do, that can I do. And man, too—but that's not the question here, is it?"

"No, my Lady," Elske smiled. Then she thought to tell Beriel, "Among the Volkaric, to become King one must win the throne away from all others, in battle, after the Volkking dies—"

"And the Death Maiden with him."

"Yes, then. For the Strydd, the captains strip naked, except for their swords."

"Naked?"

"Clothed in their strength and courage, why should they need more?"

"The captains fight until one has conquered all the rest?"

"Yes. Then all serve the new Volkking, and all belongs to him."

Beriel paced, and every now and then stopped to lean against something, concentrating on her labor.

"They do then make some small sounds?" she asked.

"My Lady, if you will be soundless that will keep you safest. And the babe will—"

"I've told you, I will know nothing of this babe."

"Yes, my Lady," Elske said. She explained to Beriel, "I can tell them you are ill, but to keep you safe we must give no suspicion of what illness it is that keeps you in your chamber."

Beriel agreed without argument. She paced, and said, "In a battle for the crown, I would stand the victor. Against my brother. Guerric plies his sword as if he were a strengthless girl, with a girl's cowardly heart. He keeps his horse to a trot, lest he fall off. He loves sweet cakes better than his land. He isn't fit to be King, and yet he is the King's preferred heir."

"A man who brings others to rape his sister, that man isn't fit to be King," Elske said. "Even were he a brave and strong swordsman, he would not be fit."

"Neither, I think, is that man fit who drags a girl child behind him into death," Beriel remarked.

"It is the way of the Volkaric that the Volkking take a maiden to serve him in his death, and offer him her body for his comfort in Death's halls. Is it the way in your Kingdom that a Prince should lack heart in fighting? And seek to shame his blood sister?"

There was no answer. Beriel waited out a pain, then said,

"I have another brother, and sisters, and they are not poisoned as Guerric is, with envy and fear of me. I have a good brother, Aidenil." Beriel smiled, thinking of this brother. "My sisters, too, are gentle and obedient. Only in Guerric does ambition rage."

"And in you, also, my Lady."

"Do you say I'm no better than he?" Beriel demanded, displeased.

Elske said, "I say nothing of better."

"And why should I not be Queen? And is not revenge the action of a Queen?"

"Whatever you do will be the action of a Queen," Elske said, and Beriel subsided. Later, in the deep night, as the pains came more swiftly, "My mother, who should have saved me, has always betrayed me," Beriel said. She still refused to sit, or to lie on her bed. Elske knew that soon it would be good for her mistress to take off her gown, and good for Elske to take the white linens from off the bed—lest either be soiled in a manner that could not be explained away. Elske had already called for a bowl of water, as if for washing, and set it on the stove to heat. She had called also for a jug of wine.

"I had no grandmother to save me, as you did," Beriel said. Then she stopped speaking, to place her hands flat against the window and stare out, as she breathed deeply.

There came the time when Beriel consented to take off her gown, and lie down upon the stripped bed, and then the time when she could think of nothing but the labor working upon her body. She opened her mouth, but made no cry. Elske wiped the sweat from her mistress's face and neck. That was all Elske could do, as the long night wore on. She could sit beside her mistress and dry her sweat and later her tears. Elske's hands were bruised in Beriel's clasp, that long night.

In the morning, she waited by her own antechamber door until the house servants brought food, and drink. "My Lady is unwell," she told them, whispering as if Beriel slept at last behind her closed door, after a night's illness. "She must have quiet."

"Shall we send for the housekeeper?" they asked, well-trained servants in a well-run household.

"Not yet," Elske answered. "She is not so feverish for that. Leave her to me, and to quiet."

Elske knew that if darkness did not come before the babe, her own dangers would be multiplied. Climbing out of the window in daylight would increase her chances of being seen, as would crossing the snowy lawn and gardens into the woods by day; but waiting for darkness would increase the chance of the babe's presence being detected at the villa.

And if the babe were born in daylight and couldn't be quieted, then Elske would have no choice. She would take it into another room and silence it; and at dark she would walk out over the ice until she came to one of the fisherman's huts, and the fishing hole within, through which a newborn babe with its soft bones could be forced. No one would ever know.

Beriel was beyond caring if it was daylight or dark and Elske—sitting at her mistress's side, meeting Beriel's blue gaze with calmness—watched pain wash over her mistress's body until the girl wept, tears as silent as the cries that came mutely from her howling mouth. Elske couldn't take time to look away, to know what time of day it was, if dark or light. They were near the end, she thought.

Beriel drew her knees up and Elske—speaking almost in Tamara's soft remembered voice—urged her to push.

The blue eyes were near wild, like some wolf brought down, struggling to stand and run, except its legs would not obey its will. Beriel closed her eyes and wept with the pain, and the labor, and the silence.

And so the babe was born, the head first and hardest, followed by the narrow-shouldered body, which slipped out. Beriel lay back, panting, emptied, out of pain's reach—then her body arched stiffly one more time, to expel the afterbirth.

Using Beriel's dagger, Elske cut the cord and tied it off. Bloody and wet with its own birthing, the babe started to cry. She wrapped it around with soft cloths, and that soothed it again. It was a girl child.

Beriel lay, chest heaving, her eyes screwed shut. Her hands were fists where they lay on her breasts. Her hair lay wet and straggled around her head.

Elske laid the baby on a cloak which she had set out like a small pallet near the warmth of the stove. She took water, and washed her mistress clean, giving her clean cloths to place between her legs and catch the flow of blood there. She covered her mistress with a clean bedsheet and thrust the afterbirth into the stove. She returned to Beriel, lifting her head to give her wine.

The baby stirred, fussed.

Beriel lay abed, her face closed away from everything.

"I'm going now," Elske said, pulling on the trousers she had sewn for herself, tucking her shirt half into them. Putting her stockinged feet into her warm wolfskin boots, she took up the baby and the cloak. She set the baby down on the window-sill and settled the cloak around her shoulders, then climbed up onto the sill and jumped down into the deep snow. She reached inside to gather the baby to herself, tucking it up against her breast under the cloak. If the child would stay quiet and warm there, as if she thought herself yet unborn, then Elske could carry her safely through the darkness.

For it was deep, dark night, and her luck held—this might be a lucky child—as Elske crept out of the villa grounds and hurried along dark roadways, across the bridge that arched over the dark ice of the frozen river, then down the familiar streets of Harboring until she came to Var Kenric's house, silent and shuttered. She knocked on the door, and waited, hoping that the snow muffled the sound that was so loud in her own ears, hoping that none but the people of the house might hear. A shuttered window above her head opened, and Var Kenric looked down at her. Then Ula opened the door to her and she saw Idelle's freckled face as eager as it had been before she had been married and childless. Elske gave the child into Idelle's arms.

"A girl," she said to Taddus. He had bent over the baby's face, and only looked up to nod.

"We thank—" Var Kenric started to say and Ula was wiping at her eyes with her apron, but Elske said, "I must return," and she would not stay for food and drink, for thanks, for anything. She had done all she could here, and she would be needed by Beriel.

Darkness hid her in shadows as Elske raced back to Var Vladislav's snow-covered grounds, and climbed over the low fence, easier now without a newborn held close against her chest. She moved through trees, past stables, around the kitchen gardens—slipping like the shadow of a bird along the walls—until she was at the open window to Beriel's bedchamber.

Elske climbed back inside.

"I didn't close the window, but I'm cold," Beriel said from the bed.

Elske pulled the window in, and went to the stove to remove her boots and warm her hands, after the bitter night.

"I'm bleeding, as if it were my time," Beriel said.

"That's the way of it. Did you sleep?"

"I couldn't sleep. I did well."

"You did well, my Lady."

"I want food," Beriel said then.

"Wiser to wait for the servants to bring food in the morning," Elske advised.

"I'm very hungry."

"It's the hard work of birthing."

"What have you done with the child, then?" Beriel asked.

"I can't tell you that," Elske answered. She held her hands out over the warm stove, but she could hear Beriel stirring behind her, sitting up.

"I command you."

"I gave my word," Elske reminded her. At Beriel's silence, she turned around—and fury crashed against her like a wave thrown by a storm against the rocky coast.

"You gave your word to me and I return it to you. I ask again, what have you done with my babe?"

Elske didn't speak. This was no more than Beriel herself had warned Elske of.

"My own child, which I endured the shame of getting and the pain of birthing. Where is it now?"

Elske kept silence.

"Will you at least tell me if it was a girl child or a boy?" Beriel asked, more quietly.

"My Lady, I cannot."

Fury rose again in Beriel's eyes. "Will not, more like. It's fortunate for you that I am in your debt," she said.

"Why should you be in my debt?" Elske asked.

"Sometimes—you are so—innocent—and ignorant," Beriel answered, and this added to her anger. "I know you lived among brutes, but—" She took a deep breath and gave the order more quietly. "I am hungry, and you are my servant. I tell you to find me food, and drink. It has been more than a day since I have eaten, and if Var Vladislav's housekeeper catches you at the larder, and punishes you, remember that a better servant would have had food ready for me."

"Yes, my Lady," Elske said. She turned to leave the room.

"After all, they believe I have been feverish. When a fever passes on, the sick person is often hungry, so why should they suspect anything? Unless, you've told them—?"

Elske knew that if Beriel wished to believe ill of her, nothing Elske could say would convince her otherwise. But why should her mistress wish to distrust Elske?

And when Elske returned, carrying a tankard of ale, and some cheese, cold roasted fowl, fish pudding and bread, Beriel said to her, "You also have not eaten, have you, Elske?" Then she adjusted herself back on her pillows, as if the bed were a throne, and announced, "We must both eat." At last Beriel said, "I am afraid for my land, and for my throne," and thus ended her quarrel with Elske.

CHAPTER 12

IT WAS HARD TO PERSUADE Beriel to keep to her bed for as long as the household would expect for recovery from a feverish illness. It seemed as if the baby had been a stone in Beriel's belly, and she had needed her best strength to keep it hidden there. Now, Beriel could use her best strength for her own purposes and those required her to be out of her bed.

Elske reminded her, again and again, that she must appear to the servants to be weak, although recovering as her good appetite attested.

Beriel argued, again and again. "I gave birth as a Wolfer woman, soundless, and I think such a woman would not lie abed. Did they, among the Wolfers?"

"They did not, my Lady," Elske answered patiently.

"They must have been proud," Beriel observed from her bed. "To have given birth, so, and perhaps to a son. Did I have a son, Elske? You might at least tell me that."

Elske had given her word, and kept silent. She did, however, point out to Beriel, "The women of the Volkaric were never proud. What could a woman do to be proud of? Not win treasure for the Volkking, not fight in battle. The women couldn't hunt, either. And even when they hated—for they were good haters—it was only among themselves."

"You are quarrelsome," Beriel complained. "Go and find me some book. If I can't read it myself, then you must read it to me."

So Elske went to Var Vladislav's library, where she unexpectedly interrupted him as he sat for a painting of himself. The High Councillor was not displeased at the disturbance. When she explained who she was and that she had permission from his housekeeper to go to this room, and her purpose there, he answered impatiently, "I know, I know you, Elske. Take what you will, but I would ask your mistress, will she spare you to me, to teach me a little Souther, perhaps to tell me of the Volkaric, so I can make a use of these inactive hours?"

Elske carried that request, along with a volume of animal stories she had sometimes read to Var Jerrol's daughters, back to Beriel, who had an answer quick on her tongue. "If I say yes, will you tell me about my child?"

"No, my Lady."

Beriel then asked from her bed, "And if I say no?"

"I will obey you."

When Beriel did not say yes or no, Elske turned to leave the bedchamber. At the door Beriel called her back to say, "Very well, I give you my permission. I will also warn you, Elske, as a kind mistress. Do you know what men use flattery for?"

"For rape," Elske answered.

Beriel laughed, her ill temper flown like a bird out of the cage. She said, "We must find you some other word, in Norther and in Souther, too, some word that tells the bed pleasures a man and a woman have together. Did your Wolfer women never have pleasure of a man?"

"They had babies. They never spoke of pleasure."

"And the men?"

"They had their desire and—sometimes—they had sons."

"Among the Wolfers," Beriel said then, "if you refused to tell me what I wished to know, I would have you killed. Isn't that so? No captive among the Wolfers would dare refuse her mistress."

"Among the Volkaric, you would be but one of many women," Elske explained patiently. "You might ask one of the men to accuse me before the Volkking, but the Volkking might easily give the same justice to both, give both to the wolves and thus be rid of our quarrels."

Elske must sew, now, whenever she was in Beriel's apartments, to return Beriel's gowns to their original seams. This occupied her hands and so to save them both from tedium, also to practice her skill in Norther, Beriel read aloud from the animal tales. In the stories, the animals had speech, like men and women; like men and women they were vain, ungrateful and greedy. "This tale-teller mocks us," Beriel cried, but she was amused, not angered. "He mocks us from the greatest to the least."

When Elske was called to Var Vladislav in his library, Beriel used her to discover what the Trastaders knew about the Kingdom. As far as Elske could tell from the maps Var Vladislav collected and from the few questions he asked her, the Trastaders knew almost nothing of the Kingdom, only that Beriel claimed to be its Queen.

"As Queen, do you rule everyone in everything?" Elske asked Beriel one evening, her hands busy with needle and thread.

"I do, but also I do not," Beriel answered. "I will share rule with the law, as the Priests read it. Also there are two Earls, each given lands that together make near two-thirds of the Kingdom. The Earls have power over their lands and people, but must bend the knee to the King and serve as his vassals, just as their own vassals bend the knee to them, and serve them. But there are also royal moieties, greater than what any Earl possesses. The people serve each their own Lord, who awards them their holdings, and each Lord serves his Overlord, until it comes to the Earls, who serve the King."

"Among the Volkaric," Elske said, "all men serve the Volkking, with no other to stand between them and him."

"Among the Volkaric, then," Beriel said, "if a man is not the Volkking, he has nothing more than any other man."

Elske agreed and pointed out, "Thus each man's loyalty is to the Volkking only."

At the end of her enforced time in bed, Beriel had her plans begun. "There is only one moon of winter left to me here in Trastad, and I will use that time to my own advantage. I will have Var Jerrol to dine with me, as my guest. You will deliver my invitation, Elske, at the next Assembly. I will have him come to me two days after the next Assembly. I will not be gainsayed in this," Beriel warned. But Elske thought only to obey—except she wondered if she would find such another, master or mistress, to serve, and she wished that Beriel had not made her know how little time remained in this Courting Winter.

The next Assembly came not four days after.

New-cut greens freshened the air of the hall with their sharp, bitter fragrances, as they did at every first-quarter moon. The table was set out with ale and cheeses and breads, as well as sweet apple cakes. For entertainment, a ropedancer performed on a thick hawser hung down from one of the open beams. Held by his strong arms, his legs stiff and straight, he swung up and down the rope, turning, twisting, poising to balance weight with strength in a solitary dance as measured and slow as a ship docking.

Beriel entered to the Assembly altered in no way that could be seen, but everything about her was changed. Now everyone attended her, Adeliers both men and women, both betrothed and free, and all of the servants and the overseeing Vars as well. None could keep their eyes from noting Beriel's progress through the hall—even while each continued his own private talk and flirtations. All wished her to notice them and yet hoped also to avoid her glance. Adelinnes praised her dress and wit. Adels offered her plates of food, and their arms to escort her around the floor. These attentions Beriel received as if they were her due, and her custom.

"What illness did she have?" the servants asked Elske, who shook her head, to ask how such as she would know the name of a disease. "How is she to serve?" they asked, and did not dare hope to be answered. They pressed Elske with questions, but also now kept back a little distance from her, as if fearing to be in conversation with her. So that Var Jerrol could speak to her from behind without danger of being overheard.

"Has your mistress had a proposal, then?"

"No," Elske answered. "She wishes to dine with you."

"That likes me well. I'll send to invite her," he said, but Elske told him, "She asks you to be her guest, two days hence."

"Ah," Var Jerrol said. "So she has sent *her* servant to me.

And what have you learned about this Kingdom of hers?"

"Of the royal house, something."

"Royalty doesn't concern me. And if I know the world, this girl—however bright she glows today—will not rule in her Kingdom. For haven't they sent her here to marry her away into some distant land and bury her there? To make some lesser marriage than a Queen on her throne could command? She might do well," Var Jerrol said into Elske's ear, "to take one of these boys. If she cares for her own safety. Does she care for her own safety, do you think?"

Beriel stopped walking, and freed her arm, so that her escort could reach into his purse for a coin to put into the soft hat the ropedancer was now handing around. Beriel spoke a word to the dancer, who bowed from the waist to her, without asking her for coins; when she had turned to walk away from him, the ropedancer followed her with his eyes.

"When your Queen has gone into whatever fortune may prove to be hers," Var Jerrol said to Elske, "have you thought how alone and helpless you will be?"

Now Beriel was surrounded by Adels, like a wolf in the midst of a pack of dogs, and she freed herself from their attentions with a single glance, like a wolf keeping a pack of dogs at bay.

When Elske did not answer him, Var Jerrol said, "Tell your mistress, I accept her invitation to dine. Var Vladislav's cook has a fine hand with fish, I hear, and with the sweet pastry his master favors. Tell her, I anticipate luxurious hospitality."

All of this Elske reported faithfully, when Beriel wanted to know how Var Jerrol had received the invitation. Hearing what his questions, and concerns, and opinions were, Beriel only smiled. "I wonder what future Var Jerrol has planned for *you*," she said. "Once I've gone, I doubt you'll escape his bed. Fetch me the cook, Elske. My time here runs out and my will scampers before it. I'll have a menu, first, and then the housekeeper, and then I'll be ready for your Var Jerrol."

WHEN VAR JERROL ENTERED BERIEL'S private dining room, he looked around with pleasure. Against the dark wood of walls and floor, the table shone with the whiteness of its cloths, and gleamed with silver plates and utensils. Oil lights burned in sconces on all the walls, driving shadows from all but the lowest corners. The air was sweet with the odors of dried spices which Elske had tossed into the fire. Elske stood beside the chest, ready to pour red wine into the waiting goblets and serve the soup, which was being kept hot on top of the tile stove. Her mistress had not wanted to confide her purposes for Var Jerrol, so Elske watched this dinner unfold before her as if she were an Adelier watching an entertainment at the Assembly. Her own purpose at the dinner, she knew, was to enhance Beriel's queenliness.

Beriel entered beside Var Jerrol, so tall that she came up to his chin. Her brown hair hung down loose, and they had made one of her golden chains into a coronet. She wore her grandmother's medallion on her breast. Beriel noticed neither her maidservant's readiness nor her guest's pleasure; she merely indicated his place and allowed Elske to seat her across from him. Elske served the soup and placed a woven basket of little breads between them. She set down before each a goblet of wine so dark it seemed like a red ruby disk set in a silver ring.

"Do you always entertain in such luxury?" Var Jerrol asked and Beriel answered, "Always. But you aren't unaccustomed to being richly entertained. For you must often dine by invitation with the Adeliers, although perhaps not often with an Adelinne, and alone."

"Correct," Var Jerrol acknowledged, then reminded her, "You were less circumspect, when last you were our guest. I was led to expect something less . . . civilized."

"I would never think anyone could lead you, Var Jerrol," Beriel said, as amused as he was by their exchange. "And is it not fine weather we are enjoying?" she asked.

They discussed the spring melts, already begun, sending flat islands of ice floating out to sea. Var Jerrol explained how the fishermen in their little boats could avoid the dangers of ice, but said it would be a few sennights yet before the less agile merchant vessels would set out for the year's trading. "And to return our Adeliers to their own homelands, their futures now happily settled, as we hope," Var Jerrol said.

As the dinner progressed, soup and fowl, fish and roasted meat, plates of savories, Elske removed the empty plates from the table and exchanged them for trays from the kitchen.

"They might be enjoying spring already in your homeland," Var Jerrol said, leading the topic of the weather into a new direction. "It lies far enough to the south, doesn't it?"

"They might, but I have no way of knowing. And you will soon be opening your mines?" When Var Jerrol didn't respond, "In the Kingdom," Beriel told him, giving him something of what she knew he wanted, "spring is long and generous, a slow, sweet-smelling, soft-winded time upon the land."

"In the Kingdom, you say? Do you know, I couldn't find your Kingdom on any map?"

"And I could find my way there blindfolded." She was playing a game with him, as if he were a child.

"It is no great thing to find your way blindfolded when you travel on a ship another man captains," Var Jerrol pointed out humorously, playing his own game with her. "The ship must come to land, somewhere."

"At a small city," Beriel agreed.

"Celindon?" he guessed.

She didn't gainsay him. "I was there under close guard, to protect me from contact with its inhabitants."

"So you know nothing of it?"

"It is a city on a river."

"It must be Celindon," Var Jerrol decided. "You would have approached it from inland, traveling down that river."

"We traveled downriver for many days," Beriel agreed.

Elske didn't know what Beriel would need her to have understood, when they discussed afterwards what information had been gained in the evening. But she had to be careful not to let her attention to their talk lead her to neglect her duties.

"You traveled from your home on horseback? Or by boat?"

"On horseback," Beriel said. "The Kingdom is hidden away, as if we wished to be concealed from the rest of the world. Although merchants do find us, for the Spring and Autumn Fairs."

"Never Trastaders."

Beriel agreed. "It's odd, isn't it, that they knew to send me here for your Courting Winter?"

"To find yourself a husband," Var Jerrol said.

"What would I want with a husband?" Beriel asked, signaling for Elske to offer around the platter of fish again.

"Only if you had need of an heir."

They ate, and Elske served them, and they talked together, each maneuvering to gain much from the other, and to give little in exchange.

"If I wanted an heir, I would find myself one," Beriel told Var Jerrol.

"There are some things which, however much you desire them, you cannot be certain they wish to be found."

"Like the alchemist's stone," Beriel suggested, agreeably, "able to turn any material into gold, or like the storied black powder, or the fountain of eternal life."

"Black powder turns stone walls into dust," Var Jerrol said. "Turns living men into dead. Black powder is, I am afraid to say, easier to come by than any alchemist's stone, or waters of miracle."

"Who would desire such a weapon?" Beriel asked.

"Anyone who feared that his enemies might already possess it."

"Yes." Beriel was thoughtful. "I would give much to be able to protect my Kingdom from such weaponry. And then, a merchant might desire the weapon also, for the great profits to be made in selling it."

"A man who knows its formulation would grow powerful," Var Jerrol said, adding, "But that is a closely guarded secret."

"Oh," Beriel laughed now, as lightly as any Adelinne who had her Adel on his knees before her, "do you never think that there are too many secrets in the world?"

Elske offered Var Jerrol a platter of thick slices of roast meat, from which he served himself, with onions and carrots that had been roasted beneath it, catching up the juices as they dripped down.

"I am a great believer in secrets," Var Jerrol told Beriel. "I draw them to me, as flowers draw bees, as beauty draws the hearts of men."

"Are you here to draw my secrets from me?" Beriel asked, still teasing.

"Who would want to take anything from you, my Lady?" Var Jerrol returned the question. "Any true man would only hope to give you the choicest of his treasures, and if you were to reward him with a smile, he would count himself overpaid."

Beriel returned the smiling compliment. "As if a Var were like any ordinary man."

"Vars are but ordinary men," Var Jerrol said. "Unusual in their wealth but wealth cannot buy all you desire. Our Vars have disappointments."

"What could disappoint men of such substance?" Beriel wondered.

"You speak lightly. You think I speak lightly," Var Jerrol said. "Or perhaps, you think I speak falsely. Let me give you a plain tale, which none but I know the whole of, with a happy enough ending for a Lady's soft ears." He drank from his wine, and went on. "There is a young merchant of the city who married well—so well that he will become a Var while still a young man. In fact, now I remember myself, it was just this young man who accompanied our Elske to Trastad, and it was just his new wife she saved from attack by ruffians."

"I remember hearing something of such an incident," Beriel observed, with a glance for her maidservant.

"This young couple had no child, to their great sorrow. For she was the only surviving child of her father's house. She must have a child to inherit the wealth of the house, which otherwise must return to the Council of Trastad," Var Jerrol explained, as if this loss of wealth were the point of his story.

"To be divided among them? I can't think, then, that such a lack would be all grief to the Council," Beriel said, as if she were only hearing another tale of Trastader greed.

"That question is now moot, for the young woman has a child." Var Jerrol glanced carelessly at Beriel as he said this, and speared an onion on his fork, and ate it.

"A great happiness for her," Beriel responded with equal carelessness.

He chewed, and nodded pleasure at her kind thought. "Yes. It is that. Were her friends and family, and the young husband also, not so gratified by this turn of events, they might wonder at so secret a pregnancy, so sudden a birth, but— All is gladness where before sorrow shadowed the house, and who would deny them their happiness? So you see, our Vars are indeed ordinary men."

"Did I doubt you, that you needed to give me such proof?" Beriel inquired.

Elske poured more wine. She kept silent, but she saw the

direction of this intricate conversational dance. She saw its direction, and unease gripped her heart. Meanwhile, she gave their plates to the kitchen maid and sent the girl back to fetch the cold fowl. Meanwhile, she set out clean silver plates, one before each diner.

"I am ready to believe whatever you might tell me, Var Jerrol," Beriel continued.

"I tell you only the tale I heard," Var Jerrol concluded.

"What happiness for the young husband, this child. But I am still curious. Is it a girl child, or a boy child?" Beriel asked offhandedly, as she lifted her goblet to her lips.

So this was Beriel's purpose for Var Jerrol. Elske's heart grew chilly, to know why she had been kept ignorant.

"The child is a girl, as I hear, with a strong pair of lungs and a healthy appetite. The Varinne is already famous for her motherly devotion." Var Jerrol continued to eat, too clever to let Beriel see that he knew he had given her what she wanted from him, too clever to ask immediately for a favor in return.

"I wish her many children," Beriel said, with another glance at Elske. "And much joy of them all. But now I wonder, have they given their daughter a name?"

"I've heard that they call her Elskele, as if to honor Elske for her rescue of the Varinne, with that gratitude always fresh in their minds."

"As it should be," Beriel announced happily. "As my own

gratitude would be kept fresh, should Elske have so well served me."

This wasn't gratitude, Elske knew, even though she knew also that she had served Beriel so well, and better. She stood with her back to the table, listening, carving the fowl. She offered the platter to Var Jerrol, first, then to Beriel. The silver platter was icy cold in her hands, from having been set out in the snow, lest the fowl grow warm in the heat of the dining chamber. If this fowl were to grow warm, Elske thought, it would be from the fury that burned in her, and from the hot grief for her sworn word, now a dead thing.

Why should Beriel take from her the worth of her own word, which was all that she owned? And which Beriel herself had given to Elske, by showing her that she did own it. Although Beriel had given it to her, she now seized it back, imperiously.

The two were talking now of trade, and how it served the well-being of Trastad, or any other land. Var Jerrol asked Beriel what metal ores were to be found in the Kingdom, and what crops grew there, and if they had coins and how they were minted, how sold, what cloths, blades, books and ales. He argued that understanding of letters was best distributed freely among all who wished to learn it, although Beriel feared that knowledge would lead to discontent. They spoke of law, and Beriel wondered how the Council could govern without written laws. But he assured her, "We have custom and tradition, to be considered during any judgement. We are well-governed."

"Yet the cells are full, as I hear it, and overfull."

"We build new cells as we need them," Var Jerrol said. "They are not overfull."

As they spoke, Elske stood in the silence of her anger; for Beriel had taken Elske's word and made it valueless. Elske felt as if Beriel had walked with her out to the hillside; and she had gone with her mistress, all trusting; and Beriel had left her there for the wolves.

Elske did not know which cut more deeply, her defenselessness or her solitude.

"I'd have thought you would be using Elske to translate for you," Var Jerrol said, and Beriel answered him that she had improved her knowledge of his language, under Elske's tutelage.

Var Jerrol asked, "Do you ever think to open the door to your land?"

"I think of it," Beriel said. "I think of sending out emissaries, and merchants, and even of sending my unruly cousins to the Courting Winter. I think of giving my Kingdom a place in the greater world."

"Why should your Lords and Princes not wed outside of your Kingdom?" Var Jerrol asked. "If you were to have a brother, for example, and I a daughter both richly dowered and gently reared, might not all profit from a union between them?"

Beriel agreed. "I have brothers, that much is true, and one a worthy Prince. I will think of what you have said, you who are the eyes and ears of the Council, and a man of wisdom."

Var Jerrol bowed his head, receiving the compliment.

Beriel told him, "Mine is a land of stories, not like Trastad which is a merchant city. I think often of Jackaroo, who with his sword and his great heart brought justice to a people oppressed by poverty and misgoverned by Overlords. Jackaroo rides out only when the land has need of him, then rests in sleep under the mountains until he is needed again, to save his people." Var Jerrol smiled tolerantly and Beriel reflected the expression back at him. "I always believe, however, that if my land needs saving, I must save it myself."

"Trastad makes a generous ally," Var Jerrol told her. "But is your Kingdom in danger?"

At that question, Beriel stood. Restless, she moved to the window, to look out at the ice-clogged river. She became again a young woman, sent into courtship against her will. "I do not know," she said. "I have no reason to think so, but my father was not in health when I left and—I have been too long away."

Var Jerrol watched her the way a snake might watch a mouse. "It is a moon yet before you will set out on your return."

Beriel turned around to face him, and she was a Queen again. "It may be," she said, "that it is time for we of the Kingdom to travel outwards from our own borders, and beyond the protection of the forests that surround us, and of the mountains that ring us. If it is that time, be sure I will remember you, and I will think of the skills of Trastad."

"You mean in trade."

"And carpentry, shipbuilding, too, in your paintings and goldsmiths, your spacious houses and the tile stoves with which you heat your chambers. There is much I value in Trastad," Beriel said, holding out her white hand, "as you know well."

Var Jerrol became gallant. "When you leave us, there will be a diminishment in that sum. And more, if you think to take Elske with you."

"What happens to my maidservant does not concern you," Beriel announced, to which Var Jerrol made no quarrel. "Escort my guest to the door," Beriel commanded. "See Var Jerrol safely away, Elske."

When Elske returned, she found Beriel in the dining chamber, at the window, and looking out to where a sky of deep blue shone over the moving water, which carried its cargo of ice down to the sea. A field of ice-crusted snow sparkled white down to the water's edge and across the river more white fields held the dark forests back from little houses. Smoke rose from distant chimneys into the bright blue sky.

Beriel turned to greet Elske and her eyes shone like the sky, and her whole face was alight with her victory. "Now I, too, know where my child, my daughter, lives, and what child it is I had. Did you think you could keep a secret from me?"

Elske gathered up plates and goblets. She was expected to make her own dinner from whatever was left on the platters, but she had no appetite for this meal.

"Have you no answer?" Beriel demanded.

"None."

Elske attended to her task.

Beriel watched her, then said, "How could Var Jerrol know something so close to me and I not seek to find it out, since you must have told him."

"No." Elske denied what Beriel already knew was a false accusation.

"You need not fear my anger," Beriel promised.

Elske forced herself to respond. "I am not afraid."

"Then you're jealous. You thought that you alone could hold Var Jerrol's eyes and attentions. You thought that only your smiling ways could win him. I will not have a jealous servant, Elske."

"Nor jealous," Elske said.

Then Beriel did look long and hard at her, and Elske met the glance like a swordsman meeting a blow.

"No, you are not jealous," Beriel admitted. "But you

would have kept me in ignorance about my own child."

Elske spoke her thought, "I gave my word."

"So you did, and you kept it."

"My word was made worthless."

"But you gave it to *me*," Beriel protested. "Can I not say when you must change your word, if you gave it to *me*?"

"I thought, it was *my* word. I thought, it was *my* promise."

"Not jealous, but proud," Beriel said then.

"Why should I be proud?"

Beriel answered impatiently. "I do not know, unless it is for your charms and high-heartedness, which draw people to you. But what are those more than charms and high-heartedness? What cause for pride in these? Still, I am myself proud enough to recognize pride's face when I see it in a beryl glass. So. So." She stood taller even than before, her eyes still alight, and asked, "Are you grown too proud to be my maidservant?"

"No, my Lady," Elske said, for that was true.

"Give me your word for that," Beriel commanded.

"I have no word to give," Elske answered. "You've taken it from me, this day."

"Then I give it back, as a Queen can. Elske, you have never given birth, and neither had I when I asked for your promise. When I know that my child is cared for, named—a daughter—now I can truly leave her behind me. How could I have known my true will before she was born?"

"You could not have, my Lady," Elske said; and that, too, was true.

Elske thought, How could Beriel, who would be Queen, be asked also to know herself? Willful, imperious, unyielding—how could Beriel accept not knowing of her child, when with wit and charm she could win that knowledge? Even at the cost of Elske's word, Beriel would have her own way. Elske could not remain angry at Beriel, for how could Beriel have known how bitterly Elske would see her own little word gathered up into all the rest that a Queen possessed? As servant, Elske might have nothing but her own word and her own choices; but perhaps a Queen had no more—had less, even, if her royal word was not good, or her choices suspect. Elske would not wish to blame Beriel—but neither did she intend to give her word, her choices, into Beriel's keeping.

"And if I were to ask, would you come with me to the Kingdom? There will be others to offer you a more certain future here in Trastad," Beriel said. "If I am displaced, I cannot promise you anything but death, but still, I ask you to come with me."

"I need no promise of rewards," Elske said, making her own choice.

CHAPTER 13

BERIEL RECOUNTED THE OBSTACLES: A ship must be
found and passage negotiated. It must be decided
how they would leave Var Vladislav's villa undetected—
not that she thought the Council wished to detain her, just
that they would require her to travel at the time of their
choice, not hers. There was the question of what essen-
tials to bring, for if she was to travel unescorted, she must
travel light.

But the greatest difficulty they faced was gold. If she
wished to return to the Kingdom at her own will, Beriel
needed gold to purchase berths on a ship, and then more
gold to bribe the captain to set them ashore on the harbor-
less coast close to Pericol. There, they would need yet more
gold to purchase horses, food and safe passage from the cut-
throat who ruled that city. And even when they had arrived
in the Kingdom, who knew what preparations it would be

necessary for Beriel to purchase. For Beriel couldn't know how her land would greet her.

"I know how my brother would like to welcome me. Guerric," Beriel spoke his name as if she had her foot on his neck. "He is no question. But the others? The soldiers, Priests and Lords—they will be divided, I'd guess, they'll be uneasy, fearful to choose the losing side and thus forfeit their high positions. Some are loyal, I think, Northgate and his heir, Arborford probably. I can't know if my father still lives or what my mother might do after his death, except that she will not hope to have her daughter share the name of Queen. She is proud, and jealous. Oh yes," Beriel answered, although Elske had not spoken. "I am her true daughter."

"You have my purse," Elske offered.

"For which I thank you, and promise to repay you manifold," Beriel said. "If I live. The people will welcome me, I believe. My people, I think, know me. I trust my people," Beriel said, her chin high and her eyes shining blue.

They were in among the books and maps of the High Councillor's library, and in fact stood with a map open before them. Beriel's fingers traced the coastline between Trastad and Celindon. Elske could not find Pericol named on the map.

"All the baubles they've sent to me, these Adels, these boys, and for which I have been so grateful and smiling, a goldsmith will buy them—at his own price, but between his price and nothing my choice is easy," Beriel told Elske. "You must find the man, to conceal my interest. Wear those trousers you put on when you took my daughter—"

"You saw?"

"It was clever. In trousers, cloaked, your hair tied back like a man's, no one would take you for a girl, and unprotected. So you can move as freely as a man through Trastad, and carry these jewels safely. Take my dagger, against thieves—for danger stalks anyone seen leaving bankers or smiths alone, even a man." Beriel put her finger down on the map, on the coast north of Celindon, where a river entered the sea. "Pericol," she said. "They put me in the midst of a troop of horsemen to go through Pericol, have I told you?" And Beriel laughed at the memory. "With Guerric's hand-chosen captains in charge, and they did deliver me safely, so I have something to thank them for. I do not know if I can deliver us safely through that place," Beriel said. "But I think I might," she said.

"I can take us that far," Beriel said, and then added, without prologue or preamble, "If I have not already lost my Kingdom forever, and my people lost their chance of me, I must marry. For the heir," Beriel answered the question Elske had not asked. "Be it boy or girl, my first child will be named heir to the throne of the Kingdom."

"I will set about finding a goldsmith," Elske said.

"And a ship, too. But none must suspect us. You have a

wide and loyal acquaintance in Trastad, Elske; what help can you offer me in the matter of ships?" Beriel asked.

"None," Elske answered, truthfully.

As it happened, however, after she had exchanged baubles for coins, she ran into Nido as she walked along the docks to see what ships were being readied for embarkation, to see what goods they were to carry and hear what destination they sailed for. Elske kept her head low to hide her face and her hands hidden under the short cloak to conceal the heavy purse she carried, but Nido had no difficulty in recognizing her. He insisted on walking with her, at least as far as the bridge that joined Harboring to Logisle. He hadn't seen her for so long a time and there was much he wished to tell her. Was it that she didn't want his company? he asked. He wouldn't give her disguise away, he assured her of that, and besides, wouldn't the disguise be improved when they were two young men, walking about together?

Nido had grown taller, and had the shadow of a beard. The labors of apprenticeship hadn't dampened his spirits. His great news was that he was to be sent out as the assistant to a ship's carpenter, on one of Var Kenric's vessels. "We are fitted and stocked, and the ice has broken up. Var Kenric wants to be the first to offer goods in Celindon—I'll see Celindon again, Elske. The other time I was just a boy, the time we met you, Taddus and Father and I, when we were returning. He's ill, did you know?"

"Taddus?"

"Not Taddus, Father. Taddus counts himself the luckiest man in Trastad, now that Idelle has given him an heir. They named the girl after you, did you know that? If Taddus were not Var Kenric's heir, now, Father and Mother would worry where they might find stock, for Father will not be strong enough to travel out this summer. But Taddus supplies their shelves, and I am now placed on one of Var Kenric's ships. In only two days, or perhaps three, I'll be gone. So it is good fortune that I saw you here. What do you think of that chance, after all this time, Elske?"

Elske thought it was a fair chance, and she decided to risk Beriel's anger and spend some of these coins taking that chance. "Will your ship take passengers?" she asked.

"Ships that will bear the Adeliers back to their own lands, and carry our merchants south, will await the fairer weather."

"What if I knew of two travelers who desire to commence their journey now and don't fear foul weather?"

"My ship has a stateroom, next to the captain's quarters. But the sea is still rough, they say—and storms not unlikely. Although, less likely as we move south," Nido told her.

"I do know of two such," Elske said. "What would the charge be, for your captain?"

"I'd have to ask him, and he would have to know he wasn't setting himself or Var Kenric against the will of the Council." Nido looked like a man grown now.

"These are two the Council will not object over," Elske promised him. "There is no criminal, no traitor, no one Trastad wishes to keep within its own territory. I give you my word."

Nido studied her face. They had arrived at the bridge, and stood talking there. "Have they the Council's permission to leave the city?"

"Can two women, neither of them Trastaders, one of them impatient to be back in her own land, endanger Trastad by leaving it betimes?"

Nido thought. "And the second is you?"

"Yes."

"Can you give me the fare now, to convince my captain?"

Elske opened the purse and took out four gold coins. She put them into Nido's hands.

"It's too much," he said.

"You can return to me what you don't need."

"Or it maybe will not be enough, if you cannot show the captain your permissions," Nido said thoughtfully.

Elske gave him four more coins, and so she had spent half of Beriel's purse.

"How will I find you?" Nido asked.

"I'll be here, in this place, at this time, every day until I hear from you," Elske said.

"You'll hear from me tomorrow," Nido promised her.

�❧ ❦

SO IT WAS THAT TWO days from that time, Beriel strode up the wooden gangplank and onto the deck of the ship. Elske followed behind, wearing her warm Wolfer boots, carrying the pack in which whatever clothing they brought with them was folded.

Nido led them down a steep ladder into the belly of the ship, then through a low doorway into a low-ceilinged, narrow, short room where two high, shuttered portholes let in light. With the three of them in the room, there was barely space to move, but Nido squeezed out past them, saying hurriedly, "The captain will send me when we're far enough from land." And he was gone.

The boat moved gently under Elske. The sound of feet came from overhead. When she opened the portholes, she could see the open sky, with a few wispy clouds hurrying across it.

Beriel sat down on the bunk, to wait. Her first fury, when Elske had reported to her of the meeting with Nido, and the coins spent, and the plan laid, had faded away under her desire to return to the Kingdom. She had left behind her a letter for the High Councillor, an elaborate apology for her hasty departure, citing unease about her father who had been in poor health when she had left him, thanking Var Vladislav for his hospitality, hoping that he had intended her to take Elske with her, for that was her will. "I take with me the maidservant, Elske," Beriel had written, and then offered a guileful compliment, "Your wisdom and good judgement in choosing me this girl for servant reveals how it is that Trastad has come to such well-deserved prosperity." So Beriel completed her affairs in Trastad, and Elske—who had no affairs of her own—now sat beside her mistress on the narrow bunk, listening to the sounds of a ship being readied to sail.

Eventually, the ship drew heavily away from the dock. Unable to see, listening, Elske heard the sails being raised and knew they were on their way even before the ship came alive all around them. Elske felt the quickening and asked, "Can we go up on deck, my Lady?"

"Now you're the impatient one," Beriel observed, refusing. "Remember, your little Nido will come to tell us when that is permitted."

"He is not little anymore."

"Will you marry him?"

"Why should I marry Nido?"

"Why should you marry any man?" Beriel answered. "But you will. You are like a flower for them, and they come around like bees to suck the honey of you, the happiness. But perhaps you will not marry."

"Why should I not marry?" Elske asked her. "When I choose. Who I choose, if he chooses me. When it's a good time for marriage, then if it is good to do, why should I not do it? Yours is the dangerous case, as I think, my Lady."

"I know that, Elske. I don't know why you trouble me with it now."

Elske fell silent.

The ship rocked beneath them, like a cradle, and they swayed on the bunk. The lamp which hung down into the center of the room stayed still. Elske's skin felt cold and her mouth dry, but when Nido opened the door to call them out she stood eagerly.

The floor underfoot—moving—made her stumble clumsily. Beriel promised, "You'll get your sea legs soon, Elske, but until then, be careful. Hold on."

Elske hung on, climbing up the ladder, and scurried to the side of the boat where she could hold on to the railing. The sharp wind blew away her own chills; the taste of salt water on the air moistened her mouth and cheeks. Beriel went off with Nido to look at the section of the stern deck the captain had set aside for her particular use, but Elske stayed where she was and saw the city falling away behind them as the river emptied its waters into the open sea. They sailed out into this open water, until the islands that hugged the shore blended into the mainland, and all together they lay like a flat grey cloud along one horizon. Off to the west the sea moved empty, endless, as the boat sailed southwards. But by the time the sun was lowering itself behind the shelter of land, they had come back close to land, and they dropped anchor in a small cove on one of the islands.

After eating they went below, to sleep. Beriel's bunk had a thin straw mattress, but Elske wrapped herself around in a blanket and climbed into a hammock. This bed swayed with the waters that rocked the boat, and Elske woke many times, and slept again, until at last she could see lightening in the sky outside. Then she rolled herself quietly out of the hammock and let herself quietly out of their small room, and climbed in quiet stockinged feet up the ladder.

The ship was getting under way. Long slow waves rolled under her, lifting her bow and lowering it. The ship was like some snared bird, struggling to rise, but falling.

Elske leaned against the railing as the ship rose and fell under her. The cook had a steaming cauldron set out on his stone hob, but her stomach disliked the smell of food. She would have liked fresh water, though. She walked off-balance over to the helmsman to ask if there was any water. "Are ye blind?" he asked, laughing at his wit.

Elske could only smile, and he relented. He pointed to a barrel at the boat's midsection. A wooden ladle was tied at its side, and she thanked him.

Water cooled her mouth, and moistened it. The wind blew from behind her, lazily, and clouds covered the sky. The deck rolled under her feet, and her legs felt weak.

Elske had just seated herself on cushions provided in their section of the stern, had just closed her eyes, when she was called to answer Beriel's summons. She went slowly down the ladder, feeling that if her feet slipped on the rungs her arms would lack the strength to catch and hold her. In the dark companionway the air was close, and in their cabin, too. Beriel wanted the chamber pot emptied. "Unbolt the shutter," she instructed, "and empty it out of the porthole."

The swaying rolling surging of the ship was stronger, below, and also slower. Elske felt sick, but not with fever; it was as if she had swallowed into her stomach something which it did not wish to keep. A cold sweat misted her face. She turned around to return the chamber pot to its hook under Beriel's bunk—but brought her stomach up into it, instead.

She knew she was vomiting. She had seen men at the Volkking's feast empty their bellies of honey mead and meat. But she did not remember ever having done so herself.

"Elske! Don't—! What—?" and then Beriel laughed. "You're seasick. I never was, not even in storms. Come, you have to get into fresh air. There will be no getting over it if you stay here below. Come," and she lifted Elske onto her feet, then pushed her out the door.

Elske hauled herself back up the ladder.

It was the same clouded sky overhead and the same wood decking underfoot, and Elske fell back onto the same cushions from which she had arisen when summoned. There she spent the long day. Sometimes Beriel was nearby, and sometimes Elske dozed uneasily, and sometimes she stumbled to the barrel for a mouthful of water, and often she leaned over the railing to vomit. In the afternoon, Nido came to sit with her. He had none of his customary liveliness and she knew that he, too, had caught the seasickness. When the ship rode at anchor in protected waters that evening, Elske felt more herself, although she did not eat. Beriel offered consolation. "Seasickness only lasts a day or two in this gentle weather."

Elske waited for the named time to pass. Nido was his usual self again after only a day, and in two days had forgotten that he ever shared Elske's misery. Elske, who had never before had any such misery, had enough now to share with any who asked. She lived on deck, in the fresh air, and refused to go below, even in rain. She slept out on the deck, also, because even at anchor the ship swayed with the movement of the water. After a few days, she found she could keep some of the evening meal down. "That's a good thing, or you'd starve. The captain says there's some, the sea always brings up their stomachs," Beriel reported, scraping clean her own bowl of stewed fish.

Elske waited three days, then four, five.

Eight days, then nine, ten—

"Do you never complain?" Nido asked her. "You look like you're dying, all pale and greeny. How can you stand it?"

Elske endured. Beriel grew impatient with her, and restless, too. "This ship is twenty paces long, and I've walked it a hundred times. More than a hundred. I've explored into every cabin—although the captain was none too pleased to show me his, and he doesn't know I could find his strongbox where he thinks it's so well-concealed. I've counted every piece of cargo. Don't you want to know what we're carrying, Elske?"

"No," Elske said, but at the sight of Beriel's bored displeasure she found words in her throat to add, "Later, perhaps. Perhaps tonight."

"Tonight I'll be tired, sleepy not restless. I need to tell you now. There are a dozen barrels—hidden away under the stacks of furs. Barrels the same size as they store ale in but marked by dustings of fine, dark powder. Do you know what I think we are carrying?"

"Later," Elske answered, and Beriel went off to join Nido at his work of repairing one of the chairs from the captain's cabin.

"You look terrible," everyone said to her, and Elske smiled weakly, and nodded her agreement, unable to speak. The times she felt well enough for company, most of the others were asleep, except for whichever sailors stood the watch; those men made her companions of the journey. The ship rode quietly at night, and by dawn Elske often felt entirely well. Now that she knew sickness, she could recognize and name this well-feeling, and take pleasure in it, too. Until the ship raised anchor and set sail again.

As they moved southwards, into spring, spring rushed northwards to greet them. When they were not more than a few nights from Trastad, the night air warmed enough so that Elske was never wakened by the cold. When they were at almost two sennights' distance, Elske could smell on a light wind, blowing off the land, the sweetness of flowers. In Trastad, when a flower came into bloom, if you bent over it you could just catch its perfume. Here in the south, the air itself was flowered. "Does it always smell so, the southern air?" she asked Beriel.

"It's only spring," Beriel answered, but this was Elske's fifteenth spring, and this was more than spring.

And then one afternoon, while sunlight poured down over the deck of the ship and the sails thumped sullenly on their masts, she could see a cluster of buildings on the distant shore, where a wide river entered. Behind the houses, a dark forest spread backwards, so thick and heavy that it seemed to be pushing the little wooden buildings into the water. That day the captain lingered far out to sea, and it was almost full dark before he brought the ship close in, to anchor. Nido explained to Elske, "That town has no name, but all know to keep a distance from it. They're thieves, pirates—and they sell slaves. They can be bribed, sometimes, if your cargo means less to them than gold, but they always choose to board and take Trastader vessels."

"This is where I go ashore, Nido," Beriel announced.

"My Lady, you can't go to shore here. What kind of a man do you think my captain is, to leave two unescorted women here? What kind of a fool do you think him, to put himself in danger by lingering at this place?"

Beriel didn't hesitate. "Enough of a fool to transport barrels of what looks like ground charcoal into the south, but which someone might—or might not—guess to be black powder," she said to Nido's surprised face. Then she added, "I wonder if the Council knows what Var Kenric is shipping into the south, or why one of Var Kenric's near relatives has been given the position of assistant carpenter, when he hasn't completed four years of his apprenticeship and the requirement is for seven. I wonder if Var Jerrol—who is the eyes and ears of the Council—can have been kept ignorant of this merchandise or if it isn't, instead, his own, alone or in partnership with Var Kenric, and the Council kept blind and deaf on this matter. Tell your captain this, if he objects, and tell him that I require to be delivered onto land in the morning. Your ship is safely south of Pericol and we will make our further way by ourselves. Isn't that right, Elske?" Beriel asked.

Elske agreed. She would have agreed to anything that marked the end of this terrible journey.

CHAPTER 14

WHILE NIDO WAS ROWING THEM to shore in the morning, Elske watched the ship fall back, and away. The curved wooden sides rose high out of the water, and the tall masts stretched up into a pale sky. Nido's oars dipped and pulled in the water. He tried to persuade Beriel to sail on to Celindon, to make a safer journey from that city, but his words affected her no more than the slapping of the waves affected their little boat. When he'd pulled the little boat up onto a narrow beach, Nido gave Beriel his hand, still making his quarrels. "Leave me," Beriel answered him, and he obeyed.

Beriel was impatient. "Come along," she commanded Elske. "What are you doing?"

"Looking back," Elske said. She had looked back over the distance to flames, leaving the Volkaric, and now she looked back to sails being raised, leaving Trastad.

"It'll take us the better part of the morning to reach Pericol and I'd like to be far from that place before dark has fallen," Beriel said. "Take up the pack."

But Elske had started to undress, letting her overskirt fall to the ground.

"*Now* what are you doing?"

"Putting on the trousers. I can make you a pair, in a day; we could delay that day. It would be safer to travel as a pair of young men, wouldn't it?"

"I doubt anything could keep us safe from these citizens of Pericol who try everything—rape and robbery, and there are some who enjoy torture, or we might be sold into slavery. I know them. If Josko is still their King, I've dealt with him before, but if he has been killed—"

"Who would kill the King?"

"Any one of these cutthroats who thought he could get away with it. But Josko is strong, and cruel, a madman in a fight they say. Also, he makes fair judgements, and even thieves and pirates prefer some order in their lives, in their home city. Even thieves and pirates like to keep their possessions and women to themselves. So they allow Josko to rule over them."

"None would have dared to attack the Volkking."

"Josko has his protections. He has Wileen, and although a man might leave Josko sitting in his own blood, he knows he must then deal with Wileen—who would take revenge."

"Why would you know such people?" Elske tied her trousers at the waist.

"He held me captive the first time I came through Pericol, to go to Trastad. But Josko enjoyed a bold child. Who was a girl child. Who paid her own ransom. Who claimed to be Queen, and could make him laugh."

"Perhaps then you *should* wear trousers, my Lady, now that you aren't a child."

"A Queen," and here Beriel paused, as if troubled for the way to speak it, "must always be seen to be a Queen. I will never be otherwise." She looked at Elske, in trousers and the Wolfer boots, her shirt hanging out loose and her cloak draped over one shoulder. "You'll do for my escort, perhaps; and it is well for you to try, for I've never treated with Josko and not had soldiers nearby. Tie your hair back, and now can we go?"

They scrambled along the land's edge, which was sometimes stony outcropping, sometimes stony beach, and every now and then a shallow cove with a narrow pebbled beach at its heart. Elske followed Beriel, her feet too warm in the boots but too softened by the years in Trastad for barefooted comfort. She had the pack slung across her back, carrying Beriel's clothing as well as the maps Beriel had copied from those Var Vladislav kept. What wealth they had, Beriel carried in three purses. The lightest purse was at her waist. She had one not quite so light hidden under her skirt, at the side. The third and richest purse was in fact the hem of her skirt, which Elske had sewn up in little pockets for storage of coins, and golden chains, and the heavy medallion, the best of her wealth. Before leaving Trastad, Beriel had purchased a knife for Elske, and she carried her own; they wore their weapons sheathed, but only half hidden.

Beriel had said it was unwise to show weapons too openly in Pericol. That might be taken as a challenge, or a threat, or even a game; but games in Pericol were as deadly as challenges and threats. Also, it was unwise to appear helpless, if you wanted to reach Josko safely.

"We will have to see him," Beriel said, picking her way over the stones which the withdrawing tides had left damp and slippery. She held her skirts up, but they were still wet, and dark with mud. "Only he can offer us the mounts we need and make it easier for us to supply ourselves at a fair price. That is," Beriel laughed, "fair price in Pericol. Even the profit-mongering merchants of Trastad would be ashamed to take what the tradesmen of Pericol demand for their goods."

"Do they receive what they demand?" Elske wondered.

"It depends on how desperate the need. It's cheaper, often, to murder than to purchase; and the tradesmen know this, too."

Like the Volkking's stronghold, Pericol had no outlying farmlands, although there were a few huts—small gardens spread out before them, fishing nets spread out to dry on straw roofs—huddled together at the shore. Then there appeared a dirt path.

Beriel led Elske along this path, which kept them to single file through dense and overgrown woods before it became broad enough to walk abreast on, as it ran between crowded wooden buildings and became a muddy street. Branches and logs had been scattered along the street to make it firmer underfoot. There were no fences, no flowers, no trees in Pericol. Pericol was mud streets and log houses, two stubby docks and a single well; they could have crossed the city in no more time than it took the sun to rise.

It was midday by the time they entered the city, and the citizens were just stirring awake. Shutters were thrown open, and men called to one another from doorways, rubbing their faces and urinating. The sky had filled with clouds but the air was still warm. Elske followed Beriel.

Beriel walked without haste or hesitation, her shoulders high. Some of the men in doorways called out to her, but they did not approach. Women called out at her from windows, hooting and mocking; they called to Elske, too, as if she were a young man. Elske walked behind Beriel, as unresponsive as her mistress.

The muddy street twisted down to a broad river, where low, marshy islands floated on glassy water. On the opposite bank, more log houses could be seen. Some coracles were tied up to ramshackle docks, and some masted boats as well, such as a fisherman might take out into the sea. A sign with two gold coins painted on it hung over a doorway, and there Beriel entered.

Elske followed.

The room they entered was lit by many candles, some in lanterns hung on the walls, some standing in a pool of their own wax on wooden tables, some set into wooden rings, like the wheels of wagons, hung down from the ceiling. The air was thick with the smell of ale mingling with smoke from the open fire, odors of roasting meat, sweat, cheese, privies and damp riverside mud. The room was crowded with people, mostly men, lounging on benches along the walls, or gathered around long wooden tables.

At Beriel's entrance, the noise ceased and every eye was fixed upon her.

Beriel ignored this greeting and moved into the room, winding between tables. The noise rose up again like waves around them as Elske followed.

Beriel crossed the room towards a closed door. Following, Elske looked around at drinking men and women with their breasts half pushed out of their bodices. In a back corner, three men looked with hatred across the table at a fourth; but he was not uneasy. Near them, a man and a girl leaned back against a wall; he offered her a coin. In the shadow of the balcony, two men held a third with a knife to his throat and a hand over his mouth. The third man's eyes wept with fear and fury; his hands couldn't reach to the sword at his side, for they were pinned back behind him; his booted feet kicked out, and his captors backed away, mocking. He was a young man, bearded, and his red hair shone like fire out of the shadows in which he struggled to save his life. At one of the tables in the center of the room, a grey-haired woman—looking like one of the distinguished Varinnes of Trastad—dealt out cards to narrow-eyed men, who tossed their wagers into a bowl she had set before her. At another table, two women sat on the laps of two men and all four laughed openmouthed, and drank from tankards.

Beriel was observed, but not questioned. She was watched, but not accosted. Everything about Beriel declared that she had a purpose and a right to be where she was, going whence she went. Elske followed in the wake of Beriel's passage, looking all about her.

The door opened before Beriel had raised a fist to knock. A man stood framed in it, his face bright with greeting. His thin brown hair was tied back, his grey-brown beard was trimmed short, and his smile showed brown teeth. He held out a hand and Beriel put hers into it.

The room behind watched all of this.

The man wore a dark tunic, not clean, and tights. A sword hung at his side and he had a pair of knives in his belt. He wore golden rings on his fingers and golden hoops in his ears. Raising Beriel's hand to his mouth, and bowing over it, he watched the room behind her.

"Welcome, my Queen. I welcome you to my humble manor," he said. His voice was rich as red wine, and loud, to carry all around the tavern. "You honor me with this unexpected visit. Please, enter." He stepped back to let Beriel pass. Elske followed.

When they were through, he closed the door behind them and asked, "Was that greeting enough, Queenie? Was that the honor you looked for?"

This chamber was as large as the room they'd just crossed. A curtained bed stood at the rear, beside another closed door. Two chairs with cushioned seats and backs, and carved arms like thrones, were set out near to the fire. In one of them sat a woman, a jeweled pin in the yellow hair that tumbled in curls down onto her shoulders, her dress a bright woven blue and her stockinged feet resting on a pillow. The woman glanced at Elske without interest. It was Beriel who commanded her attention.

"I am flattered that you come to me without soldiers," the man said. "This—boy—not being, as I take it, much of a soldier."

Beriel didn't answer the man. Instead, she returned to the door through which they had just entered. She opened it wide and stood in the open doorway until the room outside fell silent again, and then she raised her arm and pointed. She motioned with that hand, and waited.

Elske could not see past her mistress. She could see only the fall of Beriel's cloak and her brown hair, hanging in a long braid down her back, and her arm raised, imperiously.

The red-haired young man, his face still wet with tears, stepped into the room, a hand on the hilt of his sword, his eyes fixed on Beriel's face as if hearing words she did not speak.

"What do you—?" their host said, but Beriel interrupted his thought.

"Did you permit the slaughter on your very doorstep, Josko? Had you given those two louts permission to take this fellow?"

"I have nothing to steal," the young man protested to Josko. His beard might be soft, and his eyes might weep, but he was no coward. "Why do they attack me? I have not a single coin."

"Oh, well," Josko answered, and a smile returned to his face. "You have youth, and good boots, that's a sweet piece of steel you carry even if it is plain-hilted—"

"They would have killed me," the young man insisted, indignant. "What kind of law do you have here?"

"As little as possible," Josko answered lightly. "What regulation there is exists to protect our own citizens. *My* own people, I should say, for this place is *my* stronghold."

"And it's not much of a place, neither," the young man

said. He might have a fox's hair, but he did not have a fox's cunning. "You ought to warn strangers."

"But would that work to my advantage?" Josko asked, patiently. "For then my people might have to turn against themselves for their livelihoods, and eventually they would have to turn on me. No, we welcome strangers to Pericol. They are our lifeblood."

The woman, who had been silent at the back of the room, rose then, and came forward to them. "This is tiresome and you are only teasing," she said. "Get on with it, Josko."

"Beriel must tell me, then, what she wanted with this fellow," Josko answered. "He's handsome enough, if you like pink cheeks. Do you think he's pretty enough for Beriel, Wileen?"

Nobody responded to this jesting.

"There's a door at the back of the room, boy," Beriel said. "Anyone who leaves through that door has Josko's hand over his head until the next daybreak. After that, you'll be fair game again. Go now," she commanded, putting up a hand to silence whatever he might have said to her, and he obeyed.

"You're in my debt now, Queenie," Josko said. "To the measure of one life."

"I have owed you a life for years now," Beriel answered, "and I begin to hope that you will never call that debt in."

"This is the gratitude of a Queen?" Josko laughed, and beside him, Wileen smiled approval.

"And I have another favor to ask of you," Beriel said. "Two

favors, if you keep careful count and that makes three, if we include the life just granted."

"By all means let it be included," Josko said. "May I offer you refreshment, and to your man, also?"

"No, but we thank you," Beriel said.

Josko and Wileen seated themselves in the two chairs before the fire, and Beriel stood before them with Elske at her shoulder, but several paces back. Elske was overly warm now, in her cape and fur boots, so close to a fire. Beriel stood in the petitioner's position, but she seemed to be granting rather than asking.

"I ask to purchase two horses from your stables, and a supply of food, too."

"You aren't going to stay with us until an escort arrives? The first ships are expected to pass within two sennights, if the weather holds. Your own escort is looked for daily," Wileen said. She leaned forward to ask, "If I were suspicious, I might think that you wished to evade the company of your own soldiers."

"Why should I trouble my soldiers when I can ride to meet them?" Beriel asked.

"I might wonder if you intend to return to your home," Wileen asked.

"There I can reassure you," Josko said. "Queenie would never give up her throne, not of her own choice, not of her own will, not alive."

"She's not the crowned Queen," Wileen pointed out. "For all that her father is dead, and buried, and she the eldest—"

"The King is dead?" Beriel demanded. "When?"

"Word reached us at winter's end, with the first who came out from the Kingdom," Wileen said.

"The King is dead, long live the King," Josko added.

"My brother is crowned." It was not a question. Beriel looked over her shoulder at Elske, for once indecisive, for the first time since Elske had known her, unsure.

"Perhaps he's not yet crowned," Josko said. "What will you do?" he asked Beriel.

"Claim my throne," Beriel said. "So I ask you for horses, and food, and I will pay you twice their worth if you can answer me speedily."

"If you can pay so much, why should I let you go?" Josko asked. "When your pockets are so thick with gold—more than you offer, I'm sure. When there might be a King in the Kingdom who would be glad to sit unopposed on his throne, why should I give you what you ask?"

"Because the gratitude of a true Queen is a treasure," Beriel answered him, "while the thanks of a false Prince come stuffed with adders. Because the King of Thieves might someday need a deeper hiding place than Pericol, and a friend to help him live comfortably there."

"A Queen's word being law in her own Kingdom," Josko observed.

"As long as the man seeking sanctuary abides by the laws of the land," Beriel answered.

Josko turned to Wileen then, to ask, "It has value, don't you think?"

She agreed, and asked, "Do we need a pass? Some written word?"

"Well thought, queen of my heart." He gave Beriel paper, ink and quill. While she wrote he asked Wileen, "But what if Guerric should be King and this paper prove worthless?"

"He'll kill her for certain, then, if she has made a public challenge, and we'll be out two horses and some food, plus the life of a nondescript young man. A bearable loss," Wileen decided.

"No; too unequal," Josko announced. He stood up. "You," he said to Elske. "Come to me."

Elske looked to Beriel, who nodded. Elske approached the man until she stood not two paces before him.

"A life for a life," he suggested. "This life for that young man's. What do you say, Queenie?"

Beriel was shaking her head. "I say, this is my proved servant, when there is no other I can trust. I do not wish to be parted from this servant."

"I do not wish it, either, Josko," Wileen said, but she spoke as if this were some small and careless thing.

"And do I obey your wishes?" Josko asked Wileen.

"You know the answer to that," she said to him.

He walked around Elske, looking her up and down, and answered Wileen. "You know that you are not my wife."

She answered him, "I don't need to be a wife to keep a man at my side."

Beriel said, "I will take my chances in the streets of Pericol before I will part with this servant."

"You would have no chance," Josko told her, amused.

Beriel said nothing, for a long time. Then she spoke. "I would have a chance."

"Leave the lad be," Wileen said to Josko.

"Lad?" he asked, and in one swift move he had a knife from his belt and with his free hand shoved Elske backwards, until he held her pinned against the wall. The point of the dagger was at her throat as sharp as a needle, and the man looked down into her eyes.

He meant rape. She could see that. There was nothing she could do against him. But he would not live long afterwards. That she promised herself, staring back into his mud-colored eyes.

And Josko released her. He lowered the knife and took his hand from her shoulder to take her by the hair at the back of her head. "This is no lad." He pulled her around to set her in front of Wileen. "Haven't you got eyes? This is a girl, and she's dangerous. I think she's even more dangerous than you are, Queenie," Josko said. "But if you want to be a lad and you can't grow a beard—I'd better cut your hair for you," he said, bringing his knife around.

"If I were you, I'd settle for stripping the girl of her boots," Wileen said with laughter in her voice. "They're worth at least one life, if you ask me. Wolfskin, is my guess, and warm enough for Wolfers in their snowy caves. How would a girl get a pair of Wolfer boots?"

Josko shoved Elske back towards Beriel. "How indeed?" he asked, and "Do you refuse me the boots?" he asked Beriel.

Beriel raised her hand, in a gesture of command, and Elske bent over, pulled off her boots one after the other, and gave them to Beriel. Beriel presented them to Josko, who set them down beside his feet. They looked like a child's boots there beside his heavy leather ones, so he picked them up, and laid them in Wileen's lap.

"I'm honored by the gift, Josko," she said. "And yes, pleased, too. You're in a generous humor to let these two pass safely."

"And horses? Food?" Beriel asked.

He held out his hand, and she gave Elske the light purse from her waist, to hold, while she reached up under her skirt to take out the heavier one. This she gave to Josko, without even counting the coins in it.

He weighed it on the palm of his hand. "Two horses from my stables, and tell the men to fetch you bread and cheese for a sennight's journey."

"How *did* you get the boots?" Wileen asked Elske.

"I am Wolfer born," she answered.

"Wolfer?" This interested Josko. "How do you know she is not a spy?" he asked Beriel.

"But she is a spy," Beriel answered him, and now she was the one laughing.

"So that's how you plan to do it," Josko said. "You'll use Wolfers."

Wileen disagreed. "Beriel wouldn't betray her own people."

"She's ambitious for the crown," Josko answered her.

"Beriel is a Queen," Wileen said. "She would never give her land over to Wolfers."

"What do you wager me?" Josko asked her, and she was thinking of her answer when Beriel interrupted their game to ask, "Do I have your leave to go?"

They both stood up, then, stood side by side. "We give you leave, Beriel, Queen that may be. And you have given us your word for safe passage, safe keeping, in need."

"You have my word," Beriel affirmed.

She left the room without looking back, and Elske followed in her stockinged feet. Beriel hesitated at the doorway, to let Elske hold it open for her.

Outside, late afternoon light filled the air and painted the river gold and red where it flowed past Pericol and out into the sea. Beriel hesitated on the covered wooden porch. The steep muddy bank fell away below them; if they had wished, they could have climbed up on the railing and jumped into the water, to join all the other men and women who had fallen out of the world from Josko's porch.

After taking a little time for thought, Beriel descended the staircase to a path along the high riverbank, with Elske following. Something stirred under the staircase and Beriel had her dagger out before she had turned. Elske also had drawn.

A man spoke as he emerged, crawling and cobwebbed. "Lady." He brushed dirt from his face and red hair, and his knees, too. He straightened up, then bowed clumsily from the waist. "My Queen. I owe you my life."

"You *are* one of my people," Beriel said. "Your name?"

"Win. I am the third son of the innkeeper at the Ram's Head."

"In Hildebrand's demesne."

"Yes, under Northgate's banner."

Beriel wore her royalty as naturally as her own skin and as she drew close to her own land, her queenliness intensified, or so it seemed to Elske, but now she turned to Elske like any girl in her delight at her own cleverness. "I thought he was. I *knew* he was mine. Tell me, Win," she demanded, turning back to where he stood red-cheeked, eyes shining. "Why have you come to Pericol, and without any coins to buy food or safety? Do you flee the law? Has winter been so harsh in Northgate's lands that younger sons must find livings outside of the Kingdom?"

"I came to protect you, my Queen."

Beriel asked no more. "Then you must travel with me. Stay hidden while we get horses and food. I'll look for you just within the forest."

He bowed, and Beriel walked on along the path, without another word for him, or a glance to see what direction he chose. Elske followed Beriel.

At the stables, the men gave Beriel a wide-backed grey palfrey and a livelier chestnut, and one seat and tack, but said that her manservant would have to ride barebacked. Beriel insisted that they find some kind of bit and reins for Elske, and they did. She insisted that Elske be given a blanket, folded, to sit on, and they found one. She insisted that the stable boy be sent for the food Josko had ordered, and he was. She required the men to find a pair of boots, of a size for her servant, and one of them ran after the stable boy to tell him that, then ran back to face Beriel.

Beriel refused to step out of the sun and into the shadowy stables, and so the two men brought the horses out for her inspection, and got them ready. Through all of this, Elske said nothing; she was a sullen lad accompanying his mistress on her willful way, a lad who could not be bothered even to raise his eyes to watch the dealings his mistress conducted.

"You'll want hobbles," the stable men told Beriel. Their greedy eyes had noted the purse at Beriel's waist. "Otherside, if these two get loose they'll come back to us like calves to their mothers at feeding time, and don't think our Josko doesn't know that."

Beriel thought hard about the question, her brow wrinkled, her mouth frowning. At last, she offered two silver coins, for two hobbles. The men were pleased. The boy returned with heavy round loaves of bread and a wheel of cheese, two strings of onions, and also a pair of heavy, much-worn boots. Elske stuffed straw into the toes, and shoved her feet into them, as she thought a boy might who resented wearing another man's boots. She put the food into the pack she carried.

"That's a fine seat Josko has given me," Beriel remarked to one of the men, and he smiled to show his three remaining teeth and tell her, "That 'tis. It belonged to the widow of a tanner, from the south, fleeing Wolfers. Josko let her pass through—in exchange for a horse and its gear, and a handful of coins, and a certain necklace of twisted gold that Wileen fancied, set with bright blue stones, as I was told. Whether she made it to the safety of Trastad we don't know. That would be up to the captain of the boat, wouldn't it?" he asked Beriel, smiling.

She didn't answer him.

"There's worse than Wolfers, to sniff out a fat widow,"

he said. "Or a proud young woman, ill-attended."

Beriel stared at him until his smile faded, and his eyes lowered to elude her gaze, and he bowed his head to her as she walked past him. "We'll walk the horses out of Pericol," she announced, "as Josko has given us safe passage through." She took the reins, and led the chestnut, which followed her without hesitation, as did Elske, leading her own mount and carrying their pack on her back.

Pericol the city ended abruptly, muddy streets becoming a thin dirt track at the last log house. Then they were on a narrow path through forest, with the river somewhere nearby but hidden from sight. Elske could smell the river, sometimes, and when Win stepped out onto the path to join them, his boots were damp from clambering along its bank. He hailed them, cheerful as a robin.

He gave his hands to help Beriel mount and held the reins while she settled into the seat, her legs to one side. Then he gave his hands to Elske. There was no way for Elske to ride comfortably or safely unless she rode astride, which suited her trousers. Win said he could trot along behind them and catch up when they halted, but Beriel did not allow that. "You would slow our progress," she said, and ordered him first to tie the pack onto her own mount and then to ride seated behind Elske.

While they traveled, they listened closely but could hear only forest sounds. It was midspring here, leaves unfurling and birds restlessly nesting and the quick quiet animals on their daytime hunts. Nobody trailed them out of Pericol. Josko's hand was over them, for the day.

They used what was left of that day to move north, putting as much distance as they could between themselves and Pericol.

CHAPTER 15

A S THEY TRAVELED NORTHWARDS, LEAFY trees and thick undergrowth separated them from the river, for the traders who used this path hoped to remain hidden from the river and its pirates. As they traveled, the sun lowered into the west, until the trees were black silhouettes against an orange sky, and still Beriel did not rein in her horse.

Win told Elske that it was seven days' journey on horseback from Pericol to the Falcon's Wing, the inn at the southernmost point of the Kingdom. "At a horse's walking gait," he said, adding, "It took me longer, but I was on foot." As they rode on into the evening he started to sing. His songs told stories: of the young hunter who chased a white doe into the forest, where she turned into a beautiful Princess, and he stayed with her forever, and was never seen again; of the soldier glad to die in battle for his King, although he also thought sadly back to his wife and children, in the village he would never see again; of Jackaroo on his winged horse, and how he disguised himself as a puppeteer and went from north to south with the fairs, to see that all was well in the Kingdom.

"And if he sees that all is well?"

"Then he goes back to sleep under the mountain, and is never seen again."

Elske laughed. "All of your songs come to the same ending—'never seen again.'"

Win was merry. "Is that not life's ending, also?"

Beriel looked around then. "This singing and chattering," she said. "It displeases me."

Elske asked, "How can it displease you?" but Win said, "I apologize, my Queen," so seriously that Elske quelled her own high spirits. After that, Win would only hum, the melody repeating and repeating, to pass the time.

Elske thought of Beriel's queenly imperiousness, and kept her thoughts her own. Beriel in desperate need in Trastad was not the same companion as Beriel riding to claim her Kingdom. And how could she be unchanged, whatever Elske might wish?

The air grew murky, thick, purpled with the shadows that were closing in around them. Still Beriel rode on, and even when night cloaked them so they could barely see one another, she did not stop. So at last Win called ahead to her, "My Queen, there is a clearing, with the firestones set and a fire built. We're a safe distance from Pericol, and it's not wise to ask the horses to walk on when none can see what lies on the path."

Beriel reined in her horse. "Here?"

"Soon," Win said, and it was no time at all until he said, "There."

In the darkness, the clearing could be felt more than seen, until Win took a tinderbox out of his purse and struck it, to start a fire. When the dry twigs and grasses had infected the sticks and logs with flame, they could see the circle of stones and the tall ring of trees that fenced a flat space, grassy underfoot. Win had hobbled the horses by then and Elske had opened the pack to remove bread and cheese. "There is water in a bucket. On one of the trees—here. I had only half of it, less than half."

Beriel had seated herself on a log, her cloak gathered around her. Elske lifted down the bucket and read, in the restless light from the fire, a notice that hung above it. "To who comes after me, Fill this for who comes after you: that none go thirsty." She carried the bucket over to Beriel, who dipped her hand into it, and drank.

"Why didn't you fill it again?" Elske asked Win, as they awaited their turn to drink. Win looked surprised, as if she were asking him some unlikely question, so she explained, "The notice asks you to refill the bucket for whoever comes next."

"You can read?"

"You cannot," Elske realized.

"He's not a Lord," Beriel explained to Elske. "Only the Lords are taught letters, and some of the Ladies if they ask to learn. As I did," she said. "Come, sit and eat. There are things I would ask you, innkeeper's son."

Win sat on the ground. Elske cut off chunks of bread, offering them to Beriel first, and then the young man, then she cut hunks of cheese. They kept the bucket of water where all could dip into it. The fire crackled and burned, the horses grazed and stamped, and all around them the forest whispered in the wind. A disk of dark sky above was filled with stars, as thick as daisies scattered in a field.

"Who are you?" Beriel asked. "Who are you, really?"

Elske had difficulty remembering that just that morning she had awakened on a ship, on the sea, all the air salty.

"I am just what I said, my Queen, the youngest son of the innkeeper at the Ram's Head."

And she had long forgotten the smoke-choked air of Mirkele's little house, and the wide skies that spread out over the treeless land of the Volkaric.

"Why would a son of the innkeeper at the Ram's Head be sent to protect me?"

Elske had no part in their talk. She was content to sit, and chew on the thick bread, and watch the skies, and listen.

"But nobody sent me, nobody knows—I don't know what they think happened to me."

"Then what have you to protect me against?"

"A plot. Against you, against your life, if you were to return unwed. He said—"

"Who said?"

"The King. Your brother. King Guerric, who was crowned at the end of winter, thirty days after his father's death."

Beriel rose, then, and walked away from the fire to stare into the thick black forest. At last, she turned, and returned to her seat. She asked then, "Said what, Win? What did he say? This King."

"It was whispers," Win answered uneasily. "I do not believe them."

"Speak it."

"They said, that you had formed a shameful alliance and were with child."

"And the man?"

"He'd been put to death, as would you have been were you not a royal Princess. Guerric said . . ." Win stopped again. "Lady, there is truth in me, even if it angers you to hear what I tell you. There are many of the people who believe you should have been crowned, and I think there must be those among the Lords, also. What I speak is treason against the King, I know, and if you tell me I must die for it, then I will."

Beriel waited.

"The land trembles, my Queen," Win took up his tale, after waiting for her silence to end. "This is more than fear of change. The new King has taken two cousins for his advisors, making the eldest his First Minister and giving the younger rule over the Priests and laws. The new King keeps the army under his own hand. The soldiers are restless—the King's courage is untested and they doubt his generalship. The Priests complain that young Lord Aymeric lacks foresight and judgement; moreover, he cannot even read the laws, having lost whatever knowledge of letters he once had. The Lords are angry when Lord Ditrik stands between them and their sworn King, to whom they owe their allegiance, and who owes them honors in return."

"And the people?" Beriel asked.

"The people are frightened. Their few coins are squeezed out of them, like cider from apples, and those who have no coins are set deeper into servitude. The people think of Jackaroo, and some dare to speak aloud of him. They hoard food in their own cellars, for themselves and their families; they begin to look on their neighbors with untrusting eyes. The people say you have forgotten them. Some say you have married the Emperor of the East, leaving the Kingdom to the ravages of your brother, and some say you have blessed the Kingdom by leaving it to its rightful King, and these two factions distrust one another. All agree that you have abandoned your Kingdom. But I knew you would not," Win said.

"How would you know that?" Beriel asked.

"You are our Queen," Win answered. "You could not abandon us. I saw you once—when you were a girl, a child—"

"How can that be, when you are yet so young?"

"My Queen, I have two or three years more than you. Do not mistake me, for all that I look young, and soft. Let others overlook me, but do not you. I saw you the once, at a hanging offered your father and his retinue for their entertainment, when they visited Earl Northgate."

"The man did not die well," Beriel remembered.

"No, not bravely. And he was a murderer who struck his victim from behind, and we all knew that of him. But his wife asked mercy for him—"

"I remember."

"For the sake of his children. The King refused it."

"Do you question the King's judgement in that?"

"No. And neither did you, except—"

"Except?" Beriel demanded.

"You sent one of your maidservants, with a purse of coins, for the family, so that they would not starve, so that the widow might have a dowry to attract another husband for herself and father for the children. You asked only that the gift be kept secret."

"What was the woman to you?" Beriel asked.

"A woman of the village, only that, but she had made an unthrifty marriage. I have a troublesome heart," Win smiled, his teeth showing in the firelight, "as my father and brothers will tell you, mother and sisters, too. My heart was troubled for the woman, and her children."

"What was the woman to you?" Beriel asked again, patient.

Win lowered his head. "The man was my uncle. None from the inn offered kindness to his wife, because they were shamed by him. He was a villain and a coward, as we all knew. But his deeds were not done by his wife, nor by his children. Were they? You knew that they were not, my Queen, even when you were a child yourself."

"So I had sealed you to me, and I never knew your face," Beriel said, not displeased.

"So it is with many of the people. You are our hope."

"Which is why you came to warn me."

"And save you, if I can. He plots your death, this Guerric, whom I will not call my King."

"It is not for you to choose who rules," Beriel reminded him.

"I choose who I serve," Win said, proudly.

"So might you change your loyalty, should you be displeased."

"I think I am loyal," Win said, so simply that Elske knew he could be trusted. "You are the firstborn and the heir under the law, unless you renounce your claim. Do you renounce your claim? If so, let me go with you, to serve you in whatever foreign land you like. If so, let us turn around now, because Guerric will not leave you alive five days within the Kingdom."

Beriel brushed aside that danger. "He cannot murder me."

"My Queen," Win said, rising up onto his knees. "You must believe me. Your safety lies in believing what I say. I am a man often trusted with another's secret joys, or fears. The short of it is that I have friends among the soldiers. They have told me this: The King has formed an escort to meet your vessel when it lands."

"As there was an escort to see me onto the ship last fall."

Elske didn't know why Beriel thwarted the telling of Win's tale, as if she needed to test Win's loyalty. So although she longed for sleep and rest, Elske kept herself awake, lest her mistress need her.

Win argued, "This escort will be different. Each soldier will be a stranger to all the others, because each man comes from a different village or city, each serves in a different company. Their orders depend on what they find when you step off the ship. Should you have a child with you, they will bring you back in chains to stand trial for your misconduct; and Guerric has ordered the Priests to prepare a case to try you by. If you have no child, then you must not arrive back in the Kingdom alive; and each soldier will be given a purse of gold. Gold is the prize the King offers to rid himself of this shamed sister. Should you bring a guard of your own hire, then it will be battle, until you and all who are with you are dead, as if by robbery."

"This is known?" Beriel demanded.

"Only by the soldiers of the King's chosen escort."

"No soldier questions the order?"

"There are enough who say that where smoke rises, there fire burns, and there are those who would save a civil war, and always there are those who wish to continue the gold that flows into their purses while Guerric rules," Win answered.

"Having less to lose, in wealth, in lands, in reputation, the people can see farther into the truth," Beriel said. "The people will support me."

"Think you?" Win asked. "Having less to lose, in wealth and lands and reputation, don't they guard their little more jealously?" But with the dangers defined, Win settled back, leaning against the log on which Beriel sat. He asked, "What will you do, my Queen?"

"I'll sleep," Beriel said. "I'll consider what you tell me. Then, sleep and waking, I'll consider further. We leave at first light," she told them.

This was the permission Elske had been waiting for, to slip down onto the ground and close her eyes.

It seemed to Elske that she had barely rested a moment when Beriel was shaking her by the shoulder, dragging her up and away from the comfort of sleep. Win refilled the bucket with water from the river and they loosed the horses. "We'll eat as we go," Beriel ordered. They were mounted and on their way before the first yellow beams of sunlight came tumbling down through the trees.

Once again Win rode behind Elske, his arms around her waist, and Beriel carried their pack behind her. Win rode silently, or sang softly to himself and Elske. There were more tales of Jackaroo, how Jackaroo dressed the bride, and how Jackaroo brought the three robbers to hanging. There was the song of a fisherman, calling to the fish as if he wooed them, and the song of an old woman after her man had died. There were children's songs in plenty. The Kingdom was a place where stories grew as plentifully as apples on a tree, Elske thought; Tamara would have been at home in the Kingdom.

On this sunlit day, far from Pericol, Beriel sometimes rode beside them and joined Win in his singing, her displeasure of the previous day forgotten. So the day's journey, although long, passed pleasantly.

That second evening, once again Beriel and Win talked about Guerric and his rule over the Kingdom, until Win said, hesitantly, "Also, my Queen. Also, there are tales from the northernmost holdings."

Elske pictured the map Beriel had shown her, the northern borders of the Kingdom up against high mountains.

"Where at the northern borders? The royal lands? Hildebrand's?"

"In Northgate's lands, under Hildebrand, but—it's cruel, my Queen."

Elske wondered what this news could be, if Win was more reluctant to speak it than he had been to tell of Guerric's plots.

"I have stomach for the cruelty of truth," Beriel said.

"A band of—wild men, thieves, monsters—"

Then Elske knew the end of his tale.

"They came out of the forests at the end of summer. They fell upon isolated holdings, one village, too. One boy glimpsed them and he ran home to tell his father of the strangers, but he found his father's holding in flames and all his family slaughtered, except for the youngest child, a girl of seven winters, and she was gone. Lord Hildebrand sent out his soldiery, and they found a number of holdings so destroyed, but they could find no battle. The enemy slipped away. The soldiers brought back one old woman in jabbering madness, who said it was the northern wind, howling, taking human form. They burn their victims like logs on a fire, while they eat and drink in its warmth."

"Do we know what they are?" Beriel asked.

"At the inn, merchants have told stories which we dismissed as the talk of men who enjoy frightening those they think simple, as fathers like to frighten their children. The merchants spoke of warrior bands, swooping down to take anything of value, gold, silver, food, clothing. They kill for the pleasure of killing and take prisoners—dark-haired women, a few men—only rarely. Although why they keep some men and slaughter others, nobody knows."

"For Wolfguard," Elske explained.

"Wolfers," Beriel said. "I thought so. I hoped not."

"These wild men speak gibberish," Win said.

"They speak Norther," Beriel told him, and said to him in Norther, "I thought the Kingdom was hidden away, safe from this danger. I hoped."

"Lady?" Win asked, uncomprehending.

"She spoke in Norther," Elske explained. "I'm Wolfer born," she explained.

"No." The firelight washed over his face like water, making shadows of his eyes, and then revealing his hidden thoughts. He stared closely at Elske, a sudden stranger. He asked Beriel, "How can that be? When you trust her."

"With my life."

Beriel gave this gift to Elske carelessly, as if to be trusted were the common fortune. But Elske opened her heart to take the gift into her care as if it were a babe.

Win made his decision. "If my Queen trusts you, then so will I," he said, and held out his hands to her. "I give you greeting, Lady Elske."

Elske took his hands in hers. This was another true servant to Beriel. "I give you greeting, Win," she said, while Beriel protested, "Elske is my servant."

Win's surprise spoke. "She can read. You trust her with your life. Her dress, hair—this is more than servant."

"If you cannot be a servant, then who will you be?" Beriel

asked Elske but answered herself, "I will think who you must be."

Win knew who he was, for Beriel. "I am in your debt for my life," he said, "so it is I who am your servant. And your soldier, too, if you need me, against your brother, against Wolfers. I am your man against any enemy who offers you harm."

"At the moment, you are my eyes and my ears in the Kingdom," Beriel said, and smiled at Elske, then asked, "But what is this Wolfguard you mentioned?"

Elske could tell her. "When the Volkking's warrior bands return in the fall, they must cross lands where wolves roam. So pairs of prisoners are bound together and set out, each night. These the wolves devour, leaving the warriors unharmed."

"The prisoners don't escape?" Win wondered.

"They're hobbled," Elske explained, and at the expression on both of their faces she added, "As we do with our horses."

"But they are men, not animals," Win protested.

"For the people of the Volkaric, they are human animals who cannot speak and have little courage, *Fruhckmen*. Would you never stake a goat to draw wolves away from your houses?"

Win said, "These Wolfers are fearless, the merchants say. They go into battle armed only with long knives, clad only in animal skins."

"I do not call it battle to attack an undefended holding," Beriel said.

"No human force can stop them," Win said.

"They were stopped in Selby," Elske told them. "My grand-mother was a girl in Selby when they fought off the Wolfers, all the men of Selby standing together. The Wolfers can be turned back," she assured Beriel. "At cost," she added. "With courage."

"The merchants say—" Win started, but then didn't fin-ish the thought.

"What do they say?" Beriel demanded, so Win told her this, also. "When you hear their cry, your heart freezes within you. Men have gone mad with fear, from just the Wolfer cry."

"And such enemies have come into my Kingdom?" Beriel cried out, as if she had taken a wound. "How will the crops be put into the fields so there will be food next winter?"

Win agreed. "Fear is plowed like salt into the farmlands of the north."

"And Sutherland?"

"The south feels far from danger. Let the wild men feed off the north, they say, thinking that will guarantee their own safety, with the rivers running between them and danger."

"Wolfers do fear water," Elske told her companions.

"And so we have Northgate's people for a Wolfguard of our own," Beriel observed bitterly, then said, "I will sleep now."

⋄ ⋄

THE LONG DAYS OF THE journey passed slowly, in sunshine, clouds or rain. Evenings were spent with whatever news from the Kingdom Win could remember, or guess at. Days held the steady thump of the horses' hooves on the packed dirt pathway and more stories, more songs, more questions from Beriel.

Elske did not need to be told when they had crossed the borders into the Kingdom. Beriel shone with it, like a sun, the Queen in her Kingdom. It was as if each breath she drew increased her pleasure, breathing that air. It was as if each hoof the chestnut planted onto that earth increased her strength. Beriel looked about her, to the broad slow-flowing river and the thick-trunked trees. She looked to the sky, less blue than her eyes.

By midday they had come to an inn, the Falcon's Wing, sleepy grey stone soaking up the spring sunlight. Beriel rode up to the doorway, and dismounted.

"My Queen," Win protested. "They will know you here."

"As they should. I must send messengers to the Earl Sutherland, my uncle, and to the King in his palace, to say when they may expect me."

"My Queen," Win said. "Do you think how this forewarning places you in harm's way?"

"I do not fear the King," Beriel said. "Rather, he should fear me."

"My Queen," Win said, "I think he does."

Beriel smiled up at him then, and offered him a hand to aid in his dismounting. "So you are more than the country onion you pretend," she said.

The three stood together, looking at the blank stone face of the building before them, and Beriel gave the order. "Announce me, Win. Tell the innkeeper of the Falcon's Wing that I have returned, and have need of messengers, and have need of fresh mounts. Tell him that we require also food for three, with his best ale. I will tell you, Win, since you concern yourself with my safety, that I will be safest riding openly to Sutherland's castle. If all know that I have set off, then all must seek out treachery should I not arrive."

She looked around her then, at the grey stone inn backed up against the tree-clogged forest, at the green meadow stretched out before them and the blue curve of river beyond; all under a bowl of sky out of which a warm and generous sun poured its light. "Is it not beautiful, my Kingdom?" Beriel asked Elske.

CHAPTER 16

THE MESSENGERS RODE OFF AT the gallop, but Beriel's party rested at the Falcon's Wing. Elske and Beriel walked across the meadow, down to the river's edge and out onto a dock, and when they returned, the innkeeper had set out a platter of baked fish for them, and bread, and onions, and tankards of his own ale. Win was fed in the inn kitchens.

At Beriel's command, Win brought their fresh mounts around. Elske, at Beriel's command, changed her garments, wearing now a dress so that she also must sit her palfrey sideways. Her hair, like Beriel's, hung loose, with only a broad ribbon to hold it back from her face. Win walked behind them until the inn was out of sight, and then once again Beriel took the pack while Win and Elske rode together at her side. As they traveled the King's Way east, Win reported what he had learned in the kitchen and the stables:

Beriel was rumored dead. Where the rumor had started,

none could say, but all had heard it. A maidservant had declared that the soldiers would be bringing a dead body back for its burial, not a bride to her wedding day nor a Queen to her people. There was sadness in her telling, and in the hearing, too, for Beriel had been well-beloved.

There were rumors of a terrible army attacking the north, Wolfers, wild men; but Sutherland's domain was in no danger as long as Earl Northgate's farms and villages satisfied their blood lust. The Wolfers were a destruction from which none escaped. Lands they crossed lay barren—choked with blood, blackened with fires. People lay slaughtered, and worse. Lest they lay hands on him, and his Kingdom founder, the King had taken his court and his soldiers into Arborford, where two armies would give him twice the might, rumor said.

The King had fled for his own safety, the cook muttered over her pastry.

Another rumor reported that the King had a weapon that could spit out fire like a dragon, and when he turned this against the Wolfers they would be driven back. This new weapon burned hotter than fire, and had teeth that could rip a soldier into pieces of flesh that even his own mother wouldn't recognize. With this weapon, the King would preserve his Kingdom, and the people in it. Only King Guerric could save them, rumor said.

Thus, a groom reasoned, if this Lady of Win's was Beriel,

Beriel alive, she would cause civil war. The Kingdom would be split over the question of King or Queen. Its men would be taken off into armies, and killed or crippled, the crops would suffer, all would go hungry—and the wonderful new weapon would be turned on its own people. Wolfers from without and the royal family from within: Destruction threatened at every turn of the wheel.

But if this Lady was not Beriel, then there was hope. And how could this be the Princess, and her dead in that far city where she had gone to seek her husband, since none in the Kingdom could satisfy her proud heart? No, this was not the Princess.

"What did you say to that?" Beriel asked Win.

"I said only that I rode with my Queen, who would separate rumor from fact, and deal with these Wolfers."

"You promised much," Beriel remarked, not displeased. She turned to Elske to ask, "Do you think Guerric has the black powder?" but it was Win who answered, "I think not. I think nobody in the Kingdom knows more of the black powder than— What is it? What? My Queen, what have I said to offend you?"

"What do you know of this weapon?" Beriel demanded.

He reminded her, "Merchants come to an inn. However quietly men may talk among themselves, he who serves them will overhear."

"You serve the inn's tables? But you are a son of the house, not a servant," Beriel protested.

"Among the people, as among the Lords, however different the labors, a son does the work of the house."

Beriel accepted this, and now wanted to know, "What do you hear of the black powder?"

"They say that in the cities of the south, there are those who possess it. They speak of a captain who has made himself a Prince over many cities by its power, and none dare oppose him, for the destruction he can visit upon them. He aims to give his son a royal bride—"

"I have danced with this son, I think," Beriel said. "I did not know he was to be such a King but if he rules as stupidly as he courts, he will lose all that his father has won. Do my people fear the black powder?"

Win answered apologetically, "Your people fear everything, my Queen. If it is not the terror of the black powder, then it is dread of the consequences of Guerric's crowning or the dread of the consequences of your return. Fear spreads like a plague, and especially in the north where the Wolfers have struck." Then his face grew thoughtful, quiet, and he added, "Or perhaps fear is least in the north, for there they know what dangers they face. Imagined terrors are more fearsome than known, think you, my Queen?"

"I think I will see what awaits us at Sutherland's castle," Beriel decided, and urged her horse on, leading them.

Elske followed her mistress. She knew little of the Kingdom and its ways and had not been sent among the women of the inn, to gather their rumors. She didn't know how she might now help her mistress. There was that in Elske for which this was a gall, and she felt like a sail bereft of wind, a useless thing.

They traveled quickly, not stopping except for what quick refreshment an inn might offer, for fresh horses, for a few hours of sleep out under the open sky, to awake damp with dew. A little more than a day from the Falcon's Wing, they skirted a walled city, and then the King's Way took them across gently rolling lands, through the occasional village. Everywhere, the fields were being tilled and household gardens were being dug over. People came to the roadside to see them pass, as they rode north to Earl Sutherland's castle. None cried out in welcome, but their eyes were fixed on Beriel.

Beriel looked neither to right nor to left, but she saw everything and later would ask Win if he drew the same conclusions from the same rows of brown earth—"Is it not late for the crops to be going in?"—and the same faces—"Were they not used to be more merry? When I was a child, I thought them carefree."

Elske's impression was that nobody need go hungry here in the Kingdom, with its farms and herds, and Win told her that in his own northern lands there were lakes filled with fish, as well. There was room, and food, for all who might be born into this rich land.

And Beriel, riding always ahead, always now at a canter, was born to be Queen in the Kingdom. Even the horses she rode, which neither tired nor stumbled, seemed to take from her the strength to travel on, day after day, until at last they rode between the high stone gateposts into Earl Sutherland's castle.

They were expected there, and escorted across the yards, and welcomed on the doorstep by the Earl himself, a tall, broad man, grey-haired, with a kindly expression. He looked with brief curiosity at Win and at Elske, then gave his full attention to his niece. He took her by the hand as she stood before him, to say, "Beriel, I give you greeting."

"Sir, I give you greeting," she answered.

They met as equals, not as Earl and niece, neither as Queen and vassal. There was no bowing of the head or bending of the knee from one to the other, although Beriel wore her travel-worn cloak and the Earl a green shirt with a golden falcon stitched onto it, on his breast a medallion like the one Beriel now carried in her pack.

"Welcome to Sutherland's castle," he said. "You are welcome into my home. The servants will bring in your chests. Where are your chests?" he asked.

"I travel in haste, for I have heard much to disturb me," Beriel answered him.

"Will you not rest a night under my care?" the Earl asked. "Will you not take a meal with us? For you look travel weary and travel stained, Niece. I promise you your safety, here in my castle," he told her. "Also," he said, and his face looked suddenly tired, "I would have your advice on some matters of importance. To the Kingdom, Niece, for the Kingdom. You are right to think that these are parlous times."

"More even than you might yet know, Uncle," Beriel said, as if in warning, but gently.

"May we not advise one another, Niece?"

Beriel assented, and turned to Win, telling him to see to their horses and refresh himself against their continued journey. Then Beriel summoned Elske to her side. "My handmaiden," she said. "Elske."

"I give you greeting," Elske said, and curtseyed—as she would have to a Varinne—and the Earl answered her courteously, "I give you greeting, Elske." She was close enough to see relief in his eyes, and she thought she could guess what need Beriel had for a handmaiden. Her spirits lifted, when Beriel had a use for her.

"I am glad to see you decently attended, Niece," the Earl said. "I had heard rumors that the situation was otherwise."

Beriel acknowledged neither the warning given, nor the offense offered. "My man will wait out here, after he is fed," was her response. "I need fresh horses. Can you supply us?"

"Of course," the Earl answered. He summoned servants and sent them ahead, while he escorted Beriel through the arched doorway into the castle, with Elske at her mistress's shoulder.

ଓ ଞ

BATHED, WEARING FRESH CLOTHING FROM shift to dress, they joined the Earl in a large dining hall. Chairs were set around three sides of the table, which had been drawn up close to the dying fire. Elske was seated beside Beriel, and next to Beriel sat a Lady who must be the Earl's wife, for she, too, wore the medallion. The Earl was catty-corner to his wife, and down the length of the table from him sat a young man, his son. While the servants placed food and drink before them, nobody spoke.

The Earl's Lady, her faded hair held back from her face by golden combs, looked from Beriel to the Earl, as if she sensed trouble there; and the young man—tall and slim, with his mother's fine face—watched only his own hands, which rested beside his plate. They ate of smoked pig meat and onions, carrots, a cold fowl and some bitter greens. When their plates had been cleared from the table, the Earl asked, "Well, Niece?" and drank from his goblet of wine.

"Guerric is crowned," Beriel began.

After some thought the Earl remarked, "You ever were desirous to be the Queen."

"I am the firstborn, the eldest."

"But not male."

"In the history of Sutherland, as was made the law of the Kingdom, the firstborn inherited, be it woman or man. This was my own mother, your sister, who gave the Earldom into your inheritance when she chose instead to marry my father and be his Queen."

The Earl nodded, agreeing.

"The Priests allowed my mother her inheritance of the Earldom, and gave her the power to name her successor."

The Earl pointed out, "You have not been named successor."

"I should have been," Beriel argued. "Until my father lay dead, none ever dared name Guerric, for fear of the law."

The Earl nodded, but "Will you have a civil war?" he asked.

"I will have my crown," she answered.

"To do that, you must turn traitor to the crowned King."

"A usurper is himself a traitor. It is no treason to take the crown from him."

The Earl considered. Elske, watching the faces around the table, thought that the Earl's son was troubled, uneasy, although not about the question of King or Queen; and she guessed she knew what he had to trouble him. The Earl's Lady listened, and often leaned forward, with her mouth moving as if to speak; but she uttered no words.

At last the Earl said, "You want troops. But, Niece, I have bent the knee to Guerric and am his vassal. Even if I accept your claim, I cannot, in honor, send troops against him."

Beriel considered this. She decided, "I will not ask dishonor of you."

"I will gladly give you troops to go against the Wolfers," the Earl offered.

"Hasn't the King already sent an army into the north?"

"Guerric orders Northgate to defend his lands as best he can, and has left those royal villages unprotected that lie in the north. The soldiery Guerric has, he keeps close about him, and he has taken his army eastwards, to bring Arborford under his will."

Beriel asked, "Lord Arbor refuses the King soldiers?"

"Arborford goes its own way, and ever has."

"Yet, is not Lord Arbor your vassal?" Beriel asked.

"He is," the Earl said.

"You have not required him to give Guerric his soldiery?"

"Arbor's vow is to me, to protect me in need. I have no need," the Earl pointed out.

Beriel considered this. The room was still, except for the Earl's Lady restless in her chair. Elske could not think what Beriel was planning, except there would be a revenge on this young man, with his shining pink cheeks, who could not look at his cousin's face.

Beriel changed the topic of conversation, then. "My brother plots my death, as I hear."

At this the young man told his father, "This is what I reported to you."

The Earl nodded at him and told Beriel, "It is for this reason our Aymeric has been sent home in disgrace—sent by his own brother, who is now the King's First Minister. Because Aymeric won't conspire to your murder."

Beriel stared at the young man, then, until his whole face burned red. It seemed to Elske that shame sat on his shoulders like the Volkking on his throne; and it seemed to Elske just that Aymeric should carry that weight, for all that it crushed and crippled him.

Beriel spoke boldly then to her uncle, "You will have heard rumors that I was with child, last fall, when I left the Kingdom."

"I see no child," the Earl answered.

"You would not have known whether to believe the rumors," Beriel said. "Aunt?"

The Earl's Lady looked at her husband, who awaited her answer. She said nothing.

"I ask you, Aunt," Beriel repeated.

"I must speak, when this—girl—requires?" the Lady asked her husband. "When I must keep silent about important matters, of Kingship and the promotion of my son into a rank higher than I had dreamed, of—"

Beriel interrupted the complaint. "I have asked you."

"If I must speak, and speak truly, I did think you had the look. Last fall. I wondered. And you were—you were often angry, when you were a child, impatient, but last fall you were uncontrolled. I did wonder if you were with child. But who in this Kingdom cares for what a woman thinks, what a woman knows? So I held my tongue—and begged the maidservants to overlook your spitefulness. It was not too soon for me when you rode out of my gates, with your guard—although none asked me if your visit was to my taste, not before it happened, nor after."

The Earl looked as if he wished to silence his wife, and their son was almost smiling at this tirade; but Beriel remained courteous. "I thank you for your silence, Aunt. But I have a story to tell, and it is not a tale to lighten your hearts. May I speak of it?" she asked the Earl.

"You may," the Earl answered.

His wife said, "No." His son's chair scraped on the stone floor.

Beriel addressed her uncle. "In the spring of last year, a year ago—or perhaps a little more than a year— In the spring," Beriel said, pale but keeping her eyes fixed on her uncle's face, "there were men let into my apartments. At the palace, and the door was locked behind them. So that I couldn't escape them. Night after night, they came. And raped me." She kept her eyes on the Earl when she asked, "Is this so, Aymeric?"

"Yes," he whispered.

Silence settled over the table.

Beriel watched her uncle. Elske, that she might report what she observed, watched the other two, both as still as deer, startled into fear. The fire whispered to itself.

"I don't—" the Earl's Lady started to say but her husband interrupted her again to inquire, "Who would have wished such disgrace on you?"

"My brother," Beriel said. "Guerric," she said. "The King."

"She accuses our son, our Aymeric, of this—vileness," the Earl's Lady said, and warned Beriel, "I will hate you forever if you accuse my son."

Beriel gave Elske a troubled glance.

"I would not wish your hatred, Aunt," Beriel said.

But it was not the hatred that troubled her, Elske knew.

"Then that's an end on it," the Earl's Lady declared. "I will forget what you have said."

Elske saw what troubled Beriel: The Earldom would be divided by the hatred of the Earl's Lady for Beriel, if Beriel were Queen and had accused the Lady's sons of rape. Beriel could not speak openly without risking a necessary ally; and that was what troubled her.

"I will accuse Aymeric," Elske said.

All turned to her.

"I will accuse both of your sons," Elske said, to the Earl.

"I cannot credit it," he said, but Elske could see that he half-believed her.

"Why would Beriel lie about such a thing?" Elske asked.

"To be Queen!" the Earl's Lady cried.

"In the Kingdom, must a woman be raped before she can be Queen?" Elske asked.

"She has always hated my sons, with a jealous hatred."

Elske said, "She has hated Guerric thus, and he her. But not your sons."

"Why doesn't she accuse her brother, then?" the Lady demanded, furious.

"She does," Elske said, and turned back to the Earl, who was studying Aymeric's bent head. "If I had a son," Elske said, "I would not wish this shame on him. I would not wish to leave him in his shame."

The Earl nodded.

"If I had a daughter," Elske said, "I would wish to keep her safe from such shame." The Earl's Lady said nothing.

At last, the Earl spoke. "Aymeric," he said. "My son. I ask you if this accusation is true. I ask you to tell me only what is true, because I will take your word in this."

"Tell him it's not true," urged the young man's mother.

Aymeric raised his unhappy eyes to Elske's and said, "Lady, it is true. I did that thing."

"He's just a boy," the Earl's Lady explained to Elske.

"And your brother?" the Earl demanded.

Aymeric looked at Beriel for the first time. "Lady," he said. "I would give an arm not to have used you so. If I could, I—" His words stumbled, halted.

"You cannot, Cousin," Beriel answered him.

"Whatever revenge you wish," Aymeric said, "even my life—"

"No!" cried the Earl's Lady.

"And your brother, Ditrik?" the Earl asked again, more sternly.

"I cannot speak of my brother. I have given my word," Aymeric told his father.

"Which means he extracted a promise from you," his father said, "and that means there was need of a promise. But I can at least be glad you were stripped of honors and sent home. I can know that my heir is not such a villain as to become another man's hired murderer."

"Aymeric cannot be your heir," Beriel announced.

"Who—?" the Earl started to demand.

"Have you no other sons? I think you have one other, and daughters, too, although they are young."

"Who are you to say who cannot—or can—be Earl Sutherland?" the Earl demanded.

"I am your rightful Queen," Beriel answered. "Aymeric has shamed his name, dishonored it."

"He has shamed *you*," the Earl's Lady said. "And you wish revenge."

"But he has not dishonored me," Beriel said quietly. "The dishonor is not mine, for all they wished it so, and tried to make it so. As to revenge," Beriel said, in a voice that turned her aunt's face pale with fear, and respect. Beriel took a breath, and said it again, "As to revenge, I think his own heart has been taking my revenge upon Aymeric. I need no more."

"And for Ditrik?" the Earl asked.

"Ditrik has sought my death," Beriel answered. "He is a traitor."

Elske remembered Beriel locked into her chambers in Trastad, as if she were a criminal. She remembered Beriel standing naked in her pride, in the bath, in her shame, with the child pushing her belly out. She remembered the silence of those laborious hours of birth. "He is *Fruhckman*," Elske said.

The Earl sighed deeply, accepting. "The word is foreign, like the lady, but I know its meaning. We must lay what plans we can, Niece."

"Yes," Beriel agreed, and she spoke in a new voice, ready to make her plans with the Earl. "Your captains have sworn their allegiance to you, as I think. If I can win them to my cause, will your vow to the false King be broken?" she asked.

But before the Earl could answer this, the doors into the hall burst open and a young man strode into the room. He wore leather armor and carried a long sword, sheathed, at his belt. His dark brown hair clung to his forehead and neck, wet with sweat. Beardless, he had not shaven, so his face was shadowed. His strides, in booted feet, carried him swiftly up to the table.

"My Lord Earl, I must speak with you," he said, noticing none of the others in the room.

The Earl rose and the younger man bowed slightly, impatiently, while the Earl said, "I give you greeting, Lord Dugald. What brings you—?"

"I need troops," the man interrupted. "Forgive me the lack of courtesies, but—my father has sent me—he sent first to the King, who has denied us. Wolfers are poised to pour down into our lands, like crows circling over a wounded bear, and our people are— Can you give me any soldiers? I must be answered, and quickly, for I have been away too long, and I would not have my men defend the holdings and villages and my sword not raised with theirs, and my life not given with theirs, if needs must. What say you, my Lord?"

"I will give you soldiers, and weapons, horses, and supplies, also," the Earl said.

The dark-haired man went down on his knee, then, in gratitude. He was white-faced, and trembling with fatigue, Elske saw. She rose from her chair, so that he might sit. He accepted this place, without thanks.

"Do you not greet *me*?" Beriel asked him. "Am I so much changed, my Lord Dugald?"

He turned to her, surprised. "Beriel? And alive? Why did you leave us to this fortune?"

"The fortune of the Wolfers?" Beriel asked. "Or the fortune of this King?"

He did not hesitate. "Both," he said, "and one as ill as the other. I take it, then, that the rumors were false?" This was a blunt man, and privileged to speak plainly.

"Are not rumors most often false?" Beriel asked him, teasing. "I am as you see me, Dugald," she said, neither lying nor telling the truth.

"I see little, blinded as I am with tiredness and hunger,"

he answered, with a little upwards lifting of the ends of his mouth, to make it a pleasantry. "And it's many days' ride before me, back to my own lands, where . . ."

"But first you must rest," Beriel told him. "You'll be of little use to your soldiery if you ride so exhausted." He opened his mouth to argue but she raised a hand to silence him, and he obeyed her command. "Moreover," Beriel announced, "I have need of good counsel here, as I determine how to make my claim on the throne. So I ask you to sit, take some rest, take refreshment, and give me the benefit of your counsel. Grant me this, Lord Dugald."

"It is granted, Beriel," he said. "But I will not deliberate overlong," he warned her with a smile.

The Earl's Lady rose then, to give order for food, and the Earl asked Elske to take that empty seat before he turned to the newcomer, to explain where they had arrived in their talk. Elske could feel Beriel's anger at being left out of the men's talk, as if she had nothing to contribute, as if it didn't concern her. The newcomer was too engrossed to even notice Beriel's growing fury, as he leaned in front of her to hear what the Earl was saying. Elske couldn't help but smile, although she *could* help laughing where any might hear it.

When Elske smiled, the newcomer turned his head to her. Quickly, she made her expression solemn, but his stone-brown eyes stayed on her. "Has our Aymeric brought home a bride, then?" Lord Dugald asked. "And the stories of the

King's dissatisfactions with you, are they then also false? Will you, too, come to my aid?"

This man would not long be diverted from his own purposes, Elske noted.

"She is not my wife," Aymeric said, "although I might do much worse than such a stranger. For you are a foreigner, aren't you?" he asked Elske. "From the great city of Trastad, I think, for that was a Norther word you spoke, was it not? *Fruhckman?*" he repeated it, with a sad smile.

Lord Dugald did not smile. He put a hand on his sword's hilt, as if Elske had drawn on him. "It *is* a Norther word. Who are you?" he demanded of Elske.

She did not look away. "Elske," she said.

"Wolfer?"

"Yes."

She studied him as closely as he studied her, and thought she could trust him to see into the truth of her.

He shifted in the chair. "Are you not afraid I will slay you?"

"Why should I fear you, when your care is for your people?" she asked him.

"And my lands, also—for I am the Earl that will be," he told her, then, "How came you here?" he asked.

"I am the Queen's handmaiden."

"Oh—ho—Beriel, so that is how the river runs," he laughed. "So you will be Queen?"

But she would not be jested with on this point. Solemnly, she answered him. "I will. And will you bend the knee to me?"

Lord Dugald, too, grew solemn. "My Queen, I will. Whom even Wolfers serve, she has my sworn loyalty. As you always did, from when we were children. Northgate is ever for the law, and thus for the Queen."

Beriel rose then and placed her right hand on his left shoulder. "I accept your sword, Dugald, heir to Earl Northgate. Now, then," she said, and turned to them all, taking her place once again at the head of the council of war, "let us lay our plans. For we waste time here, while the Kingdom is being wasted around us. What is your choice, Uncle? Will you let me speak before your soldiers to win them to my cause?"

It didn't take long for the decisions to be reached. The Earl's soldiery was divided into three parts. One part would remain where they were, for although the Earl didn't think his own lands were in danger, Beriel would not have him defenseless. The second part was given for Lord Dugald's use. The third part of the army—those who chose so, if any did—would ride with Beriel, to confront Guerric at Arborford, to ask him to bring the question of the succession before the law or, if he required it, to do battle with him. Beriel expected battle, although the two men chided her for bloodthirstiness; she argued that she knew her brother, knew what he was capable of, and would trust him only when she had buried him.

It did not please them to hear her speak so. The Earl told her she did not mean the words she spoke, but Lord Dugald only looked at her thoughtfully. Elske believed Beriel, and hoped to ride into battle before her mistress, or beside her, and wondered which place would enable her to better protect the Queen.

Aymeric would ride with Beriel, as her herald. He would bear letters to the First Minister and to the King, ordering the two before the law to answer certain charges. "If I die in this, then the dishonor I have done you, my father, and you, my Queen that will be, and to myself, also—then all will be paid," Aymeric said, as if he almost hoped for death.

With them also, to his dismay and deep pleasure, would go Win. When he protested to Beriel that he should ride with Lord Dugald to the Ram's Head, to stand with his family and his neighbors in need, she reminded him that he had vowed to serve *her*, and argued that she needed his service now even more than when he first pressed it upon her. If he chose to go home she would not bar his way; but her own will was to have him at her side, someone she could trust absolutely. Hearing her will, Win did not hesitate to promise his life to his Queen.

A brief speech won many of Sutherland's soldiers to her cause. Elske watched from the background how Beriel stood up tall on a mounting block to look over the men, and pick out their captains with her glance. She said only: "I am the Queen that will be. I am the rightful Queen under the law, and I ride to place my claim before this cowardly false King. Who rides with me?" Her voice carried easily as a falcon in flight over the assembled soldiers. She stood high-shouldered and unafraid. There was that about her that all recognized, and trusted, and wished to follow.

To her surprise, and chagrin, Elske was sent with Lord Dugald and his soldiers. "You must," Beriel told her. "I order it. You will understand the Wolfers more than our own people can. At least you can speak their tongue, so that if it comes to treating, you can speak for us."

"The Volkaric do not make treaties," Elske said. "If they have sent war bands, they will overrun what they can and avoid those places that can defend themselves. Like wolves, they disappear into the safety of the forests and hills and come out of hiding to attack where they are least expected and will be most weakly opposed. Once they have entered your land, all you can do is warn your people to flee the danger," she told Lord Dugald. "In the autumn, they will carry their booty back to the Volkking, and then you will have time to arm and train your people, for their own defense. But there is nothing I can do at this time against the Wolfers, my Lady. Let me ride with you."

Win added his voice to her pleas. "Aye, and whatever

Elske undertakes goes well. For did you not come out of this castle with an army to ride behind you and the Earl's own son in your service? Take Elske with you."

At his words, Beriel's blue eyes grew hard and she would not be persuaded. So Elske rode out of Sutherland's castle at the side of Lord Dugald, with an army at their backs. Beriel had already left, for Arborford.

Watching that army take one broad roadway while she herself rode with another army down the other, Elske felt what must be fear curl its wolf claws into her heart. For what if Beriel were to die, in claiming her throne? In battle or by treachery, what if Beriel's life were lost? What if they were never to meet again?

CHAPTER 17

THEY MARCHED AWAY FROM SUTHERLAND'S city with two bands of soldiery, the smaller loyal to Lord Dugald, the larger serving the Earl. The two soldieries camped separately from one another, strangers and mistrustful. Each ate from its own supplies and tended to its own animals, and arms.

Dugald gave Elske the use of his own tent and himself slept on the open ground, with his soldiers; but they shared a fire, and food, and they rode side by side, all the days of the march.

He was a good companion for a journey with urgent business. He might talk or he might ride silent, but he never complained nor did he forget to ask after her comfort, thirst, hunger or desire to rest. While he did not sing and jest, as Win had, still the hours in his company did not drag. He spoke of his father's land, which he would inherit, and the people of it—less pleasure-loving than those of the south but staunch, and true-hearted. "There are those who say that the land in the north, with its dark forests and icy lakes, its rocky soil, too, is not hospitable, but I have ever found it kind." He spoke of the history of the Kingdom, its treacheries and disasters, its great Kings and Earls, and Jackaroo, too. He explained its laws and described the great wheel of the year with its plantings and harvestings, its fairs; they discussed how a Lord could assist in the well-being of his people.

Elske enjoyed the company of this Lord. But when he called her Lady for the time that made it too many times, she asked him, "Do you not remember I am no Lady?"

At that, he gainsayed her, for all around to hear. "My Queen so calls you when she names you her handmaiden, which is her Lady-in-Waiting." And he smiled, to ask her, "Will you set me against my Queen?" He smiled, making his courtly request, and she saw no falsehood in his smile. Also, there was a different request in his eyes, asking her to trust him in this, and follow his lead, as if they were moving through the steps of a dance, together.

Elske had neither will nor reason to quarrel with Lord Dugald, and so she acquiesced.

During the day, Dugald and the countryside they crossed diverted Elske, but at night, even in the privacy of the tent, she could not rest for long. Tired from the day's exertions, she'd fall immediately asleep, but in the dark of night she would awaken, and think of Beriel. Her thoughts made her restless, so she'd wrap herself around with her cloak and leave the tent.

Sentries grew accustomed to her, and watched for her. They greeted her. "A cool night, my Lady, sit here by our fire." She learned their names and the names of their fathers, too, mothers, sisters, sweethearts. She asked after their brothers. She learned about the cities or villages where they had lived, and the work of their fathers' holdings, shepherd and pigman, blacksmith, weaver, farmer, fisherman. "The lakes of the north are as full of fish as a goodwife's stew," they told her, when she was surprised to hear of fish, here, so far from the sea. They were surprised to hear that there was a way of smoking fish, as if it were pig, to preserve it. Most of these soldiers were younger sons, ambitious to be named sergeants so that they could take a wife, and be given one of the little houses the cities of the north kept for the particular use of a soldier's family. The one thing they never spoke of was the battles ahead. Elske guessed that the depth of their silence reflected the depth of their dread.

Eventually, Elske also wandered into the camps of Earl Sutherland's men, and they also welcomed her. These southern men worried less than their northern counterparts about doing battle with the Wolfers; they spoke of it carelessly, jestingly, as confident and eager as Adels before a ball, as if the Wolfers were a game.

The soldiers looked out for Elske, and Dugald often brought their well-wishes back to her from his twice-daily inspection tours. Lord Dugald was a useful man, Elske thought; and she had never met with such a man before. He carried messages gladly, without any pride of place to interfere, whether the word traveled from captain to captain or soldier to soldier. He could deal with the stone caught in a horse's shoe or set a broken bone as easily as he detailed men to gather fuel or encouraged them at the arduous march. The soldiers came to him with their quarrels and their desires, and he answered their needs. Elske had seen his dark brown head bent over a needle and thread, mending a tear in his own blue tunic—on the chest of which Northgate's bear, standing, had been emblazoned. Like his soldiers, Elske came to trust the Earl's heir in all things; and Sutherland's soldiers, too, soon followed him confidently.

All this he achieved without—apparently—even thinking of it. He did not make his own cleverness known, or his strength, power or position. Those who served Lord Dugald did not so much follow him as find him at their shoulder, ready to assist or to give succor or just to hear them. Thus it was he listened to Elske, as if he wished to understand even that which she could not put into words. However, his thoughts did not always march with hers, as when he pointed out, "There will now be another Death Maiden, won't there?" The grim sorrow in his voice caused her to turn her head so that she might see his face. But he was staring ahead, towards the hills they approached. So Elske, who had never thought of her, must remember this next, unknown Death Maiden, without Tamara to protect her, and must feel a sorrow that matched his own for this unmet child, and for herself, too, as she had not known herself to be.

Dugald was like a beryl glass, showing Elske herself. "You have been so many things," he once exclaimed, "and seen so much of the world. Do you never think how wonderful it is, what you have seen and done, all that you know? And now you are here to make a lighter time of this strenuous march, and help us know what awaits us. For which I thank you, Elske. My soldiers are less fatigued of body and fearful of heart than they would have been were you not with us. Me, as well. You have shone in my days like the sun in the sky," he said, and she laughed, then, at his courtly extravagance here in the rough life of a marching army, and at her pleasure in his good opinion.

They had forded the great river and were camped on its western banks the evening that Elske unknowingly risked the loss of that valued good opinion. It was a mild evening. They had just set up camp, the fires lit, refreshing water taken by men and animals; they had not yet eaten. Dugald was conferring with the captains and Elske walked to the riverbank, where the water rippled golden under a burnished sky. Some of Sutherland's soldiers were about to wade into the water and she asked them if they knew how to swim.

"Aye, Lady," they answered, so she asked them if they would teach her. "Nay, Lady, why should you know that?" they said, answering her neither yes nor no as they stood barefooted, wearing only shirts and trousers, halted in their undressing by her arrival, wary as foxes.

"I wish to know," she said. "The Queen that will be, Beriel, was taught it by fishermen."

They looked at one another, and thought to say, "What would you wear, Lady? If you try to swim in those skirts, you'll drown for sure, and what Lord Dugald would do to us I don't like to think. It would be a quick hanging, if we were lucky."

"Can I not wear what you do?" Elske asked.

"Lady, we swim without clothing."

"Naked?"

"How else?"

Elske could not answer, never having seen a man either unclothed or swimming.

"I'll give her my shirt," one of the soldiers volunteered.

"How can we watch over her, when we are naked? Not watching, how can we be sure of her safety?" they asked one another.

"And why should our Elskeling not learn to swim, or have anything else she wishes?"

So they took off only their shirts and stood in a circle around her, with their backs to her, while she removed her own clothing until she wore only a shift. She put on the soldier's green shirt, which reached below her knees. Then she moved down into the water among her guard of soldiers.

This was a sandy-bottomed river and Elske stepped barefooted into the water, which rose steadily as she walked out into it, cool against her ankles, then calves, then knees. The green shirt grew heavy with water, and what was cool on her feet was cold enough on her belly to make her gasp.

They walked her out until the water reached her breasts and then told her, if she was not afraid to try, that she might lie down on it. "Lie on your belly. Lift your face," they advised her.

Elske bent her knees, but could not persuade her feet to leave the river bottom.

"Push off," her teachers advised her, laughter in their voices, and eagerness for her to learn. "Push yourself towards the shore where the water grows shallower."

Elske filled her chest with air and pushed off. Almost, she stayed on top of the water, before she began to sink, and her feet scrabbled beneath her to stand on firm sand again. But her *almost* had given her a sense of it, and soon she floated easily, and even rolled over onto her back to look up into the sky while she floated on top of the water, swimming.

The soldiers were pleased with themselves, and with her.

"Our Elskeling can do anything she sets her spirit on, can't she?" they asked one another. "Now, Lady," they told her. "You must learn how to paddle with your hands, and kick with your feet, so that—like a boat with its oars—you can steer yourself whither you will. And then you will know how to swim."

"Yes," Elske said, and smiled so widely, to know that she had thought she already knew what she did not, that her mouth filled with water, and she coughed so hard to get it out that she forgot to keep her chest filled with air, and she had to stand up, and stop swimming as she choked, chest-deep in the river, her wet hair plastered to her shoulders.

This was what Dugald saw, as he came searching for her. Seeing this, he rushed down to the water's edge, bellowing orders to the soldiers, bellowing orders to Elske, his anger whipping out in all directions.

The soldiers scurried out of the river and gathered up their clothing. "We only—" "It wasn't—" He would deal with them later, Dugald promised them, and would not hear their protests. "My Lord, you know we wouldn't—" He sent them back to their captains, at a run.

When the soldiers had gone, he called again for Elske to get out of the water.

She, too, protested. "But I can swim."

"Just obey me," he commanded. He waited on the shore with his boots on and his cloak held out to wrap around her. He scolded her, even as she walked through the water towards him. "It isn't decent for a Lady to be so undressed among men, and the soldiers bare-chested—"

"They told me, usually they swim naked but they didn't today, because of my presence. They gave me a shirt so I wouldn't be naked. They've done nothing wrong," Elske said as she accepted his cloak. She picked up her own clothing from where it lay folded on the long riverside grasses. "And I've done nothing wrong."

The man at her side was dark-faced. "I don't know what is permitted in Trastad, how their women behave, but in the Kingdom no Lady would see men bare-chested, nor would she let them see her so unclothed—"

"I am neither a Lady nor a Trastader." He had no reason to speak so to her, and she had no reason to be courteous to his anger.

"Neither would any woman of the people," Dugald went on, ignoring her. "You are as blind and willful as Beriel."

"Beriel is not blind," Elske answered him. "She is no more willful than she must be."

He escorted her back to their fire, and neither one of them spoke to the other. Elske withdrew into her tent, to change into dry clothing, but she did not remain there. Instead— being careful to tell one of the soldiers in which direction she would go, lest Dugald think she had been cowed by his anger—she walked away from the river, along a path out into the countryside, until she stood beside the dark furrows of a plowed field.

The sky was darkening from the east but still glowed blue gold in the west, where a horizon as uneven as the sea's showed hills, rising up. The mountains, she knew, lay out of sight, beyond; if she could see them, they would be covered still with snow. It was as if Dugald's troops were the army of spring, hurrying to catch up with her and escort her safely through the land from which winter's troops were retreating.

He spoke behind her. "Lady, I give you greeting."

Elske turned around, and found that her ill humor had left her. "I give you greeting, Lord Dugald," she answered. When he stepped up beside her to look out over the fields, she saw how dark his eyes were, as dark as the deep rocks in the land of the Volkaric, as unchanging as earth.

"This is my father's land," he said to her. "It will be mine, in my time, if I live. The soldiers call you Elskeling. Does that offend you?"

"Why should it offend me?"

Dugald smiled at her then, and said, "And I, if I were to request it—with courtly flourishes, with songs and flowers—could I ask you to teach me to swim? Not now, but at some future time, when the men have forgotten how they trespassed against your dignity."

"The soldiers would make better teachers," Elske said,

and with a teasing smile of her own reminded him, "You would all be men together as is proper."

He shrugged.

"But," she said, then stopped, then decided to speak, "Why should you ask me to teach you what I barely know myself?"

The steady eyes looked down into hers and he told her, "Because I am afraid to learn, afraid to drown learning it. But I think you are someone I would trust to show me how to enter the water and not die there. I think my fear and my life would be safe with you. Because I think that when Beriel left us last fall Guerric didn't expect her to return. I think," he said again, his eyes now on the distances of his land so that whatever was written on her face might go unread. "Perhaps, if there is any truth to the rumors of a man in her bed and a baby in her belly, that Beriel has trusted herself to you, and you have served her well. So I think that what we call *proper* doesn't signify to you. Although this freedom could make you dangerous, especially to those whose secrets you keep, it is difficult for me to believe that you are a danger to me, or my land, or my Queen. On the other hand, it could make you a true heart. I can believe that your heart is true."

"I think it is," Elske agreed, accepting his arm and the apology of his request, and—most gladly—his good opinion.

WITH THE ARMY STRETCHED OUT behind, they left the river. The King's Way ran north between low fences, through

rough, brown fields. Dugald asked Elske about the Wolfers, telling her, "I've chased after one of the war bands, and raised my sword to its rear guard, and I have fought against those who buy the time for their fellows to escape. They don't fear death as we do."

She agreed. "They fear only the Volkking, and the shame of cowardice."

"And what do you fear, Elske?"

Elske considered, to give him the true answer. "I fear for the safety of Beriel."

"Not for your own safety? Not for mine?"

Elske considered. "No," she answered.

His shout of laughter caused the nearby soldiers to fall silent, so he spoke more quietly to tell her, "When we are at Hildebrand's city, there will be a council of war. I think, I would wish people to know you are Wolfer, so that we can hear your advice about our enemy. I give my pledge for your safety," he promised.

The army traveled at some speed along the King's Way, passing solitary cottages, farmhouses with their outbuildings, inns and villages. Sometimes, people gathered to watch them pass, and all their faces seemed stilled by fear. They feared even to hope, Elske thought. The green shirts of the soldiers from the south at least earned a look of surprise, and a man might whisper into his neighbor's ear, or point out to a child Northgate's heir.

At the Ram's Head Inn, Elske slept under a roof, in her own chamber. She dined with Dugald, waited on by the red-headed innkeeper, Win's brother.

Their host could not speak four words without putting in "my Lord" or "my honored Lord." His wife bustled in and out, as he apologized for the simple fare—"Had we known, my honored Lord, that you would dine with us, my Lord"—but dared to hope that the inn's wine, "made from the family vineyard, would please my noble Lord." He offered clean napkins, his wife offered a chair to make Lord Dugald more comfortable, until finally Dugald tried to divert his hosts by saying, "I have news of your brother, if you would hear it."

They stood with their hands folded in front of their aprons, to hear, and what they heard gave them unease. The innkeeper pulled ruminatively at his red beard, but his wife could not hold her tongue. "He ever did seek to serve that Princess," she said, to her husband. "She magicked him that summer, over the hanging of your uncle, and you know how Win is. Stubborn-hearted."

"He's ever been too quick to pity," the host agreed, sadly.

Elske spoke up. "Win is loyal to his Queen."

"Aye, and it'll be just that loyalty that will get him a traitor's death," Win's brother said. "And if I know my brother, he'll say she's done him fair."

"If that's what he gets, I'll be hanged beside him," Dugald told them and their host asked uneasily, "What mean you, my Lord?"

Dugald answered plainly. "I mean that if a brother seizes the crown from his sister who is the firstborn, then *he* is the traitor, as are all who follow him."

"Aye, and I know nothing of that," the wife said. "But I know they're cowards who follow Guerric into the safety of Arborford, and leave their own people undefended."

Her husband tried to shush her. "Here is Northgate's heir," he pointed out, "and he brings soldiers from Sutherland to join his father's army, to protect us."

"Aye, and there's no protection against these Wolfers," she lamented. "They move secretly, and in packs, they never stand to fight. And it is the worse, now, for now they take revenge, too." She turned to Dugald, "They eat the flesh of children!" she cried. "Women who fall into their hands go mad with pain, and shame, and fear, before they die. You must promise me, you'll slay me, Husband—I'll slay my daughters, I can do that—if those—"

"Hush," he tried to soothe her frenzy. "I'll not keep you here if they come close."

"You fool! They give no warning. Do you think the pig-man would not have sent his daughter away? You saw the bodies, Husband. It's you who are the dreamer and fool, not Win. His enemy fights honestly—and speaks his language.

Maybe he was the clever one, to leave you here without his arm at such a time—"

"She is afraid," the host apologized. "My Lord, I ask you to remember that our children are young, and she is afraid for them. We'll leave you, my honored Lord, to your dinner."

"Don't tell me there's nothing to fear!" his wife cried.

The host bowed to Lord Dugald, and bowed to Elske, too, as he drew his wife out of the long room, leaving them alone.

Dugald lifted his spoon and dipped it into his bowl of meat stew, but he didn't eat. Elske did not even lift her spoon.

"I need a map," Dugald said, but not to her. "Hildebrand will have one."

He took a bite then, chewed and swallowed. He drank a swallow of the wine. "I've let myself make a pleasure journey, and my people in danger."

He drank of the wine again, and poured more from the pitcher into his goblet. Then he did raise his face, his eyes as mute as boulders, to ask Elske, "How could you be as you are and have lived among Wolfers?"

Elske shook her head. She could not answer his question.

"Tell me," Lord Dugald insisted.

If he wished to insist, then Elske wished to make the attempt. "I was a girl," she said, "and among the Volkaric—" but he interrupted her, "Who are these Volkaric?"

"Those whom you call Wolfers. Among the Volkaric," she began again, and this time he did not interrupt her, "women are nothing, useless in battle, useless to win treasure. They remain near their houses—as do the women of Trastad, both the great Varinnes and their servants—to sew and scrub and cook, to care for children. Among the Volkaric, the best of a woman is to bear sons. I lived among the Volkaric as women everywhere live," Elske told Dugald. "Except Beriel," she said. Then she added, "All women except Beriel, who would be Queen."

As she spoke, Dugald looked into her face, and looked still into her face. "How could they ask your death of you, being who you are?" he asked, but it was a protest, not a question. "And how could they ask you to know what your death was to be?"

"If it were kept a secret," Elske explained, "there would have been no revenge on my grandmother. I was their revenge on her. Whenever anyone saw me, they remembered how my death would come and so our life was better when all knew what my death would be."

"It was ill done," Dugald said plainly. He asked her then, "So you would have no secrets?"

"My Lord?"

"It is a simple question, a simple policy: Do you believe secrets should be kept, and that the people should be kept in ignorance?"

Elske considered what secrets she had known, and kept, and which she had spoken of, before she said, "I believe that there are some secrets dangerous to their possessors, should they be known." She was thinking of the secret of the black powder, which she held unbeknownst to any other, not even Var Jerrol, who had assumed she could not comprehend what she had heard; for otherwise—this she knew—he would have had her killed. "And surely those who do not know secrets can live most easily, in this world. For the day, at least."

"For the day," he echoed, doubtfully.

"It is not a simple question," she told him.

"You've heard of the black powder," he told her.

Elske didn't wonder how he knew that of her. She just answered him truthfully. "Yes."

"A deeply kept secret, and no man knows where it comes from so that he may get it for his own use, even against Wolfers," Lord Dugald said.

Elske corrected him. "Men know where it comes from, and where to buy it, and even how to make it. I learned how to make it," she told him, trusting him, "from a man who revealed the ingredients and their proportions before he died. He gave up his secret so that he would live, but he died because he no longer possessed it. This was among the merchants of Trastad."

Lord Dugald looked into her face again. "Is this a secret that should be kept?"

"I think, no," she answered.

"But the people," he said, and waved his hand in the

direction of the door through which the host and his wife had withdrawn. "If the people are so afraid of Wolfers—who are only men after all—how much will they be crazed by fear of the black powder, which is a hundred times more heartless than any Wolfer, and is moreover magic?"

"It is not magic," Elske told him. "Any man might make it."

"Can we? Have we the time?" Lord Dugald asked, and when she shook her head he smiled ruefully. "Well, it's too dangerous a weapon to take lightly up, as if it were no more than a pretty dagger. And the Wolfers do not stand as still as city walls, so it could not serve against them. Yet I would like to be so strongly weaponed."

"Beriel also wishes to have it," Elske said. "Ask of me what help you need, for the Wolfers must not come killing here. In Beriel's Kingdom. In Northgate's lands."

"Can they be stopped?" he asked. He answered his own question, "How can I know unless I make the attempt? Are you willing to die in this cause, Elske?"

"Yes."

"Because it is Beriel's cause," he said. "Well, so am I, although I cannot be so willing for *you* to die. On some Wolfer blade or at the end of a traitor's rope, we may all die in Beriel's cause."

Elske had never seen a man hanged, but she saw in her mind Dugald so dangling, dead, and her heart twisted in her chest.

"Elske?" he asked, watching her face. "What is it? Did you not know the dangers you faced?"

"I knew my danger," she said, "but—"

"As Beriel knows hers, I promise you. It is in Beriel's cause, and that is a good one," he reassured her. "Few understand this of her, but I have known her from a child and seen how she masks her true heart. I know that if one of her people bleeds, Beriel bleeds. If fire scorches the land, Beriel has the scar. Can you ride through the night, Elske?"

"Yes," she said, and he was not surprised at her answer.

CHAPTER 18

THE LORDS AND THEIR CAPTAINS gathered together in Hildebrand's great hall, where the long table had a map unrolled onto it. The Lords were seated in high-backed chairs, and their captains stood behind them. Lord Dugald had Elske seated beside him.

A fire burned in the great fireplace, taking the chill off the air, and the stone walls of the hall were hung with woven carpets. Through the unshuttered windows a mild blue sky shone over the low roofs of Hildebrand's city. The army waited beyond the city walls for the decisions being debated now, in this hall, and Elske would have felt more at ease among the soldiers.

Lord Hildebrand was an aging man, his thin hair silvery, his cheeks sunken; he coughed, and drank wine to soothe his throat, and kept his eye on Dugald, to learn the younger man's thoughts. Hildebrand's heir, a square-jawed man of middle years, sat the length of the table from his father, and kept his eyes on the map as if only his vigilance kept it flat on the table. One of Dugald's brothers, Thorold, had been sent by the Earl, and with him came four other Lords, all younger sons, all bringing troops in response to Northgate's appeal.

The map showed the whole Kingdom, and the men discussed how they might defend it. Troops were kept in plenty to guard the cities, but there was no protection for the villages, nor for the isolated holdings, all easy prey. The map showed these habitations and villages, as well as the cities. Northgate's demesne spread between the river to the east and the foothills to the west; mountains bordered the northern parts and thick forests guarded the south. Lakes were plentiful among the wooded foothills. The map did not mark the cities of the south, Celindon and Selby, nor the northern city of Trastad. Pericol was only a phrase: HOUSES HERE. It was as if in all the world, there was only this Kingdom.

White pebbles marked the places where the Wolfers had struck at the end of the last summer, and these were all gathered in the southern and western parts of Northgate's lands. For each homestead or village looted, burned, destroyed, there was a white pebble on the map. There was no marking for the lives lost. The men studied the map to see where a fortress might be built, to be garrisoned to patrol and guard the western and southern borders; or wouldn't a line of walled castles make a stronger defense?

Looking at the map, Elske could guess that the Wolfers had entered the Kingdom from the south, although she didn't know how they had found their way to its borders, whether they had been led by some trader who hoped by the favor to gain his life, or if some Wolfer bands, lost and wandering homewards, had stumbled into this unknown land. She guessed that there had been at least three Wolfer bands entering together and then, when they saw what lay before them, separating, each to pursue its own chances. They would have joined up again where they had parted, to return together to the Volkking.

None of the men asked her thoughts.

In any case, her thoughts were more with Beriel than here in this hall. Messengers from the east had told of two great armies moving towards one another, and war declared between the King's army and the Queen's. They said a battle was only a few days off. Dugald had told Elske how armies fight: The troops formed into lines, to dash against one another until one or the other mass of men yielded. Elske had thought of the seawalls of Trastad, and the waves rolling up against the great cut stones, and breaking themselves upon the walls; except that there was no victory or retreat between the seawalls and the waves, and in battle men die. In battle, Dugald had told her, the air rang loud, as the soldiers cried out to one another to ask or promise aid, to warn, to threaten, to curse their enemies, to curse their luck. The air rang thick with the sounds of fighting, steel clanging against steel, the pounding hooves of the war horses, the men's shrieks of fury and fear and pain.

"Have you been in battle?" she had asked him.

"No," he said. "No, I have not. But I have asked those who have, or their fathers; we have few battles in the Kingdom, although there have been occasional rebellions. I asked because I like to know what might lie ahead to unman me at the very time when I most need my courage. Knowledge blunts the blade of fear," he said.

"Yes," Elske had agreed.

"Although there are those who would prefer to run blind into danger. But you are not one of those, are you, Elske?" he had asked, as if his mouth could taste honey in her name, and Elske had felt confused, as if she had stepped from darkness into blinding day. It took a little time for her to ask him, "How are men persuaded to enter such battles?"

Dugald shrugged his shoulders. "They fight to defend their homes or keep their vows, to gain revenge. Men will fight for profit, too, and also to stand for a Queen whose throne has been usurped. Do not your Wolfers go into battle? And are they not men?"

"Wolfers swoop in, seize, kill, then return into their hiding places," she had answered him. "They fight no battles. They are war bands, raiders—not armies."

"They are cowards, who attack only the weak."

"Not cowards," Elske had told him.

Now, seated in this long hall while the men debated how to do battle against Wolfers, Elske could only wish that Beriel was facing a Wolfer war band, and not the army of trained soldiers led by her brother who hated her. The Wolfers would know Beriel's quality, at one glance, and their choice would be quick—either to take her back to the Volkking, or to cut her throat across. They might not know the word but they would respond to Beriel as to a Queen.

But this brother did not have a Wolfer nature. He feared Beriel, that she was the Queen; and what he might do, in his fear—

Elske felt her heart race at the unfinished thought.

Beside her, quietly, Dugald asked, "What troubles you, my Lady?"

"I think of Beriel," she told him. If Beriel lived, Elske would serve her, but if Beriel were dead . . . Elske would not abandon Beriel's Kingdom to this false King. She thought, imagination as swift as a falcon falling onto its prey, that she would become Jackaroo, riding to free the land of its King, or perhaps she would find her own army. There was this younger brother, Aidenil, and he could be placed on the throne. Her own future decided should Beriel not survive her war, Elske could attend to Hildebrand's son, asking, "Who is this girl, Lord Dugald? Why does she sit with us?"

"To give us counsel."

Hildebrand shifted in his chair, and let out his breath in a *pfftt* sound. "Women at a council of war?" he asked. "Go call your mother, my boy, and you might ask your wife, too," he laughed.

Hildebrand's son had already started to rise and obey when his father laughed, at which he sat down, red-faced. Hildebrand coughed, and when he could speak again turned back to Dugald. "My Lord, you are too young to remember— but your father, the Earl, he could tell you. This is one of those ideas out of the south, a Sutherlandish notion. In my father's time, there was a woman who advised the Earl Sutherland in his council; and they said she had an equal voice. I suppose it might have been possible in those earlier days, when there were no real dangers to face. But if my mother had had a voice, during the droughty years of my childhood when there was such unrest among the people, and armed robbers in the forests and hills—if there had been a woman on my father's council, I don't like to think what evil might have happened. It was hard enough times as it was, without a woman's voice to make quarrels. So, despite your bright eyes, my dear, and the pleasure a pretty girl always gives me, I must ask you to leave us."

Dugald put a hand on Elske's arm to hold her beside him.

"Lord Dugald," Hildebrand protested. "What does she know of war?"

"Nothing," Dugald answered. Then, with a glance at

Elske, he explained to the gathered Lords, "But she is Wolfer born and Wolfer raised."

"A Wolfer? The enemy—" "Wolfer? A spy—" "Witch—"

The words were whispered around the room, and answered by the name "Elskeling," spoken reassuringly by Dugald's captains, that she should not be afraid. But Elske was not afraid of what might happen in this room.

"I give my word for her," Dugald said, in warning and promise.

Lord Hildebrand spoke to Elske, then. "Would you betray your own people?"

"They are no longer my people," Elske told him.

He made the *pfftt* sound again and asked her, "Who are your people?"

"I have a Queen. Beriel," she answered.

"If she lives," one of the young Lords muttered.

Dugald reminded them, "We have our own dire necessity. We have a Kingdom to preserve, if we can."

Elske could speak to that. "They will go no farther than this," she said, and traced the two rivers that divided Earl Northgate's lands from the King's holdings, and Sutherland's. "It is only this countryside the Wolfers will attack."

"How can you know this so surely?" a doubting Lord demanded.

"Wolfers fear deep water, and never cross it nor go out upon it," Elske said.

"This is true?" Dugald asked her, although he already believed her.

"True," she promised, promising every man there.

"So King Guerric need never have fled into the east," someone said, and "He could not have known," another answered.

Lord Hildebrand announced his plan. "We have the numbers to overwhelm them. They are only bands of wild men, and we have trained soldiers. I say, Lord Dugald leads the army into the west to engage these Wolfers in battle."

"I say, we make a line of our soldiers, along this border," Thorold suggested. "So many soldiers will make a wall of men to keep the Wolfers out."

"I say, we divide our troops, and let them roam as Wolfers, to fight and destroy the enemy wherever he might be found," said another.

"Elske?" Dugald asked her.

She shook her head, and tried to explain. "The war bands are as hard to track as a pack of wolves. They move separately, each going its own way under its own captain, except when they first enter a land, and make the camp at which they will gather again, to leave the land together. You might stand in a castle with your soldiers at the ready all summer long and never see a single Wolfer. Yet if you stretch your soldiers into a thin line, each of your men will be weak and alone—and those the Wolfers will attack."

"If the enemy will not engage us in our numbers, how do we fight him?"

"If you know where they gathered together last fall, before leaving the Kingdom—do you know where that is?" she asked.

"Isn't it too late?"

"Have you had word of attacks?" Dugald asked Hildebrand, who shook his head; there had been no word. "How early in spring do they leave their own lands, Elske?" he asked.

"The land of the Volkaric lies northwards from the Kingdom, and they will leave in early spring, but not so soon as to be caught by a late winter storm. Then they must travel into the south, to find again their way into the Kingdom, through the forest, as I guess."

In her mind, she could see the long-bearded Wolfers, knives at their sides, racing up through the thick forest into this newfound land. She could see their speed and eagerness, how they hungered for the slaughter and the stealing. How each captain hoped to carry back to the Volkking the richest treasures, and give to him the greatest honor, and gain from that an eminence over all the other Volkaric warriors. Elske never doubted the boldness of the Wolfers, and their willingness to die in the chance of standing proud before the Volkking. She didn't think these bushy-bearded soldiers of the Kingdom had that same wild courage.

These people of the Kingdom did not know the enemy they faced. Elske drew her attention back to the questions Hildebrand's son asked. "Lady," he began again, "these Wolfers—" He looked about him, as if hoping some other man would ask it. But no other man offered. "Their cry freezes the heart, and— What can we tell our soldiers? To keep them from cowardice, which will not only defeat but also shame them. Do you know the cry?"

Elske did.

"Do you know how we might guard ourselves against its power?"

"What can be so fearful in a sound that comes from men's throats," Elske asked, "any more than a dog's bark? But you might ask your soldiers to answer in kind. The Wolfers give themselves courage, following their own voices into battle. If your soldiers have the same voices, why should they not find the same courage?"

"Can you teach us?" one of the captains asked, and "Yes," Elske agreed.

One of the young Lords had been studying the map. "They gathered here," he said, now. "In my father's lands, beside this lake. Lady, following their spoor we found campfires—" There was something in his eyes that sorrowed Elske, as if he had seen that which would never leave off troubling him, every day of his life, and every night. "Lady," he asked again, "these men had taken— We found a creature, like a doll, at one of the holdings, only . . . It had been made out of the family, the limbs of children, the woman's body. Lady, these were goatherders. Not soldiers. Not armed." He had placed his memory out on the table before all of them. They wished to look away from it, but knew they had to stay and face what he had seen. They were angry at him, displeased. The silence in the long room grew heavy, the air cool despite the warming fire.

A captain asked, "What kind of men are they?"

"Not men at all," another captain answered. "They are animals."

"Lady?" they asked her, as much fearful as furious.

Elske shook her head. She could not answer, did not know.

The young Lord insisted. "As if death were a game."

So Elske answered him. "When men have drunk too much honey mead together, as the Wolfers love to do, or wine, or ale, and more so if they have passed some danger together, then they will do such things as they would otherwise not think of. Even Wolfers, accustomed as they are to battle and blood, can be made more wild by blood and drink and the fear with which their victims look at them." She looked around at the smooth-shaven Lords in their blue shirts, the bearded captains wearing metal breastplates.

They did not wish to meet her glance, and their faces were wiped clear of any expression. So she knew they had seen men behave so, and had perhaps themselves done that of which they would not willingly speak.

She turned to Dugald, to his rock-grey eyes. "Yes," he said. "They do. We do."

Around the two of them, the other men breathed out, and each might have been thinking to himself that whatever he might have done in the past, which he would never tell, he would not act so again in future. Dugald, by his words that did not deny, freed them, as from the spell of their own actions. As if their own actions were the enchantress and it must take Dugald to break her spell.

Thorold asked then, "What do they want, these Wolfers? Why do they deal so cruelly with our people, who are not soldiers and must, I think, surrender as soon as they see the Wolfers come?"

Elske did not know how to explain the people of the Volkaric to the people of this rich and pleasant land. "They want victory in the fight, to prove their courage. They want to take treasure, to please their appetites for food and drink, to rape women. They are as much children as men. They are as much animals as thieves, and murderers. They are like wolves, except for the treasure they seek, coins and jewels, swords and knives, cloths, dark-haired girls."

"If it is treasure they want, why don't they attack the cities where they'd find booty in abundance? These holdings are poor and the cities, especially the castles of the Lords, have greater wealth, so why don't they go after those places?"

"They will," Elske promised.

This caused another chilled quiet, until Lord Hildebrand asked the question of the meeting, again. "Can you tell us how to stop them, Elske?"

Beriel had sent her here, to protect this countryside. Elske had few sword skills, and she was no Queen to hearten men for their own deaths. She could fight beside the soldiers, and that would be her choice, but more help than that she could not give them. The rest they must find for themselves.

"You know where they had gathered together before they left the Kingdom?" she asked the young Lord.

"As I said." His finger pointed again to the map. "It seemed the Wolfers had rested there several days."

"Then that is where they will enter the Kingdom," Elske told the men. "That is where you will find them massed like an army."

"And there we can use our own army on them," a captain said, his voice glad. "If not when they enter, then when they leave the Kingdom. Just let them be gathered together, and we'll be on them like wolves on sheep."

The hall was suddenly lit with hope. The men pointed out routes, arguing, and made requests of Hildebrand for supply wagons, and Lord Dugald promised that the treasury of Earl Northgate would stand open for this cause. "That's the way, then," they said to one another, and "My men are ready to move out," and "All haste, my Lord," they said. Until Hildebrand raised his doubting eyes to Elske and asked, "So, we must trust you to betray your own people?"

"Not her people," Dugald's captains said, but Hildebrand insisted, "How do we know that? She has a plausible face, granted, but do we thus put all our lives in her hands?"

Again, Elske needed to explain what they could not understand. "I cannot betray the Wolfers. I can only betray the Volkking. The warriors are only his arms and fingers and hands, each man belonging only to the Volkking, and ruled by him. He is the spider in the web; if you take off a strand of the web, the spider only spins another. The web traps moths for the spider to eat, not for itself. I cannot be a traitor to these people and I have already betrayed the Volkking. You have no need to doubt me."

But they wanted to know just how she had betrayed this Volkking, so she explained about the role of the Death Maiden, and her grandmother's revenge on the people of the Volkaric. And from that, with the days of the journey into the hills to polish and improve it, came Lord Dugald's plan of battle.

CHAPTER 19

IN A SILVERY DAWN, MIST floated on the glassy surface of the lake and rose up into brightening air. All around, forests darkened the sides of the encircling hills. In the far meadow, the night's campfires were black circles and the sleeping Wolfers short, black lines.

Soldiers of the Kingdom slipped among the trees, invisible, horseless, wordless. Silently, they circled around the lake, approaching the meadow from both sides.

Across the black and bottomless water, a small boat moved. Elske sat in the bow. Dugald—with his back to her—rowed. He had wrapped the oars in cloth, to muffle their sound. He himself and Elske, too, were wrapped around with long cloaks.

The air was damp, chill. Those birds that woke before the sun sang their brief songs, their voices cutting sharp as knife blades through the still air.

Elske's boat glided with only the tiniest ripples of sound, through the still water.

The sun rose up into the sky behind the eastern hills and the lake's surface turned pale gold, and the mists rose up gold and white.

The night before, as they stood in the short reeds, the coracle at their feet, Elske and Dugald had looked across the black surface of the lake to the many, many campfires—almost a reflection in yellow of the many, many white stars scattered across the black skies above—and they had spoken in whispers to one another, "At halfway, do you think?" It was at that point, they'd agreed, that Elske should stand up in the bow of the boat, and make herself visible.

Dugald, her ferryman, would be hidden behind her.

Their hope was to distract the Wolfers. They hoped that the sight of Elske—some of the men might think they recognized her—gliding towards their camp across the surface of the water, would seize their attention so that the Wolfers would not discover the approaching army until it was too late to do anything more than stand, and fight. They hoped that by the end of morning the soldiers would have driven the Wolfers out of the Kingdom. Elske—and Lord Dugald, too, who would let no other man take his part—would alarm and attract the Wolfers by gliding right up into their midst.

When the time was right, Elske would give the signal for the attack. Until they heard that signal, the soldiers were under the strictest orders of silence. It was Dugald who would tell her when the time was right, another part he would let no other man take.

"The Queen put her into my care," he said, over and over. "Elske is mine to guard."

Neither he nor Elske spoke aloud what they both knew, and all the others also understood: The two in the little boat would be alone in the midst of the enemy when battle was engaged. Elske was the staked goat, to draw the enemy out, and Lord Dugald perforce staked with her.

The boat drew the sun's gold after it across the wide lake, as a Lady would the train of her fine gown. The boat moved forward through the fading mist, so that it would seem—when Elske stood—that she floated upon mist, not water.

Halfway across, at a whisper from Dugald, she stood up. The round-bottomed coracle rocked under her bare feet and she heard Dugald's intaken breaths, his unspoken fear, before the boat rocked itself into safe balance again.

Balanced, Elske dropped her cloak. This was what she had told no one. As naked as the Death Maiden entering to the Volkking, Elske stood in the bow of the boat. Her dark hair flowed down over her back.

Dugald rowed steadily, quietly. His back was turned to her, so he could not see Elske, nor the beginnings of movement among the men on the shore. The men stirred. Their voices sounded, clear across the water, groaning, laughing, quarreling.

Elske stood motionless and the boat glided under her feet.

A few of the Wolfers rose. She was not close enough to see their faces and know if she knew them. They rubbed at their arms and looked about them. One man pointed, at her, and his neighbor responded by turning around to look. A muffled wave of voices rolled towards her, almost a greeting. Slowly, the Wolfers drew together in their numbers. Slowly, gathering, their eyes all fixed on her, they approached the water's edge.

They could not believe their eyes.

They were there in their hundreds, twenty and more of the raiding parties, come to scour this fat land clean of its goodnesses. In their hundreds they drew towards the edge of the lake, as if towards the Volkking's carved throne on the day he distributed the year's takings. But on this day, they faced not the man on the throne but a naked girl, her arms at her side, being carried magically towards them on water.

And on this morning, they drew their long knives out of the scabbards. Their long beards hung down narrow from their chins and their wolf eyes were wild.

The boat glided forward, towards them, towards their center, and the boldest of them stepped out into the water.

Elske stood with her dark hair loose over her shoulders.

There was a time of absolute silence. Silence hung over the scene like a knife. And then the sun broke free of the hills, to rise up into the sky as if it were a ball of flames, ignited, lighting everything.

"Now," Dugald said quietly, and Elske opened her throat.

The Wolfer war cry rose up out of her chest, out of her mouth and into the air where it twisted, and clawed its way up. Her cry howled out over the water and into the trees.

Before that sound had left the sky, an answering, echoing cry from the throats of hundreds of unseen soldiers rolled like a fog out of the trees.

On the shore, the Wolfers looked to one another, unable to know, undecided and leaderless. The motionless Death Maiden approached them, coming ever closer.

Their eyes were on Elske, wild with confusion and doubt; then their faces turned from her to the trees, out of which soldiers emerged, howling endlessly as they marched into battle, attacking in orderly lines.

Turning to face the soldiers on their left and turning to face the soldiers on their right, turning to face Elske, turning back to see soldiers, the Wolfers turned their backs to the lake, the Death Maiden, and the army. They fled.

They ran in packs across the meadow grass, faster than the more heavily armored soldiers could go. They crossed the meadow and melted into the trees, as fleet as wolves.

The soldiers hesitated, unprepared for this response.

Elske raised her cry again and—trained to this—they answered her, louder and more clear here in the open air. Then their captains ordered them after the enemy in his flight. Giving the Wolfer cry, the captains led their men in the pursuit.

Then it was that the coracle scraped its bottom on the sandy lake bottom.

Elske lost her balance, and stumbled forward. Clutching at the rounded side of the little boat, she tumbled sideways and the boat rocked.

Dugald leapt out of the boat, then, and in the same motion turned, drawing his sword to fight—as he expected—to his death. But he could see no enemy to engage. He could see only his own soldiers, some alert and watching on the meadow, some racing into the distant woods, and then he saw Elske crouched naked in the bow of the boat.

"What—?" he asked her, as he covered her with his own cloak. "Where—?"

Elske climbed onto her knees, and then—the cloak wrapped around her—out of the boat and into the shallow water.

"Elske! What has happened?" he demanded. The water rose almost to the top of his leather boots, and he clambered quickly onto dry land. There, he reached out a hand to her, if she might need it.

Shivering from excitement, her teeth chattering with

victory and with fear dispelled, as if she stood barefooted in a snowstorm before the lighted doorway of her grand-mother's little house, Elske felt laughter rise up in her. "I said, they are children. I said, I think—" She shivered violently.

"Bring drink for the Lady," Dugald called to a group of watching soldiers.

She was given a leather flask filled with a liquid that burned down into her stomach, and warmed her. She drank it eagerly, and coughed, and laughed out loud.

"As if I led troops of dead men against them," she told Dugald. He understood her immediately, and looked off towards the trees into which the Wolfers had fled.

"What shall we do, Lord Dugald?" a captain asked and Dugald gave the order, "Pursue, and do not take prisoners. Let me march with you, to see how the battle goes."

"There is no battle, my Lord," the captain pointed out.

ALL THE MORNING, ELSKE WAITED alone beside the quiet lake, while those soldiers left on guard there rested on the ground behind her, joking and jovial now. She could hear complaints that they had missed their chance to prove their courage and skill, matched by rough reminders that they had also missed their chance at death and wounding. "To be prepared for bloodshed, and know you have the courage for it, but not to be put in the way of it—now there's a soldier's dream," more than one said. "This is our Elskeling's way of war," they said and called out, "Lady, I'll be your soldier on any cause."

"The battle won and not a man lost," they rejoiced.

It was midday before Dugald returned to break her solitude. He'd left a troop of his own soldiers following the Wolfer trail as the war band dashed headlong, stopping neither for drink nor food, back into the south, fleeing the Kingdom. "They're not likely to come back against us," he decided. "We can sleep easy upon the question of Wolfers."

"Unless they have changed their natures, I think we can," Elske agreed.

"And you did not guess what they would think?"

"How could I guess more than that seeing me they might be stunned with surprise, and therefore taken at a disadvantage? You know that was my thought. How could I guess that they would run from me?"

"I think it was the armies in the forest they ran from."

"Thinking they were armies of dead men, and deathless."

"Did you know that you would be naked?" he asked her then.

"I knew I must be. As the Death Maiden is, when she enters to the Volkking." She also knew he would have forbidden it and so she had kept silent. Just as she had known his fear of drowning when he insisted on being her boatman, and kept silent. Now she waited for his sentence on her.

"You did not tell me that you would be naked."

"You would have stopped me, I think," she said.

"I think I would have tried to stop you, and you would have persuaded me of the need," he corrected her. "Elske," he said and then said her name again, "Elske. I never tire of your surprises. You know that."

That, she hadn't known.

"I can warm my hands in the grey of your eyes, as in the warmth of wolf fur. I warm my heart at the sound of your name. Elske, if I have my way, I will have you with me every day of my life, as long as I live," he told her, and added, "Also, in my bed."

Elske had not known that, either.

"Will you have me?" he asked, and before she had time to say yes, he said, "For husband, I mean. Do you want me for your husband?"

"How could I not want you?" she asked him. "For husband, but—"

"Why?" he interrupted.

This she could answer easily. "Because you are true-hearted," she explained, "and brave. And useful—in many ways—and you desire to be useful to people. Because"—she didn't know how to say this in the more delicate southern language, in a way that would be decent to him; the feeling being so unfamiliar to her, and confusing to her, and understanding as she now did how rape was not the right word for her feeling—"because I would be in your bed with you, and both naked, even if it is not decent," she said and then, when he shouted with laughter, she remembered, "because of your laughter."

When he wrapped his arms around her and lifted her up into his embrace, the soldiers around them looked away, mumbling to one another, shuffling their boots into the dirt, coughing and spitting, before they gave way and stared.

When Dugald set her apart, it was only to hold out both his hands to her and say, "I offer you my heart, Lady, my hand, my title and my lands. Give me your word that you will take them."

"I promise you," Elske said, almost unable to breathe for gladness, almost as if she were drowning, with his hands held in her own strong grasp.

CHAPTER 20

THE ARMY UNDER LORD DUGALD returned woundless the way they had come. At every village and inn they were greeted by welcoming crowds, for their story preceded them. Elske grew accustomed to hearing her name called out, perhaps by the children near a farmhouse, "Elske, Elskeling!" or by villagers gathered near a well, "Elskeling!" She rode at Dugald's side, once again dressed as a Lady must and riding sideways. Elske could wave, and smile, and be glad of the victory. She could be glad that through the victory, the shadows of fear had been lifted from this land, with its stony fields and the flocks of sheep and goats which grazed on its hills, with its dark-eyed sturdy people, who cheered for the soldiers as they marched past in file, and cheered for their Earl that would be, and called her by name, "Elske!"

Dugald chose not to disband his army until he knew the

outcome of the royal contest, so he sent messengers out ahead, to find what news they could, and received them without delay when they returned, and questioned them closely. For these interviews Elske was with him, although, "Beriel does not concern me as she does you," he remarked.

"Beriel is your lawful Queen."

"And I will be her loyal vassal," he said. "But if she dies in battle, she cannot be my Queen and I must be vassal to another, and that with a good heart—if my lands are to prosper. She rules you almost as a sister, bound in blood. Let us hope she will approve our marriage."

"How could she not?" Elske asked.

"Beriel's is a Queen's royal will," Dugald said. "But first, there is the question of the throne to be settled, for if Beriel is slain or taken—"

All along the King's Way, messengers met them with news, in Hildebrand's city, in inn yards and at the ford of the river. The reports of these messengers sometimes echoed and sometimes contradicted one another:

There was to be joined a great battle, with many soldiers risked on both sides.

There was to be a duel, because Beriel had challenged Guerric, offering a fight to the death. Her brother would not accept her challenge, claiming she mocked him, being a woman, claiming that a victory in such combat would be shame.

A later messenger told them the armies had taken up positions on opposite sides of a broad valley, where the sleepy little river meandered lazily through grassy meadows.

Dugald rode on towards the King's City, encountering the messengers who rode to tell him that a fierce battle raged, the green grass turned into mud by the booted feet of the soldiery while the little river turned red with men's blood. They told him, Guerric delayed the start of battle, and delayed again, while Beriel chafed at the postponement of the chance to prove her claims. They told him, Beriel was slain, taken captive, hanged as a traitor without her royal privilege of the ax.

No, it was Beriel's army that had won the victory. The number of dead exceeded the number of those left alive, including the wounded.

No, King Guerric had set an ambush for his ambitious sister, and trapped her and all of her royal guard, too. Thus the battle ended in victory for Guerric.

No, the Queen had found and slain her brother and enemy. She rode now at the head of those who had survived her victory. She carried the severed head of Guerric on a tall pole, that all might know her power and her right.

All the messengers agreed that many lives had been lost. Most reported victory for Beriel so Dugald and Elske moved forward with hope.

Their way led them now beside the river, and they set up

their camps in the sweet spring evenings, the army around them. "You have not taught me to swim," Dugald reminded Elske, who by then knew enough propriety to answer, "When we are alone, my Lord. When we are alone and by one of the lakes, for didn't you promise me that I would have a house at the lakeside to be my marriage gift?"

"I did, and you will." They were watching night settle gentle as falling snow down over the silver river and the green land. "Let Beriel be Queen," Dugald said, then, "and I will ask no more for my perfect contentment. And did you ever think you would be an Earl's wife, Elske?"

"No," she said, for she had never thought of being any man's wife.

Dugald was in a robust pride that evening. "Has another man—any other man—asked to give you the honor of his name?"

"Yes," she said.

This surprised him. "Who was he? One of the Wolfers?"

"The men of the Volkaric have no wives," she explained, meaning to tease him. "Besides, I was the Death Maiden, and belonged to the Volkking."

This reminder drove the pride from Dugald, who took her naked hand in his own bare fingers to say, "Then who was this other man? Must I be jealous? Or were there many men, and I must be jealous of them all?"

"Be jealous of none," Elske reassured him.

The river nuzzled into the long grasses at its shallow banks, and Elske's skirts swished in echoing sound. From behind them came the voices of their soldiers. "In two days' journey," Dugald told Elske, "we'll be at the King's City and know what fortune awaits the Kingdom."

"I'll be glad when the cheering's done," Elske admitted.

But when the two armies met together and joined into one on the jousting field outside the walls of the King's City, the cheers of the citizens for their soldiers and their Queen, and the cheers of the soldiers for their victories and their Queen, for Northgate's heir, and Elske, too, choked the air. Beriel stood on the King's pavilion, where all might see her, tall and high-shouldered, one arm bandaged close to her chest, this being one of the deep wounds she had taken in battle, and leaning on a carved wooden stick for the other. She turned and turned, showing her face to all in the crowd that surrounded her. Her eyes shone blue, and her bandages shone white as she stood before her people. She wore no crown, not yet having been anointed; but Beriel had never needed any crown to be the Queen.

The soldiers of Dugald's army, both those of his father's house and those of Sutherland's, lifted Elske up onto the platform, that she might stand with Beriel, but the two could not say any words to one another, for the roar of voices. They clasped hands, once, before the voices called them apart. "Beriel!" the people cheered, and the soldiers, too. "Long live the Queen! Long life to our Warrior Queen!" Voices of men and women and children, Lords and people, all mingled together. "Elske!" they cheered, "Elske of the deathless battle, Elskeling!"

At first, Beriel and Elske stood back-to-back, like Wolfguard. With Elske to balance against, Beriel could drop her stick and raise her good arm up into the air.

Louder cried the crowd, in its joy at the double victory and in honor of these two. The two were filled with the cries of the people as the sails of a ship fill with wind, and Elske, too, raised an arm in answer to the people's joy in Beriel, and honor to them both.

When they turned to face one another again, each with her own name and the other's ringing in her ears, Beriel stepped back. She held out her right hand to Elske, palm down. She wore on that hand the royal signet. Her eyes were like the blue sea when it reflected back the light of the midday sun.

This was Beriel in her full power. This was Beriel, Queen.

Elske took the hand in her own, and when the crowd saw that it cheered more loudly, and gladly, "Elskeling!"

Beriel's hand pressed hard down on Elske's. "Kneel," she commanded. "Kneel to me."

But why should Beriel need Elske kneeling before her? Still, Elske sank down to her knees before her Queen, and pressed her forehead to the hand which she held, to show loyalty, to give honor, in servitude, and all gladly.

Now the crowd cheered Beriel's name, over and over, tirelessly.

Before Elske could rise, Beriel signaled to five men who stood close by the pavilion's steps. They were richly dressed, and two were also bandaged; they came forward to surround her. This guard, with the Queen in their midst, descended the steps and stepped into the crowd, which parted to give the Queen passage.

Win was not one of this close guard. Left on her knees on the pavilion floor, Elske wondered what had befallen the young man, wondered if he lived. She had just stepped back onto the ground, when one of the guard returned to tell her, "The Queen requires your attendance, my Lady. With no more time lost, my Lady. That is the Queen's will."

"I obey and follow," Elske assured him, and he was away to rejoin the Queen.

WIDE WOODEN DOORWAYS OPENED TO let Elske enter the reception chamber where Beriel was holding court. A tall-backed throne, with carved arms and legs, stood on a raised dais at the far end of the room, and there Beriel sat.

Beriel saw Elske enter, but made no sign; she was giving public thanks and praise to the captains and Lords of Northgate's army, who were called up one by one to receive her hand and swear their allegiances.

Elske looked around her, while she waited her time to be called forward. The wooden floors in this hall gleamed with polish, each plank fitted tight against its neighbors. The long windows were unshuttered, letting fresh, sun-warmed air fill the hall. But Elske did not see Win among the courtiers gathered in this room, nor among the soldiery.

Beriel called for Dugald, heir to Earl Northgate. He knelt before her and she thanked him for driving the Wolfers out of her lands, and she proclaimed him first among her loyal Lords. Then she rose up from the throne and asked him for his arm so that he might escort her through a doorway behind the dais, thus ending the ceremony of thanks.

At the opened door, Beriel sent one of her hovering Ladies-in-Waiting to Elske, to tell Elske that she, too, was required in this private conference with the Queen. Elske followed the woman's broad skirts and stepped through the door held open for her. Elske hoped to find Win waiting within. But Win was not there in the small paneled room. Dugald and Beriel sat across from one another at a table, and there was no one to occupy the fourth chair.

"Be seated," Beriel told Elske. "Now, Dugald, give me your report. Tell me how we stand with the Wolfers."

"We stand free of them," Dugald told her. "They think they were met by the Death Maiden and her army of the deathless dead. That at least is our guess, my Queen, and if that is so, Elske tells me it will be many years before they dare the Kingdom again, and maybe forever."

"I don't think you should promise us forever, Elske."

Elske protested, "I have promised nothing, my Lady."

"I can offer you no honors that would equal your worth," Beriel said to Dugald.

Dugald answered her. "I seek no honors."

"Sought or unsought, you have gathered honors about you," Beriel answered. "Rumors unsaddled their horses in my courtyards before you dismounted your own, tales of a bloodless victory, of a naked maiden before whose brightness Wolfers flee. My own wars don't make such a pretty story."

"Nor such an easy one," Dugald agreed. "What of Guerric, what of the battle? For we, also, have dined on rumors."

At the question, Beriel leaned towards Elske with a mischievous smile, as if they were back in Trastad and she the Fiendly Princess again. "Guerric put a price on my head—a fortune in gold coins and land rights, which he offered for my capture alive. If dead, then only coins. But many coins," Beriel announced, as if that pleased her.

Her next thought did not please her. "He would have suborned his own soldiers into murderers. He hoped to corrupt those who had pledged their swords to me. He was a fool."

"Ah, he *was*?" Lord Dugald asked, seizing on the clue, but Beriel would tell her own story in her own way.

"I had an army to defeat, trained and weaponed, led by experienced captains. I had my own men to use—and not to waste. Our battle plan was to attack at three points, in three equal parts, two at their flanks—where they were spread thin, not expecting attack there; and I led the third part of my soldiers into the waiting center of their line."

"On horseback?"

"At first, but after the first clash I dismounted. Sideseated is a weak position from which to wield a sword. So I fought among my soldiers, beside my own men. Elske, I think I am more of a Wolfer than you."

"I think you are," Elske agreed.

"I have walked into battle," Beriel told Elske proudly. "I have had soldiers ready to follow me to their deaths, and many did die in my cause. I have had a man's heart at the end of my blade, and watched the life leave his body, and pulled my sword free for the next enemy. And my courage did not fail me," Beriel announced. "I have had my revenge," she told Elske.

"On Guerric?" Dugald asked.

Beriel told Elske, "I was too late to be the man who slew Ditrik. But I watched him fight, and lose, and lie open-eyed as the sword came down into his throat. He knew I watched. He died bravely, which I will be able to tell my uncle, the Earl Sutherland, that harmony may grow between our houses. And I return Aymeric to his father, his honor restored as much as it can be, earned back to him by his sword. So that is finished."

"What of Guerric, the crowned King?" Dugald asked again.

"The usurper," Beriel corrected him, then told him, "Guerric surrendered his sword to one of my captains. Of course, when he saw he could neither defeat me nor escape me. He was ever a coward—what was the word, Elske? The Wolfer word, like spitting."

"*Fruhckman,*" Elske said, and could wait no longer for her own question. "But where is Win? I would have thought to find him here. Is he dead?"

"Not dead," Beriel answered. "Win was at my side throughout the battle, and took wounds—although none deep. He was at my side afterwards, when I visited the wounded and walked among the dead of both armies. And Win was at my side when they brought Guerric to me, my wounds freshly bound and my cheeks still wet with grief. Guerric offered me the ring, and the throne, and asked in exchange for his life. He asked only for his own life. The lives of all the others he gave into my hands. He offered me only what was mine by right, and my lands still wet with the blood of our soldiers."

"Where will you send him for his exile?" Dugald asked.

"I took our father's ring. I had already won the throne. What need to treat with him? Guerric ever hated me as much as I learned to hate him, and he knew I wished him dead." She stood up from her chair and went to the window, leaning heavily on the stick, to look out over her city before she turned to tell them, "So then he thought to make my men doubt me. He accused me of being possessed by insatiable appetites for the men around me. To have them in my bed— Why do you smile in that insolent way, my Lord?" Beriel demanded.

"Anyone who knows you must know the falseness of that charge," Dugald answered. "I know you from childhood, and you have ever been more quick to quarrel than to kiss— and if ever you did kiss any man, even as a willful girl, it was not me. And yet," he said, "I'd swear you were my fond cousin."

"As I am," Beriel smiled. "As you are mine, I hope. But Guerric claimed to know of his own experience men I had called to my chamber, and claimed to be one of those himself, and he said he could prove by his knowledge of my private body that he spoke the truth. He called me unworthy, and would have said worse, except that Win cut his throat and silenced him forever."

Nobody spoke in the little room. Almost, they might not have been breathing.

"Knowingly," Beriel said slowly, as if they could not understand it spoken otherwise, "Win slew the anointed King."

"High treason," Dugald said.

Elske didn't understand them. "Can it be treason to defend the honor of your Queen?" she asked. "Can it be treason to slay a traitor? Guerric was the usurper, wasn't he? And he had sought your life, Beriel, in battle and before, also, as Win told us."

Dugald and Beriel spoke as if Elske were not present. "The Priests will have to read the law over him. My Queen, will you lose your throne?"

"I gave no order for Guerric's death," Beriel answered.

Elske cried, "Will Win die for taking your revenge?"

Beriel told Dugald, "Guerric's death Win's own loyal heart offered to me."

"You will speak to the Priests for him?" Dugald asked.

"Can your Kingdom's law condemn the man who defends his Queen?" Elske protested.

"I cannot speak. The Queen cannot. The Queen must not attempt to influence the Priests, as they apply the law."

"What will happen to Win?" Elske demanded, and at last they looked at her.

"She wouldn't let him be hanged," Dugald said.

Beriel answered precisely. "If I could lawfully save him, I would. He has given me the only cheer I have found in all of this bloody claiming of my throne. If I can lawfully save him, trust me, I will."

"You must," Elske told her.

"There is no must for a Queen," Beriel answered sharply, and this silenced them all. After a time, Beriel rose. "You may leave me, now."

Disregarding the command, Dugald said, "My Queen, I ask your blessing on my marriage."

Beriel asked, with royal displeasure, "You are wed?"

"Not wed. Promised," he answered, and looked her steadily in the eye.

"Promised," Beriel echoed him. "To whom promised?"

"I have offered and I have been accepted," Dugald said, with unconcealed happiness.

Beriel lost patience. "Name her."

"My Queen, she is Elske."

"Elske? Of course it is Elske." Beriel sounded apologetic when she said, "But, Dugald, you are to marry my sister—whichever sister you prefer—and thus join Northgate's house as close to the throne as is Sutherland's," she said. "Elske will go with my brother Aidenil to Trastad. There you must help Aidenil, Elske, to establish a merchant bank so that he can trade, as the Trastaders do, and accumulate wealth for our royal house as well as make commercial connections in whatever cities and lands the bank does business. Var Jerrol will aid in this, Elske, for your sake. Undoubtedly, he will offer hospitality to my princely brother. You will be there to help Aidenil make our way in this new world, with your connections to the Council, and to Var Kenric's family. You will be my Ambassador to Trastad, Elske," Beriel announced, then turned to Dugald. "So you see, Elske cannot be your wife. I have need of her."

Dugald warned her, "I know you, Beriel. We have been children together, and I know how your heart is."

"Do you contravene my will? Do you seek to rule me?" she demanded.

Dugald did not shrink from her anger. "I seek to remind you to rule yourself. If you will make your two truest supporters into a meal for your pride, then your reign promises ill."

"You count yourself one of my truest men?"

"I speak of Win," Dugald said. "You have nothing to fear from Elske, Beriel."

"Have you forgotten that she is Wolfer?"

At that, Dugald laughed, then at the look on Beriel's face, answered more diplomatically, "Let us add her wild blood to our own, then, to give ours new strength."

"Dugald, you know my house. We have had new blood, my grandfathers both gave new blood to the house, and my grandmother, too, and look what it has brought—"

"Beriel, it has brought us you. I have known you from a child, and you were ever worthy to be my Queen," Dugald answered her, and she turned from him.

She said to Elske, "I had thought you would be my voice in Trastad, and my watchdog over all of my many interests there. I thought to honor you."

Once again they kept silence, until Beriel broke it. "Leave us, Lord Dugald," she ordered. He hesitated, with a glance at Elske, but obeyed.

Beriel sat down again. Into the quiet she spoke as if her heart wept. "How can you betray me so?"

Elske knew that it was fear that dug long fingers into her neck. "My Queen, how have I done that?" she asked.

"You have allowed my Earl to give you his heart."

"How is that betrayal?" Elske asked.

"You have been a servant in Trastad, and you would marry my Earl? You have gone naked before soldiers, and all have seen you naked, and you would marry my Earl? You are a Wolfer, and you would marry my Earl?"

All of this was true. But it was not the whole truth of her, as Beriel must remember.

Beriel said now, more quietly, "Why will you not go to Trastad, where honors will be showered upon you?"

There were no words in Elske's throat waiting to be spoken.

"I know Dugald," Beriel said. "We were children together, and I know his nature. It must be you who refuses him, for he will not give you up. If you were my sister, and I forbade the match, you must obey me. If you marry him, his mother—I know her—will hate you."

Elske said, "I'm not afraid of the hatred of women."

"The men, too, his Lords, they will despise you and pity

him for having such a wife. What will you do, Elske, when people do not smile upon you? For people have ever smiled on you, and been glad of you."

Elske did not speak her thoughts aloud, for she did not wish to quarrel.

Now Beriel warned her, "You'll always be a stranger where you live. In my Kingdom."

They sat across from one another at the table, like two merchants negotiating a trade. Elske answered plainly. "I have never been other than an outsider where I have lived. But my children will be born in the Kingdom."

"Your children also will be outsiders," Beriel announced.

"Are the people of the Kingdom as blind, and foolish, as the people of the Volkaric? I cannot believe that," Elske said, no longer concealing anger; and then she reminded the Queen, "I have given Dugald my word."

"Your word? What is your word next to my will?" Beriel demanded. Then she lowered her forehead down onto her folded hands, and rested there a long time. When she raised her face, she was resolute, but to what, Elske could not guess. "So you are determined to take from me the most worthy man of the Kingdom?"

"How do I take him from you by marrying him?" Elske argued, reminding Beriel, "It was one of your sisters you spoke of for his wife, not yourself."

"You cannot be such an innocent!" Beriel cried out angrily.

"I know my debt to you, Elske, but you go too far with me in this. Oh, I won't forbid you. If you will marry against my will, so be it. So. You will be Northgate's Lady, and I will be sorry for it all the days of my life," Beriel promised. "And sometimes," she promised, "you will be sorry, too. For we will be parted now."

Elske had feared Beriel's death, but she did not fear to be parted from her now. Her young mistress she would have grieved for, and revenged, but this imperious and jealous Queen had no need of such service as Elske could give her.

"You have been my servant and now you will be my Earl's Lady," Beriel said, as if this thought gave her unwelcome amusement. "And who knows what you might be next, when fortune's wheel has already raised you so high."

Elske promised what she could. "You will always be my Queen. Your child and heir will always be my royal sovereign."

"And what husband must I marry to bear his children, that there will be an heir for the Kingdom?" Beriel cried.

"Why not Win?" Elske asked.

Beriel had her answer ready. "Win is one of the people and not even the firstborn son. He has nothing to give me."

Beriel had desired the throne, and been born to it, and she had earned it, too, but in the matter of her own husbanding she seemed as foolish as any other girl. "Win has no ambition more than to serve you; he will never ask more honors than those you choose to give him. He would never let himself shame you. And he has given you your brother's tongue, silenced."

Beriel listened closely to Elske's words, but still she made protest. "If he hangs? Would you wish me wed to a traitor, and a dead man?"

"No," Elske smiled. "Not if he hangs." But why should Win hang, when he was no traitor? Elske would not stand by, to watch Win die; there would be a way to save him, and she would find it.

Beriel acknowledged then, "I have spoken of marriage to Win. You should know that he refused me, for the dishonor his birth would bring to me. He will be my servant, and he will die if I need his life from him, but he refuses to be my husband and bed partner, even though he says his heart is mine, forever, and swears that he will never wed another. So, you see, even if the Priests find him innocent under the law, I may not marry Win."

Beriel rose now to return to the window where she looked out again to whatever she could see. "Even as we speak here, the Priests argue his life," she said. "I think they will decide for me. But until that question is settled, I require you with me."

"I will obey you, my Queen," Elske said.

"In that, but not in the other," Beriel said bitterly. She

gave Elske no time to answer, but turned on her stick to sweep out of the room.

ELSKE SAT FOR A TIME alone, to understand that if she wished, she might renounce Dugald and regain the Queen's favor; and to understand that she did not wish it. Also, she thought of Win. When she re-entered the hall, it was crowded with courtiers, both Lords and Ladies, several captains still wearing their light armor, and a few Priests. Servants stood along the walls. People spoke in low voices, waiting, watching the Queen. Beriel sat enthroned, lost in thought.

Elske searched for Dugald in the crowd but could not see him. She heard a woman whisper that Beriel would be crowned now, today, that there were none left to keep her from the throne, for her mother was already sent into exile in the care of Earl Sutherland. Another woman's voice answered that since this young Queen had rid the land of two evils—civil war and Wolfers—she herself was ready to bend the knee to her. And hope for the best, a third woman added, as we did when the usurper was crowned, only hope, as we must always do who are only observers in the events, we who are women. The first voice whispered that she counted that her good fortune, and the other two laughed softly.

A knocking at the great doors echoed through the hall. The company fell silent and all turned towards the sound. A steward stood before the now-opened doors to call out that the delegation of Priests awaited Beriel's pleasure. At the far end of the hall, she rose up from her throne, to stand tall and pale. "Give them entry," she commanded.

Three men in dark robes preceded one who wore a robe embroidered with colored threads, and the company parted to let them come before the young Queen. The last, most important man had a mouth turned sternly downwards at the ends. He knelt before Beriel and his voice sounded like a bell, or a drum, reverberating through the room. "My Queen, we are prepared to give judgement."

"Rise, High Priest Ellard," Beriel commanded, and "Bring forward the prisoner," she called. Win was led in, his hands bound before him and his leather soldier's shirt stained dark. He wore the dirt of imprisonment, but his face lighted up to see Beriel, and he bowed to her before his guard escorted him up to stand before her.

Elske waited beside the dais, her hands clasped together, fingers wound around fingers. In the whole room, only Win seemed at ease, as if to face the hangman was a matter of little importance, or a joke, as if he had stood so a hundred times before. She still could not see Dugald, not among the courtiers, not among the soldiers, nor at the back of the hall or beneath the windows. She moved closer to Win, close enough to see how he watched his Queen.

Elske had moved close enough to attack the soldiers who

stood beside Win, and take one of their knives in their first surprise at being so assaulted, and by a woman. With a knife, Elske could cut the rope that bound Win's hands, and also give a weapon into his hands. If Win were named traitor, then that was what she would do.

That no one might guess her intentions, she hid her hands behind her back. Something was placed into them, something with a handle, and Dugald's voice was soft in her ear. "So we are both armed. But I do not think that she will let him hang," the soft voice said. Elske grasped the knife behind her, and waited.

For a moment, Beriel lingered in front of her throne, her gown cloth-of-gold, her face as stern as the face in a painting, her bandages shining white. When she sat again, the High Priest drew his breath to speak.

All waited to hear.

The Priest's face was masked as a falcon's.

Elske wrapped her fingers tight around the knife she held, and considered Win's guard. The soldiers were young, and paid little attention to their prisoner, being caught up with the great events unfolding before them. Then Elske considered the rest of the company. These Lords were not even carrying swords. Elske guessed that their response to danger would be to protect their Ladies, amid shrieks and curses and rushings to safety. The captains were few, and many from the northern army; those would never attack her, nor Dugald. And Beriel, the only worthy enemy in the room, had but one good arm—besides needing a stick to walk on, for she had but one good leg. Beriel was no danger to her.

"Will you have our judgement?" the Priest asked Beriel.

"We will," she answered.

"Prisoner"—he turned to Win—"you have put yourself under the shelter of the law for your life or for your death. Do you understand this?" he asked.

"I do," Win answered, boldly.

"Then I give the law's judgement upon you." Now the Priest kept his eyes on Win, as if they were alone. Win listened to the Priest's words, but watched his Queen. "As to the accusation of treason, the law finds you not guilty, for the reason that the man—Guerric, Prince of this royal house—had usurped his sister's rightful place, and set out false rumor of her, and moreover for the reason that he had himself plotted the death of a royal Princess. Thus the man was a traitor and death his just punishment. These things are proven and determined," the Priest said.

The court sighed and clapped its palms together to signify approval. Neither Beriel nor Win responded, however. They remembered the second charge.

"As to the accusation of murder," the Priest said now. "You slew the man before many witnesses, and never sought to conceal the deed, nor deny it; however, the law finds you not guilty of murder. A soldier may not murder his enemy, or we must hang every man returned living from battle. A soldier kills but does not murder. This is the law."

Then Win did smile, and so did the Queen. He smiled for her and she smiled to fill up the room with the light of her pleasure.

Elske felt the knife being taken out of her hands so that she might clap, and be no different from her neighbors.

Beriel rose again, then. Clothed in gold she announced to all, "I will be crowned before I sleep again, for my land must not be left without its anointed ruler. I will be crowned this afternoon," she announced, and the room cheered her.

She allowed them this, then raised her hand for silence again. "There are two," she said, "and they have served me in my greatest need, at risk of all the little they had. To these two I would offer a Queen's reward. Elske," Beriel called. "Where are you, my servant Elske?"

"I am here, my Queen." Elske stepped forward to kneel down again before Beriel.

"Elske, I will ask my cousin and my Earl that will be, Lord Dugald, heir to Northgate, to husband you, and give to you the protection of his name and his lands," Beriel announced. "Dugald, this I ask of you, to take Elske for wife."

People murmured, and Elske felt their eyes on her bent neck. She thought she knew Beriel's purposes, and she hoped this would be the Queen's only revenge. And why should Beriel ask for more than that revenge?

"For all that the girl is Wolfer born, and Wolfer raised," Beriel continued, and at that the courtiers gasped softly, "I am in her debt. I ask you to pay that debt for me. Will you obey me in this, Lord Dugald?"

Dugald answered without hesitation, "My Queen, I will." This taught Elske the words to use, so when Beriel asked for her obedience also in this matter Elske said in a voice that rang as clear as his, "My Queen, I will."

Satisfied, Beriel turned to the second matter at hand. "Win," she called out, though he stood right before her. "Win, son of the innkeeper at the Ram's Head, who have been true in my service when I did not even know you served me, of you I ask more than you have already given, which has been even the offer of your life. Of you I ask also a marriage. I ask you to take the hand of your Queen," Beriel called out. "Yes, in marriage, to be her consort and her guard, advisor, husband, Prince. Will you obey me in this, Win?"

His cheeks flamed as red as his hair, almost, but Win could not, without shaming her, refuse; and so he must give his will over to hers. "My Queen, I will."

Then Beriel called for wine. Waiting, standing before her carved throne, she announced to the hall, "There remains yet one third matter of loyalty that must be settled."

"She will throw her glove down before them all," Dugald said into Elske's ear.

"And how could she do otherwise?" Elske asked softly.

347

Beriel accepted a golden goblet from her servant and held it out that he might pour red wine into it. The courtiers murmured uneasily, waiting for her next words. When she raised the goblet high, they fell silent.

"Today," Beriel announced in a voice that rang into every corner of the great hall, "on this day of my crowning, I offer to all of my Lords an amnesty."

Many voices breathed out sighs of relief and gratitude.

"After this day," Beriel announced, "this day of my crowning, if you serve me well I will never seek to know what you might have said or done before this day. To this I give you the word of your rightful Queen. But hear me now," she warned them. "In exchange I require your perfect obedience."

Beriel turned then, the goblet still raised, to the right, to the left, back to the front, so that she might look down on the whole assemblage and every man and woman in it. The goblet glinted in the light. She said, more solemnly but no less ringingly, "Too many have paid too great a price that I might be your Queen for any to offer me less than that perfect obedience. And I, too, have paid dearly for my throne and crown," she said. Her blue eyes looked briefly at Elske, and then Beriel made the toast herself. "May this Kingdom flourish under my rule, in all the years I am Queen."

They all echoed and answered her, "Long life to the Queen."

Elske's voice was one among many, in that well-wishing

which was also a long farewell. When she could raise her voice to call "Long life to Queen Beriel," Elske must part from her mistress and companion, since Dugald was her choice. So Elske would make her own gladness after the sorrow of this farewell.

EPILOGUE

IN THE HISTORY OF THE Kingdom, these things are told:

—How Beriel, called the Warrior Queen, extended the borders of the Kingdom eastwards to the sea at Pericol, and as far south as Selby. How her armies also conquered the barren lands of the west, obliterating the primitive tribe of the Volkaric. In two major military campaigns, the first against Pericol and then into the west, the second—with an army more seasoned by warfare and experienced in success—into the south, Beriel led her forces to victory after victory. Part of the reason for this was her weaponry, since Beriel almost from the first possessed gunpowder. Another factor that contributed to her military success was her soldiers' loyalty to her. Beriel was as well a gifted strategist and fearless general; she rode into battle at the head of her own troops; she asked no hardship of them she did not herself endure.

—How for five years after her first double victory, over the Volkaric war bands that were preying on the Kingdom and over a rebellious brother, Beriel's forces went undefeated. That first, most famous, military victory was achieved without a single wound being received by a single soldier of the Kingdom.

—How for the opening years of her brief reign Beriel conquered, but at the end lost much of the territory she had taken. Nonetheless, enough remained in her control to add substantially to the increasing power and wealth of the Kingdom.

—How through Beriel, the Kingdom gained a port on the sea. Although her last years as Queen were devoted to defensive warfare, as the cities of the south fought free of her domination, she held Pericol, and built up its defenses as well as its docks. Pericol remained the basis of the Kingdom's maritime power. The Queen was among those killed in the great explosion of the magazines there, which destroyed a third of that city; she left a male heir who ascended to the throne when he had attained his twelfth year.

—How the shift from an agricultural to a mercantile economy was begun during Beriel's reign, not only as a result of the military victories and the growth of Pericol as a center for shipping and shipbuilding, but also with the discovery of copper and iron ores in the northern Kingdom.

The development of these resources was the work of the Earl Northgate, and made him the most powerful man of the Kingdom, whose personal fortune exceeded even that of the royal house. At the same time, the Earl established around himself a court dedicated to learning and to civilized graces, into which any man of integrity and ability was welcomed. There were those who maintained that the merchants who flocked to trade with the Kingdom did so not so much for the profits as for the honor of being received at Northgate's court, and the pleasures of time spent there. In the annals of the time, it is sometimes referred to as the Court of Light and sometimes as the Court of Elske [*sic*]. During the long rule of this distinguished Earl, Northgate was the premier city of the Kingdom.

—How Gwyniver the Great, granddaughter of both Queen Beriel and the Earl Northgate—whose daughter had married the young King thus joining together the two great families of the Kingdom—ascended to her throne at the age of fourteen. The year of her crowning marks the beginning of the Thirty-Seven Year Peace, which extended into the sixth year after her death. Scholar, linguist, diplomat and gifted economist, Gwyniver forged a series of alliances— through marriages, through trade monopolies, through the threat of arms—among the great cities of the south as well as the emerging cities of the north, as far away as Trastad. Gwyniver is also known as the founder of the University, and as a patron of artists, musicians, minstrels, mediciners and craftsmen of all callings. During her reign the laws of the Kingdom were codified and the seasonal sitting of justices in trial instituted, as well as the profession of Speaker for the Accused. She established Pericol as the royal seat, and welcomed Ambassadors from all over the known world, thus continuing the anti-isolationist movement begun in her grandparents' day. She absorbed customs from other lands into her own government—such as guilds of craftsmen as in Celindon and the local governing Council as in Trastad. She had a reputation for wild courage, and tireless curiosity. Her citizens, from the greatest to the least, all lived without fear of want or of tyranny. In the reign of Gwyniver the Great, the Kingdom's Ambassadors were welcome wherever they journeyed, received with honor even at the court of the Emperor of the East. Under the rule of this Queen, the Kingdom enjoyed its golden age.

TURN THE PAGE FOR A LOOK AT THE FIRST BOOK IN
CYNTHIA VOIGT'S TILLERMAN CYCLE SERIES

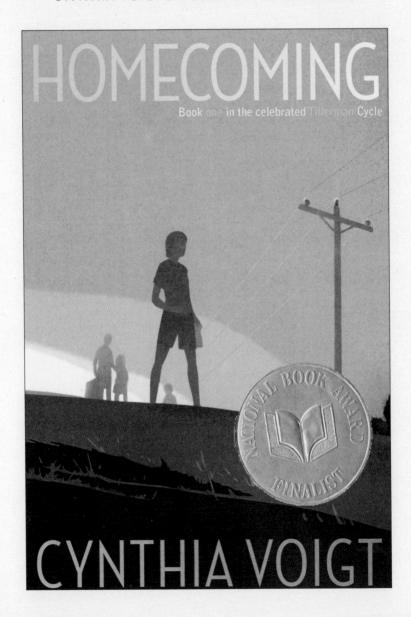

The woman put her sad moon-face in at the window of the car. "You be good," she said. "You hear me? You little ones, mind what Dicey tells you. You hear?"

"Yes, Momma," they said.

"That's all right then." She slung her purse over her shoulder and walked away, her stride made uneven by broken sandal thongs, thin elbows showing through holes in the oversized sweater, her jeans faded and baggy. When she had disappeared into the crowd of Saturday morning shoppers entering the side doors of the mall, the three younger children leaned forward onto the front seat. Dicey sat in front. She was thirteen and she read the maps.

"Why'd we stop?" asked James. "We're not there yet. We've got food. There's no reason to stop." James was ten and wanted everything to have a reason. "Dicey?"

"I dunno. You heard everything she said, same as I did. You tell me."

"All she said was, *We gotta stop here.* She didn't say why. She never says why, you know that. Are we out of gas?"

"I didn't look." Dicey wanted some quiet for thinking. There was something odd about this whole trip. She couldn't put her finger on it, not yet. "Why don't you tell them a story?"

"What story?"

"Cripes, James, you're the one with the famous brain."

"Yeah, well I can't think of any stories right now."

"Tell them anything. Tell them Hansel and Gretel."

"I want HanselnGretel. And the witch. And the candy house with peppermint sticks," Sammy said, from the backseat. James gave in without a quarrel. It was easier to give in to Sammy than to fight him. Dicey turned around to look at them. Maybeth sat hunched in a corner, big-eyed. Dicey smiled at her and Maybeth smiled back. "Once upon a time," James began. Maybeth turned to him.

Dicey closed her eyes and leaned her head back. She put her feet on the dashboard. She was tired. She'd had to stay awake and read maps, to find roads without tolls. She'd been up since three in the morning. But Dicey couldn't go to sleep. She gnawed away at what was bothering her.

For one thing, they never took trips. Momma always said the car couldn't run more than ten miles at a stretch. And here they were in Connecticut, heading down to Bridgeport. For one thing.

But that might make sense. All her life, Dicey had been hearing about Momma's aunt Cilla and her big house in Bridgeport that Momma had never seen, and her rich husband who died. Aunt Cilla sent Christmas cards year after year, with pictures of baby Jesus on them and long notes inside, on paper so thin it could have been tissue paper. Only Momma could decipher the lacy handwriting with its long, tall letters all bunched together and the lines running into one another because of the long-tailed, fancy z's and f's and g's. Aunt Cilla kept in touch. So it made sense for Momma to go to her for help.

But driving off like that in the middle of the night didn't make sense. That was the second thing. Momma woke them all up and told them to pack paper bags of clothing while she made sandwiches. She got them all into the old car and headed for Bridgeport.

For a third—things had been happening, all at once. Things were always bad with them, but lately worse than ever. Momma lost her checker's job. Maybeth's teacher had wanted a meeting with Momma that Momma wouldn't go to. Maybeth would be held back another year. Momma said she didn't want to hear about it, and she had ripped up every note, without reading any of them. Maybeth didn't worry her family, but she worried her teachers. She was nine and still in the second grade. She never said much, that was the trouble, so everybody thought she was stupid. Dicey knew she wasn't. Sometimes she'd come out and say something that showed she'd been watching and listening and taking things in. Dicey knew her sister could read and do sums, but Maybeth always sat quiet around strangers. For Maybeth, everyone in the world was a stranger, except Momma and Dicey and James and Sammy.

Momma herself was the fourth thing. Lately she'd go to the store for bread and come back with a can of tuna and just put her hands over her face, sitting at the table. Sometimes she'd be gone for a couple of hours and then she wouldn't say where she had been, with her face blank as if she couldn't say. As if she didn't know. Momma didn't talk to them anymore, not even to scold, or sing, or make up games the way she used to. Except Sammy. She talked to Sammy, but even then they sounded like two six-year-olds talking, not one six-year-old and his mother.

Dicey kept her feet on the dash, and her body slouched down. She looked out through the windshield, over the rows of parked cars, to where the sky hung like a bleached-out sheet over the top of the mall buildings. Bugs were spattered all over the windshield and the sky promised a heavy, hot day. Dicey slid still further down on the seat. Her skin stuck to the blue plastic seat covers.

James was describing the witch's house, listing the kinds of candy used for various parts of the building. This was the part James liked best in Hansel and Gretel, and he always did it a little differently from the time before. Picturing the almond Hershey bar roof and the shutters made of cinnamon licorice sticks, Dicey did fall asleep.

She woke covered with sweat from the hot sun pouring in through the windshield. She woke hungry. Maybeth was singing softly, one of Momma's songs, about making her love a baby with no crying. "I fell asleep," Dicey said. "What time's it?"

"I dunno," James said. "You've been asleep a long time. I'm hungry."

"Where's Momma?"

"I dunno. I'm hungry."

"You're always hungry. Go ask someone what time it is, okay?"

James climbed out of the car. He crossed to the walkway and stopped a man in a business suit. "Twelve thirty," James reported.

"But that means I slept for more than two hours," Dicey protested.

"I'm going to eat," Sammy announced from the backseat. He opened the bag of food and pulled out a sandwich before Dicey could say anything.

"What do you want me to do?" James asked, looking into Dicey's face. His narrow little face wore a worried expression. "Want me to go look for her?"

"No," Dicey said. (*Now* what had Momma gone and done.) "Sammy, give Maybeth a sandwich too. Let her choose for herself. Then pass the bag up here."

When everyone had a sandwich, and James had two, Dicey reached a decision. "We have to wait here for a while more," she said. "Then we'll do something. I'm going to take a walk and see if I can find her."

"Don't you go away too," Maybeth said softly.

"I'll be right where you can see me," Dicey said. "I'll stay on the sidewalk—see?—just like a path in front of the stores. Then maybe later we can all go into the mall and look in the stores. You'd like that, wouldn't you?" Maybeth smiled and nodded her golden head.

Dicey did her best thinking when she walked. On this warm June afternoon, she walked so fast and thought so hard, she didn't even see the people going past her. If Momma went past she'd say something, so Dicey wasn't worried about that.

She was worried that Momma had wandered off. And would not come back.

("You always look for the worst," Momma had often told her. "I like to be ready," Dicey answered.)

If Momma was gone . . . But that wasn't possible. Was it? But if she was, what could they do? Ask for help, probably from a policeman. (Would he put them in homes or orphanages? Wouldn't that be just what the police or some social worker would do?) Go back to Provincetown, they could go back home. (Momma hadn't paid the rent, not for weeks, and it was almost summertime, when even their old cabin, set off alone in the dunes, could bring in a lot of money. Mr. Martinez wasn't sympathetic, not when it came to money, not when it came to giving something away for free. He'd never let them stay there to wait for Momma.) They could go on to Bridgeport. Dicey had never seen Aunt Cilla—Great-Aunt Cilla. She knew the name and address, because Momma had made her write it down four times, on each paper bag, in case something happened: Mrs. Cilla Logan, 1724 Ocean Drive, Bridgeport, Connecticut. Aunt Cilla was family, the only family Dicey knew about.

The sun beat down on the parking lot and heated up the air so even in the shaded walkway Dicey was hot. The kids must be hot too, she thought, and turned to get them.

Momma must have gone away on purpose. (But she loved them, loved them all.) Why else the addresses on the bags? Why else tell them to mind Dicey? (Mothers didn't do things like going off. It was crazy. Was Momma crazy?) How did she expect Dicey to take care of them? What did she expect Dicey to do? Take them to Bridgeport, of course. (Dump it all on Dicey, that was what Momma did, she always did, because Dicey was the determined sort. "It's in your blood," Momma said, and then wouldn't explain.)

Anger welled up in Dicey, flooded her eyes with tears, and now she was swept away with the determination to get the kids to Bridgeport. Well, she'd do it somehow, if she had to.

Momma wasn't at the car when Dicey returned, so Dicey said they'd wait for her until the next morning.

"Where'll we sleep?" Sammy asked.

"Right here—and no complaints," Dicey said.

"Then Momma will come back and we'll go on tomorrow?" Sammy asked.

Dicey nodded.

"Where is Momma? Why's she taking so long?" James asked.

"I dunno, James," Dicey answered. Maybeth was silent, staring.

After a few minutes, Dicey hustled them all out of the car and trailed after them as they entered the mall.

The mall was built like a fortress around a huge, two-story enclosed street, where store succeeded store, as far as you could see. At one end of the central section was a cage of live birds in a little park of plastic trees and shrubs. The floor of their cage was littered with pieces of popcorn and gum wrappers. At the other end, the builders had made a waterfall through which shone different colored lights. Outside, beyond the covered sidewalk that ran like a moat around the huge building, lay the huge, gray parking lot, a no-man's-land of empty cars.

But here inside was a fairyland of colors and sounds, crowded with people on this Saturday afternoon, artificially lit and planted. Inside was a miniature city where endless diversions from the work-day world offered everything delightful. If you had money, of course. And even without money, you could still stare and be amazed.

They spent a long time wandering through stores, looking at toys and records and pianos and birthday cards. They were drawn to restaurants that exuded the smell of spaghetti and pizza or fried chicken, bakeries with trays of golden doughnuts lined up behind glass windows, candy stores, where the countertop was crowded with large jars of jelly beans and sourballs and little foil-covered chocolates and peppermints dipped in crunchy white frosting; cheese shops (they each had two free samples), where the rich smell of aged cheeses mingled with fresh-ground coffee, and hot dog stands, where they stood back in a silent row. After this, they sat on a backless bench before the waterfall, tired and hungry. Altogether, they had eleven dollars and fifty cents, more than any one of them had ever had at one time before, even Dicey who contributed all of her babysitting money, seven dollars.

They spent almost four dollars on supper at the mall, and none of them had dessert. They had hamburgers and french fries and, after Dicey thought it over, milkshakes. At that rate, they could have one more meal before they ran out of money, or maybe two more. It was still light when they returned to the car. The little ones horsed around in the back, teasing, wrestling, tickling, quarreling and laughing, while Dicey studied the map. People walked by their car, vehicles came and went, and nobody paid any attention to them. In parking lots, it's not unusual to see a car full of kids waiting.

At half-past eight, Dicey herded everybody back into the mall, to use the bathrooms they had found earlier. Later, Sammy and Maybeth fell asleep easily, curled up along the backseat. James moved up to the front with Dicey. Dicey couldn't see how they were both to sleep in the front seat, but she supposed they would manage it. James sat stiffly, gripping the wheel. James had a narrow head and sharp features, a nose that pointed out, pencil-thin eyebrows, a narrow chin. Dicey studied him in the darkening car. They were parked so far from the nearest lamppost that they were in deep shadows.

With her brothers and sister near, with the two youngest asleep in the backseat, sitting as they were in a cocoon of darkness, she should feel safe. But she didn't. Though it was standing still, the car seemed to be flying down a highway, going too fast. Even the dark inside of it was not deep enough to hide them. Faces might appear in the windows at any time, asking angry questions.

"Where's Momma gone?" James asked, looking out at the night.

"I just don't know," Dicey said. "Here's what I think, I think if she isn't back by morning we ought to go on to Bridgeport."

"On our own?"

"Yes."

"How'll we get there? You can't drive. Momma took the keys."

"We could take a bus, if we have enough money. If we don't, we'll walk."

James stared at her. Finally he spoke. "Dicey? I'm scared. I feel all jiggly in my stomach. Why doesn't Momma come back?"

"If I knew, James, I'd know what to do."

"Do you know the way?"

"To Bridgeport? I can read a map. Once we get there, we can ask directions to Aunt Cilla's house."

James nodded. "Do you think she's been killed? Or kidnapped?"

"Rich people get kidnapped; not Momma. I'm not going to think about what might have happened to her, and I don't think you should, either."

"I can't help thinking about it," James said in a small voice.

"Don't tell Sammy or Maybeth," Dicey warned.

"I wouldn't. I know better. You should know I'd know better than that."

Dicey reached out and patted him on the shoulder. "I do know," she said.

James grabbed her hand. "Dicey? Do you think Momma meant to leave us here?"

"I think Momma meant to take us to Bridgeport, but—"

"Is Momma crazy?"

Dicey turned her head to look at him.

"The kids said so, at school. And the way the teachers looked at me and loaned me their own books and talked to me. And Maybeth. Craziness can run in families."

Dicey felt a great weight settle on her shoulders. She tried to shrug it off, but it wouldn't move.

"Dicey?"

"She loves us," Dicey muttered.

"But that's the only reason I can think of that might be true."

"There's nothing wrong with Maybeth. You know that."

"It runs in families. Hereditary craziness."

"Well, you don't have to worry about it, do you? You're the smart one, with A's in school and the science projects that get entered in the state contest."

"Yeah," James said. He settled his head back on the seat.

"Listen, I'm going to go to a phone and see where the bus station is and call them up to find out how much tickets cost. You lay low."

"Why?"

Dicey decided to tell him the truth. "Just in case. I mean, three kids in a car in a parking lot at night . . . See, James, I think we've got to get to Bridgeport and I just don't know what would happen if a policeman saw us. Foster homes or something, I dunno. I don't want to risk it. But one kid . . . and I'm pretty old so it doesn't look funny."

"Okay. That sounds okay."

"We've got to get to Bridgeport."

James thought about that, then nodded his head. "I never listened much to Momma's talk about her. What will she be like, Aunt Cilla?"

"Rich," Dicey said.

"It would be a long walk," James said.

"Long enough," Dicey agreed. She got out of the car fast.

It was full dark, an overcast night. The parking lot was nearly empty; only two cars besides theirs remained. Dicey wondered how many cars were left in the other three parking lots that spread out from the other sides of the building. It felt as empty as all of space must be. She hoped there were cars in each lot. The more cars there were, the safer their car was for them.

Dicey headed confidently for the walkway, as if she had every right to be where she was, as if she had an important errand to run, as if she knew just where she was going. She remembered a telephone at the far end of the building. It wasn't a real phone booth, but a kind of cubicle hung up on the wall, with an open shelf underneath to hold the directory. James could probably see her from the car, if he looked for her. From that distance, she would look small.

The walkway was lit up, and the store windows were lit, so she moved through patches of sharp light. At the phone, she took out the directory to look up bus companies in the yellow pages. She ran her finger down the names, selected one that sounded local and reached into her pocket for change.

She heard footsteps. A man approached her, in a uniform like a policeman's, but tan not blue, and without the badge. He took his time getting to her, as if he was sure she'd wait, sure of his own strength to hold her, even at that distance. He moved like he thought she was afraid of him, too afraid to run.

"Hey," the man said. His shirt had the word "Security" sewn onto it. Where his belly sagged, the shirt hung out over his pants. He carried a long-handled flashlight. He wore a pistol at his belt.

Dicey didn't answer, but she didn't look away.

"Hey kid," he said, as if she had shown signs of running and he needed to halt her. He was heavy, out of shape. He had a pig-person face, a coarse skin that sagged at the jowls, little blue eyes and pale eyebrows, and a fat, pushed-back nose. When he came up next to her, Dicey stepped back a pace, but kept her finger on the number in the book.

"You lost?"

"Naw. I'm making a phone call."

"Where do you live?"

"Just over there," Dicey said, pointing vaguely with her free hand.

"Go home and call from there. Run along now. If you were a girl, I'd walk you over, but—"

"Our phone's broken," Dicey said. "That's why my mom sent me here."

The guard shifted his flashlight, holding it like a club. "Phones don't break. How's a phone break?"

"We've got this dog that chews things up. Slippers, papers, you know. He chewed the phone. The cord, actually, but it's all the same—the phone's broken."

"Are you bulling me?"

"I wish I was."

"What's your name, kid?"

"Danny."

She felt funny, strange, making up lies as quickly and smoothly as if she'd been doing it all her life.

The man took a piece of gum out of his pocket, unwrapped it, folded it in half and stuck it into his mouth, chewing on it a couple of times.

"Danny what?"

"Tillerman." Dicey couldn't make up a new last name, except Smith, and nobody would believe that even if it was true.

"You don't look more than ten. Isn't it late to be out?"

Dicey shrugged.

The guard grew suspicious. "Who're you calling?"

"The bus company. My sisters and me are going down to Bridgeport some time soon, to stay with my aunt."

He chewed and thought. "Sometime soon wouldn't send you out after ten at night to phone. What's the rush?"

"My mom just got back from the clinic and she's gonna have her baby, any day now the doctor said, and my aunt needs to know what time the buses arrive so she can meet us on Monday. So's we can take a bus it's good for her to meet. My mom asked me to come find out so's she can call first thing in the morning, before my aunt goes to church. It's hard for my mom to get around now—you know."

"Where's your father?"

"Gone."

"Gone where?"

"Dunno. He just up and went, way back, last winter."

The guard nodded. He reached in his pocket and pulled out the pack of gum. He offered a piece to Dicey, but she shook her head.

"Can I call now, mister?"

"Sure thing," he said. "I wouldn't have bothered you except that there've been some windows broken around here. We think it's kids. I'm the security guard. I've got to be careful."

Dicey nodded. She inserted the coins and slowly dialed the numbers, hoping he'd go away. But he stood there and listened. Behind him lay the parking lot, a vast open space where occasional clumps of planted bushes spread long shadows over the ground.

An impersonal voice answered. Dicey asked about tickets to Bridgeport, how much they cost.

"From where to Bridgeport."

Dicey grabbed at a name. "Peewauket." That was what the map said. She pronounced it Pee-Walk-It. The guard, listening narrowed his eyes.

"From Peewauket?" the voice asked, saying it Pwuk-it.

"Yeah."

"Two dollars and forty-five cents a person."

"What's the rate for children?"

"The same. The charge is for the seat. Unless you've got a child under two."

"What time do buses run?"

"Every other hour, from eight to eight."

Dicey thanked the voice and hung up the phone. She stood with her arms hanging down at her sides, waiting for the guard to leave.

He was studying her with his little piggly eyes. He held his flashlight now in one hand and slapped it into the palm of the other. "You better get back now," he said and then added, "You didn't write anything down."

"I've got a good memory."

"Yeah? I'll give you a test." His body blocked the way to the safe darkness of the parking lot. "You don't remember anything about broken windows in the mall, do you? For instance, just one for instance, at Record City."

"I don't know what you're talking about."

"I wonder about that. I really wonder, Danny. You said Danny, didn't you? Tillerman, wasn't it? You see, we figure it was probably kids did it, account of nothing's been stolen. Or maybe just one kid did it, that's what I'm thinking."

Dicey glared at him. "I said I don't know anything about that."

He put one arm out to bar her in, resting his hand against the side of the phone. "I can't think of why I should believe you. Nope, now I come to think of it, I don't think I do believe you. The only question in my mind is, what do I do with you?"

Dicey thought fast, then acted just as fast. She lifted her right knee as if to hit him in the groin where she knew it would hurt bad. He lowered his arm and stepped back, to protect himself. In that one second while he was off balance, Dicey took off. She sprinted into the darkness of the parking lot. As soon as she was in the cover of the shadows, she turned left around the corner of the building, away from their car. He thundered after her.

Dicey ran smoothly. She was used to running on beaches, where the sand gave way under your feet and each thrust of your legs was hindered. Running over asphalt was easier. Dicey pulled away from her pursuer. His steps were heavy and his breathing was heavy. He was out of shape and too fat to catch up with her. She had time to crouch behind one of the little islands of green that decorated the parking lot. She had on a dark shirt and jeans, her face was tanned and her hair brown; she was confident nothing would give her away.

He stopped by the front entrance shining his flashlight out over the parking lot, like one bright eye. Dicey watched him. He listened, but his chest was heaving so much that she was sure he couldn't hear anything but the blood pounding in his ears. She smiled to herself.

"You haven't got a chance," he called. "You better come out now, kid. You're only making it worse."

Dicey covered her mouth with her hand.

"I know you now. We'll find you out," he said. He turned quickly away from the parking lot and looked farther along the front of the

mall. He hunched behind the flashlight. He used the beam like a giant eye, to peer into the shadows. "There you are! I can see you!" he cried.

But he was looking the wrong way. Dicey giggled, and the sound escaped her even though she bit on her hand to stop it.

He turned back to the parking lot, listening. Then he swore. His light swooped over the dark lot, trying to search out her hiding place. "Danny? I'm gonna find you."

Dicey moved softly away on soundless sneakers through the covering shadows. He continued to call: "I'll remember your face, you hear? You hear me? Hear me?"

From halfway across the parking lot, safe in her own speed and in shadows, Dicey stopped. Her heart swelled in victory. "I hear you," she called softly back, as she ran toward the empty road and the patch of woods beyond.

Much later, when she returned to the car, James awoke briefly. "Everything's okay," Dicey whispered, curling down onto the cold seat to sleep.

Plant Stems: Physiology and Functional Morphology

Edited by

Barbara L. Gartner

Department of Forest Products
Oregon State University
Corvallis, Oregon

Academic Press

San Diego   New York   Boston   London   Sydney   Tokyo   Toronto

Cover photograph: Bur oak, *Quercus macrocarpa* Michx, located in the floodplain of the Missouri River near McBaine, Missouri. Photograph courtesy of Dr. F. Duhme.

This book is printed on acid-free paper. ∞

Copyright © 1995 by ACADEMIC PRESS, INC.

All Rights Reserved.
No part of this publication may be reproduced or transmitted in any form or by any means, electronic or mechanical, including photocopy, recording, or any information storage and retrieval system, without permission in writing from the publisher.

Academic Press, Inc.
A Division of Harcourt Brace & Company
525 B Street, Suite 1900, San Diego, California 92101-4495

United Kingdom Edition published by
Academic Press Limited
24-28 Oval Road, London NW1 7DX

Library of Congress Cataloging-in-Publication Data

Plant stems: physiological and functional morphology / editor, Barbara L. Gartner.
   p.   cm. -- (physiological ecology series)
  Includes index.
  ISBN 0-12-276460-9
  1. Stems (Botany) 2. Tree trunks. I. Gartner, Barbara L.
 II. Series: Physiological Ecology.
 QK646.P58   1995
 581.4'95--dc20   95-2197
                                   CIP

PRINTED IN THE UNITED STATES OF AMERICA
95 96 97 98 99 00 BB 9 8 7 6 5 4 3 2 1

Contents

Part I
Roles of Stem Architecture in Plant Performance

1. Plant Stems: Biomechanical Adaptation for Energy Capture and Influence on Species Distributions
Thomas J. Givnish

2. Opportunities and Constraints in the Placement of Flowers and Fruits
Donald M. Waller and David A. Steingraeber

v

Part II
Roles of Stems in Transport and Storage of Water

Part IV
Roles of Stems in Preventing or Reacting to Plant Injury

Part V
Synthesis

Contributors

Numbers in parentheses indicate the pages on which the authors' contributions begin.

John P. Bryant (365), Institute of Arctic Biology, University of Alaska, Fairbanks, Alaska 99775

Barbara L. Gartner (125), Department of Forest Products, Oregon State University, Corvallis, Oregon 97331

A. Malcolm Gill (323), Centre for Plant Biodiversity Research, C.S.I.R.O., Division of Plant Industry, Canberra City, A.C.T. 2601, Australia

Thomas J. Givnish (3), Department of Botany, University of Wisconsin, Madison, Wisconsin 53706

N. E. Grulke (343), USDA/Forestry Sciences Laboratory, Corvallis, Oregon 97331

Thomas M. Hinckley (409), College of Forest Resources, University of Washington, Seattle, Washington 98195

N. Michele Holbrook (151), Department of Organismic and Evolutionary Biology, Harvard University, Cambridge, Massachusetts 02138

E. R. Ingham (241), Department of Botany and Plant Pathology, Oregon State University, Corvallis, Oregon 97331

W. Dieter Jeschke (177), Julius-von-Sachs-Institut, Lehrstuhl für Botanik I, Universität Würzburg, D-97082 Würzburg, Germany

C. H. Anthony Little (281), Canadian Forestry Service-Maritimes, Fredericton, New Brunswick, Canada E3B 5P7

Claus Mattheck (75), Kernforschungszentrum Karlsruhe, Institut für Materialforschung II, 76021 Karlsruhe, Germany

A. R. Moldenke (241), Department of Entomology, Oregon State University, Corvallis, Oregon 97331

Erik T. Nilsen (223), Department of Biology, Virginia Polytechnic Institute and State University, Blacksburg, Virginia 24061

John S. Pate (177), Department of Botany, University of Western Australia, Nedlands, Western Australia 6907, Australia

Richard P. Pharis (281), Department of Biological Sciences, University of Calgary, Calgary, Alberta, Canada 2TN 1N4

Kenneth F. Raffa (365), Department of Entomology, University of Wisconsin, Madison, Wisconsin 53706

Paul J. Schulte (409), Department of Biological Sciences, University of Nevada, Las Vegas, Nevada 89154

Louis Shain (383), Department of Plant Pathology, University of Kentucky, Lexington, Kentucky 40546

John S. Sperry (105), Department of Biology, University of Utah, Salt Lake City, Utah 84112

Joel P. Stafstrom (257), Department of Biological Sciences, Northern Illinois University, DeKalb, Illinois 60115

David A. Steingraeber (51), Department of Biology, Colorado State University, Fort Collins, Colorado 80523

Aart J. E. Van Bel (205), Department of Plant Ecology and Evolutionary Biology, University of Utrecht, 3584 CA Utrecht, The Netherlands

Donald M. Waller (51), Department of Botany, University of Wisconsin, Madison, Wisconsin 53706

James A. Weber (343), United States Environmental Protection Agency, Environmenal Research Laboratory, Corvallis, Oregon 97333

Brayton F. Wilson (91), Department of Forestry and Wildlife Management, University of Massachusetts, Amherst, Massachusetts 01003

Preface

The stem serves as a physical link between the below- and aboveground organs of the plant and between tissues produced in the past and in the present. A stem's very location makes it a key structure for understanding whole-plant biology because a stem can act as a buffer between organs that do not touch, such as root and leaf, two leaves, or leaf and fruit. Historically, however, the stem has been treated as a weight-bearing pole ("support," "structural material") or as a passive, water-bearing conduit ("pipe"). Consequently, many researchers have overlooked activities that occur in the stem while concentrating on the biology of the more obviously active organs such as leaves or roots. The purpose of this book is to synthesize ideas and insights on stems from disparate fields, to help students and specialists visualize trade-offs among various stem roles, and to stimulate more study of the stem in the whole-plant context. Such work is needed in a broad taxonomic array of plants and growth forms: culms of graminoids; stems of forbs and herbaceous perennials; and the trunks, branches, twigs, petioles, and rachises of palms, cacti, aquatic plants, hemiepiphytes, vines, shrubs, and trees.

Stems perform an enormous variety of roles. Typically, these roles have been studied in spatial and temporal isolation, but there is now enough information to link various subfields of stem biology and to consider the trade-offs that occur among roles. Stems are physical connectors between the terminal organs, lengtheners to aid in competition, spacers to control canopy and reproductive display, and supporters to hold the canopy off the ground. Some stems externally channel nutrient-rich water ("stemflow") toward their root system; they also harbor organisms that may be responsible for much of the nutrition within the stemflow. Internally, stems transport, store, release, and direct water, nutrients, and organic compounds selectively to different parts of the canopy or to the root system. Stems fix and respire carbon, they produce and respond to growth substances, and they contain zones of radial and longitudinal development. They harbor quiescent meristems and they protect the shoot from environmental and pathogenic injury. Upon their death, stems become substrate and habitat for a large web of organisms that contributes greatly to the biodiversity and functioning of the ecosystem.

Stem form is particularly accessible and illustrative in woody plants. The development and structure of the persistent secondary tissues are available for retrospective study, and woody plants, unlike herbaceous ones, have time (years, rather than a few seasons) to elaborate stems with well-tuned physiological, structural, and developmental strategies. This history that is "archived" into the structure of the plant may constrain its function, because the configuration and physiology that were adaptive for a young plant or one in, for example, a shady environment, may be less adaptive for the older plant or the plant whose canopy emerges into the sun. This means that until the plant becomes reproductive, the features produced at an earlier stage must be nonlethal for the plant in the present. Such considerations of historical constraints are relevant if the stems last the lifespan of the plant (e.g., excurrent trees and some lianas), but irrelevant if the stem's lifespan is short relative to the plant's lifespan (some shrubs and branches of umbrella-shaped trees). We may learn that in comparison to species with a throw-away stem strategy, species with long plant lifespans relative to stem lifespans have syndromes involving high plasticity for development of new growth, generalist tissues that function over a broad environmental range, high factors of safety against physiological or mechanical failure, and/or a large investment in defense or protection.

In the face of anticipated human-caused changes to most environments, we need not only a baseline understanding of whole-plant biology, but also predictive capabilities for how plants will react to perturbations. More research on trunks, branches, and twigs is important for our baseline understanding of plant biology—the diversity, ecology, physiology, and development of life. There is also a large economic value to better comprehension of trees because they provide food, fiber, building products, chemicals, shade, and habitat for people and structure, food, protection, and cover for many other species.

This book represents the results of interactions and discussions at a small workshop in Newport, Oregon. It is organized into four sections and a synthesis: roles of stem architecture in plant performance, roles of stems in water transport and storage, roles of live stem cells in plant performance, and roles of stems in preventing or reacting to plant injury. The synthesis "stemmed" from debate and discussion by the authors and a few dozen other workshop participants. Each chapter indicates the types of information we now have and the types of information we lack. The authors cover many stem functions, although the list is not exhaustive, and the focus is on terrestrial woody tree stems, primarily of temperate and boreal zones. A book such as this, which aims to cover the stem from its structural through its physiological and ecological functions, necessarily presents only one point of view per topic. Whereas the authors include physiologists, ecologists, entomologists, biomechanicians, and pathologists, most have a functional or adaptive viewpoint but not an explicitly evolutionary perspective.

A century ago, the link between form and function was central to many biological investigations. Arguably, this link is even more important to contemporary biologists than it was to our predecessors. Today's tools and instrumentation for studies of physiology, development, and processes at a large range of scales bring us back to questions of what is the structure that is being developed, why is it there, how does it function, and what pressures caused it to evolve. In the long run, I hope this book will help ecologists, evolutionary biologists, physiologists, developmental biologists, geneticists, paleobiologists, and molecular biologists unravel the mechanisms and processes that allow organisms and ecosystems to function.

BARBARA L. GARTNER

Acknowledgments

This material is based in part on work supported by the USDA's Cooperative State Research Service, National Research Initiative Competitive Grants Program, jointly sponsored by Plant Responses to the Environment, and Plant Growth and Development (Agreement 93-37100-9063). The workshop and project were also supported by the USDA Special Grant on Wood Utilization; the Division of Energy Biosciences, DOE Office of Basic Energy Sciences (06–93ER20128); and the Biofuels Feedstock Development Division, DOE Biofuels Division (19X-SP670V). I thank Bart Thielges for securing additional funds from the College of Forestry and the Research Office, both at the Oregon State University.

For help with the scientific and technical programs of the workshop I thank Toni Gwin, Katy Kavanagh, Mike Unsworth, and Nan Vance, as well as graduate students Jeanne Panek, Mike Remmick, NaDene Sorensen, Amy Tuininga, and Maciej Zwieniecki. I thank Bill Carlson, Chuck Crumly, Tom Hinckley, Hal Mooney, Ian Sussex, and Jim Weber for advice and discussion. I also thank the participants who took time from their lives and, in some cases, funding from their own projects or pockets to help make possible the workshop and this publication. Finally, I thank my family for their patience.

I

Roles of Stem Architecture in Plant Performance

1

Plant Stems: Biomechanical Adaptation for Energy Capture and Influence on Species Distributions

Thomas J. Givnish

I. Introduction

It is fitting that this symposium on plant stems be held in the Pacific Northwest, where many of the tallest trees in the world—coastal redwood, Sitka spruce, Douglas fir—grow. Their ancient, towering stems are among the most massive on earth, monuments to the ever-escalating struggle for light among plants, and to the enduring mechanical designs wrought by natural selection.

These forest giants, like all green plants, depend on photosynthetic light capture for the energy they need to grow and reproduce. The support skeleton of a plant—its stems, petioles, and analogous structures—play three vital roles in capturing light, providing the means (1) to arrange, orient, and support foliage efficiently, (2) to overtop competitors and invade new space, and (3) to carry water and nutrients to the leaves, and sugars and starches to other plant organs (Givnish, 1986a). These three functions—**support**, **competition**, and **transport**—are arguably the most important roles of a plant stem and other support structures, given the fundamental importance of photosynthesis, and the preponderance of leaves vs other organs (such as flowers, fruits, or domatia) in the biomass borne by the stem. **Transport** may be the least important of these functions for self-supporting plants, at least in terms of the biomass required, given the ability of vines and other structural parasites to move massive amounts of water and nutrients through slender stems (Gartner *et al.*, 1990; Ewers *et al.*, 1991;

Schultz and Matthews, 1993; see Sperry [5], Gartner [6], Pate and Jeschke [8], and Van Bel [9] in this volume for more thorough discussions of adaptations for transport).

The form, biomechanical properties, and growth dynamics of stems have important implications for a plant's rate of growth and competitive ability, and play a crucial but often overlooked role in adapting plants for different conditions and influencing their ecological distribution (Givnish, 1986b, 1988; King, 1986). This chapter explores some of the trade-offs and underlying constraints on stem adaptations for energy capture, and analyzes how such adaptations may limit the distribution of species along gradients and shape the structure and physiognomy of plant communities. Such analyses provide important insights into the determinants of plant stature, crown geometry, phyllotaxis, the location of tree lines, the zonation of aquatic plants, and the shift in understory dominance from shrubs to herbs along forested gradients.

II. Constraints on Optimal Stem Allocation, Form, and Growth Dynamics

The primary functions of support and competition impose four principal constraints on stem adaptations for energy capture: (1) mechanical stability, (2) mechanical safety, (3) photosynthetic efficiency, and (4) whole-plant growth and competitive ability. Each of these constraints is discussed briefly below.

A. Mechanical Stability

If the energetic investment plants make in stems is to be of any use, the stems must at least be able to bear their own weight (perhaps with the assistance of hosts) and avoid collapse, tearing, or other forms of mechanical failure (McMahon, 1973; King and Loucks, 1978; Long *et al.*, 1981; King, 1981, 1986; Givnish, 1986a,c). This requirement for mechanical stability imposes minimum design constraints on the size and mechanical properties of stems, and hence on the amount of energy allocated to stems. Stems must satisfy one of three specific stability constraints, depending on the most important kind of mechanical stress they face.

1. Compressive Structures   Compressive structures, such as the main stems of most self-supporting trees and herbs, must resist the compressive and tensile stresses (forces per unit cross-sectional area) imposed by the static and dynamic loads resulting from the weight of the stem and associated foliage. The principal constraint on vertical stems and tree trunks appears to be the avoidance of elastic toppling, caused by the stem being insuffi-

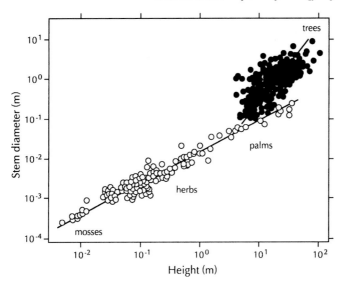

Figure 1 Allometry of stem diameter vs height for data compiled by Niklas (1993a) on "herbaceous" species, including mosses, herbs, and palms (○), and trees (●). Lines are least mean square regressions: ln $y = 0.78$ ln $x - 4.25$ ($r^2 = 0.95$; $p < 0.001$ for 188 df) for nonwoody plants, and ln $y = 1.86$ ln $x - 5.63$ ($r^2 = 0.54$; $p < 0.001$ for 418 df) for trees. The slopes of reduced major axis regressions (LaBarbara, 1986) are 0.72 for nonwoody plants and 1.37 for trees; avoidance of elastic buckling would favor a slope of 1.5 provided that Young's modulus is proportional to stem tissue density (McMahon, 1973). McMahon found a closer approach to the 3/2 power law for a larger data set of trees (including all of the points analyzed by Niklas), but did not present a statistical analysis.

ciently thick or stiff to pull its own mass back to a vertical position when deflected (McMahon, 1973; McMahon and Kronauer, 1976; King, 1981, 1991). As predicted by Greenhill (1881) and McMahon (1973), the stem diameter of woody plants scales roughly as the 3/2 power of their height (Fig. 1). Niklas (1993a,b) has found that the diameter of "herbaceous" plants (including mosses, herbs, and palm trees) scales roughly linearly with their height (Fig. 1). Niklas argues that this difference in scaling arises because the tight correlations among tissue density, stiffness (i.e., Young's modulus), and strength (i.e., modulus of rupture) seen in wood break down for the parenchyma of herb stems and the sclerenchyma of palm stems, and because the material properties of such stems vary systematically with stature.

   With either scaling law, stem volume and biomass must increase rapidly with plant stature. Not only does total stem mass increase rapidly with height, but so does the fraction of a plant's annual production devoted to building stem tissue, imposing a fundamental constraint on the biology of

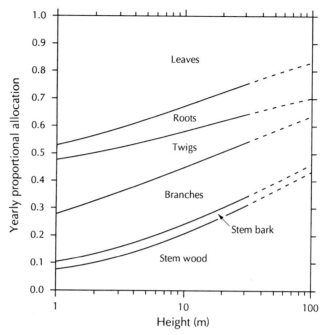

Figure 2 Allometry of annual biomass allocation in woody plants as a function of height, derived from equations for shrubs and trees up to 30 m tall given by Whittaker and Woodwell (1968). Dashed lines represent extrapolation of trends beyond range of data studied by the original authors. Formulas used are as follows: (1) stem wood production = 7.602 dbh$^{2.0828}$; (2) stem bark production = 2.474 dbh$^{1.8073}$; (3) branch and branch bark production = 14.839 dbh$^{1.8069}$; (4) twig production = 34.313 dbh$^{1.6526}$; (5) leaf production = 14.01512 dbh$^{1.6526}$ [71% of the leaf and twig fraction for *Liriodendron* (Whittaker *et al.*, 1963)]; (6) root production = 0.2 × (production of stem wood and bark, branch wood and bark, twigs); and (7) shoot height = 177.05 dbh$^{0.7042}$. dbh = Diameter at breast height (m).

self-supporting plants (Givnish, 1982, 1988). Studies by Whittaker and Woodwell (1968) on temperate shrubs and trees up to 30 m tall showed that the fraction of annual production committed to stems increases sharply with plant height, and that the fraction committed to productive foliage declines in roughly parallel fashion (Fig. 2). In addition, the fractional allocation to stems in plants of a given height should increase with the size of the mechanical stresses imposed on stems by nonvertical posture, crown mass, wind or water movement, and loading by snow or ice.

2. Tensile Structures Tensile structures, such as kelp stipes, water lily petioles, or calabash fruit peduncles, must resist mainly stretching forces, not compression or bending. In such structures, stem diameter is unrelated to stem length and instead scales as roughly the cube root of the leaf or fruit mass they bear (Fig. 3). The reason for this cube root scaling law is obscure,

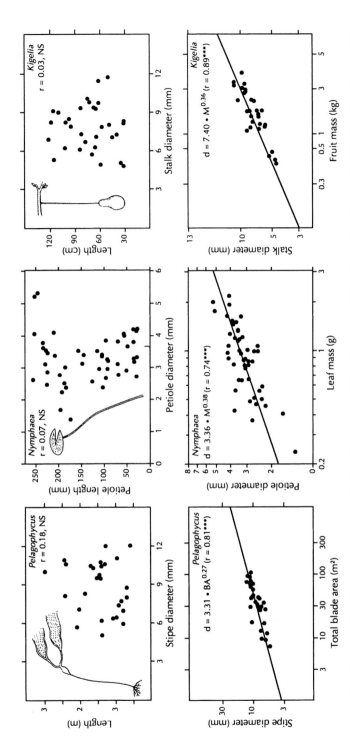

Figure 3 Allometry of tensile plant structures, including elk kelp stipes (*Pelagophycus*), water lily petioles (*Nymphaea*), and calabash fruit peduncles (*Kigelia*). Top: Diameter of these tensile structures shows no relationship to their length. Bottom: Diameter scales roughly as the cube root of the loading inferred from blade area, leaf mass, or fruit mass. (Data for *Kigelia* and *Pelagophycus* from Givnish, 1995; data for *Nymphaea* from Peterson *et al.*, 1982; data for *Pelagophycus* from Givnish, 1995).

insofar as resistance to static loads would imply a square root law. Resistance to torsional stresses could impose a cube root scaling law, but measurements made by Peterson *et al.* (1982) on a variety of structures tend to exclude this possibility. As an alternative hypothesis, I suggest that resistance to "necking" under dynamic loads might generate the observed relationship of stem diameter to load. If a linear, imperfectly elastic structure (e.g., a licorice stick) is suddenly subjected to tension, it often narrows—or necks—at one point. This increases the stress (force per unit area) experienced by the material in the neck, making it the focus of further extension under stress and the most likely point of failure. The ability of the neck to withstand a dynamic load before it is "drawn" to the breaking point should be roughly proportional to its volume, and hence, to the cube of the diameter of the structure.

Whatever its basis, the cube root scaling law implies that, at a given leaf mass, the absolute allocation to tensile structures should increase in proportion to their length. Hence, the relative allocation to such structures vs leaves should increase with their length, although more slowly than in compressive structures. Indeed, as a general rule, tensile structures are more slender (and less costly) than compressive structures of the same length and bearing a similar load: they need act only as tethers, not as self-supporting beams.

3. Climbing Structures In climbing structures, including the stems of vines and other climbing plants, tensile stresses predominate, but the loads are usually supported by the host at more than one point. Consequently, such structures may be even more slender than equivalent tensile structures. Flexibility and other traits that allow climbing plants to survive catastrophic stresses due to slippage, or host death, are crucial (Putz and Holbrook, 1991; Fisher and Ewers, 1991). Vines often display anomalous patterns of secondary thickening that generate cable-like stems, with strands of woody tissue in a matrix of parenchyma. Such stems combine tensile strength with flexibility; in addition, the parenchyma act as preformed failure zones that absorb much of the force of a fall without rupturing essential xylem or phloem (Putz and Holbrook, 1991). Scaling laws for vine stems appear to be unknown, but their stems are generally more slender than those of self-supporting species (Putz, 1983; Ewers *et al.,* 1991; Gartner, 1991a); studies by Gartner (1988) and Putz and Holbrook (1991) indicate that vine stem material is often less stiff as well.

B. Mechanical Safety

The requirement for stem safety arises from stochastic variation in the size of the mechanical stresses faced by a plant. The probability of surviving such stresses for a given amount of time should increase with stem allocation above that required to ensure mechanical stability under the least stressful conditions. Almost all self-supporting plants that have been studied show some "safety factor" by which their diameter (or material stiffness) exceeds the minimum required to avoid elastic toppling in still air (e.g., see McMahon, 1973; McMahon and Bonner, 1983; King, 1981, 1986, 1987, 1990; Chazdon, 1986, 1991).

C. Photosynthetic Efficiency

The requirement for photosynthetic efficiency imposes constraints on stem form and branching pattern, on the basis of their effects on leaf arrangement and orientation, and the impact that these have on the rates of photosynthesis and transpiration (Givnish, 1984, 1986a, 1988). Self-shading is likely to reduce both photosynthesis and the costs of transpiration. The resulting decrements to photosynthesis are likely to be especially severe in shady environments; the benefits of reduced transpiration are likely to be particularly great in dry and/or sunny environments (Givnish, 1984).

D. Whole-Plant Growth and Competitive Ability

Finally, the requirements for whole-plant growth and competitive ability impose constraints on the maximum rate of net carbon gain by a plant and its ability to overtop other plants. Increased allocation to support tissue decreases the potential net carbon uptake by a plant by decreasing its investment in productive foliage, and increasing its energetic "overhead" in unproductive stem tissue (Givnish, 1986a,b, 1988). On the other hand, increased allocation to support tissue can increase the ability of a plant to overtop other plants, allowing it to gain access to greater amounts of light while depriving competitors of the same (Horn, 1971; Givnish, 1982; Gaudet and Keddy, 1988; Tilman, 1988).

In general, we might expect that natural selection should favor stems whose form, biomechanical properties, and growth dynamics maximize carbon gain, competitive ability, and safety, and minimize the costs of stem construction and maintenance. However, conflicts among the constraints affecting these factors clearly make it impossible to optimize all factors simultaneously. The traditional optimality criterion used for analyzing traits that affect energy capture, namely, maximal carbon gain in a given physical environment (Horn, 1971; Givnish, 1979, 1986d; Mooney and Gulmon, 1979), will not work for stem adaptations. As Givnish (1982) noted, the very stem strategy (i.e., zero investment) that maximizes the potential rate of whole-plant carbon gain will minimize the ability to compete for light and the actual rate of carbon gain, at least in crowded environments, by keeping leaves at ground level.

As a preliminary hypothesis, I suggest that natural selection should favor stems that maximize whole-plant growth in the presence of competitors, and permit survival between catastrophic disturbances. Under uncrowded conditions in which competition for light is unimportant, this criterion should approach that of maximizing carbon gain; under crowded conditions, of maximizing height growth; and under disturbed conditions, of favoring low safety factors in fast-growing, shade-intolerant species and high safety factors in slow-growing, shade-tolerant species.

On the basis of this optimality criterion, the optimal form, biomechanical properties, and growth dynamics of stems in a particular ecological context should be set by five major trade-offs involving the constraints already discussed (Table 1). These trade-offs involve the balance between (1) safety vs growth and competitive ability, (2) growth vs photosynthetic requirements, (3) mechanical vs photosynthetic efficiency, (4) initial vs continuing costs, and (5) structural parasitism vs self-support. Each of these trade-offs is discussed below, and the resulting implications for ecological trends in stem form, resource allocation, and growth dynamics are analyzed.

III. Energetic Trade-Offs and Predicted Trends

A. Safety versus Growth and Competitive Ability

The trade-off involving the balance between safety vs growth and competitive ability arises because stems with a higher margin of biomechanical safety have higher rates of survival (or can withstand greater stresses), at the cost of either lesser stature or greater allocation to stem tissue at a given height. The latter should have a deleterious effect on competitive success, resulting in slower rates of whole-plant growth in mass and/or reduced height. Two predictions follow directly from this trade-off.

1. Adaptation to Different Degrees of Mechanical Stress   In general, species adapted to environments with a high degree of mechanical stress should be competitively excluded from less stressful environments; species adapted to the latter should be unable to survive, even in the absence of competition, in mechanically stressful sites. This prediction is vividly supported by Johnson's (1991) study of the distribution and biomechanical properties of woody plants found in avalanche tracks in the Rocky Mountains. Johnson found that variation in stem diameter, not stem material stiffness or strength, explained the ability of plants to avoid stem rupture via bending during avalanches. The analysis predicted that only stems less than 6 cm in diameter should survive avalanches, and field observations confirmed this. Short, shrubby stems of glandular birch (*Betula glandulosa*) and glaucous willow (*Salix glauca*) were able to survive avalanches by bending to the ground without snapping, but the taller, thicker stems of Engelmann spruce (*Picea engelmannii*) and lodgepole pine (*Pinus contorta*) were stronger but less flexible: the outer portions of their stem cross-sections generated greater stresses when bent, exceeded the modulus of rupture, and snapped.

However, Engelmann spruce and lodgepole pine are able to overtop glandular birch and glaucous willow in 15 to 20 years. Thus, high on steep slopes, where avalanches occur frequently, birch and willow dominate the tracks, but spruce and pine dominate the surrounding matrix. At lower elevations on gentler slopes, avalanches are less frequent and spruce and pine dominate the avalanche tracks as well. This case nicely illustrates how the biomechanical properties of plants, and specifically the trade-off between safety and competitive ability, can limit their ecological distribution and shape community structure. Another study (Sufling, 1993) suggests even broader ramifications: at high elevations, the structure of avalanche tracks creates fire breaks and helps reduce the landscape-scale frequency of fire, helping fire-sensitive vegetation dominate the matrix between the tracks.

Another case that may involve the trade-off between safety and competitive ability involves the remarkable convergence on narrow, willow-like leaves (Fig. 4) and highly flexible branches in rheophytes, the woody plants that dwell along the shores of streams, torrents, and spates (Ridley, 1893; Beccari, 1902, 1904; Merrill, 1945; van Steenis, 1967, 1981; Whitmore, 1984). Van Steenis (1981) suggested that such leaves and pliant branches may be an adaptation to reduce drag during flash floods, serving to align the plant body with the streamlines and (in modern terminology) reducing form and pressure drag. This argument seems plausible, and similar arguments have been made for drag reduction in seaweeds with elongate fronds and flexible stipes (e.g., see Wainwright *et al.*, 1976; Koehl and Wainwright, 1977; Vogel, 1981). However, convincing hydrodynamic data to test this intriguing idea in rheophytes have yet to be gathered, and the potential down sides of the rheophytic habit, such as the tendency of highly flexible branches to "weep" and be unable to hold leaves far from the main bole, remain to be explored.

2. *Relation to Successional Status and Longevity*

A second general prediction emerging from the safety vs growth trade-off is that shade-intolerant, fast-growing, short-lived pioneer species should have lower biomechanical safety margins than shade-tolerant, long-lived species of comparable stature. If a shade-intolerant plant is overtopped because it invests too heavily in stems, it will soon die, whereas a shade-tolerant plant can survive. Low safety margins result in higher rates of growth in pioneer species, but are a liability in longer-lived species, which are more likely to be exposed to a greater range of mechanical stresses during their lifetime.

Work by King (1981, 1986) provides an excellent illustration of these principles. King found that short-lived, shade-intolerant, early successional aspen growing in dense stands had low safety margins: their stem diameters

Table 1 Summary of the Five Principal Trade-Offs Involving Stem Traits Discussed in Text

Trade-off	Basis	Prediction(s)
Mechanical safety vs growth and competitive ability	Stems with a higher margin of biomechanical safety have higher rates of survival or withstand greater stresses, at the cost of lesser stature or greater allocation to stem tissue at a given height	1. Species adapted to a high degree of mechanical stress should be competitively excluded from less stressful environments; species adapted to the latter should be unable to survive in mechanically stressful sites, even in the absence of competition 2. Shade-intolerant, short-lived pioneers should have lower mechanical safety margins than shade-tolerant, long-lived species of similar stature
Growth vs photosynthetic requirements	Taller plants have an advantage in competing for light, but must allocate more to unproductive support tissue. The competitive advantage of greater stature is greatest where coverage is dense	3. Productive, infrequently disturbed habitats favor heavy allocation to stem tissue and high stature, at least among late-successional dominants. Tall plants may be unable to survive in unproductive habitats a. In herbs, leaf height should increase with the density of competing foliage b. In woody plants, maximum height should be strongly influenced by the height-dependent pattern of allocation to support tissue c. Treelines should occur where low levels of light, soil moisture, or temperature strongly limit photosynthesis and cause woody plants to reach their energetic break-even point close to the ground. Woody plants should generally also be unable to invade sodden soils, given the constraints on aerenchyma function imposed by secondary thickening d. Emergent, floating, and submersed herbs should dominate progressively deeper bands of water, reflecting the relationship between stature and support costs at a given depth seen across growth forms

Category	Description	Predictions
Initial vs continuing costs	Woody tissue has a higher initial cost of construction than mechanically equivalent herbaceous tissue, but lower continuing costs because only a fraction must be replaced each year	4. Tall, woody plants should be less shade tolerant than shorter or more herbaceous species 5. Dominance in temperate forest understories should shift from shrubs to herbs in moving toward moister, more fertile, shadier sites 6. Compound leaves should be favored in gap-phase succession or in seasonally arid environments that favor deciduous foliage, where there is an advantage in bearing short-lived twigs/rachises
Photosynthetic vs mechanical efficiency	Branching patterns and leaf arrangements that reduce leaf overlap and competition for light often require more investment in stem tissue, or involve exposure to greater irradiance and transpiration	7. Shade-adapted plants should be plagiotropic and show distichous phyllotaxis, and sun-adapted plants should be orthotropic and show spiral phyllotaxis 8. Branching angles should minimize both leaf overlap and structural costs, if possible 9. Efficient leaf packing in shade-adapted, distichous species favors alternate leaves (or anisophylly in lineages with opposite leaves), as well as asymmetric leaf bases
Self-support vs structural parasitism	Structural parasites allocate far less to stems to achieve a given height than do self-supporting plants, resulting in greater rates of vertical and horizontal growth. However, vines require self-supporting hosts on which they climb, their slender stems make them vulnerable to certain environmental stresses, and their climbing mechanism enables them to climb only certain kinds of hosts	10. Vines should be most common in frequently disturbed habitats with an intermediate amount of coverage by self-supporting plants; they should be rare in arid, nutrient-poor, and/or fire-swept environments 11. Tendril climbers should ascend hosts of the finest diameter; twiners, hosts of greater diameter; and adhesive-root climbers, hosts of the greatest diameter 12. In habitats where vines are abundant, hosts should evolve traits that deter climbing by vines, such as frequently shed compound leaves or shaggy, exfoliating bark

Figure 4   Willow-like leaves of rheophytes (after Merrill, 1945): (A) *Neonauclea angustifolia* (Rubiaceae); (B) *Gagraea stenophylla* (Loganiaceae); (C) *Garcinia linearis* (Guttiferae); (D) *Syzygium neriifolium* (Myrtaceae); (E) *Saurania angustifolia* (Actinidiaceae); (F) *Eyrcibe stenophylla* (Convolvulaceae); (G) *Hamonoia riparia* (Euphorbiaceae); (H) *Eugenia mimica* (Myrtaceae); (I) *Atalantia linearis* (Rutaceae); (J) *Psychotria acuminata* (Rubiaceae); (K) *Tetranthera salicifolia* (Lauraceae).

were only about 50% greater than the minimum calculated as necessary to avoid elastic toppling. By contrast, long-lived, shade-tolerant, slower growing sugar maple had a much higher safety factor: its stems were 100 to 500% thicker than the toppling limit. Interestingly, the sugar maple safety factor increased with stature and age (Fig. 5). King (1986) argued that this might reflect greater height competition among sugar maples early in development. As an alternative hypothesis, I would propose that high safety factors are incompatible with growth in deep shade, and that sugar maple increases its safety factor only when it is energetically affordable (see Section III,B,3 for additional discussion).

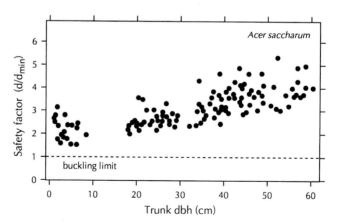

Figure 5   Safety factor (d/d_{min}) as a function of height in sugar maple (after King, 1986). Actual stem diameter d is always greater than the critical diameter d_{min} needed to avoid elastic buckling (*sensu* McMahon, 1973).

Stems of equal height and safety are less costly when constructed of wood of low density (Wainwright *et al.*, 1976; King, 1986). Wood strength is proportional to its density (McMahon, 1973). But, while denser woods are stiffer, they impose a proportionally greater bending moment in stems of a given height, on the basis of the greater mass of wood above a given point. Therefore the critical diameter for stems of a given height to resist elastic toppling is unaffected by wood density (McMahon, 1973; contrary to Horn, 1971). Consequently, the energetic cost of achieving a given height is minimized by constructing stems of the lowest density wood possible.

However, there is a negative correlation between wood density and stem breakage, at least in tropical trees (Putz *et al.*, 1983); denser woods may provide a better combination of strength and flexibility with which to resist rupture caused by the stem stresses induced by strong winds (King, 1986). In addition, denser woods (and other long-lived structural materials) often confer greater resistance to attack by fungi and/or insects (Bultman and Southwell, 1976; King, 1986; see also Shain [17] and Bryant and Raffa [16] in this volume). Hence, based on a trade-off between growth and safety from biological attack (not mechanical failure, *contra* Horn, 1971), we might expect short-lived pioneers to have light, energetically inexpensive wood that allows rapid height growth, whereas long-lived, late successional species should have dense, expensive, highly lignified wood that is herbivore resistant, as observed (Horn, 1971; Long *et al.*, 1981). Gap-phase trees such as hickories (*Carya*), ashes (*Fraxinus*), walnuts (*Juglans*), or black locust (*Robinia*), which are early successional in that they invade well-lit forest openings but usually defer reproduction until they reach the canopy before the surrounding trees close the gap, have an intermediate strategy, with soft sapwood, pithy twigs, and inexpensive rachises, and a light but strong, secondarily lignified, attack-resistant heartwood.

Palms and other arborescent monocotyledons lack secondary thickening (Hallé *et al.*, 1978). Hence, they potentially face a chronic problem of declining safety, with crown height increasing while stem diameter remains roughly constant. Studies by Rich (1987), however, indicate that some palms avoid this problem by (1) increasing the density and strength of stem tissue over time within a given cross-section, and (2) increasing the diameter of the stem cross-section over time via enlargement and proliferation of existing tissues (e.g., see Horn, 1971).

B. Growth versus Photosynthetic Requirements

The inevitable conflict between stem safety and plant growth in an unproductive environment leads us naturally to a consideration of a second (and ecologically extremely important) stem trade-off, that of balancing growth and photosynthetic requirements. As a general principle, taller plants have an advantage in competing for light, but must allocate more to unproductive support tissue. The competitive advantage of increased stature is greatest where coverage is dense, on moist, fertile, infrequently disturbed sites. But the energetic demands of tall plants may exclude them from less productive sites. Given that the return to a plant with a particular stature is strongly dependent on the heights of its competitors, and vice versa, a game theoretic approach will often be needed to assess the costs and benefits of stature and allocation to height growth (see Givnish, 1982, 1986b; Makälä, 1985; King, 1991).

1. Leaf Height in Forest Herbs   One prediction that follows immediately from the preceding principle is that productive, infrequently disturbed habitats should favor heavy allocation to stem tissue and great stature, at least among late successional dominants. Strong qualitative support for this prediction comes from the rapid evolution of increased stature in several lineages of land plants soon after their appearance in the Silurian and Devonian (Tiffney, 1981; Knoll, 1984; Tilman, 1986), and the evolution of the woody habit and arborescence in several modern lineages of island plants derived from herbaceous ancestors (Carlquist, 1965, 1970; Givnish *et al.*, 1995).

The first quantitative support for the predicted relationship of stem allocation to coverage and environmental conditions came from the Givnish (1982, 1986b) game theoretical analysis of optimal leaf height in forest herbs. Many forest herbs have annual, essentially determinate shoots. The proportion of above-ground biomass they devote each year to leaf tissue declines with leaf height (Fig. 6, left), reflecting the disproportionate in-

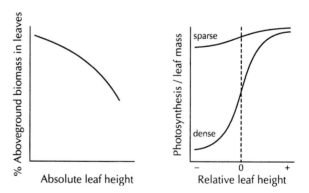

Figure 6   Energetic trade-offs associated with the evolution of leaf height in herbaceous plants. *Left:* Taller herbs must allocate more resources to support tissue in order to remain mechanically stable, resulting in a decline in the fraction of above-ground productivity allocated to leaves with increasing leaf height. *Right:* Balanced against this structural cost is the expected photosynthetic advantage, averaged over many shoots of the same height, of holding leaves higher than those of a competitor. This advantage is small in areas of sparse herbaceous cover, and larger where cover is denser (after Givnish, 1982).

crease in stem or petiole mass required to maintain mechanical stability. This decline in allocation to leaf tissue with height is a cost of stature that is independent of competitive context (but can depend on other environmental factors, such as windiness).

The benefits of stature, by contrast, are context dependent. If a plant holds its foliage much above the height of its competitors, then its expected rate of photosynthesis per gram of leaf actually built (averaged over many shoots of the same height) will be the maximum for the prevailing conditions (Fig. 6, right). If a plant holds its foliage lower, its expected photosynthetic rate will be reduced by an amount that depends on the density of coverage by competitors. If coverage is sparse, then a short plant is unlikely to be next to (and hence, under) a competitor, and therefore the expected rate of photosynthesis will vary little with relative leaf height. If, on the other hand, coverage is dense, then a short plant will likely be under a competitor, and the expected rate of return will increase sharply with relative leaf height. Plants should evolve the capacity to develop taller and taller stems until the photosynthetic benefit each obtains by a small height increment is just balanced by the structural cost of that increment (Givnish, 1982, 1986b).

The resulting prediction is that more productive conditions, and specifically, denser coverage within the herb layer, favor taller herbs, whether in forests or more open habitats like prairies. The data compiled by Givnish (1982) and Menges (1987) are in accord with this qualitative prediction. In addition, the average increase in leaf height with coverage accords quantitatively with predictions based on the observed allometry of support tissue (Fig. 7). Many rare herbs are short in stature; their uncommonness may, in part, reflect the rarity in the landscape of the chronically unproductive, low-coverage microsites (e.g., bogs, cliffs, densely shaded *Thuja* forests) that favor them (Givnish, 1982; see also Grubb, 1984, 1986; Keddy, 1990).

An interesting spinoff of the leaf height model involves the distribution of herbs with arching stems, including many woodland members of the Liliaceae such as *Polygonatum, Smilacina,* and *Disporum* (Givnish, 1986b). These arching herbs are mechanically less efficient than umbrella-like forest herbs, requiring more stem tissue to support a fixed amount of leaf tissue at a particular height above level ground. However, on slopes arching plants orient strongly downhill, creating the possibility of an energetic advantage (Fig. 8). As the inclination of a slope or the lateral spread of an arching herb increases, the height of an upright herb that could hold foliage in the same position as an arching herb rooted uphill also increases. On the basis of the allometry of support tissue in arching vs erect herbs, Givnish (1986b) calculated that arching herbs should achieve competitive superiority on slopes steeper than roughly 15 to 25°. The distribution of arching herbs in a virgin forest in the Great Smoky Mountains was generally

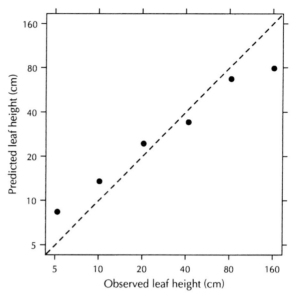

Figure 7   Predicted vs observed leaf height in forest herbs, based on studies by Givnish (1982, 1986b). The *x* coordinate of each point corresponds to the maximum leaf height (5, 10, 20, 40, 80, or 160 cm) defining a group of herbaceous species found at the study transect. The *y* coordinate of each point corresponds to the ESS leaf height predicted by the Givnish (1982, 1986b) model for the average of the coverages in which the corresponding herbaceous species are found. All predictions assume that shaded leaves respire, on an average lifetime basis, at roughly the same rate as unshaded leaves photosynthesize. The predictions for the upper two height classes are based on the allometry of late summer species, which dominate those height classes; the predictions for the remaining classes are based on the allometry of early summer species, which otherwise predominate.

in accord with these predictions (Fig. 9). *Polygonatum* tends to dominate steeper slopes than those dominated by *Smilacina*, as expected from its more horizontal inclination.

2. Optimal Allocation to Stem Tissue in Woody Plants   King (1981, 1991) has explored constraints on stem allocation in trees using both ordinary optimality and game theory. In 1981, King used the allometry of aspen stems and crowns to determine the allocation between bole and crown that maximized the rate of height growth, which King assumed would be favored in crowded stands. Zero allocation to bole results in zero height growth, as does 100% allocation; therefore optimum height growth occurs at some intermediate allocation. King found that aspen operates close to the expected allocation (Fig. 10). The crown diameter-to-crown height ratio of 0.34 seen in aspen (and presumably set to maximize upward growth) is close to that inferred by Givnish (1986c) from data compiled by O'Neill and DeAngelis (1981) for a variety of fully stocked, single- and mixed-species

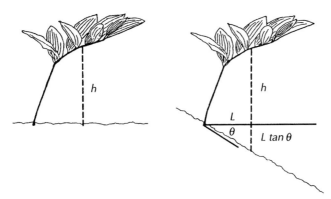

Figure 8 *Left:* Arching herbs hold the centroid of their leaf mass at a height *h* and a horizontal distance *L* from their point of attachment to the ground, and are mechanically less efficient than umbrella-like herbs holding leaves at the same height over a horizontal surface. *Right:* However, on slopes arching herbs characteristically orient downhill (Givnish, 1986b), forcing umbrella-like herbs to build stems of height $h + L \tan \theta$ in order to hold leaves in the same position as arching herbs on a slope of inclination θ. Above a critical slope inclination (ca. 15 to 25°) determined by the allometries of support tissue in umbrella-like vs arching herbs, arching herbs are mechanically more efficient, allocating less to support tissue than umbrella-like herbs of effectively equivalent stature; species with a greater horizontal length *L* at a given height *h* gain an advantage on steeper slopes. (After Givnish, 1986b.)

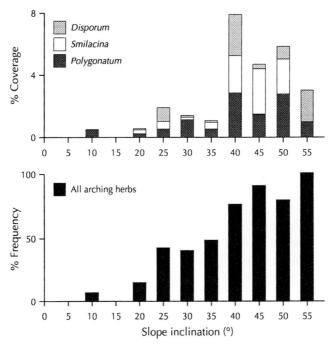

Figure 9 Distribution of arching herbs along a gradient of slope inclination *q* in the Great Smoky Mountains (after Givnish, 1986b). *Top:* Average percent coverage by *Disporum lanuginosum, Polygonatum biflorum,* and *Smilacina racemosa. Bottom:* Percent of quadrats with arching herbs present.

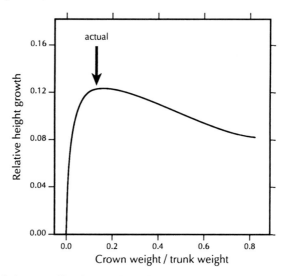

Figure 10   Relative rate of height growth predicted for fixed ratios of biomass allocation to crown vs bole in aspen (*Populus tremuloides*) (after King, 1981). Arrow indicates actual allocation ratio (0.13), which results in an expected rate of height growth that is 99% of that at the predicted ratio (0.17) atop a broad optimum.

forests, suggesting that plants in crowded stands are generally designed so as to maximize height growth. Givnish (1986c) used this fact, and the biomechanical constraints on stem mass imposed by the elastic toppling limit, to provide the first mechanistic explanation of the $-3/2$ self-thinning law; subsequently, Norberg (1988), Weller (1989), and Osawa and Allen (1993) published related models and analyses on this theme. The $-3/2$ power law relating average plant mass to density, in turn, should be a key determinant of forest productivity, together with the photosynthetic rate and allometry of resource allocation.

The King (1981) model predicted that the optimal allocation between crown and bole should not vary with environmental conditions. Some increase in the crown diameter-to-height ratio may occur in shade-adapted trees as a result of an adaptive shift from a multilayered to a monolayered array of branches (Horn, 1971), with a consequent increase in the length of the few remaining branches. However, any such increase would be modest, given that the ratio of biomass allocation to crown vs bole would remain fixed, and that branch biomass B increases steeply with branch length L ($B \propto L^3$ or L^4; King, 1981). Givnish (1988) argued that shade-adapted trees in uncrowded understories should have substantially broader crowns at a given height than sun-adapted trees in crowded canopies, on the basis of the relative benefits and costs of growing upward vs outward. If an understory tree is surrounded, on average, by few neighbors and is well below the canopy, an increment in canopy height will have little impact on the expected photosynthesis by its canopy. A comparable increment to canopy diameter should, however, have a dramatic impact on total photosynthesis by increasing total canopy area. In addition, near a crown radius-to-height ratio of 0.17, the cost of a given length increment to the branches should be many times less than a comparable height increment to the bole, based on the scaling of bole and branch masses as roughly the third or fourth power of their lengths. The data compiled by Givnish (1988) for the crown width-to-height ratios of "champion trees" adapted to shaded vs unshaded conditions are compatible with the predictions of this model: shade-tolerant understory species had a mean crown diameter-to-height ratio of 1.16 ± 0.48 ($n = 9$), whereas shade-intolerant canopy species had a mean ratio of 0.66 ± 0.21 ($n = 10$) ($p < 0.005$, one-tailed t test, 17 df).

In 1991, King presented a game theoretic model for maximum tree height, based on earlier work by Givnish (1982) and Mäkälä (1985), and using the empirical relation of wood production to tree height. King (1991) concluded that trees should cease vertical growth short of their physiological maximum, at a point at which the photosynthetic benefits of further increments in height relative to competitors are outweighed by the structural costs. He found good agreement between observed and "predicted" tree heights for several tree species, but the results should be viewed with the understanding that (1) the predicted maxima are necessarily close to the observed maxima; (2) the predicted maxima could be made arbitrarily close to the physiological (i.e., actual) maxima, depending on how disadvantageous it is to be shaded; and (3) the "predictions" are essentially regression models of growth vs height, and do not account for maximum tree height in terms of fundamental processes or constraints.

Tilman (1988) presented the results of a supercomputer simulation (ALLOCATE) involving competition for light and soil resources among size-structured plants, and found that the optimal allocation to stems increased in more productive, less disturbed habitats (Fig. 11). Tilman used this model to account qualitatively for trends in the stature of prairie plants along soil fertility gradients at Cedar Creek, Minnesota, and for general trends in the stature and physiognomy of forests along moisture and fertility gradients. Although not acknowledged by Tilman (1988), several of his predictions had already been made by Givnish (1982) and Grubb (1986), on essentially the same grounds. More importantly, ALLOCATE produces a maximum limit on tree height only by balancing growth with disturbance; in the absence of the latter, there is no limit to tree height because Tilman assumed no allometry in the annual allocation to stem mass with stem height (even though an allometry of total stem mass was incorporated). Most importantly, and as a direct consequence of the assumption

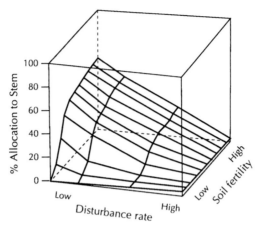

Figure 11   Optimal fractional allocation of biomass to stems as a function of disturbance rate and soil fertility, as predicted by the ALLOCATE model. (After Tilman, 1988.)

of allocational isometry, the Tilman (1988) model does not permit short and tall plants with similar photosynthetic characteristics to coexist, and thus fails to account for the ubiquitous stratification of forests into tree, shrub, and herb layers.

In my view, the trade-off between growth and photosynthetic requirements provides a fundamental explanation for maximum tree height, forest stratification, and several other ecological phenomena. Specifically, I predict that *tall plants* may be unable to survive in unproductive or frequently disturbed habitats, on the basis of their high energetic overhead. The effect of stature on minimum energy requirements may be responsible for patterns in maximum tree height, the position of tree lines, shade tolerance, the stratification of forests, and the depth zonation of aquatic growth forms.

3. Maximum Tree Height   Givnish (1988) showed how data on photosynthesis and the allometry of allocation to stems and other organs could be used to predict the maximum height of tulip poplar (*Liriodendron tulipifera*), the tallest tree in eastern North America, as well as expected trends in its shade tolerance with crown height. The mass-specific rates of photosynthesis and respiration in tulip poplar do not vary substantially over a wide range of irradiances, allowing whole-plant performance to be approximated from leaf-level gas exchange and whole-plant energy allocation (see Fig. 12). The traditional light compensation point (the irradiance at which the instantaneous rates of leaf photosynthesis and respiration just balance) is 12 μmol m^{-2} sec^{-1}, roughly 0.6% of full sunlight. If one includes night leaf respiration and the construction cost of the leaves amortized over the

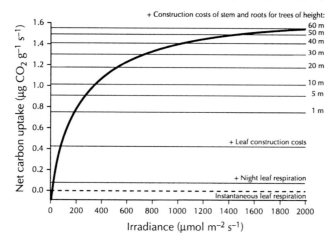

Figure 12   Effective leaf compensation point in *Liriodendron tulipifera* as a function of the inclusion of various respiratory costs. The curve is the instantaneous rate of net leaf photosynthesis, plotted as a function of irradiance I [$P = P_{max} I/(I + k) - R$, where $P_{max} = 1.83$ μg g^{-1} s^{-1}, $k = 236$ μmol m^{-2} s^{-1}, and $R = 82$ ng g^{-1} s^{-1}], yielding the observed maximum net rate of 1.55 μg g^{-1} s^{-1} at 2000 μmol m^{-2} s^{-1} [Fig. 3 in Givnish (1988) erroneously assumed $P_{max} = 1.63$ μg g^{-1} s^{-1}, yielding incorrect estimates of maximum height at intermediate irradiance; however, the limiting heights given in the text for 2000 μmol m^{-2} s^{-1} were based on the actual maximum rate of photosynthesis and were correct]. The dashed line is the instantaneous rate of net leaf respiration; the intersection of this line with the photosynthetic curve marks the traditional compensation point. The solid lines represent the cumulative respiration rates associated with night leaf respiration, leaf construction, and construction of support and root tissue for a 6.5-month growing season (see text and Givnish, 1988); the corresponding points of their intersection with the photosynthetic curve mark the effective compensation points associated with including each additional source of respiration.

growing season, the energetic break-even point jumps to roughly 5% full sunlight. Finally, if one includes stem and root costs [estimated from the Whittaker and Woodwell (1968) allometric allocation functions], then a 1-m-tall sapling requires 10% full sunlight, and the maximum height at which energetic break-even can take place, even in full sunlight, is 60 m, roughly the actual maximum height tulip poplar achieves in nature.

Obviously, there are many factors other than allocational shifts that may limit tree height, such as (1) drops in leaf photosynthesis with stature due to more negative leaf water potentials, (2) greater exposure to drought or wind damage, or even (3) the balance of growth and disturbance described by Tilman (1988) (see also Wilson [4] in this volume). But the tulip poplar model was the first to demonstrate quantitatively that the allometry of allocation to support tissue places realistic limits on tree height. In addition, it showed that differences in stature can have a far more profound effect on minimum light requirements than any adaptation at the leaf level, changing whole-plant light needs by two and a half orders of magnitude (see Fig. 13A).

4. Differential Distribution of Shrubs versus Herbs along Forested Gradients   As noted by Givnish (1984, 1988) and Raven (1986), the lower light requirements of shorter plants (e.g., herbs and shrubs) provide a simple mechanism that permits them to persist under a canopy of taller species, even if all have leaves with the same photosynthetic characteristics. The differing energetic requirements of woody vs herbaceous plants may also help explain the shift from shrub to herb dominance in forest understories, often seen in moving from xeric to mesic sites in eastern North America (Whittaker, 1956; Curtis, 1959). Shrubs, being taller than herbs and having stems constructed of costly wood, should have higher whole-plant compensation points than herbs (Givnish, 1988), and may be able to persist mainly on xeric sites, where drought, soil infertility, and/or fire maintain a relatively open tree canopy. Shrubs, being taller than herbs, rooting in the same soil horizon, and casting shadows that move little as the sun moves across the sky, may suppress herb growth by competition. On mesic sites, by contrast, the dense tree canopy may lower understory light levels below the minimum required by shrubs, allowing herbs with shorter, less expensive stems to predominate. This hypothesis has important implications not only for trends in the relation of forest strata to each other, but also for overall forest diversity, given the far greater number of herb species than those of shrubs or trees in most temperate regions.

5. Arctic, Alpine, Desert, and Aquatic Tree Lines   The limit on tree height imposed by the allometry of allocation to support tissue may also provide an explanation for arctic, alpine, and desert tree lines. If, for the moment, we cast tulip poplar in the role of a green Everyman (using its physiological parameters as other aspects of the environment or resource allocation are varied), we find that maximum tree height drops to near ground level if the growing season is 2 months or less (Fig. 13B), as it is in many arctic and alpine areas (Grace, 1987), or if root allocation exceeds 150 to 200% of leaf allocation (Fig. 13C), as it does in many deserts (Schulze, 1982). Extreme soil infertility also favors heavy allocation to roots (see Mooney and Gulmon, 1979; Tilman, 1988) and may foster dominance by shrubby species even on well-drained, low-elevation, tropical sites with abundant rainfall year round, such as the bana woodlands of southern Venezuela (Bongers *et al.*, 1985). Short plants have other putative advantages that may help determine tree lines, such as their location within the ground boundary layer and consequent exposure to warm microclimates and protection from icy blasts in arctic or alpine areas (Bliss, 1982; Chapin and Shaver, 1982; Richards and Bliss, 1986; Grace, 1987; Hadley and Smith, 1987), or reduced

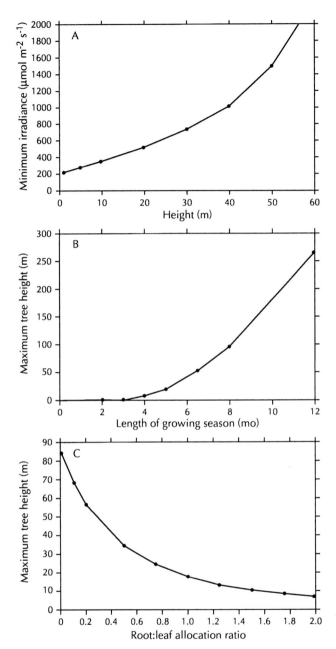

Figure 13 Predictions of the *Liriodendron* model. (A) Shade tolerance (minimum irradiance required for energetic break-even) as a function of height in *Liriodendron tulipifera,* using the model shown in Fig. 12; (B) maximum plant height as a function of the length of the growing season; and (C) maximum plant height as a function of the root:leaf allocation ratio. Graphs (B) and (C) show the trends expected in full sunlight if all other parameters in the *Liriodendron* model are held constant.

stem evaporation in deserts (Walter, 1973). But these simulations suggest that allocational allometry alone may play an important role in determining the position of tree lines. Arguments by Tranquillini (1979) to the contrary should be reconsidered, because Tranquillini failed to account for shifts in the cost of building and maintaining stems with plant height in his research on alpine tree lines.

Note that an increase in the length of the photosynthetic season much beyond the 6.5 months assumed in the tulip popular model generates predictions of unrealistically tall trees (Fig. 13B). Yet even the forest giants of the Pacific Northwest do not exceed ca. 100 m in height, in spite of holding their needles for at least 2 years (Waring and Franklin, 1979). How can we account for this apparent discrepancy between theory and reality? One important factor that must be included in a more realistic model is the reduced photosynthetic rates observed in old trees (Yoder *et al.,* 1994). Another factor to include is the negative correlation between leaf longevity and photosynthetic rate across species (Orians and Solbrig, 1977; Williams *et al.,* 1989; Reich *et al.,* 1992; Reich, 1993). Longer growing seasons favor taller plants in the tulip poplar model (Fig. 13B) by decreasing the amortized cost of constructing a gram of leaf tissue and associated shoot and root tissues; incorporating the decrease in photosynthesis with leaf life span would reduce the expected increase in plant stature. In theory, it should be possible to apply the tulip poplar model to *Sequoiadendron,* the tallest tree on earth, by using its photosynthetic and allometric parameters. Additional realism could be added to the tulip poplar model by incorporating (1) daily and seasonal variation in irradiance, (2) variation in the length of the photosynthetically active period induced by variation in soil moisture, and (3) dependence of the length of the growing season on root allocation, and vice versa (see Cowan, 1986).

Although it is often overlooked, there is a fourth kind of tree line (in addition to the three just discussed) characteristic of the transition from well-drained to sodden, saturated soils. Bogs, pond edges, marshes, and shallow fresh and salt water are all generally devoid of trees and dominated by herbaceous plants. Exceptions to this rule include mangroves (Tomlinson, 1986) and bald cypress swamps. Why are herbaceous plants generally so dominant on chronically sodden soils?

Soil anoxia is a key challenge faced by plants on such soils, and most species either have aerenchyma that carry oxygen to the roots, or restrict their rooting to shallow soil where oxygen is directly available. Tall, shallowly rooted trees on wet, mucky soils may be mechanically unstable. In addition, at higher latitudes, the mechanical damage associated with ice formation and movement may act to exclude plants with permanent aboveground parts from areas with standing water. However, a more general constraint may be the inability of most woody plants to maintain functional aerenchyma. Many plant species on wet soils have air channels that carry oxygen from their leaves and/or shoots to their roots, thereby enabling the latter to function in a hostile, anaerobic soil environment. In herbs, this path is easily maintained: each petiole (or annually replaced shoot) bears aerenchyma in its pith, and portions of its outer surface (or those of leaves to which it is directly connected) exchange gases directly with the atmosphere (e.g., see Sculthorpe, 1967; Dacey, 1981). In woody plants, however, normal secondary growth (i.e,. addition of xylem and phloem on the inner surface of the circumferential cambium, and addition of bark on the outer surface) would interrupt the connection of the aerenchyma to the surface of the shoots and/or the petioles of new leaves, and thus interrupt oxygen flow to the roots. Intriguingly, several of the woody plants that do grow in constantly sodden soils (e.g., mangroves) bear pneumatophores of determinate growth or display anomalous patterns of secondary thickening (Tomlinson, 1986) that may obviate this problem.

6. *Zonation of Aquatic Plants*   The allometry of allocation to support may also provide an explanation for the characteristic depth zonation of aquatic growth forms. In ponds, small lakes, and slow-flowing streams around the world, emergent herbs with aerial leaves dominate shallow water (typically 0 to 1 m), floating-leaved species dominate deeper water water (<ca. 4 m), and submersed species dominate deeper water yet (<18 m) (Sculthorpe, 1967; Hutchinson, 1975; Spence, 1982; Singer *et al.,* 1983; Wetzel, 1983). Emergents may gain a competitive edge in shallow water by holding their leaves higher than those of water lilies or other floating-leaved plants, but the more massive allocation by emergents to self-supporting petioles may exclude them from deeper water. At some depth, the cost of building and maintaining even the slender, tether-like petioles of floating-leaved species (together with associated leaf and root tissue) will exceed photosynthetic income, and only submersed species (which need not build long petioles to reach the surface of the water) will survive (Givnish, 1995). My group is currently testing this hypothesis and several related predictions, using an integrated series of comparative observations, allocational studies, and experimental field transplants and reciprocal removals.

C. Initial versus Continuing Costs

A third major trade-off affecting stem adaptations involves the balance between initial vs continuing costs, and often entails the contrast between permanent and temporary support skeletons. The main point is that woody tissue has a higher initial construction cost for stems of a given length or height than mechanically equivalent herbaceous tissue, but only a small fraction of the total support structure must be built each year in woody plants.

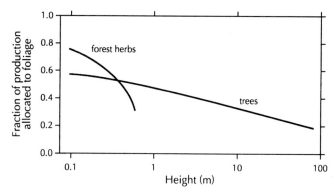

Figure 14 Proportion of annual above-ground biomass production allocated to foliage as a function of plant height (after Givnish, 1988). The curve for trees is based on allometric regressions given by Whittaker *et al.* (1963) and Whittaker and Woodwell (1968) (see caption to Fig. 2). The curve for forest herbs is based on the data of Givnish (1982) for early summer species that arrange their foliage in an umbrella-like arrangement. Late summer species, which typically occur in gaps and are exposed to greater levels of light availability (Givnish, 1987), have narrower crowns with several overlapping layers of leaves, and hence allocate more to leaf tissue at a given height. As shown, umbrella-like forest herbs are mechanically more efficient than woody plants below a height of roughly 0.5 m; the cross-over point for late summer species (and presumably, for other sun-adapted herbs) is roughly 1 m.

1. Shade Tolerance of Herbaceous and Woody Plants

Two predictions that follow directly from this principle are that (1) short plants should be herbaceous, and taller plants should be woody, and (2) herbs should be more shade tolerant than woody plants of the same stature. The proportion of above-ground biomass annually allocated to leaves decreases with plant stature but at different rates in herbs and woody plants, starting higher in shade-adapted herbs before dropping below that in woody plants at about 0.5 m (Fig. 14); the cross-over point is about 1 m for sun-adapted herbs. The reason for the evolutionary ascendance of woody plants is simply that, even though their support tissue is more expensive than that of herbs of the same height, they build only a portion of their stem per year and do not discard previous increments to the support skeleton (Givnish, 1988). The greater shade tolerance of herbs and its ecological implications have already been discussed (see Section III,B,4).

2. Compound versus Simple Leaves

Givnish (1978) analyzed the potential advantages and disadvantages of compound leaves in woody plants, and concluded that they should be favored (1) in gap-phase succession, and other situations in which height growth is at a premium, and (2) among deciduous species in seasonally arid environments. Central to this analysis is the assumption that the herbaceous rachises of compound leaves have a lower initial cost of construction than woody twigs that support a mechanically equivalent array of simple leaves. A. Monk and the author have re-

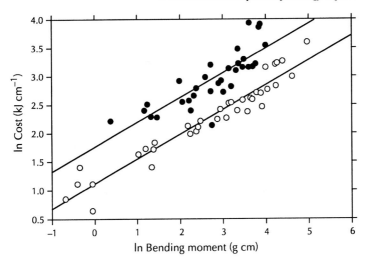

Figure 15   Construction costs (kJ cm^{-1}) of twigs bearing the simple leaves of *Ulmus rubra* (●) and rachises bearing leaflets of the compound leaves of *Juglans nigra* (○) as a function of the bending moments (g cm) on twig or rachis cross-sections created by the weight of laminae and support tissue distal to those cross-sections (A. Monk and T. Givnish, unpublished data). Lines represent least mean square regressions. The intercept of the *Juglans* regression is significantly less ($p < 0.05$, ANCOVA) than that for *Ulmus*, indicating that, at least for this pair of species, the initial construction cost of rachises is less than that for twigs bearing comparable loads.

cently gathered data that support this assumption (Fig. 15). Fully expanded compound leaves were collected from six species, and annual twigs with attached foliage were collected from six species with simple leaves. Lever arms were measured, and the fresh and dry masses of individual leaves/leaflets and intervening portions of rachises/twigs determined. Tissue construction costs (kJ g^{-1}) of rachises and twigs were estimated using the technique of Williams *et al.* (1987, 1989). Tissue cost per unit length (kJ cm^{-1}) of each segment of a twig or petiole was then plotted against the bending moment exerted on that segment, and the regression lines for simple and compound leaves compared; one pairwise comparison is shown in Fig. 15. As expected, the energetic cost of supporting a given load is lower for rachises than for twigs.

   Therefore, rachises do have a lower initial cost of construction than woody twigs. In addition, in deciduous species the rachises are shed during the unfavorable season and, unlike twigs, do not then transpire or respire (Givnish, 1978, 1984). On the other hand, rachises must be rebuilt in ensuing seasons, whereas twigs generally do not and form the core for more massive branches. Therefore compound leaves are essentially cheap, throwaway branches, having a low initial cost of construction but large continuing costs of replacement. Compound leaves should be favored in gap-phase succession because of the premium on height growth: plants should show little lateral growth (which would divert energy from the leader), and such side branches as are built should be short-lived (as a result of their being rapidly shaded by new branches overhead), and hence built as cheaply as possible (Givnish, 1978). Most genera of trees in the northeastern United States that possess compound leaves are, as expected, early or gap-phase successional (Givnish, 1978, 1984). Examples include Kentucky coffee tree (*Gymnocladus dioicus*), Hercules club (*Zanthoxylum clava-herculis*), devil's walking stick (*Aralia spinosa*), black locust (*Robinia pseudo-acacia*), mountain ash (*Sorbus americana*), sumacs (*Rhus*), walnuts (*Juglans*), and most ashes (*Fraxinus*) and hickories (*Carya*).

Compound leaves should also be favored in seasonally arid environments that favor deciduous foliage, as a cost-effective means of reducing residual transpiration (and respiration, in tropical and subtropical areas with a warm dry season) after the leaves are shed (Givnish, 1978, 1984). Indeed, as expected, compound-leaved species are common in deserts and semi-deserts, tropical seasonal dry forests, and in the upper strata of rain forests. The increased proportion of compound-leaved species in the upper layers of tropical forests is associated directly with the increase in the fraction of deciduous species with compound leaves, and the effective size (width) of simple leaves or leaflets of compound leaves does not differ significantly in a given layer (Givnish, 1978). As expected, the proportion of compound-leaved species is low in seasonally arid environments that favor evergreen foliage, such as mediterranean scrub.

D. Photosynthetic versus Mechanical Efficiency

In general, we would expect that branching patterns and leaf arrangements that reduce leaf overlap and competition for light often do so at the expense of increased investment in stem tissue, and entail exposure to greater irradiance and transpirational demand (Givnish, 1984, 1986a).

1. Plagiotropy versus Orthotropy   One important prediction based on these considerations involves the fundamental organization of shoots in sun and shade: shade-adapted plants should be plagiotropic, and sun-adapted plants should be orthotropic (Givnish, 1984). Plagiotropic shoots are horizontal twigs with leaves arranged distichously in a planar array, and are indeed common in shade-adapted plants; orthotropic shoots are erect, bear spiral leaf arrays, and are generally common in well-lit habitats (Hallé *et al.,* 1978; Leigh, 1972, 1990).

As organs of energy capture, plagiotropic shoots minimize self-shading, and so are well adapted to shady conditions in which light is strongly limiting. Orthotropic shoots self-shade more, but should require less stem tissue to support the same or greater leaf mass. Consequently, they may confer an advantage in well-lit situations, in which light less strongly limits photosynthesis and self-shading may reduce water loss (Givnish, 1984). Data on the comparative mechanical efficiency of orthotropic and plagiotropic axes are urgently needed, however (see also Wilson [4] in this volume).

As organs of growth, orthotropic shoots may yield an advantage to sun-adapted plants, directing growth upward and helping to prevent overtopping. Plagiotropic shoots direct growth outward and may be favored in shade-adapted species: increasing total leaf area may be a more certain means of raising whole-plant carbon gain than growing taller for plants that grow far below the canopies of others (Givnish, 1984, 1988).

2. *Optimal Branching Angles*   Another prediction related to the balance between photosynthetic and mechanical efficiency is that branching angles should minimize both leaf overlap and structural costs, if possible. For example, Honda and Fisher (1978) and Fisher and Honda (1979a,b) showed that branching angles in *Terminalia catappa* (Combretaceae) are close to those that minimize the overlap between the leaf clusters borne at the nodes of that tree's highly regular pattern of branching (Fig. 16). It is not

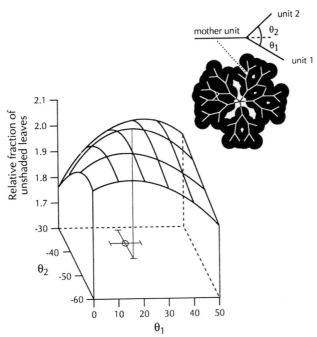

Figure 16   Predicted vs observed branching angles in *Terminalia catappa* (Combretaceae) (after Honda and Fisher, 1978). *Terminalia* branches are more or less horizontal, and bear a circular rosette of leaves at each node. According to Honda and Fisher (1978), the optimal branching angles of daughter shoots from parental axes (inset) are those that maximize the relative area of unshaded, nonoverlapping foliage; the observed means and standard deviations of these angles are indicated on the *x,y* plane. The total area covered by foliage at the optimal branching angles is shaded in the inset, which closely approaches the *Terminalia* branching pattern.

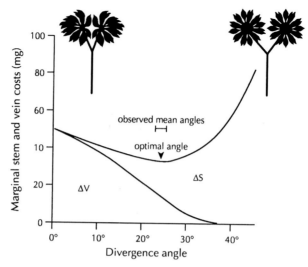

Figure 17   Predicted vs observed branching angle in reproductive shoots of *Podophyllum peltatum* (Berberidaceae) (after Givnish, 1986b). The optimal divergence angle occurs at 24.0°, where the sum of the marginal costs (i.e., additional costs over minimum) of veins (ΔV) and petioles (ΔS) is minimized. As the divergence angle increases, marginal vein costs decrease because the leaves can be radially more symmetric and still not overlap, reducing lever arm lengths and the total biomass allocated to veins for a fixed leaf mass. However, marginal petiole costs increase with divergence angle, reflecting the greater length of such petiole required to hold the leaves at a given height.

clear, however, why selection favors minimization of leaf overlap in *Terminalia* without regard to mechanical costs (Givnish, 1986a). For *Podophyllum*, Givnish (1986b) was able to show that the branching angle between the two leaf-bearing axes of the sexual shoots minimized total support costs, subject to the constraint of no overlap between the leaves (Fig. 17).

3. Alternate versus Opposite Leaves, Anisophylly, and Asymmetric Leaf Bases For different shoot orientations and branching patterns, selection should favor the phyllotaxis that minimizes self-shading and/or structural costs, at least under relatively moist or shaded conditions (Horn, 1971; Givnish, 1984, 1986a). In orthotropic shoots, a spiral phyllotaxis with an angle of 137° between successive leaves may be favored because it minimizes self-shading (Leigh, 1972), or possibly because it results in the most efficient packing of primordia on an expanding shoot apex (Green, 1992).

For shade-adapted, plagiotropic shoots a distichous, alternate leaf arrangement may be best (Fig. 18). The tightest packing of convex, bilaterally symmetric leaf bases is possible on a triangular, not square, grid (Givnish, 1984). This packing results in fewer uncovered gaps, for which the plant has paid in terms of stem tissue; it should by particularly adaptive in shade-

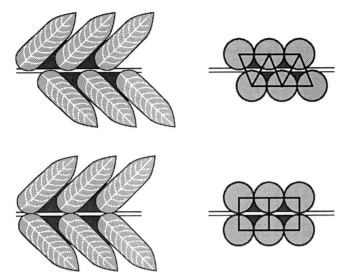

Figure 18   Packing of alternate and opposite leaves in a planar array (left) and packing of disks on triangular vs rectangular grids (right). Note the smaller amount of uncovered space in the close packing of leaf bases or disks on a triangular (alternate) grid. For circles, alternate packing reduces the area uncovered by 44%. (After Givnish, 1986b.)

adapted plants that are growing close to their energetic limits. Interestingly, shade-adapted members of some groups that are invariably characterized by opposite leaves (e.g., Gesneriaceae, Melastomaceae) approach the alternative leaf arrangement through anisophylly, in which one leaf is much smaller than the other at a node, with the position of the larger leaf alternating from one side of the twig to the other (Fig. 19).

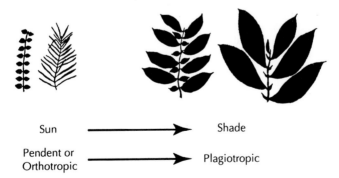

Sun ⟶ Shade

Pendent or
Orthotropic ⟶ Plagiotropic

Figure 19   Anisophylly in *Columnea* (Gesneriaceae). Sun-adapted species with pendent or erect shoots (e.g., *C. microphylla* and *C. linearis*) are isophyllous; shade-adapted species with horizontal shoots and broader leaves (*C. harrisii and C. sanguinea*) are markedly anisophyllous and approach an efficient mosaic of alternative leaves. (After Givnish, 1986b.)

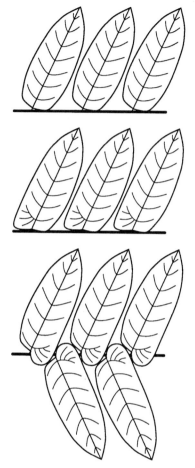

Figure 20   *Top:* Efficient packing of bilaterally symmetric leaves in a planar array; note gap adjacent to proximal side of leaf base. *Middle:* Increased efficiency of packing with asymmetric leaf bases in which an additional area is supported by the basal secondary vein on the proximal side. *Bottom:* Same, but additional area is supported by the distal side of the leaf base. (After Givnish, 1986b.)

Even an alternate leaf arrangement will leave some space near a branch uncovered if the leaf bases are bilaterally symmetric (Fig. 20). Not surprisingly, several shade-adapted groups with plagiotropic shoots (e.g., *Anisophyllea, Begonia,* and *Ulmus*) are characterized by asymmetric leaf bases that appear to provide a final refinement of leaf packing, and such asymmetric leaves seem generally to be restricted to plagiotropic groups adapted to extreme shade (see Givnish, 1984).

Additional issues involving the balance between photosynthetic and mechanical efficiency include (1) the ecological significance of different shapes of trees crowns (Paltridge, 1973; Brunig, 1976; Givnish, 1984; Niklas and Kerschner, 1984; Terborgh, 1985; Niklas, 1986, 1992; Morgan and Cannell, 1988; Cannell and Morgan, 1989; Sprugel, 1989; Kuuluvainen, 1992), and the importance of branching angles in generating them (Davidson and Remphrey, 1990; Remphrey and Davidson, 1991; de Reffye *et al.*, 1991; Fisher, 1992), (2) the adaptive value of the branched vs unbranched habit (Givnish, 1978; Meinzer and Goldstein, 1986; Givnish *et al.*, 1986, 1995), (3) the significance of plasticity in branching (Fisher and Hibbs, 1982; Waller and Steingraeber, 1985; Grime *et al.*, 1986), (4) the function of the long-shoot/short-shoot system (Büsgen and Münsch, 1929), and (5) the implications of different patterns of self-pruning (Bassow and Ford, 1990; Ford *et al.*, 1990; Brooks *et al.*, 1991; Sprugel *et al.*, 1991). These issues suggest many fertile areas for future research, but space does not permit their consideration here.

E. Self-Support versus Structural Parasitism

Several predictions arise from the final trade-off involving self-support vs structural parasitism: structural parasites allocate far less to stems to achieve a given height than do self-supporting plants, resulting in greater rates of vertical and/or horizontal growth. However, vines require self-supporting hosts on which they climb. Gartner (1991b) showed that vinelike and shrubby forms of poison oak (*Toxicodendron diversilobum*) allocate similar amounts of energy to foliage vs stems, but that the vinelike form is able to produce much longer stems for the same investment; Niklas (personal communication) has compiled data suggesting a similar trend across species. Putz (1984a) reported that vine seedlings that were experimentally supplied with a trellis grew much taller than control seedlings. Furthermore, Putz and Holbrook (1991) noted that 25% of the woody seedlings in several tropical forests are climbing species, while Putz *et al.* (1984) observe that liana-infested hosts suffer a much higher rate of mortality than liana-free hosts.

Three interesting predictions emerge from this trade-off, bearing on the distribution and climbing adaptations of vines, and the evolution of anti-vine defenses by self-supporting plants (Givnish, 1984; Putz, 1984b; Putz and Holbrook, 1991; Givnish, 1992). These are detailed below.

1. Ecological Distribution of Vines   Vines should be most common in frequently disturbed habitats with an intermediate amount of coverage by self-supporting plants; they should be rare in arid, nutrient-poor, and/or fire-swept environments. A moderate amount of disturbance (relative to the growth rate of self-supporting plants) creates a shifting mosaic of horizontally and vertically distributed gaps; vines, by virtue of their low allocation to stem tissue per unit length, have a natural advantage in "mobility" (i.e., growth rate) toward such energy-rich microsites. Too high a rate of disturbance, of course, could eliminate the hosts on which vines climb or make them so rare that host–vine encounter rates plummet.

A shortage of water or nutrients may reduce the competitive advantage of vines by forcing all plants, structural parasites as well as self-supporting species, to allocate heavily to roots, reducing the relative growth advantage of vines (Givnish, 1984). Vines will also lose their competitive edge if low resource availability limits the abundance of tall, self-supporting hosts (Gartner, 1991b). Finally, the slender stems of vines might become a liability in a fire-swept landscape, given their much higher surface area-to-volume ratio and likelihood of kindling (see Givnish *et al.*, 1986; Putz and Mooney, 1991; Gill [14], this volume).

These structurally related principles explain most, but not all of the broad patterns of vine abundance. Vines, and especially woody lianas, are a characteristic feature of tropical rain forests (Gentry, 1991), and are especially common in gaps and along forest edges (Hegarty and Caballé, 1991). Up to 52% of individual trees in some rain forests bear lianas in their crowns (Putz, 1984a; Gentry, 1991), and lianas can account for 36% of total leaf production (Ogawa *et al.*, 1965). As expected, they are most common on highly fertile soils, and less common on extremely infertile substrates (Proctor *et al.*, 1983; Putz and Chai, 1987; Gentry, 1991). Interestingly, vines are particularly frequent in rain forests with a marked dry season (Hueck, 1981; Balee and Campbell, 1989) or that are seasonally inundated (Gentry, 1991); both inundation and drought stress probably create a more open canopy, but data on this point are currently unavailable. The sparseness of vines on tropical islands has been ascribed to the abundance of wind dispersal in vines, and its limited powers to move seeds long distances (Gentry, 1991).

Vines are less common in temperate forests, and rare in desert, mediterranean scrub, boreal forest, and tundra (Gentry, 1991; Rundel and Franklin, 1991). Presumably, the poor evolutionary fortunes of vines in these habitats may be partly ascribed to limitations of transport rather than support structure: seasonal drought or freezing temperatures are likely to place vines at a particular disadvantage, given their dependence on xylem vessels with exceptionally wide diameters (Carlquist, 1991), which are highly efficient but cavitation prone (see Sperry [5] in this volume). In addition, the pervasive role of fire in mediterranean scrub and boreal forest (as well as soil infertility in the latter), probably has also placed vines at a disadvantage.

In temperate forests of the eastern United States (as exemplified by those of Wisconsin; Curtis, 1959), vines are most common in flood-plain forests, where gaps are created frequently and levels of soil moisture and fertility are generally high. They are secondarily abundant in drier oak forests, where the canopy is kept open by drought and fire, in accord with one but not another of our predictions. In mesic forests, vines are generally restricted to tree-fall gaps and woodland edges (Gysel, 1951).

Gentry (1983) argued that the abundance of large woody lianas in tropical forests and their near absence at higher latitudes may explain the surprising tendency for litter production to increase toward the equator while wood production decreases or remains constant. Tropical lianas occupy a large fraction of the canopy while being attached to relatively slender stems, and can thus produce substantial amounts of leaf tissue while contributing little to wood production.

An oft-overlooked form of structural parasitism occurs in clump-forming plants (e.g., many grasses), in which individual shoots lean on each other and derive some of their support from neighboring shoots. This phenomenon could be considered a form of structural mutualism and deserves further study. It should be noted, however, that this form of mutualism is stable only if support continues to be provided by neighbors. If some are removed or buckle under heavy winds, then shoots near the exposed edge can become unstable and lead to a catastrophic spread of buckling throughout the stand. Such failure ("lodging") occurs frequently in grain crops struck by heavy winds when nearly ripe. On a larger scale, the shelter from winds provided by neighboring forest trees probably also results in structural mutualism; the downwind propagation of alternating bands of dead and live trees in high-elevation fir forests ("fir waves" or the Shinozaki phenomenon; Sprugel, 1976, 1984; Sprugel and Bormann, 1981) is a striking manifestation of what can happen when such mutualism is disrupted.

2. Climbing Adaptations   Biomechanical constraints dictate that tendril climbers can ascend on hosts of the finest diameter; twiners, on hosts of greater diameter; and adhesive-root climbers, on hosts of the greatest diameter. Putz and Holbrook (1991) argue that the minimum host diameter that tendrils or twining stems can grasp is set by their minimum radius of curvature, and hence ultimately by their diameter. Tendrils, being more slender than the stems of most twining vines, can thus climb more slender hosts. Maximum host diameters are set by the maximum radius of curvature of twining shoots and the length of tendrils; climbers with adhesive roots can climb hosts of any diameter (Putz and Holbrook, 1991). Data compiled by Putz (1984b) and Putz and Chai (1987) for rain forest lianas in Panama and Borneo support these predictions, but they remain to be confirmed for other communities.

3. Host Defenses against Structural Parasites   In habitats with abundant vines, hosts should develop characteristics that deter climbing by vines, such as frequently shed compound leaves or shaggy, exfoliating bark. Woody lianas that can reach the canopy are a major threat to the life of their host, given their high growth rates and substantial leaf area (see Featherly, 1941; Lutz, 1943; Gysel, 1951; Kira and Ogawa, 1971; Putz *et al.*, 1984; Stevens, 1987; Hegarty, 1991; Putz, 1991). It is therefore not surprising that some hosts appear to have evolved countermeasures to deter climbing by structural parasites (Janzen, 1966; Maier, 1982; Putz *et al.*, 1984; Putz and Holbrook, 1986; Rich *et al.*, 1987; Hegarty, 1991; Givnish, 1992).

Janzen (1973), Putz *et al.* (1984), and Putz and Holbrook (1986) argued that ant bodyguards can remove or destroy vines growing on their hosts in tropical forests; Janzen (1966, 1973) provided detailed observations showing that this actually happens in *Acacia* and *Cecropia*. Putz *et al.* (1984) suggested that large compound leaves may help to shed vines when they are discarded; Maier (1982) and Rich *et al.* (1987) presented evidence that supports this view. Several additional hypotheses regarding antivine defenses were reviewed by Hegarty (1991). Those for which there was at least some empirical support included (1) stems with fragile spines (Maier, 1982), (2) highly flexible stems (Putz, 1984b; Rich *et al.*, 1987), and (3) retention of dead leaves (Page and Browney, 1986).

It is interesting, however, that many of the trees in the eastern United States with exfoliating or unusually knobby bark [river birch (*Betula nigra*), shagbark hickory (*Carya ovata*), sweet gum (*Liquidambar styraciflua*), sycamore (*Platanus occidentalis*), swamp white oak (*Quercus bicolor*), and hackberry (*Celtis* spp.)] occur in mainly (or in the case of shagbark hickory, secondarily) in flood-plain forests, where vines are particularly prevalent. Givnish (1992) suggested that such bark may serve to shed vines by shedding their support points at frequent intervals, in analogy to the argument of Putz *et al.* (1984) regarding compound leaves. Sycamore is especially interesting in that it appears to shed its bark most frequently on the branches and upper one-third of its bole, in the sunlit portions that would be especially susceptible to invasion and overgrowth by wild grape (T. J. Givnish, personal observation).

There are two salient ecological questions regarding the interactions between structural parasites and self-supporting hosts that remain unresolved. These involve frequency dependence and host ascendancy. Clearly, the competitive advantage of vines should be frequency dependent, decreasing with the increasing abundance of vines vs hosts (Givnish, 1992). Such a relationship could be one of the most important factors setting the equilibrium abundance of vines and hosts, but such a relationship has yet to be studied experimentally.

In addition, it is not clear why dense stands of trees (or herbs) are not generally invaded by vines that grow slowly and are shade adapted when young, ascend the stems of their hosts en masse, and then become sun-adapted and expand rapidly when they reach the canopy. If such plasticity were to evolve in structural parasites, it could spell the doom of forests and of self-supporting plants generally; imagine the destructive capacity of a shade-tolerant kudzu (*Pueraria*) or banana-poka (*Passiflora*)! Perhaps such a doomsday scenario is implausible for some as yet unknown physiological reason, or perhaps such scenarios are regularly enacted, but the destructive potential of the parasite burns out the local supply of hosts and, hence, its own population. Hairston *et al.* (1960) asked, "Why is the earth green?" If we can now answer this question, on the basis of our improved understanding of plant–herbivore interactions, perhaps we should ask the parallel question (whose answer would require a more thorough understanding of host–vine interactions than we now possess): "Why are green plants tall and self-supporting?" While several of the considerations raised in this chapter (see Sections III,A–D) clearly explain why competition favors tall plants, the issue of the competitive and evolutionary balance between vines and hosts leaves a tantalizing paradox to be resolved.

Finally, the competitive balance between self-supporting plants and structural parasites may be shifting. Phillips and Gentry (1994) report that the rates of the death and replacement of individual trees in tropical forests have accelerated in the last few decades. Elevated levels of CO_2 greatly enhance the photosynthesis and growth of vines, as expected from their high area-specific stem conductivity (see Sperry [5] in this volume) and low allocation to stem tissue at a given height to length: Condon *et al.* (1992) found that a three-fold increase in CO_2 concentration to 1000 ppm created up to a 78% increase in photosynthesis and a 710% increase in height growth by two cucurbitaceous vines. Phillips and Gentry (1994) propose that such dramatic increases in vine growth, together with the tree-killing capabilities of many tropical lianas, may be responsible for the observed increase in tree turnover, and may presage even greater tree death in tropical forests in the future as global atmospheric levels of CO_2 continue to rise.

IV. Conclusion and Coda

Stem biomechanics and resource allocation are important but often overlooked factors in determining trends in the composition, structure, dynamics, and productivity of plant communities. Mechanical stability, safety, photosynthetic efficiency, and impact on whole-plant growth and competitive ability are the most important constraints on the optimal pattern of allocation to support tissue, and create a series of trade-offs with context-dependent benefits and costs. Superior competitors can be excluded by mechanically stressful environments that favor safe but short or slow-growing species, which are in turn excluded by faster growing species in less frequently or violently disturbed habitats. Safe but slow-growing trees with relatively massive allocation to stem tissue (as a result of greater wood density, or greater diameter at a given height) are at a disadvantage early in succession, but outlive faster growing pioneers; they dominate later in succession by virtue of their greater resistance to large, infrequent mechanical stresses and/or chronic attacks by predators of support tissue, such as termites and fungi.

The balance of growth and biomechanical efficiency is a pivotal determinant of plant stature, with key implications for the maximum height of trees and herbs, the location of tree lines, the stratification of forests, and the zonation of aquatic vegetation. Tall plants are competitively dominant but have a higher energetic "overhead," excluding them from unproductive and/or frequently disturbed habitats; short plants allocate relatively little to support and have a competitive advantage in sparse vegetation where they are unlikely to be overtopped. Wood has a higher initial cost than herbaceous parenchyma, but is retained as part of a permanent support skeleton, yielding an energetic advantage in plants more than about 0.5 m tall. Stature and woodiness have a far larger impact on shade tolerance than leaf-level photosynthetic adaptations, with profound ramifications for forest stratification. The pattern of allocation between tree crown and bole that maximizes height growth has important implications for crown width-to-height ratios in closed forests and, hence, for tree density, the dynamics of self-thinning, and (ultimately) forest productivity.

The balance between mechanical and photosynthetic efficiency helps determine patterns of leaf arrangement, leaf shape, and branching angles. Orthotropic (erect) axes with spiral phyllotaxis are favored in sunny sites, whereas plagiotropic (horizontal) axes with distichous phyllotaxis are favored in shadier environments. Stem branching angles minimize leaf overlap and support costs. Shade-adapted plants have an alternate, distichous leaf arrangement (or approach it through anisophylly) that minimizes the uncovered area near branches; asymmetric leaf bases occupy space near the branch even more efficiently, and are frequent in plagiotropic species of extreme shade.

Finally, the balance of the benefits and disadvantages of structural parasitism helps set trends in the relative abundance of vines vs self-supporting hosts. Vines are common in productive but frequently disturbed habitats, particularly in the tropics; their susceptibility to cavitation (due to the volume of their large-bore, highly efficient vessels) in environments with frequent freeze-thaw cycles, and their special vulnerability to fire (due to their slender stem diameters) may restrict their abundance elsewhere. Tendril-climbing vines can ascend the most slender hosts; twining vines, thicker hosts; and vines with adhesive roots, the thickest hosts. Self-supporting plants in habitats with a high frequency of vines show a variety of defenses against structural parasites, including ant bodyguards, compound leaves, retention of dead leaves, and exfoliating bark. However, it is not yet clear what sets the ecological and evolutionary balance between self-supporting plants and structural parasites, and it is possible that rising levels of atmospheric CO_2 are altering the competitive balance in favor of vines, at least in tropical forests.

What could be termed *biomechanical ecology*—the study of how the form, mechanical properties, and growth dynamics of the support skeleton of an organism influence its ability to survive and compete in different environments—promises to be as productive an area of intellectual inquiry in plant ecology in the 1980s and 1990s as physiological ecology has been in the 1960s, 1970s, and 1980s. Publications on the biomechanical ecology of terrestrial plants (many of which are reviewed in this chapter) have burgeoned in the last 10 years. These parallel a rich and growing tradition of insightful studies on the biomechanical ecology of sessile marine organisms (e.g., Koehl and Wainwright, 1977; Vogel, 1977; Branch and Marsh, 1978; Tunnicliffe, 1981; Sebens, 1982; Denny *et al.*, 1985, 1989; Koehl, 1986; Denny, 1988; Koehl and Alberte, 1988; Holbrook *et al.*, 1991; Sebens and Johnson, 1991), with which terrestrial plant ecologists should become familiar. Future developments in biomechanical ecology will undoubtedly involve several of the general topics discussed in this chapter, as well as some that have been little examined [e.g., adaptations for "aggressive" mechanical competition, such as the "flailing" of opponents by highly flexible sea palms (Paine, 1979), or the generation of forces by forest herbs to penetrate leaf litter (Campbell *et al.*, 1992)]. One feature, however, that is likely to remain a hallmark of the most innovative studies is a focus on the context specificity of the benefits and costs associated with particular traits, and the role this context specificity plays in determining species distributions. Context specificity is the key feature that distinguishes biomechanical ecology from pure biomechanics, and allows insights derived from functional morphology and biomechanics to illuminate ecological and evolutionary issues.

Acknowledgments

This research was supported in part by NSF Grant DEB-9107379. I thank Kenneth Systma, who provided helpful comments on a preliminary draft.

References

Balee, W., and Campbell, D. (1989). Evidence for the successional status of liana forest (Xingu River Basin, Amazonian Brazil). *Biotropica* **22,** 36–47.

Bassow, S. L., and Ford, E. D. (1990). A process-based model of carbon translocation in trees: An exploration of the branch autonomy theory. *Silva Carelica* **15,** 77–87.

Beccari, O. (1902). "Nelle Foreste di Borneo." Florence, Italy.

Beccari, O. (1904). "Wanderings in the Great Forests of Borneo." London.

Bliss, L. G. (1982). Alpine. *In* "Physiological Ecology of North American Plant Communities" (B. F. Chabot and H. A. Mooney, eds.), pp. 41–65. Chapman & Hall, New York.

Bongers, F., Engelen, D., and Klinge, H. (1985). Phytomass structure of natural plant communities on spodosols in southern Venezuela: The bana woodland. *Vegetatio* **63,** 13–34.

Branch, G. M., and Marsh, A. C. (1978). Tenacity and shell shape in six *Patella* species: Adaptive features. *J. Exp. Mar. Biol. Ecol.* **34,** 111–130.

Brooks, J. R., Hinckley, T. M., Ford, E. D., and Sprugel, D. G. (1991). Foliage and dark respiration in *Abies amabilis:* Variation within the canopy. *Tree Physiol.* **9,** 325–338.

Brunig, E. F. (1976). Tree forms in relation to environmental conditions: An ecological viewpoint. *In* "Tree Physiology and Yield Improvement" (M. G. R. Cannell and F. T. Last, eds.), pp. 139–156. Academic Press, London.

Bultman, J. D., and Southwell, C. R. (1976). Natural resistance of tropical American woods to terrestrial wood-destroying organisms. *Biotropica* **8,** 71–95.

Büsgen, M., and Münsch, E. (1929). "The Structure and Life of Forest Trees." John Wiley & Sons, New York.

Campbell, B. D., Grime, J. P., and Mackey, J. M. L. (1992). Shoot thrust and its role in plant competition. *J. Ecol.* **80,** 633–641.

Cannell, M. G. R., and Morgan, J. (1989). Branch breakage under snow and ice loads. *Tree Physiol.* **5,** 307–317.

Carlquist, S. (1965). "Island Life." Natural History Press, New York.

Carlquist, S. (1970). "Hawaii: A Natural History." Natural History Press, New York.

Carlquist, S. (1991). Anatomy of vine and liana stems: A review and synthesis. *In* "The Biology of Vines" (F. E. Putz and H. A. Mooney, eds.), pp. 53–71. Cambridge University Press, Cambridge.

Chapin, F. S., III, and G. R. Shaver. (1982). Arctic. *In* "Physiological Ecology of North American Plant Communities" (B. F. Chabot and H. A. Mooney, eds.), pp. 16–40. Chapman & Hall, New York.

Chazdon, R. L. (1986). Light variation and carbon gain in an understory palm. *J. Ecol.* **74,** 995–1012.

Chazdon, R. L. (1991). Plant size and form in the understory palm genus *Geonoma:* Are species variations on a theme? *Am. J. Bot.* **78,** 680–694.

Condon, M. A., Sasek, T. W., and Strain, B. R. (1992). Allocation patterns in two tropical vines in response to increase atmospheric CO_2. *Funct. Ecol.* **6,** 680–685.

Cowan, I. R. (1986). Economics of carbon fixation in higher plants. *In* "On the Economy of Plant Form and Function" (T. J. Givnish, ed.), pp. 133–170. Cambridge University Press, New York.

Curtis, J. T. (1959). "The Vegetation of Wisconsin." University of Wisconsin Press, Madison, Wisconsin.

Dacey, J. W. H. (1981). Pressurized ventilation in the yellow waterlily. *Ecology* **62,** 1137–1147.

Davidson, C. G., and Remphrey, W. R. (1990). An analysis of architectural parameters of male and female *Fraxinus pensylvanica* in relation to crown shape and crown location. *Can. J. Bot.* **68,** 2035–2043.

Denny, M. W. (1988). "Biology and the Mechanics of the Wave-swept Environment." Princeton University Press, Princeton, New Jersey.

Denny, M. W., Daniel, T. L., and Koehl, M. A. R. (1985). Mechanical limits to size in wave-swept organisms. *Ecol. Monogr.* **55,** 69–102.

Denny, M. W., Brown, V., Carrington, E., Kraemer, G., and Miller, A. (1989). Fracture mechanics and the survival of wave-swept macroalgae. *J. Exp. Mar. Biol. Ecol.* **127,** 211–228.

de Reffye, P., Dinouard, P., and Barthélemy, D. (1991). L'arbre—biologie et developpement.

In "Modélisation et Simulation de l'Architecture de l'orme du Japon *Zelkova serrata* (Thunb.) Makino (Ulmaceae): La Notion d'Axe de Reférénce" (C. Edelin, ed.), pp. 251–266. Naturalia Monspeliensia 1991, Suppl. Ser. A7. Université Montpellier II, Montpellier, France.

Ewers, F. W., Fisher, J. B., and Fichtner, K. (1991). Water flux and xylem structure in vines. *In* "The Biology of Vines," (F. E. Putz and H. A. Mooney, eds.), pp. 127–160. Cambridge University Press, Cambridge.

Featherly, H. I. (1941). The effect of grapevines on trees. *Okla. Acad. Sci. Proc.* **21**, 61–62.

Fisher, J. B. (1992). How predictive are computer simulations of tree architecture? *Int. J. Plant Sci.* **153**, S137–S146.

Fisher, J. B., and Ewers, F. W. (1991). Structural responses to stem injury in vines. *In* "The Biology of Vines" (F. E. Putz and H. A. Mooney, eds.), pp. 99–124. Cambridge University Press, Cambridge.

Fisher, J. B., and Hibbs, D. E. (1982). Plasticity of tree architecture: Specific and ecological variations found in Aubréville's model. *Am. J. Bot.* **69**, 690–702.

Fisher, J. B., and Honda, H. (1979a). Branch geometry and effective leaf area: A study of *Terminalia catappa*. I. Theoretical trees. *Am. J. Bot.* **66**, 633–644.

Fisher, J. B., and Honda, H. (1979b). Branch geometry and effective leaf area: A study of *Terminalia catappa*. II. Survey of real trees. *Am. J. Bot.* **66**, 645–655.

Ford, E. D., Avery, A., and Ford, R. (1990). Simulation of branch growth in the Pinaceae: Interactions of morphology, phenology, foliage productivity, and the requirement for structural support, on the export of carbon. *J. Theor. Biol.* **146**, 15–36.

Gartner, B. L. (1988). Functional morphology and architecture in conspecific lianas and shrubs. *Bull. Ecol. Soc. Am.* **69**, 142.

Gartner, B. L. (1991a). Structural stability and architecture of vines vs. shrubs of poison oak, *Toxicodendron diversilobum*. *Ecology* **72**, 2005–2015.

Gartner, B. L. (1991b). Relative growth rates of vines and shrubs of western poison oak, *Toxicodendron diversilobum* (Anacardiaceae). *Am. J. Bot.* **78**, 1345–1353.

Gartner, B. L., Bullock, S. H., Mooney, H. A., Brown, V. B., and Whitbeck, J. L. (1990). Water transport properties of vine and tree stems in a tropical deciduous forest. *Am. J. Bot.* **77**, 742–749.

Gaudet, C. L., and Keddy, P. A. (1988). A comparative approach to predicting competitive ability from plant traits. *Nature* (London) **334**, 242–243.

Gentry, A. H. (1983). Lianas and the "paradox" of contrasting latitudinal gradients in wood and litter production. *Trop. Ecol.* **24**, 63–67.

Gentry, A. H. (1991). The distribution and evolution of climbing plants. *In* "The Biology of Vines" (F. E. Putz and H. A. Mooney, eds.), pp. 3–49. Cambridge University Press, Cambridge.

Givnish, T. J. (1978). On the adaptive significance of compound leaves, with particular reference to tropical trees. *In* "Tropical Trees as Living Systems" (P. B. Tomlinson and M. H. Zimmermann, eds.), pp. 351–380. Cambridge University Press, Cambridge.

Givnish, T. J. (1979). On the adaptive significance of leaf form. *In* "Topics in Plant Population Biology" (O. T. Solbrig, P. H. Raven, S. Jain, and G. B. Johnson, eds.), pp. 375–407. Columbia University Press, New York.

Givnish, T. J. (1982). On the adaptive significance of leaf height in forest herbs. *Am. Nat.* **120**, 353–381.

Givnish, T. J. (1984). Leaf and canopy adaptations in tropical forests. *In* "Physiological Ecology of Plants of the Wet Tropics" (E. Medina, H. A. Mooney, and C. Vasquez-Yánes, eds.), pp. 51–84. Dr. Junk, The Hague, the Netherlands.

Givnish, T. J. (1986a). Economics of support. *In* "On the Economy of Plant Form and Function" (T. J. Givnish, ed.), pp. 413–420 Cambridge University Press, Cambridge.

Givnish, T. J. (1986b). Biomechanical constraints on crown geometry in forest herbs. *In* "On the Economy of Plant Form and Function" (T. J. Givnish, ed.), pp. 525–583. Cambridge University Press, Cambridge.

Givnish, T. J. (1986c). Biomechanical constraints on self-thinning in plant populations. *J. Theor. Biol.* **119**, 139–146.

Givnish, T. J. (1986d). On the use of optimality arguments. *In* "On the Economy of Plant Form and Function" (T. J. Givnish, ed.), pp. 3–9. Cambridge University Press, Cambridge.

Givnish, T. J. (1987). Comparative studies of leaf form: Assessing the relative roles of selection pressures and phylogenetic constraints. *New Phytol.* **106** (Suppl.), 131–160.

Givnish, T. J. (1988). Adaptation to sun vs. shade: A whole-plant perspective. *Aust. J. Plant Physiol.* **15**, 63–92.

Givnish, T. J. (1992). Nature green in leaf and tendril. *Science* **256**, 1339–1341.

Givnish, T. J. (1995). Manuscript in preparation.

Givnish, T. J., McDiarmid, R. W., and Buck, W. R. (1986). Fire adaptation in *Neblinaria celiae* (Theaceae), a high-elevation rosette shrub endemic to a wet equatorial tepui. *Oecologia* **70**, 481–485.

Givnish, T. J., Sytsma, K. J., Smith, J. F., and Hahn, W. S. (1995). Molecular evolution, adaptive radiation, and geographic speciation in the largest endemic genus of Hawaiian plants, *Cyanea* (Campanulaceae: Lobelioideae). *In* "Hawaiian Biogeography: Evolution on a Hot Spot Archipelago" (W. L. Wagner and V. Funk, ed.), pp. 288–337. Smithsonian Institution Press, Washington, D.C.

Grace, J. (1987). Climatic tolerance and the distribution of plants. *New Phytol.* **106** (Suppl.), 113–130.

Green, P. D. (1992). Pattern formation in shoots—a likely role for minimal energy configuration of the tunica. *Int. J. Plant Sci.* **153**, S59–S75.

Greenhill, A. G. (1881). Determination of the greatest height consistent with stability that a vertical pole or mast can be made, and of the greatest height to which a tree of given proportions can grow. *Proc. Cambridge Philos. Soc.* **4**, 65–73.

Grime, P. J., Crick, J. C., and Rincon, J. E. (1986). The ecological significance of plasticity. *In* "Plasticity in Plants" (D. H. Jennings and A. Trewavas, eds.). Society for Experimental Biology Symposium, No. 40, pp. 5–29, Cambridge University Press, Cambridge.

Grubb, P. J. (1984). Some growth points in investigative plant ecology. *In* "Trends in Ecological Research in the 1980's" (J. H. Cooley and F. B. Golley, eds.), pp. 51–74. Plenum Press, New York.

Grubb, P. J. (1986). Problems posed by sparse and patchily distributed species in species-rich plant communities. *In* "Community Ecology" (J. Diamond and T. J. Case, eds.), pp. 207–225. Harper & Row, New York.

Gysel, L. W. (1951). Borders and openings of beech-maple woodlands in southern Michigan. *J. For.* **49**, 13–19.

Hadley, J. L., and Smith, W. K. (1987). Influence of krummholz mat microclimate on needle physiology and survival. *Oecologia* **73**, 82–90.

Hairston, N. G., Smith, F. E., and Slobodkin, L. B. (1960). Community structure, population control, and competition. *Am. Nat.* **94**, 421–425.

Hallé, F., Oldeman, R. A. A., and Tomlinson, P. B. (1978). "Tropical Trees and Forests: An Architectural Analysis." Springer-Verlag, Berlin.

Hegarty, E. E. (1991). Vine-host interactions. *In* "The Biology of Vines" (F. E. Putz and H. A. Mooney, eds.), pp. 357–375. Cambridge University Press, Cambridge.

Hegarty, E. E., and Caballé, G. (1991). Distribution and abundance of vines in forest communities. *In* "The Biology of Vines" (F. E. Putz and H. A. Mooney, eds.), pp. 313–335. Cambridge University Press, Cambridge.

Holbrook, N. M., Denny, M. W., and Koehl, M. A. R. (1991). Intertidal trees—consequences of aggregation on the mechanical and photosynthetic properties of sea palms (*Postelsia palmae-formis* Ruprecht). *J. Exp. Mar. Biol. Ecol.* **146**, 39–67.

Honda, H., and Fisher, J. B. (1978). Tree branch angle: Maximizing effective leaf area. *Science* **199**, 888–890.

Horn, H. S. (1971). "The Adaptive Geometry of Trees." Princeton University Press, Princeton, New Jersey.

Hueck, K. (1981). Vegetationskarte von Sudamerika: Mapa de la Vegetacíon de America del Sur. G. Fischer, Stuttgart, Germany.

Hutchinson, G. E. (1975). "A Treatise on Limnology," Vol. III. Limnological Botany. John Wiley & Sons, New York.

Janzen, D. H. (1966). Coevolution of mutualism between ants and acacias in Central America. *Evolution* **20**, 249–275.

Janzen, D. H. (1973). Dissolution of mutualism between *Cecropia* and its *Azteca* ants. *Biotropica* **5**, 15–28.

Johnson, E. A. (1991). The relative importance of snow avalanche disturbance and thinning on canopy plant populations. *Ecology* **68**, 43–53.

Keddy, P. A. (1990). Competitive hierarchies and centrifugal organization in plant communities. *In* "Perspectives on Plant Competition" (J. B. Grace and D. Tilman, eds.), pp. 265–290. Academic Press, New York.

King, D. A. (1981). Tree dimensions: Maximizing the rate of height growth in dense stands. *Oecologia* **51**, 351–356.

King, D. A. (1986). Tree form: Height growth, and susceptibility to wind damage in *Acer saccharum. Ecology* **67**, 980–990.

King, D. A. (1987). Load bearing capacity of understory treelets of a tropical wet forest. *Bull. Torrey Bot. Club* **114**, 419–428.

King, D. A. (1990). The adaptive significance of tree height. *Am. Nat.* **135**, 809–828.

King, D. A. (1991). The allometry of trees in temperate and tropical forests. *Res. Explor.* **7**, 342–351.

King, D. A., and Loucks, O. L. (1978). The theory of tree bole and branch form. *Radiat. Environ. Biophys.* **15**, 141–165.

Kira, T., and Ogawa, H. (1971). Assessment of primary productivity in tropical and equatorial forests. *In* "Productivity in Forest Ecosystems: Proceedings of Brussels Symposium 1969" (P. Duvigneaud, ed.), pp. 309–321. UNESCO, Paris.

Knoll, A. H. (1984). Patterns of extinction in fossil record of vascular plants. *In* "Extinctions" (M. Nitecki, ed.), pp. 21–67. University of Chicago Press, Chicago.

Koehl, M. A. R. (1986). Seaweeds in moving water: Form and mechanical function. *In* "On the Economy of Plant Form and Function" (T. J. Givnish, ed.), pp. 603–634. Cambridge University Press, Cambridge.

Koehl, M. A. R., and Alberte, R. S.. (1988). Flow, flapping, and photosynthesis of *Nereocystis luetkana:* A functional comparison of undulate and flat blade morphologies. *Mar. Biol.* **99**, 435–444.

Koehl, M. A. R., and Wainwright, S. A. (1977). Mechanical adaptations of a giant kelp. *Limnol. Oceanogr.* **22**, 1067–1071.

Kuuluvainen, T. (1992). Tree architectures adapted to efficient light utilization: Is there a basis for latitudinal gradients? *Oikos* **65**, 275–284.

LaBarbara, M. (1986). The evolution and ecology of body size. *In* "Patterns and Processes in the History of Life" (D. M. Raup and D. Jablonski, eds.), pp. 69–98. Springer-Verlag, Berlin.

Leigh, E. G., Jr. (1972). The golden section and spiral leaf arrangement. *In* "Growth by Intussusception" (E. S. Deevey, ed.), pp. 161–176. Archon Press, Hamden, Connecticut.

Leigh, E. G., Jr. (1990). Tree shape and leaf arrangement: A quantitative comparison of montane forests, with emphasis on Malaysia and south India. *In* "Conservation in Developing

Countries: Problems and Prospects" (J. C. Daniel and J. S. Serrao, eds.), pp. 119–174. Oxford University Press, Bombay, India.

Long, J. N., Smith, F. W., and Scott, D. R. M. (1981). The role of Douglas fir stem sapwood and heartwood in the mechanical and physiological support of crowns and development of stem form. *Can. J. For. Res.* **11**, 459–464.

Lutz, H. J. (1943). Injuries to trees caused by *Celastrus* and *Vitis. Bull. Torrey Bot. Club* **70**, 436–439.

Maier, F. E. (1982). Effects of physical defenses on vines and epiphyte growth in palms. *Trop. Ecol.* **23**, 212–217.

Makälä, A. (1985). Differential games in evolutionary theory: Height growth strategies of trees. *Theor. Popul. Biol.* **27**, 239–267.

McMahon, T. A. (1973). Size and shape in biology. *Science* **179**, 1201–1204.

McMahon, T. A., and Bonner, J. T. (1983). "On Size and Life." W. H. Freeman & Co., New York.

McMahon, T. A., and Kronauer, R. E. (1976). Tree structures: Deducing the principle of mechanical design. *J. Theor. Biol.* **59**, 443–466.

Meinzer, F., and Goldstein, G. (1986). Adaptations for water and thermal balance in Andean giant rosette plants. *In* "On the Economy of Plant Form and Function" (T. J. Givnish, ed.), pp. 381–411. Cambridge University Press, Cambridge.

Menges, E. R. (1987). Biomass allocation and geometry of the clonal forest herb *Laportea canadensis:* Adaptive responses to the environment or allometric constraints? *Am. J. Bot.* **74**, 551–563.

Merrill, E. D. (1945). "Plant Life of the Pacific World." Macmillan, New York.

Mooney, H. A., and Gulmon, S. L. (1979). Environmental and evolutionary constraints on the photosynthetic characteristics of higher plants. *In* "Topics in Plant Population Biology" (O. T. Solbrig, S. Jain, G. B. Johnson, and P. H. Raven, eds.), pp. 316–337. Columbia University Press, New York.

Morgan, J., and Cannell, M. G. R. (1988). Support costs of different branch designs: Effects of position, number, angle, and deflection of laterals. *Tree Physiol.* **4**, 303–313.

Niklas, K. (1986). Computer-simulated plant evolution. *Sci. Am.* **254** (3), 78–86.

Niklas, K. J. (1992). "Plant Biomechanics." University of Chicago Press, Chicago.

Niklas, K. J. (1993a). The scaling of plant height —a comparison among major plant clades and anatomical grades. *Ann. Bot.* **72**, 165–172.

Niklas, K. J. (1993b). Influence of tissue density-specific mechanical properties on the scaling of plant height. *Ann. Bot.* **72**, 173–179.

Niklas, K., and Kerschner, V. (1984). Mechanical and photosynthetic constraints on the evolution of plant shape. *Paleobiology* **10**, 79–101.

Norberg, R. Å. (1988). Theory of growth geometry of plants and self-thinning of plant populations: Geometric similarity, elastic similarity, and different growth modes of plant parts. *Am. Nat.* **131**, 220–256.

Ogawa, H., Yoda, K., Ogino, I., and Kira, T. (1965). Comparative ecological studies on three main types of forest vegetation in Thailand. II. Plant biomass. *Nature Life South-East Asia* **4**, 49–80.

O'Neill, R. V., and DeAngelis, D. L. (1981). *In* "Dynamic Properties of Forest Ecosystems" (D. E. Reichle, ed.), pp. 411–449. Cambridge University Press, Cambridge.

Orians, G. H., and Solbrig, O. T. (1977). A cost-income model of leaves and roots with special reference to arid and semiarid areas. *Am. Nat.* **111**, 677–690.

Osawa, A., and Allen, R. B. (1993). Allometric theory explains self-thinning relationships of mountain beech and red pine. *Ecology* **74**, 1020–1032.

Page, C. N., and Browney, P. J. (1986). Tree fern skirts: A defence against climbers and large epiphytes. *J. Ecol.* **74**, 787–796.

Paine, R. T. (1979). Disaster, catastrophe, and local persistence of the sea palm *Postelsia palmaeformis. Science* **207**, 685–687.

Paltridge, G. W. (1973). On the shape of trees. *J. Theor. Biol.* **38**, 111–137.

Peterson, J. A., Benson, J. A., Ngai, M., Morin, J., and Ow, C. (1982). Scaling in tensile "skeletons": Structures with scale-independent length dimensions. *Science* **217**, 1267–1270.

Phillips, O. L., and Gentry, A. H. (1994). Increasing turnover through time in tropical forests. *Science* **263**, 954–959.

Proctor, J., Anderson, J., Chai, P., and Vallack, H. (1983). Ecological studies in four contrasting lowland rain forests in Gunung Mulu National Park, Sarawak. I. Forest environment, structure, and floristics. *J. Ecol.* **71**, 237–260.

Putz, F. E. (1983). Liana biomass and leaf area of a "tierra firme" forest in the Rio Negro basin, Venezuela. *Biotropica* **15**, 185–189.

Putz, F. E. (1984a). Natural history of lianas on Barro Colorado Island, Panama. *Ecology* **65**, 1713–1724.

Putz, F. E. (1984b). How trees avoid and shed lianas. *Biotropica* **16**, 19–23.

Putz, F. E. 1991. Silvicultural effects of lianas. *In* "The Biology of Vines" (F. E. Putz and H. A. Mooney, eds.), pp. 493–501. Cambridge University Press, Cambridge.

Putz, F. E., and Chai, P. (1987). Ecological studies of lianas in Lambir National Park, Sarawak, Malaysia. *J. Ecol.* **75**, 523–531.

Putz, F. E., and Holbrook, N. M. (1986). Notes on the natural history of hemiepiphytes. *Selbyana* **9**, 61–69.

Putz, F. E., and Holbrook, N. M. (1991). Biomechanical studies of vines. *In* "The Biology of Vines" (F. E. Putz and H. A. Mooney, eds.), pp. 73–97. Cambridge University Press, Cambridge.

Putz, F. E., and Mooney, H. A., eds. (1991). "The Biology of Vines." Cambridge University Press, Cambridge.

Putz, F. E., Coley, P. D., Lu, K., Montalvo, A., and Aiello, A. (1983). Uprooting and snapping of trees: Structural determinants and ecological consequences. *Can. J. For. Res.* **13**, 1011–1020.

Putz, F. E., Lee, H. S., and Goh, R. (1984). Effects of post-felling silvicultural practices on woody vines in Sarawak. *Malays. For.* **47**, 214–226.

Raven, J. A. (1986). Evolution of plant life forms. *In* "On the Economy of Plant Form and Function" (T. J. Givnish, ed.), pp. 421–492. Cambridge University Press, Cambridge.

Reich, P. B. (1993). Reconciling apparent discrepancies among studies relating life span, structure and function of leaves in contrasting plant life forms and climates: "The blind men and the elephant" retold. *Funct. Ecol.* **7**, 721–725.

Reich, P. B., Walters, M. B., and Ellsworth, D. S. (1992). Leaf life-span in relation to leaf, plant, and stand characteristics among diverse ecosystems. *Ecol. Monogr.* **62**, 365–392.

Remphrey, W. R., and Davidson, C. G. (1991). Crown shape variation in *Fraxinus pensylvanica* (Vahl) Fern.: Its relation to architectural parameters including the effect of shoot-tip abortion. *In* "L'Arbre—Biologie et Developppment" (C. Edelin, ed.), pp. 169–180. Naturalia Monspeliensia 1991, Suppl. Ser. A7. Université Montpellier II, Montpellier, France.

Rich, P. M. (1987). Developmental anatomy of the stem of *Welfia georgii, Iriartea gigantea,* and other arborescent palms: Implications for mechanical support. *Am. J. Bot.* **74**, 792–802.

Rich, P. M., Lum, S., Muñoz, E. L., and Quesada, A. M. (1987). Shedding of vines by the palms *Welfia georgii* and *Iriartea gigantea.Principes* **31**, 31–40.

Richards, J. H., and Bliss, L. C. (1986). Winter water relations of a deciduous timberline conifer, *Larix lyalli* Parl. *Oecologia* **69**, 16–24.

Ridley, H. N. (1893). On the flora of the eastern coast of the Malay Peninsula. *Trans. Linn. Soc. Bot.* **3**, 267–408.

Rundel, P. W., and Franklin, T. (1991). Vines in arid and semi-arid ecosystems. *In* "The Biology of Vines" (F. E. Putz and H. A. Mooney, eds.), pp. 337–356. Cambridge University Press, Cambridge.

Schultz, H. R., and Matthews, M. A. (1993). Xylem development and hydraulic conductance in sun and shade shoots of grapevine (*Vitis vinifera* L.)—evidence that low light uncouples water transport capacity from leaf area. *Planta* **190**, 393–406.

Schulze, E.-D. (1982). Plant life forms and their carbon, water, and nutrient relations. *In*, "Encyclopedia of Plant Physiology" (O. L. Lange, P. S. Nobel, C. B. Osmond, and H. Ziegler, eds.), New Series, vol. 12A, pp. 615–676. Springer-Verlag, Berlin.

Sculthorpe, C. D. (1967). "The Biology of Aquatic Vascular Plants." Edward Arnold, London.

Sebens, K. P. (1982). The limits to indeterminate growth: An optimal size model applied to passive suspension feeders. *Ecology* **63**, 209–222.

Sebens, K. P., and Johnson, A. S. (1991). Effects of water movement on prey capture and distribution of reef corals. *Hydrobiology* **226**, 91–101.

Singer, R., D. A. Roberts, and Boylen, C. W. (1983). The macrophytic community of an acidic lake in Adirondack (New York, U.S.A.): A new depth record for aquatic angiosperms. *Aq. Bot.* **16**, 49–57.

Snedecor, G. W., and Cochran, W. G. (1989). "Statistical Methods," 8th Ed. Iowa State University Press, Ames, Iowa.

Spence, D. H. N. (1982). The zonation of plants in freshwater lakes. *Adv. Ecol. Res.* **12**, 37–126.

Sprugel, D. G. (1976). Dynamic structure of wave-regenerated *Abies balsamea* forest in the northeastern United States. *J. Ecol.* **64**, 889–912.

Sprugel, D. G. (1984). Density, biomass, productivity, and nutrient-cycling changes during stand development in wave-regenerated balsam fir forests. *Ecol. Monogr.* **54**, 165–186.

Sprugel, D. G. (1989). The relationship of evergreenness, crown architecture, and leaf size. *Am. Nat.* **133**, 465–479.

Sprugel, D. G., and Bormann, F. H. (1981). Natural disturbance and the steady state in high-altitude balsam fir forests. *Science* **211**, 390–393.

Sprugel, D. G., Hinckley, T. M., and Schaap, W. (1991). The theory and practice of branch autonomy. *Annu. Rev. Ecol. Syst.* **22**, 309–334.

Stevens, G. C. (1987). Lianas as structural parasites: The *Bursera simaruba* example. *Ecology* **68**, 77–81.

Sufling, R. (1993). Induction of vertical zones in subalpine valley forests by avalanche-formed fuel breaks. *Landscape Ecol.* **8**, 127–138.

Terborgh, J. (1985). The vertical component of plant species diversity in temperate and tropical forests. *Am. Nat.* **126**, 760–776.

Tiffney, B. H. (1981). Diversity and major events in the evolution of land plants. *In* "Paleobotany, Paleoecology, and Evolution" (K. J. Niklas, ed.), Vol. 2, pp. 193–230. Praeger, New York.

Tilman, D. (1986). Evolution and differentiation in terrestrial plant communities: The importance of the soil resource:light gradient. *In* "Community Ecology" (J. Diamond and T. J. Case, eds.), pp. 359–380. Harper & Row, New York.

Tilman, D. (1988). "Resource Competition and Community Structure." Princeton University Press, Princeton, New Jersey.

Tomlinson, P. B. (1986). "The Botany of Mangroves." Cambridge University Press, New York.

Tranquillini, W. (1979). "Physiological Ecology of the Alpine Timberline." Springer-Verlag, Berlin.

Tunnicliffe, V. (1981). Breakage and propagation of the stony coral *Acropora cervicornis*. *Proc. Natl. Acad. Sci. U.S.A.* **78**, 2427–2431.

van Steenis, C. G. G. J. (1967). Autonomous evolution in plants. *Gard. Bull. Sing.* **29**, 103–126.

van Steenis, C. G. G. J. (1981). "Rheophytes of the World: An Account of the Flood-Resistant Flowering Plants and Ferns and the Theory of Autonomous Evolution." Sijthoff and Noordhoof, Alphen aan den Rijn, the Netherlands.

Vogel, S. (1977). Current-induced flow through living sponges in nature. *Proc. Natl. Acad. Sci. U.S.A.* **74**, 2069–2071.

Vogel, S. (1981). "Life in Moving Fluids." Willard Grant Press, Boston.

Wainwright, S. A., Briggs, W. D., Currey, J. D., and Gosline, J. M. (1976). "Mechanical Design in Organisms." Edward Arnold, London.

Waller, D. M., and Steingraeber, D. A. (1985). Branching and modular growth: Theoretical models and empirical patterns. *In* "Population Biology and Evolution of Clonal Organisms" (J. B. C. Jackson, L. W. Buss, and R. E. Cook, eds.), pp. 225–257. Yale University Press, New Haven, Connecticut.

Walter, H. (1973). "Vegetation of the Earth," 2nd Ed. Springer-Verlag, Berlin.

Waring, R. H., and Franklin, J. F. (1979). Evergreen coniferous forests of the Pacific Northwest. *Science* **204**, 1380–1386.

Weller, D. E. (1989). The interspecific size-density relationship among crowded plant stands and its implications for the $-3/2$ power rule of self-thinning. *Am. Nat.* **133**, 20–41.

Wetzel, R. G. (1983). "Limnology," 2nd Ed. W. B. Saunders, Philadelphia, Pennsylvania.

Whitmore, T. C. (1984). "Tropical Rain Forests of the Far East," 2nd Ed. Oxford University Press, Oxford.

Whittaker, R. H. (1956). Vegetation of the Great Smoky Mountains. *Ecol. Monogr.* **26**, 1–80.

Whittaker, R. H., and Woodwell, G. M. (1968). Dimension and production: Relations of trees and shrubs in the Brookhaven Forest, New York. *Ecology* **56**, 1–25.

Whittaker, R. H., Cohen, N., and Olson, J. S. (1963). Net production relations of three tree species at Oak Ridge, Tennessee. *Ecology* **44**, 806–810.

Williams, K., Percival, F., Merino, J., and Mooney, H. A. (1987). Estimation of tissue construction cost from heat of combustion and organic nitrogen content. *Plant Cell Environ.* **10**, 725–734.

Williams, K., Field, C. B., and Mooney, H. A. (1989). Relationships among leaf construction cost, leaf longevity and light environment in rainforest plants of the genus *Piper. Am. Nat.* **133**, 198–211.

Yoder, B. J., Ryan, M. G., Waring, R. H., Schoettle, A. W., and Kaufmann, M. R. (1994). Evidence of reduced photosynthetic rate in old trees. *For. Sci.* **40**, 513–527.

2

Opportunities and Constraints in the Placement of Flowers and Fruits

Donald M. Waller and David A. Steingraeber

I. Introduction

Plant stems create the scaffold on which flowers and fruits must be distributed. Both passive agents of pollination and dispersal (e.g., wind) and active animal pollinators and dispersers will tend to favor flowers and fruits in some locations over those elsewhere. This immediately creates a selective environment that can be expected to have strongly modified patterns of flower placement and phenology. Such selection may also influence plant architecture via stem growth and placement. Stems are, after all, only a seed's way of producing more seeds.

While most biologists agree that it would be naive to expect flowers or fruit to be distributed randomly on or along plant stems, few have inquired into how plant architecture may have been modified to serve reproductive rather than photosynthetic ends. Ecological assessments of plant form have instead tended to treat plants as vegetative bodies composed only of roots, stems, and leaves. Such analyses typically approach their problem as one of optimally allocating root, stem, and leaf tissue to the functions of supply, transport, and leaf display for photosynthesis (see Givnish [1] in this volume, and Givnish, 1986). While such approaches may suffice to analyze immature stages of plant growth, they neglect possible opportunities or constraints influencing plant structure via the need to reproduce successfully. In effect, they view flowers and fruit as accessories placed on the vegetative lattice, like Christmas ornaments on a tree.

Conversely, those interested in plant reproductive ecology have tended to ignore plant structure and the details regarding how flowers and fruits are attached to plant stems. Those researching reproductive ecology assume that natural selection modifies floral and fruit characteristics mainly in response to external environmental factors, that is, pollination and dispersal vectors, local biotic and abiotic circumstances, and the ultimate genetic consequences of inbreeding and outbreeding. While this work has ranged widely to address sexual selection, functional gender, mate choice, and mating system variation (Lloyd, 1976; Stephenson, 1981; Stephenson and Bertin, 1983; Willson and Burley, 1983; Marshall and Folsom, 1991), its preoccupation with external factors has tended to obscure the roles played by internal structural and physiological factors. Any complete understanding of plant reproduction must also include some understanding of how plant form, stem structure, and physiological supply influence pollinator attraction, pollinator movement, interfruit competition, and fruit dispersal.

In this chapter, we consider how stem placement and growth affect flowering and fruiting and vice versa. What opportunities do stems and trunks provide for the placement of flowers and fruit? Are flowers and fruits placed optimally to achieve high rates of pollination and dispersal, or does their placement reflect the constraints of structural support and physiological supply? How do developing flowers and fruits, in turn, influence stem growth and placement?

We first assess the opportunities that stems and trunks provide for placing flowers and fruits within the plant body, reviewing how the success of pollination, fruit set, and dispersal can vary over various positions within the plant. We then describe how structural and physiological costs may constrain flower and fruit placement and the size that reproductive structures can attain. Our goal is to explore how internal and external constraints interact to influence the placement of flowers or fruits. While the work reviewed here is sufficient to dispel the belief that plant stems and reproductive structures are autonomous, we need further work to explore just how plant structure influences and constrains patterns of plant reproduction. We therefore conclude by discussing how further research could help elucidate how vegetative and reproductive growth interact. Throughout this chapter, we use the terms "flowers" and "fruits" in the broad sense to refer to the structures bearing ovules and seeds in both angiosperms and gymnosperms.

II. Adaptive Opportunities in Flower and Fruit Placement

Stems and trunks provide three services to the flowers and fruits they support: structural support, vascular supply via phloem and xylem, and a competitive crown with which to compete with neighboring plants. Because natural selection favors traits that increase the number of ovules fertilized, we expect flowers to be produced at a time and in a location and quantity that makes them accessible to wind or their animal pollinators. Similarly, we expect seeds and the fruits encasing them to be produced at times and places that make them available to their dispersal agents. Furthermore, while making their flowers and fruits available to pollinators and dispersers, we expect plants to protect these structures from mechanical damage and potential seed predators.

These expectations reflect the adaptive paradigm used to frame hypotheses in evolutionary biology. Maximizing fitness should not be expected to maximize each trait that contributes to fitness, however. Rather, evolutionists attempt to analyze the web of correlations and trade-offs that constrain patterns of stem growth, branching, flowering, and fruiting within the context set by patterns of heritability and life history theory. Simplistic analyses of either plant architecture or reproductive patterns run the risk of ignoring important interactions that occur between the vegetative and reproductive structures of plants. In contrast, comprehensive evolutionary analyses should attempt to assess how both vegetative and reproductive traits contribute to overall reproductive success. Such studies typically confront the trade-offs that usually exist between growth and reproduction. Most simply, we may choose to analyze the trade-offs between growth and reproduction via techniques commonly used in allocation studies. Alternatively, one could extend the analysis to consider the detailed effects of plant structure such as stem placement or stem size (see Section VII). In Section II,A–E we lay out the many conspicuous external factors that favor placing flowers and fruit into particular locations.

A. Access to Sunlight

Because sinks generally draw on the nearest sources, flowers and developing seeds draw photosynthate mostly from nearby leaves. Such local patterns of supply imply that reproductive structures located in the upper canopy, adjacent to highly productive leaves, will generally enjoy greater rates of photosynthate supply than those borne lower within the crown (assuming there is no compensatory increase in flower density in such locations). We therefore could expect higher flowers adjacent to sunlit leaves and their seeds and fruits to grow faster, to a larger size, and with more success than reproductive structures located elsewhere in the plant. In contrast, we expect that more shaded flowers or those located at some distance from productive leaves to develop more slowly or be less capable of setting seed. As a consequence, we expect selection to have favored patterns of development that concentrate flowers in more sunlit canopy positions.

As gardeners well know, it is the case in many species that flowering is controlled by levels of irradiance (Lyndon, 1992). This pattern is particularly conspicuous in common herbaceous plants of the forest understory, such as *Aster macrophyllus,* where flowers are rare except in gaps. Other shrubs and herbs also tend to flower in the more sunlit locations or to cluster their flowers in more sunlit portions within their canopy. Similarly, most trees wait to flower until they reach the canopy and typically flower or fruit most abundantly on their uppermost branches. While it is tempting to interpret these patterns in physiological terms, they could also reflect the fact that such locations often favor pollination (see the next section).

Flowers located in exposed canopy locations may also produce more or larger seeds relative to shaded flowers (e.g., Janzen, 1977). In the woodland annual, *Impatiens capensis,* capsules higher in the canopy and closer to the main stem produce larger seeds (Waller, 1982). Because larger seeds enjoy higher fitness as seedlings, such positional effects on seed size and number could strongly favor placing flowers in sunnier locations.

B. Access to Wind for Pollination and Dispersal

We expect male flowers in wind-pollinated species to be placed in high and exposed locations to better disperse their pollen. In this context, leaves and stems represent impediments that by decreasing wind velocity interfere with effective pollen dispersal. Thus, it is not surprising that many conifers (e.g., *Abies balsamifera* and *Pinus banksiana*) rely on erect or pendant ovulate cones to capture pollen at some distance from twigs and dense foliage. The terminal flowering spikes of rushes, sedges, grasses, and cattails also serve to elevate wind-pollinated flowers above leaves and the slower moving air currents associated with the boundary layer next to the ground. The protruding exserted anthers of most wind-pollinated species provide further access to the wind and may be structurally designed to facilitate agitation in turbulent air currents.

Wind pollination can be further enhanced in deciduous species if flowering occurs before leaf-out or after leaf fall. Amentiferous catkins in many deciduous trees appear early in spring at a time of frequent gusty winds and before leaf-out (e.g., *Betula, Corylus, Carya, Fagus,* and *Quercus*). For wind pollination to work efficiently in these species, a dense cloud of pollen must be produced to ensure reasonable pollination success. Thus, it is not surprising that wind pollination is associated with flowering synchrony, high plant density, and correspondingly low species diversity. These trends reach their acme with the monocarpic bamboos, which grow in dense populations for decades before flowering synchronously and setting massive numbers of seeds (Janzen, 1976).

Once wind-borne pollen has been dispersed, it must reach a receptive stigma to succeed. Thus, we expect female flowers in such species also to occur in locations that expose them to air currents. The stems and foliage of a plant could play an important role if they enhance local eddies and updrafts or otherwise modify air currents so as to enhance pollen deposition onto their stigmas. For example, in *Simmondsia* (jojoba), leaves arranged above the branch may create vortices that help direct pollen onto the ovulate flowers dangling below (Niklas and Buchmann, 1985). Niklas (1984, 1985) has also proposed that ovulate cones modify local air currents so as to precipitate airborne pollen from the air onto their stigmas and even that ovulate cones in *Pinus* are constructed so as to preferentially precipitate pollen of their own species.

The subsequent dispersal of seeds or fruit by wind should also favor locating female flowers in high and exposed locations. Plants releasing windborne seeds and fruit usually do place flowers in locations accessible to the wind, as in the pendant infructescences of cottonwood (*Populus*). Erect stems on many herbs and the culms on graminoids clearly serve to elevate the seeds above the boundary layer of air near the ground, extending their dispersal range. In acaulous rosette species such as *Tragopogon*, *Taraxacum*, and *Cypripedium acaule*, stems serve primarily to enhance dispersal and may even elongate after flowering. Greater dispersal enhances fitness by allowing colonization of distant sites, decreasing sibling competition, and allowing some escape from seed predators (Janzen, 1969, 1971; Howe and VanderKerckhove, 1980; Wright, 1983) or diseases (Gilbert *et al.*, 1994).

Fruit shape, winged appendages, and asymmetry also clearly contribute to dispersal potential (Augspurger, 1986). It would be interesting in this context to explore how particular fruit structures perform when they encounter plant canopies. For example, when spinning samaras hit leaves or twigs that interrupt their rotation, they often drop vertically for some distance before regaining their rotation (McCutchen, 1977; Green, 1980). Perhaps certain designs of wind-dispersed seed perform better within forest canopies, or particular types of crowns, than others.

C. Access to Animal Pollinators and Dispersers

Animal pollinators and dispersers can be expected to discriminate among flowers (inflorescences) and fruits (infructescences) within and among plants in accord with principles of optimal foraging theory (Waddington, 1979; Pyke, 1981). We should therefore expect first that plants will tend to place flowers and fruits where they are most likely to be visited. Second, we might expect plants to place flowers where they are likely to receive pollen that enhances the genetic quality of their offspring and to place fruits where they are likely to receive high-quality dispersal (i.e., to appropriate "safe sites").

Animal pollinators and dispersers do appear to respond to many aspects of flower and fruit size, aggregation, location, and concentration (Howe and Smallwood, 1982; Howe and Westley, 1988). As expected, bees tend to favor large clumps of flowers with correspondingly large rewards (Heinrich, 1979; Schmitt, 1983; Denslow, 1987). Toucans and other bird species visiting nutmeg trees (*Virola surinamensis*) are sensitive to both fruit size (removing fewer of the larger fruits) and fruit quality (favoring fruits with a higher proportion of edible aril; Howe and VanderKerckhove, 1980). Birds may also favor fruits that are longer and skinnier (Mazer and Wheelwright, 1993). More than 60% of the fruits in the Australian shrub, *Telopea speciosissima*, were derived from flowers in the top third of the inflorescence, apparently due to better pollinator visitation rather than better vascular supply (Goldingay and Whelan, 1993). If heavy pollinators and dispersers tended to favor sturdy perches consistently, selection may have favored the placement of flowers and fruits along stout branches or even the trunk, providing a possible explanation for cauliflory (van der Pijl, 1972; Faegri and van der Pijl, 1979; Jacobs, 1988).

Aerial pollinators and fruit dispersers are also more likely to notice flowers and fruit located away from nearby stems and leaves. They may also find it easier to approach such structures without hitting branches with their wings. In such cases, we might expect flowers or fruits to be placed above or below layers of foliage via erect or pendant pedicels or peduncles. This may help to explain why so many short-statured woodland herbs arrange their flowers and fruits either terminally (e.g., *Maianthemum canadense*, *Trillium erectum* and *T. grandiflorum*, *Cypripedium*, and *Smilacina racemosa*) or dangle them beneath their leaves (e.g., *Polygonatum* and *Trillium cernuum*). Fruit dispersers also appear to respond sensitively to fruit spacing (Levey *et al.*, 1984). Where specialized pollinators or dispersers favor larger and more conspicuous aggregations of flowers or fruit, there may be selection for synchronous and massive displays. These tendencies reach extremes in certain species of *Agave* (Schaffer and Schaffer, 1979) and palms (Tomlinson and Soderholm, 1975), in which selection by animal pollinators appears to have favored both the monocarpic life history and the construction of giant stems supporting a massive inflorescence.

Many animal-pollinated trees and shrubs produce flowers or inflorescences suspended away from their foliage, making them both more conspicuous and reducing the likelihood that winged pollinators would collide with woody branches. Seasonally deciduous animal-pollinated tropical trees often flower during the dry season when they lack leaves, enhancing animal access to their flowers [e.g., *Tabebuia ochracea* (Gentry, 1983) and *Ceiba pentandra* (Baker, 1983)]. In bat-pollinated tropical trees such as *Ceiba*, *Pseudobombax*, *Kigelia pinnata* (sausage tree), and *Adansonia digitata* (baobab), the large, short-lived, white or drab-colored flowers unfold at dusk and are suspended accessibly on stems above or below the branches. In a survey of the bird-dispersed genus *Coprosma* in New Zealand, Lee *et al.* (1994) noted considerable color variation among fruit over the 33 species. Interestingly, larger leaved species exhibited the most conspicuous contrast between fruit and foliage. Such an association might reflect either the greater likelihood of larger leaves hiding fruit or the correlation one might expect given that larger leaves produce shadier conditions that reduce contrast.

Aside from this work on the conspicuous effects of flower and fruit placement, we encountered only a few studies investigating how stem location or the details of inflorescence architecture influence reproductive success. Work with *Asclepias,* however, suggests that inflorescence architecture and flower position can directly affect patterns of pollination and fruit set (Wyatt, 1982). It would be interesting to assess gradients of selection in such systems (see Section VII).

D. Protection from Flower and Seed Predators

Structures that enhance dispersal by making fruit more accessible to frugivores may simultaneously increase the chance that these seeds will be taken by seed predators. Thus, the arrangement of flowers on stems may sometimes have more to do with making flowers or fruit less, rather than more, accessible. Seed and fruit predators take a great toll of the total reproductive output in many plant species and often appear capable of even greater depredations except for the existence of particular defense mechanisms (Janzen, 1971; DeSteven, 1983; Benkman *et al.,* 1984; Hainsworth *et al.,* 1984; Menges *et al.,* 1986). Under such circumstances, selection may even favor reduced rates of dispersal if doing so effectively increases fruit survival. Denslow and Moermond used captive tanagers and manakins to evaluate the quantitative nature of this trade-off in experiments with neotropical bird-dispersed fruit (Denslow and Moermond, 1982; Moermond and Denslow, 1983). By titrating the proximity of berry clusters against fruit preferences they demonstrated that fruit preferences could be overridden by making the nonpreferred berries more accessible. They also noted that actual patterns of berry placement are often inconvenient for frugivores, presumably reflecting selection exerted by seed predators.

The extrafloral nectaries found in many, particularly tropical, species have been interpreted as defensive in that the ants typically attracted to the nectaries patrol the plant and remove or kill larvae and other insects that may threaten flowers or developing fruits in addition to vegetative structures (Bentley, 1977; Bentley and Elias, 1983). For instance, ants visiting sepal-surface nectaries in *Ipomoea leptophylla* significantly decrease damage to flowers by grasshoppers, as well as seed losses caused by bruchid beetles (Keeler, 1980). In some cases, postflowering activity of floral nectaries can similarly attract ants whose presence significantly enhances seed set (Keeler, 1981). Likewise, the sticky stems of *Tofieldia glutinosa* may serve to slow or trap potential flower or fruit predators. The thick husk that envelops many nuts, or the astringent or poisonous substances in many fruits or seed coats (e.g., cyanide in apple seeds and almonds), are even more conspicuous examples of the need to protect vulnerable plant embryos.

Fruits placed at the tips of slender branches or on the ends of elongate peduncles become less accessible, particularly to heavier bodied terrestrial animals that may also be reluctant to venture out to exposed locations that might increase the risk of predation. Presumably, their avian dispersers are less discouraged, although they may still be inconvenienced. In such cases, the construction costs of producing elongate stems might be repaid by the increase in seed dispersal they could ensure. Stems may also serve directly to protect fruit. In the New Zealand divaricate shrub, *Melicytus alpinus,* fruit are hidden beneath low branches, making them less conspicuous, in this case to destructive avian predators, while they remain accessible to lizard dispersers (Webb and Kelly, 1993). Some inflorescence architectures may be less vulnerable to predation than others. Where such protection is ineffective, we expect infructescence structure simply to accelerate rates of fruit dispersal.

E. Gambits to Improve the Genetic Quality of Offspring

Many aspects of the placement of flowers along stems appear to represent adaptations not just to ensure successful pollination, but also to minimize self-fertilization or to facilitate crossing with other plants. Pollination biologists have studied the spatial and sequential patterns of flower presentation in many species to document the many diverse and often subtle ways in which such patterns increase the efficiency of pollination or reduce selfing (Faegri and van der Pijl, 1979; Real, 1983; Weiss, 1991). Inflorescence architecture, patterns of flower development, and the distribution of nectar rewards often function together to enhance pollen transfer (Weberling, 1989). Even when genetic self-incompatibility mechanisms are present, many plants benefit from these tactics by enhancing pollen export, intercepting more foreign pollen, and/or preventing the clogging of their own stigmas with selfed pollen. Despite the complexity of these effects, pollination biologists have now begun to dissect the contributions of inflorescence architecture within this context (Wyatt, 1982).

III. Functional Constraints on Reproduction

Stems provide both a lattice from which to hang flowers and fruits and the vascular system that supplies these organs with the resources they require. For trees and other plants whose stems ramify to fill space and support leaves through a dispersed crown, this lattice provides differing conditions for flower placement. Plants with fewer stems or more constrained patterns of growth present a more restricted set of opportunities. In Section III,A–C, we consider some of the principal functional (physiological) constraints on reproduction imposed by plant stems.

A. Plant Life Histories and the Overall Allocation of Resources

Perhaps the most basic constraint that potentially limits the production of flowers and fruits is the primary tenet of resource allocation: limited materials allocated to one structure or process are unavailable for other, competing uses. Most analyses of life history center on the fundamental trade-offs thought to exist between such competing demands within organisms, for example, sexual reproduction vs somatic growth, current reproduction vs survival, or current vs future reproduction (Cole, 1954; MacArthur and Wilson, 1967; Pianka, 1976; Horn, 1978; Stearns, 1992). Stearns (1992) claims that the best-confirmed fundamental phenotypic trade-off relevant to life history theory is the one between reproduction and growth. When juveniles must compete closely among themselves or with larger neighbors, we expect natural selection to favor juvenile traits that augment growth and immediate survival rather than early reproduction ("K-selection"). We therefore expect seedlings of perennials to allocate their limited resources exclusively to vegetative structures that would help them to attain a secure position. Even simple optimality models of annual life histories predict that plants should allocate resources exclusively to vegetative growth before initiating reproduction (Cohen, 1971, 1976). Evolutionary biologists further expect patterns of growth and reproduction to depend on the behavior of surrounding plants. Thus, it is not surprising that the mean height of herbaceous plants increases in more productive locations where the density of potential competitors increases, as game theory would predict (Givnish, 1982).

In spite of the widespread acceptance that a fundamental trade-off exists between reproduction and somatic growth, there are questions regarding the general applicability of this trade-off to plants (Bazzaz and Reekie, 1985; Reekie and Bazzaz, 1987c). Reproductive structures are often green and photosynthetic, and therefore capable of supplying a significant fraction of their total energetic and carbon costs (Bazzaz *et al.,* 1979; Reekie and Bazzaz, 1987a). When reproductive structures carry out photosynthesis, they clearly benefit from exposure to adequate levels of light (see Section II,A). There is a further difficulty in assessing just which structures and activities constitute the reproductive effort of a plant: in addition to the production of flowering and fruiting structures, reproduction also involves the production of additional stem material, as well as the photosynthetic gain and respiratory loss of carbon from these structures. Furthermore, allocation of resources to reproduction can result in an increase in the photosynthetic rates of vegetative parts due to increased sink strength of the reproductive structures (Reekie and Bazzaz, 1987a; Reekie and Reekie,

1991). Realistic assessments of reproductive effort in plants should include measures or estimates of all of these components, and simple measures of biomass allocation are insufficient to represent the actual allocation of carbon to reproductive effort (Reekie and Bazzaz, 1987a). An additional problem is the determination of the proper "currency" of allocation to be used. For the concept of resource allocation to be meaningfully applied, some resource(s) must be in limited supply. On the basis of experiments with *Agropyron repens*, Reekie and Bazzaz (1987b) suggest that total carbon is the most appropriate currency, because carbon integrates the allocation patterns of other resources and carbon allocation tends to be biased toward the most limiting resources. Experiments with *A. repens* (Reekie and Bazzaz, 1987a,c) and *Oenothera biennis* (Reekie and Reekie, 1991) indicate that reproduction does not necessarily result in decreased vegetative growth as long as the resources allocated to reproduction are small relative to the total resource base of the plant.

The ultimate currency with which to measure life history trade-offs is that of evolutionary fitness (successful reproduction). Any trait can be evaluated in these terms by measuring the partial correlation between it and a suitable index of overall fitness (the basis for phenotypic selection analysis; see Section VII). Trade-offs among somatic and reproductive characters are represented in the (usually negative) genetic correlations between them. Such approaches capture, better than energetic analyses, the lost opportunity costs involved with reproduction. To avoid the time and expense of estimating genetic correlations directly, it may be reasonable in ecological studies to substitute partial phenotypic correlations between the traits, controlling for the effects of plant size. Clearly, detailed examination of a wider range of species will help us determine more fully the nature and extent of the potential trade-off between reproduction and growth in plants.

B. When Do Stems and Foliage Interfere with Flowers or Fruit?

When flowers and fruits are produced and displayed in close proximity to stems and foliage, there is the potential for the vegetative structures to interfere with and constrain pollination and/or dispersal. As discussed previously, positioning of flowers and fruits away from foliage, or producing flowers and fruits when leaves are absent, often increases the efficiency of pollination or dispersal by either wind (Section II,B) or animals (Section II,C). In instances in which seeds are dispersed by ballistic release from fruits, nearby foliage can intercept the seeds and thereby limit dispersal distances. In many plants, the ballistic fruits are positioned so that such interference is minimized (Ridley, 1930; van der Pijl, 1972). For instance, in *Ricinus communis* (castor oil plant), fruits are held on semierect peduncles at the top of the plant, with the fruits at an angle of 45° to the horizon.

In the case of *Hevea brasiliensis* (para rubber), the fruits hang downward from branches, and seeds can be dispersed as far as 40 yards away when they are ejected from a fruit (Ridley, 1930).

Many tropical trees exhibit flagelliflory, in which the flowers and/or fruits are suspended away from the foliage on long peduncles. In most such cases, the plants are either pollinated or dispersed (or both) by bats, and the pendant position of the flowers or fruits allows the bats easy access. Conversely, if flowers and fruits are in close proximity to foliage, especially in the distal regions of the shoot where stems are smaller in diameter and, hence, mechanically weaker (see Section IV,B below), the activity of bats and other large-bodied pollinators and dispersers will be severely impeded.

C. Vascular Constraints on Supply

Because resources are transported to flowers and fruits via the vascular tissues (xylem and phloem), the distribution and functional capabilities of these tissues could potentially constrain reproduction. In general, the pedicels and peduncles of reproductive structures are well vascularized, and high rates of translocation often occur in their phloem (Crafts and Crisp, 1971). Flowers and fruits generally act as strong sinks; consequently, pathways of connection (via phloem) between reproductive structures and their carbohydrate sources are likely to be of primary importance in determining the supply of resources normally available to flowers and fruits.

There has been a growing realization over the past decade that patterns of carbon transport are not uniformly integrated among all parts of the plant. Rather, portions of plants often function as semiautonomous "integrated physiological units," or IPUs (Watson and Casper, 1984; Watson, 1986), especially during the growing season (Sprugel *et al.,* 1991). The localized patterns of resource supply and movement that characterize IPUs are the result of specific anatomical patterns of connection among the individual vascular bundles within the plant. Nearby structures, especially those in the same orthostichy or longitudinal series along a stem (e.g., a leaf and its associated axillary bud, branch, or reproductive structure), usually maintain close vascular connection, because their vascular bundles insert into the same bundle or portion of vascular tissues in the stem. If relatively discrete vascular bundles are maintained longitudinally within the stem, sectorial restriction of carbon transport can result.

The localized restriction of carbon transport within IPUs highlights the importance of positional relationships between reproductive structures and their carbon sources. Flowers and fruits located closer to the stem often receive more resources than do structures more distal (Watson and Casper, 1984), resulting in higher seed set or seed mass in the more proximal fruits (Maun and Cavers, 1971; Wyatt, 1982; Stanton, 1984; Nichols, 1987). Furthermore, the sources supplying the majority of carbon to reproductive structures are usually the nearest leaves. For instance, Flinn and Pate (1970) found that the majority of carbon in seeds of *Pisum arvense* was supplied from the adjacent leaf and its stipules, and that a substantial part of the remainder was supplied by photosynthesis within the fruit itself, primarily by refixing internal CO_2 produced in seed respiration. The localized nature of carbon supply to flowers and fruits also suggests that these structures will often respond sensitively to local circumstances or disturbances. Localized defoliation has been shown to decrease the mass of nearby reproductive structures in some species (Tuomi *et al.*, 1988, 1989; Marquis, 1991). In other instances, however, defoliation of individual branches does not reduce fruit production on the branch, suggesting that the fruits are being supplied either by stores within the stem or by other branches (Obeso and Grubb, 1993). Nonetheless, it is clear that plants often are functionally segmented into largely separate IPUs, which can severely constrain the carbon sources normally available to support reproduction.

IV. Biomechanical Factors Influencing the Placement of Flowers and Fruits

In addition to supplying resources to reproductive structures, stems also function in mechanically supporting flowers and fruits. The tissues most often involved in providing such support are the vascular tissues, xylem and phloem, which function simultaneously in resource supply and mechanical support (see Gartner [6] in this volume for further discussion of these trade-offs). More specifically, cells in these tissues with thick, secondary walls (vessel members, tracheids, and fibers in xylem; fibers in phloem), along with sclerenchymatous ground tissue, provide the majority of this support. In Section IV,A–C, we examine the role of stems in providing biomechanical support for reproductive structures.

A. How Can Support Costs Be Minimized?

Because the cells with thickened walls that function in support are costly to produce, a rather obvious way that support costs can be reduced is by reducing the size of supporting pedicels and peduncles, especially if the mass of flowers and fruits to be supported is small. This suggests that compaction, reduction, and branching of inflorescences, such as in spikes, umbels, cymes, racemes, and their compound forms, provide efficient structural support to smaller flowers and fruits. A second, equally obvious way in which support costs can be reduced is by using other structures or a supportive medium such as water (as in floating aquatics like *Nelumbo*) for support. Vines that trail along the ground, such as many members of the Cucurbitaceae (pumpkins, squashes, and gourds), simply place their massive fruits on the ground, obviating the need for stems to provide support.

B. How Do Stems Support Great Expansions in Fruit Mass?

Many fruits increase greatly in mass as they develop, resulting in ever-increasing loads on supporting structures. In many instances, the distalmost stems and twigs of a shoot, which are slender and have not undergone significant secondary growth, may be too weak to provide adequate support for large fruits. In such cases, the number and sizes of fruits produced along shoots may be constrained, or reproductive structures may be confined to nonelongating stems (short shoots) that insert on older and more thickened stems, as is seen in *Ginkgo* and many fruiting trees (e.g., apple, pear, cherry, peach, and plum).

As fruits increase in mass, it becomes increasingly difficult to support them in an upright position, and fruits generally become pendant under the load of their mass. Pendant fruits and infructescences must therefore be supported by their pedicels and peduncles, which act as support cables as well as supply conduits. In some cases, such as *Mangifera* (mango) and *Musa* (banana), inflorescences may initially be fairly erect before bending as the load increases. If pendant fruits rotate or twist, as when buffeted by wind, the supporting stems are subjected to torsional moments in addition to the tensile stresses (Peterson *et al.*, 1982).

C. How Should Stems Supporting Flowers and Fruits Be Designed?

We might expect that pedicels and peduncles will exhibit structural features that facilitate the simultaneous functional demands of supply and support discussed above. These stems should be well vascularized and capable of increasing the amounts of vascular tissues present as fruits grow in size and the concomitant supply and support demands increase. As fruits grow and become pendant, the supporting stems should respond by producing tissues with high tensile strength. Ideally, the stems would exhibit developmental flexibility such that they sense the increasing structural load and add new tissues in response to the magnitude of the load. In this regard, Niklas (1992, p. 49) discusses the early work of Vöchting, who found that the pedicels of squash fruits suspended from a trellis contained significantly more vascular tissue than did pedicels of comparable fruits produced on the ground. We would also expect that the supportive tissues produced (xylem, phloem, and sclerenchyma) would be arranged in anatomical patterns that allow some flexibility and rotation while maintaining functional integrity for both support and supply. The functional anatomy of pedicels and peduncles would appear to be a fruitful topic for additional investigation.

The following assessment by Tomlinson (1990, p. 335) regarding palms seems applicable in a broader context:

> "The ability of the inflorescence axis to support large fruit loads depends on the distribution and efficiency of mechanical tissues. A knowledge of translocation efficiency into developing fruits depends on an understanding of phloem structure. . . . It is surprising that this aspect of palm structure is almost totally neglected."

V. Can Flower Placement Constrain Stem or Shoot Growth?

The placement of stems clearly constrains where flowers can and cannot appear within a plant. The converse, that particular patterns of placement of reproductive structures might constrain stem growth, seems inherently much less likely. Although we expect vegetative and reproductive growth to draw on a common and limited pool of photosynthetic resources, this represents only an overall, quantitative constraint on stem growth. Yet it is also the case that flowers and shoots both derive from meristems, which might themselves be a limiting resource in some situations. In such cases, differentiation of a floral bud or inflorescence axis could represent an irretrievable commitment of resources restricting the potential for stem growth (at least in that part of the plant).

Although trade-offs between vegetative and reproductive growth are evident in many plants, only a few studies, mostly of herbaceous plants, demonstrate internal competition for meristems. In the annual *Floerkia proserpinacoides,* for example, plants typically produce axillary shoots from their basal nodes, then switch to producing flowers at some point. Those plants that switch to producing flowers on earlier nodes produce more fruit sooner, but do not grow as large, or produce as many total fruit, as plants that sustain their vegetative growth longer (Smith, 1984). Meristems devoted to flowers in water hyacinth (*Eichhornia crassipes*) (Watson, 1984) and *Polygonum arenastrum* (Geber, 1990) also appear to limit the potential for vegetative growth. Several reviews consider the question of meristem limitation and the associated idea that some plants may be divided up into more or less autonomous "integrated physiological units" (see Section III,C), within which meristem competition could often be important (Watson and Casper, 1984; Diggle, 1992; Marshall and Watson, 1992).

One case in which we would expect flowers to interfere directly with stem growth is when flowers/inflorescences are terminal, terminating shoot growth along that axis. Such limitation is conspicuously evident in monoaxial plants such as the palms, which typically support only a single terminal meristem. Monocarpic flowering in *Corypha elata* ends a prolonged period of vegetative growth in an extraordinary burst of flowering and fruiting, producing an estimated 1×10^7 flowers and 2.5×10^5 fruit on 5.3 km of flower-bearing axes before the plant dies (Tomlinson and Soderholm, 1975). Where terminal flowers are side-stepped by new branches, however, such interference may be rare. In trees such as smooth sumac (*Rhus glabra*) with determinate shoot axes [such as in the architectural models of Leeu-wenberg or Troll (Hallé *et al.*, 1978)], terminal growth ceases whether or not an inflorescence is formed and an indeterminate and sometimes large number of daughter branches sprout along the previous year's growth. Because woody plants generally support many vegetative axes and an excess of buds, many of which normally remain dormant, they are unlikely to offer many cases in which flower placement severely constrains the potential for shoot growth.

VI. How Are Flower Types Influenced by Flower Placement?

Many plant species can produce more than one type of flower at a time, either via cleistogamy or by varying flower gender (Darwin, 1877). In all these cases, there appear to be regular patterns regarding which flowers are produced where (or when). We therefore explore these patterns in order to assess their adaptive value within the context established by the architecture of the plant.

A. Cleistogamous and Chasmogamous Flowers

Many species produce both cleistogamous (CL) flowers, which remain closed and are capable only of self-fertilization, and open, chasmogamous (CH) flowers capable of exchanging pollen with other individuals (Uphof, 1938; Lord, 1981). Cleistogamous flowers commonly appear in characteristic locations, such as at the base of spikes within the leaf sheath in many cleistogamous grasses (Campbell *et al.*, 1983). Botanists since Darwin have noted that CL flowers frequently appear more abundantly under conditions that can be described as adverse. In *Viola*, for example, CH flowers appear early in the spring when light and moisture are abundant whereas the CL flowers develop under the shadier and usually drier conditions of midsummer. In *Impatiens*, CH flowers develop on the top and periphery of larger plants in more sunlit locations, whereas CL flowers form abundantly in the axils of interior and lower branches and may be the only flowers produced on small plants (Waller, 1980). Short days seem to favor cleistogamy in *Collomia* (Lord, 1980). These regular patterns suggest that floral buds are programmed to respond to gradients in some physiological or hormonal cue within the plant.

In many CL plants, there appears to be a hierarchical pattern of reproductive investment with smaller or suppressed plants (or parts of plants) using cleistogamy as an assured means of reproduction under adverse growing conditions. The regular association of CH flowers with favorable growing conditions suggests that CL flowers could represent an adaptation to the slower rates of flower development in suppressed plants, or parts of plants (Waller, 1988). Because CL flowers develop faster and require fewer resources, they allow reproduction under circumstances when limited time or energy resources could otherwise prevent seed set.

B. Flowers in Amphicarpic Plants

Although less common than cleistogamy, amphicarpy, or the ability to produce subterranean seeds, may also represent a mechanism to assure reproduction in the face of particular environmental threats such as fire or seed predators. Typically, these underground seeds are much larger, germinate readily, and yield seedlings of high fitness (McNamara and Quinn, 1977). In producing such seeds, however, opportunities for cross-pollination and wide dispersal are clearly restricted.

Plants that produce subterranean seeds produce either aerial flowers capable of cross-fertilization, which then bury themselves to ripen seeds (e.g., *Arachis hypogaea,* the peanut) or subterranean flowers that must self-fertilize (e.g., hog peanut, *Amphicarpaea bracteata*). As in many CL plants, amphicarpic plants appear to express a rather strict hierarchy of reproductive investment. In hog peanut, for example, all plants invest first in subterranean CL flowers placed on cotyledary axils which act to replace the plant *in situ.* Subsequent resources are allocated next in additional subterranean CL flowers produced along the stem, then aerial CL flowers, and finally aerial CH flowers (Schnee and Waller, 1986). The result is that floral type depends critically on where within the stem system the floral bud lies and only the largest plants outcross.

C. Flower Gender and Position

As with cleistogamy, flower gender in monoeciou splants is often dependent on position within the plant and the influence of environmental variables, probably as mediated by plant hormones (Chaihkhyan and Khrianin, 1987). In many conifers, female cones tend to be produced at the top or periphery of the crown and above the male cones. Such displacement could be favored by selection either to reduce the amount of self-fertilization (Section II,E) or to produce female cones in the most productive part of the canopy (Section II,A). In lodgepole pine it appears that meristems with the least shading produce female cones, meristems with intermediate shading produce male cones, and those most shaded produce only needles (Smith, 1981). While such patterns appear to have adaptive value, they also make plants vulnerable to having their patterns of sexual allocation disrupted by herbivory (Whitham and Mopper, 1985; Allison, 1990). Sexual expression in many angiosperms also appears dependent on position within the plant or on external conditions (Bertin, 1982; Bertin and Newman,

1993). Striped maple (*Acer pensylvanicum*), a subcanopy tree, generally remains exclusively male until a gap occurs, bringing high light and a gender switch to female flowering and fruiting, followed by death (Hibbs and
Fischer, 1979).

Thus, we see that plant structure and postition of the bud within the
crown strongly influence patterns of reproductive allocation in many species. Meristems often respond sensitively to local variation in the internal
physiological and external environmental conditions within the plant by
varying their rate of growth and often the type of organ produced.

VII. Prospects for Further Research: Exploring Trade-Offs

We have seen that plants use stems to place their flowers and fruits into a
variety of locations in, above, and below their canopy, primarily in response
to the selection generated by their pollinators and dispersers. Scientists analyzing plant architecture have often ignored flowers and fruit, while those
analyzing reproductive strategies usually choose to ignore plant structure
and patterns of development. While stems serve as adaptive platforms for
flowers and fruits, they also constrain flower and fruit placement and success. The interplay of selective forces is sometimes obvious, but in other
cases it is difficult to discriminate among alternative explanations without
experiments or careful comparative work.

Many of these questions can be addressed by obtaining further empirical
data or straightforward experimentation. To address how differences in
flower type or seed and fruit size are generated, one could manipulate local
conditions within the plant by removing leaves or flower buds, shading, adding local light via fiber optics, adding hormones, or perhaps even molecular
genetic manipulations. As more of this work is done, it may also be possible
to follow the fate of the flowers and fruits thereby produced in order to
determine whether the observed patterns are adaptive. Similar experiments
might reveal whether particular patterns of flower and fruit presentation in
inflorescences and infructescences affect pollination and dispersal success.
Even without manipulating plants, it should often be possible to use naturally occurring variation to explore questions concerning how the success
of male and female flowers varies with respect to their position within mo-
noecious plants. Plants with their flowers or fruit in unusual locations, such
as on their trunks or below ground, may provide particularly provocative
cases for further experimental work.

As this work proceeds, we will also need to address questions regarding
the nature and extent of the trade-offs that may exist between stem characteristics and the many traits that contribute to successful flowering and
fruiting. In general, there are two approaches. Some adopt an engineering
approach, analyzing the direct and indirect costs and benefits of various

traits often in terms of structure or energy in lieu of the ultimate currency of successful reproduction (Givnish, 1986; Niklas, 1992). Such approaches can illuminate key aspects of plant structural design and often make explicit predictions that can be quantitatively tested. They also make the implicit assumption that selection can operate simultaneously on several different traits (termed "quasi-independence" by Lewontin, 1978). To better assess patterns of resource allocation within plants, it would be especially useful to have better estimates of the energetic costs of synthesizing various types of structural tissue and the costs of photosynthate transport, storage, and remobilization.

A second and more evolutionarily powerful approach to analyzing trade-offs among traits employs the tools of quantitative genetics. Under this approach, empirical measurements of genetic correlations among traits or responses to selection are substituted for assumptions of independence among traits and theoretical projections of how traits should interact. Under the classic model, partial regressions of fitness onto particular traits reveal the sign and intensity of selection on each trait, with the overall response to selection dependent on the variance–covariance structure among the traits (Lande, 1982; Lande and Arnold, 1983). Constraints acting to limit selection for any particular trait are reflected in the existence of negative genetic correlations between various traits, collectively comprising the genetic variance–covariance matrix. These correlations among traits reflect both overall energetic constraints as well as more fundamental structural and developmental constraints (including genetic correlations arising from associations among loci).

While intrinsically powerful, analyses of evolutionary response based on quantitative genetic relationships require considerable data and are correspondingly scarce. Nevertheless, it would be of great interest to use such approaches to investigate the exact nature of the trade-offs between particular patterns of flower placement and the associated costs of structural support. We could also ask the following: how evolutionarily labile (or constrained) are patterns of flower placement and fruit development? Is there some underlying structural or physiological factor that constrains seeds in some conifers and oaks to take 2 or 3 years to ripen? We could also use comparative data from related species to determine whether the genetic correlations we observe within species are maintained across species in a way that would suggest that they represent longer term, rather than local or short-term, evolutionary constraints.

References

Allison, T. D. (1990). The influence of deer browsing on the reproductive biology of Canada yew (*Taxus canadensis* Marsh.). II. Pollen limitation: An indirect effect. *Oecologia* **83**, 530–534.

Augspurger, C. K. (1986). Morphology and dispersal potential of wind-dispersed diaspores of neotropical trees. *Am. J. Bot.* **73,** 353–363.

Baker, H. G. (1983). *Ceiba pentandra* (kapok tree). *In* "Costa Rican Natural History" (D. H. Janzen, ed.), pp. 212–215. University of Chicago Press, Chicago.

Bazzaz, F. A., and Reekie, E. G. (1985). The meaning and measurement of reproductive effort in plants. *In* "Studies on Plant Demography: A Festschrift for John L. Harper" (J. White, ed.), pp. 373–387. Academic Press, London.

Bazzaz, F. A., Carlson, R. W., and Harper, J. L. (1979). Contributions to reproductive effort by photosynthesis of flowers and fruits. *Nature (London)* **279,** 554–555.

Benkman, C. W., Balda, R. P., and Smith, C. C. (1984). Adaptations for seed dispersal and the compromises due to seed predation in limber pine. *Ecology* **65,** 632–642.

Bentley, B. L. (1977). Extrafloral nectaries and protection by pugnacious bodyguards. *Annu. Rev. Ecol. Syst.* **8,** 407–427.

Bentley, B. L., and Elias, T. S., eds. (1983). "The Biology of Nectaries." Columbia University Press, New York.

Bertin, R. I. (1982). The ecology of sex expression in red buckeye. *Ecology* **63,** 445–456.

Bertin, R. I., and Newman, C. M. (1993). Dichogamy in angiosperms. *Bot. Rev.* **59,** 112–152.

Campbell, C. S., Quinn, J. A., Cheplick, G. P., and Bell, T. J. (1983). Cleistogamy in grasses. *Annu. Rev. Ecol. Syst.* **14,** 411–441.

Chaihkhyan, M. K., and Khrianin, V. N. (1987). "Sexuality in Plants and Its Hormonal Regulation." Springer-Verlag, Berlin.

Cohen, D. (1971). Maximizing final yield when growth is limited by time or limiting resources. *J. Theor. Biol.* **33,** 299–301.

Cohen, D. (1976). The optimal timing of reproduction. *Am. Nat.* 110, 801–807.

Cole, L. C. (1954). The population consequences of life history phenomena. *Q. Rev. Biol.* **29,** 103–137.

Crafts, A. S., and Crisp, C. E. (1971). "Phloem Transport in Plants." W. H. Freeman, San Francisco.

Darwin, C. (1877). "Different Forms of Flowers of Plants of the Same Species." J. Murray & Co., London.

Denslow, J. S. (1987). Fruit removal from aggregated and isolated bushes of the red elderberry, *Sambucus pubens. Can. J. Bot.* **65,** 1229–1235.

Denslow, J. S., and Moermond, T. C. (1982). The effect of accessibility on rates of fruit removal from tropical shrubs: An experimental study. *Oecologia* **54,** 170–176.

DeSteven, D.(1983). Reproductive consequences of insect seed predation in *Hamamelis virginiana. Ecology* **64,** 89–98.

Diggle, P. (1992). Development and the evolution of plant reproductive structures. *In* "Ecology and Evolution of Plant Reproduction" (R. Wyatt, ed.), pp. 326–355. Chapman & Hall, New York.

Faegri, K., and van der Pijl, L. (1979). "The Principles of Pollination Ecology." Pergamon Press, New York.

Flinn, A. M., and Pate, J. S. (1970). A quantitative study of carbon transfer from pod and subtending leaf to the ripening seeds of the field pea (*Pisum arvense* L.). *J. Exp. Bot.* **21,** 71–82.

Geber, M. (1990). The cost of meristem limitation in *Polygonum arenastrum:* Negative genetic correlations between fecundity and growth. *Evolution* **44,** 799–819.

Gentry, A. H. (1983). *Tabebuia ochracea* ssp. *neochrysantha. In* "Costa Rican Natural History" (D. H. Janzen, ed.), pp. 335–336. University of Chicago Press, Chicago.

Gilbert, G. S., Hubbell, S. P., and Foster, R. B. (1994). Density and distance-to-adult effects of a canker disease of trees in a moist tropical forest. *Oecologia* **98,** 100–108.

Givnish, T. J. (1982). On the adaptive significance of leaf height in forest herbs. *Am. Nat.* **120,** 353–381.

Givnish, T. J., ed. (1986). "On the Economy of Plant Form and Function." Cambridge University Press, Cambridge.

Goldingay, R. L., and Whelan, R. J. (1993). The influence of pollinators on fruit positioning in the Australian shrub *Telopea speciosissima* (Proteaceae). *Oikos* **68,** 501–509.

Green, D. S. (1980). The terminal velocity and dispersal of spinning samaras. *Am. J. Bot.* **67,** 1218–1224.

Hainsworth, F. R., Wolf, L. L., and Mercier, T. (1984). Pollination and pre-dispersal seed predation: Net effect on reproduction and inflorescence characteristics in *Ipomopsis aggregata*. *Oecologia* **63,** 405–409.

Hallé, F., Oldemann, R. A. A., and Tomlinson, P. B. (1978). "Tropical Trees and Forests: An Architectural Analysis." Springer-Verlag, Berlin.

Heinrich, B. (1979). "Bumblebee Economics." Harvard University Press, Cambridge, Massachusetts.

Hibbs, D. E., and Fischer, B. C. (1979). Sexual and vegetative reproduction of striped maple (*Acer pensylvanicum*). *Bull. Torrey Bot. Club* **106,** 222–227.

Horn, H. S. (1978). Optimal tactics of reproduction and life history. *In* "Behavioural Ecology: An Evolutionary Approach" (J. R. Krebs and N. B. Davies, eds.), 1st Ed., pp. 411–429. Blackwell Scientific Publications, Oxford.

Howe, H. F., and Smallwood, J. (1982). Ecology of seed dispersal. *Annu. Rev. Ecol. Syst.* **13,** 201–228.

Howe, H. F., and VanderKerckhove, G. A. (1980). Nutmeg dispersal by tropical birds. *Science* **210,** 925–926.

Howe, H. F., and Westley, L. C. (1988). "Ecological Relationships of Plants and Animals." Oxford University Press, New York.

Jacobs, M. (1988). "The Tropical Rain Forest: A First Encounter." Springer-Verlag, Berlin.

Janzen, D. H. (1969). Seed eaters versus seed size, number, dispersal, and toxicity. *Evolution* **23,** 1–27.

Janzen, D. H. (1971). Seed predation by animals. *Annu. Rev. Ecol. Syst.* **2,** 465–492.

Janzen, D. H. (1976). Why bamboos wait so long to flower. *Annu. Rev. Ecol. Syst.* **7,** 347–391.

Janzen, D. H. (1977). Variation in seed size within a crop of a Costa Rican *Mucuna andreana* (Leguminosae). *Am. J. Bot.* **64,** 347–349.

Keeler, K. H. (1980). The extrafloral nectaries of *Ipomoea leptophylla* (Convolvulaceae). *Amer. J. Bot.* **67,** 216–222.

Keeler, K. H. (1981). Function of *Mentzelia nuda* (Loasaceae) postfloral nectaries in seed defense. *Am. J. Bot.* **68,** 295–299.

Lande, R. (1982). A quantitative genetic theory of life history evolution. *Ecology* **63,** 607–615.

Lande, R., and Arnold, S. J. (1983). The measurement of selection on correlated characters. *Evolution* **37,** 1210–1226.

Lee, W. G., Weatherall, I. L., and Wilson, J. B. (1994). Fruit conspicuousness in some New Zealand *Coprosma* (Rubiaceae) species. *Oikos* **69,** 87–94.

Levey, D. J., Moermond, T. C., and Denslow, J. S. (1984). Fruit choice in neotropical birds: The effect of distance between fruits on preference patterns. *Ecology* **65,** 844–850.

Lewontin, R. C. (1978). Adaptation. *Sci. Am.* **239,** 212–230.

Lloyd, D. G. (1976). The transmission of genes via pollen and ovules in gynodioecious angiosperms. *Theor. Popul. Biol.* **9,** 299–316.

Lord, E. M. (1980). Physiological controls on the production of cleistogamous and chasmogamous flowers in *Lamium amplexicaule* L. *Ann. Bot.* **44,** 757–766.

Lord, E. M. (1981). Cleistogamy: A tool for the study of floral morphogenesis, function, and evolution. *Bot. Rev.* **47,** 421–449.

Lyndon, R. F. (1992). The environmental control of reproductive development. *In* "Fruit and Seed Production: Aspects of Development, Environmental Physiology, and Ecology" (C. Marshall and J. Grace, eds.), pp. 9–32. Cambridge University Press, New York.

MacArthur, R. H., and Wilson, E. O. (1967). "The Theory of Island Biogeography." Princeton University Press, Princeton, New Jersey.

Marquis, R. J. (1991). Physiological constraints on response by *Ostrya virginiana* (Betulaceae) to localized folivory. *Can. J. Bot.* **69**, 1951–1955.

Marshall, C., and Watson, M. A. (1992). Ecological and physiological aspects of reproductive allocation. *In* "Fruit and Seed Production: Aspects of Development, Environmental Physiology and Ecology" (C. Marshall and J. Grace, eds.), pp. 173–202. Cambridge University Press, New York.

Marshall, D. L., and Folsom, M. W. (1991). Mate choice in plants: An anatomical to population perspective. *Annu. Rev. Ecol. Syst.* **22**, 37–63.

Maun, M. A., and Cavers, P. B. (1971). Seed production and dormancy in *Rumex crispus*. II. The effects of removal of various proportions of flowers at anthesis. *Can. J. Bot.* **49**, 1841–1848.

Mazer, S. J., and Wheelwright, N. T. (1993). Fruit size and shape: Allometry at different taxonomic levels in bird-dispersed plants. *Evol. Ecol.* **7**, 556–575.

McCutchen, C. W. (1977). The spinning rotation of ash and tulip tree samaras. *Science* **197**, 691–692.

McNamara, J., and Quinn, J. A. (1977). Resource allocation and reproduction in populations of *Amphicarpum purshii* (Gramineae). *Am. J. Bot.* **64**, 17–23.

Menges, E. S., Waller, D. M.,and Gawler, S. C. (1986). Seed set and seed predation in *Pedicularis furbishiae*, a rare endemic of the St. John River. *Am. J. Bot.* **73**, 1168–1177.

Moermond, T. C., and Denslow, J. S. (1983). Fruit choice in neotropical birds: effects of fruit type and accessibility on selectivity. *J. Anim. Ecol.* **52**, 407–420.

Nichols, M. (1987). Spatial pattern of ovule maturation in the inflorescence of *Echium vulgare:* Demography, resource allocation and the constraints of architecture. *Biol. J. Linn. Soc.* **31**, 247–256.

Niklas, K. J. (1984). The motion of windborne pollen grains around conifer ovulate cones: Implications on wind pollination. *Am. J. Bot.* **71**, 356–374.

Niklas, K. J. (1985). The aerodynamics of wind pollination. *Bot. Rev.* **51**, 328–386.

Niklas, K. J. (1992). "Plant Biomechanics: An Engineering Approach to Plant Form and Function." University of Chicago Press, Chicago.

Niklas, K. J., and Buchmann, S. L. (1985). Aerodynamics of wind pollination in *Simmondsia chinensis* (Link) Schneider. *Am. J. Bot.* **72**, 530–539.

Obeso, J. R., and Grubb, P. J. (1993). Fruit maturation in the shrub *Ligustrum vulgare* (Oleaceae): Lack of defoliation effects.*Oikos* **68**, 309–316.

Peterson, J. A., Benson, J. A., Ngai, M., Morin, J., and Ow, C. (1982). Scaling in tensile "skeletons": Structures with scale-independent length dimensions. *Science* **217**, 1267–1270.

Pianka, E. R.(1976). Natural selection of optimal reproductive tactics. *Am. Zool.* **16**, 775–784.

Pyke, G. (1981). Optimal foraging in nectar-feeding animals and coevolution with their plants. *In* "Foraging Behavior: Ecological, Ethological, and Psychological Approaches" (A. C. Kamil and T. D. Sargent, eds.), pp. 19–38. Garland STPM Press, New York.

Real, L., ed. (1983). "Pollination Biology." Academic Press, London.

Reekie, E. G., and Bazzaz, F. A. (1987a). Reproductive effort in plants. 1. Carbon allocation to reproduction. *Am. Nat.* **129**, 876–896.

Reekie, E. G., and Bazzaz, F. A. (1987b). Reproductive effort in plants. 2. Does carbon reflect the allocation of other resources? *Am. Nat.* **129**, 897–906.

Reekie, E. G., and Bazzaz, F. A. (1987c). Reproductive effort in plants. 3. Effects of reproduction on vegetative activity. *Am. Nat.* **129**, 907–919.

Reekie, E. G., and Reekie, J. Y. C. (1991). The effect of reproduction on canopy structure, allocation and growth in *Oenothera biennis.J. Ecol.* **79**, 1061–1071.

Ridley, H. N. (1930). "The Dispersal of Plants throughout the World." L. Reeve & Co., Ashford, Kent, England.

Schaffer, W. M., and Schaffer, M. V. (1979). The adaptive significance of variations in reproductive habit in Agavaceae. II. Pollinator foraging behavior and selection for increased reproductive expenditure. *Ecology* **60**, 1051–1069.

Schmitt, J. (1983). Density-dependent pollinator foraging, flowering, phenology, and temporal pollen dispersal patterns in *Lianthus bicolor. Evolution* 37(6), 1247–1257.

Schnee, B. K., and Waller, D. M. (1986). Reproductive behavior of *Amphicarpaea bracteata* (Leguminosae), an amphicarpic annual. *Am. J. Bot.* **73**, 376–386.

Smith, B. H. (1984). The optimal design of a herbaceous body. *Am. Nat.* **123**, 197–211.

Smith, C. C. (1981). The facultative adjustment of sex ratio in lodgepole pine. *Am. Nat.* **118**, 297–305.

Sprugel, D. G., Hinckley, T. M., and Schaap, W. (1991). The theory and practice of branch autonomy. *Annu. Rev. Ecol. Syst.* **22**, 309–334.

Stanton, M. L. (1984). Developmental and genetic sources of seed weight variation in *Raphanus raphanistrum* L. (Brassicaceae). *Am. J. Bot.* **71**, 1090–1098.

Stearns, S. C. (1992). "The Evolution of Life Histories." Oxford University Press, Oxford.

Stephenson, A. G. (1981). Flower and fruit abortion: Proximate causes and ultimate functions. *Annu. Rev. Ecol. Syst.* **12**, 253–279.

Stephenson, A. G., and Bertin, R. I. (1983). Male competition, female choice, and sexual selection in plants. *In* "Pollination Biology" (L. Real, ed.), pp. 109–149. Academic Press, New York.

Tomlinson, P. B. (1990). "The Structural Biology of Palms." Oxford University Press, Oxford.

Tomlinson, P. B., and Soderholm, P. K. (1975). The flowering and fruiting of *Corypha elata* in South Florida. *Principes* **19**, 83–99.

Tuomi, J., Vuorisalo, T., Niemelä, P., Nisula, S., and Jormalainen, V. (1988). Localized effects of branch defoliations on weight gain of female inflorescences in *Betula pubescens. Oikos* **51**, 327–330.

Tuomi, J., Vuorisalo, T., Niemelä, P., and Haukioja, E. (1989). Effects of localized defoliations on female inflorescences in mountain birch, *Betula pubescens* ssp. *tortuosa. Can. J. Bot.* **67**, 334–338.

Uphof, J. C. T. (1938). Cleistogamic flowers. *Bot. Rev.* **4**, 21–49.

van der Pijl, L. (1972). "Principles of Dispersal in Higher Plants." Springer-Verlag, Berlin.

Waddington, K. D. (1979). Optimal foraging: On flower selection by bees. *Am. Midl. Nat.* **114**, 179–196.

Waller, D. M. (1980). Environmental determinants of outcrossing in *Impatiens capensis* (Balsaminaceae). *Evolution* **34**, 747–761.

Waller, D. M. (1982). Factors influencing seed weight in *Impatiens capensis* (Balsaminaceae). *Am. J. Bot.* **69**, 1470–1475.

Waller, D. M. (1988). Plant morphology and reproduction. *In* "Plant Reproductive Ecology: Patterns and Strategies" (J. Lovett Doust and L. Lovett Doust, eds.), pp. 203–227. Oxford University Press, New York.

Watson, M. A. (1984). Developmental constraints: Effect on population growth and patterns of resource allocation in a clonal plant. *Am. Nat.* **123**, 411–426.

Watson, M. A. (1986). Integrated physiological units in plants. *Trends Ecol. Evol.* **1**, 119–123.

Watson, M. A., and Casper, B. B. (1984). Morphogenetic constraints on patterns of carbon distribution in plants. *Annu. Rev. Ecol. Syst.* **15**, 233–258.

Webb, C. J., and Kelly, D. (1993). The reproductive biology of the New Zealand flora. *Trends Ecol. Evol.* **8**, 442–447.

Weberling, F. (1989). "Morphology of Flowers and Inflorescences." Cambridge University Press, Cambridge.

Weiss, M. R. (1991). Floral colour changes as cues for pollinators. *Nature (London)* **354**, 227–229.

Whitham, T. G., and Mopper, S. (1985). Chronic herbivory: Impacts on architecture and sex expression of pinyon pine. *Science* **228**, 1089–1091.

Willson, M. F., and Burley, N. (1983)."Mate Choice in Plants." Princeton University Press, Princeton, New Jersey.

Wright, J. S. (1983). The dispersion of eggs by a bruchid beetle among *Scheelea* palm seeds and the effect of distance to the parent palm. *Ecology* **64**(5), 1016–1021.

Wyatt, R. (1982). Inflorescence architecture: How flower number, arrangement, and phenology affect pollination and fruit set. *Am. J. Bot.* **69,** 585–594.

3

Biomechanical Optimum
in Woody Stems

Claus Mattheck

I. Trees as Sailboats

Swaying trees in a heavy storm may remind us of sailboats that are safely moored in a harbor. The leaves collect the wind load, which passes through a filigreed system of delicate twigs and small branches into the thicker primary branches and into the stem. The stem carries the wind bending moment into the root plate, where the load acts in reverse order on the primary roots, on the thinner roots, and on the fine roots, through which it enters the soil. At a certain distance from the tree the soil alone must take up the entire wind load.

During natural selection, there were trade-offs among canopy shape, stem shape, plant competition, and whole-plant carbon gain (see also Givnish [1] in this volume). On the one hand, selection for light interception (especially in the face of competition) would favor tall, broad canopies with little leaf overlap. On the other hand, selection for a mechanically sound structure would favor shorter plants, those sufficiently streamlined to minimize bending stresses, those that resist unavoidable loads and stresses, and/ or those that function with a minimum of support material (wood).

This chapter elucidates the author's view of how trees have been meeting these mechanical requirements established by nature. Emphasis is on stems, and a few remarks will be made on the junctions of stems with branches or roots.

The mechanical problem is solved by an optimum mechanical design. The characteristics of such a design, and the differences between biological design and engineering design are discussed below.

II. Human-Made Engineering Design versus Grown Biomechanical Design

Any mature engineering component is the result of a number of improvements that are made as the engineer learns from the deficiencies of the previous design. This technical evolution, as one may call it, may be influenced by ever new inventions and ideas. The human-made designs are not subject to the slow, step-by-step process that biological components are bound to undergo.

Engineering components can neither respond to loads and stresses nor adapt to changes in loads and stresses by adequate self-corrections. Once manufactured, the engineered component is subject to loads and failures but has no mechanism for response to these. In contrast, "grown" biomechanical components such as tree stems react to weak points such as cracks, and repair mechanical defects as long as the plants are vigorous and vital.

Trees may improve in design through development of new tissue. Improvements in the design of trees may be induced by pure mechanical or by biological phenomena or processes. Wood cannot be removed once the tree has produced it, nor does it shrink in underloaded areas. The shape that a tree develops in the course of time hence documents its entire load history, and provides the observer with a biomechanical diary. The additional wood can be interpreted as a reaction to mechanical events or interventions such as changes in loads or stresses, or mechanical injuries.

The advantages of the adaptive potential of biological components are evident. For the purpose it serves in trees, biological design is superior to engineered components on account of its local stress detection ability, its adaptive growth and shape optimization in accordance with the detected changes in loads and stresses, and its self-repair ability, that is, the repair of detected defects and the avoidance of deterioration.

The disadvantages of human-made engineering components compared with the ingenious biological structures are irrevocable, definitive, non-adaptive designs, the inability to repair defects actively; and the indifference to critical loads that may cause severe failures. The adaptive growth of trees follows some basic laws of self-optimization. These basic laws are discussed below.

III. Optimum Mechanical Design

Studies of over 400 biological structures and structural details have shown that 2 complementary processes enable the tree to keep stresses low at any point on the surface or inside: (1) the minimization of external loads through minimization of the lengths of lever arms (principle of minimum lever arms), and (2) an even stress distribution on the surface of the tree (constant stress axiom).

The principle of minimum lever arms is easily understood regarding a tree whose center of gravity (S) is displaced laterally (Fig. 1). The tree turns its unfavorably long lever arms toward the load axis to minimize the bending moment. Hartmann (1942), Mattheck (1991), and Timell (1986) are among the authors who investigated the formation and action of reaction wood.

Lever arms can also be corrected passively, that is, through spiral grain, and through reduction of the crown on the windward side with spiral grain as part of the flexibility strategy of the tree (Mosbrugger, 1990). Any long lateral branch at right angles to the wind direction leads a torsional moment into the tree. The tree increasingly twists the branch in the wind direction, thus reducing the lever arm on which the wind load acts. As everybody can see in nature, this twisting movement produces a stem with spiral grain whose wood fibers are realigned with the force flow or, to be more precise, with the principal tensile stress trajectories. The tree will not change this direction of the grain. It would fail if it were twisted the wrong way, and would slacken or split lengthwise like a rope twisted in the wrong direction. However, spiral grain can also occur under the influence of strong genetic control mechanisms (Harris, 1988).

Growth or just elastic bending of the peripheral parts of the crown in the wind direction, that is, reduction of the sail area exposed to the wind, is another manifestation of the flexible response of trees to external loading. It was found, in addition, that certain mechanisms in the area of the leaves and needles reduce the wind drag coefficient as the wind load increases (Mayhead, 1973).

Trees that are too stiff and inflexible to "win by yielding" experience a reduction of their crowns on the windward side. Such reductions are cumulative losses that the tree suffers when its leaves are dried up by the wind and when branches growing in an unfavorable direction break.

The principle of minimum lever arms is helpful but cannot completely eliminate the stresses that act on trees. These unavoidable stresses that the tree must bear are coped with through yet another rule described by the constant stress axiom (Mattheck, 1991, 1993), which was observed for *Picea* trees (Metzger, 1893). According to this axiom, the stresses on the surface

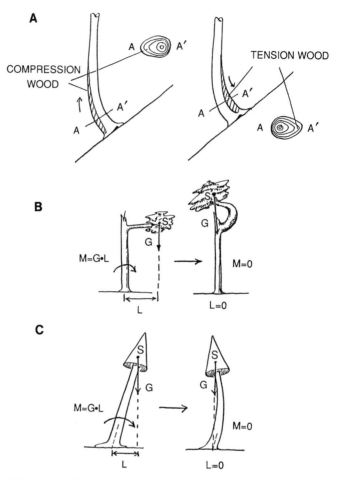

Figure 1 Minimization of lever arms through active formation of reaction wood. (A) Reaction wood in gymnosperms (left) and angiosperms (right). (B) Growth trajectory by which a side branch becomes the new leader, decreasing the lever arm (L) such that the bending moment (M) decreases (G is the weight of the canopy part, and S is its center of gravity). (C) Growth trajectory of a leaning tree, decreasing the lever arm of its canopy.

of biological load carriers are distributed evenly, that is, there are neither overloaded areas (predetermined breaking points) nor underloaded areas (waste of material).

Components that are designed in compliance with the axiom of constant stress are as light as possible and as strong as necessary. Computer methods developed at the Karlsruhe Nuclear Research Center (Karlsruhe, Germany) enable the engineer to let components grow in size (Mattheck, 1993;

Mattheck *et al.*, 1992). Components that are "manufactured" by applying this axiom are lighter and may endure more than 100 times as many load cycles as nonoptimized components without breakage. German industry increasingly relies on the applicability to human-made components of the natural design rule of trees (Mattheck, 1993).

IV. The Design Principle in Trees

These examples of trees elucidate the phenomenon of optimum mechanical designs that avoid avoidable stresses and distribute unavoidable stresses evenly.

A. Stem Tapering and Wind Load

The taper of the stem $\Delta D/h$ (where D is the diameter and h is the distance to the effective point of wind attack) was found to be related to the shape and location of the canopy with respect to the wind (Fig. 2). Using *Picea*, Metzger (1893) observed that the stresses along stems appear constant owing, presumably, to some adjustment during development of the form of the stem relative to that of the crown. Other authors preferred to formulate this principle of uniform load distribution in terms of constant strain (Ylinen, 1952), presumably because strains can be measured more easily than stresses. In spite of these different formulations there is general

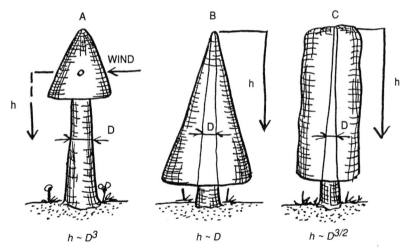

Figure 2   The form of the crown determines the form of the stem. (A) Below the crown (conical canopy; Metzger 1893); (B) within the crown (conical canopy); (C) within the crown (right cylindrical canopy).

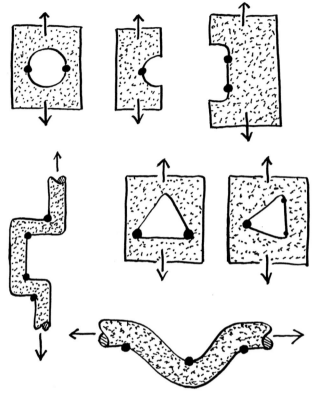

Figure 3　Nonoptimized notches cause notch stresses (●). The arrows show the direction of forces.

agreement that the shape of the stem is influenced by the crown shape and, hence, by the axial distribution of the wind load. The shape of the stem leads to a uniform stress distribution.

B. Branch Junctions and Tree Forks

A branch with large leaf area per unit length or with many leaves at the tip will experience major wind loads. By the nature of branch systems, the branch will divert the force flow from its axis down the stem axis. This force flow diversion causes high notch stresses (Fig. 3) in nonoptimized components.

The designs of branch junctions and forks appear to have no local stress concentrations due to shape optimization (Mattheck and Vorberg, 1991; Mattheck, 1993). The tree fork in Fig. 4 conforms with the computer-generated shape that has no notch stress at all. If, instead, the fork had a semicircular shape, stresses would be 1.4 times as high. The same optimi-

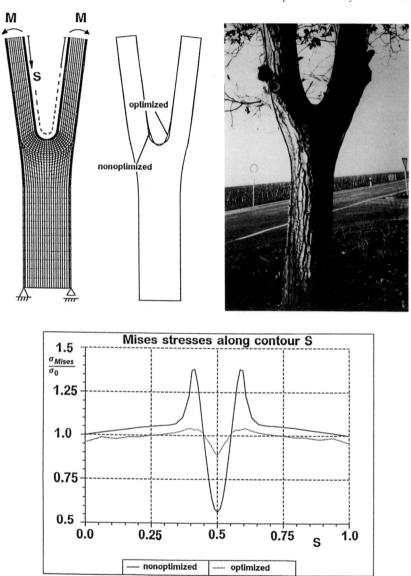

Figure 4   Tree forks are shape-optimized notches without notch stresses (for explanation, see Mattheck and Vorberg, 1991).

zation applies to vigorous branches whose lengths are comparable to those of the leading shoots. We have found that optimization is less pronounced in low-vigor branches. The bases of these branches are even surrounded with collars, that is, with predetermined breaking points in the form of circular notches. This phenomenon is most pronounced around the bases of dead branches or stubs.

C. Shape-Optimized Root–Stem Junctions

The wind load, which may come to several metric tons and which acts on lever arms that may be 80 m in length, causes a high bending moment at the butt of the stem. This bending moment is distributed over the roots to be borne ultimately by the soil alone at the edge of the root plate. Both the shear strength of the root–soil interface and that of the soil itself are factors that determine the size of the root plate. As in the case of tree forks (see 4.2 above), notch stresses at the stem–root junction (Mattheck, 1993) are completely absent, which again supports the constant stress axiom.

Preferential wind directions stimulate an increase in the tensile strength of roots on the windward side. Stokes (1994) showed experimentally that spruce roots on the windward side are thicker and longer than the remaining roots. This phenomenon makes sense regarding the laws of basic mechanics plus Mohr–Coulomb's law of soil mechanics (Mattheck and Breloer, 1993). According to the latter, the shear strength of soil increases with the pressure that the shear surfaces exert on one another. This pressure is weaker on the windward than on the leeward side because the roots are lifted rather than depressed by the wind. The tree as a structure requires longer and thicker roots for reinforcement where soil shear strength is insufficient. These reinforcement roots can ensure an optimum load-bearing capacity of the root–soil "composite material" even on the windward side. This is presumably stimulated by soil movements that are larger at the windward side than in the compacted soil on the lee side.

Again using basic mechanics and Mohr–Coulomb's law, one can explain several other natural phenomena. Thicker and larger roots form on the upslope side of a tree (Mattheck and Breloer, 1993, 1995). When the vertical sinker roots of a tree are anchored at some distance from the stem, the lateral root is subjected to enormous tensile and bending stresses. Whereas the tensile part of the bending stresses is added to the axial tensile stresses on the upper side of the roots, the compressive bending stresses and the axial tension neutralize one another on the lower side. As a result, wood is added to the upper but not to the lower side of the root, and buttress roots are finally formed (Fig. 5).

Computer simulations at the Karlsruhe Nuclear Research Center (Mattheck, 1993) showed that lateral roots that are anchored with sinker roots far away from the stem indeed form a buttress root on the windward side when they are conditioned for a state of constant stress. It was found that the thickest tree rings are formed where the mechanical stresses are greatest (upper side of the roots), and that little xylem is added where the stresses are weakest (lower side of the roots). Field studies confirm this.

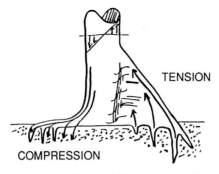

Figure 5 Buttress roots form on the windward side in the case of flat roots whose lateral roots exhibit sinker roots at a certain distance from the stem. This is due to the combination of tensile stresses and bending stresses, which leads to maximum stresses and a maximum tree ring thickness on the upper side and to minimum stresses and minimum tree ring thicknesses on the lower side of the roots.

D. Optimum Fiber and Ray Arrangement for Radial and Axial Strength

Wood is susceptible to failure due to shear stresses. The tree reduces the probability of failure due to shear by arranging the wood fibers along the force flow, that is, along the principal stress trajectories, which are entirely free of shear stresses. Engineering components that were manufactured on the basis of computer simulations of this stress-adapted fiber arrangement mechanism bore much higher loads than conventional composite materials (R. Kriechbaum and C. Mattheck, unpublished data).

The mechanically controlled formation of spiral grain, described above, is a vivid example of the minimum shear stresses between the fibers. The coiled tensile stress trajectories in a twisted cylinder coincide with the axial alignment of the cells in wood. It is probable that the genetically controlled spiral grain that is often observed in horse chestnut is adapted to the prevailing stresses purely accidentally. Longitudinal splits due to inappropriate loading thus occur more frequently. According to Kübler (1991), spiral grain also ensures a circumferential distribution of water and assimilates when individual roots or branches have lost their vitality.

Another comprehensive study by Kübler is dedicated to growth stresses and their distribution in trees (Kübler, 1991). While axial tensile stresses act on the surface, the pith of the tree is subjected to axial pressure. The tensile stress in the outermost growth rings delays or even avoids failure due to fiber buckling on the compression side of bending.

Most authors emphasize the storage and transport functions of rays but neglect their mechanical function. Albrecht *et al.* (1995) examined three ash trees (*Fraxinus excelsior*) and showed the mechanical significance of the rays. They found a strict correlation between the fractometer-measured lateral strength (Mattheck and Bethge, 1994) and the internal lateral stresses,

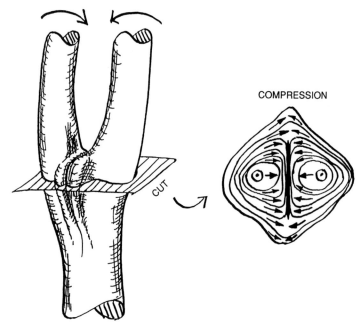

Figure 6   The tree rings are arranged perpendicular to the plane interface of two stems that form a narrow fork.

which were calculated by applying the finite-element method. Moreover, they found a strong positive correlation between ray size or ray abundance and the maximum lateral-strength fractometer value: larger or more abundant rays give greater strength to wood when pulled in the radial direction.

E. Optimum Shape of Growth Rings

The fibers of which the growth rings are composed are arranged along the major force flow in the axial direction. Shear-free lines are also preferred developmentally in the circumferential direction, as shown by the perpendicular arrangement of tree rings on contacting surfaces (Fig. 6, Mattheck, 1993). This perpendicular tree ring arrangement is also observed (C. Mattheck, personal observation) when adjacent branches of a tree fork grow together in the presence of contacting stones or other external objects.

V. Safety Factors

The failure of trees in spite of the mechanical optimization of their outer shape and inner architecture may be surprising. The safety factor of trees explains why breakage of these perfectly designed structures cannot always be avoided.

The safety factor is defined as follows (Currey, 1984):

$$S = \text{fracture stress/service stress} = \sigma_{crit}/\sigma_0$$

Fracture stresses are the stresses required to break the tree longitudinally or transversely. They are much higher parallel to the grain than transversely to it (Lavers, 1983). Service stresses σ_0 are the "everyday" stresses that the tree experiences. The tree conforms with the axiom of constant stress by producing thicker tree rings where the service stresses are higher on a time average.

The safety factor S is a measure of the mechanical safety margins of trees under normal service loads. According to Alexander (1981) and Currey (1984), S is in the range of 3 to 4 for the bones of mammals. Because animals run about and must carry each extra kilogram for a lifetime, it seems only natural that trees, being firmly anchored, can afford more weight, hence somewhat greater safety factors.

Mattheck *et al.* (1993b) determined the safety factor of trees by systematic notching. Rectangular windows were punched diametrically through various deciduous and coniferous stems. The window edges were filed smooth to obtain defined notch radii. Those trees with windows extending over about a third of the stem diameter survived whereas those with larger windows failed. Finite-element calculations revealed a 4.5-fold service stress increase on account of the punched windows. It can be inferred that trees do not break unless stresses increase by a factor of 4.5. This gives a longitudinal safety factor of ≥ 4.5, which is somewhat above the value reported for the mammal bones. Hollow trees are an exception to this rule and are treated separately below (Section VI).

Bending stresses that exceed the safety factor (thus causing failure) occasionally occur, but natural selection has not favored stem production for such rare events. Alexander (1981) explains this apparent insufficiency for bones. Biological designs could certainly resist the highest loads imaginable but the cost of preserving such "safe" species would be too high.

VI. Relevance of Hollow Spaces and Cavities to Safety of Trees

When a water hose is bent, its cross-section flattens and becomes more flexible. A hollow tree with a modest tangential strength splits longitudinally at a very early stage of cross-sectional flattening, and collapses into segments (C. Mattheck, personal observation). The hollow stem is unable to resist bending stresses and finally fails as its cross-section collapses. "Dev-

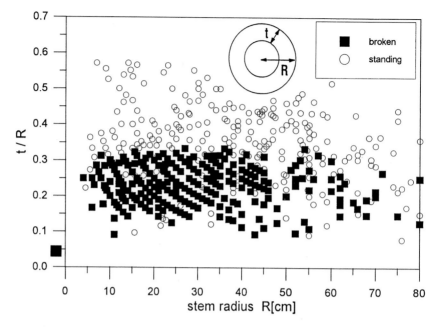

Figure 7 The critical wall thickness (t)-to-radius (R) ratio seems to be $t/R = 0.3 \ldots 0.32$. No significant failure was found above this value. (■) Broken; (○) standing.

il's ears" (peaks of standing xylem that remain in place after tree failure) may reveal that decay has spread and has already attacked the xylem rings in the compact areas above the cavity.

We sought to learn the critical sizes of hollow spaces and cavities to avoid tree breakage that could threaten nearby structures or inhabitants. This failure criterion was investigated through field measurements of hollow trees (Fig. 7, Mattheck and Breloer, 1993; Mattheck *et al.*, 1993a). We measured the wall thickness t of the hollow shell and the outside radius R as well for 800 trees that have survived so far, and for broken hollow trees.

The solid squares in Fig. 7 represent the hollow trees that failed, and the open circles symbolize the hollow trees that remained standing. Hollow spaces were found to be critical when their sizes amounted to about 70% the size of the radius. Seventy percent and sometimes, if rarely, 68% may cause trees with full crowns and fully developed diameters to fail as a result of cross-sectional collapsing. Trees whose crowns are strongly reduced may even remain upright despite the presence of rot stem in cavities 85–90% the size of their stem radius (Mattheck and Breloer, 1993).

The service stress of a solid tree is σ_0. A critical hollow space whose size is 70% the size of the radius gives an increase in stresses of only $\sigma/\sigma_0 = 1.3$, which is much smaller than the calculated safety factor of 4.5 given in Section V. Only wide open cross-sections fully use their mechanical safety margins through $\sigma/\sigma_0 = 4.5$. This is when both bending fracture and cross-sectional collapsing may occur. Closed cross-sections collapse under much lower loads long before the value of 4.5 is reached. This is due to the change in cross-sectional bending resistance when the stem collapses into timber boards.

The criterion $t/R = 0.3$ applied to all of the European and North American hardwoods and softwoods considered (Mattheck *et al.*, 1993a). A field study conducted in Australia corroborated this result for eucalyptus trees <4 m in diameter (C. Mattheck, personal observation). These findings may be explained by the fact that the bending stress in a hollow shell does not depend on the material used.

The bending stress calculated by applying the simple Bernoulli bending theory increases only a little for small hollows but quickly rises when the hollow is more than 70% of the radius. This is an initial hypothetical explanation that requires deeper understanding. However, it is not really necessary to provide further proofs because the field studies reflect how the failure criterion works in nature. Therefore, the failure criterion $t/R = 0.3$ can be used as an empirical result for practical tree assessment.

VII. Repair of the Damaged Optimum

It was shown above how trees optimize their outer shape and inner architecture to reduce the probability of failure. What happens, however, if the developed optimum is disturbed by external impacts? For example, what will occur if mechanical defects modify the developed form of a plant? Wounds that injure the wood usually cause high notch stresses (see Section IV, A and B) as the force flow is diverted. Results from experiments (Mattheck, 1993) are consistent with the hypothesis that high notch stresses are detected by the cambium, and are reacted to by formation of a tree ring that is thickest where the stresses are highest. In the areas of highest stresses the tree attaches the most material for most effective and rapid wound healing. Predetermined breaking points that threaten the tree are repaired first and fastest.

Local stress concentrations may also be caused by mechanical contacts. If, for example, a stone presses against a tree or becomes stuck in a tree fork, the tree instantaneously enlarges the contact surface to grow around the intruding stone. The material that the tree attaches distributes the contact force over a larger surface. The contact stresses are reduced, and the state of even stress distribution is restored (Mattheck, 1991, 1993).

New contact stresses develop as the material surrounds the stone from both sides and joins. The new contact surface is enlarged as well and welds as the tree rings coming from both sides melt into one smooth contour without kinks. The enclosed bark, however, will have the effect of a crack if the contacting partners are torn apart (Mattheck, 1993; Mattheck and Breloer, 1993).

The additional material that the tree attaches to limit its risk of failure due to internal defects can be interpreted as a warning signal in the body language of trees. Any material that seems to be out of place or grown in excess can be regarded as symptomatic of a defect.

The interpretation of these defect symptoms was systematized through development of the visual tree assessment (VTA) method at the Karlsruhe Nuclear Research Center (Mattheck and Breloer, 1993, 1995). This method is based on a catalog of symptoms that assigns external symptoms to internal defects. The severity of the defects is evaluated, and failure criteria are defined. The VTA catalog also includes a library of the known cases of tree failure due to breakage and windthrow.

A failure criterion for evaluation of decayed parts was introduced in Section VI. The risk of stem breakage increases greatly if a hollow space occupies an area >68% of the stem radius.

Cracks in vertical trees are another type of defect. However, trees that were cut longitudinally from the butt to a point at shoulder level by use of a chain saw during field studies 2 years ago still stretch their branches to the light today. On the other hand, cracks due to lignin creep in leaning trees often cause the crack surfaces to slip on each other and may quickly lead to tree failure. As a defect symptom, ribs that form in front of each crack are warning signals. Progressive lean due to shear deformation is indicated by transverse cracks in the bark on the upper side, and by bellows-type folds in the bark and perturbations on the lower side of the slanting tree right above the root buttress.

Progressive lean of a stem must be expected to advance when no reaction wood is formed to actively check the existing creep potential. In the case of deciduous trees, this counteraction reminds one of a tensile rope that shortens on its upper side and tightens continuously. If this tightening tension is not produced, the tree keeps on leaning and falls when it reaches a critical stress. In this sense, tension wood formation by leaning trees is a repair activity that compensates for progressive lean of the stem.

VIII. Summary

The following statements summarize the main points of this chapter.

Trees are like sailboats. They consist of crown (sail), stem (mast), and root plate (hull). The development of these parts is well coordinated during natural tree growth.

In contrast to human-made structures, trees, being biological components, are often able to modify their designs and make repairs whenever changes in the loads and stresses demand adaptation.

An optimum mechanical design lessens avoidable loads to the greatest extent possible and evenly distributes unavoidable ones (constant stress axiom).

The stems represent a mechanical optimum with respect to tapering, branch and root junctions, and inner architecture.

The safety factor of tree stems is $S \geq 4.5$.

Field studies suggest that hollow stems with wall thickness to radius ratios above 0.3 do not break as a result of hollowness. However, any tree can break when its safety margin decreases because of overloads.

Defective trees (those whose structure has been damaged, e.g., by mechanical impacts) repair themselves. The mechanical defects can be inferred from the repair material that the tree produces. This repair material forms the basis of a body language of trees, which can be used by people to evaluate the stability of urban trees.

Future work by the author's team will focus on the optimum distribution of mechanical properties such as stiffness and strength inside the tree.

Acknowledgments

I am grateful to Mrs. Dagmar Gräbe for her help in the preparation of the figures, and to Mrs. Heidi Knierim, who translated the German manuscript. I also thank Dr. Robert Archer, Dr. John Sperry, and Dr. Brayton Wilson for their comments on the manuscript.

References

Albrecht, W., Bethge, K., and Mattheck, C. (1995). Is lateral strength in trees controlled by lateral stress. *J. Arboricult.* **21**(2), 83–87.

Alexander, M. (1981). Factors of safety in the structure of animals. *Sci. Prog. (Oxford).* **67**, 109–130.

Currey, J. (1984). "The Mechanical Adaptation of Bone." Princeton University Press, Princeton, New Jersey.

Harris, J. (1988). "Spiral Grain and Wave Phenomena in Wood Formation." Springer-Verlag, Berlin.

Hartmann, F. (1942). Das statische Wuchsgesetz bei Nadel—und Läubbaumen,"pp. 111. Springer-Verlag, Wien.

Kübler, H. (1987). Growth stresses in trees and related wood properties. *For. Abstr.* **48**, 131—189.

Kübler, H. (1991). Function of spiral grain in trees. *Trees Struct. Funct.* **5**, 125–135.

Lavers, G. M. (1983). "The Strength Properties of Timber." HMSO, London.

Mattheck, C. (1991). "Trees—The Mechanical Design." Springer Verlag, Heidelberg and New York.

Mattheck, C. (1993). "Design in der Natur," 2nd Ed. Rombach Verlag, Freiburg, Germany.

Mattheck, C., and Bethge, K. (1994). A guide to fractometer tree assessment. *Arborist's News* **3**, 9–12.

Mattheck, C., and Breloer, H. (1993). "Handbuch der Schadenskunde von Bäumen." Rombach Verlag, Freiburg, Germany.

Mattheck, C., and Breloer, H. (1995). "The Body Language of Trees." HMSO, London.

Mattheck, C., and Vorberg, U. (1991). The biomechanics of tree fork design. *Bot. Acta* **104**, 399–404.

Mattheck, C., Bethge, K., and Erb, D. (1992). Three-dimensional shape optimization of a bar with a rectangular hole. *Fatigue Fract. Eng. Mater. Struct.* **15**, 347–351.

Mattheck, C., Bethge, K., and Erb, D. (1993a). Failure criteria for trees. *Arboricult. J.* **17**, 201–209.

Mattheck, C., Bethge, K., and Schäfer, J. (1993b). Safety factors in trees. *J. Theor. Biol.* **165**, 185–189.

Mayhead, G. (1973). Some drag coefficients for British forest trees derived from wind tunnel studies. *Agric. Meteorol.* **12**, 123–130.

Metzger, K. (1893). Der Einfluß des Windes als maßgeblicher Faktor für das Wachstum der Bäume. In "Mündener Forstliche Hefte," Springer-Verlag, Berlin.

Mosbrugger, V. (1990). "The Tree Habit in Land Plants." Lecture Notes in Earth Sciences. Springer-Verlag, Berlin.

Stokes, A. (1994). Responses of young trees to wind: Effects on root architecture and anchorage strength. Ph.D. thesis. University of York, York, England.

Timell, T. E. (1986). "Compression Wood in Gymnosperms." Springer-Verlag, Berlin and New York.

Ylinen, A. (1952). Über die mechanische Schaftform der Bäume," Silva Fennica, Helsinki, Finland.

4

Shrub Stems: Form and Function

Brayton F. Wilson

I. Introduction

Shrubs have smaller stems than trees and shrubs, shrubs often have multiple stems, and they can grow where trees cannot survive. These three facts raise many questions about shrub stems that center around the issue of whether selection resulted in short, woody, multiple-stemmed plants that happened to be tolerant of stress, or whether selection for stress tolerance resulted in short, woody, multiple-stemmed plants. This chapter summarizes much of what we know about shrub stems and the shrub form. We need to know more about shrubs not only because they are important world-wide, but also because clarifying the biology of shrub structure, growth, and function will help us to understand other plants.

A. Definitions of Shrubs

Shrubs are defined on the basis of stem characteristics as intermediate in the continuum from herbs to trees. Definitions of shrubs are necessarily arbitrary and often reflect the regional bias of the investigator. Rundel (1991) gave an ecological definition of shrubs as "low woody plants with multiple stems." Orsham (1989) used a more restrictive definition of shrubs as "plants with lignified stems not developing a distinct trunk. The stems branch from their basal part above or below the soil surface." Woodiness of the stem eliminates most herbs from the shrub definition. Shrubs are shorter than trees. They are also upright, as opposed to prostrate woody plants, and self-supporting, as opposed to vines. Some shrub species never develop multiple stems from underground buds, even after injuries. Some shrubs branch profusely at the base and do not have a main stem, yet other shrubs may have distinct main stems clearly differentiated from the branches.

B. Habitats of Shrubs

Shrubs often dominate in areas of high environmental stress such as shrub deserts (water stress), shrub tundra (cold, nutrient and wind stress), shrub wetlands (soil oxygen stress), shrubs on nutrient-deficient soils, or fire-dependent communities (Rundel, 1991). Forest shrubs occur throughout the world and are limited by tree competition, primarily for light, but also by root competition (Riegel *et al.*, 1992).

An interesting question is whether forest shrubs are adapted to grow in these relatively benign environments or whether they were originally adapted for high-stress environments outside the forest and secondarily invaded the forest. Californian chaparral shrub taxa apparently originated in forests under warm temperate conditions with summer rainfall (Axelrod, 1989). These taxa had basic structural features that permitted their success after the change to a high-stress, summer-dry mediterranean climate.

C. Evolution of Shrubs

Stebbins (1972) concluded that arid-land shrubs have arisen independently in many different taxa from both herbs and trees. Given this multiple origin of shrub form, generalizations are probably doomed to failure. Even so, two alternative hypotheses are proposed here about the adaptive nature of shrub form.

The first hypothesis is that shrub form is an adaptation based on the design strategy of relatively small, low-investment, low-risk, "throwaway" stems that are expendable in high-stress environments (comparable to throwaway compound leaves, Givnish, 1978; and [1] in this volume; Stevens and Fox, 1991). A shortened life cycle for each stem and the ability to produce new stems after the death of old ones would be associated with such a design. Under this hypothesis, specific stress adaptations would be secondary, after shrub form had developed.

The second hypothesis is that adaptations for surviving high stress imposed the shrub form. A possible example would be a species with small vessels that increase drought resistance. These vessels would also increase water stress under optimal conditions, thus restricting growth and inducing the shrub habit.

II. Stem Hydraulics and Adaptations to Drought

A. Stem Hydraulics

Stem adaptations to stress often involve trade-offs among different organs in the plant, or among different functions of the stem. Leaves or roots often have adaptations for drought avoidance or tolerance (Orsham, 1972; Nilsen *et al.*, 1984; Newton and Goodin, 1989a;b). These adaptations may be different between trees and shrubs (DeLucia and Schlesinger, 1991). The stem adaptations vary widely depending on the adaptations of other organs. The woods of shrubs, vines, and trees seem to exhibit different trade-offs. Wide, long vessels are efficient for conduction, but risky for embolisms from freezing, and from low water potentials if they have large pores in the pit membranes (Sperry, [5] in this volume). Zimmermann and Jeje (1981) measured vessel lengths in mesic forest trees (seven species) and shrubs (four species). The diffuse porous trees had maximum vessel lengths of 20–50 cm. The vessels of most of the shrubs (all diffuse porous) were <50 cm long, but a few vessels in each species were >1 m long. Farmer (1918) found no consistent differences in the specific conductivity (volume cm^{-2} min^{-1}) between deciduous shrub and tree stems. Several studies have examined the differences in wood structure or water conductivity between trees, shrubs, and vines (Baas and Schweingruber, 1987; Chiu and Ewers, 1992; Ewers *et al.*, 1990; Gartner, 1991a). The general conclusions were that shrubs tend to have narrower, shorter vessels than do trees or vines. Shrubs, compared to vines, have wider stems with more vessels, so that the leaf-specific conductivities (conductivity of the stem divided by the distal leaf area) of the vine and shrub forms are about the same.

B. Case History: The California Chaparral

The southern California chaparral is a shrub ecosystem that has been studied intensively. It is subjected to summer drought and frequent fires.

The woods of chaparral shrubs appear to have anatomical adaptations for drought (Carlquist, 1989). Many species have wood specialized for high conductivity when water is available (simple perforation plates, wide earlywood vessels), but also specialized for safety during drought periods (narrow latewood vessels, vasicentric tracheids). Adaptations in the wood allow some stems to be subjected to very low water potentials without developing embolisms (Kolb and Davis, 1994).

Shallow-rooted shrubs of the chaparral may reach leaf water potentials of -8 to -9 MPa during the summer, among the lowest values recorded anywhere (Gill and Mahall, 1986). Deep-rooted species can essentially avoid water stress problems and maintain leaf water potentials above -1.1 MPa

(Davis and Mooney, 1986). Those species developing low water potentials may be vulnerable to stem embolisms. Some chaparral shrub stems are vulnerable to stem embolisms at the relatively high stem water potentials of -1.5 MPa, yet other species are not vulnerable to embolisms until they reach -11 MPa (Davis *et al.*, 1993). In many cases in woody plants the lowest water potential a species normally encounters is near the water potential at which severe embolisms occur (see Sperry, 1995). Kolb and Davis (1994) have shown that two species that develop water potentials of -8 MPa have different mechanisms for survival. By the end of the dry season the summer-deciduous *Salvia mellifera* had lost 78% of its hydraulic conductivity through embolisms, while the evergreen *Ceanothus megacarpus* had lost only 17% of its hydraulic conductivity. *Salvia mellifera* apparently survives by forming new xylem and new shoots each spring. *Ceanothus megacarpus* survives by being extremely resistant to embolism formation.

III. Stem Height and Form

Height is the major distinction between shrubs and trees. Height is correlated with stem mechanical design (taper, length, angle, and material properties) and stem longevity, and may be related to stem number. These factors are discussed with the cautionary note that causality is unknown. For example, Givnish ([1] in this volume) discusses how allocation within a plant can limit maximum plant height. Did reduced height growth in shrubs cause reduced allocation of carbohydrates to the stem, or did reduced allocation to the stem cause reduced height growth? Did selection result in rapid stem turnover to maintain low stature, or did selection for rapid turnover result in low stature?

A. Stem Number

Allocation to stem growth is relatively low in shrubs compared to trees. In multiple-stemmed shrubs there may be complex interactions both among stems and between stems and below-ground storage. Competition for stored materials between stems of the same clone might be expected to limit height growth. In *Vaccinium myrtillus*, clipping shoots did not affect the number of new shoots, but did reduce both the growth of new shoots and the new growth on old shoots (Tolvanen *et al.*, 1994).

B. Stem Taper

Wood production by cambial activity in trees is generally distributed so that bending strains are uniform along the stem (Mattheck, [3] in this volume). This distribution of cambial activity results in stems with taper from tip to base because the bending stresses are greatest at the base and the stem must thicken to reduce surface strains. In trees that are guyed or supported to eliminate wind sway, bending strains are reduced or eliminated. These trees may not thicken enough at the base to keep from breaking when the support is removed (Jacobs, 1954). Strain is not the only factor in determining stem form because in low light, trees or their branches may have no cambial activity at the base where surface strains are highest (Bormann, 1965; Reukema, 1959). Supported vines have little stem taper and allocate more growth to elongation and cambial activity near the tip (Gartner, 1991c). *Toxicodendron diversilobum* grows as a vine when supported externally, but as a shrub when not supported (Gartner, 1991b). Similarly, reduced thickening of shrub stems might result from support by adjacent stems of the same clone. Shrubs appear to be intermediate in the distribution of cambial activity between trees and vines. The ratio of height to diameter is often lower in shrubs than in trees, so that they bend under relatively low loads (King, 1987). Shrub stems may have nonuniform surface strains because they are comparable to suppressed, or supported, trees.

C. Length or Height of Stems

The rate of shoot elongation, the angle of shoot growth, and the death of shoots could all determine maximum shrub height. Elongation rates could decrease with increasing height, reaching zero at maximum height, suggesting that elongation is some function of height. Elongation rates could stay relatively high, but shoots above the maximum height could die back. For example, *S. mellifera* elongates more each year than does cooccurring *C. megacarpus*, yet is shorter because the shoots die back each year (Kolb and Davis, 1994). Wind-shaped trees and shrubs are common where exposed shoots are killed.

Height growth would also decrease when stems lean toward the horizontal even though elongation continues. Shrub stems frequently are leaning. Leaning may result from passive bending due to self-weight and inadequate stem thickening. Alternatively, active shifts from vertical to angled growth could result from the formation of reaction wood to bend a vertical stem down (Hallé *et al.*, 1978).

Understory shrubs are relatively free from wind forces, but they are prone to having branches or whole trees fall on top of them, bending the shrub stems over or breaking the terminal shoots (Gartner, 1989). Most understory plants have preventitious buds that grow vertically after such events, so that height growth is interrupted only temporarily.

Internal water stress could limit height growth through several mechanisms. Hydraulic resistance could accumulate rapidly along the stem as it becomes longer or taller. Another factor is that most of the resistance of a shoot system is in the small-diameter twigs (Yang and Tyree, 1993). If a shrub is highly branched, then the taller shrubs would have many small-diameter twigs and many branch junctions, both of which could offer increased resistance to water flow and decreased water potential at the leaves and growing shoots (Tyree and Alexander, 1993). One might, therefore, expect a rapid drop in water potential toward the tips of highly branched shrubs with small leaves and thin twigs (characteristic of dry sites), with a relatively low drop in water potential in shrubs with large leaves, thick twigs, and few branch junctions.

The effect of shade on height of shrubs is unclear. Shrubs in shady environments experience not only reduced light intensity and changed light quality compared to open grown individuals, but they may also be exposed to less wind, which might tend to increase height growth (Neel and Harris, 1971). Understory shrubs usually grow faster in canopy gaps than in the shade (Hicks and Hustin, 1989; Runkle, 1982). Yet, studies of the understory shrub *Gaultheria shallon* in the Pacific Northwest (Messier *et al.,* 1989; Bunnell, 1990; Smith, 1991) and six shrub species in South Africa (Holmes and Cowling, 1993) found that the shade-grown plants were taller than open-grown plants. In shade-tolerant or midtolerant trees optimum height growth is generally at less than full light (Spurr and Barnes, 1980, p. 129). For shrubs, the light shade of canopy gaps may stimulate elongation whereas height growth would be inhibited under completely open conditions.

D. Stem Longevity

The short life span of individual stem ramets could limit the height of shrubs. If stems live only a few years they cannot become tall unless they elongate extremely rapidly over those few years. Shrub stems that are sprouts may grow very rapidly for the first year. *Sambucus canadensis* sprout stems may grow more than 2 m the first year, but elongation rates slow rapidly and most stems only live 5 or 6 years (B. F. Wilson, personal observation).

IV. Architectural Strategies

A. Multiple vs. Single Stems

The multistemmed character results from the growth of buds from below ground level to form new stems (ramets). Multiple-stemmed shrubs can survive death of individual stems because the underground portion of the plant survives to sprout and form replacement stems. In contrast, the single-stemmed shrubs do not produce new stems. They may survive severe drought by sacrificing some branches rather than the whole plant (Parsons *et al.,* 1981). When the stem is killed by fire, single-stemmed shrubs are adapted for production of abundant seedlings rather than new sprouts from buried buds as in multiple-stemmed species.

In the California chaparral most genera form multiple-stemmed shrubs, but 46 (79.3%) of the *Ceanothus* species and 59 (78.7%) of the *Arctostaphylos* species form single-stemmed shrubs (Wells, 1969). Although multiple-stemmed shrubs can survive indefinitely as a clone by producing new stems, single-stemmed shrubs die when the stem dies. Single-stemmed shrubs may live only 9 to 15 years (*Baccharis pilularis*, Hobbs and Mooney, 1986), or they may survive more than 100 years (*Ceanothus crassifolius*; Keeley, 1992). In forests most shrub species are multiple-stemmed, although a few species may sprout infrequently (e.g., *Vaccinium corymbosum*; Pritts and Hancock, 1985).

The underground buds of multiple-stemmed shrubs may be on the basal part of the primary shoot (lignotubers, root crowns, or burls), or they may be distributed along rhizomes (Tappeiner, 1971; Tappeiner *et al.*, 1991), or new shoots may form from branches that have layered (O'Keefe *et al.*, 1982; Gartner, 1989).

Release of basal buds is related to cessation of apical growth at the end of the summer in *Corylus* and to winter-imposed dormancy in *Sambucus* (Champagnat, 1978). The new stems may remain interconnected or eventually become separated into independent ramets. The rate of lateral expansion of a clone depends on the rate of expansion of the organ that bears the buds. Clones from root crowns remain compact, [e.g., *Corylus* (Tappeiner, 1971) or *Alnus* (Huenneke, 1987)], but clones formed from rhizomes or layered branches may spread rapidly (>2 m/year in the rhizomatous *Rhus*; Gilbert, 1966).

Populations of stems from multiple-stemmed shrubs generally have a large number of young stems and an exponential decrease in stem numbers with increasing age (e.g., Stohlgren *et al.*, 1984). This distribution indicates a continuous production of new stems with a constant mortality rate over their life span. As a result, clone age often exceeds maximum stem age and may be unlimited (e.g., Vasek, 1980). Even more buds may be released if the top of the shrub is killed, for example by fire. Thus, apparently some buds escape apical dominance and grow out each year despite the presence of vigorous stems, whereas other buds are inhibited by the living stems and may be released only if the stems are killed. There is always the possibility that new adventitious buds and shoots may be formed after a disturbance (Gill [14] in this volume).

B. Development of Shrub Stems

The distinction between stems and branches arises through the dominance and thickening of a single series of axes (Hallé *et al.*, 1978). Usually shrub stems are sympodial with axes from a succession of lateral meristems. Under natural conditions injury to terminal meristems and shoots is common. Terminal meristems may also abort, or flower, or lose apical control of lateral shoots even though they persist.

A common form of development in shrub stems occurs when stems bend, or are bent, toward the horizontal. Horizontal growth is usually associated with reduced elongation and release of buds that grow to form vigorous, vertical shoots (Hallé *et al.,* 1978; Schulze *et al.,* 1986). The vertical shoot then thickens to form the main stem while the distal part of the older parent shoot grows slowly and becomes a branch. The process may be repeated, forming a series of arching stem segments (e.g., *Sambucus,* Champagnat, 1978).

Lack of apical dominance or apical control leads to a highly branched system with growth diffused over many small, slow-growing twigs without a main stem. Loss of the terminal apical meristem by abortion, flowering, or browsing may lead to forking of the stem if two or more lateral shoots escape apical control. Such forking is common in opposite-leaved shrubs such as *Viburnum* spp. or *Cornus* spp., but also occurs in alternate-leaved shrubs such as *Rhus typhina* (Leeuwenberg's model, as described by Hallé *et al.,* 1978). Major stem forks may also form occasionally without loss of the terminal when a lateral branch grows at about the same rate as the parent shoot.

C. Architecture for Leaf Display

The display of leaves in a shrub crown is determined primarily by the architecture of the shoot system (Givnish, 1995; Waller and Steingraeber, [2] in this volume). Pickett and co-workers have described aspects of the architecture of the eastern forest shrubs *Lindera benzoin, Viburnum acerifolium, V. dentatum,* and *V. prunifolia* (Pickett and Kempf, 1980; Kempf and Pickett, 1981; Veres and Pickett, 1982; Nicola and Pickett, 1983). In high light these shrubs had vertical stems with branches at angles, but in the shade the shrubs tended to have cantilevered stems with the terminal parts nearly horizontal and with horizontal branches with very little overlap among leaves. These species exemplify Horn's (1971) model of the shade-adapted leaf monolayer.

When a stem forms a horizontal cantilever with the crown toward the end of the stem, the bending moment from the weight of the crown is at a maximum. Maintaining horizontal growth in a leaning stem requires more allocation to stem thickening than would be needed for vertical growth. In contrast, *Vaccinium ovalifolium* in coastal Alaska forms the minimum-cost monolayer in the shade (Alaback and Tappeiner, 1991): young *V. ovalifolium* develops an evergreen, prostrate monolayer under a dense overstory. Three to 4 years after release by high light, it grows upright and becomes deciduous.

V. Future Areas for Research

The nature of shrubs as short and, usually, multiple-stemmed plants makes them especially suitable for investigating some aspects of woody plant biology. Shrub species reach a lower maximum height, and reach their maximum height much faster, than do trees. Do they reach a maximum height because of allocation patterns and carbon balance, because of hydraulic or mechanical constraints associated with height, or because of some genetic growth pattern unrelated to the above factors? Most shrub species have clonal growth with multiple stems. How do shrubs regulate new stem production and how do stems interact within a clone?

Shrubs are also excellent organisms for the study of adaptations to stress because they often survive in high-stress environments. Desert and chaparral species will continue to be studied to elucidate mechanisms for drought resistance, while forest shrubs have marked architectural adaptations for survival under low light.

Shrub stems will be studied because shrubs are important throughout the world as sources of food, fuel, forage, and fiber. Stems themselves may be the product. Where leaves or fruits are the products, the stems serve a vital role in support, leaf display, and the transport of materials between roots and leaves. The structure and function of the stem drastically affect the growth of the whole plant. The resilience of shrubs after injury, because of their ability to produce new stems, makes them ideally suited for frequent harvesting as crops.

Acknowledgments

I thank S. D. Davis, E. T. Nilsen, and J. Stafstrom for their helpful comments on this chapter.

References

Alaback, P. B., and Tappeiner, J. C. (1991). Response of western hemlock (*Tsuga heterophylla*) and early huckleberry (*Vaccinium ovalifolium*) seedlings to forest windthrow. *Can. J. For. Res.* **21,** 534–539.

Axelrod, D. I. (1989). Age and origin of the chaparral. *In* "The California Chaparral: Paradigms Reexamined" (S. C. Keeley, ed.), pp. 7–20. Nat. Hist. Museum Los Angeles County Sci. Ser. **34.**

Baas, P., and Schweingruber, F. H. (1987). Ecological trends in the wood anatomy of trees, shrubs and climbers from Europe. *IAWA Bull.* **8,** 245–274.

Bormann, F. H. (1965). Changes in the growth pattern of white pine trees undergoing suppression. *Ecology* **46,** 269–277.

Bunnell, F. L. (1990). Reproduction of salal (*Gaultheria shallon*) under forest canopy. *Can. J. For. Res.* **20,** 91–100.

Carlquist, S. (1989). Adaptive wood anatomy of chaparral shrubs. *In* "The California Chaparral: Paradigms Reexamined" (S. C. Keeley, ed.), pp. 25–36. *Nat. Hist. Museum Los Angeles County Sci. Ser.* 34.

Champagnat, P. (1978). Formation of the trunk in woody plants. *In* "Tropical Trees as Living Systems" (P. B. Tomlinson and M. H. Zimmermann, eds.), pp. 401–422. Cambridge University Press, Cambridge.

Chiu, S.-T., and Ewers, F. W. (1992). Xylem structure and water transport in a twiner, a scrambler, and a shrub of *Lonicera* (Caprifoliaceae). *Trees* **6,** 216–224.

Davis, S. D., and Mooney, H. A. (1986). Water use patterns of four co-occurring chaparral shrubs. *Oecologia* **70,** 172–174.

Davis, S. D., Kolb, K. J., Jarbeau, J. A., and Redtfeldt, R. A. (1993). Water stress and xylem dysfunction in chaparral shrubs of California. *Ecol. Soc. Am. Bull. Supp.* **74,** 209.

DeLucia, E. H., and Schlesinger, W. H. (1991). Resource use efficiency and drought tolerance in adjacent Great Basin and Sierran plants *Ecology* **72,** 51–58.

Ewers, F. W., Fisher, J. B., and Chiu, S.-T. (1990). A survey of vessel dimensions in stems of tropical lianas and other growth forms. *Oecologia* **84,** 544–552.

Farmer, J. B. (1918). On the quantitative differences in the water-conductivity of the wood in trees and shrubs. 1. The evergreens. 2. The deciduous plants. *Proc. R. Soc. London Ser. B* **90,** 218–250.

Gartner, B. L. (1989). Breakage and regrowth of *Piper* species in rain forest understory. *Biotropica* **21,** 303–307.

Gartner, B. L. (1991a). Stem hydraulic properties of vines vs shrubs of western poison oak, *Toxicodendron diversilobum. Oecologia* **87,** 180–189.

Gartner, B. L. (1991b). Structural stability and architecture of vines vs. shrubs of poison oak, *Toxicodendron diversilobum. Ecology* **72,** 2005–2015.

Gartner, B. L. (1991c). Relative growth rates of vines and shrubs of western poison oak, *Toxicodendron diversilobum* (Anacardiaceae). *Am. J. Bot.* **78,** 1435–1353.

Gilbert, E. (1966). Structure and development of sumac clones. *Am. Midl. Nat.* **75,** 432–445.

Gill, D. S., and Mahall, B. E. (1986). Quantitative phenology and water relations of an evergreen and a deciduous chaparral shrub. *Ecol. Monogr.* **56,** 127–143.

Givnish, T. J. (1978). On the adaptive significance of compound leaves, with particular reference to tropical trees. *In* "Tropical Trees as Living Systems" (P. B. Tomlinson and M. H. Zimmermann, eds.), pp. 351–380. Cambridge University Press, Cambridge.

Hallé, F., Oldeman, R. A. A., and Tomlinson, P. B. (1978). "Tropical Trees and Forests: An Architectural Analysis." Springer-Verlag, New York.

Hicks, D. J., and Hustin, D. L. (1989). Response of *Hamamelis virginiana* L. to canopy gaps in a Pennsylvania oak forest. *Am. Midl. Nat.* **121,** 200–204.

Hobbs, R. J., and Mooney, H. A. (1986). Community changes following shrub invasion of grassland. *Oecologia* **70,** 508–513.

Holmes, P. M., and Cowling, R. M. (1993). Effects of shade on seedling growth, morphology and leaf photosynthesis in six subtropical thicket species from the eastern Cape, South Africa. *For. Ecol. Manage.* **61,** 199–220.

Horn, H. S. (1971). "The Adaptive Geometry of Trees." Princeton University Press, Princeton, New Jersey.

Huenneke, L. F. (1987). Demography of a clonal shrub, *Alnus incana* ssp *rugosa* (Betulaceae). *Am. Midl. Nat.* **117,** 43–56.

Jacobs, M. R. (1954). The effect of wind sway on the form and development of *Pinus radiata* D. Don. *Aust. J. Bot.* **2,** 35–51.

Keeley, J. E. (1992). Recruitment of seedlings and vegetative sprouts in unburned chaparral. *Ecology* **73,** 1194–1208.

Kempf, J. S., and Pickett, S. T. A. (1981). The role of branch length and angle in branching pattern of forest shrubs along a successional gradient. *New Phytol.* **87,** 111–116.

King, D. A. (1987). Load bearing capacity of understory treelets of a tropical wet forest. *Bull. Torrey. Bot. Club* **114,** 419–428.

Kolb, K. J., and Davis, S. D. (1994). Drought tolerance and xylem embolism in co-occurring species of coastal sage and chaparral. *Ecology* **75,** 648–659.

Messier, C., Honer, T. W., and Kimmins, J. P. (1989). Photosynthetic photon flux density, red: far-red ratio, and minimum light requirement for survival of *Gaultheria shallon* in western red-cedar—western hemlock stands in British Columbia. *Can. J. For. Res.* **19,** 1470–1477.

Neel, P. L., and Harris, R. W. (1971). Motion-induced inhibition of elongation and induction of dormancy in *Liquidambar. Science* **173,** 58–59.

Newton, R. J., and Goodin, J. R. (1989a). Moisture stress adaptations in shrubs. *In* "Biology and Utilization of Shrubs" (C. M. McKell, ed.), pp. 365–383. Academic Press, New York.

Newton, R. J., and Goodin, J. R. (1989b). Temperature stress adaptations in shrubs. *In* "Biology and Utilization of Shrubs" (C. M. McKell, ed.), pp. 384–402. Academic Press, New York.

Nicola, A., and Pickett, S. T. A. (1983). The adaptive architecture of shrub canopies: Leaf display and biomass allocation in relation to light environment. *New Phytol.* **93,** 301–310.

Nilsen, E. T., Sharifi, M. R., and Rundel, P. W. (1984). Comparative water relations of phreatophytes in the Sonoran Desert of California. *Ecology* **65,** 767–778.

O'Keefe, J. F., Saunders, K., and Wilson, B. F. (1982). Mountain laurel: a problem in northeastern forests. Presented at Northern Logger Timber Proceeding, July 15, 1982.

Orsham, G. (1972). Morphological and physiological plasticity in relation to drought. *In* "Wildland Shrubs—their Biology and Utilization," pp. 245–254. *U.S. Forest Service General Technical Report* INT-1.

Orsham, G. (1989). Shrubs as a growth form. *In* "Biology and Utilization of Shrubs" (C. M. McKell, ed.), pp. 249–265. Academic Press, New York.

Parsons, D. J., Rundel, P. W., Hedlund, R. P., and Baker, G. A. (1981). Survival of a severe drought by a non-sprouting chaparral shrub. *Am. J. Bot.* **68,** 973–979.

Pickett, S. T. A., and Kempf, J. S. (1980). Branching patterns in forest shrubs and understory trees in relation to habitat. *New Phytol.* **86,** 219–232.

Pritts, M. P., and Hancock, J. F. (1985). Lifetime biomass partitioning and yield component relationships in the highbush blueberry *Vaccinium corymbosum* L. (Ericaceae). *Am. J. Bot.* **72,** 446–452.

Reukema, D. L. (1959). Missing rings in branches of young Douglas fir. *Ecology* **40,** 480–482.

Riegel, G. M., Miller, R. F., and Krueger, W. C. (1992). Competition for resources between understory vegetation and overstory *Pinus ponderosa* in northeastern Oregon. *Ecol. Appl.* **2,** 71–75.

Rundel, P. W. (1991). Shrub life forms. *In* "Responses of Plants to Multiple Stresses" (H. A. Mooney, W. E. Winner, E. J. Pell, and E. Chu, eds.), pp. 345–370. Academic Press, New York.

Runkle, J. R. (1982). Patterns of disturbance in some old-growth forests of North America. *Ecology* **63,** 1533–1546.

Schulze, E.-D., Kuppers, M., and Matyssek, R. (1986). The role of carbon balance and branching pattern in the growth of woody species. *In* "On the Economy of Plant Form and Function" (T. J. Givnish, ed.), pp. 585–602. Cambridge University Press, Cambridge.

Smith, N. J. (1991). Sun and shade leaves: Clues to how salal (*Gaultheria shallon*) responds to overstory stand density. *Can. J. For. Res.* **21,** 300–305.

Spurr, S. H., and Barnes, B. V. (1980). "Forest Ecology." John Wiley & Sons, New York.

Stebbins, G. L. (1972). Evolution and diversity of arid-land shrubs. *In* "Wildland Shrubs—Their Biology and Utilization," pp. 111–121, U.S. Forest Service General Technical Report INT-1.

Stevens, G. C., and Fox, J. F. (1991). The causes of treeline. *Annual Rev. Ecol. Syst.* **22,** 177–191.

Stohlgren, T. J., Parsons, D. J., and Rundel, P. W. (1984). Population structure of *Adenostoma fasciculata* in mature stands of chamise chaparral in the southern Sierra Nevada, California. *Oecologia* **64,** 87–91.

Tappeiner, J. C. (1971). Invasion and development of beaked hazel in red pine stands in northern Minnesota. *Ecology* **52,** 514–519.

Tappeiner, J. C., Zasada, J., Ryan, P., and Newton, M. (1991). Salmonberry clonal and population structure: The basis for persistent cover. *Ecology* **72,** 609–618.

Tolvanen, A., Laine, K., Pukonen, T., Saari, E., and Havas, P. (1994). Responses to harvesting intensity in a clonal dwarf shrub, the bilberry (*Vaccinium myrtillus* L.) *Vegetatio* **110,** 163–169.

Tyree, M. T., and Alexander, J. D. (1993). Hydraulic conductivity of branch junctions in three temperate tree species. *Trees* **7,** 156–159.

Vasek, F. C. (1980). Creosote bush: Long-lived clones in the Mojave desert. *Am. J. Bot.* **67,** 246–255.

Veres, J. S., and Pickett, S. T. A. (1982). Branching pattern of *Lindera benzoin* beneath gaps and closed canopies. *New Phytol.* **91,** 767–772.

Wells, P. V. (1969). The relation between mode of reproduction and extent of speciation in woody genera of the California chaparral. *Evolution* **23,** 264–267.

Yang, S., and Tyree, M. T. (1993). Hydraulic resistance in *Acer saccharum* shoots and its influence on leaf water potential and transpiration. *Tree Physiol.* **12,** 231–242.

Zimmermann, M. H., and Jeje, A. A. (1981). Vessel-length distribution in stems of some American woody plants. *Can. J. Bot.* **59,** 1882–1892.

II

Roles of Stems
in Transport and Storage
of Water

5

Limitations on Stem Water Transport and Their Consequences

John S. Sperry

I. Introduction

Mechanical support and long-distance transport are two of the most obvious functions of stems. Vascular tissue, which makes up most of the stem in plants with secondary growth, plays a major role in both functions. Overproduction of vascular tissue relative to requirements for support and transport represents a waste of resources; underproduction may place restrictions on growth. The chapters by Mattheck [3], Gartner [6], and Givnish [1] in this volume discuss constraints of stem support on plant size and shape. Implications of stem phloem transport are discussed by Pate and Jeschke [8] and Van Bel [9] in this volume. This chapter considers interactions between stem water transport, xylem structure, vegetative phenology, and stomatal regulation of gas exchange.

II. Importance of Stem Water Transport

The significance of stem water transport is apparent in its influence on leaf water status and, ultimately, in how leaf water status is linked to the regulation of gas exchange and other leaf-level processes affecting whole-plant carbon gain. The abundance of xylem conduits specialized for longitudinal flow suggests an efficient transport system offering minimal frictional resistance. However, a number of studies have shown that a large fraction of the decrease in leaf water potential caused by transpiration results from the hydraulic resistance of stem xylem (reviewed in Tyree and Ewers, 1991).

Water flow through stems generally conforms to Darcy's law where volume flow rate ($\Delta v/\Delta t$) is a function of the hydraulic conductance (k; reciprocal of resistance) and the pressure difference between the ends of the flow path (ΔP):

$$\Delta v/\Delta t = k\ \Delta P \tag{1}$$

Although osmotic forces contribute to water flow into the root xylem (Passioura, 1988) and may influence water flow from leaf xylem to mesophyll cells (Canny, 1993), longitudinal transport in mature stem xylem introduces no symplastic barriers and osmotic potential does not participate in driving flow (Pickard, 1981). Stem k has been shown to be independent of ΔP over a 0.07 to 2.8 MPa range (Sperry and Tyree, 1990); this is consistent with water being nearly incompressible, and conduit walls being inflexible. Exceptions occur when pressure gradients alter pit membrane geometry (Sperry and Tyree, 1990) or cause cavitation and air blockage (Kelso *et al.*, 1963).

The hydraulic conductance of a stem [k; i.e., $(\Delta v/\Delta t)/\Delta P$, Eq. (1)] depends on stem length, transverse area of xylem, number and size distribution of xylem conduits, and extent of cavitation. Length can be factored out by expressing xylem flow rate per pressure gradient, $\Delta P/l$, rather than per ΔP, where l is the stem length. This gives the hydraulic conductivity (k_h). Dividing k_h by transverse xylem area gives a length- and area-specific conductivity ("specific conductivity," k_s) that is a useful measure of conducting efficiency. Either k or k_h can also be expressed per leaf area supplied to give leaf-specific conductance or conductivity, respectively (Tyree and Ewers, 1991); in this chapter leaf-specific conductance (k_l) will be used. The k_l of a defined flow path determines the associated ΔP at a given transpiration rate (E; per leaf area) for steady state conditions:

$$\Delta P = E/k_l \tag{2}$$

Hydraulic conductance of shoot xylem accounts for 20 to 60% of the total ΔP in the soil-to-leaf continuum in transpiring trees (Hellkvist *et al.*, 1974; Yang and Tyree, 1993; Sperry and Pockman, 1993) and crop plants (Moreshet *et al.*, 1987; McGowan *et al.*, 1987; Saliendra and Meinzer, 1989). In woody plants, most of this pressure drop in shoots occurs in the minor branches because k_l decreases as branch diameter decreases (Gartner, [6] in this volume; Zimmermann, 1978; Tyree and Ewers, 1991; Yang and Tyree, 1993).

III. Limits on Stem Water Transport: Cavitation

The importance of shoot k_l on leaf water status increases dramatically in response to drought and freezing stress because of physical limitations on xylem transport. According to the generally accepted cohesion theory (Dixon and Joly, 1895), water is pulled from the soil to the leaves to replace what evaporates through stomata. This places water inside the xylem conduits under negative pressure. At pressures below vapor pressure liquid water is in a "metastable" state and vulnerable to rapid transition to the stable vapor phase (cavitation). The result is a gas-filled (embolized) conduit that does not conduct water. The fact that significant negative pressures exist in the xylem indicates that nucleating sites for the phase change are relatively absent within the plant apoplast.

Nevertheless, as Milburn was the first to demonstrate (Milburn, 1966; Milburn and Johnson, 1966), xylem cavitation does occur in plants under stress. Xylem cavitation occurs by independent mechanisms during water stress and during freezing and thawing of xylem sap (Scholander *et al.*, 1961; Hammel, 1967). Cavitation is usually quantified by acoustic detection (e.g., Dixon *et al.*, 1984), or by how much the embolized conduits reduce the hydraulic conductance of the xylem ("percent loss k" or "embolism"; Sperry *et al.*, 1988a).

The cavitation response of a plant unambiguously limits the xylem pressure range over which water transport is possible. The remainder of this chapter concerns mechanisms of cavitation in stems caused by freezing and water stress and the implications of cavitation for adaptation to environmental stress.

IV. Freezing and Cavitation

A. Mechanism

Seasonal measurements of naturally occurring ("native") embolism in temperate trees have shown it is often most extensive during winter, and that its increase is correlated with number of freeze-thaw episodes rather than degrees of frost (Sperry *et al.*, 1988b, 1994; Cochard and Tyree, 1990; Wang *et al.*, 1992; Sperry, 1993). The simplest explanation for this is the induction of cavitation by freeze-thaw cycles. Freezing of xylem sap produces air bubbles inside the conduits because dissolved air in the sap is insoluble in ice. On thawing, these bubbles form potential nucleating sites (Hammel, 1967).

Other possible mechanisms causing winter embolism include sublimation of ice from frozen vessels, and water stress resulting from transpiration when soil is cold or frozen. The latter is most likely in evergreens, and the mechanism is discussed in Section V,A. Embolism by sublimation has been observed in branches where bark has been abraded (J. S. Sperry, unpublished data); however, there is little evidence for extensive sublimation from intact branches. Prolonged and severe midwinter freezes in Alaska were associated with stable and relatively low embolism (Sperry *et al.,* 1994).

The likelihood of a freeze-thaw cycle causing cavitation depends on the maximum radius of the gas bubbles formed in the conduit (r_b), and the xylem pressure following the thaw (P_x, relative to atmospheric; Oertli, 1971; Yang and Tyree, 1992). The internal pressure in a spherical bubble (P_b, relative to atmospheric, but above vacuum) is given by:

$$P_b = 2T/r_b + P_x \qquad (3)$$

where T is the surface tension of water (Yang and Tyree, 1992). Assuming the xylem sap is saturated with air at atmospheric pressure, if P_b is greater than the atmospheric pressure (i.e., > 0), gas will dissolve into the xylem sap and diffuse through the liquid to the atmosphere (or be carried away by bulk flow) and the bubble will disappear. This will be true for $P_x > -2T/r_b$. When $P_x \leq -2T/r_b$, the bubble will expand. If the expansion does not alter P_x, it will continue unchecked until the xylem conduit is embolized.

B. Relation to Conduit Size

From the above it can be predicted that larger xylem conduits will tend to be more vulnerable to cavitation by the freeze-thaw mechanism than smaller ones (Zimmermann, 1983; Ewers, 1985). This is because their larger water volume results in larger air bubbles after freezing. The larger the r_b value, the less negative is the P_x causing bubble expansion. Because the number of gas molecules dissolved in a water-filled conduit is a direct function of the conduit volume, the r_b of bubbles freezing out should generally be proportional to the cube root of the conduit volume $(V_c)^{1/3}$. The P_x causing bubble expansion should therefore be proportional to $-1/(V_c)^{1/3}$.

Although empirical data on vulnerability to cavitation by freezing are limited, they support the expected proportionality (Wang *et al.,* 1992; Sperry and Sullivan, 1992; Lo Gullo and Salleo, 1993; Sperry *et al.,* 1994). Figure 1a (solid circles) is a plot of conduit volume vs $-P_x$ causing 50% loss in hydraulic conductance in stems undergoing a single freeze-thaw cycle under controlled conditions. Species that have been measured span the range of conduit volumes from low (conifer tracheids) to high (earlywood ring-porous vessels). The slope of the log–log relationship is -0.34, which is close to the expected value of -0.33 (long dashed line) for proportionality of $-P_x$ to $1/(V_c)^{1/3}$. However, more data from large-vesselled species (i.e., $V_c > 10^{-10}$ m^3) are needed to confirm this proportionality.

Much of the early interest in winter cavitation centered on conifers

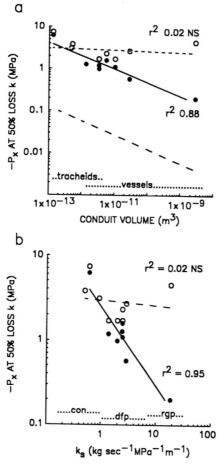

Figure 1 (a) The relationship between conduit volume and the xylem pressure (P_x) required to induce 50% loss in hydraulic conductance. Each data point represents a different species. There is no correlation between volume and cavitating pressure for cavitation induced by water stress ($\bigcirc$). There is a correlation between volume and cavitating pressure for cavitation caused by water stress in combination with a freeze-thaw event ($\bullet$). The slope of the freeze-thaw relationship ($\bullet$) is equal to the predicted slope (dashed line), but actual conduits cavitate at pressures an order of magnitude or more lower than predicted (from Sperry *et al.*, 1994; Sperry and Sullivan, 1992). (b) Relationship between specific conductivity (k_s) and xylem pressure (P_x) required to induce 50% loss of hydraulic conductance (k) for the same species as in (a). There is no correlation between cavitation pressure and k_s for water stress-induced cavitation ($\bigcirc$). There is a correlation between cavitation pressure and k_s for freeze-thaw-induced cavitation ($\bullet$) (from Sperry *et al.*, 1994). The range of k_s for conifers (con), diffuse–porous (dfp), and ring–porous (rgp) trees is shown.

(Hammel, 1967; Sucoff, 1969). Most conifers studied have been entirely resistant to freeze-thaw-induced cavitation regardless of the number of cycles experienced. In these conifers, freeze-thaw cycles induce no more cavitation than does negative pressure alone. Apparently bubble radii are small enough that pressures required to expand them are lower than what causes cavitation by the water-stress mechanism discussed in Section V,A. In support of this, conifers that are relatively resistant to cavitation by negative pressure do show cavitation in response to freeze-thaw cycles (e.g., *Juniperus scopulorum;* Sperry and Sullivan, 1992).

As discussed by Hammel (1967) and others (e.g., Sucoff, 1969; Sperry and Sullivan, 1992; Robson and Petty, 1993), pressures causing embolism by freeze-thaw cycles are much more negative than expected from predictions based on conduit volume (Fig. 1a, dashed line) or measurements of bubble radii in frozen conduits (Sucoff, 1969; Robson *et al.,* 1987). The reason may involve the expansion of water during freezing. This will tend to increase the pressure of surrounding liquid water, especially if the resistance to flow away from the freezing zone is high. This causes positive xylem pressures that can persist until all the ice disappears and thawing is complete (Robson and Petty, 1987). During the thaw, bubbles will dissolve relatively quickly into the degassed liquid xylem sap. Therefore, when negative pressures are restored after the thaw (by the return to original water volume), bubbles will be smaller than predicted on the basis of air content of the xylem conduit prior to freezing. Pressures required to expand them would be more negative than expected.

The amount of embolism occurring during a freeze-thaw cycle may also depend on the rate of thawing (Sperry and Sullivan, 1992). Faster thaws would give bubbles less time to dissolve and cause cavitation at less negative pressures. Slower thaws would do the opposite. Degrees of frost per se should be irrelevant to the amount of cavitation. These predictions have been confirmed in work by Davis and co-workers on chaparral shrubs (Langan and Davis, 1994).

C. Implications for Evolution of Woody Plants

The causal link between vulnerability to freezing-induced cavitation and conduit size may have constrained the evolution of vascular systems and foliar phenology in woody plants of the temperate zone and other frost-prone regions. The selective pressure for increased conduit size is generally assumed to be increased conducting efficiency. The wider the conduit, the greater the conductance as predicted by the Poiseuille equation (Zimmermann, 1983). The longer the conduit, the fewer pit membranes need to be crossed; pit membranes can add substantial flow resistance (Calkin *et al.,* 1986). This is empirically evident from the fact that conifers have lower k_s values than diffuse-porous trees, which in turn have lower values than ring-porous species (Fig. 1b, *x* axis). However, the trade-off between conduit size and freezing vulnerability would tend to restrict the evolution of large-size conduits in above-ground stems, or otherwise select for traits mitigating the effects of winter embolism.

1. Evergreen Plants   These considerations predict that evergreen phenology, small-volume conduits, and low conducting efficiency (e.g., low k_s) would be coupled for temperate zone woody plants. Small conduits would confer greater resistance to cavitation caused by freezing, and would be necessary to extend the growing season. However, low k_s would mean lower canopy water loss rates per xylem transverse area and pressure gradient. To the extent that water loss rates are coupled to stomatal conductance, this would reduce the potential for canopy CO_2 uptake. The advantage of small conduits for evergreen woody plants in temperate areas may explain the putative loss of vessels (i.e., return to tracheid-based xylem) in certain primitive angiosperm clades (Young, 1981). Although the current range of these plants (tropical montane) does not suggest a temperate origin, conditions may have differed during their evolution.

Another advantage of tracheids may be the ability to refill after cavitation in the absence of positive pressures in the xylem (Borghetti *et al.*, 1991; Sobrado *et al.*, 1992; Sperry, 1993; Sperry *et al.*, 1994). This refilling may occur even when pressures are more negative than the minimum predicted to allow bubble dissolving by capillary forces [e.g., P_x from Eq. (3); Borghetti *et al.*, 1991]). If this is the case, the mechanism is unknown.

It is unclear whether evergreen temperate angiosperms with vessels have restricted vessel sizes and relatively low k_s as predicted. Certainly there are no evergreen ring-porous trees and few evergreen vines in the temperate zone (Teramura *et al.*, 1991). Notably, the vessels of the evergreen vine *Lonicera japonicum* are much narrower than cooccurring deciduous vines in the southeastern United States, and survival of winter leaves is less in exposed than protected sites (Teramura *et al.*, 1991). If large vessels are present in evergreen plants, complete cavitation of the vascular system would severely restrict the stomatal conductance of the overwintering foliage. Transpiration from these leaves could not resume until new vessels were produced or embolized ones were refilled. In the interim, smaller latewood vessels and/ or vasicentric tracheids (Carlquist, 1988) could be important in keeping buds and tissues hydrated.

2. Deciduous Plants   In contrast to evergreens, deciduous woody plants would be predicted to have relatively large-volume conduits with higher conducting efficiency. Refilling of embolized xylem prior to bud break by root or stem pressures occurs in many diffuse-porous species [*Vitis* spp. (Scholander *et al.*, 1957; Sperry *et al.*, 1987); *Acer saccharum* (Sperry *et al.*, 1988b); *Betula cordifolia* (Sperry, 1993); *Betula occidentalis, Alnus crispa*, and *A. incana* (Sperry *et al.*, 1994)]. Other diffuse-porous trees appear incapable of refilling [e.g., *Fagus* spp. (Sperry, 1993); and *Populus* spp. (Sperry *et al.*, 1994)]. To the extent that they become embolized over winter and rely on the previous year's sapwood for water transport, their stomatal conductances and/or leaf area may be limited by winter embolism. For example, Borghetti *et al.* (1993) found a relationship between increased late-winter embolism, delayed budbreak, and reduced growth rate among ecotypes of *Fagus sylvatica.*

Refilling of overwintering xylem of ring-porous species does not seem to occur (Ellmore and Ewers, 1986; Cochard and Tyree, 1990; Sperry *et al.*, 1994). Late in the spring, ring-porous species produce their large earlywood vessels at the same time the leaves are maturing. The width of these vessels creates sufficient transport capacity within a single growth ring to supply the entire crown (Ellmore and Ewers, 1986). The disadvantage of the ring-porous pattern may be extreme susceptibility to early fall or late spring frosts. This is consistent with their delay of 2 weeks or more in leafing out compared to cooccurring diffuse-porous trees (Wang *et al.*, 1992).

3. Range Limits   The response of stem transport to freeze-thaw cycles may be particularly important in the distribution of species growing near the boundaries between freezing and nonfreezing habitats. Any evergreen species relying primarily on large volume conduits for transport would be severely impaired as the frequency of freeze-thaw cycles increased. This would be true regardless of the freezing tolerance of the living tissue. In contrast, there may be little adaptive difference in xylem anatomy related to the freeze-thaw problem between low and high temperate latitudes because the number of freeze-thaw cycles tends to be much less at higher latitudes (Sperry *et al.*, 1994).

V. Water Stress and Cavitation

A. Mechanism

The nucleating event for cavitation caused by water stress has been the focus of considerable speculation and research. Several hypotheses have been proposed ranging from mechanical shock to cosmic rays (Oertli, 1971; Milburn, 1973; Pickard, 1981).

Experimental evidence overwhelmingly supports the air-seeding hypothesis originally advanced by Renner (1915), and more recently by Zimmermann (1983). According to this explanation, cavitation occurs when air from outside the conduit is aspirated through water-filled pores in the xylem conduit wall. A modification of Eq. (3) to account for adhesion between water and the pore wall describes the relationship between pore diameter and the minimum pressure difference (ΔP_{crit}) between xylem water and air pressure required to displace a gas–water meniscus in the pore:

$$\Delta P_{crit} = (2T \cos a)/r_p \tag{4}$$

where a is the contact angle between meniscus and pore wall, and r_p is the radius of the pore. Pressure differences lower than ΔP_{crit} can be maintained because of cohesive and adhesive forces (i.e., hydrogen bonding) within water and between water and cell walls. When ΔP reaches ΔP_{crit}, the air–water meniscus withdraws from the wall pore and an air bubble of radius $r_b = r_p$ is sucked into the xylem conduit. If $P_x \leq -2T/r_b$, then the bubble will expand and cause cavitation [Eq. (3)]. This will usually be the case because a = 0° for cell walls (Nobel, 1991), and ΔP results entirely from negative P_x. Initially, the cavitated conduit would be chiefly vapor filled. Relatively quickly (minutes to hours; Yang and Tyree, 1992), air would diffuse into the embolized conduit and cause pressures to rise near atmospheric.

The air-seeding hypothesis has been discounted by some (Oertli, 1971; Pickard, 1981) on the grounds that cell wall pores are too narrow to account for observed cavitation pressures. The limiting (i.e., maximum r_p) wall pores, however, are not in the wall proper, but in the interconduit pit membranes. These pits facilitate water flow between conduits, and pores in their membranes are often relatively large (e.g., maximum r_p of 0.01 to 0.22 μm; Van Alfen *et al.*, 1983; Siau, 1984). These pits function as check valves preventing the spread of gas from cavitated and embolized conduits (Zimmermann, 1983). In pit membranes lacking a torus (most angiosperms), the check-valve function results from the ΔP sustained by the gas–water meniscus in pit membrane pores. When a torus is present (most gymnosperms), the check-valve function results from deflection of the impermeable (i.e., nonporous) torus over the pit aperture (Dixon, 1914).

According to the air-seeding hypothesis, interconduit pits will have a ΔP_{crit} at which they fail as check valves and allow gas to propagate throughout the vascular system. For pits without a torus, this would be a function of the pore sizes and can be estimated from Eq. (4). When a torus is present, ΔP_{crit} would be determined by the strength (or probably more precisely, the modulus of elasticity) of the margo portion of the membrane that holds the torus in sealing position (Sperry and Tyree, 1990). Slippage of the torus from the pit aperture would result in air seeding and cavitation.

The strongest evidence for air seeding comes from testing its prediction that embolism can be induced not only by lowering the xylem pressure inside the functional xylem conduits, but also by raising the air pressure around the xylem conduits (and inside embolized ones). As shown in Fig. 2, the positive air pressure required to cause a given amount of cavitation when xylem pressures are atmospheric (e.g., Fig. 2, solid symbols) accu-

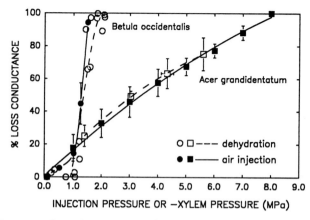

Figure 2   Percentage loss in hydraulic conductance vs xylem pressure (open symbols), and vs air injection pressure (solid symbols) for stems of *Betula occidentalis* (circles) and *Acer grandidentatum* (squares) (Sperry and Saliendra, 1994; Alder *et al.*, 1995).

rately predicts the negative xylem pressure required to cause the same amount of cavitation under atmospheric air pressures (e.g., Fig. 2, open symbols). Whether the air is pushed or pulled into the xylem conduits, ΔP_{crit} is the same. The only difference is that when air is pulled in, it nucleates cavitation; when it is pushed in there is no cavitation (i.e., P_x = atmospheric pressure) and embolism arises from water displaced by the continued entrance of air. The same correspondence has been found in conifers and angiosperms with a wide range of vulnerability to cavitation (Sperry and Tyree, 1990; Cochard *et al.*, 1992; Jarbeau *et al.*, 1995; Sperry and Saliendra, 1994; Alder *et al.*, 1995). Incidentally, these experiments provide evidence for substantial negative pressures in plants that is independent of, but consistent with, pressure bomb estimates (as questioned by Zimmermann *et al.*, 1993).

B. Relation to Conduit Size

In contrast to cavitation caused by freeze-thaw events in which conduit size is directly related to cavitation vulnerability (Fig. 1a, solid circles), there is no such relationship across taxa for cavitation caused by water stress (Fig. 1a, open circles; Tyree and Dixon, 1986; Sperry and Sullivan, 1992; Sperry *et al.*, 1994). Tracheids or small vessels can be as vulnerable as large vessels; large vessels can be as resistant as tracheids. This means pit membrane permeability is independent of conduit size across taxa, and that conduit size itself has no direct influence on cavitation by negative pressure alone. This is true even between individuals of a species (Sperry and Saliendra, 1994). Within a single stem or individual, however, conduit diameter does correlate with vulnerability to water stress-induced cavitation (Salleo and Lo Gullo, 1989a,b; Sperry and Tyree, 1990; Lo Gullo and Salleo, 1991; Hargrave *et al.*, 1994; Sperry and Saliendra, 1994) because the larger conduits have pit membranes more permeable to air (Sperry and Tyree, 1990).

C. Safety Margins

The vulnerability of stem xylem to cavitation by water stress varies widely across taxa and correlates with the minimum xylem pressures developed in nature (Fig. 3, solid line). The safety margin against complete failure of stem water transport (Fig. 3, compare solid vs dashed line; Tyree and Sperry, 1988) is narrow (ca. 0.4–0.6 MPa) in plants developing less negative pressures (> -2.0 MPa) but increases to several megapascals in plants experiencing lower pressures. Safety margins in root xylem may be even less than in stems (Sperry and Saliendra, 1994; Alder *et al.*, 1995).

Why do small margins of safety exist? The advantage of maximizing stomatal conductance for increased carbon gain will favor low xylem pressures at a given hydraulic conductance [Eq. (5), below]. However, the 100% cavitation pressure could in principle be well below physiological pressures for many species, giving them a generous buffer (i.e., 100% cavitation occurs at < -16 MPa in *Larrea tridentata*; Pockman and Sperry, 1994). Although narrow safety margins could have resulted from a trade-off between cavitation resistance and conducting efficiency, there is no evidence for this trade-off from comparisons across taxa (Fig. 1b, open circles; see also Cochard, 1992; Tyree *et al.*, 1994) because conduit size does not directly influence

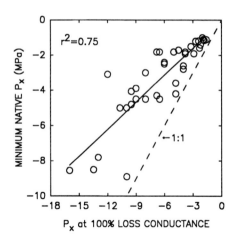

Figure 3 Xylem pressure (P_x) required to induce 100% cavitation vs minimum pressure observed in the field. Dashed line indicates 1:1 relationship. (Data from Davis *et al.*, 1990; Neufeld *et al.*, 1992; Tyree *et al.*, 1991; Kolb and Davis, 1994; Sperry *et al.*, 1988c, 1994; Pockman and Sperry, 1994; Alder *et al.*, 1995; D. Piccotino, K. J. Kolb, and J. S. Sperry, unpublished observations.)

vulnerability to cavitation by water stress (Fig. 1a, open circles). Perhaps there is an inherent advantage to cavitation that explains why many plants function so "close to the edge" (Section V,E).

D. Implications for Stomatal Responses to Water Stress

The limitations on xylem pressure and hydraulic conductance created by cavitation have important implications for how stomata "sense" water stress and regulate leaf xylem pressure (equivalent to leaf water potential, ψ_{pl}, for xylem sap with negligible osmotic potential). To control ψ_{pl}, stomata must exhibit a feedback response to xylem pressure (i.e., via changes in cell volume and/or turgor), and/or a feed-forward response to parameters influencing this pressure. Applying Eq. (2) to the soil–plant hydraulic continuum and solving for ψ_{pl} gives:

$$\psi_{pl} = \psi_s - (g_l \, \Delta N_{wv})/k_l \qquad (5)$$

where ψ_s is soil water potential [in Eq. (2), $\Delta P = \psi_{pl} - \psi_s$], g_l is the leaf conductance to water vapor (per leaf area), ΔN_{wv} is the driving force for evaporation from the leaf or canopy [in Eq. (2), $E = g_l \, \Delta N_{wv}$], and k_l is the leaf-specific hydraulic conductance of the soil–leaf flow path. The plant influences ψ_{pl} via changes in stomatal conductance (g_s) that in turn alter g_l. Boundary layer conductance (g_b) also influences g_l, but the plant has no direct short-term control over this component.

The safety margin from cavitation places obvious constraints on stomatal regulation of transpiration and ψ_{pl}. This is illustrated by comparing two common tree species of the western United States. *Betula occidentalis* branch xylem (stem diameter, 4–5 mm) has a threshold-type relationship between loss of conductance and xylem pressure ("vulnerability curve") with 100% loss of conductance occurring at -1.75 MPa (Fig. 4, solid squares). It occupies riparian habitat and its stomata maintain a narrow ψ_{pl} range between -1.0 and -1.4 MPa on clear days (Fig. 4, solid bar, upper x axis) despite changes in ψ_s, ΔN_{wv}, and k_l (Sperry *et al.*, 1993; Saliendra *et al.*, 1995). This "isohydric" behavior (Tardieu, 1993) is necessary because there is only a 0.3 to 0.7 MPa buffer between midday ψ_{pl} and pressures causing complete cavitation. Stems in the field seldom develop more than 10% loss of conduction (Sperry *et al.*, 1993). In contrast, *Acer grandidentatum* branch xylem (stem diameter, 5–8 mm) has a shallow-sloped vulnerability curve with 100% loss of conductance occurring at -8.0 MPa (Fig. 4, open symbols). It grows over a wide range in ψ_s, and its midday ψ_{pl} varies from -1.25 MPa in riparian areas to -4.4 MPa (and probably more negative) in dry upland sites (Fig. 4, open bar on upper x axis). Vulnerability curves do not vary between wet and dry sites (Fig. 4, compare open circles and squares), and its "nonisohydric" behavior is accommodated by at least a 3.6 MPa buffer from complete cavitation. However, stems can develop as much as 50% loss of conductance in drier sites (Alder *et al.*, 1995).

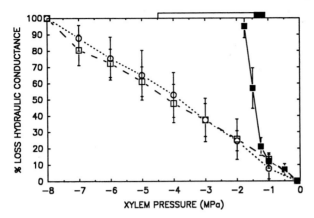

Figure 4 Contrasting safety margins from cavitation in two tree species of stream valleys in the western United States. Percentage loss in hydraulic conductance of stem xylem vs xylem pressure shown for *Betula occidentalis* (■) and *Acer grandidentatum* (○, □). Range of midday ψ_{pl} under clear conditions is shown by bar on the upper x axis: solid bar, *B. occidentalis*; open bar, *A. grandidentatum*. Safety margin from complete cavitation is the difference (in MPa) between ψ_{pl} and the xylem pressure causing 100% loss of conductance. The small safety margin in *B. occidentalis* corresponds with its strictly riparian habitat and isohydric regulation of ψ_{pl}. Native cavitation seldom exceeds 10%. The larger safety margin in *A. grandidentatum* corresponds with its tolerance of riparian and upland habitat and non-isohydric regulation of ψ_{pl}. Vulnerability curves did not differ between upland (□) and riparian (○) sites, and lower ψ_{pl} at drier sites was associated with up to ca. 50% loss of conductance in stems. (From Sperry and Saliendra, 1994; Alder *et al.*, 1995.)

Although all plants must avoid complete cavitation to continue gas exchange, many, like *A. grandidentatum* (Fig. 4), have linear or shallow-sloped vulnerability curves and may show progressive cavitation during drought [e.g., *Populus tremuloides* (Sperry *et al.*, 1991), *Salvia mellifera* (Kolb and Davis, 1994), *Adenostoma sparsifolium* (Redtfeldt and Davis, 1995), and *Artemisia tridentata* (K. J. Kolb and J. S. Sperry, unpublished observations)]. The few crop species examined have similarly shaped vulnerability curves and cavitate extensively during the day even when well watered; the xylem appears to refill at night by root pressure (Tyree *et al.*, 1986; Neufeld *et al.*, 1992). Even *B. occidentalis*, which avoids cavitation in its shoot xylem (Fig. 4), develops significant cavitation in its more vulnerable root xylem under normal conditions (Sperry and Saliendra, 1994).

The occurrence of partial cavitation has direct bearing on how stomata "sense" water stress and avoid an uncontrolled drop in ψ_{pl}. If there is no change in g_s (for constant ΔN_{wv} and ψ_s), cavitation would cause ψ_{pl} to drop by decreasing k_l [Eq. (5)]. This could lead to more cavitation and lower k_l and a positive feedback cycle causing "runaway" cavitation until all xylem is embolized (Tyree and Sperry, 1988). In fact, g_s tends to adjust in proportion to changes in k_l so that bulk ψ_{pl} remains nearly constant. This occurs whether k_1 is reduced by partial stem cavitation, stem notching, or root pruning; or whether k_1 is increased by partial defoliation (Teskey *et al.*, 1983; Meinzer and Grantz, 1990; Meinzer *et al.*, 1992; Sperry *et al.*, 1993).

This isohydric response to changing k_1 could result from a feed-forward signal linking k_1 to g_s because g_s appears to vary independently of ψ_{pl}. The same logic has been used to propose feed-forward responses of stomata to ψ_s via chemical signals transported from roots and to ΔN_{wv} via epidermal transpiration or humidity sensing (Farquhar, 1978; Davies and Zhang, 1991). In the case of k_1, however, it is difficult to imagine a feed-forward response more rapid than the almost immediate influence of k_1 on ψ_{pl} (pressure changes can propagate through xylem at up to the speed of sound in water; Malone, 1993).

It is more likely that the isohydric response of plants to k_1 results from a sensitive feedback loop between ψ_{pl} and g_s. The pressure bomb is often used to measure ψ_{pl}, and it gives only a crude volume-averaged estimate. It cannot resolve small-scale changes in time and space to which stomata may be responding. Pressure probe measurements of mesophyll turgor during humidity changes have revealed the presumed feed-forward response of leaves to humidity is more consistent with a fine-scale feedback loop (Nonami *et al.*, 1990). Experiments with *B. occidentalis* suggest this is true of short-term stomatal responses to k_1 as well as ΔN_{wv} and ψ_s (Saliendra *et al.*, 1995).

E. Advantages of Cavitation

Why does partial cavitation occur? The theoretical analysis by Jones and Sutherland (1991) predicts it is necessary for maximizing g_s in species with shallow-sloped vulnerability curves and large safety margins from cavitation. However, steeper-sloped curves allow maximum g_s without cavitation and the question remains why shallow-sloped vulnerability curves exist. Furthermore, this analysis did not account for the interaction between g_s and k_1 that minimizes short-term changes in ψ_{pl} (Teskey *et al.*, 1983; Meinzer and Grantz, 1990; Meinzer *et al.*, 1992; Sperry *et al.*, 1993).

Reduced hydraulic conductance from xylem cavitation during a day or season of soil water depletion could result in two advantages as compared to no cavitation and constant plant hydraulic conductance: (1) the release of water from cavitating xylem conduits may buffer leaf water status (Dixon *et al.*, 1984; Lo Gullo and Salleo, 1992); (2) a measured drop in plant conductance beginning early in a drought may at once conserve soil water and facilitate its extraction.

The second point is speculative and requires explanation. A reduction in plant hydraulic conductance from cavitation will cause stomatal closure and reduced transpiration over the short term (to maintain constant ψ_{pl}, see Section V,D). This will not only conserve soil water, but by moderating its extraction rate it will reduce the drop in soil hydraulic conductance associated with water depletion (Hillel, 1980). If there were no drop in plant conductance when water potential gradients were causing soil conductance to drop sharply, positive feedback could ensue, causing severe loss of soil conductance analogous with runaway cavitation in plant xylem. Partial cavitation in xylem may cause total soil–plant hydraulic conductance to be higher over a drought period than if plant conductance remained high and unchanged. Stomatal conductance would also be maximized over the interval.

Although competition for soil water would favor rapid water uptake, this would be self-defeating if it entailed an uncontrolled drop in soil-to-root conductance. For a given life history (i.e., annual, suffrutescent or drought-deciduous perennial, evergreen perennial, etc.) and rooting profile there may be only one optimal balance between plant and soil conductances to optimize soil water uptake and stomatal conductance over the required period. For this benefit of reduced xylem conductance to be meaningful, the hydraulic conductance must be restored when soil is recharged with water. This could result from new xylem production after seasonal droughts, or from refilling of embolized xylem by nightly root pressures as documented in crop species (Tyree *et al.*, 1986; Neufeld *et al.*, 1992).

While cavitation in perennial stems may be partial in response to drought stress, complete cavitation in more ephemeral organs may eliminate water transport with advantageous consequences. An extreme example of the feedback between plant and soil hydraulic conductance occurs in the response of smaller cactus and agave roots to soil drought (North *et al.*, 1992). As soil water potential and conductance drop, cavitation in specific tracheids at the junction between lateral and major roots plays an important role in hydraulically isolating the plant from the drying soil. This prevents backward flow of water from the plant into the soil and allows these desert succulents to maintain a favorable water balance. Hydraulic conductance in major roots and the stem is preserved.

Similarly, the rachis xylem of *Juglans regia* is significantly more vulnerable than the stem xylem (Tyree *et al.*, 1993). During drought, complete cavitation in the leaf may induce abscission and protect the necessarily more permanent stem xylem from complete cavitation. Thus, a controlled form of runaway cavitation in ephemeral organs may promote survival of more permanent stems during extreme drought. Gartner ([6] in this volume) describes other examples of hydraulically mediated changes in canopy architecture.

The role of cavitation in controlling water use may explain why many plants experience limited safety margins from failure of water transport. Cavitation may not represent a limitation on gas exchange as much as an additional means of regulating it. The shape of the vulnerability curve with respect to the pattern of stomatal regulation, water availability, and plant life history may have important consequences for adaptation to different habitats. The "limitation" imposed by cavitation may have evolved as a mechanism to moderate water use as it becomes less available in a given niche.

VI. Conclusions

The study of stem water transport has revealed previously unsuspected constraints on whole plant-level processes including drought survival, stomatal control, foliar phenology, and freezing tolerance. In particular, the occurrence of extensive xylem cavitation in stems and roots forces a new perspective on the stomatal regulation of water loss. The importance of cavitation for changing whole-plant hydraulic conductance, and the dependence of stomatal conductance on hydraulic conductance, reveals a link that can potentially explain variation in water use efficiency, drought survival, and signaling processes linking water stress to the stomatal reaction. The general goal of research in this area continues to be understanding how water transport capability in the xylem and other parts of the soil–plant continuum may facilitate and/or limit adaptive responses of the whole plant to the environment.

References

Alder, N. N., Sperry, J.S., and Pockman, W. T. (1995). Root and stem xylem embolism, stomatal conductance, and leaf turgor in *Acer grandidentatum* populations along a moisture gradient. *Oecologia.* (submitted).

Borghetti, M., Edwards, W. R. N., Grace, J., Jarvis, P. G., and Raschi, A. (1991). The refilling of embolized xylem in *Pinus sylvestris. Plant Cell Environ.* **14,** 357–369.

Borghetti, M., Leonardi, S., Raschi, A., Snyderman, D., and Tognetti, R. (1993). Ecotypic variation of xylem embolism, phenological traits, growth parameters, and allozyme characteristics in *Fagus sylvatica. Funct. Ecol.* **7,** 713–720.

Calkin, H. W., Gibson, A. C., and Nobel, P. S. (1986). Biophysical model of xylem conductance in tracheids of the fern *Pteris vittata. J. Exp. Bot.* **37,** 1054–1064.

Canny, M. J. (1993). The transpiration stream in the leaf apoplast: Water and solutes. *Philos. Trans. R. Soc. London B* **341,** 87–100.

Carlquist, S. (1988). "Comparative Wood Anatomy: Systematic, Ecological, and Evolutionary Aspects of Dicotyledon Wood." Springer-Verlag, Berlin.

Cochard, H. (1992). Vulnerability of several conifers to air embolism. *Tree Physiol.* **11,** 73–83.

Cochard, H., and Tyree, M. T. (1990). Xylem dysfunction in *Quercus*: Vessel sizes, tyloses, cavitation and seasonal changes in embolism. *Tree Physiol.* **6,** 393–407.

Cochard, H., Cruziat, P., and Tyree, M. T. (1992). Use of positive pressures to establish vulnerability curves: Further support for the air-seeding hypothesis and implications for pressure-volume analysis. *Plant Physiol.* **100,** 205–209.

Davies, W. J., and Zhang, J. (1991). Root signals and the regulation of growth and development of plants in drying soil. *Annu. Rev. Plant Physiol. Mol. Biol.* **42,** 55–76.

Davis, S. D., Paul, A., and Mallare, L. (1990). Differential resistance to water stress induced embolism between two species of chaparral shrubs: *Rhus laurina* and *Ceanothus megacarpus*. *Bull. Ecol. Soc. Am.* **71,** 133.

Dixon, H. H. (1914). "Transpiration and the Ascent of Sap in Plants." Macmillan, London.

Dixon, H. H., and Joly, J. (1895). On the ascent of sap. *Philos. Trans. R. Soc. London B* **186,** 563–576.

Dixon, M. A., Grace, J., and Tyree, M. T. (1984). Concurrent measurements of stem density, leaf and stem water potential, stomatal conductance, and cavitation on a sapling of *Thuja occidentalis* L. *Plant Cell Environ.* **7,** 615–618.

Ellmore, G. S., and Ewers, F. W. (1986). Fluid flow in the outermost xylem increment of a ring-porous tree, *Ulmus americana. Am. J. Bot.* **73,** 1771–1774.

Ewers, F. W. (1985). Xylem structure and water conduction in conifer trees, dicot trees, and lianas. *Int. Assoc. Wood Anat. Bull.* **6,** 309–317.

Farquhar, G. D. (1978). Feedforward responses of stomata to humidity. *Aust. J. Plant Physiol.* **5,** 787–800.

Hammel, H. T. (1967). Freezing of xylem sap without cavitation. *Plant Physiol.* **42,** 55–66.

Hargrave, K. R., Kolb, K. J., Ewers, F. W., and Davis, S. D. (1994). Conduit diameter and drought-induced embolism in *Salvia mellifera* (Labiateae). *New Phytol.* **126,** 695–705.

Hellkvist, J., Richards, G. P., and Jarvis, P. G. (1974). Vertical gradients of water potential and tissue water relations in Sitka spruce trees measured with the pressure chamber. *J. Appl. Ecol.* **7,** 637–667.

Hillel, D. (1980). "Fundamentals of Soil Physics." Academic Press, New York.

Jarbeau, J. A., Ewers, F. W., and Davis, S. D. (1995). The mechanism of water stress induced xylem dysfunction in two species of chaparral shrubs. *Plant Cell Environ.* **18,** 189–196.

Jones, H. G., and Sutherland, R. A. (1991). Stomatal control of xylem embolism. *Plant Cell Environ.* **14,** 607–612.

Kelso, W. C., Jr., Gertjejansen, R. O., and Hossfeld, R. L. (1963). The effect of air blockage upon the permeability of wood to liquids. *Univ. Minn. Agric. Res. Stat. Tech. Bull.* No. 242.

Kolb, K. J., and Davis, S. D. (1994). Drought-induced xylem embolism in two co-occurring species of coastal sage and chaparral of California. *Ecology* **75,** 648–659.

Langan, S. J., and Davis, S. D. (1994). Xylem dysfunction caused by freezing and water stress in two species of co-occurring chaparral shrubs. *Bull. Ecol. Soc. Am.* **75,** 126.

LoGullo, M. A., and Salleo, S. (1991). Three different methods for measuring xylem cavitation and embolism: A comparison. *Ann. Bot.* **67,** 417–424.

LoGullo, M. A., and Salleo, S. (1992). Water storage in the wood and xylem cavitation in 1-year-old twigs of *Populus deltoides* Bartr. *Plant Cell Environ.* **15,** 431–438.

LoGullo, M. A., and Salleo, S. (1993). Different vulnerabilities of *Quercus ilex* L. to freeze- and summer drought-induced xylem embolism: An ecological interpretation. *Plant Cell Environ.* **16,** 511–519.

Malone, M. (1993). Hydraulic signals. *Philos. Trans. R. Soc. London B* **341,** 33–39.

McGowan, M., Hector, D., and Gregson, K. (1987). Water relations of temperate crops. *In* "Proceedings of International Conference on Measurement of Soil and Plant Water Status," pp. 289–297. Utah State University Press, Logan, Utah.

Meinzer, F. C., and Grantz, D. A. (1990). Stomatal and hydraulic conductance in growing sugarcane: Stomatal adjustment to water transport capacity. *Plant Cell Environ.* **13,** 383–388.

Meinzer, F. C., Goldstein, G., Neufeld, H. S., Grantz, D. A., and Crisosto, G. M. (1992). Hydraulic architecture of sugar cane in relation to patterns of water use during development. *Plant Cell Environ.* **15,** 471–477.

Milburn, J. A. (1966). The conduction of sap. I. Water conduction and cavitation in water stressed leaves. *Planta* **65,** 34–42.

Milburn, J. A. (1973). Cavitation studies on whole *Ricinus* plants by acoustic detection. *Planta* **112,** 333–342.

Milburn, J. A, and Johnson, R. P. C. (1966). The conduction of sap. II. Detection of vibrations produced by sap cavitation in *Ricinus* xylem. *Planta* **69**, 133–141.

Moreshet, S., Huck, M. G., Hesketh, J. D., and Peters, D. B. (1987). Measuring the hydraulic conductance of soybean root systems. *In* "Proceedings of International Conference on Measurement of Soil and Plant Water Status," pp. 221–228. Utah State University Press, Logan, Utah.

Neufeld, H. S., Grantz, D. A., Meinzer, F. C., Goldstein, G., Crisosto, G. M., and Crisosto, C. (1992). Genotypic variability in vulnerability of leaf xylem to cavitation in water-stressed and well-irrigated sugarcane. *Plant Physiol.* **100**, 1020–1028.

Nobel, P. S. (1991). "Physicochemical and Environmental Plant Physiology." Academic Press, San Diego.

Nonami, H., Schulze, E. D., and Zeigler, H. (1990). Mechanisms of stomatal movement in response to air humidity, irradiance and xylem water potential. *Planta* **183**, 57–64.

North, G. B., Ewers, F. W., and Nobel, P. S. (1992). Main root-lateral root junctions of two desert succulents: Changes in axial and radial components of hydraulic conductivity during drying. *Am. J. Bot.* **79**, 1039–1050.

Oertli, J. J. (1971). The stability of water under tension in the xylem. *Z. Pflanzenphysiol.* **65**, 195–209.

Passioura, J. B. (1988). Water transport in and to roots. *Annu. Rev. Plant Physiol. Mol. Biol.* **39**, 245–265.

Pickard, W. F. (1981). The ascent of sap in plants. *Prog. Biophys. Mol. Biol.* **37**, 181–229.

Pockman, W. T., and Sperry, J. S. (1994). The relationship between vulnerability to cavitation and the annual range of soil water potential in woody perennial vegetation of the Sonoran Desert. *Bull. Ecol. Soc. Am.* **75**, 182.

Redtfeldt, R. A., and Davis, S. D. (1995). Further evidence of niche segregation between two congeneric, co-occurring species of *Adenostoma* in California chaparral. *Ecoscience* (submitted).

Renner, O. (1915). Theoretisches und Experimentelles zur Kohasionetheorie der Wasserbewegung. *Jahrb. Wiss. Bot.* **56**, 617–667.

Robson, D. J., and Petty, J. A. (1987). Freezing in conifer xylem. I. Pressure changes and growth velocity of ice. *J. Exp. Bot.* **38**, 1901–1908.

Robson, D. J., and Petty, J. A. (1993). A proposed mechanism of freezing and thawing in conifer xylem. *In* "Water Transport in Plants under Climatic Stress" (A. Raschi, M. Borghetti, and J. Grace, eds.), pp. 75–85. Cambridge University Press, Cambridge.

Robson, D. J., McHardy, W. J., and Petty, J. A. (1987). Freezing in conifer xylem. II. Pit aspiration and bubble formation. *J. Exp. Bot.* **39**, 1617–1621.

Saliendra, N. Z., and Meinzer, F. C. (1989). Relationship between root/soil hydraulic properties and stomatal behaviour in sugarcane. *Aust. J. Plant Physiol.* **16**, 241–250.

Saliendra, N. Z., Sperry, J. S., and Comstock, J. P. (1995). Influence of leaf water status on stomatal response to humidity, hydraulic conductance, and soil drought in *Betula occidentalis*. *Planta* (in press).

Salleo, S., and Lo Gullo, M. A. (1989a). Different aspects of cavitation resistance in *Ceratonia siliqua*, a drought-avoiding Mediterranean tree. *Ann. Bot.* **64**, 325–336.

Salleo, S., and Lo Gullo, M. A. (1989b). Xylem cavitation in nodes and internodes of *Vitis vinifera* L. plants subjected to water stress. Limits of restoration of water conduction in cavitated xylem conduits. *In* "Structural and Functional Responses to Environmental Stresses" (K. H. Kreeb, H. Richter, and T. Hinckley, eds.), pp. 33–42. Academic Publishing, The Hague, the Netherlands.

Scholander, P. F., Ruud, B., and Leivestad, H. (1957). The rise of sap in a tropical liana. *Plant Physiol.* **32**, 1–6.

Scholander, P. F., Hemmingsen, E., and Garey, W. (1961). Cohesive lift of sap in the rattan vine. *Science* **134**, 1835–1838.

Siau, J. F. (1984). "Transport Processes in Wood." Springer-Verlag, New York.

Sobrado, M. A., Grace, J., and Jarvis, P. G. (1992). The limits to xylem embolism recovery in *Pinus sylvestris* L. *J. Exp. Bot.* **43**, 831–836.

Sperry, J. S. (1993). Winter xylem embolism and spring recovery in *Betula cordifolia, Fagus grandifolia, Abies balsamifera,* and *Picea rubens. In* "Water Transport in Plants under Climatic Stress" (A. Raschi, M. Borghetti, and J. Grace, eds.), pp. 86–98. Cambridge University Press, Cambridge.

Sperry, J. S., and Pockman, W. T. (1993). Limitation of transpiration by hydraulic conductance and xylem cavitation in *Betula occidentalis. Plant Cell Environ.* **16**, 279–288.

Sperry, J. S., and Saliendra, N. Z. (1994). Intra- and inter-plant variation in xylem cavitation in *Betula occidentalis. Plant Cell Environ.* **17**, 1233–1241.

Sperry, J. S., and Sullivan, J. E. M. (1992). Xylem embolism in response to freeze-thaw cycles and water stress in ring-porous, diffuse-porous, and conifer species. *Plant Physiol.* **100**, 605–613.

Sperry, J. S., and Tyree, M. T. (1990). Water stress induced xylem cavitation in three species of conifers. *Plant Cell Environ.* **13**, 427–436.

Sperry, J. S., Holbrook, N. M., Zimmermann, M. H., and Tyree, M. T. (1987). Spring filling of xylem vessels in wild grapevine. *Plant Physiol.* **83**, 414–417.

Sperry, J. S., Donnelly, J. R., and Tyree, M. T. (1988a). A method for measuring hydraulic conductivity and embolism in xylem. *Plant Cell Environ.* **11**, 35–40.

Sperry, J. S., Donnelly, J. R., and Tyree, M. T. (1988b). Seasonal occurrence of xylem embolism in sugar maple (*Acer saccharum*). *Am. J. Bot.* **75**, 1212–1218.

Sperry, J. S., Tyree, M. T., and Donnelly, J. R. (1988c). Vulnerability of xylem to embolism in a mangrove vs. an inland species of Rhizophoraceae. *Physiol Plant.* **74**, 276–283.

Sperry, J. S., Perry, A., and Sullivan, J. E. M. (1991). Pit membrane degradation and air embolism formation in ageing vessels of *Populus tremuloides* Michx. *J. Exp. Bot.* **42**, 1399–1406.

Sperry, J. S., Alder, N. N., and Eastlack, S. E. (1993). The effect of reduced hydraulic conductance on stomatal conductance and xylem cavitation. *J. Exp. Bot.* **44**, 1075–1082.

Sperry, J. S., Nichols, K. L., Sullivan, J. E. M., and Eastlack, S. E. (1994). Xylem embolism in ring-porous, diffuse-porous, and coniferous trees of northern Utah and interior Alaska. *Ecology* **75**, 1736–1752.

Sucoff, E. (1969). Freezing of conifer xylem sap and the cohesion-tension theory. *Physiol. Plant.* **22**, 424–431.

Tardieu, F. (1993). Will increases in our understanding of soil-root relations and root signalling substantially alter water flux models? *Philos. Trans. R. Soc. London* **B341**, 57–66.

Teramura, A. H., Gold, W. G., and Forseth, I. N. (1991). Physiological ecology of mesic, temperate woody vines. *In* "Biology of Vines" (F. E. Putz and H. A. Mooney, eds.), pp. 245–286. Cambridge University Press, Cambridge.

Teskey, R. O., Hinckley, T. M., and Grier, C. C. (1983). Effect of interruption of flow path on stomatal conductance of *Abies amabilis. J. Exp. Bot.* **34**, 1251–1259.

Tyree, M. T., and Dixon, M. A. (1986). Water stress induced cavitation and embolism in some woody plants. *Physiol. Plant.* **66**, 397–405.

Tyree, M. T., and Ewers, F. W. (1991). The hydraulic architecture of trees and other woody plants (Tansley Review No. 34). *New Phytol.* **119**, 345–360.

Tyree, M. T., and Sperry, J. S. (1988). Do woody plants operate near the point of catastrophic xylem dysfunction caused by dynamic water stress? Answers from a model. *Plant Physiol.* **88**, 574–580.

Tyree, M. T., Fiscus, E. L., Wullschleger, S. D., and Dixon, M. A. (1986). Detection of xylem cavitation in corn under field conditions. *Plant Physiol.* **82**, 597–599.

Tyree, M. T., Snyderman, D. A., Wilmot, T. R., and Machado, J. L. (1991). Water relations and hydraulic architecture of a tropical tree (*Schefflera morototoni*). *Plant Physiol.* **96**, 1105–1113.

Tyree, M. T., Cochard, H., Cruziat, P., Sinclair, B., and Ameglio, T. (1993). Drought-induced leaf shedding in walnut: Evidence for vulnerability segmentation. *Plant Cell Environ.* **16,** 879–882.

Tyree, M. T., Davis, S. D., and Cochard, H. (1994). Biophysical perspectives of xylem evolution: Is there a tradeoff of hydraulic efficiency for vulnerability to dysfunction? *IAWA Bull.* **15,** 335–360.

Van Alfen, N. K., McMillan, B. D., Turner, V., and Hess, W. M. (1983). Role of pit membranes in macromolecule-induced wilt of plants. *Plant Physiol.* **73,** 1020–1023.

Wang, J., Ives, N. E., and Lechowicz, M. J. (1992). The relation of foliar phenology to xylem embolism in trees. *Funct. Ecol.* **6,** 469–475.

Yang, S., and Tyree, M. T. (1992). A theoretical model of hydraulic conductivity recovery from embolism with comparison to experimental data on *Acer saccharum. Plant Cell Environ.* **15,** 633–643.

Yang, S., and Tyree, M. T. (1993). Hydraulic resistance in *Acer saccharum* shoots and its influence on leaf water potential and transpiration. *Tree Physiol.* **12,** 231–242.

Young, D. A. (1981). Are the angiosperms primatively vesselless? *Syst. Bot.* **6,** 313–330.

Zimmermann, M. H. (1978). Hydraulic architecture of some diffuse-porous trees. *Can. J. Bot.* **56,** 2286–2295.

Zimmermann, M. H. (1983). "Xylem Structure and the Ascent of Sap." Springer-Verlag, New York.

Zimmermann, U., Haase, A., Langbein, D., and Meinzer, F. C. (1993). Mechanisms of long-distance water transport in plants: A re-examination of some paradigms in the light of new evidence. *Philos. Trans. R. Soc. London* **B341,** 19–31.

6

Patterns of Xylem Variation within a Tree and Their Hydraulic and Mechanical Consequences

Barbara L. Gartner

I. Introduction

Xylem is nonuniform in its structure and function throughout the plant stem. Xylem structure varies from pith to bark, from root to apical meristem, from stem to branch, at nodes vs internodes, and at junctions of branches, stems, or roots compared to the internodal regions nearby. At smaller scales, anatomy varies systematically within one growth ring and it varies among the layers of the cell wall. Xylem properties vary by the plane in which they are examined, owing to cell shape, cell orientation, and the orientation of microfibrils in the cell walls. As concluded by Larson (1967, p. 145), "more variability in wood characteristics exists within a single tree than among [average values for] trees growing on the same site or between [average values for] trees growing on different sites."

This structural heterogeneity results in spatial variation in hydraulic and mechanical performance of the xylem. Whereas wood technologists have long acknowledged the importance of wood variability (e.g., Northcott, 1957; Dadswell, 1958; Larson, 1962; Cown and McConchie, 1980; Beery et al., 1983; Megraw, 1985; Schniewind and Berndt, 1991), this heterogeneity often has been overlooked by botanists, who have tended to view stems as homogeneous organs ("biomass") with only a passive role in the biology of the plant. This chapter details the patterns of variation in xylem structure found within a woody plant, and emphasizes what is known and what is not known about the functional consequences of this variation for shoot water movement and mechanics.

II. Typical Patterns of Xylem Variation

This section reviews the typical structure of xylem within a tree, but the reader should refer to other sources such as Panshin and de Zeeuw (Ch. 7, 1980) or Koch (pp. 305–349, 1985) for more detailed descriptions. There is more information on softwood (gymnosperm) than hardwood (woody angiosperm) anatomy, and therefore many of the paradigms of wood anatomy are based on softwoods. In fact, most of that research has probably occurred in only two genera, *Pinus* and *Pseudotsuga*. In spite of the extreme differences in xylem anatomy of softwoods and hardwoods, the wood in both types of plant apparently fulfills the same basic functions. Softwood xylem is made of about 90–94% tracheids by volume, with most of the remaining cells in ray parenchyma (Petric and Scukanec, 1973), whereas hardwoods have a much greater variety of cell types and configurations. Hardwoods can have libriform fibers, tracheids, and vasicentric tracheids (all in the same size range as softwood tracheids), vessel elements (up to an order of magnitude wider than tracheids), and numerous types of parenchyma cells and arrangements (Panshin and de Zeeuw, 1980). Vessel volume in North American hardwood tree species ranges from 6 to 55%, with 29–76% fiber volume, 6–31% ray volume, and 0–23% volume of axial (longitudinally oriented) parenchyma (French, 1923, as cited in Panshin and de Zeeuw, 1980). Tracheids, which are cells with closed ends, range from 1 to 7 mm long (Panshin and de Zeeuw, 1980). Vessels, which are made of stacks of open-ended vessel elements, are variable in length. In diffuse-porous species, most vessels are shorter than 10 cm, but in ring-porous species many of the vessels are longer, with the longest frequently as long as the stem itself (Zimmermann and Jeje, 1981).

Within a growth ring there are systematic changes in cell length, frequency of cell type, and cell wall structure (Panshin and de Zeeuw, 1980), but the most apparent differences are in xylem density and the abruptness of density changes within a ring. In general, ring-porous hardwoods (e.g., *Fraxinus, Quercus,* and *Ulmus*) and abrupt-transition softwoods (e.g., the hard pines, such as *Pinus taeda* and *P. rigida*) have the most abrupt change in density across the growth ring, followed by gradual-transition softwoods (e.g., *Picea*) and then diffuse-porous hardwoods (e.g., *Acer, Alnus,* and some *Populus*). Softwoods can have 500% denser wood in latewood than earlywood (*Thuja plicata;* p. 271 in Panshin and de Zeeuw, 1980) and even a diffuse-porous hardwood can have 10–20% denser wood at the end of the growth ring than at the beginning (*Populus* × *euroamericana;* Babos, 1970).

Wood near the pith (called core wood, juvenile wood, or crown-formed wood) differs anatomically from that nearer the bark (called outer wood, mature wood, or stem-formed wood; reviewed in Panshin and de Zeeuw, 1980; Megraw, 1985; Zobel and van Buijtenen, 1989). Outer wood has

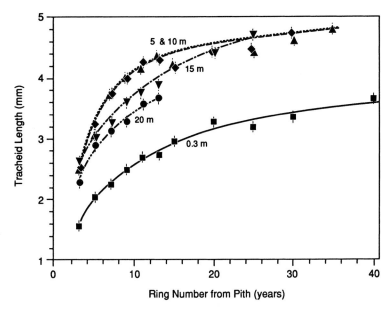

Figure 1 Variation in tracheid length as a function of cambial age and height in *Pinus taeda* (mean of 33 trees). Tracheid length increases with increasing cambial age (ring number from the pith), and its value at any cambial age is a function of height. [Reprinted from Megraw (1985) with permission from TAPPI.]

longer (Fig. 1), sometimes wider (Olesen, 1982) longitudinal cells than core wood. In *Alnus rubra*, a species showing no variation in density from pith to bark (Harrington and DeBell, 1980), the average fiber length increased by 39% from the first to the twentieth growth ring, where it leveled off (H. Lei and B. L. Gartner, unpublished observations). In ring-porous hardwoods (e.g., *Quercus alba;* Phelps and Workman, 1994) and some softwoods, outer wood has a lower proportion of latewood. However, outer wood has a higher proportion of latewood than does core wood in the majority of softwoods [e.g., *Pinus taeda* (Megraw, 1985) and *Pseudotsuga menziesii* (Abdel-Gadir *et al.*, 1993)]. In addition, outer wood often has narrower growth rings than core wood, thicker latewood cell walls, and a lower incidence of spiral grain (cells oriented at a consistent angle to vertical) or compression wood (see below).

This radial (pith-to-bark) variation results from wood produced by a cambium at one height that increases in age with each growth ring (Fig. 2, transect A). As shown by Duff and Nolan (1953), woody plants also exhibit variation in the vertical axis, whether cambial age is held constant (Fig. 2, transect B), or whether wood is produced in the same year but by cambia of different ages (Fig. 2, transect C). As a first approximation, the same

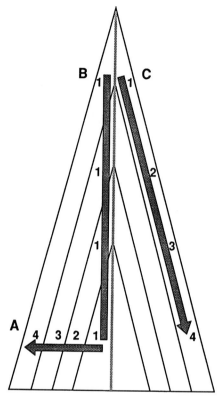

Figure 2   Schematic diagram of a longitudinal section of a 4-year-old stem, showing sampling transects (numbers represent years from pith at a location; stippled line represents the pith). (A) Wood produced by the same cambium at one height with increasing cambial age and during different years; (B) wood produced by cambia of the same age but with differing height and during different years; (C) wood produced by cambia of increasing age and decreasing height during the same year.

pattern is found in the vertical direction (transect C) as in the radial direction (transect A) because the younger cambium (at the tip or center of the tree) makes different products than does the older cambium (at the base or perimeter of the tree).

The pattern of variation due to vertical position not related to cambial age (Fig. 2, transect B) depends on the taxon, and is superimposed on the variation due to cambial age (transect A) to give the actual patterns of transect C. Common patterns in transect B are an increase in tracheary diameter from the base of the stem to near the base of the live crown, then a decrease to the apex (Dinwoodie, 1961), or a steady decrease from the base of the stem to its apex. For hardwoods, vessel density increases as vessel diameter decreases within an individual (Larson, 1962). The parallel patterns of anatomy along transects A and C (Fig. 2) may not pertain to axial or ray parenchyma: in hardwoods, the amount and type of parenchyma may be highly variable within the individual, with the highest proportions reported at the base of the stem (e.g., Patel, 1965; also see Pate and Jeschke [8] in this volume).

Typical heartwood (following the softwood paradigm) has no living cells, is nonconductive, and develops in the oldest xylem. Sapwood has some living cells, is conductive, and occupies the outer sheath of a stem, or the entire cross-section in a younger plant. An old tree may have core wood that is heartwood and core wood that is sapwood, and outer wood that is heartwood and outer wood that is sapwood. In softwoods, the conversion of sapwood into heartwood always involves death of the cytoplasm of all living cells, which may include longitudinal or ray parenchyma, and fiber cells. In hardwoods, the transition may be less distinct, with some cells remaining alive in the inner region, known as "ripewood" rather than heartwood (Hillis, 1987). Depending on the taxon, conversion can also involve many of the following (Hillis, 1987): a decrease in sugars and starches; embolism of the tracheary elements; a decrease in moisture content in softwoods, or an increase or decrease in moisture content in hardwoods (Table 3–3, p. 3-10, U.S. Forest Products Laboratory, 1987); deposition of secondary chemicals onto nearby cell walls; or production of tyloses into tracheary cell lumens.

The wood in branches is different from the wood in main stems. This degree of difference must depend on the growth form of the plant, but more research is needed to clarify this point. Compared to main stems, branches have shorter, narrower tracheary elements (Ikeda and Suzaki, 1984), generally denser wood (but in some reports, less dense wood), narrower growth rings, and more numerous rays (Table I). Vessel density is higher but vessel volume is lower in branches than trunks (Fegel, 1941; and see Table I). The stem–branch and branch–branch junctions are commonly sites of decreased diameter of tracheary elements (Salleo *et al.*, 1982b), but other anatomical patterns have also been described (see Section III,D). Table I also shows that roots have different anatomical characteristics than stems. Moreover, unlike stems, roots rarely possess reaction wood (Wilson and Archer, 1977). In fact, there may be more within-plant variability in secondary xylem structure between roots and other plant parts than within the shoot; the magnitude and functional significance of these differences need more research.

Reaction wood develops in response to gravity where stems or branches are out of their vertical "equilibrium positions" (Wilson and Archer, 1977). Reaction wood is usually present on the underside of branches or leaning stems in softwoods (compression wood), and on the upper side of branches or leaning stems in hardwoods (tension wood). Opposite wood, with its own

Table I   Comparative Anatomy of Root, Trunk, and Branch
for Diffuse- and Ring-Porous Hardwoods and Softwoods[a]

Characteristic	Diffuse-porous hardwoods			Ring-porous hardwoods			Conifers		
	Root	Trunk	Branch	Root	Trunk	Branch	Root	Trunk	Branc[h]
Specific gravity	0.46	0.49	0.54	0.46	0.54	0.57	0.38	0.36	0.49
Growth rings/cm	7.9	4.6	9.8	9.4	5.1	10.2	7.9	5.9	15.0
Tracheid diameter (μm)							30	27	31
Vessel diameter (μm)	90	100	71	78	60	40			
Vessel density (No./mm^2)	22	54	60	48	118	200			
Vessel volume (%)	13	27	18	29	27	22			
Ray volume (%)	19	14	15	16	11	13	5	5	5

[a]Specific gravity is based on oven-dried weight and fresh volume. There were four ring-porous species (*Fraxinus americana*, *F. nigra*, *Ulmus americana*, and *Quercus borealis* var *maxima*), eight diffuse-porous species (*Prunus serotina*, *pensylvanica*, *Betula lutea*, *Populus tremuloides*, *Tilia americana*, *Fagus grandifolia*, *Acer saccharum*, and *A. rubrum*), and eight coniferous species (*Pinus strobus*, *Pinus resinosa*, *Picea rubens*, *Picea mariana*, *Larix laricina*, *Tsuga canadensis*, *Abies balsamea*, and *Thuja occidentalis*). (From Fegel, 1941.)

unique anatomical and mechanical properties, may develop in the same growth ring but on the opposite side of the reaction wood (see discussion in Wilson and Archer, 1977). Growth rings may be wider on the side with reaction wood than opposite wood. Another type of wood, flexure wood, results from repetitive motion of the gymnosperm stem, not from a permanent offset (Telewski, 1989), and it has slightly higher density and smaller cell lumens than normal wood.

Compression wood has higher density, thicker cell walls, different cell wall ultrastructure, and often smaller diameter cell lumens than normal wood. The earlywood/latewood transition of compression wood becomes gradual in species with abrupt transitions in their normal wood, and it becomes abrupt in species with gradual transitions in their normal wood (Panshin and de Zeeuw, 1980). Tension wood has lower vessel density, narrower vessels, different cell wall ultrastructure in the fiber, and less ray or longitudinal parenchyma than normal wood, with most modifications in the beginning of the growth ring (Scurfield, 1973; Panshin and de Zeeuw, 1980). There appears to be a gradation in anatomy from opposite to normal to reaction wood, such that distinctions among the three may be somewhat arbitrary (Dadswell and Wardrop, 1949).

III. Variation in Water Transport

The anatomical variation just described results in systematic variation in efficiency of water transport through the stem. The hydraulic properties discussed here are hydraulic conductivity (k_h) and specific conductivity (k_s), in the axial direction, as follows:

$$k_h = V/[t(\Delta P/l)] \tag{1}$$

$$k_s = k_h/A_{stem} \tag{2}$$

where V is the volume of water, t is time, ΔP is the pressure difference between the two ends of the stem segment, l is length of the stem segment, and A_{stem} is stem cross-sectional area. The variable A_{stem} can be defined to include only the portion of the stem that later conducted stain, all sapwood, or the whole stem cross-section (including or excluding the pith). Hydraulic conductivity (k_h) is a measure of how much water comes out of a stem segment (diameter unspecified) per unit time per pressure gradient. Specific conductivity (k_s) is a measure of how much water a stem segment will transport per unit time per pressure gradient, normalized by its cross-sectional area. If a twig and a trunk of the same length were made of hydraulically identical material, the trunk would have higher k_h than the twig but the same k_s. The effects of wood anatomy on xylem embolism are considered by Sperry ([5] in this volume).

A. Within a Growth Ring

Most research on hydraulics within a growth ring has focused on hardwoods. The hydraulic function of different parts of a hardwood growth ring is controlled by their anatomy: vessel diameter (flow is proportional to radius to the fourth power; Poiseuille's law), vessel density, time span over which vessels are conductive given their environment, permeability of intervessel pits, and vessel lengths. Ring-porous species usually have the same vessel density throughout the growth ring (Carlquist, 1988), with wider vessels at the beginning than the end of the growth ring. On that basis one would expect much higher specific conductivity (k_s) of wood at the beginning of the growth ring. Indeed, Ellmore and Ewers (1985) calculated that for the ring-porous species *Ulmus americana*, 96% of the flow would be through the beginning of the growth ring if flow were governed by Poiseuille's law alone.

The ring-porous habit involves production of xylem with two spatially separated hydraulic strategies in each growth ring (high k_s with short functional life span, and low k_s with long functional life span), whereas the diffuse-porous habit results in a more uniform tissue (intermediate k_s, variable life span). Within an individual, the wider vessels conducted water for a shorter period than the narrower vessels (Salleo and Lo Gullo, 1986; Hargrave *et al.*, 1994). Ring-porous species (with some wide long vessels) were much more susceptible to freezing-induced embolism than were diffuse-porous species (with only narrow, short vessels; Sperry and Sullivan, 1992). Of 43 north-temperate tree species sampled in late winter, the ring-porous species were the most embolized followed by diffuse-porous species and then conifers (Wang *et al.*, 1992). Interestingly, the date of leafing out was inversely related to the degree of late winter embolism: the least embolized species were the fastest to leaf out (Wang *et al.*, 1992). A common xylem pattern in regions with a mediterranean climate is to have smaller vessels and tracheids that are interwoven among the larger vessels, purportedly to provide some water throughout the canopy once the larger vessels have embolized owing to drought (Carlquist, 1985). The double-staining experiments of Hargrave and colleagues (1994) support this hypothesis with evidence for spatial intermingling of large embolized vessels and smaller non-embolized ones in droughted, but not in irrigated, *Salvia mellifera,* a chaparral shrub.

Even in conifers there is evidence of two spatially separated hydraulic strategies: pit membranes of earlywood tracheids are more likely to "aspirate" (indicating that the conduit has embolized) than the pit membranes of latewood (Wardrop and Davies, 1961). The current interest in temporal and spatial patterns of embolism in softwoods shows that there is much to learn even about the hydraulic strategy of woods as simple in structure as softwoods.

There are numerous other intraring xylem arrangements in hardwoods besides ring-porous and diffuse-porous, such as those characterized by vessel grouping (solitary, chains, or bands), ray frequency and type, or presence and pattern of longitudinal parenchyma (Carlquist, 1988). Except for the surveys documenting the proportion of a flora that may contain them (e.g., Carlquist and Hoekman, 1985; Baas and Schweingruber, 1987), these arrangements have been little studied in an ecological context. Function, within-individual variability, and the degree of plasticity in exhibiting these arrangements are largely unknown.

B. From Pith to Bark

Outer wood has a higher k_s value than core wood because of the radial gradient in anatomy resulting from development (see Section II) and because the center of an old stem has heartwood. This results in the portion of the stem with the highest k_s being the closest to the external environment, and thus the most vulnerable to fluctuating temperatures, physical injury, and attack by biotic agents.

Water does not flow readily between growth rings (Ewart, 1905; Ellmore and Ewers, 1985). In softwoods, pits are larger and more frequent in the radial walls of tracheids than in the tangential walls (Koran, 1977; Panshin and de Zeeuw, 1980), promoting water movement within a growth ring rather than between growth rings. Nonetheless, *Picea mariana* has tangential pitting in tracheids of the last four rows of latewood and the first row of earlywood (Koran, 1977), facilitating some water flow between growth rings.

1. Developmental Changes The radial changes in anatomy that occur during cell development (e.g., increasing vessel and tracheid lengths and widths, alteration in earlywood to latewood ratio) have been well described, but their effects on hydraulics have not. The experiments to determine the pattern of radial changes in k_s are not done easily, because xylem position and age are confounded. There should be an increase in k_s going from pith to bark, owing to tracheary dimension alone (this is especially true in hardwoods), but the outcome could be different, for example, if the ratio of earlywood to latewood increases with radius (e.g., a ring-porous *Quercus*) rather than decreases (e.g., a *Pseudotsuga menziesii*).

2. Heartwood and Sapwood Heartwood supports no appreciable water flow, and therefore all the axial flow occurs in the sapwood. However, not all zones of sapwood have the same k_s: there is an abrupt increase in embolized tracheids in the sapwood adjacent to the sapwood/heartwood boundary (Hillis, 1987). Sperry and colleagues (1991) discovered that pit membranes are partially degraded in the older vessels of *Populus tremuloides* near the boundary of the ripewood (see Section II) and the sapwood. This degradation lowers the xylem tensions required for embolism and may initiate heartwood formation.

The costs or benefits of spatial patterns of sapwood area have been only rarely studied from the plant's perspective (Ryan, 1989). Apparent benefits of a large sapwood cross-sectional area are that it permits high stem k_h and thus maintenance of a large leaf area, and that it permits storage and reuse of water (Waring and Running, 1978; and see Holbrook [7] in this volume), nutrients, and carbohydrates. An apparent cost is the maintenance respiration for the larger volume of xylem parenchyma (Ryan, 1990; Ryan *et al.*, 1995).

C. From Root to Crown

The hydraulic trends from base to tip of a stem (e.g., Booker and Kininmonth, 1978) reflect the anatomical variation, with higher k_s in locations that have a higher proportion of earlywood and wider conducting elements. If the species produces distinct core wood, then the top of the tree will differ hydraulically from the base of the tree (see Fig. 2). Empirically, researchers have generally found the pattern of k_s reported by Farmer (1918a, p. 223): "Young or immature wood always gives a relatively low reading [of k_s] and of quite uncertain value." This finding is in spite of the fact that a typical growth ring has a higher proportion of earlywood near the top of a tree than near the base (Larson, 1962). In the shrub *Toxicodendron diversilobum,* the k_s of apical segments of wood (2–3 years old) averaged 45% of that of basal segments of wood (averaging 10.5 years old; Gartner, 1991a). To characterize the hydraulic strategy of a plant will require research throughout its lifetime on its transpiration rates and stem transport capabilities resulting from growth, development, and injury.

The shortness of average vessels and tracheids protects a stem from losing much of the hydrosystem from a point injury or a single embolism. This feature explains the results of double saw-cut experiments (described at least as far back as 1806; see Zimmermann, 1983), in which the foliage remains alive despite a cut half-way through the trunk on one side, and a cut half-way through the trunk on the opposite side a few centimeters higher. Nonetheless, experiments in noninjured trees have shown that sap generally spreads very little laterally from the rank and file of vessels or tracheids in which it enters (reviewed in Kübler, 1991), although in some species that rank and file may have a characteristic path of ascent (e.g., spiral to the right, spiral to the left, or winding; Vité and Rudinsky, 1959).

D. Between Stems, Branches, and Nodes

Consistent with their smaller tracheary elements, branches generally have lower k_s values than their parent axis (e.g., Ewers and Zimmermann, 1984a,b; Gartner, 1991a). Moreover, there is usually a localized decrease in calculated or measured k_s for junctions between a branch and its lower order stem (e.g., Ewers and Zimmermann, 1984b), nodes vs internodes in young stems (Farmer, 1918b; Rivett and Rivett, 1920; Salleo *et al.*, 1982a,b; Tyree *et al.*, 1983; Salleo and Lo Gullo, 1986), the branch and the reproductive parts (Darlington and Dixon, 1991), and the branch and its deciduous leaves (Larson and Isebrands, 1978). Two possible causes of this decreased k_s are a greater proportion of mechanical tissue at branch junctions (see Section IV,A,2), and selection for segmentation (Section III,E). Lower k_s at junctions can result from various anatomical combinations such as a decrease in diameter and number of vessels in the leaf–branch abscission zone of *Populus deltoides* (Larson and Isebrands, 1978), an increase in vessel diameter but a decrease in vessel numbers in nodes vs internodes of *Vitis* (Salleo *et al.*, 1982b), or a discontinuity between vessels in the vegetative and the reproductive stem of *Rosa hybrida* (Darlington and Dixon, 1991).

E. Segmentation and the Relationship between Wood Anatomy, Hydraulics, and Architecture

The segmentation hypothesis of plant hydraulics (Zimmermann, 1978, 1983) states that the hydraulic architecture of a plant (the geometry and performance of its xylem relative to its distribution of ports of water loss, mainly the leaves) permits certain zones of the plant to survive drought stress while other zones die. Regardless of the hydraulic architecture of the plant, distal axes will have more negative water potentials than will proximal axes during steady state transpiration. But hydraulic constrictions, thought to result from the arrangement and structure of xylem cells, may enhance cavitation in some localities relative to others. Organs such as branches (e.g., Kolb and Davis, 1994), fruits (e.g., Darlington and Dixon, 1991), leaves (e.g., Sperry, 1986), or above-ground shoots (e.g., Aloni and Griffith, 1991) that are distal to zones of hydraulic constriction will die under conditions of severe water stress. These deaths will decrease the evaporative area supplied by the parent axis, promoting its survival.

The amount of water that actually flows through a stem depends on its xylem conductance and its flow rate. Conductance is controlled by the wood structure, whereas flow rate is controlled at least in part by leaf-level factors such as leaf number, size, and albedo; stomatal aperture and density; and sensitivity of the stomata to the environment. Given the function of xylem in supplying water for transpiration, one would expect some relationship between stem water transport and transpiration. The Huber value (Huber, 1928) was one such relationship, describing the ratio of stem area (including heartwood) to leaf area (or mass) in a plant. The pipe model (Shinozaki *et al.*, 1964) suggested that a unit of sapwood will supply water for one unit of leaf area. A more refined relationship, that of leaf-specific conductivity (k_1), takes into account the conductivity of that sapwood:

$$k_1 = k_h / A_{leaf} \qquad (3)$$

This value describes how conductive the wood is relative to the potential evaporative surface, the leaf area (A_{leaf}). For a given order branch and height, k_1 can be relatively constant for different individuals or species in the same environment, even when other factors differ, such as k_s (Fig. 3) (Gartner, 1991a; Chiu and Ewers, 1992; Kolb and Davis, 1994), rooting

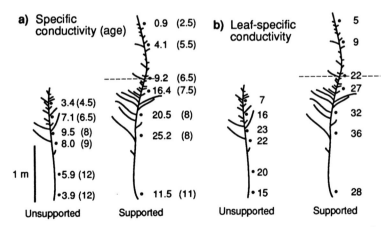

Figure 3   (a) Specific conductivity (k_s, 10^{-3} m^2 sec^{-1} MPa^{-1}) and (b) leaf-specific conductivity (k_1, 10^{-7} m^2 sec^{-1} MPa^{-1}) of two neighboring *Toxicodendron diversilobum* shoots, one shrubby (unsupported) and one viney (supported). Above the dashed line, the vine is unsupported. Stem age is shown in parentheses. Whereas k_s is much higher in supported than unsupported individuals for a given aged segment, k_1 does not vary significantly. [Modified from Gartner (1991a) with permission from Springer-Verlag.]

depth (S. D. Davis, personal communication), growth form (Fig. 3) (Gartner, 1991a; Chiu and Ewers, 1992), wood structure (Shumway *et al.*, 1993), or total path resistance (Shumway *et al.*, 1993). Undoubtedly, better relationships will be established for stem/leaf hydraulic function to indicate the hydraulic design criteria of plants.

It is unknown whether the crown physiology, phenology, and architecture drive development of the stem hydraulics (Larson, 1962), the reverse, or whether both occur in a feedback loop (Ford, 1992). Nonetheless, stem architectural development is clearly related to k_s and k_l in many reported cases. Branches have lower k_l than lower order stems and trunks. Tyree and Alexander (1993) argue that the lower k_l of branches, not the localized constrictions of k_h or k_s at branch junctions, contributes most to segmentation. Larson and Isebrands (1978) explained the death and abscission of deciduous leaves according to principles consistent with the segmentation hypothesis. Darlington and Dixon (1991) describe anatomy of the sympodial species *R. hybrida,* in which one lateral becomes reproductive (with vessels discontinuous from the main shoot) while the other remains vegetative (with vessels continuous with the rest of the plant body). This arrangement allows continued vegetative growth during drought at the expense of reproductive growth. Farmer (1918b) said that in ash trees (no scientific name given), the leader is replaced by a lateral almost annually. Measurements by Farmer showed that the lateral (which will become the leader) has a higher k_s than the leader (which will lose dominance). Similarly, *Tsuga canadensis* has weak apical control (its leader is replaced by a lateral in at least 31% of the years; Hibbs, 1981) and there is little hydraulic difference between the tip of the main stem and the lateral branches (Ewers and Zimmermann, 1984b). In contrast to ash and *T. canadensis,* sycamore (no scientific name given) has a persistent leader and its k_s remains higher than the k_s of its laterals (Farmer, 1918b). A vigorous *Abies balsamea* tree with strong apical control had higher k_l along the main stem, and particularly at the apex, than did less vigorous individuals having lower apical control (Ewers and Zimmermann, 1984a).

IV. Variation in Stresses, Structure, and Density

A. Stress Distributions

Stems experience short- and long-term stress (force per unit area) from a variety of causes such as gravity, wind, weight of snow or a maturing fruit, removal of a branch, partial failure of the anchorage system, or growth and development (the latter classified as "growth stress"; Jacobs, 1945). The effect that a force has on the structure depends on where the force is applied, the material properties of the structure, the geometry of the structure, and the degree to which it is "fixed" (unmovable) at its base. Note that the material properties of wood are variable on scales from 10^{-3} to 10 m and that as a first-order approximation, wood density is positively and nearly linearly correlated with strength properties (Table 4-8, p. 4-28, U.S. Forest Products Laboratory, 1987).

One of the ways in which a plant senses the environment is through stress, most likely through sensing the strain (relative change in length of a line in a deformed body) that stress generates. The strain could indicate, for example, that a stem is flexing (perhaps from wind), the stem has little compressive or tensile stress (as in the case of a vine on an external support), or the stem is leaning.

1. Typical Normal Stress Distributions   This discussion deals with normal (not shear) stresses: radial, axial, and bending. At the scale of the growth ring, the denser wood bears more of the stress than less dense wood if both have the same strain, because the denser wood has more cell wall material per cross-sectional area. Therefore, a plant with large intraring variation in density will have a more variable axial stress distribution than a plant with relatively uniform density.

For a tapered columnar beam of a homogeneous material, the normal bending stress throughout the cross-section is at a maximum at the surface. However, for at least part of the season there will be higher axial and bending stresses in the preceding year's latewood than in the current growth (earlywood) and at the vascular cambium (the contribution of bark will be variable). The mechanical theory of uniform stress states that at each height a woody stem develops a cross-sectional shape that tends to equalize the average bending plus axial stresses (Morgan and Cannell, 1994; see also Mattheck [3] in this volume). This theory, combined with the previous statement, suggests that the time-averaged bending stress at the cambium at a given height is somewhat lower than the time-averaged bending stress several millimeters toward the pith. However, this stress diminution probably has a trivial effect on wood development because at the wind speeds likely to be encountered most of the time in most forests, the majority of the stress is axial, not bending (Morgan and Cannell, 1994), and because the same phenomenon occurs throughout the entire circumference.

The vertical location of peak stress depends on the geometry of the beam, where the load is applied, and whether the force is acting in compression, bending, or torsion (see texts on theory of beam column for analytical solutions, e.g., Chajes, 1974; Chen and Atsuta, 1976, 1977). Leiser and Kemper (1973) modeled bending stress for young trees with wind loads on the canopy, and concluded that stress is maximum in the lowest one-third of the height if the stem is moderately tapered, grading to the very base if the stem is a right cylinder. In actual trees, normal bending stresses are also concentrated at locations where the stem cross-section is eccentric. Within the canopy, bending stresses are concentrated at junctions between branches or between branches and stems, but some of the hypothetical stress concentration at the branch–stem junction is dissipated by the orientation of the grain (e.g., Mattheck, 1990; Hermanson, 1992).

Options for lowering stresses on the structure (tree) are to decrease the stress encountered or to increase the resistance to the stresses. The first option, decreasing the normal stress encountered, can be accomplished by means such as occupying a less windy site, reducing leaf area to decrease wind or snow load, remaining shorter to project a shorter lever arm, being lighter in weight, or modifying branches to prevent their blowing to one side of the stem, thereby causing a large overturning moment. The second option, increasing resistance to the stresses, can be accomplished by having stiffer material or a greater resisting area (becoming wider).

2. Radial, Tangential, and Axial Growth Stresses   The maturation of sequential sheaths of xylem cells produces stress in the older xylem along each of the three axes. The static stresses at any location change as the plant grows because that location changes its position relative to the perimeter of the stem. Cell walls can be thought of as fiber-reinforced composites, with cellulose as the fiber and lignin as the matrix. The microfibrils are oriented in helices with distinct angles of ascent in the different cell wall layers (Wardrop and Preston, 1947). These angles, which direct many of the physical properties of wood (Cave and Walker, 1994), are under both environmental and genetic control (Wardrop and Preston, 1950). Mathematical models have shown that the stresses generated during maturation are consistent with the explanation that as cell walls mature, the microfibrils shorten and the matrix between them swells (Archer, 1987). Thus, the orientation of the microfibrils and the quantity of lignin should play major roles in the direction and magnitude of stresses generated.

Tangential stress is tensile at the center of a stem, zero at about half the radius, and compressive at the cambium (Fournier *et al.*, 1994). Radial stress is also tensile at the center of the stem but declines to zero at the cambium (Fournier *et al.*, 1994). Nonetheless, Hejnowicz (1980) shows for both hardwoods and softwoods that the small radial stresses near the cambium facilitate intrusive growth of developing axial cells.

Some species, such as *Eucalyptus* and *Fagus*, develop large axial growth stresses. This condition is well documented because of the nuisance and danger to loggers: during sawing the saw commonly becomes stuck in the stem, and occasionally an enormous longitudinal segment of wood will burst out of the bole. Axial growth stresses are compressive in the center of a woody stem and decline with distance from the pith to become tensile in about the outer third of the radius (e.g., Boyd, 1950; and see Fig. 4). In some species, the maximum compressive stresses near the center of the stem are much lower than those determined from theory (Fig. 4), with the extra stress probably dissipated through viscoelastic creep (Boyd, 1950) and/or minute compression failures (Dadswell, 1958). There are many

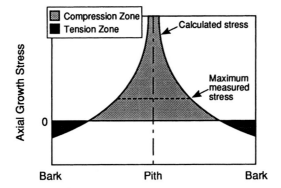

Figure 4 Theoretical distributions of axial growth stress across the cross-section of a tree stem. The dashed line shows maximum measured longitudinal stresses, which are much lower than those calculated from theory. [Modified from Boyd (1950) with permission from the *Australian Journal of Applied Science.*]

ways in which tree stems may fail, but if the first failure occurs on the compressive (downhill) side of the tree, then the growth stresses should act to help trees resist breakage: the tension prestressing will reduce the total compressive bending stress on the downhill side of the tree compared to the case with no such tension prestressing (Boyd, 1950).

Reaction wood relies on the generation of growth stresses and the firm bonding of adjacent cells for its action (Wilson and Archer, 1977). The mechanism of stress generation is thought to be similar to that discussed above for cell maturation in general. Compression wood, on the lower side of a leaning stem, has microfibrils in the S2 layer of the cell wall oriented at about 45° with respect to the cell axis; normal wood generally has microfibrils at about 10–20° (Dadswell and Wardrop, 1949). The bulking of the cell wall during maturation causes the cells to attempt to elongate (Scurfield, 1973), and concomitantly a tension develops along the microfibrils, also causing cells to attempt to elongate. These processes place a tensile force on the lower side of the stem that will tend to right the stem (Archer, 1987). Furthermore, a small reorientation of the stem can shift the canopy enough such that it has a shorter lever arm and/or is more evenly balanced over the root crown. The generation of compressive forces during cell wall maturation in tension wood derives from the tension generated along the microfibrils (Okuyama *et al.,* 1990; Yamamoto *et al.,* 1993), which are in a near axial orientation (Wardrop and Dadswell, 1955). These compressive forces on the upper side of the leaning stem will tend to pull the stem upright.

There remain many puzzles about reaction wood, normal wood, opposite wood, flexure wood, and the wood of branches vs stems. The lumens of conducting cells are narrower in reaction wood than normal wood, but the increment of wood is wider (Scurfield, 1973); what is the effect on supply of water to the foliage? Rays and other parenchyma are less abundant in tension wood (Scurfield, 1973); is less parenchyma needed, is the parenchyma more efficient, or is the plant made more vulnerable in some way by its reduced parenchyma volume? Why do some species have a greater tendency to produce reaction wood than others, and what accounts for the numerous patterns of reaction wood, especially in angiosperms (Wilson and Archer, 1977; Panshin and de Zeeuw, 1980)? How much of typical branch wood is actually a type of reaction wood? More research is needed on the incidence, magnitude, generation, and location of normal stresses in stems, their roles in development, and their consequences for the biology of the plant.

B. Within a Growth Ring

Within-growth ring variation in density will affect mechanics, although the extent to which these variations are important to the biology of a plant is unknown. Trees with distinct annual growth rings have significantly denser latewood than earlywood, even if diffuse-porous (Section II). The seasonal patterns of wood production and density are less understood in plants lacking annual rings. One approach to understanding the functional significance of different patterns of wood within a growth ring is to model wood as a laminate having low and high stiffness areas (corresponding to the earlywood and latewood) to predict modulus of elasticity and zones of failure (reviewed in Bodig and Jayne, 1982). A second approach is to determine empirically the effect of natural variation in anatomy (e.g., proportion of ray or earlywood tissue) on a mechanical property (e.g., modulus of elasticity, maximum stress and strain) of wood when tested in a certain axis (e.g., Schniewind, 1959; Beery *et al.*, 1983; Bariska and Kucera, 1985). These approaches could be used by botanists to gain insights on evolutionary costs or constraints of different wood patterns. Wood technologists have used neither the correlative nor the modeling approach exhaustively, perhaps because most engineering needs are met by tabulated values of allowable strengths based on performance standards. The tables themselves (e.g., U.S. Forest Products Laboratory, 1987) are not directly relevant to tree physiologists because the origin of the wood usually is not stated, and because the values represent moisture contents of in-service lumber (8–15%; mass of water in wood/wood dry mass) rather than moisture contents found in live trees (≥30%).

The case of earlywood provides a simple example of a mechanical function of a specialized pattern of xylem cells. Because the earlywood zone has relatively thin cell walls, it contributes little to the axial strength of wood (Dinwoodie, 1975). Earlywood has a lower tensile axial breaking strength than does latewood, and earlywood fails brashly (perpendicular to the cell axis), breaking the cells, whereas latewood failures are jagged, following a path between cells, such that few cells break (Kennedy and Ifju, 1962; Nordman and Qvickström, 1970).

A second example of mechanical function related to the pattern of xylem cells comes from research on lianas. Müller (1866, as cited in Haberlandt, 1914, pp. 690–696) hypothesized that the cable-like construction of some lianas, in which longitudinal strands of conducting tissue are separated from one another by parenchyma, makes use of the different strengths of these tissues, with parenchyma acting as padding for the conducting tissues should the liana sway (by wind) or fall (by failure of its external support). In support of this hypothesis, Putz and Holbrook (1991) found that liana stems withstood much more torsional stress (they could be twisted through more revolutions) before water stopped flowing than did tree stems of similar diameter. A quick glance through an atlas showing cross-sections of diverse dicotyledonous woods (e.g., Schweingruber, 1990; Ilic, 1991) or the Obaton (1960) treatise on "anomalous" patterns in wood production in lianas demonstrates the plethora of xylem patterns. Our understanding of the functional significance of any of these patterns is almost nil.

C. From Pith to Bark

The radial gradient in xylem density appears to fall into several different patterns. It is unknown whether the typical pattern of a species results from selection for some biomechanical and/or hydraulic optimum, whether it is a plastic response to the changing environment perceived by the changing plant, or whether it is developmentally controlled but unrelated to selection for mechanics or hydraulics. The general pattern for hard pines, *Larix*, *Pseudotsuga*, and the mid- to high-density diffuse-porous hardwoods is low-density wood near the pith, with an increase in density for some number of years, and then a leveling off or a decline in the rate of increase (summarized in Panshin and de Zeeuw, 1980, and Zobel and van Buijtenen, 1989). Many tropical hardwood species appear to have lower density near the pith than those from temperate zones, while attaining similar densities to temperate-zone species in the outer wood (Wiemann and Williamson, 1989; Butterfield *et al.*, 1993). With this pattern, the core wood is weaker in tension and compression and more flexible (lower modulus of elasticity) than outer wood.

Tsuga heterophylla and some of the low-density diffuse-porous hardwoods such as *Populus* tend to have highest density at the pith with a gradual decrease toward the bark. For softwoods in the Cupressaceae and most soft pines the general pattern is high density near the pith, a dip in density for several growth rings, and then an increase again to a constant or slowly increasing value (Panshin and de Zeeuw, 1980; Zobel and van Buijtenen, 1989).

Many vines have a fourth pattern, that is, production of denser wood where they are self-supported and less dense wood around this dense core once they find support (Haberlandt, 1914; Carlquist, 1991; Gartner, 1991a). Ring-porous hardwoods often show the same pattern as do vines, caused by outer wood having a higher proportion of the growth ring occupied by wide vessels (summarized in Zobel and van Buijtenen, 1989). Last, some diffuse-porous tree species such as *Alnus rubra* appear to have no change in density with age (Harrington and DeBell, 1980) or growth rate (H. Lei and B. L. Gartner, unpublished data).

Models on mechanical trade-offs of stem width and wood density (see Givnish [1] in this volume) in tandem with models on the effects of density and stem width on water conduction could help explain the range of wood densities and stem widths in nature. A small decrease in wood density may result in a small decrease in the ability of a stem to resist compression and bending (e.g., Gartner 1991b), but a large increase in specific conductivity (Gartner, 1991a). Such a negative correlation between sapwood k_s and wood density has been reported for *Pinus radiata* (Booker and Kininmonth, 1978).

The several percent higher density of heartwood than sapwood that results from deposition of secondary compounds should have no direct effect on the mechanics of the live tree. However, the secondary compounds make the heartwood more resistant to decay. A solid stem (i.e., interior not decayed) is more stable than a hollow one, particularly if the outer layer is O shaped rather than C shaped (broken; Ch. 9 in Chen and Atsuta, 1977). Thus, one mechanical justification for protection of heartwood from decay is that heartwood provides mechanical stability in case the sapwood layer becomes disrupted.

D. From Root to Crown

The pattern of xylem density from the base to the tip depends mainly (but not always entirely) on the pattern found from pith to bark because the vertical profile reflects the simultaneous production of outer wood at the base (if a plant is old enough) and core wood at the tip. In hardwoods, the magnitude of density variation with height is relatively low compared to softwoods (Zobel and van Buijtenen, 1989). Descending the stem within the growth ring produced in the same year (Fig. 2, transect C), density of hardwoods can decrease (as in a ring-porous species), increase, or increase and then decrease. The common pattern for hard pines and *Pseudotsuga* is greater density at the base than the tip (Panshin and de Zeeuw, 1980; Zobel and van Buijtenen, 1989). Denser wood at the base of a stem, together with the widening of the stem base that is often observed (butt swell), can contribute to mitigating the stress concentration there.

E. Between Stems and Branches

Branches often have denser wood than do stems (Fegel, 1941; and see Table I), meaning that branch material is stronger on a volumetric basis than stem wood. At least in softwoods, larger diameter branches have higher density than smaller diameter ones, branches have higher density near their base than toward their tip, and knots have very high density (Fig. 5) (Hakkila, 1969). The presence of reaction wood at branch junc-

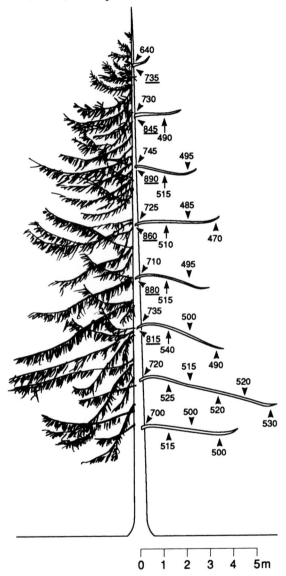

Figure 5 Variation in wood density (kg/m³) within and between branches in *Picea abies*. Along one branch, density is highest at the knot (the junction of branch and main stem; underlined values) and decreases toward the branch tip. Between branches, density is highest in large, more basal branches. [Modified from Hakkila (1969) with permission from the Finnish Forest Research Institute.]

tions may partially explain the lower k_s value there than in normal wood, although reaction wood is not always present at branch junctions.

V. Conclusions

Xylem in stems and branches is constructed of nonuniform material that is systematically distributed throughout a plant. In some cases, the nonuniformity allows the material to function mechanically and hydraulically in manners appropriate to its location such that it contributes to the success of the plant. Different aspects of the variation are probably controlled by the environment, cambial age, distance from the leaves, physiological status of the plant, and even plant size, for size may contribute to the scale of environmental fluctuations that the plant senses. This chapter has emphasized optima for mechanics and hydraulics separately, but the trade-offs between the two (Long *et al.*, 1981; Gartner, 1991a) must be considered more fully. In the ranges of wood densities and water demands that plants have, we do not even know whether there are trade-offs between mechanics and hydraulics, partly because one must define the hydraulic and mechanical criteria in order to try such analyses.

Little is known about the effect on plant function of different combinations or patterns of xylem cell types (e.g., vessel groupings or parenchyma banding in relation to vessels). Baseline surveys of ecological wood anatomy provide starting points for experimental work on relationships between wood structure, environment, and growth form. For example, in different regional floras it has been reported that vines tend to have more paratracheal parenchyma than do trees (Carlquist, 1991), shrubs have more vessels per grouping and a higher incidence of vasicentric tracheids than do trees (Carlquist and Hoekman, 1985), and shrubs are less commonly ring-porous than are trees (Baas and Schweingruber, 1987). What clues do these patterns give us to relate structure to function, and physiology to habitat and population biology? What are the most common xylem patterns in areas that are arid (Lindorf, 1994), have frequent freeze-thaw cycles, have short growing seasons, are subject to frequent fires, have cyclic herbivore outbreaks? How does the wood compare in congeners that are drought deciduous, evergreen, and winter deciduous? How does ramet demography relate to xylem anatomy: do short-lived stems have throw-away xylem strategies compared to long-lived stems? Are there syndromes of bark/xylem anatomy? Thin-barked species may be more susceptible to physical and biotic injury to the sapwood; do these species tend to have more parenchyma or other xylem adaptations to mitigate damage?

Experimental research is beginning to elucidate the physiological, ecological, and structural roles of stem xylem. Like the roots, leaves, and flowers, the stem profoundly influences the biology of the plant. Further studies in the physiological ecology of wood can impart new insights into areas such as physiology, plasticity, demography, and patterns and dynamics of architecture. Such research will also benefit efficient production and utilization of forest products, manipulation of woody crops, and management of forested lands.

Acknowledgments

I thank Bob Leichti and John Sperry for valuable discussion, and Frank Dietrich, Missy Holbrook, Bob Leichti, Claus Mattheck, John Sperry, and Bill Wilson for comments on the manuscript. I appreciate the financial support of the USDA Special Grant for Wood Utilization Research.

References

Abdel-Gadir, A. Y., Krahmer, R. L., and McKimmy, J. D. (1993). Intra-ring variations in mature Douglas-fir trees from provenance plantations. *Wood Fiber Sci.* **25**, 170–181.

Aloni, R., and Griffith, M. (1991). Functional xylem anatomy in root-shoot junctions of six cereal species. *Planta* **184**, 123–129.

Archer, R. R. (1987). On the origin of growth stresses in trees. 1. Micro mechanics of the developing cambial cell wall. *Wood Sci. Technol.* **21**, 139–154.

Baas, P., and Schweingruber, F. H. (1987). Ecological trends in the wood anatomy of trees, shrubs and climbers from Europe. *IAWA Bull.* **8**, 245–274.

Babos, K. (1970). Faserlängen- und Rohdichteverleilung innerhalb der Jahrringe einer Robustapappel. *Holztechnologie* **11**, 188–192.

Bariska, M., and Kucera, L. J. (1985). On the fracture morphology in wood. 2. Macroscopical deformations upon ultimate axial compression in wood. *Wood Sci. Technol.* **19**, 19–34.

Beery, W. H., Ifju, G., and McLain, T. E. (1983). Quantitative wood anatomy—relating anatomy to transverse tensile strength. *Wood Fiber Sci.* **15**, 395–407.

Bodig, J., and Jayne, B. A. (1982). Material organization. *In* "Mechanics of Wood and Wood Composites," pp. 461–546. Van Nostrand Reinhold, New York.

Booker, R. E., and Kininmonth, J. A. (1978). Variation in longitudinal permeability of green radiata pine wood. *N.Z. J. For. Sci.* **8**, 295–308.

Boyd, J. D. (1950). Tree growth stresses. II. The development of shakes and other visual failures in timber. *Austr. J. Appl. Sci.* **1**, 296–312.

Butterfield, R. P., Crook, R. P., Adams, R., and Morris, R. (1993). Radial variation in wood specific gravity, fibre length and vessel area for two Central American hardwoods, *Hyeronima alchorneoides* and *Vochysia guatemalensis:* Natural and plantation-grown trees. *IAWA J.* **14**, 153–161.

Carlquist, S. (1985). Vasicentric tracheids as a drought survival mechanism in the woody flora of southern California and similar regions: Review of vasicentric tracheids. *Aliso* **11**, 37–68.

Carlquist, S. (1988). "Comparative Wood Anatomy: Systematic, Ecological, and Evolutionary Aspects of Dicotyledon Wood." Springer-Verlag, New York.

Carlquist, S. (1991). Anatomy of vine and liana stems: A review and synthesis. *In* "The Biology of Vines" (F. E. Putz and H. A. Mooney, eds.), pp. 53–71. Cambridge University Press, Cambridge.

Carlquist, S., and Hoekman, D. A. (1985). Ecological wood anatomy of the woody southern California flora. *IAWA Bull.* **6**, 319–347.

Cave, I. D., and Walker, J. C. F. (1994). Stiffness of wood in fast-grown plantation softwoods: The influence of microfibril angle. *For. Prod. J.* **44**, 43–48.

Chajes, A. (1974). "Principles of Structural Stability Theory." Prentice-Hall, Englewood Cliffs, New Jersey.

Chen, W. F., and Atsuta, T. (1976). "Theory of Beam-Columns," Vol. 1: In-Plane Behavior and Design. McGraw-Hill, New York.

Chen, W. F. and Atsuta, T. (1977). "Theory of Beam-Columns," Vol. 2: Space Behavior and Design. McGraw-Hill, New York.

Chiu, S.-T., and Ewers, F. W. (1992). Xylem structure and water transport in a twiner, a scrambler, and a shrub of *Lonicera* (Caprifoliaceae). *Trees* **6**, 216–224.

Cown, D. J., and McConchie, D. L. (1980). Wood property variations in an old-crop stand of radiata pine. *N.Z. J. For. Sci.* **10**, 508–520.

Dadswell, H. E. (1958). Wood structure variations occurring during tree growth and their influence on properties. *J. Inst. Wood Sci.* **1**, 11–33.

Dadswell, H. E., and Wardrop, A. B. (1949). What is reaction wood? *Aust. For.* **13**, 22–33.

Darlington, A. B., and Dixon, M. A. (1991). The hydraulic architecture of roses (*Rosa hybrida*). *Can. J. Bot.* **69**, 702–710.

Dinwoodie, J. M. (1961). Tracheid and fiber length in timber—a review of the literature. *Forestry* **34**, 125–144.

Dinwoodie, J. M. (1975). Timber—a review of the structure-mechanical property relationship. *J. Microsc.* **104**, 3–32.

Duff, G. H., and Nolan, N. J. (1953). Growth and morphogenesis in the Canadian forest species. I. The controls of cambial and apical activity in *Pinus resinosa* Ait. *Canadian Journal of Botany* **31**, 471–513.

Ellmore, G. S., and Ewers, F. W. (1985). Hydraulic conductivity in trunk xylem of elm, *Ulmus americana*. *IAWA Bull.* **6**, 303–307.

Ewart, A. J. (1905–1906). The ascent of water in trees. *Philos. Trans. Soc. London Ser. B* **198**, 41–85.

Ewers, F. W., and Zimmermann, M. H. (1984a). The hydraulic architecture of balsam fir (*Abies balsamea*). *Physiol. Plant* **60**, 453–458.

Ewers, F. W., and Zimmermann, M. H. (1984b). The hydraulic architecture of eastern hemlock (*Tsuga canadensis*). *Can. J. Bot.* **62**, 940–946.

Farmer, J. B. (1918a). On the quantitative differences in the water-conductivity of the wood in trees and shrubs. I. The evergreens. *Proc. R. Soc. London Ser. B* **90**, 218–232.

Farmer, J. B. (1918b). On the quantitative differences in the water-conductivity of the wood in trees and shrubs. II. The deciduous plants. *Proc. R. Soc. London Ser. B* **90**, 232–250.

Fegel, A. C. (1941). Comparative anatomy and varying physical properties of trunk, branch, and root wood in certain northeastern trees. *Bull. N.Y. State Coll. For. Syracuse Univ. Tech. Publ.* **14**(55), 5–20.

Ford, E. D. (1992). Control of tree structure and productivity through the interaction of morphological development and physiological processes. *Int. J. Plant Sci.* **153**, S147–S162.

Fournier, M., Bailleres, H., and Chanson, B. (1994). Tree biomechanics: Growth, cumulative prestresses, and reorientations. *Biomimetics* **2**, 229–251.

French, G. E. (1923). Untitled M.S. thesis. New York State College of Forestry, Syracuse, New York; as cited in Panshin and de Zeeuw (1980).

Gartner, B. L. (1991a). Stem hydraulic properties of vines vs. shrubs of western poison oak, *Toxicodendron diversilobum*. *Oecologia* **87**, 180–189.

Gartner, B. L. (1991b). Structural stability and architecture of vines vs. shrubs of poison oak, *Toxicodendron diversilobum*. *Ecology* **72**, 2005–2015.

Haberlandt, G. (1914). "Physiological Plant Anatomy" (M. Drummond, transl.). Macmillan, London.

Hakkila, P. (1969). Weight and composition of the branches of large Scots pine and Norway spruce trees. *Commun. Inst. Forestalis Fenniae (Helsinki)* **67** (6).

Hargrave, K. R., Kolb, K. J., Ewers, F. W., and Davis, S. D. (1994). Conduit diameter and drought-induced embolism in *Salvia mellifera* Greene (Labiateae). *New Phytol.* **126**, 695–705.

Harrington, C. A., and DeBell, D. S. (1980). Variation in specific gravity of red alder (*Alnus rubra* Bong.). *Can. J. For. Res.* **10**, 293–299.

Hejnowicz, Z. (1980). Tensional stress in the cambium and its developmental significance. *Am. J. Bot.* **67**, 1–5.

Hermanson, J. (1992). "A Finite Element Analysis of the Influence of Curvilinear Orthotropy on the State of Stress in a Plate with a Hole." M.S. thesis. University of Washington, Seattle, Washington.

Hibbs, D. E. (1981). Leader growth and the architecture of three North American hemlocks. *Can. J. Bot.* **59**, 476–480.

Hillis, W. E. (1987). "Heartwood and Tree Exudates." Springer-Verlag, New York.

Huber, B. (1928). Weitere quantitative Untersuchungen über das Wasserleitungssystem der Pflanzen. *Jahr. Wiss. Bot.* **67**, 877–959.

Ikeda, T., and Suzaki, T. (1984). Distribution of xylem resistance to water flow in stems and branches of hardwood species. *J. Jpn. For. Soc.* **66**, 229–236.

Ilic, J. (1991). "CSIRO Atlas of Hardwoods." Crawford House Press, Bathurst, New South Wales, Australia.

Jacobs, M. R. (1945). "The Growth Stresses of Woody Stems." Bulletin 28. Commonwealth Forestry Bureau, Canberra, Australia.

Kennedy, R. W., and Ifju, G. (1962). Applications of microtensile testing to thin wood sections. *Tappi* **45**, 725–733.

Koch, P. (1985). "Utilization of Hardwoods Growing on Southern Pine Sites," Vol. I: The Raw Material. Agricultural Handbook No. 605. USDA Forest Service, Washington, D.C.

Kolb, K. J., and Davis, S. D. (1994). Drought tolerance and xylem embolism in co-occurring species of coastal sage and chaparral. *Ecology* **75**, 648–659.

Koran, Z. (1977). Tangential pitting in black spruce tracheids. *Wood Sci. Technol.* **11**, 115–123.

Kübler, H. (1991). Function of spiral grain in trees. *Trees* **5**, 125–135.

Larson, P. R. (1962). A biological approach to wood quality. *Tappi* **45**, 443–448.

Larson, P. R. (1967). Silvicultural control of the characteristics of wood used for furnish. *In* "Proc. 4th TAPPI For. Biol. Conf. New York," pp. 143–150. Pulp and Paper Research Institute of Canada, Pointe Claire, Quebec.

Larson, P. R., and Isebrands, J. G. (1978). Functional significance of the nodal constricted zone in *Populus deltoides* Barts. *Can. J. Bot.* **56**, 801–804.

Leiser, A. T., and Kemper, J. D. (1973). Analysis of stress distribution in the sapling tree trunk. *J. Am. Soc. Hortic. Sci.* **98**, 164–170.

Lindorf, H. (1994). Eco-anatomical wood features of species from a very dry tropical forest. *IAWA J.* **15**, 361–376.

Long, J. N., Smith, F. W., and Scott, D. R. M. (1981). The role of Douglas-fir stem, sapwood and heartwood in the mechanical and physiological support of crowns and development of stem form. *Can. J. For. Res.* **11**, 459–464.

Mattheck, C. (1990). Why they grow, how they grow: The mechanics of trees. *Arboricult. J.* **14**, 1–17.

Megraw, R. A. (1985). "Wood Quality Factors in Loblolly Pine: The Influence of Tree Age, Position in Tree, and Cultural Practice on Wood Specific Gravity, Fiber Length, and Fibril Angle." TAPPI Press, Atlanta.

Morgan, H., and Cannell, M. G. R. (1994). Shape of tree stems—a re-examination of the uniform stress hypothesis. *Tree Physiol.* **14**, 49–62.

Müller, F. (1866). *Botanische Zeitung.* As cited in Haberlandt, G. (1914).

Nordman, L. S., and Qvickström, B. (1970). Variability of the mechanical properties of fibers within a growth period. *In* "The Physics and Chemistry of Wood Pulp Fibres" (D. H. Page, ed.), pp. 177–209. STAP No. 8.

Northcott, P. T. (1957). Is spiral grain the normal growth pattern? *For. Chron.* **33**, 335–352.

Obaton, M. (1960). Les lianes ligneuses a structure anormale des forêts d'Afrique occidental. *Ann. Sci. Nat. Ser.* **12**, 1–219.

Okuyama, T., Yamamoto, H., Iguchi, M., and Yoshida, M. (1990). Generation process of growth stresses in cell walls. II. Growth in tension wood. *Mokuzai Gakkaishi* **36**, 797–803.

Olesen, P. O. (1982). The effect of cyclophysis on tracheid width and basic density in Norway spruce. *In* "Forest Tree Improvement," No. 15. Denmark.

Panshin, A. J., and de Zeeuw, C. (1980.) "Textbook of Wood Technology: Structure, Identification, Properties, and Uses of the Commercial Woods of the United States," 4th Ed. McGraw-Hill, New York.

Patel, R. N. (1965). A comparison of the anatomy of the secondary xylem in roots and stems. *Holzforschung* **19**, 72–79.

Petric, B., and Scukanec, V. (1973). Volume percentage of tissues in wood of conifers grown in Yugoslavia. *IAWA Bull.* **2**, 3–7.

Phelps, J. E., and Workman, E. C., Jr. (1994). Vessel area studies in white oak (*Quercus alba* L.). *Wood Fiber Sci.* **26**, 315–322.

Putz, F. E., and Holbrook, N. M. (1991). Biomechanical studies of vines. *In* "The Biology of Vines" (F. E. Putz and H. A. Mooney, eds.), pp. 73–97. Cambridge University Press, Cambridge.

Rivett, M., and Rivett, E. (1920). The anatomy of *Rhododendron ponticum* L. and *Ilex aquifolium* L. in reference to specific conductivity. *Ann. Bot.* **34**, 525–550.

Ryan, M. G. (1989). Sapwood volume for three subalpine conifers: Predictive equations and ecological implications. *Can. J. For. Res.* **19**, 1397–1401.

Ryan, M. G. (1990). Growth and maintenance respiration in stems of *Pinus contorta* and *Picea engelmannii. Can. J. For. Res.* **20**, 48–57.

Ryan, M. G., Gower, S. T., Hubbard, R. M., Waring, R. H., Gholz, H. L., Cropper, W. P., and Running, S. W. (1995). Woody tissue maintenance respiration of four conifers in contrasting climates. *Oecologia* (in press).

Salleo, S., and Lo Gullo, M. A. (1986). Xylem cavitation in nodes and internodes of whole *Chorisia insignis* H. B. et K. plants subjected to water stress: Relations between xylem conduit size and cavitation. *Ann. Bot.* **58**, 431–441.

Salleo, S., Rosso, R., and Lo Gullo, M. (1982a). Hydraulic architecture of *Vitis vinifera* L. and *Populus deltoides* Bartr. 1-year-old twigs. I. Hydraulic conductivity (LSC) and water potential gradients. *Giorn. Bot. Ital.* **116**, 15–27.

Salleo, S., Rosso, R., and Lo Gullo, M. (1982b). Hydraulic architecture of *Vitis vinifera* L. and *Populus deltoides* Bartr. 1-year-old twigs. II. The nodal regions as "constriction zones" of the xylem system. *Giorn. Bot. Ital.* **116**, 29–40.

Schniewind, A. P. (1959). Transverse anisotropy of wood: A function of gross anatomical structure. *For. Prod. J.* **9**, 350–359.

Schniewind, A. P., and Berndt, H. (1991). The composite nature of wood. *In* "Wood Structure and Composition" (M. Lewin and I. S. Goldstein, eds.), pp. 435–476. Marcel Dekker, New York.

Schweingruber, F. H. (1990). "Anatomy of European Woods." Paul Haupt Berne and Stuttgart Publishers, Stuttgart, Germany.

Scurfield, G. (1973). Reaction wood: Its structure and function. *Science* **179**, 647–655.

Shinozaki, K., Yoda, K., Hozumi, K., and Kira, T. (1964.) A quantitative analysis of plant form—the pipe model theory. I. Basic analyses. *Jpn. J. Ecol.* **14**, 97–105.

Shumway, D. L., Steiner, K. C., and Kolb, T. E. (1993). Variation in seedling hydraulic architecture as a function of species and environment. *Tree Physiol.* **12**, 41–54.

Sperry, J. S. (1986). Relationship of xylem embolism to xylem pressure potential, stomatal closure, and shoot morphology in the palm *Rhapis excelsa. Plant Physiol.* **80**, 110–116.

Sperry, J. S., and Sullivan, J. E. M. (1992). Xylem embolism in response to freeze-thaw cycles and water stress in ring-porous, diffuse-porous, and conifer species. *Plant Physiol.* **100,** 605–613.

Sperry, J. S., Perry, A., and Sullivan, J. E. M. (1991). Pit membrane degradation and air-embolism formation in ageing xylem vessels of *Populus tremuloides* Michx. *J. Exp. Bot.* **42,** 1399–1406.

Telewski, F. W. (1989). Structure and function of flexure wood in *Abies fraseri*. *Tree Physiol.* **5,** 113–121.

Tyree, M. T., and Alexander, J. D. (1993). Hydraulic conductivity of branch junctions in three temperate tree species. *Trees* **7,** 156–159.

Tyree, M. T., Graham, M. E. D., Cooper, K. E., and Bazos, L. J. (1983). The hydraulic architecture of *Thuja occidentalis*. *Can. J. Bot.* **61,** 2105–2111.

U.S. Forest Products Laboratory (1987). "Wood Handbook: Wood as an Engineering Material." USDA Forest Service Agriculture Handbook 72. U.S. Government Printing Office, Washington, DC.

Vité, J. P., and Rudinsky, J. A. (1959). The water-conducting systems in conifers and their importance to the distribution of trunk injected chemicals. *Contrib. Boyce Thompson Inst.* **20,** 27–38.

Wang, J., Ives, N. E., and Lechowicz, M. J. (1992). The relation of foliar phenology to xylem embolism in trees. *Funct. Ecol.* **6,** 469–475.

Wardrop, A. B., and Dadswell, H. E. (1955). The nature of reaction wood. IV. Variations in cell wall organization of tension wood fibers. *Aust. J. Bot.* **3,** 177–189.

Wardrop, A. B., and Davies, G. W. (1961). Morphological factors relating to the penetration of liquids into wood. *Holzforschung* **15,** 129–141.

Wardrop, A. B., and Preston, R. D. (1947). The submicroscopic organization of the cell wall in conifer tracheids and wood fibres. *J. Exp. Bot.* **2,** 20–30.

Wardrop, A. B., and Preston, R. D. (1950). The fine structure of the wall of the conifer tracheid. V. The organization of the secondary wall in relation to the growth rate of the cambium. *Biochim. Biophys. Acta* **6,** 36–47.

Waring, R. H., and Running, S. W. (1978). Sapwood water storage: Its contribution to transpiration and effect upon water conductance through the stems of old-growth Douglas-fir. *Plant Cell Environ.* **1,** 131–140.

Wiemann, M. C., and Williamson, G. B. (1989). Radial gradients in the specific gravity of wood in some tropical and temperate trees. *For. Sci.* **35,** 197–210.

Wilson, B. F., and Archer, R. R. (1977). Reaction wood: Induction and mechanical action. *Annu. Rev. Plant Physiol.* **28,** 23–43.

Yamamoto, H., Okuyama, T., and Yoshida, M. (1993). Generation process of growth stresses in cell walls. V. Model of tensile stress generation in gelatinous fibers. *Mokuzai Gakkaishi* **39,** 118–125.

Zimmermann, M. H. (1978). Hydraulic architecture of some diffuse-porous trees. *Can. J. Bot.* **56,** 2286–2295.

Zimmermann, M. H. (1983). "Xylem Structure and the Ascent of Sap." Springer-Verlag, New York.

Zimmermann, M. H., and Jeje, A. A. (1981). Vessel-length distribution in stems of some American woody plants. *Can. J. Bot.* **59,** 1882–1892.

Zobel, B. H., and van Buijtenen, J. P. (1989). Variation among and within trees. *In* "Wood Variation: Its Causes and Control," pp. 72–131. Springer-Verlag, New York.

7

Stem Water Storage

N. Michele Holbrook

I. Introduction

Plants face an uncertain environment in terms of water availability. Not only are rainfall events unpredictable, but soil water may be depleted via surface runoff, deep drainage, uptake by neighboring plants, or evaporation from the soil surface. The demand for water by a plant may also vary depending on environmental conditions and the phenological stage of the plant. One way of dealing with imbalances in supply and demand is to acquire resources when they are plentiful for use when they are scarce. In economic terms, storage forms a viable strategy when the benefits of having access to a reserve during periods when the market price is high outweigh costs incurred in their collection and maintenance plus the loss of any profits that might have accrued from utilizing those resources at a previous date (Chapin *et al.*, 1990). Water stored within a plant's tissues represents a resource to which the individual plant has exclusive rights, but carries with it the costs of constructing and maintaining the structural components required to hold and protect this reserve. In contrast, the common reservoir of water in the soil does not require any expenditure in terms of physical containment, but the degree of control that a plant exerts over its access to this resource is comparatively low. All plant tissues contain some water that can be withdrawn given a sufficient driving force. Thus, all parts of the plant provide some degree of water storage. This chapter focuses on the ecological and physiological significance of stem water storage.

Understanding the contribution of water stored within the stem to the overall water economy of the plant requires consideration of the following questions: (1) how much water is in the stem?, (2) how available is this water?, and (3) how important is it? The first is determined by growth form and stem construction—how big is the stem and how much water does it hold? The second question focuses on how the water is held within the stem and the difficulty in accessing stem water stores. The final question refers to the contribution of stem water stores to the plant in relation to changes in soil water availability and evaporative losses. Because storage alters only the temporal disposition of a resource, rather than its total amount, it is important to examine the dynamics of resource utilization in relation to changes in supply and demand. In particular, the paradox or design criterion for effective storage is that the reserves must be readily available when needed, but not so easily accessed that they are depleted prior to the onset of conditions warranting their storage.

Why should a plant store water? One answer is to allow carbon uptake from the atmosphere when the soil is dry. Most plants use water in tremendous quantities, with the majority of this being lost to the atmosphere. Under favorable environmental conditions, the amount of water passing through most plants each day is so vast as to preclude the possibility of using stored water to supply such demands. In general, a strategy of utilizing stored water to promote carbon gain appears to require intrinsically low transpiration rates, a large stem volume to leaf area ratio, or both. In this regard, plants from arid environments that combine the low transpiration rates characteristic of crassulacean acid metabolism (CAM), with extensive stem parenchyma and limited surface area are exceptionally well suited to rely on stored water for photosynthetic activity. A second role for water storage is to buffer against damage due to desiccation in specific portions of the plant. Tissues targeted for protection could include reproductive structures, xylem conduits, or meristems. Stem water storage may also place constraints on plant activities. For example, the presence of a large fraction of living tissues within the stem of a woody plant may increase its susceptibility to successful invasion by pathogens.

II. Approaches to Studying Stem Water Storage

Stems are difficult to study. They are bulky, heterogeneous, and rarely amenable to destructive sampling without substantially compromising the integrity of the plant. A variety of techniques, both invasive and non-invasive, have been used to measure stem water content (Table I). Each method has limitations and the problem of scaling point measurements to the entire stem remains a serious challenge. Furthermore, understanding

Table I Comparison of Techniques for Measuring Stem Water Content

Technique	Destructive?	Requires empirical calibration?	Appropriate for field studies?	References
Increment cores	Yes	No	Yes	Waring and Running (1979); Brough et al. (1986)
Dendrometer bands	No	Yes	Yes	Hinckley et al. (1978)
Electrical resistance	Invasive	Yes	Yes	Dixon et al. (1978); Borchert (1994c)
Thermal conductance	Invasive	Yes	Yes	Goulden (1991)
Capacitance measures	No, some applications require invasive configuration	Yes	Yes	Holbrook et al. (1992)
γ-ray absorption	No	Yes (information on the wood matrix density)	No given current technology	Edwards and Jarvis (1983); Brough et al. (1986)
Magnetic resonance	No	No	No given current technology	Reinders et al. (1988); Veres et al. (1991)
Water potential	Invasive or requires subsampling	Yes	Difficulties with temperature gradients	Goldstein and Meinzer (1983); Nobel and Jordan (1983)

the significance of stem water storage requires more than simply documenting the presence of water in the stem. The inherently dynamic nature of water storage means that this reservoir must be examined within the context of the whole plant's water use. The basic components necessary to examine the contribution of stem water storage are straightforward and include: determination of water uptake from the soil, water loss by the entire canopy, and changes in stem water content. Unfortunately, all of these quantities can be difficult to measure under natural conditions.

A. Root-Excision and Pot Experiments

One way around the difficulties associated with constructing the water budget of an intact plant is to determine the contribution of water withdrawn from stem tissues to the total evaporative loss when soil water uptake has been eliminated (root-excision) or the exploited soil volume has been physically limited (pot experiments). Root-excision experiments with trees indicate that stem water stores are capable of supporting preexcision water loss rates for only one to two days (Roberts, 1976; Running, 1980; Holbrook and Sinclair, 1992b). Once the stomata do close, however, stem water reserves may serve to maintain the foliage at their initial level of hydration for many weeks (Running, 1980; Holbrook and Sinclair, 1992b). Container-grown plants are particularly amenable to studies of stem water storage because of the relative ease of determining both whole-plant transpiration (by changes in weight) and whole-plant water uptake (from changes in soil water content), with the contribution of stem water stores being inferred from their difference (Holbrook and Sinclair, 1992b). Pot experiments, however, are generally limited to fairly small plants and are subject to influences on physiological processes associated with restricted rooting volume.

B. Modeling

Empirical studies of stem water storage are frequently augmented with models that stimulate the dynamics of stem water storage. Models of non-steady-state water flow through plants based on an electric circuit analog have been used to simulate the contribution of stem water stores over a broad range of conditions (Hunt and Nobel, 1987; Nobel and Jordan, 1983). The continuous flows and storage locations within the intact plant, however, must be mapped onto a finite number of discrete components. This approach has been successfully applied to a variety of plants including desert perennials (e.g., Calkin and Nobel, 1986; Schulte and Nobel, 1989; Schulte et al., 1989), conifers (e.g., Tyree, 1988), and dicotyledonous trees (e.g., Tyree et al., 1991). In many cases empirical parameterization of the capacitance and transfer resistance of individual organs (leaves, roots, stem) under laboratory conditions may be easier than the simultaneous measurement of total fluxes within an intact plant. Furthermore, models frequently provide insight into complex interactions because they permit estimation of variables that are difficult or impossible to measure, although this same feature poses a major difficulty in terms of model validation.

C. Time Series Analysis

Any out-of-phase or storage term will alter the temporal dynamics of the response parameters relative to the driving variables (Fig. 1). Examination of how variables such as transpiration and stem water potential change over time (time-series analysis) thus provides information on the contribution of stored water. A simple example of this is to use measurements of sap flow after sundown to infer a net withdrawal of water from stem tissues during the day (Morikawa, 1974). A substantial time lag in the propagation of water potential along the stem also indicates the net movement of water in or out of storage (Hellkvist *et al.*, 1974; Hinckley *et al.*, 1978). In practice, the

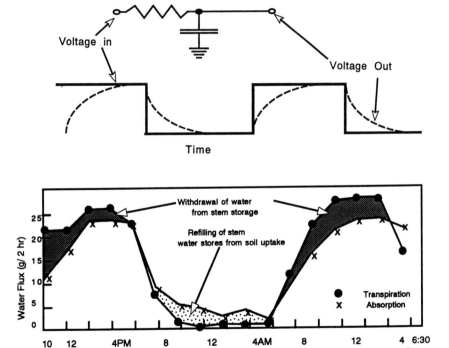

Figure 1 Effect of capacitance on the temporal dynamics of response variable relative to input parameters. In both cases the response (output voltage, water uptake) lags the driving force (input voltage, transpiration). (Upper) low pass filter. (Lower) transpiration (●) and water uptake (absorption) (×) of *Pinus taeda* as a function of time. Lower portion of figure reprinted with permission from Kramer (1937).

propagation of water potential along the stem generally has been inferred from changes in stem diameter (Wronski *et al.*, 1985; Milne *et al.*, 1983; Dobbs and Scott, 1971). Measurement of the amplitude and phase relations between the rate of water loss from leaf surfaces and water potential at various points along the stem can be used to parameterize a simple electrical-analog model of within-plant water flows and thus to calculate the capacitance of the stem (Wronski *et al.*, 1985; Milne *et al.*, 1983). Alternatively, comparison of time lags determined at various points within a single tree are valuable in determining the structure of the resistor/capacitor network by providing information on which portions of the crown and stem can be treated as a single unit in terms of their contribution to water flow and which should be included in the model as separate components (Milne *et al.*, 1983).

D. Comparative Studies

In some cases it may be possible to compare individuals of the same species that differ primarily in their capacity for stem water storage. Plants in which the crown geometry and total leaf area stay relatively constant as the stem increases in height are well suited for this approach. Comparison of Andean giant rosette plants (*Espeletia timotensis*) of different heights and thus varying leaf area/stem volume indicated a substantial influence of stem water storage on both leaf water relations and plant survivorship during the dry season (Goldstein *et al.*, 1985). Differences in dry season photosynthetic activity (as indicated by diel fluctuations in titratable acidity) in the arborescent cacti (*Opuntia excelsa*) that were related to plant size may indicate the contribution of water stored within the trunk and major branches (Lerdau *et al.*, 1992). A related approach contrasts two subspecies that differ in the amount of pectin-like accumulations in their basal leaves to examine the influence of extracellular polysaccharides on water storage and physiological activity during periods of drought (Morse, 1990).

III. Structural Features Influencing Stem Water Storage

The water storage capacity of plant tissues is defined as the amount of water that can be withdrawn for a given change in driving force (water potential) and is generally referred to as the tissue's capacitance, in keeping with the electrical circuit analogy for water movement within plants (Powell and Thorpe, 1977; Jarvis, 1975; Tyree and Jarvis, 1982; Fig. 1). In practice, capacitance is determined as the change in water content per unit change in water potential (Fig. 2). For comparative purposes, capacitance is usually normalized either by sample volume or in relation to the transpiring sur-

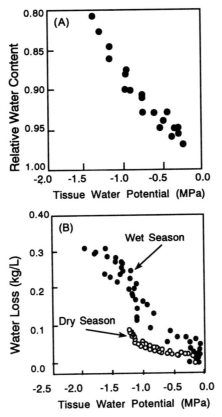

Figure 2 Water potential isotherms for the dehydration of *Schefflera morotoni* stems collected during the wet (●) and dry (○) season. Water content expressed as percentage of initial value (A) or normalized by tissue volume (B). Changes in slope (capacitance) with increasing water loss reflect the successive importance of capillary, elastic, and cavitation release as water storage mechanisms. Reprinted with permission from Tyree *et al.* (1991).

face area (Table II). Size, however, is often the major parameter determining water storage capacity. For example, most of the 1000-fold variation in total capacitance among leaves, stems, and roots of three sympatric desert perennials was due to differences in organ size; capacitance per unit volume varied by only a factor of two (Nobel and Jordan, 1983). It is important to emphasize that capacitance is not a fixed parameter, but one that varies with water potential (Table II). This is especially true for stems because they are structurally heterogeneous and the relationship between capacitance and water potential may differ among storage mechanisms (see below).

In terms of water storage, stem tissues can be differentiated according to

Table II Stem Capacitance of Selected Species

Species	Capacitance (kg liter^{-1} MPa^{-1})	Water potential range (MPa)	Water potential technique	Reference
Tsuga canadensis	0.40	0 to −0.2	*In situ* psychrometer	Tyree and Yang (1990)
	0.019	−0.5 to −2.0		
	0.22	−2.8 to −3.4		
Thuja occidentalis	0.46	0 to −0.2	*In situ* psychrometer	Tyree and Yang (1990)
	0.017	−0.5 to −2.0		
	0.09	−2.2 to −3.0		
Acer saccharum	1.02	0 to −0.2	*In situ* psychrometer	Tyree and Yang (1990)
	0.02	−0.5 to −3.0		
	0.068	−3.5 to −5.0		
Pseudotsuga menziesii[a]	0.85	0 to −0.5	Vapor equilibration with salt solutions	Waring and Running (1978)
	0.28	−0.5 to −1.0		
Malus pumila[b]	1.8 to 2.4 × 10-2 kg/kg MPa	0 to −4.0 MPa	Dehydration isotherm of cut trees	Landsberg *et al.* (1976)
Schefflera morototoni	0.03 (dry season)	−0.2 to −1.0	Pressure chamber	Tyree *et al.* (1991)
	0.20 (wet season)			
Ochroma pyrimidale	0.062 (dry season)	−0.15 to −1.0	*In situ* psychrometer	Machado and Tyree (1994)
	0.134 (rehydrated)[c]			
Pseudobombax septenatum	0.078 (dry season)	−0.15 to −1.0	*In situ* psychrometer	Machado and Tyree (1994)
	0.047 (rehydrated)			
Ferocactus acanthodes	0.11	0 to −1.0	Pressure chamber	Hunt and Nobel (1987)
Espeletia spp.	0.07	0 to −1.0	Thermocouple psychrometer chambers	Goldstein *et al.* (1984)

[a]Estimated from figure.
[b]Where stems are 50% water by weight.
[c]Collected during the dry season.

whether the available water is primarily intra- or extracellular. Intracellular water storage results from the ability of semipermeable membranes to concentrate osmotically active solutes. The water-release properties of tissues containing a large fraction of living cells are determined primarily by the mechanical properties of the cell wall (Tyree and Jarvis, 1982; Tyree and Yang, 1990): cells with highly elastic walls undergo substantial changes in volume in response to small changes in total water potential (i.e., have a high capacitance), whereas cells with rigid walls experience large changes in potential with only a small change in water content. Extracellular water storage (also referred to as inelastic storage; Tyree and Yang, 1990) includes water retained within intercellular spaces and the lumen of embolized xylem elements (capillary storage *sensu* Zimmermann, 1983), water released by the cavitation of intact conducting elements, and changes in the water content of extracellular polysaccharides (e.g., mucilage, latex). In terms of the temporal dynamics governing the recharge and discharge of water from storage, both capillary and intracellular or elastic storage are reversible (i.e., show little hysteresis). Cavitation, on the other hand, may frequently be effectively irreversible or reversible only upon attainment of conditions enabling embolism repair (Tyree and Sperry, 1989).

A. Intracellular Water Storage

Intracellular water storage in stems can occur in the pith, the phloem and extracambial region, and the sapwood. Because elastic water storage/release results from changes in cell volume, the surrounding tissues must be able to accommodate these movements either by being themselves flexible or by the presence of intercellular air spaces (Carlquist, 1975). Xylem characteristics of stem succulents that may permit large fluctuations in stem volume include widening of pits, loss of fibers, and widely spaced annular or helical thickening of xylem vessels (Carlquist, 1962, 1975; Gibson, 1973). The available water fraction of parenchymatous tissues is generally considered to equal the water deficit at which the cells lose turgor (e.g., Goldstein *et al.*, 1984). Minimizing the withdrawal of water beyond this point would be particularly important for plants that rely on turgor pressure for the mechanical integrity of their stem (e.g., Niklas and O'Rourke, 1987). On the other hand, capacitance arising from the exchange of intracellular water (Δ[cell water content]/Δ[water potential]) is greatest for water deficits that exceed the turgor loss point (i.e., when losses in turgor pressure no longer contribute to decreases in water potential). In terms of effective water storage, however, the increased intrinsic, or volume-normalized, capacitance at large water deficits must be balanced by any impairment of cellular function(s) due to loss of turgor and increasing dehydration.

In most plants the volume occupied by the pith is too small to act as a significant site for water storage. A major exception occurs in plants with large apical meristems, such as the giant rosette plants of tropical alpine regions in which the diameter of the pith may exceed 10 cm (Hedberg, 1964; Goldstein *et al.*, 1984). Pith water storage sufficient to supply total plant water loss for up to 7 weeks are reported in trees of arid regions (e.g., *Idria columnaris* [Fouquieriaceae] Nilsen *et al.*, 1990). Many cacti have a substantial volume of parenchyma interior to the vascular cylinder. Members of the tribe Pachycereeae (subfamily Cactoideae) have their woody cylinder divided into parallel (fastigiate) vertical rods that can be spread apart and thus permit the development of a pith as large as 20 cm in diameter (e.g., *Carnegiea gigantea;* Gibson and Nobel, 1986). The water storage parenchyma that forms the central region of cladodes of *Opuntia* species (e.g., Goldstein *et al.*, 1991b) should also be considered developmentally as pith tissue. Arborescent members of the genus *Jacaratia* (Caricaceae) show an unusual form of stem development in which delayed radial expansion of xylem parenchyma results in a soft central region with an extremely high water content surrounded by a relatively thin outer cylinder of dense wood (Paoli and Pagano, 1988; Holbrook and Putz, 1992). Although not developmentally a true pith, the parenchymatous matrix that surrounds the vascular bundles of many monocotyledonous stems may result in substantial elastic water storage provided that there are sufficient intercellular air spaces to accommodate the volume changes (Carlquist, 1988; Tomlinson, 1990; Holbrook and Sinclair, 1992a).

The phloem and cambial regions of the stems of most plants are of relatively small volume such that their ability to serve as sites for water storage is generally limited. Furthermore, the essential functions of the cells in this region make it unlikely that the hydration of other portions of the plant at the expense of this zone would be adaptive. Nevertheless, variations in xylem tension will result in water being withdrawn from or recharged to the phloem and cambium. Greater than 90% of diurnal fluctuations in the diameter of tree stems may be attributed to changes in the water content of the phloem and cambium (Whitehead and Jarvis, 1981; Lassoie, 1979; Jarvis, 1975). In most plants such changes in external dimension may be more valuable as an index of stem water potential than as a measure of stem water extraction (e.g., Klepper *et al.*, 1971; Parlange *et al.*, 1975; McBurney and Costigan, 1984). Many cacti, however, have a substantial capacity for water storage in the stem cortex. Large primary rays that pass through openings in the vascular cylinder maintain a parenchymatous connection between the pith and the cortex (Gibson and Nobel, 1986). A major disadvantage associated with water storage near the exterior of the stem is water loss to the atmosphere. Parenchymatous water storage near the stem surface in C_3 stem succulents of arid regions (e.g., *Fouquieria columnaris* [Fouquieriaceae]; *Pachycormus discolor* [Anacardiaceae]) is protected from desiccation by a translucent periderm which permits the passage of light energy necessary for refixation of respiratory CO_2, but markedly reduces water loss (Franco-Vizcaíno *et al.*, 1990; Nilsen *et al.*, 1990; see Nilsen [10], this volume).

Almost all plants contain some living cells within the sapwood that could function in water storage (see Carlquist, 1988, for exceptions). Parenchyma cells located adjacent to xylem elements or within xylem rays, however, are frequently lignified and may be physically constrained from marked deformation by surrounding xylem elements. The contribution of living cells to the water storage capacity of the woods of temperate trees may be limited; Tyree and Yang (1990) estimate that water withdrawn from living cells in stems of *Thuja occidentalis* contribute <6% of the total daily transpirational water loss. Sapwood water content varies considerably among species, with much of this variation occurring in tropical habitats (Borchert, 1994a,b). Such interspecific differences in stem water content are inversely correlated with wood density (grams of dry mass per cubic centimeter; Barajas-Morales, 1987; Schulze *et al.*, 1988), supporting the idea that tropical trees with high stem water contents may have an abundance of thin-walled cells capable of elastic water storage (Carlquist, 1988; Borchert, 1994a).

The relatively high fraction of sapwood parenchyma observed in some tropical trees arises from a variety of structural modifications. Proliferation of axial parenchyma to form wide apotracheal bands is reported in stems of *Apeiba* (Tiliaceae; den Outer and Schutz, 1981), *Cecropia* (Cecropiaceae; Carlquist, 1988), *Bursera* (Burseraceae; Nilsen *et al.*, 1990), *Chorisia* (Bombacaceae; Metcalfe and Chalk, 1950), *Erythrina* (Fabaceae; Cumbie, 1960), and *Adansonia* (Bombacaceae; Fisher, 1981). The latter are drought-deciduous trees that flower during the dry season (Carlquist, 1988). In extreme cases of "parenchymatization" there can be a total replacement of imperforate tracheary elements with axial parenchyma (e.g., *Carica* (Caricaceae), *Brighamia* (Campanulaceae), many Crassulaceae; Carlquist, 1988; Fisher, 1980). Mechanical constraints associated with stem stability, however, may limit the proliferation of soft tissues in the stems of tall trees. Arborescent cacti typically have dense wood with many, nucleate fibers, sparse axial parenchyma, and lignified ray cells; shorter genera characteristic of more open habitats produce wood lacking fibers and having unlignified axial and ray parenchyma (Mauseth, 1993). Some species (e.g., *Browningia candelaris*) have a dimorphic construction in which the axial parenchyma is lignified in the trunk but not in the branches (Mauseth, 1993). Even nonsucculent, leaf-bearing cacti (e.g., *Pereskia*) have a tendency to form occasionally bands of axial parenchyma (Bailey, 1962; Carlquist, 1988).

B. Extracellular Water Storage

Capillary water storage and cavitation release provide mechanisms for extracellular water storage in highly lignified regions of the stem (Zimmermann, 1983; Tyree and Yang, 1990). Capillary water storage occurs in embolized xylem elements (fibers, tracheids, vessels) and in intercellular spaces where water is retained due to surface tension. As the hydrostatic pressure of water held by capillary forces is inversely proportional to the radius of curvature of the gas–water interface, the amount of water released from capillary storage will be greatest at water potentials near zero and decline sharply as xylem water potential falls. Thus, although the amount of capillary water storage within a stem can be substantial (e.g., Waring and Running, 1978), it will be largely depleted before stem water potentials fall below −0.6 MPa (Tyree and Yang, 1990). Cavitation, on the other hand, occurs predominantly at low water potentials when a gas bubble is sucked into a water-filled conducting element (Tyree and Sperry, 1989). There can be no doubt that cavitation release results in the net withdrawal of water from the stem (Tyree and Yang, 1990; Lo Gullo and Salleo, 1992). Its role in water storage, however, must be assessed in light of the resulting decrease in hydraulic conductivity and the potential for embolism repair (see Sperry [5], this volume). Under conditions of severe drought when stomata are closed and soil water uptake is minimal, water released by cavitation may aid in survival by preventing the desiccation of meristematic tissues (Dixon *et al.*, 1984; Tyree and Yang, 1990).

A "typical" conifer stem is often described as being capable of supporting 5- to 10-fold more hours of transpiration than a typical hardwood tree, with this difference being doubled in comparison with herbaceous plants (e.g., Jarvis, 1975; Chaney, 1981). The large stems and low transpiration rates of many conifers certainly play an essential role in this pattern. From the point of view of understanding the influence of stem structure on water storage capacity, however, the question arises as to whether or not there are fundamental differences between hardwoods and conifers in their capacity for cavitation repair. If refilling occurs more readily in conifers than in hardwoods, then cavitation release may play a correspondingly more important role in terms of stem water storage in conifers. Seasonal variations in sapwood water content often exceed 40% (by dry weight) in coniferous trees (e.g., Chalk and Bigg, 1956; Gibbs, 1958; Waring and Running, 1978). Laboratory studies indicate that such large changes in water content will be accompanied by marked declines in hydraulic conductivity (Waring and Running, 1978; Puritch, 1971) and thus may reflect a substantial degree of cavitation (Waring and Running, 1978). Recent studies suggest that cavitation repair in conifers may occur over a wider range of conditions than reported for dicotyledonous species (Edwards *et al.*, 1994; Sperry *et al.*, 1994). The mechanism of such refilling, however, remains unknown and further studies of embolism repair in both hardwoods and conifers are needed to determine the degree to which water release by cavitation is a reversible process.

Compared with the sapwood, the heartwood appears to be relatively limited in terms of effective water storage (Hinckley *et al.*, 1978). Heartwood formation results from numerous physiological and biological changes, including the death of any living cells and, with some exceptions, a decline in water content (Chalk and Bigg, 1956; Clark and Gibbs, 1957; Stewart, 1966, 1967; Whitehead and Jarvis, 1981; see Gartner [6], this volume). Seasonal variation in water content is generally much less pronounced in the heartwood than in the sapwood (Clark and Gibbs, 1957; Gibbs, 1958), perhaps reflecting hydraulic separation between the living portions of the stem and the heartwood.

Extracellular polysaccharides may form an important mechanism for water storage where abundant due to their hydrophilic character (Morse, 1990; Robichaux and Morse, 1990). Both the water-holding capacity and specific capacitance of such biological colloids are extremely high (Wiebe, 1966; Morse, 1990). Mucilage constituted 14% of the dry weight of *Opuntia ficus-indica* cladodes but held 30% of the water within the water storage parenchyma (Goldstein *et al.*, 1991a). Dehydration isotherms of mucilage extracted from *O. ficus-indica* showed that over 60% of this water could be removed without an appreciable decrease in water potential (Goldstein *et al.*, 1991a). Water storage by extracellular polysaccharides has been shown to buffer photosynthetic tissues against the development of short-term water deficits (Morse, 1990; Robichaux and Morse, 1990; Goldstein *et al.*, 1991b). In addition, the high capacitance of mucilage in *O. ficus-indica* cladodes may help prevent freezing damage by facilitating extracellular ice nucleation and delaying cellular water loss (Goldstein and Nobel, 1991). The stems of many plants (e.g., Moraceae, Euphorbiaceae, Musaceae) contain anastomosing canals filled with a watery latex. Such plants bleed copiously when wounded, with the concentration, rate, and duration of exudation being related to plant water status (Milburn *et al.*, 1990). Latex canals could form an important site of apoplasmic water storage (Parkin, 1990), although this possibility has not been investigated (Buttery and Boatman, 1976; Downton, 1981). However, bananas produce large amounts of latex within their stems and maintain high levels of stem hydration when subject to drought, supporting this conjecture (Kallarackal *et al.*, 1990).

C. Root Hydraulic Properties

Maintenance of a high stem water content in conjunction with very dry soils requires that the roots play a role analogous to that of the stomata in preventing water loss to the environment. In particular, the success of desert succulents requires the ability to restrict water loss from stem-to-soil during periods of drought (Nobel and North, 1993). Rectifier-like behavior has been observed in both desert succulents and tropical epiphytes (e.g., Nobel and Sanderson, 1984; Ewers *et al.*, 1992; North and Nobel, 1994); low hydraulic conductivity at the soil/root interface when the soil is dry prevents water from leaking out of the bottom of the plant when it is most needed for survival. While the structural and physiological nature of this adaptation lies outside the scope of this chapter, the essential contribution of this behavior to effective stem water storage in very dry regions must be emphasized.

IV. Ecological Significance of Stem Water Storage

A. CAM: Stem Water Storage in Relation to Photosynthetic Pathway

Environments in which periods of high soil water availability are unpredictable, infrequent, and of short duration represent conditions well suited to within-plant water storage provided that net carbon gain can be sustained at very low total water loss rates. Desert plants whose growth form can accommodate relatively large volumes of water typically exhibit the high water-use efficiency associated with night-time stomatal opening characteristic of crassulacean acid metabolism. This combination of morphological and physiological adaptations allows photosynthetic carbon gain in many CAM plants to be less affected by variation in soil water status. For example, water stored within the stems of *Ferrocactus acanthodes* (Cactaceae) was sufficient to supply transpirational water loss for 40 days after uptake from the soil had ceased (Nobel, 1977). The influence of stem storage on the productivity of CAM plants markedly differs from the majority of C_3 and C_4 plants, where stem water is primarily an adaptation enabling survival of extreme conditions.

In addition to its role in buffering the plant from variations in soil moisture availability, water storage forms an important component of CAM metabolism. Substantial accumulation of organic acids within the vacuole requires a high cellular water content and thus a means of maintaining the chlorenchyma well hydrated while at the same time mobilizing water from either internal stores or the soil. Decreases in osmotic potential due to malate formation in the chlorenchyma results in a significant driving force for the redistribution of internal water (Luttge, 1987; Goldstein *et al.*, 1991b). This internal cycling of water from nonphotosynthetic storage parenchyma to chlorenchyma during the night (and its reverse during the day) permits water deficits associated with stomatal opening to be promptly replenished without the development of low water potentials necessary for the rapid transport of water from the soil. Soil water uptake can thus be spread over a 24-hr period (Hunt and Nobel, 1987; Schulte *et al.*, 1989). During periods when soil water is not available, water is preferentially depleted from non-photosynthetic water storage parenchyma compared with the chlorenchyma (Barcikowski and Nobel, 1984; Goldstein *et al.*, 1991b). This decline in water content of the water storage parenchyma is accompanied by a decrease in osmotically active solutes, thus enabling the water storage parenchyma to remain a net source of water for the chlorenchyma (Goldstein *et al.*, 1991a,b).

B. Neotropical Dry Forest Trees: Stem Water Storage in Relation to Phenology

Differences in phenological behavior among neotropical deciduous forest trees corresponds with variation in wood density, a parameter inversely related to water content (Borchert, 1994a,b). In upland forest sites in Costa Rica where the water table is inaccessible during the dry season, the majority of species are deciduous during the 4- to 5-month dry season. Species with dense wood ($0.91-1.2$ g/cm^3) and low maximum stem moisture contents ($19-31$ g/g dry weight) delay leaf shedding until well into the dry season (Borchert, 1994a,b). At the time of leaf abscission, the leaf and branch water potentials of these trees are quite negative and the amount of water in their stems is substantially reduced from wet season levels (58 to 71% depleted). In contrast, species with high stem moisture content (wood density between 0.39 and 0.49 g/cm^3; maximum moisture contents of $121-171$ g/g dry mass) appear quite sensitive to drought (Borchert, 1994a,b). These species lose their leaves at the onset of the dry season and have leaf and branch water potentials, at the time of leaf abscission, that are substantially less negative than in the denser-wooded species (Borchert 1994a). Sensitivity to drought in stem succulent trees is also indicated by low stomatal conductances, strong stomatal closure in response to increased vapor pressure deficits, and relatively high leaf water potentials (Nilsen *et al.*, 1990; Medina and Cuevas, 1990; Olivares and Medina, 1992; Holbrook *et al.*, 1995).

Early leaf abscission appears at first to be in conflict with the idea that stem water storage functions to buffer plants from fluctuations in soil water availability. During the dry season, high leaf-to-air vapor pressure deficits and the necessity of acquiring water from deeper and increasingly drier regions of the soil profile would result in low leaf and xylem water potentials should transpiration rates remain unchanged. These low xylem water potentials would, in turn, lead to the movement of water from stem tissues with the result that these water reserves could become significantly depleted prior to substantial soil drying. Neotropical deciduous forest trees with high stem water contents are typically shallow-rooted compared to cooccurring species with dense wood (Holbrook *et al.*, 1995). This may reflect the impossibility of maintaining water stores within the stem for later use while, at the same time, extracting sufficient water from a drying soil profile to support high rates of transpiration. In species with early leaf abscission, stem water stores may be used to support the production and transpiration of flowers during the dry season (Borchert, 1994a). In western Mexico, deciduous species that flower during the dry season had higher stem water contents than species that flower during other times of the year (Schulze *et al.*, 1988; Bullock and Solís-Magallanes, 1990). Declines in stem moisture content during dry season flowering indicate a net loss of water from the stem (Borchert, 1994a); early leaf abscission in these species may be necessary to reserve sufficient water in the stem to support dry season flowering.

C. Tropical Alpine Rosette Plants: Stem Water Storage in Relation to Temperature

Plants of high alpine environments near the equator may experience strong diurnal changes in soil water availability due to fluctuations in soil temperature. In habitats in which giant rosette plants occur (*Espeletia* and *Senecio* species), freezing temperatures can be reached during any night of the year and diurnal fluctuations in temperature exceed seasonal variation in average daytime temperature (Goldstein and Meinzer, 1983; Hedberg, 1964). During the early morning when the sky is most likely to be clear, low soil temperatures may inhibit water uptake. This pattern of frequent droughts of short duration suggests that an aboveground water reservoir able to augment water supply to the leaves during the morning could provide a substantial degree of protection against desiccation and/or photodamage, while at the same time allowing them to make full use of incoming radiation during the sunniest portion of the day. The unusual pattern of increasing plant height with elevation may reflect the need for a larger aboveground water reservoir at higher elevations where temperature-induced limitations in soil water availability should be of longer duration (Smith, 1980; Goldstein *et al.*, 1985).

The parenchymatous pith tissue of giant rosette plants appears to provide a water reservoir capable of buffering leaf water potential during short periods of low soil water availability (Goldstein *et al.*, 1984; Goldstein and Meinzer, 1983; Fig. 3). Calculation of the amount of water available in the pith relative to average transpiration rates ($82.2 \, \text{g m}^{-2} \, \text{h}^{-1}$) indicates that *Espeletia* species with the highest relative capacitance would be able to supply transpirational water loss for a maximum of 2.5 hr (Goldstein *et al.*, 1984). When mature individuals were dug up and water was withheld from the roots for several days, the water content of the pith decreased indicating that water was moving from the pith into the transpiration stream (Goldstein and Meinzer, 1983). Excised individuals with a greater pith volume maintained leaf water potentials above the turgor loss point for a longer

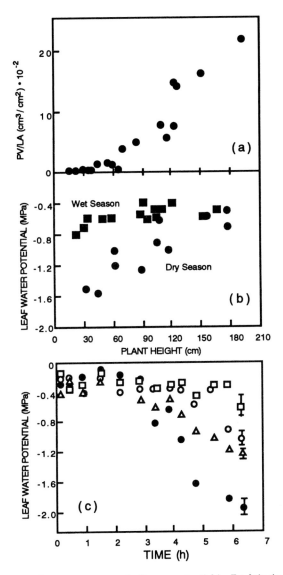

Figure 3 Effect of pith water storage on leaf water potential in *Espeletia timotensis*. (a) Relationship between the ratio of pith volume (PV) and total leaf area (LA) and plant height. (b) Relationship between leaf water potential and plant height during the wet (■) and dry (●) seasons. (c) Time course of leaf water potential following root-excision for individuals 26-(●), 40-(△), 66-(○), and 100-(□) cm tall under laboratory conditions. Reprinted with permission from Goldstein *et al.* (1985).

period than did smaller individuals (Goldstein *et al.,* 1985). Field measurements also indicate that short-statured individuals which have a small pith volume relative to their leaf area experience more negative leaf water potentials during the dry season than do taller individuals (Goldstein *et al.,* 1985; Goldstein *et al.,* 1984). High mortality rates experienced by smaller individuals may be in part due to their smaller stem water storage capacity (Goldstein *et al.,* 1985).

D. Stem Water Storage in Relation to Xylem Function

Given that water withdrawn from storage retards the propagation of low xylem water potentials through the plant, it is reasonable to consider a connection between xylem function and stem water storage. Tyree *et al.* (1991) provide evidence for a relationship between vulnerability of stem to cavitation (see Sperry [5], this volume), stem and leaf capacitances, and leaf-specific conductivity (see Gartner [6], this volume). Stems of the tropical tree *Schefflera morotoni* had the highest capacitances but were the most vulnerable to cavitation, the temperate conifer *Thuja occidentalis* had low stem capacitance and was substantially more resistant to cavitation and loss of hydraulic conductivity by embolisms, while the broad-leaved temperate species *Acer saccharum* was intermediate in both parameters (Tyree *et al.,* 1991). Dynamic models of non-steady-state water flow, however, indicated that when soil moisture was readily available, water withdrawn from stem tissues accounted for a greater fraction of daily water loss in *Thuja* (16%) than in *Schefflera* (2%). This apparent paradox arose because leaf-specific hydraulic conductivity followed the same pattern as stem capacitance (i.e., highest in *S. morotoni*, lowest in *T. occidentalis*). Gradients in water potential along the length of the stem were low in *Schefflera* compared with those of *Thuja* and *Acer,* resulting in less water being withdrawn from *Schefflera* stems.

The situation changes dramatically with soil drying (Tyree *et al.,* 1991). Reduction in xylem water potentials in *Schefflera* results in the net movement of water from stem tissues into the transpiration stream. In contrast, the species with low leaf-specific conductivity (e.g., *Thuja*) are predicted to have little additional water that can be withdrawn from stem tissues as the soils dry. Nevertheless, even in *Schefflera* Tyree *et al.* (1991) estimate that stem water stores would be depleted within 2 days with dry soils if transpiration rates remained unchanged. Reductions in water loss rates due to stomatal closure, however, should allow *Schefflera* to withstand several weeks of drought without experiencing declines in stem water potential and the associated risk of cavitation. Effective stem water storage in *Schefflera,* thus, requires a combination of high leaf-specific conductivity that prevents stem water stores from being drawn upon when the soil is wet, and stomatal regulation to moderate rates of water loss when the soil is dry.

V. Conclusions and Directions for Future Research

Stem water storage contributes to plant function in a variety of ways. Its role in maintaining high levels of photosynthetic carbon gain during periods of drought, however, is limited to plants with inherently low transpiration rates (i.e., CAM succulents and perhaps large conifers). In most plants, stem water storage appears to be most important in enabling them to survive periods of drought. In addition, stem water storage may provide a strategic reserve during limited periods of adverse environmental conditions (e.g., giant rosette plants, dry-season flowering in tropical trees). Understanding the temporal dynamics of stem water utilization requires that it be examined in the context of stomatal behavior, rooting patterns, and stem hydraulic conductivity. Because of its close proximity to the transpiring surfaces, coordination between the hydraulics and patterns of water use are necessary to prevent the depletion of stem water stores prior to the onset of extreme conditions. Current understanding of the extent and mechanism of stem water storage remains limited and additional studies are needed to examine a wider range of species and environments, as well as to explore a number of specific issues. In particular, better understanding of the mechanism of cavitation repair, improvements in methods for *in situ* measurements of stem water content, and an increased knowledge of the trade-offs associated with stem water storage are essential.

Acknowledgments

I thank C. P. Lund, E. T. Nilsen, P. S. Schulte, and J. S. Sperry for helpful comments on an earlier version and M. J. Burns for help with the figures.

References

Bailey, I. W. (1962). Comparative anatomy of the leaf-bearing Cactaceae. VI. The xylem of *Pereskia saccharosa* and *Pereskia aculeata. J. Arnold Arbor. Harv. Univ.* **43**, 376–383.

Barajas-Morales, J. (1987). Wood specific gravity in species from two tropical forests in Mexico. *IAWA Bull.* **8**, 143–148.

Barcikowski, W., and Nobel, P. S. (1984). Water relations of cacti during desiccation: Distribution of water in tissues. *Bot. Gaz.* **145**, 110–145.

Borchert, R. (1994a). Water storage in soil or tree stems determines phenology and distribution of tropical dry forest trees. *Ecology* **75**, 1437–1449.

Borchert, R. (1994b). Water status and development of tropical trees during drought. *Trees* **8**, 115–125.

Borchert, R. (1994c). Electric resistance as a measure of tree water status during seasonal drought in a tropical dry forest in Costa Rica. *Tree Physiol.* **14**, 299–312.

Brough, D. W., Jones, H. G., and Grace, J. (1986). Diurnal changes in water content of the stems of apple trees, as influenced by irrigation. *Plant, Cell Environ.* **9,** 1–7.

Bullock, S. H., and Solís-Magallanes, J. A. (1990). Phenology of canopy trees of a tropical deciduous forest in Mexico. *Biotropica* **22,** 22–35.

Buttery, B. R., and Boatman, S. G. (1976). Water deficits and flow of latex. *In* "Water Deficits and Plant Growth" (T. T. Kozlowski, ed.), Vol. IV, pp. 233–289. Academic Press, New York.

Calkin, H. W., and Nobel, P. S. (1986). Nonsteady-state analysis of water flow and capacitance for *Agave deserti. Can. J. Bot.* **64,** 2556–2560.

Carlquist, S. (1962). A theory of paedomorphosis in dicotyledonous woods. *Phytomorphology,* **12,** 30–45.

Carlquist, S. (1975). "Ecological Strategies of Xylem Evolution." Univ. of California Press, Berkeley.

Carlquist, S. (1988). "Comparative Wood Anatomy: Systematic, Ecological, and Evolutionary Aspects of Dicotyledon Wood." Springer-Verlag, Berlin.

Chalk, L., and Bigg, J. M. (1956). The distribution of moisture in the living stem in Sitka spruce and Douglas fir. *Forestry* **29,** 5–21.

Chaney, W. R. (1981). Sources of water. *In* "Water Deficits and Plant Growth" (T. T. Kozlowski, ed.), Vol. VI, pp. 1–47, Academic Press, New York.

Chapin, F. S., Schulze, E.-D., and Mooney, H. A. (1990). The ecology and economics of storage in plants. *Annu. Rev. Ecol. Syst.* **21,** 423–447.

Clark, J., and Gibbs, R. D. (1957). Studies in tree physiology. IV. Further investigations of seasonal changes in moisture content of certain Canadian trees. *Can. J. Bot.* **43,** 305–316.

Cumbie, B. G. (1960). Anatomical studies in the Leguminosae. *Trop. Woods* **113,** 1–47.

Dixon, M. A., Thompson, R. G., and Femson, D. S. (1978). Electric resistance measurement of water potential in avocado and white spruce. *Can. J. For. Res.* **8,** 73–80.

Dixon, M. A., Grace, J., and Tyree, M. T. (1984). Concurrent measurements of stem density, leaf and stem water potential, stomatal conductance and cavitation on a sapling of *Thuja occidentalis* L. *Plant, Cell Environ.* **7,** 615–618.

Dobbs, R. C., and Scott, D. R. M. (1971). Distribution of diurnal fluctuations in stem circumference of Douglas fir. *Can. J. For. Res.* **1,** 80–83.

Downton, W. J. S. (1981). Water relations of laticifers in *Nerium oleander. Aust. J. Plant Physiol.* **8,** 329–334.

Edwards, W. R. N., and Jarvis, P. G. (1982). Relations between water content, potential, and permeability in stems of conifers. *Plant, Cell Environ.* **5,** 271–277.

Edwards, W. R. N., and Jarvis, P. G. (1983). A method for measuring radial differences in water content of intact tree stems by attenuation of gamma radiation. *Plant, Cell Environ.* **6,** 255–260.

Edwards, W. R. N., Jarvis, P. G., Grace, J., Moncrieff, J. B. (1994). Reversing cavitation in tracheids of *Pinus sylvestris* L. under negative water potentials. *Plant, Cell Environ.* **17,** 389–397.

Ewers, F. W., North, G. B., and Nobel, P. S. (1992). Root-stem junctions of a desert monocotyledon and a dicotyledon: Hydraulic consequences under wet conditions and during drought. *New Phytol.* **121,** 377–385.

Fisher, J. B. (1980). The vegetative and reproductive structure of papaya (*Carica papaya*). *Lyonia* **1,** 191–208.

Fisher, J. B. (1981). Wound healing by exposed secondary xylem in *Adansonia* (Bombacaceae). *IAWA Bull.* **2,** 193–199.

Franco-Vizcaíno, E., Goldstein, G., and Ting, I. P. (1990). Comparative gas exchange of leaves and bark in three stem succulents of Baja California. *Am. J. Bot.* **77,** 1272–1278.

Gibbs, R. D. (1958). Patterns in the seasonal water content of trees. *In* "The Physiology of Forest Trees" (K. V. Thimann, ed.), pp. 43–69. The Ronald Press Company, New York.

Gibson, A. C. (1973). Wood anatomy of Cactoideae (Cactaceae). *Biotropica* **5,** 29–65.

Gibson, A. C., and Nobel, P. S. (1986). "The Cactus Primer." Harvard Univ. Press, Cambridge, MA.

Goldstein, G., and Meinzer, F. (1983). Influence of insulating dead leaves and low temperatures in an Andean giant rosette plant. *Plant, Cell Environ.* **6**, 649–656.

Goldstein, G., Meinzer, F., and Monasterio, M. (1984). The role of capacitance in the water balance of Andean giant rosette species. *Plant, Cell Environ.* **7**, 179–186.

Goldstein, G., Meinzer, F., and Monasterio, M. (1985). Physiological and mechanical factors in relation to size-dependent mortality in an Andean giant rosette species. *Acta Oecol.* **6**, 263–275.

Goldstein, G., Andrade, J. L., and Nobel, P. S. (1991a). Differences in water relations parameters for the chlorenchyma and parenchyma of *Opuntia ficus-indica* under wet versus dry conditions. *Aust. J. Plant Physiol.* **18**, 95–107.

Goldstein, G., Ortega, J. K. E., Nerd, A., and Nobel, P. S. (1991b). Diel patterns of water potential components for the Crassulacean acid metabolism plant *Opuntia ficus-indica* when well-watered or droughted. *Plant Physiol.* **95**, 274–280.

Goldstein, G., and Nobel, P. S. (1991). Changes in osmotic pressure and mucilage during low-temperature acclimation of *Opuntia ficus-indica*. *Plant Physiol.* **97**, 854–961.

Goulden, M. L. (1991). Nutrient and Water Utilization by Evergreen Oaks that differ in Rooting Depth. Ph.D. Dissertation, Stanford University, Stanford, California.

Hedberg, O. (1964). Features of afro-alpine plant ecology. *Acta Phytogeographica Suecica* **49**, 1–144.

Hellkvist, J., Richards, G. P., and Jarvis, P. G. (1974). Vertical gradients of water potential and tissue water relations in Sitka spruce trees measured with the pressure chamber. *J. Appl. Ecol.* **11**, 637–668.

Hinckley, T. M., and Bruckerhoff, D. M. (1975). The effects of drought on water relations and stem shrinkage of *Quercus alba*. *Can. J. Bot.* **53**, 62–72.

Hinckley, T. M., Lassoie, J. P., and Running, S. W. (1978). Temporal and spatial variations in the water status of trees. *For. Sci.* **24** (Suppl.) (Monograph 20).

Holbrook, N. M., Burns, M. J., and Sinclair, T. R. (1992). Frequency and time-domain dielectric measurements of stemwater content in the arborescent palm, *Sabal palmetto*. *J. Exp. Bot.* **43**, 111–120.

Holbrook, N. M., and Sinclair, T. R. (1992a). Water balance in the arborescent palm, *Sabal palmetto*. I. Stem structure, tissue water release properties and leaf epidermal conductance. *Plant, Cell Environ.* **15**, 393–399.

Holbrook, N. M., and Sinclair, T. R. (1992b). Water balance in the arborescent palm, *Sabal palmetto*. II. Transpiration and stem water storage. *Plant, Cell Environ.* **15**, 401–409.

Holbrook, N. M., and Putz, F. E. (1992). Secondary thickening in stems of *Jacaratia* (Caricaceae). *Amer. J. Bot.* **79** (Suppl.), 34.

Holbrook, N. M., Whitbeck, J. L., and Mooney, H. A. (1995). Drought responses of neotropical deciduous forest trees. *In* "Tropical Deciduous Forests" (H. A. Mooney, E. Medina, and S. H. Bullock, eds.). Cambridge Univ. Press, Cambridge, UK (in press).

Hunt, E. R., and Nobel, P. S. (1987). Non-steady-state water flow for three desert perennials with different capacitances. *Aust. J. Plant Physiol.* **14**, 363–375.

Jarvis, P. G. (1975). Water transfer in plants. *In* "Heat and Mass Transfer in the Environment of Vegetation" (D. A. deVries and N. K. van Alfen, eds.), pp. 369–394. Scripta Book Co., Washington, D.C.

Kallarackal, J., Milburn, J. A., and Baker, D. A. (1990). Water relations of the banana. III. Effects of controlled water stress on water potential, transpiration, photosynthesis and leaf growth. *Aust. J. Plant Physiol.* **17**, 79–90.

Klepper, B., Browning, V. D., and Taylor, H. M. (1971). Stem diameter in relation to plant water status. *Plant Physiol.* **48**, 683–685.

Kramer, P. J. (1937). The relation between rate of transpiration and rate of absorption of water in plants. *Am. J. Bot.* **24**, 10–15.

Kramer, P. J. (1983). "Water Relations of Plants." Academic Press, San Diego.

Landsberg, J. J., Blanchard, T. W., and Warrit, B. (1976). Studies on the movement of water through apple trees. *J. Exp. Bot.* **27**, 579–596.

Lassoie, J. P. (1979). Stem dimensional fluctuations in Douglas fir of different crown classes. *For. Sci.* **25**, 132–144.

Lerdau, M. T., Holbrook, N. M., Mooney, H. A., Rich, P. M., and Whitbeck, J. L. (1992). Seasonal patterns of acid fluctuations and resource storage in the arborescent cactus *Opuntia excelsa* in relation to light availability and size. *Oecologia* **92**, 166–171.

Lo Gullo, M. A., and Salleo, S. (1992). Water storage in the wood and xylem cavitation in 1-year-old twigs of *Populus deltoides* Bartr. *Plant, Cell Environ.* **15**, 431–438.

Luttge, U. (1987). Carbon dioxide and water demand: Crassulacean acid metabolism (CAM), a versatile ecological adaptation exemplifying the need for integration in ecophysiological work. *New Phytol.* **106**, 593–629.

Machado, J.-L., and Tyree, M. T. (1994). Patterns of hydraulic architecture and water relations of two tropical canopy trees with contrasting leaf phenologies: *Ochroma pyramidale* and *Pseudobombax septenatum. Tree Physiol.* **14**, 219–240.

Mauseth, J. D. (1993). Water-storing and cavitation-preventing adaptations in wood of cacti. *Ann. Bot.* **72**, 81–89.

McBurney, T., and Costigan, P. A. (1984). The relationship between stem diameter and water potentials in stems of young cabbage plants. *J. Exp. Bot.* **35**, 1787–1793.

Medina, E., and Cuevas, E. (1990). Propiedades fotosintéticas y eficiencia de uso de agua de plantas leñosas del bosque deciduo de Guánica: consideraciones generales y resultados preliminares. *Acta Científica (Puerto Rico)* **4**, 25–36.

Metcalfe, C. R., and Chalk, L. (1950). "Anatomy of the Dicotyledons." 2 Vols. Clarendon Press, Oxford.

Milburn, J. A., Kallarackal, J., and Baker, D. A. (1990). Water relations of the banana. I. Predicting the water relations of the field-grown banana using the exuding latex. *Aust. J. Plant Physiol.* **17**, 57–63.

Milne, R., Ford, E. D., and Deans, J. D. (1983). Time lags in the water relations of Sitka spruce. *For. Ecol. Manage.* **5**, 1–25.

Morikawa, Y. (1974). Sapflow in *Chaemaecyparis obtusa* in relation to water economy of woody plants. *Tokyo Univ. For. Bull.* **66**, 251–257.

Morse, S. R. (1990). Water balance in *Hemizonia luzulifolia:* The role of extracellular polysaccharides. *Plant, Cell Environ.* **13**, 39–48.

Niklas, K. J., and O'Rourke, T. D. (1987). Flexural rigidity of chive and its response to water potential. *Am. J. Bot.* **74**, 1033–1044.

Nilsen, E. T., Sharifi, M. R., Rundel, P. W., Forseth, I. N., and Ehleringer, J. R. (1990). Water relations of stem succulent trees in north-central Baja California. *Oecologia* **82**, 299–303.

Nobel, P. S. (1977). Water relations and photosynthesis of a barrel cactus, *Ferocactus acanthodes,* in the Colorado desert. *Oecologia* **27**, 117–133.

Nobel, P. S., and Jordan, P. W. (1983). Transpiration stream of desert species: resistances and capacitances for a C_3, a C_4, and a CAM plant. *J. Exp. Bot.* **34**, 1379–1391.

Nobel, P. S., and Sanderson, J. (1984). Rectifier-like activities of roots of two desert succulents. *J. Exp. Bot.* **35**, 727–737.

Nobel, P. S., and North, G. B. (1993). Rectifier-like behavior of root-soil systems: New insights from desert succulents. In "Water Deficits: Plant Responses From Cell to Community" (J. A. C. Smith and H. Griffiths, eds.), pp. 163–176. Bios Scientific Publishers Ltd., Oxford.

North, G. B., and Nobel, P. S. (1994). Changes in root hydraulic conductivity for two tropical epiphytic cacti as soil moisture varies. *Am. J. Bot.* **81**, 46–53.

Olivares, E., and Medina, E. (1992). Water and nutrient relations of woody perennials from tropical dry forests. *J. Vegetation Sci.* **3**, 383–392.

Paoli, A. A. S., and Pagano, S. N. (1988). Anatomy of the root, the stem and the tuberified region of *Jacaratia spinosa* (Aubl.) A.DC. (Caricaceae). *Arquivos De Biologia E Tecnologia (Curitiba).* **31**, 413–432.

Parkin, J. (1900). Observations on latex and its functions. *Ann. Bot.* **14**, 193–214.

Parlange, J.-Y., Turner, N. C., and Waggoner, P. E. (1975). Water uptake, diameter change, and nonlinear diffusion in tree stems. *Plant Physiol.* **55**, 247–250.

Powell, D. B., and Thorpe, M. R. (1977). Dynamic aspects of plant water relations. *In* "Environmental Aspects of Crop Physiology" (J. J. Landsberg and C. V. Cutting, eds.), pp. 57–73. Academic Press, London.

Puritch, G. S. (1971). Water permeability of the wood of Grand fir [*Abies grandis* (Doug.) Lindl.] in relation to infestation by the balsam wooly aphid, *Adeleges piceae* (Ratz). *J. Exp. Bot.* **22**, 936–945.

Reinders, J. E. A., Van As, H., Schaafsma, T. J., De Jager, P. A., and Sheriff, D. W. (1988). Water balance in *Cucumis* plants, measured by NMR, I. *J. Exp. Bot.* **39**, 1199–1210.

Roberts, J. (1976). An examination of the quantity of water stored in mature *Pinus sylvestris* L. trees. *J. Exp. Bot.* **27**, 473–479.

Robichaux, R. H., and Morse, S. R. (1990). Extracellular polysaccharide and leaf capacitance in a Hawaiian bog species, *Argyroxiphium grayanum* (Compositae-Madiinae). *Am. J. Bot.* **77**, 134–138.

Running, S. W. (1980). Relating plant capacitance to the water relations of *Pinus contorta*. *For. Ecol. Manag.* **2**, 237–252.

Schulte, P. J., and Nobel, P. S. (1989). Responses of a CAM plant to drought and rainfall: Capacitance and osmotic pressure influences on water movement. *J. Exp. Bot.* **40**, 61–70.

Schulte, P. J., Smith, J. A. C., and Nobel, P. S. (1989). Water storage and osmotic pressure influences on the water relations of a dicotyledonous desert succulent. *Plant, Cell Environ.* **12**, 831–842.

Schulze, E.-D., Mooney, H. A., Bullock, S. H., and Mendoza, A. (1988). Water contents of wood of tropical deciduous forest species during the dry season. *Bol. Soc. Bot. Mex.* **48**, 113–118.

Smith, A. P. (1980). The paradox of plant height in an Andean giant rosette species. *J. Ecol.* **68**, 63–73.

Sperry, J. S., Nichols, K. L., Sullivan, J. E. M., and Eastlack, S. E. (1994). Xylem embolism in ring-porous, diffuse-porous, and coniferous trees of northern Utah and interior Alaska. *Ecology* **75**, 1736–1752.

Stewart, C. M. (1966). Excretion and heartwood formation in living trees. *Science* **153**, 1068–1074.

Stewart, C. M. (1967). Moisture content of living trees. *Nature* **214**, 138–140.

Tomlinson, P. B. (1990). "The Structural Biology of Palms." Clarendon, Oxford.

Tyree, M. T. (1988). A dynamic model for water flow in a single tree: Evidence that models must account for hydraulic architecture. *Tree Physiol.* **4**, 195–217.

Tyree, M. T., and Jarvis, (1982). Water in tissues and cells. *In* "Encyclopedia of Plant Physiology" (O. L. Lange, P. S. Nobel, C. B. Osmond and H. Ziegler, eds.), Vol. 12B, pp. 35–77. Springer-Verlag, Berlin.

Tyree, M. T., and Sperry, J. S. (1989). Vulnerability of xylem to cavitation and embolism. *Annu. Rev. Plant Physiol. Mol. Biol.* **40**, 19–38.

Tyree, M. T., and Yang, S. (1990). Water-storage capacity of *Thuja*, *Tsuga* and *Acer* stems measured by dehydration isotherms: The contribution of capillary water and cavitation. *Planta* **182**, 420–426.

Tyree, M. T., and Ewers, F. W. (1991). The hydraulic architecture of trees and other woody plants. *New Phytol.* **119**, 345–360.

Tyree, M. T., Snyderman, D. A., Wilmot, T. R., and Machado, J.-L. (1991). Water relations and hydraulic architecture of a tropical tree (*Schefflera morototoni*): Data, models and a comparison with two temperate species (*Acer saccharum* and *Thuja occidentalis*). *Plant Physiol.* **96,** 1105–1113.

Veres, J. S., Johnson, G. A., and Kramer, P. J. (1991). *In vivo* magnetic resonance imaging of *Blechnum* ferns: Changes in T1 and N(H) during dehydration and rehydration. *Am. J. Bot.* **78,** 80–88.

Waring, R. H., and Running, S. W. (1978). Sapwood water storage: Its contribution to transpiration and effect upon water conductance through the stems of old growth Douglas fir. *Plant, Cell Environ.* **1,** 131–140.

Waring, R. H., Whitehead, D., and Jarvis, P. G. (1979). The contribution of stored water to transpiration in Scots pine. *Plant, Cell Environ.* **2,** 309–317.

Whitehead, D., and Jarvis, P. G. (1981). Coniferous forests and plantations. *In* "Water Deficits and Plant Growth" (T. T. Kozlowski, ed.), Vol. VI, pp. 50–153. Academic Press, New York.

Wiebe, H. H. (1966). Matric potential of several plant tissues and biocolloids. *Plant Physiol.* **41,** 1439–1442.

Wronski, E. E., Holmes, J. W., and Turner, N. C. (1985). Phase and amplitude relations between transpiration, water potential and stem shrinkage. *Plant, Cell Environ.* **8,** 613–622.

Zimmermann, M. H. (1983). "Xylem Structure and the Ascent of Sap." Springer-Verlag, Berlin.

III

Roles of Live Stem Cells in Plant Performance

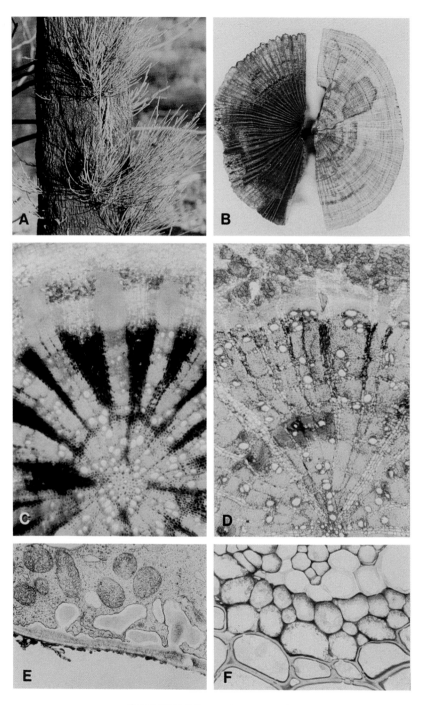

Color Plate 1 (Legend on reverse.)

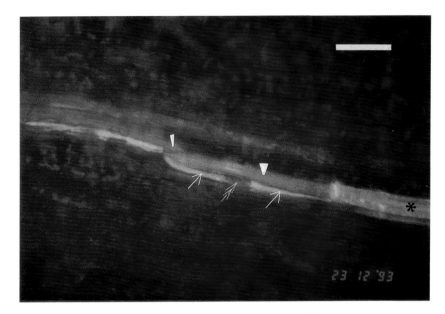

Color Plate 2 (Figure 9-4) Identification of an array of SE/CC complexes as a symplast domain. Intercellular transport of the membrane-impermeant fluorochrome Lucifer Yellow CH intracellularly injected by iontophoresis (asterisk) into a sieve element of *Vicia faba*. The fluorescent probe only moved via the sieve plates (slender arrowhead) to other sieve elements and associate companion cells (wide arrowhead). The nucleus of the companion cell (double-headed arrows) is surrounded by a vacuolar compartment that has accumulated fluorescent dye (single-headed arrows). The upper fluorescent band is a parallel sieve tube into which dye has moved via a lateral sieve plate. Bar: 50 mm.

Color Plate 1 (Figure 8-1) Structural features of stems relating to solute transfer and storage. (A) Recently burnt trunk of *Allocasuarina fraseriana*, showing growth of new photosynthetic shoots from epicormic buds under the burnt bark. (B) Iodine-treated transverse sections of the wood of the trunks of two cohabiting species of *Banksia*. *Left: Banksia illicifolia*, a resprouting species that survives fire. Note the broad starch-filled rays (black staining). *Right: Banksia prionotes*, an obligate seeder species that is killed by fire. Note the narrower rays and absence of starch. The rays of this species are used for temporary storage of minerals absorbed during winter (see text). (C) Iodine-treated transverse section of young stem of the resprouter *Banksia attenuata*, showing exceptionally broad rays packed with starch and limited starch storage also in xylem parenchyma between the rays and in the stem cortex. (D) Iodine-treated tranverse section of the burnt lower stem of the resprouter legume *Hovea elliptica*, showing depleted starch reserves associated with resprouting of the shoot after fire. Ray tissue is normally packed with starch at intensity similar to that of (C). (E) Part of a transfer cell bordering the xylem vessel of a departing leaf trace of the stem of the herbaceous species *Senecio vulgaris*, showing wall in growths, enlarged plasma membrane, dense endoplasmic reticulum, and clustered mitochondria typical of the absorptive face of transfer cells (see Gunning and Pate, 1974). (F) Group of xylem parenchyma transfer cells with purple stained wall ingrowths abutting a file of xylem conducting elements of a departing leaf trace of the stem of pea (*Pisum sativum*). The uppermost cells with thick blue stained walls are sclerenchyma between vascular traces.

8

Role of Stems in Transport, Storage, and Circulation of Ions and Metabolites by the Whole Plant

John S. Pate and W. Dieter Jeschke

I. Introduction

In terms of functioning of the whole plant, the quantitatively most important transport role of the stem is undoubtedly that of long-distance transfer of solutes and water between roots and foliar and reproductive parts of the shoot. Movement and storage of water in stems are discussed by Sperry [5], Gartner [6], and Holbrook [7] in this volume. Two fundamental types of bulk flow provide the driving forces for solute transport: the upward movement through xylem of a dilute solution of mineral ions and organic solutes from root to transpiring surfaces of the shoot, and the outward flow from photosynthesizing leaves in phloem of a concentrated, sugar-dominated stream of organic and inorganic solutes. Intensity of upward xylem traffic through different parts of the stem vasculature is determined primarily by the disposition of the xylem connections between stem and specific leaves and the relative rates of transpiration of leaves. Corresponding upward and downward flow from the same leaves in phloem is patterned principally by their respective capacities in generating photosynthate, by the sink strengths of recipient organs in consuming this photosynthate, and by the anatomical "directness" of phloem connections between each source leaf and the sink regions of the system.

The goal of this chapter is to demonstrate that stems do not function in a passive manner when mediating the transport activities mentioned above. First, because stems are mostly inactive in photosynthesis (cf. Nilsen, [10] in this volume) or uptake of minerals from the environment, their requirements for extension and secondary thickening must derive from lateral uptake of solutes from transport fluids passing through their structure. As a result phloem and xylem streams passing through the stem will be depleted in certain solutes relative to others (see Van Bel, [9] in this volume). Second, there is widespread evidence of stems functioning in short- or long-term storage of a range of substances, for example, starch and other complex carbohydrates, protein, amino compounds, and soluble and insoluble reserves containing certain essential minerals. The initial uptake and eventual mobilization of solutes relating to such reserves occurs through the agency of long-distance transport channels and again, these pathways will be correspondingly depleted or augmented in the solutes involved. Third, there are now indications that stem tissues of herbaceous species fulfill a significant function in the differential partitioning of nutrient elements. These activities, located within the stem body, involve selective exchanges of solutes between adjacent xylem and phloem streams or equally important sideways transfers from one xylem stream to another. As a result, a particular solute may be diverted away from an expected site of delivery to destinations that, in terms of sink activity, would have qualified to receive only small amounts of the solute in question. This chapter provides several examples in which integrated exchanges of this nature comprise vital and quantitatively important elements of plant functioning.

The plan of the chapter is to examine first some of the principal sites and tissue types within stems that are likely to be committed to short-distance exchanges between transport channels or to engage in storage of specific solutes or insoluble reserves. Second, a brief account is given of an empirically based modeling procedure that we have designed for the study of uptake, partitioning, and utilization of nutrient elements in whole plants. Third, employing this same approach, case studies are presented to highlight the vital role of the stem in partitioning and storage of nutrients. Last, a summary of the major conclusions to be drawn from the chapter is presented, with the goal of highlighting how little is still known of the potential role of stems in regulating the traffic of solutes and thus shaping temporal and spatial growth and storage within other parts of the plant body.

II. Anatomical Features of Stems in Relation to Storage and Internal Exchanges between Transport Channels

The storage potential of any plant organ is governed primarily by the proportions of its volume devoted to potential storage tissue as opposed to other tissue types in which significant storage is unlikely to occur. Thus, in the stems of herbaceous species, parenchyma of cortex and pith would constitute major loci of storage whereas in trunks of woody species principal storage sites would be ray tissue and other parenchyma of xylem.

Having defined the storage potential of the stem one must then ascertain the extent to which such potential is realized. This has proved difficult for soluble reserves, which are easily displaced during cutting and specimen preparation; however, where easily identifiable insoluble reserves such as starch, protein bodies, or wall polysaccharides are involved, buildup and depletion of a reserve can be readily assessed by appropriate staining procedures. The classic studies in this connection concern the seasonal buildup of starch in ray tissues of trunks of deciduous trees and the subsequent release of sugars to xylem following breakdown of starch the following spring. Another example concerns the starch reserves of the trunks of fire-resistant "resprouter" (see [14] in this volume for terminology) arboreal species of Australian ecosystems. Resprouter species often possess prolific deposits of starch in xylem parenchyma of their trunks, whereas related fire-sensitive "obligate seeder" species carry little such reserve. In many cases the storage capacity of resprouter species is augmented through development of broader rays and proportionately more interray xylem area as storage parenchyma than in corresponding seeder species (e.g., see comparison of two species of *Banksia* in Fig. 1).

Once fire has destroyed the foliage and finer twigs and shoots of a resprouter tree species, heat-resistant buds under the bark of its major branches and trunk sprout to form a clothing of densely packed leafy shoots (Fig. 1). All of these contribute initially in the generation of photoassimilates, but only a few persist to form the branches that eventually replace the prefire canopy architecture. Starch reserves are extensively utilized during the early stages of refoliation (Fig. 1) and it may take several years for stem starch to return to its prefire level (J. S. Pate, unpublished data). Similar principles apply to starch storage in roots of root-crown resprouting species, as illustrated for a broad range of southwestern Australian shrubby taxa by Pate *et al.* (1990) and Bowen and Pate (1993).

The absence of starch in ray and xylem parenchyma of trunks of obligate seeder tree species does not imply an absence of storage function. Indeed, parenchymatous tissues not replete with starch would offer ideal sites for seasonal storage of other nutrients, for example, amino acids and a range of mineral elements (see Section IV,D).

Stems of herbaceous annual species are more likely to provide a vehicle for short-distance transfers between vascular channels than for significant long-term storage. The various classes and associated sitings of specialized cells called "transfer cells" are viewed as prime candidates for both xylem-to-xylem and xylem-to-phloem exchanges in such plants. Transfer cells, with their strategically located sets of wall ingrowths and enlarged plasma membranes (see Fig. 1), are now known to occur in a wide variety of ana-

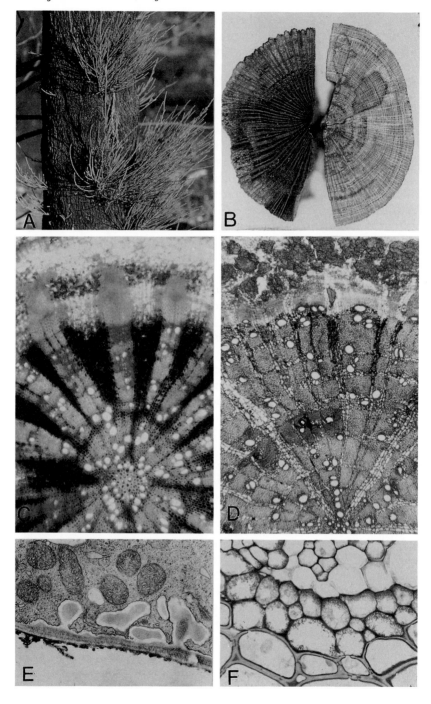

tomical and taxonomic situations throughout herbaceous taxa of the mono-cotyledons and dicotyledons (see Pate and Gunning, 1972; Gunning and Pate, 1974; and see Van Bel [9] in this volume). They are generally sus-pected, and in certain cases proved (Gunning *et al.*, 1974), to function in highly selective short-distance transport between apoplastic and symplastic compartments of plant organs, between the plant and its surrounding en-vironment, between one nuclear generation of a plant and the next, and, in certain exceptional cases, between one plant species and another organ-ism. In each of these situations the wall–membrane apparatus of the trans-fer cell is envisaged to qualify it for more effective solute exchanges per unit volume of tissue than cells not so equipped.

An especially common site for parenchyma-type transfer cells in stems is adjacent to the conducting elements of xylem of departing leaf traces (see Fig. 1 and Gunning *et al.*, 1970). Indeed, this class of transfer cell is probably much more widespread taxonomically among herbaceous species than are those associated with minor veins of leaves (Pate and Gunning, 1969) and certainly much more common than in any of the other situations described for the cell type (see Pate and Gunning, 1972; Gunning and Pate, 1974). These node-based transfer cells are suggested to function primarily in lo-calized withdrawal of solutes from xylem streams passing into the body of the node. They thus provide a potential source of nutrients for the adjacent axillary bud, both during its early growth and later when its dormancy is broken and before the emerging side branch has its vasculature connected into that of the parent stem (see Pate and Gunning, 1972). Evidence of lateral uptake of amino acids from xylem vessels by the nodal transfer cells

---

Figure 1 Structural features of stems relating to solute transfer and storage. (A) Recently burnt trunk of *Allocasuarina fraseriana*, showing growth of new photosynthetic shoots from epi-cormic buds under the burnt bark. (B) Iodine-treated transverse sections of the wood of the trunks of two cohabiting species of *Banksia*. Left: *Banksia illicifolia*, a resprouting species that survives fire. Note the broad starch-filled rays (black staining). Right: *Banksia prionotes*, an obli-gate seeder species that is killed by fire. Note the narrower rays and absence of starch. The rays of this species are used for temporary storage of minerals absorbed during winter (see text). (C) Iodine-treated transverse section of young stem of the resprouter *Banksia attenuata*, show-ing exceptionally broad rays packed with starch and limited starch storage also in xylem paren-chyma between the rays and in the stem cortex. (D) Iodine-treated transverse section of the burnt lower stem of the resprouter legume *Hovea elliptica*, showing depleted starch reserves associated with resprouting of the shoot after fire. Ray tissue is normally packed with starch at an intensity similar to that of (C). (E) Part of a transfer cell bordering the xylem vessel of a departing leaf trace of the stem of the herbaceous species *Senecio vulgaris*, showing wall in-growths, enlarged plasma membrane, dense endoplasmic reticulum, and clustered mitochon-dria typical of the absorptive face of transfer cells (see Gunning and Pate, 1974). (F) Group of xylem parenchyma transfer cells with purple-stained wall ingrowths abutting a file of xylem conducting elements of a departing leaf trace of the stem of pea (*Pisum sativum*). The upper-most cells with thick blue-stained walls are sclerenchyma between vascular traces.

of the cotyledonary node of seedlings of groundsel (*Senecio vulgaris*) derives from observations of a marked reduction in concentrations of these solutes as xylem fluid passes from leaf trace xylem of the stem into cotyledonary petioles of the seedling (see Gunning *et al.*, 1970). Similarly, in studies of vegetative shoots of white lupine (*Lupinus albus*), McNeil *et al.* (1979) have obtained autoradiographic evidence of particularly high absorption of xylem-applied ^{14}C-labeled amino acids by transfer cell complexes of departing leaf traces. Transfer cells are also encountered in phloem tissue bordering the gap caused by a departing leaf trace (see examples in Gunning *et al.*, 1970) and a potential role in nourishment of axillary buds is again indicated.

Transfer cells may also develop in the xylem of cauline traces running through internodes of herbaceous legumes (Kuo *et al.*, 1980). In most cases the internodal traces with the most prolific displays of transfer cell wall ingrowths are strictly those destined to supply the leaf subtended at the top of that internode (i.e., a lower extension of the nodal transfer cell system mentioned above). In other cases all cauline traces carry prolific investments of transfer cells throughout an internode. In some of the 21 species found positive for the trait, transfer cell development extends to secondary as well as primary xylem (Kuo *et al.*, 1980). The functional attributes of these internodal transfer cells and those of xylem and phloem of nodes are addressed in Section IV, in which quantitative models defining the role of xylem-to-xylem and xylem-to-phloem interchanges in partitioning of solutes are presented.

III. Modeling Empirically the Role Played by Stems in Partitioning, Storage, and Utilization of Specific Nutrient Elements

It is especially important for students of plant transport to possess an intimate knowledge of the vasculature of the species selected for study, to identify the types and relative amounts of solutes carried in its long-distance channels, and to assess how source and sink activities of its component organs change during growth and development. Requirements for everyday maintenance and growth should be distinguished from those concerned with storage and, by means of appropriate labeling studies, determinations should be made of how photosynthate from each source leaf is shared among currently active sink organs. Finally, when considering transport activity over a prescribed growth interval, gains or losses of dry matter or specific nutrient elements by plant parts should be assessed, and net gaseous exchanges of carbon by plant parts measured over the same study intervals. Once the above-described classes of information become available, a series of models of plant transport activity can be formulated, each depicting how a specific resource is partitioned and committed to storage or growth processes.

We use empirically based models embodying the above-mentioned classes of information in a series of case studies demonstrating quantitatively the roles played by stems in transport and cycling of solutes. Data are confined almost entirely to two herbaceous dicotyledonous species [white lupine, (*Lupinus albus*) and castor bean (*Ricinus communis*)] and a monocotyledon (barley, *Hordeum vulgare*). The first two of these bleed from cut or punctured phloem, thus enabling one to compare the composition of a series of phloem exudates with that of xylem fluid at matched exchange points within the system. Phloem sap composition can be studied in non-phloem-bleeding species such as barley by collecting phloem exudates from stylets of aphids feeding at various locations on the plant. Certain woody species bleed from cut phloem of stems (e.g., Spanish broom, *Spartium junceum;* tree tobacco, *Nicotiana glauca;* and the acorn banksia, *Banksia prionotes*), but only the last of these has been subjected to the type of modeling described above.

The modeling protocol was first used to follow fluxes of carbon and nitrogen in nitrogen-fixing plants of the herbaceous legume white lupine (Pate *et al.,* 1979a, 1980; Layzell *et al.,* 1981). Each model was based on data for C:N ratios of xylem and phloem fluids collected at relevant interchange points within the system, measurement of increments and losses of C and N from plant parts, and respiratory and photosynthetic exchanges of carbon by the same parts during a selected study interval.

The approach was then extended to follow N flow in NO_3-fed plants of white lupine (Pate *et al.,* 1979b) and castor bean (Jeschke and Pate, 1991a–c). For the latter species a sophisticated computational procedure was developed to determine the magnitude and direction of exchanges of C and N in xylem and phloem between adjacent stem segments or between a stem segment and its attached petiole. The respective effects of these internal exchanges can then be quantified in relation to dry matter gains or losses by or bulk flows of C and N in xylem and phloem through the segments in question.

A number of modeling exercises on white lupine (Jeschke *et al.,* 1985, 1987) and castor bean (Jeschke and Pate, 1991a,b; Jeschke *et al.,* 1991) have examined partitioning and cycling of other elements, especially K^+, Cl^-, Mg^{2+}, Ca^{2+}, and Na^+.

IV. Case Studies

A. Role of Stems in Partitioning of Nitrogen in White Lupine and Castor Bean

Figure 2 displays partitioning profiles for total N in symbiotically dependent white lupine (Fig. 2A) (data from Pate, 1986) and in nitrate-fed castor

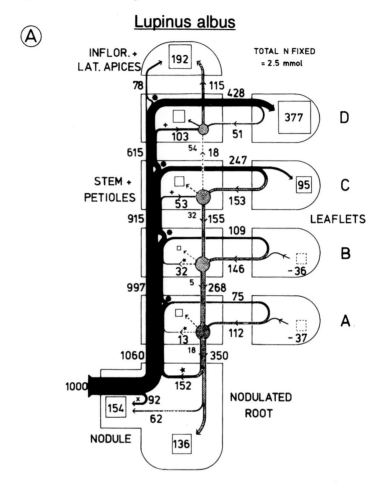

Figure 2 Role of stem tissues of two herbaceous species, white lupine (*Lupinus albus*) and castor bean (*Ricinus communis*), in partitioning of nitrogen. (A) Uptake, transport, and utilization of fixed N in symbiotically dependent lupine in a 10-day period following anthesis. (B) Partitioning of total N during midvegetative growth of castor bean, with nitrate as N source in the root medium. (C) Exchanges of nitrate and reduced nitrogen between shoot and root of castor bean, showing extents of storage of free nitrate, nitrate reduction, and incorporation of reduced nitrogen in stem and shoot. (D) More detailed flow profile for the same castor bean study as in (C) to illustrate xylem transport and organ reduction of nitrate. Nitrate is not mobile in phloem and therefore, unlike reduced N, is not retranslocated from leaves, nor does it cycle through roots. Note symbols designating various forms of intervascular exchanges in (A–C). Source references to flow models are given in text. [Redrawn from data in Layzell *et al.* (1981) and Jeschke and Pate (1991a,b).]

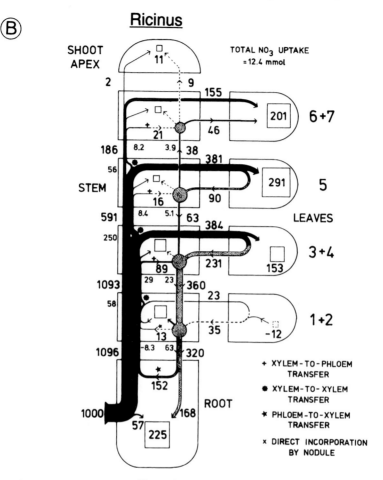

Figure 2 *Continued*

bean (Fig. 2B–D) (data from Jeschke and Pate, 1991a–c). Upper, rapidly growing leaves of both species (stratum D in Fig. 2, top four leaves in lupine, leaves 5 and 6 in castor bean) comprise the major sinks for N and in each case derive virtually all of their N through xylem. The topmost leaves and apical regions of the shoots are depicted to gain more N than that attracted on the basis of transpiration loss and to import this "additional" N exclusively by "xylem-to-xylem shuttling" in the lower regions of the stem. The magnitude of such transfers is designated in the looped pathways marked with asterisks shown in Fig. 2, each successive transfer in effect removing an amount of N from the xylem stream serving the leaf and returning the bulk

Ricinus

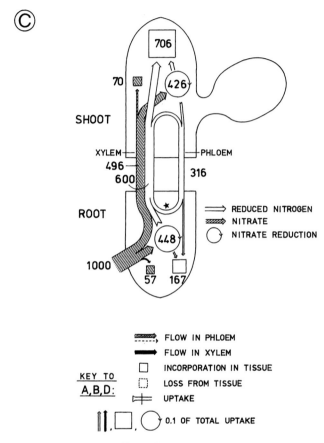

Figure 2   *Continued*

of this N to xylem traces passing further up the stem. Node-based transfer cells, prolifically developed in xylem of leaf traces of both lupine and castor bean, are implicated in this activity. Indeed, onset of wall ingrowth development in putative xylem parenchyma at a nodal complex coincides precisely with the onset of xylem-to-xylem transfer of N (Jeschke and Pate, 1991b).

As suggested for both lupine (Layzell *et al.*, 1981; Pate, 1986) and castor bean (Jeschke and Pate, 1991a), each cascade of xylem-to-xylem transfers of N up the stem functions as a concentrating mechanism through which

Ricinus

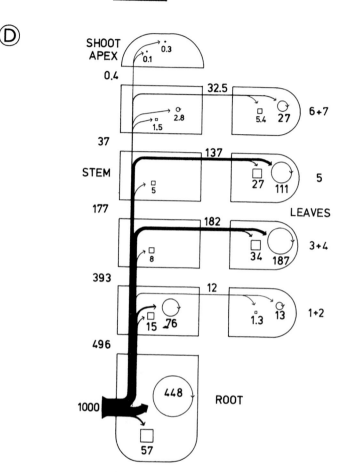

Figure 2 *Continued*

young growing leaves with high demand for N derive considerably greater amounts of N per unit water intake through xylem than do lower leaves, whose xylem supply has been correspondingly robbed of N.

By collecting vacuum-extracted tracheal xylem sap from different segments up a white lupine stem it has been found that there is a two- to four-fold increase in xylem N concentration from lowest to highest regions of the stem (Layzell *et al.*, 1981). In parallel studies on castor bean, xylem exudates have been obtained from cut midribs of leaves of otherwise intact, freely transpiring plants following application of mild pressure (0.2–

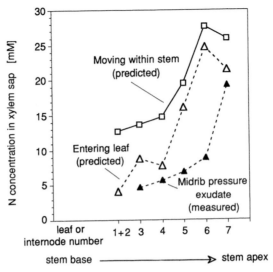

Figure 3 Predicted (open symbols) and experimentally measured (closed triangles) mean xylem concentrations of total N moving up the stem (solid lines) or entering petioles (dashed lines) of 44- to 53-day-old plants of castor bean fed 12 mol of NO_3 m and exposed to a mean salinity stress of 128 mol of NaCl m^{-3}. (Data from Jeschke and Pate, 1991a.)

0.3 MPa) to their enclosed root system. The typical set of data summarized in Fig. 3 shows a four-fold increase in measured N concentration of pressure exudates collected from the lowest to the highest leaf, and this runs more or less parallel with the corresponding gradient predicted from a modeling exercise using identical plant material. Companion predictions of concentrations of N remaining within the xylem of the stem (Fig. 3) suggest much higher concentrations at all levels than in xylem streams passing out to leaves. The generally lower values for experimentally obtained rather than predicted concentrations (Fig. 3) can be explained on the basis that pressure exudates are collected at or close to midday when high transpiration rates would dilute xylem streams greatly, whereas the predicted values refer to average flux values on a 24-hr basis.

The xylem-to-xylem transfer processes of the stem of *Ricinus* described above provide a surprisingly large share (63%) of the N requirement of the upper developing leaves (leaves 5–7, Fig. 2B), but relatively little of the N intake by the shoot apex, which is mostly fed by phloem. Comparable data for the upper four main stem leaves of *L. albus* (stratum D, Fig. 2A) also suggest a substantial input of N from the stem-concentrating mechanism, but in this case with less transfer in lower than in mid- and upper regions of the shoot, and relatively greater input to the shoot apex than in castor bean.

A further feature of the castor bean models is the considerably poorer water use efficiency in the uppermost leaves (0.8–1.7 μmol of CO_2 mmol^{-1} H_2O) than in lower leaves (4.5–6.2 μmol of CO_2 mmol^{-1} H_2O; Jeschke and Pate, 1991a). This factor, working together with higher xylem concentrations in upper than lower stem tissue, should strongly favor targeting of recently absorbed N toward regions of highest demand within a shoot.

The second equally important activity of the stem in partitioning of N is the xylem-to-phloem transfer process conducted in upper regions of its structure (marked with crosses in Fig. 2A and B). In lupine (Fig. 2A) this class of exchange exploits enriched xylem streams of the upper stem and diverts nitrogenous solutes from these to the phloem streams carrying assimilates from upper leaves to the shoot apex. The net effect is to increase greatly the amount of N that the shoot apices and inflorescences receive relative to that possible solely from their meager transpirational loss. Although relatively small proportional components of the models of Fig. 2A, xylem-to-phloem transfer by the upper stem has considerable impact on the nutrition of adjacent apical organs. Experimental proof of the significance of the process in lupine comes from the observation that the C:N ratio of the phloem sap intercepted from the petioles of leaves serving the apex is up to twice that finally entering the inflorescence. This change in ratio is almost entirely due to N enrichment of phloem translocate by xylem-to-phloem transfer of asparagine and glutamine, the two major xylem solutes of *Lupinus* (Pate *et al.*, 1979a,b).

Comparable data on *Ricinus* (Fig. 2B) indicate that xylem-to-phloem transfers of N take place throughout the stem, albeit at lesser intensity in lower than upper regions (Jeschke and Pate, 1991a,b). Comparisons of phloem composition prior to and after the exchange process suggest that the C:N molar ratio of the compounds transferred is 2.1–2.2, and amino acid analyses confirm that glutamine is involved principally. By contrast, nitrate, the other major nitrogenous solute of *Ricinus* xylem, is not transferred to phloem.

Finally, the modeling technique can be utilized to examine the role played by the stem in transport, reduction, and storage of nitrate. We use as an example data for a 9-day period in midvegetative growth of castor bean plants exposed to 12 mol of nitrate m^{-3} (see Jeschke and Pate, 1991b). A simplified model of partitioning of nitrate and reduced forms of N between shoot and root (Fig. 2C) indicates that just over half (51%) of the nitrate is reduced in the root and that much of the resulting reduced N and some unreduced NO_3^- moves to the shoot in the xylem. Storage of nitrate in shoot and root is a relatively small item in the nitrate budget. A more detailed model depicting the fate of nitrate in shoot organs (Fig. 2D) shows the stem to function in nitrate reduction to a lesser extent than leaves. As recorded for other herbaceous species (Hall and Baker, 1972; Richardson and Baker, 1982), nitrate is virtually immobile in the phloem of *Ricinus,* and therefore nitrate cycling through leaves, or between xylem and phloem in root or stem, is essentially nonexistent. The current nitrate status of a plant part can thus be assessed in terms of whether net import in xylem exceeds the observed increment in stored nitrate. If this is so, nitrate reduction must be occurring (e.g., for leaves and lower regions of the stem in Fig. 2D); if not (e.g., for petioles and upper parts of the stem in Fig. 2D), uptake leading to storage in the unreduced form must be taking place.

B. Role of Stems in Discrimination in Partitioning of K^+ versus Na^+ in White Lupine and Castor Bean

By using the modeling data for K^+ and Na^+ as presented for lupine by Jeschke *et al.* (1987) and for castor bean by Jeschke and Pate (1991c), a number of conclusions can be reached concerning the behavior of the two species under moderate salinity stress (10 mol of NaCl m^{-3} and 3.3 mol of K^+ m^{-3} in white lupine, and 128 mol of NaCl m^{-3} and 6.4 mol of K^+ m^{-3} in castor bean).

The model for K^+ in lupine (Fig. 4A) depicts the top stratum of leaves as the dominant sink for xylem-derived K^+ and the same leaves as a major source for the significant amounts of K^+ translocated back to the root, and thence, by xylem–phloem transfer, to complete the circulatory cycle between shoot and root.

By comparing the models for K^+ and Na^+ in lupine (Fig. 4A and B), it can be seen that discrimination in uptake from the medium leads to only slightly greater uptake of Na^+ over K^+, despite a threefold greater concentration in the culture solution of Na^+ over K^+. A substantial return of Na^+ occurs from shoot to root and three possible fates for this Na^+ are suggested: (1) extrusion to the medium (see Jacoby, 1979; Lauchli, 1984), (2) retention by the root, and (3) recycling back to the shoot. As shown for K^+, flow of Na^+ in xylem exceeds that in phloem, but Na^+ flow into inflorescences and lateral branches is much less than for K^+. Discriminatory phenomena favoring K^+ over Na^+ in uptake by the stem are indicated by the more than twofold increase in the $K^+:Na^+$ ratio of the xylem stream as it passes up the stem (see values in Fig. 4, and the side column in Fig. 4). This, coupled to more recycling of K^+ through roots than Na^+, leads to much greater access of K^+ to upper parts of the shoot than in the case of Na^+.

The corresponding models of K^+ and Na^+ partitioning in castor bean (Fig. 4C and D), a species substantially more salt tolerant than lupine (Jeschke and Wolf, 1988), show similar general features, but an accentuated capacity to immobilize excess Na^+ within the root. This feature, combined with zero recycling of Na^+ vs a massive (77%) recycling of K^+ between root and shoot, are principal mechanisms for selectively excluding Na^+ from the shoot. Nevertheless, lower stem tissues clearly have a backup role in excluding Na^+ from leaves and apical regions by selectively absorbing Na_k+ from the ascending xylem stream. These discriminatory processes lead to a more than 30-fold increase in the $K^+:Na^+$ ratio of the xylem stream as it passes up the stem of *Ricinus* (Fig. 4C and D).

Tolerance of high salinity by castor bean under nonlimiting K^+ supply thus comprises (1) an ability to exclude Na^+ from leaves, (2) preferential allocation of K^+ through phloem to sinks on upper parts of the shoot, (3) differential capacities for storage of the two ions in roots, and (4) marked root: shoot cycling of K^+ but not of Na^+. Some salt exclusion from leaves does occur in the salt-sensitive *Lupinus,* but this is marred by poor discrimination against Na^+ during phloem loading. Sodium ion is accordingly likely to break through into any young tissues dependent on phloem as their major source of cations. White lupine thus resembles a typical glycophyte (see the studies of Jacoby, 1964; Lauchli, 1979; Eggers and Jeschke, 1983). By contrast, the data for the highly salt-tolerant *Ricinus* suggest efficient translocation, cycling, and reutilization of K^+ as mainstays of salinity tolerance, a finding supported by observations that tolerance of salt increases with increased availability of K^+ (e.g., Chow *et al.,* 1990).

C. Uptake, Deposition, and Mobilization of Mineral Ions by Stem Tissues of Castor Bean and Barley

As shown in studies on *R. communis* (Jeschke and Pate, 1991a–c) and barley (Wolf and Jeschke, 1987; Wolf *et al.,* 1990, 1991), deposition activities of stem internodes for different ions change markedly from early stages of growth, through elongation to maturation and secondary thickening. For example, deposition of K^+ and Mg^{2+} is distinctly favored on a fresh weight basis during early growth and elongation of *Ricinus,* but Na^+ incorporation is very low at the same young stages of development. However, Na^+ deposition escalates at the start of secondary thickening of internodes, and its incorporation at this time more or less matches release of previously stored K^+. Thus, early deposition of K^+ is essentially transient storage and its subsequent release takes place mostly in exchange for Na^+. Distinctly high rates of anion (malate, chloride, sulfate, phosphate, and nitrate) incorporation are also characteristic of early growth and occur at such times in amounts closely matching the combined uptake of the major cations K^+, Mg^{2+}, and Ca^{2+}.

Further detailed modeling of the flows of mineral elements in the stem of *R. communis* (Jeschke and Pate, 1991a) allows quantification in finer detail of the exchanges of ions between tissues of a stem segment and xylem and phloem. Again, age-related differences are observed. For example, K^+ is at first taken up at exceptionally high rates from xylem by elongating internodes; its uptake from xylem and phloem then decreases strongly as internodes mature, whereas, in the hypocotyl region, K^+ appears to be

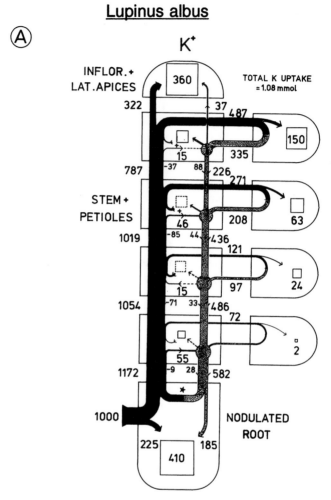

Figure 4 Contrasting profiles of uptake, partitioning, and storage of K⁺ and Na⁺ in white lupine [(A) and (B), respectively] and castor bean [C and D]. Note the much more effective exclusion of Na⁺ from upper parts of the shoot of castor bean than lupine. [Data redrawn from Jeschke *et al.*, 1987 (A and B) and from Jeschke and Pate, 1991c (C and D).]

loaded back into the xylem stream. By contrast, uptake of Na⁺ and Cl⁻ from the xylem by all internodes greatly exceeds that from phloem whereas uptake of Cl⁻ and Na⁺ from the phloem is considerably less than that of K⁺.

It has also been proved possible to examine the role of stem tissue in discriminatory transport phenomena in barley, using a modeling system based on pressure-induced xylem sap and phloem exudates from cut aphid

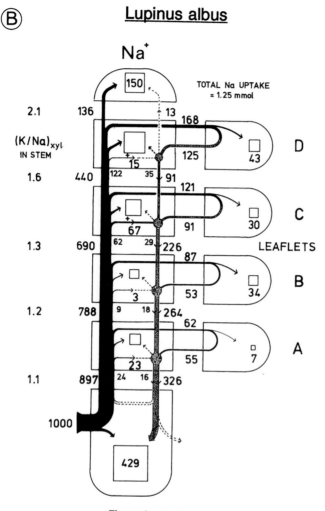

Figure 4   *Continued*

stylets (see Fig. 5 and Wolf and Jeschke, 1987; Wolf *et al.*, 1990, 1991). Before stem elongation occurs, a xylem sap of uniform composition is delivered to the variously aged leaves, but once the shoot axis elongates, Na^+,
NO_3^-, and Cl^- concentrations in xylem decrease while those of K^+ increase as the xylem stream ascends the stem. Modeling of K^+ and Na^+ flows
within salt-treated (100 mol of NaCl m^{-3}) barley indicates that the above-
described changes in xylem sap concentrations arise mostly from contrasting patterns of deposition of ions in lower stem internodes (Fig. 5). Thus,

Ricinus

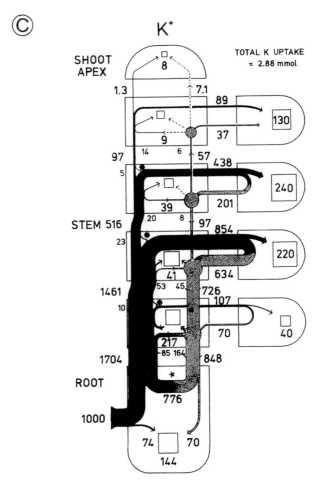

Figure 4 *Continued*

Na$^+$ is accumulated in the first (lowest) internode at 8.1 μmol/plant over a 7-day interval and at 11.8 μmol/plant in the second and third internodes while previously stored K$^+$ is released to xylem and phloem from the same parts in amounts of 5.3 and 3 μmol/plant, respectively, over the same time frame. It is likely that it is vacuolar K$^+$ that is exchanged for Na$^+$. In upper parts of barley stems both ions are deposited, but in younger internodes K$^+$ deposition exceeds that of Na$^+$.

Ricinus

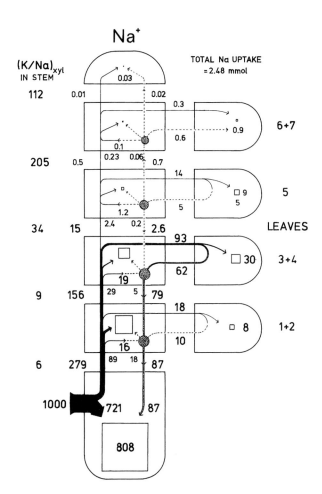

Figure 4 *Continued*

The models for K$^+$ flows in barley predict that part of the K$^+$ withdrawn from the xylem is reloaded into stem-based xylem vessels in a process analogous to the xylem-to-xylem transfers referred to above for the dicotyledonous species white lupine and castor bean. A further fraction of this K$^+$ is transferred to the phloem. These activities are highest in the midstem internodes, where 64% of total intraxylary transfer and 32% of the xylem-to-

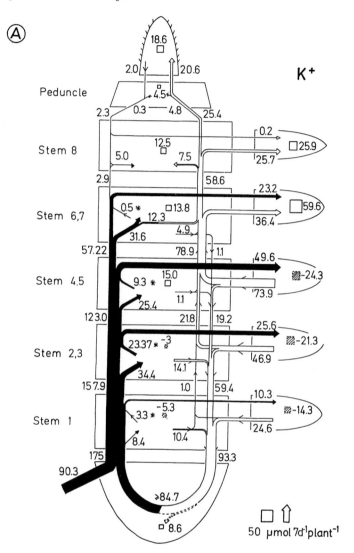

Figure 5 Models depicting contrasting patterns of flow and storage of Na$^+$ and K$^+$ in the highly salt-tolerant species barley (*Hordeum vulgare*). Discrimination involves massive storage of Na$^+$ in roots and lower stem and absence of cycling of Na$^+$ through root, and accordingly lesser transport of Na$^+$ than K$^+$ into upper parts of the shoot. (Reproduced from Wolf *et al.*, 1991.)

phloem transfers occur. However, xylem-to-xylem transfers of K$^+$ in barley are generally greater than in *Ricinus* (Fig. 4) and can amount to as much as 40% of total K$^+$ uptake (Fig. 5). In contrast, the modeling of Na$^+$ flows

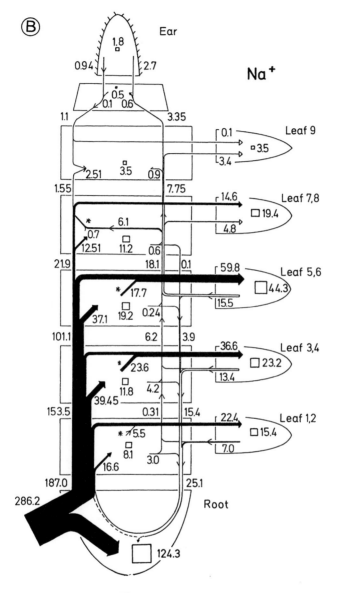

Figure 5 *Continued*

indicates that part of the Na$^+$ taken up from the xylem by the shoot is reloaded into xylem of leaf traces, thereby depleting the xylem destined for
apical shoot parts of Na$^+$ but increasing the salt (Na$^+$) load of mature and

aging leaves. Again, this activity is highest in the mature stem internodes (internodes 2 and 3), where it accounts for 50% of total xylem-to-leaf trace xylem transfer.

These ion-specific patterns of deposition, release, and xylem-to-xylem transfer in stem tissue of barley are responsible for effecting substantial changes in ion concentrations of xylem destined for differently aged leaves and thereby play a crucial role in excluding Na^+ from growing shoot parts of this highly salt-tolerant species.

D. Seasonal Partitioning and Storage in Trunks of the Tree *Banksia prionotes*

Banksia prionotes (Proteaceae) is a fire-sensitive, fast-growing tree of the nutrient-impoverished deep sands of mediterranean ecosystems of south-western Australia. It develops a markedly dimorphic root system consisting of a tap or "sinker" root through which water is drawn from the water table throughout the year, and a set of superficial lateral roots that function in uptake of nutrients during the autumn, winter, and spring months (see Pate and Jeschke, 1993). The laterals carry seasonal investments of cluster roots that function in nutrient uptake, through this cool wet period (April–October, southern hemisphere) but senesce as the soil dries out in summer. The annual extension growth of the shoot occurs during midsummer (November to February), some 4–6 months behind the peak period of uptake by lateral roots.

Xylem sap can be readily obtained from *B. prionotes* by mild vacuum extraction of segments of lateral and sinker roots or in a similar fashion from successive age segments excised from a trunk. Information can thus be obtained on the extents to which the xylem streams of lateral and sinker roots are carrying specific nutrients to the shoot and the degree to which the xylem stream ascending the trunk is enriched or depleted in specific solutes as it passes from one age segment up to the next. The trunk also bleeds from phloem when shallow incisions are made into its bark, and therefore phloem composition can also be examined through a seasonal cycle of root activity and shoot growth (see Pate and Jeschke, 1993). For the present purposes we restrict attention to transport phenomena within stems.

The broad comparison of phloem sap and xylem sap composition (Table 1) shows xylem to be much less concentrated than phloem in all solutes. Surprisingly, $K^+:Na^+$ ratios of phloem are less than those of xylem, indicating the unusually poor capacity of the phloem loading mechanism to discriminate against Na^+. Concentration ratios in phloem of phosphate to sulfate or phosphate to chloride tend to be lower than in other species, as are phloem levels of N and K^+ relative to sucrose. These features probably reflect the general deficiency of N, P, and K in the soils in which *B. prionotes* grows, and the substituting roles for ions such as sulfate, chlo-

Table I   Mean Major Solute Concentrations (m*M*)
in Midstem Phloem Sap and Stem Base
Xylem (Tracheal) Sap of *Banksia prionotes*[a]

Component	Phloem sap	Xylem sap
Sucrose	493	Absent
Total amino acids	2.35	0.53
Malate	4.28	0.42
Potassium	15.2	2.39
Sodium	24.1	1.84
Magnesium	6.36	0.55
Calcium	5.96	0.48
Phosphate	0.60	0.11
Nitrate	0.38	0.01
Chloride	26.5	2.92
Sulfate	1.06	0.25

[a]Sampled in natural habitat at Yanchep, western Australia, averaged over a 9-month cycle of uptake and growth (July 1992–February 1993). (From Pate and Jeschke, 1993.)

ride, and Na^+ in maintaining ion balance of its transport fluids under such deficiencies.

Concentrations of most solutes are found to decrease as sap ascends the xylem of the trunk during the period of maximum root uptake in winter (Pate and Jeschke, 1993). This is taken as evidence of lateral uptake into sites of storage in the trunk, probably principally into xylem parenchyma adjacent to conducting xylem. By the following October, just prior to shoot extension growth, the pattern reverses, with a tendency for higher concentrations in upper regions of the stem. This probably marks a period of remobilization of previously stored solutes back into xylem, which may then commence to function as major avenues of nourishment of new shoot tissues. By this time uptake by lateral roots has virtually ceased owing to drying of upper soil layers, and thus continued input by the root is likely to contribute significantly to new shoot growth.

Data on phloem sap composition before and during seasonal extension growth of the trunk indicate that phloem translocation is the major avenue of supply of photoassimilates from leaves serving the shoot apex and also for transfer of nutrients mobilized from older leaves whose senescence just precedes shoot extension. Nutrients accumulated in rays might also be mobilized centrifugally to phloem and thence to the stem apices along with photoassimilates from leaves. Clearly, more specific information on the seasonal storage and mobilization from different age classes of trunk segments and leaves is required before budgets for nutrient cycling can be drawn up

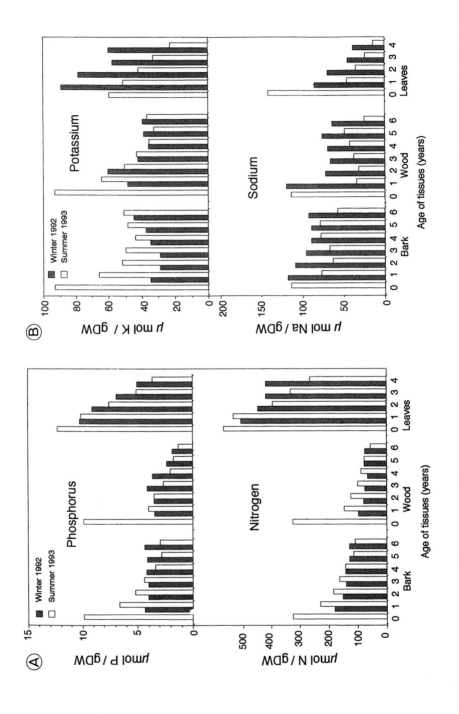

for the species, but present indications are that the trunk plays a vitally important role in such processes.

Figure 6 shows the changes in P, N, K, and Na tissue concentrations in wood, bark, and leaves of a population of 6-year-old *B. prionotes* trees sampled in winter during the main phase of nutrient uptake and again in summer during extension growth of the shoot. There are clear indications that substantial mobilization of P occurs between winter and summer from old wood, bark, and leaves and that commensurately high rates of deposition of this element occur in leaf and stem tissue of the new year's growth. By comparison, N and K mobilization from wood and bark tissues appears to be of lesser significance than that from older leaves. Substantial decreases in tissue concentrations of Na occur from old parts of trunks between winter and summer, a finding consistent with the high mobility of this element in phloem (Table I). Analyses comparing the levels of nutrients in ray and nonray tissues of the wood of mature stem tissues of *B. prionotes* provide convincing evidence of ray-specific storage of certain nutrients. Patterns of buildup and subsequent release from such tissues are currently being examined.

V. Conclusions

This chapter provides evidence of a major role of living cells of stem tissue in the transport, temporary storage, and circulation of organic and inorganic solutes within the whole plant. While much of their activity concerns essentially straight throughput of transported substances by conventional long-distance transport in xylem and phloem, they also carry out a number of subtle transfers modifying patterning of flow within a plant. Such potentially regulatory mechanisms collectively comprise temporary storage of solutes and possible exchange for others prior to remobilization from stem tissue, markedly differential rates of deposition or release of one

---

Figure 6   Concentrations of a range of nutrient elements in bark, leaves, and wood of different age segments of the trunks of 7-year-old *Banksia prionotes* trees. Data are depicted as means for (a) winter (July–September, shaded histograms), when nutrient flow from roots is fully active and mature parts of the shoot store nutrients, and for (b) the following summer (November–January, open histograms), when the shoot extension growth for the year is occurring and previously stored nutrients are being released from leaves and older bark wood of the trunk and transported in xylem and phloem toward apical regions. Note the much higher concentrations of P and N in leaves than in bark or wood and the large mobilization of Na^+ from bark and wood compared to that for other elements. Numbers refer to the current season's extension growth (0) and trunk segments 1–6 years old and leaves just expanded (0) or 1–4 years of age. (Jeschke and Pate, unpublished observations.)

solute compared to others by different age classes of tissue, and an ability at specific sites in the stem for exchanges of specific solutes to occur between xylem and phloem or between one xylem stream and another. The combined impact of these highly selective processes on plant functioning can be of considerable magnitude and results in highly effective targeting of potentially limiting nutrients such as N, P, and K^+ into young growing tissues, or, conversely, in a diversion away from sensitive young tissues of potentially damaging substances such as Na^+ and Cl^-. The spatial organization and quantitative significance of these processes can be readily visualized by means of empirical modeling. This chapter presents a number of case studies in which this is accomplished for a range of species and nutrient elements.

Information described here on the role of stems in differential partitioning of solutes is almost entirely of a descriptive nature. While the empirical modeling techniques provide a tool for examining quantitatively where each activity engaged on by the stem is located and impacts on whole-plant functioning, we remain woefully ignorant of the bases of the mechanisms that are involved and integrated throughout the life of a plant. Opportunities for further research at the cellular level are exciting and challenging, particularly in relation to the multifarious loading and unloading processes for various solutes that are clearly crucial to the programming of exchange, storage, and mobilization activities of each age and class of tissue and organ within the system. The approach, which has already been well developed in following the loading of assimilates by leaves and the unloading of assimilates by seeds and, to a certain extent, by stems of herbaceous species (see Van Bel [9] in this volume), now needs to be applied comprehensively and systematically at the whole-plant level, and especially in species whose patterns of solute flow already have been examined. Only then can we begin to understand how whole plants are organized and how one species differs from another with respect to stem functioning.

Acknowledgments

We acknowledge the financial support of the Australian Research Council (J.S.P.) and Sonderforschungbereich 251 of the Deutsche Forschungsgemeinschaft (W.D.J.). We thank Aart Van Bel for useful comments on draft versions of the manuscript.

References

Bowen, B. J., and Pate, J. S. (1993). The significance of root starch in post-fire shoot recovery of the resprouter *Stirlingia latifolia* R. Br. (Proteaceae). *Ann. Bot.* **72,** 7–16.

Chow, W. S., Ball, M. C., and Anderson, J. M. (1990). Growth and photosynthetic responses of spinach to salinity: Implications of K^+ nutrition for salt tolerance. *Aust. J. Plant Physiol.* **17**, 563–578.

Eggers, H., and Jeschke, W. D. (1983). Comparison of K^+–Na^+ selectivity mechanisms in roots of *Fagopyrum* and *Triticum*. *In* "Genetic Aspects of Plant Nutrition" (M. R. Sari'c and B. C. Loughman, eds.), pp. 223–228. Martinius Nijhoff, The Hague, the Netherlands.

Gunning, B. E. S., and Pate, J. S. (1974). Transfer cells. *In* "Dynamic Aspects of Plant Ultrastructure" (A. W. Robards, ed.), pp. 441–480. McGraw-Hill, New York.

Gunning, B. E. S., Pate, J. S., and Green, L. W. (1970). Transfer cells in the vascular system of stems: Taxonomy, association with nodes, and structure. *Protoplasma* **71**, 147–171.

Gunning, B. E. S., Pate, J. S., Minchin, F. R., and Marks, I. (1974). Quantitative aspects of transfer cell structure in relation to vein loading in leaves and solute transport in legume nodules. *Symp. Soc. Exp. Biol.* **28**, 87–126.

Hall, S. M., and Baker, D. A. (1972). The chemical composition of *Ricinus* phloem exudate. *Planta* **106**, 131–140.

Jacoby, B. (1964). Function of bean roots and stems in sodium retention. *Plant Physiol.* **39**, 445–449.

Jacoby, B. (1979). Sodium recirculation and loss from *Phaseolus vulgaris* L. *Ann. Bot.* **43**, 741–744.

Jeschke, W. D., and Pate, J. S. (1991a). Modelling of the uptake, flow and utilization of C, N and H_2O within whole plants of *Ricinus communis* L. based on empirical data. *J. Plant Physiol.* **137**, 488–498.

Jeschke, W. D., and Pate, J. S. (1991b). Modelling of the partitioning, assimilation and storage of nitrate within root and shoot organs of castor bean (*Ricinus communis* L.). *J. Exp. Bot.* **42**, 1091–1103.

Jeschke, W. D., and Pate, J. S. (1991c). Cation and chloride partitioning through xylem and phloem within the whole plant of *Ricinus communis* L. under conditions of salt stress. *J. Exp. Bot.* **42**, 1105–1116.

Jeschke, W. D., and Wolf, O. (1988). Effect of NaCl salinity on growth, development, ion distribution, and ion translocation in castor bean (*Ricinus communis* L.). *J. Plant Physiol.* **132**, 45–53.

Jeschke, W. D., Atkins, C. A., and Pate, J. S. (1985). Ion circulation via phloem and xylem between root and shoot of nodulated white lupin. *J. Plant Physiol.* **117**, 319–330.

Jeschke, W. D., Pate, J. S., and Atkins, C. A. (1987). Partitioning of K^+, Na^+, Mg^{++}, and Ca^{++} through xylem and phloem to component organs of nodulated white lupin under mild salinity. *J. Plant Physiol.* **128**, 77–93.

Jeschke, W. D., Wolf, O., and Pate, J. S. (1991). Solute exchanges from xylem to phloem in the leaf and from phloem to xylem in the root. *In* "Recent Advances in Phloem Transport and Assimilate Compartmentation" (J. L. Bonnemain, S. Delrot, W. J. Lucas, and J. Dainty, eds.), pp. 96–105. Ouest Editions, Nantes, France.

Kuo, J., Pate, J. S., Rainbird, R. M., and Atkins, C. A. (1980). Internodes of grain legumes—new location for xylem parenchyma transfer cells. *Protoplasma* **104**, 181–185.

Lauchli, A. (1979). Regulation des Salztransports und Salzausschließung in Glykophyten und Halophyten. *Ber. Dtsch. Bot. Ges.* **92**, 87–94.

Lauchli, A. (1984). Salt exclusion: An adaptation of legumes for crops and pastures under saline conditions. *In* "Salinity Tolerance in Plants. Strategies of Crop Improvement" (R. C. Staples and G. H. Toenniessen, eds.), pp. 171–187. John Wiley & Sons, New York.

Layzell, D. B., Pate, J. S., Atkins, C. A., and Canvin, D. T. (1981). Partitioning of carbon and nitrogen and the nutrition of root and shoot apex in a nodulated legume. *Plant Physiol.* **67**, 30–36.

McNeil, D. L., Atkins, C. A., and Pate, J. S. (1979). Uptake and utilization of xylem-borne amino compounds by shoot organs of a legume. *Plant Physiol.* **63**, 1076–1081.

Pate, J. S. (1986). Xylem-to-phloem transfer—vital component of the nitrogen-partitioning system of a nodulated legume. *In* "Phloem Transport" (J. Cronshaw, W. J. Lucas, and R. T. Giaquinta, eds.), pp. 445–462. A. R. Liss, New York.

Pate, J. S., and Gunning, B. E. S. (1969). Vascular transfer cells in angiosperm leaves. A taxonomic and morphological survey. *Protoplasma* **68**, 135–156.

Pate, J. S., and Gunning, B. E. S. (1972). Transfer cells. *Annu. Rev. Plant Physiol.* **23**, 173–196.

Pate, J. S., and Jeschke, W. D. (1993). *In* "Plant Nutrition—from Genetic Engineering to Field Practice" (N. J. Barrow, ed.), pp. 313–316. Kluwer Academic Publishers, Dordrecht, the Netherlands.

Pate, J. S., Layzell, D. B., and McNeil, D. L. (1979a). Modelling the transport and utilization of carbon and nitrogen in a nodulated legume. *Plant Physiol.* **63**, 730–737.

Pate, J. S., Layzell, D. B., and Atkins, C. A. (1979b). Economy of carbon and nitrogen in a nodulated and non-nodulated (NO_3-grown) legume. *Plant Physiol.* **64**, 1078–1082.

Pate, J. S., Layzell, D. B., and Atkins, C. A. (1980). Transport exchange of carbon, nitrogen and water in the context of whole plant growth and functioning—case history of a nodulated annual legume. *Ber. Dtsch. Bot. Ges.* **93**, 243–255.

Pate, J. S., Froend, R. H., Bowen, B. J., Hansen, A., and Kuo, J. (1990). Seedling growth and storage characteristics of seeder and resprouter species of Mediterranean-type ecosystems of S. W. Australia. *Ann. Bot.* **65**, 585–601.

Richardson, R. T., and Baker, D. A. (1982). The chemical composition of cucurbit vascular exudates. *J. Exp. Bot.* **33**, 1239–1247.

Wolf, O., and Jeschke, W. D. (1987). Modelling of sodium and potassium flows via phloem and xylem in the shoot of salt-stressed barley. *J. Plant Physiol.* **128**, 371–386.

Wolf, O., Munns, R., Tonnet, M. L., and Jeschke, W. D. (1990). Concentrations and transport of solutes in xylem and phloem along the leaf axis of NaCl-treated *Hordeum vulgare*. *J. Exp. Bot.* **41**, 1131–1141.

Wolf, O., Munns, R., Tonnet, M. L., and Jeschke, W. D. (1991). The role of the stem in the partitioning of Na^+ and K^+ in NaCl-treated barley. *J. Exp. Bot.* **42**, 697–704.

9

The Low Profile Directors of Carbon and Nitrogen Economy in Plants: Parenchyma Cells Associated with Translocation Channels

Aart J. E. Van Bel

I. Introduction

The mechanisms of long-distance transport are essentially similar in xylem and phloem: both are mass flow processes driven by pressure gradients set up by differences in water potential. Gradients in hydrostatic or turgor potentials are responsible for the translocation in xylem and phloem, respectively. In the past, the overwhelming appearance of the vascular channels and the painstaking efforts to master the fundamentals of long-distance transport have narrowed our view. Disproportionate value has been attached to water mass flow as the motive force of solute translocation. An example of this line of thinking was that different mass flow rates of phosphorus and tritiated water in sieve tubes were presumed to be incompatible with mass transfer in the phloem (Peel, 1970). Different rates of mass transfer, however, turned out to be due to differential lateral escape of the solutes from the channels. This was demonstrated by experiments in which mixtures of tritiated water and radiolabeled sugars and amino acids were perfused through xylem vessels under gravity. In spite of the unequivocal mass flow character of the perfusion, the longitudinal displacement strongly differed among sugars, among various amino acids, and between the solutes and the tritiated solvent (Van Bel, 1974, 1976, 1978).

There is now widespread evidence that the cells adjacent to the extremes of the long-distance channels strongly affect the sap composition. Root parenchyma cells in the xylem and minor vein companion cells in the phloem release large amounts of solutes into the translocation channels. Thus, the activities of the cells associated with the termini of the translocation channels, rather than the mass flow of water, determine the bulk movement of solutes within the channels.

The fraction of the channels adjoined by these highly active cells, however, is small in comparison with the entire channel length. In terms of distance, the channel coverage of these cells is low: intermediary cells and transfer cells adjoin the sieve elements less than about once every 1000 μm in the minor veins. This constitutes about 1% of the vascular path in small herbs and far less than 0.1% in larger herbs, shrubs, and trees. Therefore, the channel-associated cells along the transport pathway may have an impact on the nature and quantity of the translocate that has been largely overlooked. It may, therefore, be expected that parenchyma cells along xylem vessels (xylem parenchyma, ray cells) and sieve tubes (companion cells, phloem parenchyma) govern solute translocation in major veins, petioles, stems, and major roots (Fig. 1).

The effects of the inconspicuous channel-associated cells on C and N economy are dramatic (Fig. 1), as pointed out elsewhere (see Pate and Jeschke [8] in this volume). In this chapter, the underlying cellular mechanisms that govern uptake from and release into the channels are explored. The conclusion is that variations in cellular metabolism and intercellular organization of the channel-associated parenchyma lead to different strategies in C and N distribution (Fig. 1) that, in turn, appear related to growth form and habitat range.

II. Channel-Associated Cells in Xylem: Involvement in N Economy

An example of the impact of the channel-associated cells is the effect of vessel-associated cells on the distribution of organic N over the plant. In many plants, considerable quantities of amino acids are translocated through the xylem vessels. Investigations with two woody plants (*Ligustrum ovalifolium* and *Salix alba*), an herb (*Lycopersicon esculentum*), and a graminoid (*Cyperus papyrus*) have shown the magnitude of control that vessel-associated cells exert on the removal of amino acids from the transpiration stream. ^{14}C-Labeled amino acids were offered to the stem base of excised *Cyperus* shoots (Fig. 2a and b) and *Ligustrum* twigs (Fig. 2f) or were perfused through cut stem segments of *Lycopersicon* (Fig. 2c and d) and *Salix* (Fig. 2e).

The differential distribution of the apoplast marker inulin [14C]carboxylic acid (exclusively moving through the nonliving plant compartment)

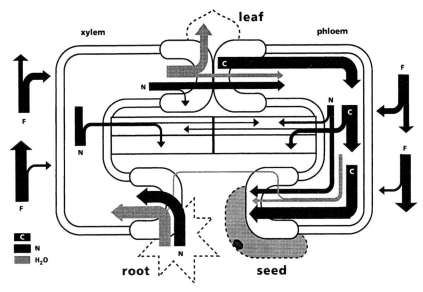

Figure 1 The impact of channel-associated cells on the distribution of carbon (C) and nitrogen (N). Water movement through the transport channels is the driving force of the long-distance transport of organic C and N. The mass flow volume both in xylem and phloem results from the differences in water potential between the termini of the system. The solute content of channel sap depends on the activities of the channel-associated cells, at the termini as well as along the translocation path. Nitrogen is released into vessels by the xylem parenchyma cells in the roots and is partly withdrawn from the xylem stream by the vessel-associated cells. The proportion of nitrogen arriving at the leaves depends on the uptake/release balance of the vessel-associated cells in combination with transfer and deposition activities of the vascular parenchyma. In mature leaves, a major part of the nitrogen is transferred and enters the phloem along with the carbon. Along the pathway to the terminal sinks, nitrogen and carbon are partly withdrawn from the sieve tubes. The degree of escape again depends on the uptake/release balance of the sieve tube-associated cells and the adjoining elements. Flux diagrams (F), to the left and right, illustrate the impact of high (top) and low (bottom) net uptake along the transport channels on the distribution of N and C, respectively.

and ^{14}C-labeled amino acids showed that, in *Cyperus,* the major part of the amino acids was sequestered in the symplasmic compartment (i.e., the living portion of the cellular network). The apparent increase in vessel volume near the cluster of top leaves (Fig. 2a) may be due to anastomosing of the vascular bundles there, as suggested by the high inulin content. The ^{14}C profile along the stem is logarithmic, indicating a first-order process (Horwitz, 1958). In light of the absorption by the symplast, the first-order kinetics results from carrier-mediated uptake. The aberrant behavior of glutamic acid (Fig. 2a) is ascribed to an increase in pH of the vessel sap along the stem resulting from the withdrawal of glutamic acid. A high pH strongly

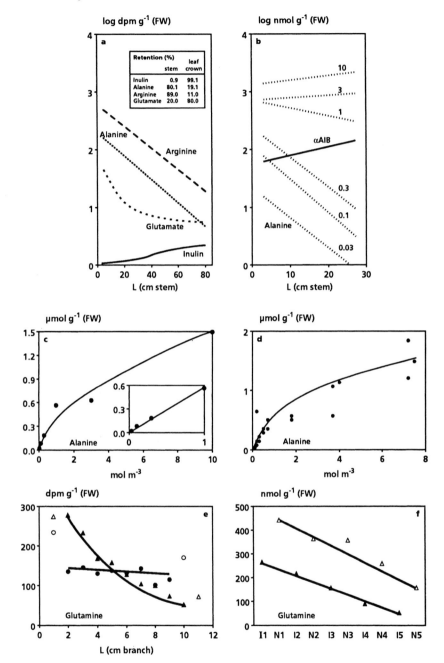

reduces the carrier-mediated uptake of acid amino acids, and the pH optimum of glutamic acid uptake is lower than that of other amino acids (King and Hirji, 1975; Van Bel and Hermans, 1977; McCutcheon and Bown, 1987).

Carrier-mediated amino acid uptake from the xylem vessels is confirmed by the retention profiles of different alanine concentrations fed to cut stem bases of *Cyperus* (Fig. 2b). Up to a concentration of 1 mol m^{-3} alanine, the retention corresponds with the concentration (Fig. 2b). Above 1 mol m^{-3}, the angle of the retention profile declines and the retention does not increase linearly with the concentration (Fig. 2b). The horizontal profile (zero-order kinetics) for 3 mol m^{-3} alanine (Fig. 2c) points to carrier saturation between 1 and 3 mol m^{-3}, with a Michaelis–Menten affinity constant (K_m) of about 1 mol m^{-3}. An extended absorption surface near the cluster of leaves (Fig. 2a) could explain the rising curves for 10 mol m^{-3} alanine and 1 mol m^{-3} α-aminoisobutyric acid (α-AIB), which has an apparently low K_m (Fig. 2b). Alanine uptake from the xylem vessels in *Lycopersicon* showed similar retention profiles, shifting in slope with the concentration (Van Bel *et al.*, 1979). The apparent K_m for alanine uptake from the xylem vessels in *Lycopersicon* (1.7 mol m^{-3}; Fig. 2d) is close to the K_m value in *Cyperus* (Fig. 2c). The nature of the linear component in the uptake kinetics (Fig. 2c and d) is not entirely clear.

As in *Cyperus* and *Lycopersicon*, the retention profile for glutamine in *Salix* was much steeper at the lower concentration (6 $\times$ 10^{-3} mol m^{-3}; Fig. 2e), at which a logarithmic decline was evident (Fig. 2e). The glutamine retention by the internodal end segments is not taken into consideration,

---

Figure 2 Retention of xylem-transported ^{14}C-labeled amino acids along various stems. Amino acids were administered to cut shoots via transpiration [*Cyperus* (a–c) and *Ligustrum* (f)] or to excised internodes by perfusion [*Lycopersicon* (d) and *Salix* (e)]. After xylem transport of the radiotracers, the xylem vessels were chased with demineralized water. (a) Log-plotted ^{14}C retention profiles (dpm, disintegrations per minute) of a basic, a neutral, and an acidic radiolabeled amino acid and the xylem transport marker inulin [^{14}C]carboxylic acid administered to cut *Cyperus papyrus* shoots (redrawn from Van Bel, 1989). The retention per unit length of stem tissue is a measure for the withdrawal from the xylem by the vessel-associated cells. Inset: Proportional distribution of each compound over stem and leaf crown after chasing with water. (b) Log-plotted ^{14}C profiles of several alanine concentrations ranging from 0.03 to 10 mol m^{-3} and 1 mol m^{-3} α-aminoisobutyric acid (α-AIB) in *Cyperus* shoots. (c) Concentration dependence of alanine uptake by the vessel-associated cells in *Cyperus* shoots. The data are the transformed results of (b). (d) Concentration dependence of alanine uptake by the vessel-associated cells in *Lycopersicon* internodes (redrawn from Van Bel *et al.*, 1979). (e) Retention profiles of ^{14}C-labeled glutamine (▲, 6 $\times$ 10^{-3} mol m^{-3}; ●, 6 mol m^{-3}) in excised *Salix alba* branch segments (redrawn from Van Bel, 1989). The values at the top and bottom (open symbols) are not taken into account as glutamine was also taken up at the cut surface. (f) Retention profiles of ^{14}C-labeled glutamine (1 mol m^{-3}) in nodes (N, △) and internodes (I, ▲) of cut *Ligustrum ovalifolium* branches.

because uptake by the cut surfaces added to the uptake from the vessels (Fig. 2e). A linearly declining retention profile was also observed for gluta-mine uptake in *Ligustrum* twigs (Fig. 2f). The absence of a logarithmic char-acter of retention here (Fig. 2e) may be due to N-cycling processes at the nodes. A relatively high retention by the nodal regions, as was reported before for *Lycopersicon* (Van Bel, 1984), is assigned to a larger anastomosing uptake surface or a more intensive uptake by nodal transfer cells (Pate and Gunning, 1972) or a combination of both.

The collective ^{14}C retention profiles sketch a general outline of the with-drawal of organic N by vessel-associated cells. (1) amino acids are intensely and selectively withdrawn from the vessels; (2) the retrieval is carrier medi-ated both in monocotyledons (Fig. 2a–c) and dicotyledons (Fig. 2d and e); (3) the absorption is a proton-driven mechanism located in the plasma membrane of the vessel-associated parenchyma cells (Van Bel and Van der Schoot, 1980); (4) the withdrawal is more intense in the nodal than in the internodal regions (Fig. 2f; Van Bel, 1984); and (5) the escape rate per unit of stem length seems to be high. At least 80% of the ^{14}C-labeled amino acids is withdrawn from the vessels in the *Cyperus* stems (inset, Fig. 2a). This per-centage does not reflect the actual and absolute retrieval from the xylem stream, as the ^{14}C uptake does not provide information about the concur-rent release of unlabelled amino acid into the xylem sap. The strong reten-tion shows, at least, that the vessel-associated cells are capable of back-cycling amino acids during upward translocation and that their release/withdrawal achievements may be substantial.

III. Channel-Associated Cells in Phloem: Background and Concept

A. New Elements in Münch's Pressure Flow Hypothesis

The role of the channel-associated cells seems even more vital in phloem than in xylem translocation. First, the parenchyma cells (companion cells) adjoining the channels are metabolically strongly involved in maintaining the transport units (sieve elements) in a functional state. Second, the sol-utes are not passively carried by the transport stream, but generate the mass flow themselves by osmotic attraction of water. Thus, the physiology of the channel-associated cells is crucial to the Münch concept of mass flow (Fig. 3A). With progressive study on the sieve element–companion cell (SE/CC) complexes, the views on phloem loading, transport, and unload-ing have changed dramatically with consequent adaptations of the mass flow concept (Fig. 3B–D).

Compelling evidence has been obtained for different modes of phloem loading (Fig. 3B) in different species (Van Bel *et al.*, 1992, 1994). In apo-

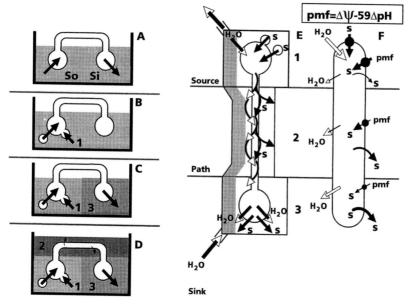

Figure 3 Phloem transport by the pressure flow mechanism. (A) The original Münch hypothesis, in which differences in osmotic potential at the source So and sink Si ends of the symplast generate the mass flow. Photoassimilates are accumulated by the sieve tubes in the source and released in the sink, creating an osmotic pressure gradient. (B) Modification (1): Insertion of various modes of phloem loading with possibly different pressure flow properties. Attached source signifies symplasmic phloem loading, detached source apoplasmic phloem loading. (C) Modification (3): The importance of a high rather than a low osmotic potential in the sink apoplast for efficient phloem transport. This modification highlights the turgor gradient as the driving force of phloem transport. (D) Modification (2): A dynamic volume flow through essentially leaky instead of impermeable pipes. The solute content and, implicitly, the turgor, are controlled by release/retrieval systems in the SE/CC complexes of the transport phloem. (E) Elaboration of (D): Tentative model of phloem transport in which differential solute release/retrieval balances along the phloem pathway control the influx/efflux of water (S, sugar). (F) Putative PMF gradient along the source-to-sink phloem pathway, causing gradual loss of solutes and commensurate amounts of water toward the sink, where a massive release of water and solutes takes place.

plasmic phloem loading, photosynthates are released from the mesophyll domain into the apoplasmic space before being accumulated by the SE/CC complexes. In the symplasmic variant, photosynthate is transferred from mesophyll to SE/CC complexes via an entirely plasmodesmatal conduit. New models have been developed to bring this mode of loading into conformation with the mass flow concept (Turgeon, 1991; Gamalei et al., 1994). Furthermore, various composite forms of symplasmic and apoplasmic phloem loading operating within one species have been postulated (Gamalei, 1990; Van Bel, 1992, 1993a).

As for the sink regions, a diversity of phloem unloading mechanisms is beginning to emerge with the novelty that the apoplasmic osmotic potential may be highly negative in the sinks (Fig. 3C). According to this observation, the source–sink turgor gradient of the sieve elements rather than the osmopotential gradient in the phloem sap is the major determinant of mass flow through the sieve tubes (Patrick, 1990, 1991; Wolswinkel, 1990).

Simultaneously, the concept of phloem transport in petioles and stems has become much more dynamic (Fig. 3D). In contrast to the assumption of Münch, the sieve tubes are not analogous to hermetically sealed pipes. The SE/CC complexes along the pathway (major veins, petioles, and stems) lose considerable amounts of sugar, part of which is retrieved (Eschrich *et al.*, 1972; Aloni *et al.*, 1986; Minchin and Thorpe, 1987; Grimm *et al.*, 1990; Schulz, 1994). This behavior reflects the dual function of the transport phloem. Photosynthetic products must be retained within the sieve tubes to nourish the terminal sinks. Concomitantly, the heterotrophic stem parenchyma, the cambium in particular, also requires a supply of food. The dualism in function must be met by a highly sophisticated and rigorously regulated release/retrieval mechanism in the SE/CC complexes (e.g., Van Bel, 1993b).

B. Symplasmic Isolation of Sieve Element–Companion Cell Complexes in Transport Phloem and Its Role in Maintaining Sugar Concentration in Sieve Tubes

The release/retrieval balance of sugars is probably controlled by carrier systems in the plasma membrane of the SE/CC complexes (reviewed by Van Bel, 1993b). Carrier kinetics of sucrose uptake have been identified by ^{14}C tracer studies and electrophysiological measurements in isolated phloem strips (Wright and Fisher, 1981; Daie, 1987; Van der Schoot and Van Bel, 1989; Grimm *et al.*, 1990). To overcome the uphill substrate gradient, the sugar carriers are energized by free energy of the electrochemical proton gradient (proton motive force, PMF). The PMF is composed of the outside–inside pH gradient (ΔpH) and the membrane potential ($\Delta \psi$) as follows: $PMF = \Delta \psi - RT/F \cdot \ln[H_o^+]/[H_i^+] = \Delta \psi - 59\Delta pH$. The membrane potential, in turn, is the sum of a diffusional and an electrogenic component. Both elements of the membrane potential have been recognized in the SE/CC-complexes (Wright and Fisher, 1981; Van der Schoot and Van Bel, 1989) The electrogenic proton gradient is created by ATPases located in the plasma membrane of the SE/CC complex. When the proton motive force is equivalent to the inside–outside chemical potential of a sugar, maximal sugar accumulation has been attained. At equilibrium, $PMF = -RT/F \cdot \ln[S_i]/[S_o]$ or $PMF = -59 \log[S_i]/[S_o]$. In dependence of the PMF, the accumulation factor of uncharged substrate molecules (with $[S_i]$ being the inside concentration and $[S_o]$ the outside concentration) thus is $\log[S_i]/[S_o] = -PMF/59$. In particular because of the high pH of the sieve tube sap, and the consequent steep ΔpH, the PMF over the SE/CC plasma membrane could enable sugar accumulation by factors ranging between 10^4 and 10^6.

As a consequence, local differences in PMF along the phloem pathway could cause a gradient in the release/retrieval balance in successive SE/CC complexes, thereby imposing a net retrieval gradient along the pathway (Fig. 3E and F). Such a gradient would combine a volume flow mechanism (the dynamic version of the mass flow) with a decreasing turgor toward the sinks. In light of the PMF-driven character of the retrieval, a PMF gradient from source to sink is expected (Fig. 3). Circumstantial evidence for a decreasing PMF from the leaves (the sources) to the roots (the major sink) was reported for *Phaseolus* and *Ricinus*. In *Phaseolus,* a tip-to-base increase of the apoplasmic sugar content was observed (Minchin and Thorpe, 1984). The tip-to-base increase of sugar in the phloem apoplast is consistent with a tip-to-base pH decrease with a corresponding drop in sugar content of the sieve tube sap in *Ricinus* (Vreugdenhil and Koot-Gronsveld, 1989). The pH gradient seems to coincide with the sugar gradient (Vreugdenhil and Koot-Gronsveld, 1989) and the PMF (Van Bel, 1993b). In contrast to the above findings, investigations on the membrane potential of the SE/CC complexes in successive internodes of *Lupinus* were inconclusive with respect to the existence of a PMF gradient along the stem phloem (Van Bel and Van Rijen, 1994).

For optimal functioning of the release/retrieval systems, a certain degree of symplasmic isolation of the SE/CC complexes in the transport phloem seems appropriate. Symplasmic exchange of solutes with adjacent cells is difficult to reconcile with strict control of the resorption by membrane-bound carriers of the SE/CC complex. In addition, maintenance of the extravagantly high pH of the sieve tube sap may be difficult, if an open communication channel exists between SE/CC complex and the surrounding cells. Moreover, symplasmic discontinuity would assist in creating the osmotic disparity between SE/CC complex and phloem parenchyma.

The inferred symplasmic discontinuity between SE/CC complex and phloem parenchyma is supported by a range of observations:

1. The plasmodesmatal frequencies between the SE/CC complex and the adjoining elements are significantly lower than those at the other interfaces of phloem elements (Hayes *et al.,* 1985; Van Bel and Kempers, 1991; Wood, 1993).

2. Fluorescent probes injected intracellularly into the sieve element moved longitudinally to other sieve elements and to the companion cells, but never to other phloem elements (Fig. 4; Van der Schoot and Van Bel, 1989; Van Bel and Kempers, 1991; Oparka *et al.,* 1992; Van Bel and Van Rijen, 1994). Movement of dye, injected into phloem parenchyma cells, to

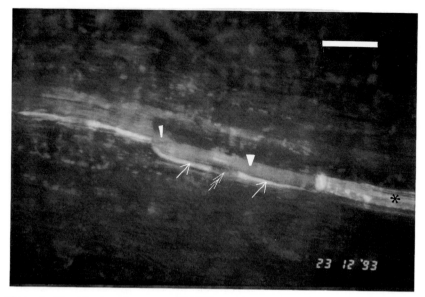

Figure 4 Identification of an array of SE/CC complexes as a symplast domain. Intercellular transport of the membrane-impermeant fluorochrome Lucifer Yellow CH intracellularly injected by iontophoresis (asterisk) into a sieve element of *Vicia faba*. The fluorescent probe only moved via the sieve plates (slender arrowhead) to other sieve elements and associate companion cells (wide arrowhead). The nucleus of the companion cell (double-headed arrow) is surrounded by a vacuolar compartment that has accumulated fluorescent dye (single-headed arrows). The upper fluorescent band is a parallel sieve tube into which dye has moved via a lateral sieve plate. Bar: 50 mm.

the SE/CC complexes, or vice versa, has never been observed (Van Bel and Kempers, 1991; Van Bel and Van Rijen, 1994).

3. The electrical conductance between adjacent phloem parenchyma cells was 10 times higher than that between SE/CC complexes and phloem parenchyma (Fig. 5; Van Bel and Van Rijen, 1994).

4. The membrane potentials of the SE/CC complex and the phloem parenchyma often differ by ≥ 20 mV (Sibaoka, 1962; Van Bel, 1993b; Van Bel and Van Rijen, 1994). The data fall into two categories (Fig. 6). In the first group (*Lupinus, Senecio,* and *Vicia*), the membrane potential of the SE/CC complexes is similar or significantly more negative than that of the phloem parenchyma (Fig. 6). In this group, the $\Delta\psi_{\text{SE/CC complex}}/\Delta\psi_{\text{phloem parenchyma}}$ ratio is significantly higher than 1. In the second group (*Epilobium, Lamium,* and *Ocimum*), the ratio is just the opposite (Fig. 6). It appears that the membrane potentials of the phloem parenchyma mainly account for the shift in the ratios (Fig. 6). The potential importance of this pattern is discussed in Section VI, after more background on phloem loading physiology is presented in Sections IV and V.

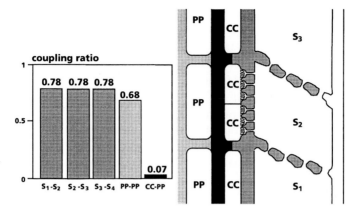

Figure 5 Differential electrical resistance between sieve elements (S), companion cells (CC), and phloem parenchyma (PP) in the stem phloem of *Lupinus luteus* (constructed after Van Bel and Van Rijen, 1994). The electrical coupling ratio is the quotient of the membrane depolarization in the current-injected cell and the membrane depolarization in the neighboring cell. S_1, S_2, and S_3 are successive sieve elements.

	SE/CC complex	(n)	Phloem parenchyma	(n)		Minor vein type
Lupinus luteus	-106.1 ± 4.3	27	-84 ± 4.5	10	**	2
Senecio viscosus	-127 ± 8.7	6	-68 ± 11.1	6	**	2
Senecio vulgaris	-123 ± 21.1	8	-131 ± 28.9	5	ns	2
Vicia faba	-121 ± 3.4	15	-104 ± 3.5	11	**	2
Epilobium angustifolium	-78 ± 16.5	8[a]	-98 ± 11.6	8	ns	1
	-71 ± 16.0	3[b]	-149 ± 8.8	5	**	1
Lamium album	-52 ± 3.1	20	-87 ± 9.1	12	**	1
Ocimum basilicum	-78 ± 3.8	12	-102 ± 3.1	24	***	1

Figure 6 Membrane potentials ($-\text{mV} \pm \text{SD}$, n = number of measurements) of SE/CC complexes and phloem parenchyma in the transport phloem of diverse dicotyledons. The qualification of minor vein type refers to the symplasmic (type 1) or apoplasmic (type 2) minor vein configuration in the leaf as outlined in Section IV,A. The volume of the circular bodies (on the right) represents the presumptive source capacity, and the arrows represent the proportional distribution of carbohydrate to axial (oblique arrow) and terminal (vertical arrow) sinks. For *Epilobium*, the data for the external (*a*) and internal (*b*) phloem are given.

IV. Channel-Associated Cells in Phloem Loading Zone: Loading Mechanisms and Potential Consequences

A. Ultrastructural Differences in Minor Vein and Mode of Phloem Loading

Different mechanisms of phloem loading have been discovered. Originally, the concept of multiprogrammed phloem loading was purely hypothetical and was based on the differences in ultrastructure and architecture between the minor veins in various plant families (Gamalei, 1989). Notably, the ultrastructure of the companion cell has been used to discriminate the minor vein configuration types. Universal features of the companion cells are the intensely branched mitochondrial network and the dense cytoplasmic matrix. The companion cells (intermediary cells) with abundant symplasmic connectivity (in type 1 minor veins; Gamalei, 1989) contain extensive vesicular labyrinths, likely made of endoplasmic reticulum. Chloroplasts are absent and other organelles are small and scarce (Gamalei, 1990). Companion cells with sporadic or virtually no plasmodesmata (in type 2 minor veins; Gamalei, 1989) contain several small vacuoles and chloroplasts embedded in an exceptionally dense cytoplasmic matrix (Gamalei, 1990). Companion cells with hardly any plasmodesmatal contacts (transfer cells) often possess conspicuous cell wall invaginations (Gamalei, 1989).

Physiological evidence obtained in about 40 species shows that the minor vein configuration corresponds with the mode of phloem loading (Van Bel *et al.*, 1992, 1994). The species with a continuous symplasmic pathway between mesophyll and SE/CC complex in the minor vein perform symplasmic phloem loading, whereas those with symplasmic discontinuity between mesophyll and SE/CC complex execute apoplasmic phloem loading. Identical results were obtained in experiments with leaf disks with the lower epidermis stripped away (Van Bel *et al.*, 1992) or whole leaves (Van Bel *et al.*, 1994).

B. Transport Sugars and Mode of Phloem Loading

Another characteristic difference between symplasmically and apoplasmically loading species is the dissimilarity in transport sugars. Whereas apoplasmic loaders transport sucrose exclusively, the sieve tube translocate of symplasmic loaders often contains large amounts of galactosyl sugars such as raffinose, stachyose, and verbascose (Zimmermann and Ziegler, 1975; Gamalei, 1985). Because the galactosyl sugars are more viscous than sucrose, the viscosity-to-concentration ratio of sucrose may be more favorable for mass transfer of organic C (Lang, 1978) and for the development of an appreciable turgor gradient between source and sink (Van Bel, 1993a). Some evidence exists that the linear velocity of phloem transport is higher in plants with apoplasmic minor vein configuration (Gamalei, 1990). If the apoplasmic mode of phloem loading generates a greater pressure gradient than the symplasmic mode, this phenomenon alone could account for a more efficient transport to terminal sinks (Gamalei, 1990; Van Bel and Visser, 1994).

V. Channel-Associated Cells in Phloem Transport Zone

Linking the data on the membrane potentials of the cell elements in transport phloem (Fig. 6) with the multiprogrammed concept of phloem loading reveals a remarkable correlation. A coincidence emerges between the vein typology (and implicitly the mode of phloem loading) and the $\Delta\psi_{SE/CC\ complex}/\Delta\psi_{phloem\ parenchyma}$ ratio in the transport phloem (Fig. 6). In type 1 species, this ratio tends to be lower than 1, whereas the opposite holds for type 2 species (Fig. 6). Admittedly, the restricted number of species and families (Fig. 6) only allows speculations on the existence and the significance of such an association (Fig. 6).

In light of the PMF-driven absorption of sugars, the $\Delta\psi_{SE/CC\ complex}/\Delta\psi_{phloem\ parenchyma}$ ratio should be indicative of the relative cell-specific capacity of the SE/CC complexes and the phloem parenchyma to retrieve sugars. The competitive capacity of the SE/CC complex for retrieving sugars from the apoplast (Fig. 6) should decline with a decreasing $\Delta\psi_{SE/CC\ complex}/\Delta\psi_{phloem\ parenchyma}$ ratio. By contrast, the competitive strength of the phloem parenchyma increases with such a decrease. As predicted by the release/retrieval model (Fig. 3F), a higher sugar accumulation by the phloem parenchyma and other axial sinks should occur in species with $\Delta\psi_{SE/CC\ complex}/\Delta\psi_{phloem\ parenchyma}$ ratios < 1 rather than in those with ratios > 1 (Fig. 6).

Provided that the correlation between the mode of loading and the behavior of the transport phloem is causal, a diagram emerges (Fig. 7). Expressed in physiological terms, symplasmic phloem loading (as in type 1 species) is linked with a reduced retrieval capacity of the transport phloem and a high accumulatory capacity of the axial sinks (Fig. 7). The opposite (low retrieval capacity, low accumulatory capacity of the axial sinks; Fig. 7) would be true for species with apoplasmic phloem loading (type 2 species).

A shift in the relative strength between axial and terminal sinks potentially leads to different distribution patterns of C and N (suggested in Van Bel and Visser, 1994). The ratio between the sink strengths of the axial and terminal sinks likely directs the distribution of organic C and N. Strong axial sinks may evoke a relative accumulation of material in petioles and stems and may reduce the outgrowth of terminal sinks. The high investment of material in stem tissues would preclude the formation of photosynthetic tissue or result in photosynthetic tissue with a lower N content, both of which would retard plant growth.

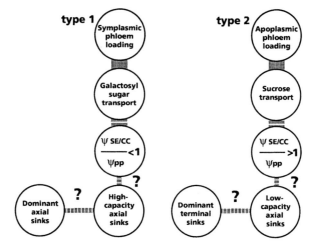

Figure 7   Correlation diagram of phloem loading, phloem transport, and assimilate distribution. The cardinal link in the diagram is the emerging correlation between the mode of phloem loading and the $\psi_{SE/CC\ complex}/\psi_{phloem\ parenchyma}$ ratio (membrane potential of the SE/CC complex divided by the membrane potential of the phloem parenchyma). Crucial is the assumption that the $\psi_{SE/CC\ complex}/\psi_{phloem\ parenchyma}$ ratio is a determinant of the assimilate distribution between axial and terminal sinks. When the ratio is <1, the competitive strength of the phloem parenchyma is high relative to the SE/CC complexes in view of the presumptive PMFs. The axial sinks in type 1 species will profit from the favorable $\psi_{SE/CC\ complex}/\psi_{phloem\ parenchyma}$ ratio, provided that the metabolic or storage capacity is commensurate with the higher supply. The opposite is presumed to be true with regard to the terminal sinks in type 2 species where the ratio is >1.

The collective activities of the channel-associated cells are not necessarily the only or principal determinants of C and N distribution or of consequent growth rates. The correlation diagram (Fig. 7) is based on a transport-physiological view of the distribution events. Obviously, many other determinants are involved in the actual distribution of C and N and the resultant relative growth rate (Lambers and Poorter, 1992). One may take this chapter as a plea to evaluate experimentally the importance of the channel-associated cells for the distribution of C and N in plants.

VI. Ecological Strategies and Operation of Channel-Associated Cells

The speculation is advanced here that variations in phloem architecture and physiology are correlated with one another (Fig. 7), which would provide different strategies for the distribution of organic matter, with potential consequences for the relative growth rate (RGR). According to this concept, C and N distribution is determined by integrative functioning of all cells associated with the phloem (including the cells in source and path) rather than by competition between the sinks alone.

Is there any evidence that phloem physiology, organic matter distribution, RGR, and growth strategy may be linked in a way that is meaningful in terms of survival? As hardly any research has been done in this direction and as it seems to be a subject full of pitfalls, only a few speculations on emerging contours may be permitted.

In herbs, the mode of phloem loading is associated with the climate zone (Gamalei, 1991; Van Bel and Gamalei, 1992; Turgeon *et al.*, 1993), with species with symplasmic phloem loading prevalent in the tropics and subtropics and with apoplasmic phloem loading prevalent in temperate and boreal zones (Gamalei, 1991; Van Bel and Gamalei, 1992). This geographical distribution suggests a coincidence between temperature and the loading physiology. A differential temperature sensitivity of symplasmic and apoplasmic phloem loading has been substantiated (Gamalei *et al.*, 1992, 1994; Turgeon *et al.*, 1993). Symplasmic phloem loading appeared to be knocked out at temperatures below 10°C, owing to closure of the plasmodesmata (Gamalei *et al.*, 1994). The temperature-induced elimination would explain the scarce occurrence of herbaceous species with a symplasmic minor vein configuration in temperate and boreal zones as well as in mountainous regions (Gamalei, 1990; Van Bel and Gamalei, 1992). These habitats are dominated by herbs executing apoplasmic phloem loading, which continues to be operative at temperatures a few degrees above the freezing point (Gamalei *et al.*, 1992).

The dominant symplasmic vein configuration in northern hemisphere temperate-zone trees (Gamalei, 1989) does not conform with a universal association between climate and mode of phloem loading. It raises the question as to how these species with a symplasmic configuration survive the temperate conditions; the trees may be able to switch to apoplasmic phloem loading when the temperature drops below 10°C by using an "overflow mechanism" (Van Bel, 1992). When the temperature falls below the point at which the plasmodesmata between mesophyll and intermediary cells close, sugars may leak from the mesophyll cells and be absorbed by carriers of the SE/CC complex.

If sugar concentration and sugar species determine pressure flow (Section IV,B) and, hence, the C allocation patterns (Fig. 7), the mode of phloem loading might influence the growth strategy. For instance, herbaceous plants in temperate habitats with a relatively short growing season would benefit from apoplasmic phloem loading being related to a high sugar retention capacity of the sieve tubes in the transport phloem (Fig. 7). These properties would lead to rapid and dominant C channeling to the terminal sinks and an inherently high RGR. Conversely, a low pressure flow coupled with a high leakage capacity of the transport phloem would enable growth strategies seen in low-RGR species in response to stress factors (Grime, 1979). It would allow a higher investment in structural adaptations (such as woody stems) and defense mechanisms against environmental assaults.

An interesting prospect to be investigated is the existence of various strategies combining structure and physiology that impact the distribution of organic matter. The channel-associated cells play the major role in these syndromes of phloem physiology that may be associated with the climate and/or the growth strategy. Despite its presumptive syndrome-bound behavior, the phloem remains a dynamic system with numerous control points for the distribution of organic matter. Future investigations have the potential to elucidate the significance of the emerging structural/physiological variety for the survival capacity of plants under specific environmental conditions.

Acknowledgments

The contributions of José Wilmering (Fig. 2b and c), Sylvia Toet (Fig. 2b and c), Ankie Ammerlaan (Fig. 2e), Kristel Perreijn (Fig. 2f), Jayand Achterberg (Fig. 4), Harold van Rijen, Jan Kees van Amerongen, and Frits Kelling (Fig. 6) are gratefully acknowledged. Critical reading of the manuscript by Drs. Dieter Jeschke, John Pate, and Hendrik Poorter is highly appreciated. The author is also much indebted to Marjolein Kortbeek and Dick Smit for excellent artwork.

References

Aloni, B., Wyse, R. E., and Griffith, S. (1986). Sucrose transport and phloem unloading in stem of *Vicia faba:* Possible involvement of a sucrose carrier and osmotic regulation. *Plant Physiol.* **81**, 482–486.

Daie, J. (1987). Sucrose uptake in isolated phloem of celery is a single saturable system. *Planta* **171**, 474–482.

Eschrich, W., Evert, R. F., and Young, J. H. (1972). Solution flow in tubular semipermeable membranes. *Planta* **107**, 279–300.

Gamalei, Y. V. (1985). Characteristics of phloem loading in woody and herbaceous plants. *Fiziol. Rast.* **32**, 866–875.

Gamalei, Y. V. (1989). Structure and function of leaf minor veins in trees and herbs. A taxonomic review. *Trees* **3**, 96–110.

Gamalei, Y. V. (1990). "Leaf Phloem" (in Russian). Nauka, Leningrad.

Gamalei, Y. V. (1991). Phloem loading and its development related to plant evolution from trees to herbs. *Trees* **5**, 50–64.

Gamalei, Y. V., Pakhomova, M. V., and Sjutkina, A. V. (1992). Ecological aspects of phloem export. I. Temperature. *Fiziol. Rast.* **39**, 1068–1079.

Gamalei, Y. V., Van Bel, A. J. E., Pakhomova, M. V., and Sjutkina, A. V. (1994). Temperature effects on the ER-conformation and starch accumulation in leaves with the symplasmic minor vein configuration. *Planta* **194**, 443–453.

Grime, J.P. (1979). "Plant Strategies and Vegetation Processes." John Wiley & Sons, New York.

Grimm, E., Bernhardt, G., Rothe, K., and Jacob, F. (1990). Mechanism of sucrose retrieval along the phloem path—a kinetic approach. *Planta* **182**, 480–485.

Hayes, P. M., Offler, C. E., and Patrick, J. W. (1985). Cellular structures, membrane surface areas and plasmodesmatal frequencies of the stem of *Phaseolus vulgaris* L. in relation to radial photosynthate transfer. *Ann. Bot.* **56**, 125–138.

Horwitz, L. (1958). Some simplified mathematical treatments of translocation in plants. *Plant Physiol.* **33**, 81–93.

King, J., and Hirji, R. (1975). Amino acid transport systems of cultured soybean root cells. *Can. J. Bot.* **18**, 2088–2091.

Lambers, H., and Poorter, H. (1992). Inherent variation in growth rate between higher plants: A search for physiological causes and ecological consequences. *Adv. Ecol. Res.* **23**, 187–261.

Lang, A. (1978). A model of mass flow in the phloem. *Aust. J. Plant Physiol.* **5**, 535–546.

McCutcheon, S. L., and Bown, A. W. (1987). Evidence for a specific glutamate/H^+ cotransport in isolated mesophyll cells. *Plant Physiol.* **83**, 691–697.

Minchin, P. E. H., and Thorpe, M. R. (1984). Apoplastic phloem unloading in the stem of bean. *J. Exp. Bot.* **35**, 538–550.

Minchin, P. E. H., and Thorpe, M. R. (1987). Measurement of unloading and reloading of photo-assimilate within the stem of bean. *J. Exp. Bot.* **38**, 211–220.

Oparka, K. J., Viola, R., Wright, K. M., and Prior, D. A. M. (1992). Sugar transport and metabolism in the potato tuber. *In* "Carbon Partitioning within and between Organisms" (C. J. Pollock, J. F. Farrar, and A. J. Gordon, eds.), pp. 91–114. Bios, Oxford.

Pate, J. S., and Gunning, B. E. S. (1972). Transfer cells. *Annu. Rev. Plant Physiol.* **23**, 173–196.

Patrick, J. W. (1990). Sieve element unloading: Cellular pathway, mechanism and control. *Physiol. Plant.* **78**, 298–308.

Patrick, J. W. (1991). Control of phloem transport to and short-distance transfer in sink regions: An overview. *In* "Recent Advances in Phloem Transport and Assimilate Compartmentation" (J. L. Bonnemain, S. Delrot, W. J. Lucas, and J. Dainty, eds.), pp. 167–177. Ouest Editions, Nantes, France.

Peel, A. J. (1970). Further evidence for the relative immobility of water in sieve tubes of willow. *Physiol. Plant.* **23**, 667–672.

Schulz, A. (1994). Phloem transport and differential unloading in pea seedlings after source and sink manipulations. *Planta* **192**, 239–248.

Sibaoka, T. (1962). Excitable cells in *Mimosa. Science* **137**, 226.

Turgeon, R. (1991). Symplastic phloem loading and the sink-source transition in leaves: A model. *In* "Recent Advances in Phloem Transport and Assimilate Compartmentation" (J. L. Bonnemain, S. Delrot, W. J. Lucas, and J. Dainty, eds.), pp. 18–22. Ouest Editions, Nantes, France.

Turgeon, R., Beebe, D. U., and Gowan, E. (1993). The intermediary cell: Minor vein anatomy and raffinose oligosaccharide synthesis in the Scrophulariaceae. *Planta* **191**, 446–456.

Van Bel, A. J. E. (1974). Different translocation rates of ^{14}C-L-alanine (U) and tritiated water through the xylem vessels of tomato stems. *Acta Bot. Neerl.* **23**, 305–313.

Van Bel, A. J. E. (1976). Different mass transfer rates of labeled sugars and tritiated water in xylem vessels and their dependency on metabolism. *Plant Physiol.* **57**, 911–914.

Van Bel, A. J. E. (1978). Lateral Transport of Amino Acids and Sugars during Their Flow through the Xylem. Ph.D. thesis. University of Utrecht, Utrecht, the Netherlands.

Van Bel, A. J. E. (1984). Quantification of the xylem-to-phloem transfer of amino acids by use of inulin ^{14}C-carboxylic acid as xylem transport marker. *Plant Sci. Lett.* **35**, 81–85.

Van Bel, A. J. E. (1989). Vessel-to-ray transport: Vital step in nitrogen cycling and deposition. *In* "Fast Growing Trees and Nitrogen Fixing Trees" (D. Werner and P. Müller, eds.), pp. 222–231. Gustav Fischer, Stuttgart, Germany.

Van Bel, A. J. E. (1992). Different phloem-loading machineries correlated with the climate. *Acta Bot. Neerl.* **41,** 121–141.

Van Bel, A. J. E. (1993a). Strategies of phloem loading. *Annu. Rev. Plant Physiol. Plant Mol. Biol.* **44,** 253–281.

Van Bel, A. J. E. (1993b). The transport phloem. Specifics of its functioning. *Prog. Bot.* **54,** 134–150.

Van Bel, A. J. E., and Gamalei, Y. V. (1992). Ecophysiology of phloem loading in source leaves. *Plant Cell Environ.* **15,** 265–270.

Van Bel, A. J. E., and Hermans, H. P. (1977). pH dependency of the uptake of glutamine, alanine and glutamic acid in tomato internodes. *Z. Pflanzenphysiol.* **84,** 413–418.

Van Bel, A. J. E., and Kempers, R. (1991). Symplastic isolation of the sieve element-companion cell complex in the phloem of *Ricinus communis* and *Salix alba* stems. *Planta* **183,** 69–76.

Van Bel, A. J. E., and Van der Schoot, C. (1980). Light-stimulated biphasic amino acid uptake by xylem parenchyma cells. *Plant Sci. Lett.* **19,** 101–107.

Van Bel, A. J. E., and Van Rijen, H. V. M. (1994). Microelectrode-recorded development of the symplasmic autonomy of the sieve element/companion cell complex in the stem phloem of *Lupinus luteus* L. *Planta* **192,** 165–175.

Van Bel, A. J. E., and Visser, A. J. (1994). Phloem transport, C/N allocation and interspecific differences in relative growth rate. *In* "A Whole Plant Perspective on Carbon-Nitrogen Interactions" (J. Roy and E. Garnier, eds.), pp. 143–159. Academic Publishing, The Hague, the Netherlands.

Van Bel, A. J. E., Mostert, E., and Borstlap, A. C. (1979). Kinetics of L-alanine escape from xylem vessels. *Plant Physiol.* **63,** 244–247.

Van Bel, A. J. E., Gamalei, Y. V., Ammerlaan, A., and Bik, L. P. M. (1992). Dissimilar phloem loading in leaves with symplasmic or apoplasmic minor-vein configurations. *Planta* **186,** 518–525.

Van Bel, A. J. E., Ammerlaan, A., and Van Dijk, A. A. (1994). A three-step screening procedure to identify the mode of phloem loading in intact leaves. Evidence for symplasmic and apoplasmic phloem loading associated with the type of companion cell. *Planta* **192,** 31–39.

Van der Schoot, C., and Van Bel, A. J. E. (1989). Glass microelectrode measurements of sieve tube membrane potentials in internode discs and petiole strips of tomato (*Solanum lycopersicum* L.). *Protoplasma* **149,** 144–154.

Vreugdenhil, D., and Koot-Gronsveld, E. A. M. (1989). Measurements of pH, sucrose and potassium ions in the phloem of castor bean (*Ricinus communis*) plants. *Physiol. Plant.* **77,** 385–388.

Wolswinkel, P. (1990). Recent progress in research on the role of turgor-sensitive transport in seed development. *Plant Physiol. Biochem.* **28,** 399–410.

Wood, R. M. (1993). Transfer of photosynthates and potassium in the elongating stem of *Phaseolus vulgaris* L. Ph.D. thesis. University of Newcastle, Newcastle, Australia.

Wright, J. P., and Fisher, D. B. (1981). Measurement of the sieve tube membrane potential. *Plant Physiol.* **67,** 845–848.

Zimmermann, M. H., and Ziegler, H. (1975). List of sugars and sugar alcohols in sieve-tube exudates. *In* "Phloem Transport" (M. H. Zimmermann and J. Milburn, eds.), pp. 480–503. Encyclopedia of Plant Physiology. New series, Vol. I. Springer-Verlag, Heidelberg, Germany.

10

Stem Photosynthesis: Extent, Patterns, and Role in Plant Carbon Economy

Erik T. Nilsen

I. Introduction

Leaves are the dominant photosynthetic organ in most species, although photosynthesis can occur in every plant organ, including stems, fruits, flowers, and roots. Among these alternative photosynthetic organs, stems most frequently contribute a significant proportion of whole-plant carbon gain. In fact, stems can often be the primary photosynthetic organ in desert species (Gibson, 1983; Nilsen *et al.,* 1989). Other than leaves and stems, only roots (in the case of some orchid species such as the ghost orchid) rarely, can serve as the primary photosynthetic organ.

Research on photosynthesis by stems originated in the early twentieth century with observations of stem chlorophyll and stem stomata (Cannon, 1905, 1908). Since then many studies have been done on the nature, magnitude, and responsiveness of photosynthetic stems. Before about 1950, studies concentrated on the description of green stem anatomy, measurement of chlorophyll in stem tissue, and documentation of stomata in epidermal layers. During the period of 1950–1970, many researchers measured the magnitude of photosynthesis in stems and calculated the potential contribution of stems to whole-plant carbon gain compared with that of leaves. During 1970–1990, most research concentrated on the comparison between leaf and stem photosynthetic responsiveness to environmental parameters. Most recently, questions about adaptation and acclimation to

Table I   Characteristics of Stem Photosynthesis for Three Generalized Classes
of Species with Chlorophyllous Stem Tissue

Characteristic	Stem photosynthesis	Corticular photosynthesis	CAM stem photosynthesis
Photosynthetic pathway	C_3	C_3	CAM
Stomatal abundance	Frequent	Absent	Frequent
Leaf abundance/ phenology	None–ephemeral	Present	Vestigial
Succulence	Absent	Occasional	Common
Palisade layer	Multiple	Absent	Present
Net photosynthesis	$6-12\ \mu\text{mol m}^{-2}\text{ sec}^{-1}$ (day)	Negative	$10-20\ \mu\text{mol m}^{-2}\text{ sec}^{-1}$ (night)

habitat conditions have become the dominant subjects of research on photosynthetic stems.

Species with photosynthetic stems can be categorized into three classes based on the structural and physiological patterns of the CO_2 diffusion pathway into the stem chloroplast. Those classes include CAM (crassulacean acid metabolism) stem photosynthesis, corticular photosynthesis, and stem photosynthesis (Table 1). This classification scheme is based on both the terminology used in past research on photosynthetic stems and the differences in physiology and anatomy among the three classes.

CAM photosynthesis is a group of physiological pathways, similar to the C_4 pathway, commonly found in leaves and stems of succulent species (Osmond et al., 1982; Ting, 1985). This terminology is selected because the most unusual aspect of stem physiology in this class of plants is the CAM photosynthetic pathway. Many of these species have few, small, vestigial leaves, and photosynthetic succulent stems (e.g., many cacti, and desert euphorbias). The stem photosynthetic organ has abundant stomata (relative to those taxa performing corticular photosynthesis) that open during the night. Leafy members of the cactus family (in the subfamily Perskioideae) perform all CAM photosynthesis by leaves (Nobel and Hartsock, 1986). In members of the subfamily Opuntioideae leaves perform C_3 photosynthesis while stems perform CAM (Nobel and Hartsock, 1986), as do members of some other succulent taxa (Lange and Zuber, 1977; Ting et al., 1983). In addition, leaves and stems of some CAM species can switch between the C_3 pathway under cool and moist conditions and CAM under hot and dry conditions (Winter et al., 1978; Bloom and Troughton, 1979).

Photosynthesis by bark tissues was first referred to as corticular photosynthesis by Strain and Johnson (1963); it had previously been referred to as bark photosynthesis (Pearson and Lawrence, 1958). Corticular photosynthesis is characteristic of the cortex of new shoots in many species, the ray parenchyma cells in the wood of many shrubs and trees, and the bark of a smaller number of woody species (Schaedle, 1975). This class of species with photosynthetic stems is present in a large number of habitats, but it has been documented most frequently in temperate-zone trees. Corticular photosynthesis may be most common in temperate deciduous species because photosynthetic stems reduce winter respiratory carbon drain. However, there are also species from desert environments that perform corticular photosynthesis (Mooney and Strain, 1964; Nedoff *et al.*, 1985; Franco-Vizcaino *et al.*, 1990; Schmitt *et al.*, 1993). Several other points concerning the ecophysiological significance of photosynthetic stems are discussed below (see Section V).

Characteristically, the epidermis of stems with corticular photosynthesis has no or very few stomata. Carbon dioxide diffuses to the cortical chlorenchyma either from the ambient air (through surface cracks or lenticels), the inner spaces of the stem, or inner tissues of the stem. The net photosynthetic rate of stems with corticular photosynthesis is zero to slightly negative. Thus, the primary role of corticular photosynthesis appears to be in the reutilization of respired carbon dioxide from nonphotosynthetic tissues, although chloroplasts in cortical tissues may be significant in other ways as well (discussed in Section V).

In this treatment, the term *stem photosynthesis* is restricted to define the third class of species with photosynthetic stems. In this class, carbon gain occurs by the C_3 pathway through abundant stomata in the stem epidermis (Table I). These stomata open and close in a manner similar to that of C_3 leaves. Carbon fixation occurs in a chlorenchyma tissue just below the epidermis. Furthermore, the chlorophyllous tissue has an anatomy reminiscent of leaf palisades and spongy mesophyll (Gibson, 1983; Comstock and Ehleringer, 1988), and this class of photosynthetic stems is characterized by response curves to climatic conditions (temperature, light, CO_2, etc.) similar to those of C_3 leaves. Stem photosynthesis is found in a large number of families, both herbaceous and woody species, and is commonly found in species that inhabit stressful sites such as deserts, and early successional sites.

None of these three classes of photosynthesis is restricted to stems. For example, CAM photosynthesis is the dominant photosynthetic process in cactus stems, but cacti also have leaves that perform CAM and there are other species that perform CAM in leaves but not stems (members of the Crassulaceae and Aizoaceae). Corticular photosynthesis is also performed by roots, inflorescences, flowers, and submerged aquatics. Stem photosynthesis presents many similarities to C_3 leaf photosynthesis.

Although species with photosynthetic stems are found in a large number of ecosystems and habitats, studies have concentrated on species from desert (40 species) and temperate forest habitats (12 species), accounting for more than 90% of the research articles on this topic. Studies on stem photosynthesis in vines or species from tropical thorn woodlands are uncommon. Comparisons among species with photosynthetic stems from a broad array of habitats are required for a thorough understanding of the diverse ecological significance of photosynthetic stems.

The purpose of this chapter is to consolidate the state of knowledge about photosynthetic stems, and to provide a baseline of information for further research efforts. The chapter is focused on stem photosynthesis because corticular photosynthesis (Schaedle, 1975; Wiebe, 1975) and CAM stem photosynthesis (Kluge and Ting, 1978; Ting, 1985) have been reviewed elsewhere. The chapter begins with evolutionary and taxonomic aspects of plants with prominent photosynthetic stems, then covers the structure and function of photosynthetic stems. In conclusion, the chapter considers the various forms of ecophysiological significance of photosynthesis by stems. The general theme of this chapter is to illustrate the inadequacy of the current state of knowledge for describing or understanding the diversity of structure, function, and ecological significance of photosynthetic stems and to suggest areas for further research.

II. Extent of Stem Photosynthesis

A. An Evolutionary Perspective

The earliest land plants were most likely derived from a family of green algae, probably a group similar to the extant Characeae (Stewart and Rothwell, 1993). These were aquatic multicellular algae whose upright stems were the dominant photosynthetic organs. Stems were also the dominant organ for photosynthesis in early terrestrial vascular plants (about 400 million years ago), because the earliest terrestrial vascular plants (*Cooksonia* and those in the Rhynophyta) performed photosynthesis exclusively by stem tissue, as they had no leaves or roots (Stewart and Rothwell, 1993). In fact, several of the currently surviving groups of ancient plant taxa employ stem photosynthesis exclusively (Ephedraceae, Equisitaceae, and Psilotaceae). The family Psilotaceae is an unusual group because one member (*Psilotum nudum*) is virtually leafless and performs stem photosynthesis exclusively, while species in the other genus of the Psilotaceae (*Tmesipteris*) utilize leaf photosynthesis. Some evolutionary biologists believe that members of the family Psilotaceae may not be as ancient as was previously assumed because of the morphology and anatomy of *P. nudum* (Bierhorst, 1977; Wagner and Smith, 1993). Nevertheless, there is no question that photosynthesis in stems is an ancient characteristic of plants dating back to the origin of land plants.

Although photosynthetic stems are an ancient characteristic of plants, there is no simple association between the evolutionary age of current taxa and the presence of photosynthetic stems. Species representing diverse evolutionary heritages have photosynthetic stems. Published reports document at least 26 families that contain species with stem photosynthesis. In addition, corticular photosynthesis has been studied in six different families and CAM stem photosynthesis in four families. In some cases, most members of a family have prominent[1] photosynthetic stems (Fabaceae, Ephedraceae, and Cactaceae), whereas in other families (Asteraceae, Rhamnaceae, and Scrophulariaceae) prominent stem photosynthesis is common, and in others it may be infrequent (Fagaceae, Cornaceae, and Rutaceae). Furthermore, a wide array of unrelated species in the American deserts have converged on a basic anatomical structure for photosynthetic stems (Gibson, 1983). The nonuniform distribution of species with photosynthetic stems among families of plants suggests multiple evolutionary events leading to the prominence of this trait. Even within one genus it is not uncommon to have a dominance of leafy species with one or a few leafless members surviving only on photosynthetic stems. For example, the genus *Prosopis* has approximately 60 species of which 1 (*P. kuntzii*) is leafless. Thus, in some cases the evolutionary lineage conserved this character, whereas in other cases prominent stem photosynthesis is a derived character within the group.

B. Habitat Requirements

Species with prominent photosynthetic stems are found in a diversity of ecosystems. Microphyllous leaves are often borne by species with photosynthetic stems; not surprisingly, then, photosynthetic stems are common in desert habitats. However, photosynthetic stems also are found on tropical trees, temperate deciduous trees, conifers, vines, and many species in disturbed habitats. In general, stem photosynthesis is found in hot, dry sites with high irradiance (Gibson, 1983). The relatively high occurrence of stem photosynthesis in these habitats is most likely due to the effectiveness of vertical stems in reducing the energy load on the photosynthetic apparatus in high-light environments.

III. Nature of Stem Photosynthetic Apparatus

A. Structure of Photosynthetic Stems

The diversity of taxonomic types, and classes of photosynthetic stems, results in a large diversity of structural characteristics. In general, most photosynthesis occurs in the outer few millimeters of stem in a cortical chlorenchyma tissue. Species with stem chlorenchyma that do not develop a superior cork layer are frequently found in deserts (Gibson, 1983) or other high-light sites. The epidermal tissues may be one or several cell layers thick and the stomata may have a variety of spatial orientations (Gibson, 1983). Stomata are commonly arrayed in columns parallel to the the long axis of the stem. In addition, the stomata are often sunken, in crypts, or covered with trichomes (Gibson, 1983).

Most woody species with stem photosynthesis have a thick chlorenchyma of densely packed cells. The chlorenchyma cells are often long when mature, resembling the palisade cells of leaves, with small substomatal chambers (Fig. 1). In herbaceous or woody species, the stem may have an anatomy similar to that of the leaf on the same plant (Comstock and Ehleringer, 1988). The chlorenchyma often contains or is subtended by corticular parenchyma (Fig. 1), sclerenchyma, or collenchyma, particularly in rushlike stems (Gibson, 1983). There is a large diversity of anatomical patterns in species with stem photosynthesis, which, with the exception of examples in the North American deserts (Gibson, 1983), have yet to be explored in an ecophysiological sense.

Species with corticular photosynthesis also carry out most photosynthesis in the cortical chlorenchyma; however, stomata are absent on the epidermis, and a cork layer develops soon after stem maturation. In some cases,

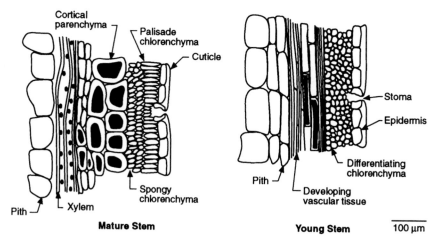

Figure 1   Chlorenchyma and related tissues associated with stem photosynthesis in a suffrutescent chaparral plant from California (*Lotus scoparius*). Young shoots are less than 1 month old, and mature shoots are 14 months old. Note the appearance of palisade chlorenchyma in mature shoots, and the size of substomatal chambers. Cortical parenchyma cells are filled with a mucilage-like substance.

the cork layer develops unevenly over the stem surface, resulting in stripes or patches where light can easily penetrate to chloroplasts in the cortex (Nedoff *et al.*, 1985). Chloroplasts that are deeply imbedded in the ray parenchyma of woody stems can also potentially contribute to corticular photosynthesis (Larcher *et al.*, 1988).

The ultrastructure of stem chloroplasts has been examined in only six species covering both stem and corticular photosynthetic classes (Adams and Strain, 1968; Kriedeman and Buttrose, 1971; Wiebe *et al.*, 1974; Nedoff *et al.*, 1985; Larcher *et al.*, 1988; Rascio *et al.*, 1991). No consistent patterns in stem chloroplast ultrastructure can be gleaned from the available literature. However, it has been reported that relative to leaf plastids the stem plastids may contain a large amount of starch (Kriedeman and Buttrose, 1971), little appressed thylakoid (Wiebe *et al.*, 1974), extensive appressed thylakoids (Nedoff *et al.*, 1985; Rascio *et al.*, 1991), or frequent osmiophilic globules (Adams and Strain, 1968).

B. Biochemical Components

The biochemical components of stem chloroplasts have been evaluated primarily in comparison with leaves. These studies have been limited to measures of chlorophyll, diagnostic gas exchange, and chlorophyll fluorescence kinetics. The first has a long historical record whereas the latter two techniques have been employed only in a few more recent studies. In fact, little is known about the biochemical characteristics of stem chloroplasts.

Many measurements of chlorophyll concentration have been made for stems (Schaedle, 1975, and citations therein). If these values are expressed on a stem surface area basis, stems have chlorophyll concentrations comparable to that of leaves on the same plant. In addition, the ratio of chlorophyll *a* and chlorophyll *b* is similar to that of leaves (Nilsen and Bao, 1990).

Some characteristics of the electron transport chain in stem chloroplasts have been determined by chlorophyll fluorescence techniques (Nedoff *et al.*, 1985; Larcher *et al.*, 1988; Franco-Vizcaino *et al.*, 1990; Rascio *et al.*, 1991; Larcher and Nägele, 1992), oxygen evolution (Ehleringer and Cooper, 1992), and by light response curves (Osmond *et al.*, 1987; Comstock and Ehleringer, 1988; Nilsen *et al.*, 1989; Nilsen, 1992a,b; Nilsen and Karpa, 1994).

Chlorophyll fluorescence kinetics of stem tissues have been studied only in species with corticular photosynthesis. However, gas exchange techniques have been used to study stem photosynthesis. Quantum yield of stem tissue is low [0.01–0.015 mol of CO_2 mol^{-1} PAR (photosynthetically active radiation)] compared with that of leaves (0.025–0.045 mol of CO_2 mol^{-1} PAR) when measured by steady state CO_2 gas exchange techniques (Comstock and Ehleringer, 1988; Nilsen *et al.*, 1989; Nilsen, 1992a). In contrast, quantum yield measured by oxygen electrode techniques is the same (approximately 100 mmol of O_2 mol^{-1} PAR) in stem and leaf tissue (Osmond *et al.*, 1987; Ehleringer and Cooper, 1992). The contrasting results obtained by CO_2 uptake or O_2 evolution may be due in part to the high CO_2 concentration used in oxygen electrode techniques. If stem chloroplasts could acclimate to lower light due to the shading effect of the epidermal tissues one would expect a higher quantum yield compared with leaves on the same plant. Quantitative studies of chloroplast density in stem cortical cells or the density of photochemical components in stem chloroplasts will help clarify the relationships between quantum yield of leaves and stems.

The only technique used to evaluate carbon reduction aspects of photosynthesis in stem chloroplasts as of this date has been CO_2 response curves (Fig. 2). In all reported cases, the CO_2 saturated rate of stem photosynthesis is lower than that for leaves (Osmond *et al.*, 1987; Comstock and Ehleringer, 1988; Nilsen *et al.*, 1989; Nilsen, 1992b). The low CO_2 saturated rate of stem photosynthesis compared to leaves could be due to many factors, including limitation by electron transport capacity, limitation by triose phosphate utilization, or limitation by ribulose 1,5-bisphosphate (RUBP) regeneration, but there is currently no evidence to support any of these mechanisms. The photosynthetic rate at low CO_2 concentration indicates that stem chlo-

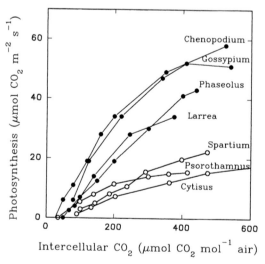

Figure 2 Stem photosynthetic responses to intercellular carbon dioxide concentration in several species performing stem photosynthesis (open symbols) or leaf photosynthesis (solid symbols) in similar habitats. (Data are redrawn from the following sources: *Spartium* and *Cytisus* from Nilsen and Karpa, 1994; *Psorothamnus* from Nilsen *et al.*, 1989; *Chenopodium* and *Larrea* from Pearcy and Ehleringer, 1984; *Gossypium* from Osmond *et al.*, 1982; *Phaseolus* from von Caemmerer and Farquhar, 1981.)

roplasts have a relatively low quantity of Rubisco (ribulose-bisphosphate carboxylase, EC 4.1.1.39) or a low activation state of Rubisco compared with leaves. This is suggested by the low mesophyll conductance (slope of photosynthesis vs intercellular CO_2 concentration at low CO_2 concentration) for stems compared with that of leaves (Fig. 2). Clearly, many aspects of the biochemistry of stem photosynthesis require further research before the physiological functions of stem photosynthesis can be understood.

C. Responses of Stem Photosynthesis to Resource Variation

Thermal responses of stem photosynthesis have been measured in a number of species from several different habitats (Fig. 3). Thermal optima are commonly between 20 and 30°C, and some species from cooler environments (*Cytisus*) have cooler thermal optima for stem photosynthesis compared with those from warmer environments (Fig. 3). In all cases, the thermal optimum range is broad (the temperature range in which stem photosynthesis is above 90% of its maximum rate), frequently encompassing 15°C. Most frequently the optimum temperature for stem photosynthesis reflects the ambient temperature of early growing season conditions (Adams

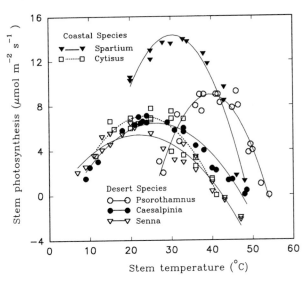

Figure 3 Temperature response curves for several species performing stem photosynthesis during the summer months. These species represent a gradient from coastal (cooler) to desert (warmer) sites. (□) *Cytisus scoparius,* a coastal species (Nilsen and Karpa, 1994); (▼) *Spartium junceum,* an inland mountain chaparral species (Nilsen and Karpa, 1994); (▽) *Senna armata,* a high-elevation (650 m) desert shrub from the Mojave; (●) *Caesalpinia virgata,* a low-elevation (50 m) shrub from the Sonoran Desert (Nilsen and Sharifi, 1994a); (○) *Psorothamnus spinosus,* a low-elevation (− 70 m) tree from the Sonoran Desert (Nilsen *et al.*, 1989).

and Strain, 1969; Depuit and Caldwell, 1975; Comstock and Ehleringer, 1988; Nilsen and Karpa, 1994; Nilsen and Sharifi, 1994b). In contrast to this evidence for adaptation of stem photosynthesis to the prevailing thermal conditions, there is little evidence for seasonal acclimation: a seasonal change in the thermal optimum for stem photosynthesis has been found in one Mojave Desert species while three other species from various habitats had no seasonal acclimation (Nilsen and Karpa, 1994; Nilsen and Sharifi, 1994b).

Stem conductance of species with stem photosynthesis responds linearly to atmospheric vapor pressure (Osmond *et al.*, 1987; Nilsen *et al.*, 1989; Nilsen, 1992a; Nilsen and Karpa, 1994; Nilsen and Sharifi, 1994a). In general, measurements of stem conductance to water vapor in natural systems are low, between 50 and 200 mmol m^{-2} sec^{-1} (Nilsen *et al.*, 1993), which is similar to that for conifer foliage. However, the slope of decreasing conductance with increasing vapor pressure deficit can be similar to that of deciduous leaves (Osmond *et al.*, 1987; Nilsen 1992a).

Seasonal acclimation of the relationship between stem stomatal conductance and atmospheric vapor pressure occurs in some desert species (e.g., *Caesalpinia* in Fig. 4). High conductances occur at the lower vapor pressures during the winter and spring, and there is a rapid decrease in conductance with increasing vapor pressure deficit. In contrast, stem conductance dur-

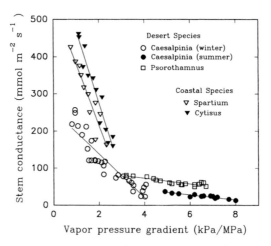

Figure 4 Vapor pressure response curves for summer stem conductance of several species from different habitats, and winter stem conductance for one species. Two species are from coastal habitats [*Cytisus scoparius* (▼) and *Spartium junceum* (▽), redrawn from Nilsen *et al.* (1993)], and three species are from desert habitats [*Caesalpinia virgata* in winter (○) and summer (●) (Nilsen and Sharifi, 1994a), and *Psorothamnus spinosus* (□), redrawn from Nilsen *et al.*, 1989].

ing the summer is lower and there is little response of conductance to vapor pressure.

The response between stem conductance and atmospheric vapor pressure may be related to habitat, as has been shown for leaves of some species (Mooney and Chu, 1983). Species from cool, moist, coastal habitats have greater stem conductance and a greater sensitivity to vapor pressure than those from desert habitats (Fig. 4). The differences in vapor response curves for stem conductance among species from different habitats may not be due to the impacts of water potential because many of these species have similar shoot water potential but different seasonal vapor pressure deficit responses (Nilsen and Karpa, 1994; Nilsen and Sharifi, 1994a).

Generally, stem photosynthesis has been shown to be sensitive to water stress (Nilsen, 1992a; Bossard and Rejmanek, 1992), but less sensitive than is leaf photosynthesis (Comstock and Ehleringer, 1988; Nilsen, 1992a). Thus, at low water potential the relative importance of carbon gain by stems increases compared to that of leaves. However, there are differences among species. For example (Nilsen and Karpa, 1994; Nilsen and Sharifi, 1994b), stem photosynthesis decreased with water potential in a similar manner for two coastal broom species (*Cytisus scoparius* and *Spartium junceum*), but water potential had minimal impact on stem photosynthesis in two desert species (*Senna armata* and *Caesalpinia virgata*). In contrast, when compared to the same species at high water potential stem photosynthesis of the desert species *Hymenoclea salsola* decreased by 38% with a shoot water potential of -2.3 MPa (Comstock and Ehleringer, 1988), and was more susceptible to photoinhibition (Ehleringer and Cooper, 1992).

The association between tissue nitrogen concentration and stem photosynthesis is not consistent among species. In some cases an excellent relationship between bulk stem nitrogen concentration and stem photosynthesis has been reported (Nilsen and Karpa, 1994). However, in other species a weak or no correlation between stem nitrogen concentration and stem photosynthesis was reported (Comstock and Ehleringer, 1988; Comstock *et al.*, 1988; Nilsen and Sharifi, 1994b). This variable association between stem nitrogen and stem photosynthesis among species may be due to the low variance in nitrogen concentration of stems in deserts and the high variance of other environmental characteristics. Furthermore, a bulk stem nitrogen analysis may miss the changing allocation of nitrogen between the chlorenchyma and the xylem parenchyma (see Pate and Jeschke [8] in this volume) and therefore obscure the relationship between chlorenchyma nitrogen and stem photosynthesis.

In an experiment in which nitrogen availability was varied and other factors held constant, there was a significant decrease in stem photosynthesis with a decrease in stem nitrogen (Nilsen, 1992b). Although the nitrogen concentrations and photosynthetic rates of these stems were lower than in leaves on the same plant, the slope of the relationship between nitrogen concentration and photosynthesis was the same for leaves and stems (Nilsen, 1992b). Controlled studies of stem photosynthetic response to stem chlorenchyma nitrogen content need to be done on both nitrogen-fixing and nonfixing species to improve our understanding of the impact of nitrogen limitation on stem photosynthesis.

IV. Ecophysiological Significance

A. Canopy Carbon Gain

In species with stem photosynthesis the stem may be the sole supplier of carbon to the plant. In some species leaves are rudimentary and extremely ephemeral (Nilsen *et al.*, 1989; Nilsen and Sharifi, 1994a); thus stems provide almost all the carbon gain. In species that have microphyllous leaves, stem carbon gain occurs in all seasons (Comstock *et al.*, 1988; Nilsen and Sharifi, 1994a), and most of the annual carbon gain by stems occurs when leaves are nonphotosynthetic or abscised.

Maximum stem photosynthesis is commonly at or below 10 μmol m^{-2} sec^{-1} in the cool and moist season when leaves are present (Table II). However, during below-optimal growth periods, both leaf and stem photosynthesis are inhibited, but stem photosynthesis is inhibited less than leaf photosynthesis (Nilsen and Bao, 1990; Nilsen, 1992a). Thus, under stressful conditions stems increase their proportional contribution to canopy carbon gain compared with leaves.

Table II   A Selection of Maximum Net Stem Photosynthesis (P_{max}) Determinations Reported for a Diversity of Species with Stem Photosynthesis during the Cool, Moist Season

Species	Habitat	Rate (μmol m^{-2} sec^{-1})	Ref.
Spartium junceum	Chaparral	7.8	Nilsen *et al.* (1993)
Cytisus scoparius	Coastal	8.7	Nilsen *et al.* (1993)
Psorothamnus spinosus	Desert	7.8	Nilsen *et al.* (1989)
Bebbia juncea	Desert	3.9	Schmitt *et al.* (1993)
Hymenoclea salsola	Desert	21.6[a]	Comstock and Ehleringer (1988)
Eriogonum inflatum	Desert	12–15	Osmond *et al.* (1987)
Cercidium floridum	Desert	2.8[b]	Adams and Strain (1969)
Senna armata	Desert	6.3	Nilsen and Sharifi (1994a)
Caesalpinia virgata	Desert	7.8	Nilsen and Sharifi (1994a)

[a]Photosynthesis calculated on a projected stem area basis.
[b]Units are converted from mg dm^{-2} hr^{-1}.

The vertical orientation of stems with stem photosynthesis may be critical for their contribution to carbon gain during the summer in desert habitats. Many species with stem photosynthesis have vertical stems in all habitats. However, there are notable exceptions in desert habitats. For example, *Cercidium floridum* and *Psorothamnus spinosus* have dense canopies with stems at a multitude of angles. In the absence of vertical orientation Ehleringer and Cooper (1992) suggest that stem photosynthesis in some species would suffer considerable photoinhibition during summer months, when stems have low water potential. Thus, the vertical orientation of stems can mitigate the high energy load of midday in the summer, preventing potential photoinhibition and allowing the maintenance of carbon gain by stems.

Many species with stem photosynthesis are nitrogen-fixing taxa (Harvey, 1972; Nilsen *et al.*,1989, 1993; Bossard and Rejmanek, 1992; Nilsen and Karpa, 1994), and root nodules require a constant supply of carbon to remain functional. Photosynthetic stems may provide a constant supply of carbon for root nodules during periods of stress that induce leaf abscission, or during periods of intense herbivory (Bossard and Rejmanek, 1992). Thus, the presence of a canopy with stem photosynthesis may prevent nodule atrophy in legumes under stressful conditions, and allow for a rapid reinitiation of nitrogen fixation following suboptimal growth conditions.

B. Water Use Efficiency

Some studies have found a lower water use efficiency in stems compared with leaves on the same plant (Depuit and Caldwell, 1975; Nilsen and Bao, 1990), whereas others have shown higher efficiency (Comstock and Ehleringer, 1988; Osmond *et al.*, 1987). The instantaneous water use efficiency patterns derived from gas exchange studies have been verified by the use of carbon isotope composition as an integrated measure of water use efficiency. In most cases, stem tissues have a lower carbon isotope discrimination than leaves on the same plant, indicating a higher water use efficiency for stems (Osmond *et al.*, 1987; Ehleringer *et al.*, 1987, 1992; Comstock and Ehleringer, 1992), although the same pattern could result from a higher temperature of stems compared with leaves on the same plant. It is possible that the chlorenchyma of photosynthetic stems is refixing some of the respired CO_2 coming from the inner tissues of the stem. In such a scenario the stem isotopic composition would be more depleted in ^{13}C, such that the stem $\delta^{13}C$ signature (O'Leary, 1993) would be similar to or more negative than the leaves. Thus, the effect of higher water use efficiency on carbon isotope composition will be counteracted by substantial refixation of respired CO_2. If the difference between the $\delta^{13}C$ signatures of stems and leaves does represent a difference in water use efficiency, then the higher water use efficiency for stems compared to leaves may be important for canopy carbon gain during the hot and dry summers in desert habitats.

C. Nutrient Use Efficiency

The only nutrient that has been investigated in relation to stem photosynthesis is nitrogen. Nitrogen use efficiency in desert taxa has been measured as 47–62 μmol of CO_2 (mol N)$^{-1}$ sec^{-1} (Comstock and Ehleringer, 1988). In a mediterranean legume, nitrogen use efficiency is approximately 40 μmol of CO_2 (mol N)$^{-1}$ sec^{-1} (calculated from data in Nilsen, 1992b). These nitrogen use efficiencies are low compared to those of leaves [in the range of 200–300 μmol of CO_2 (mol N)$^{-1}$ sec^{-1}]. The low nitrogen use efficiency of stems compared with leaves would suggest that stem photosynthesis is of lesser importance than leaf photosynthesis during nitrogen limitation. However, the ratio of stem area to leaf area increased in low soil nitrogen treatments for *S. junceum* (Nilsen, 1992b) and, when nitrogen was withheld, the concentration of nitrogen in leaf tissues decreased more than in stem tissues. Therefore, stem photosynthesis decreased less than leaf photosynthesis during whole-plant nitrogen limitation, and the proportional importance of stems to canopy carbon gain increased (Nilsen, 1992b).

V. Summary and Goals for Future Research

There are a diversity of species in many habitats that perform photosynthesis near the surface of the stem. While this trait is as old as the origin of terrestrial plants, stem photosynthesis has also developed more recently in many different phylogenetic lines. The Fabaceae and Asteraceae may be the families with the greatest diversity of stem photosynthetic species.

Cortical photosynthesis occurs in desert and temperate forest species, probably with the primary purpose of recapturing respired CO_2 from other organs. CAM stem photosynthesis occurs in succulent species to maximize water use efficiency. Stem photosynthesis is similar to C_3 leaf photosynthesis and occurs in species inhabiting a diversity of high-light sites. Stem photosynthesis can make a major contribution to plant carbon gain, particularly during periods of environmental stress.

Current research on photosynthetic stems has focused only on species from desert and temperate forest habitats. Little research has been done in comparing species from different habitats or examining the seasonal flexibility of photosynthetic stems. We know little about the biochemical regulation of stem photosynthesis, in particular the relative importance of limitations by RUBP, Rubisco, the electron transport chain, or the inorganic phosphorus pool. Furthermore, we know nothing about the impact of carbon translocation to and from the phloem (see Van Bel [9] in this volume) on the photosynthetic activity of stems.

The significance of stem photosynthesis to carbon balance during stress, and the potential importance of stem carbon gain to nodule maintenance, are critical for understanding stress tolerance in legumes, especially given the high incidence of stem photosynthesis in nitrogen-fixing species. A foundation of knowledge needs to be developed through studies of the biochemical regulation of stem photosynthesis, and its interaction with nitrogen allocation patterns among a wide variety of species and habitats. This knowledge base could then be drawn on to understand the significance of stem photosynthesis to plant evolution in many taxa (particularly the legumes), and to develop applications for improving stress tolerance in agricultural systems utilizing legumes.

Another interesting line of research concerns the other possible areas of significance of stem chloroplasts. For example, do stem chloroplasts produce enough oxygen to compensate for oxygen limitation in the inner tissues of stems? Do stem chloroplasts serve as a light sensor for young developing stems? Do stem chloroplasts provide an important nitrate reduction function in the nitrogen metabolism of stem tissues (see Pate and Jeschke [8] in this volume)?

The trade-offs between the benefits of having photosynthetic stems and the resulting constraints to plant structure and function need to be evaluated. For example, the carbon gain capacity of stems is dependent on light penetration to the chlorenchyma. Therefore, photosynthetic stems cannot have extensive cork development. What is the cost of a thin bark to stem herbivore defense (see Bryant and Raffa [16] in this volume)? Which is more important for herbivory defense: to have stem photosynthesis as a mechanism to enhance recovery from leaf herbivory, or to have an extensive bark for protection against stem insects? Stem photosynthesis requires surface stomata, but these are also the sites where fungal pathogens can enter the stem cortex. Are species with stem photosynthesis more susceptible to stem pathogens (see Shain [17] in this volume)? Canopy architecture is critical for displaying leaves in a manner that absorbs radiation optimally (see Givnish [1] in this volume). How does the absence of leaves impact the nature of canopy architecture? How does the density of canopy stems impact light penetration to photosynthetic stems? Are canopies of species with stem photosynthesis designed to maximize light absorption? It would be intriguing to use structural modeling techniques to determine the consequences of changing stem architecture on whole-canopy light absorption.

The interactions between leaves and photosynthetic stems need to be studied in order to understand the dynamics of resource use by species with both photosynthetic organs. When leaves are produced in the spring what proportion of the carbon needed for leaf construction comes from stem photosynthesis? Is stem photosynthesis correlated with reduced carbohydrate storage in the xylem? If stem photosynthesis is blocked, does this change the photosynthetic performance or longevity of leaves? When resources are accumulated by roots, how are they apportioned to stem and leaf? Does any photosynthate from leaves contribute to the maintenance cost of chlorenchyma tissues? Does the subtending layer of cortical fibers interfere with photosynthate transfer from stem chlorenchyma to phloem? Does chlorenchyma have phloem loading cells that operate similarly to that in leaves (see Van Bel [9] in this volume)? What are the interactions between stem-dwelling organisms (see Ingham and Moldenke [11] in this volume), plant nutrient availability, and stem photosynthesis?

A multitude of research questions is possible because the basic background research on stem photosynthesis is limited. As some of these questions are answered we will begin to integrate the significance of stem photosynthesis with the ecophysiology of plants.

Acknowledgments

This chapter was produced with support from the National Science Foundation Grant #BSR 91–19235 to E. T. Nilsen. Many thanks to A. Van Bel for reviewing an early draft and to A. Gibson for comments on anatomical considerations.

References

Adams, M., and Strain, B. R. (1968). Photosynthesis in stems and leaves of *Cercidium floridum:* Spring and summer diurnal field response in relation to temperature. *Oecol. Plant.* **3,** 285–297.

Adams, M., and Strain, B. R. (1969). Seasonal photosynthetic rates in stems of *Cercidium floridum* Benth. *Photosynthesis* **3,** 55–62.

Bierhorst, D. W. (1977). The systematic position of *Psilotum* and *Tmesipteris. Brittonia* **29,** 3–13.

Bloom, A.J., and Troughton, J. H. (1979). High productivity and photosynthetic flexibility in a CAM plant. *Oecologia* **38,** 35–43.

Bossard, C., and Rejmanek, M. (1992). Why have green stems? *Funct. Ecol.* **6,** 197–205.

Cannon, W. (1905). On the transpiration of *Fouqueria splendens. Bull. Torrey Bot. Club* **32,** 397–414.

Cannon, W. (1908). The topography of the chlorophyll apparatus in desert plants. *Carnegie Inst. Wash. Publ.* **98.**

Comstock, J. P., and Ehleringer, J. R. (1988). Contrasting photosynthetic behavior in leaves and twigs of *Hymenoclea salsola,* a green-twigged warm desert shrub. *Am. J. Bot.* **75,** 1360–1370.

Comstock, J. P., and Ehleringer, J. R. (1992). Correlating genetic variation in carbon isotope composition with complex climate gradients. *Proc. Nat. Acad. Sci. U.S.A.* **89,** 7747–7751.

Comstock, J., Cooper, Y., and Ehleringer, J. R. (1988). Seasonal patterns of canopy development and carbon gain in nineteen warm desert shrub species. *Oecologia* **75,** 327–335.

DePuit, E., and Caldwell, M. M. (1975). Stem and leaf gas exchange of two arid land shrubs. *Am. J. Bot.* **62,** 954–961.

Ehleringer, J. R., and Cooper, T. (1992). On the role of orientation in reducing photoinhibitory damage in photosynthetic-twig desert shrubs. *Plant Cell Environ.* **15,** 301–306.

Ehleringer, J. R., Comstock, J. P., and Cooper, T. (1987). Leaf-twig carbon isotope ratio differences in photosynthetic-twig desert shrubs. *Oecologia* **71,** 318–320.

Ehleringer, J. R., Phillips, S. L., and Comstock, J. P. (1992). Seasonal variation in the carbon isotope composition of desert plants. *Funct. Ecol.* **6,** 396–404.

Franco-Vizcaino, E., Goldstein, G., and Ting, I. P. (1990). Comparative gas exchange of leaves and bark in three stem succulents of Baja California. *Am. J. Bot.* **77,** 1272–1278.

Gibson, A. (1983). Anatomy of photosynthetic old stems of nonsucculent dicotyledons from North American deserts. *Bot. Gaz.* **144,** 347–362.

Harvey, D. M. (1972). Carbon dioxide photoassimilation in normal-leaved and mutant forms of *Pisum sativum* L. *Ann. Bot.* **36,** 981–991.

Kluge, M., and Ting, I. P. (1978). "Crassulacean Acid Metabolism." Ecology series, Vol. 30. Springer-Verlag, New York.

Kriedeman, P., and Buttrose, M. S. (1971). Chlorophyll content and photosynthetic activity within woody shoots of *Vitis vinifera* L. *Photosynthesis* **5,** 22–27.

Lange, O. L., and Zuber, M. (1977). *Frerea indica,* a stem succulent CAM plant with deciduous C_3 leaves. *Oecologia* **31,** 67–72.

Larcher, W., and Nägele, M. (1992). Changes in photosynthetic activity of buds and stem tissues of *Fagus sylvatica* during winter. *Trees* **6,** 91–95.

Larcher, W., Lutz, C., Nägele, M., and Bodner, H. (1988). Photosynthetic functioning and ultrastructure of chloroplasts in stem tissues of *Fagus sylvatica. J. Plant Physiol.* **132,** 731–737.

Mooney, H. A., and Chu, C. (1983). Stomatal responses to humidity of coastal and interior populations of a California shrub. *Oecologia* **57,** 148–150.

Mooney, H. A., and Strain, B. R. (1964). Bark photosynthesis in ocotillo. *Madroño* **17,** 230–233.

Nedoff, J., Ting, I. P., and Lord, E. (1985). Structure and function of the green stem tissue of ocotillo (*Fouquieria splendens*). *Am. J. Bot.* **72,** 143–151.

Nilsen, E. T. (1992a). The influence of water stress on leaf and stem photosynthesis in *Spartium junceum* L. *Plant Cell Environ.* **15,** 455–461.

Nilsen, E. T. (1992b). Partitioning growth and photosynthesis between leaves and stems during nitrogen limitation in *Spartium junceum. Am. J. Bot.* **79,** 1217–1223.

Nilsen, E. T., and Bao, Y. (1990). The influence of water stress on stem and leaf photosynthesis in *Glycine max* and *Spartium junceum* (Leguminosae). *Am. J. Bot.* **77,** 1007–1015.

Nilsen, E. T., and Karpa, D. (1994). Seasonal acclimation of stem photosynthesis in two invasive, naturalized legume species from coastal habitats of California. *Photosynthetica* **30,** 77–90.

Nilsen, E. T., and Sharifi, M. R. (1994a). Seasonal acclimation of stem photosynthesis in woody legume species from the Mojave and Sonoran deserts of California. *Plant Physiol.* **105,** 1385–1391.

Nilsen, E. T., and Sharifi, M. R. (1994b). Gas exchange characteristics of two stem photosynthesizing legumes growing at two elevations in the California desert. *Flora* (submitted).

Nilsen, E. T., Meinzer, F., and Rundel, P. W. (1989). Stem photosynthesis in *Psorothamnus spinosus* (smoke tree) in the Sonoran desert of California. *Oecologia* **79,** 193–197.

Nilsen, E. T., Karpa, D., Mooney, H. A., and Field, C. B. (1993). Patterns of stem photosynthesis in two invasive legume species of coastal California. *Am. J. Bot.* **80,** 1126–1136.

Nobel, P. S., and Hartsock, T. (1986). Leaf and stem CO_2 uptake in the three subfamilies of the Cactaceae. *Plant Physiol.* **80,** 913–917.

O'Leary, M. (1993). Biochemical basis of carbon isotope fractionation. *In* "Stable Isotopes and Plant Carbon–Water Relations" (J. R. Ehleringer, A. E. Hall, and G. D. Farquhar, eds.), pp. 19–26. Academic Press, San Diego.

Osmond, C. B., Winter, K., and Ziegler, H. (1982). Functional significance of different pathways of CO_2 fixation in photosynthesis. *In* "Physiological Plant Ecology II. Water Relations and Carbon Assimilation" (O. L. Lange, P. S. Nobel, C. B. Osmond, and H. Ziegler, eds.), pp. 479–548. Springer-Verlag, Berlin.

Osmond, C., Smith, S., Gui-Ying, B., and Sharkey, T. (1987). Stem photosynthesis in a desert ephemeral, *Eriogonum inflatum.* Characterization of leaf and stem CO_2 fixation and H_2O vapor exchange under controlled conditions. *Oecologia* **72,** 542–549.

Pearcy, R. W., and Ehleringer, J. R. (1984). Comparative ecophysiology of C_3 and C_4 plants. *Plant Cell Environ.* **7**, 1–13.

Pearson, L., and Lawrence, D. (1958). Photosynthesis in aspen bark. *Am. J. Bot.* **45**, 383–387.

Rascio, N., Mariani, P., Tommasini, E., Bodner, M., and Larcher, W. (1991). Photosynthetic strategies in leaves and stems of *Egeria densa. Planta* **185**, 297–303.

Schaedle, M. (1975). Tree photosynthesis. *Annu. Rev. Plant Physiol.* **26**, 101–115.

Schmitt, A. K., Martin, C. E., Loeschen, V. S., and Schmitt, A. (1993). Mid-summer gas exchange and water relations of seven C_3 species in a desert wash in Baja California, *Mex. J. Arid Environ.* **24**, 155–164.

Stewart, W. N., and Rothwell, G. W. (1993). "Paleobiology and the Evolution of Plants." Cambridge University Press, New York.

Strain, B., and Johnson, P. (1963). Corticular photosynthesis and growth in *Populus tremuloides. Ecology* **44**, 581–584.

Ting, I. P. (1985). Crassulacean acid metabolism. *Annu. Rev. Plant Physiol.* **28**, 355–377.

Ting, I. P., Sternberg, L. O., and DeNiro, M. J. (1983). Variable photosynthetic metabolism in leaves and stems of *Cissus quadrangularis* L. *Plant Physiol.* **71**, 677–679.

von Caemmerer, S., and Farquhar, G. D. (1981). Some relationships between the biochemistry of Photosynthesis and the gas exchange of leaves. *Planta* **153**, 376–387

Wagner, W. H., Jr., and Smith, A. R. (1993). Pteridophytes. *In* "Flora of North America" (N. R. Morin, ed.), Vol. 1, pp. 247–266. Oxford University Press, New York.

Wiebe, H. (1975). Photosynthesis in wood. *Physiol. Plant.* **33**, 245–246.

Wiebe, H., Al-Saadi, H. A., and Kimball, S. (1974). Photosynthesis in the anomalous secondary wood of *Atriplex confertifolia. Am. J. Bot.* **61**, 444–448.

Winter, K., Lüttge, U., Winter, E., and Troughton, J. H. (1978). Seasonal shift from C_3 photosynthesis to crassulacean acid metabolism in *Mesembryanthemum crystallinum* growing in its natural environment. *Oecologia* **34**, 225–237.

11

Microflora and Microfauna on Stems and Trunks: Diversity, Food Webs, and Effects on Plants

E. R. Ingham and A. R. Moldenke

I. Introduction

Complex ecosystems exist on the surfaces of plants (Campbell, 1985; Andrews and Hirano, 1992; Stephenson, 1989). These ecosystems exhibit significant spatial variability, daily and seasonal cycles, and successional processes. The abundance, activity, function, and species diversity or community composition of each organism group on the surface of a plant vary greatly depending on plant species, plant health, abiotic factors, and the presence of other organisms, especially predators. In general the groups that comprise plant surface ecosystems are (1) bacteria and fungi growing on plant exudates or surface cells, (2) epiphytes such as algae, bryophytes, vines, and parasitic plants, (3) pathogens including virus, bacteria, fungi, and possibly protozoa, (4) predators of these first three groups, including protozoa that feed on bacteria, nematodes that feed on bacteria and fungi, and microarthropods/insects such as mites and spiders that feed on fungi, nematodes, and other insects. Larger organisms could be considered part of this plant surface foot web, but the focus of this chapter is limited to organisms that live their entire life on the surface of plants.

This chapter focuses on the phyllosphere, that is, the above-ground surfaces of the plant including stems and trunks. The phyllosphere food web has not been studied extensively, and thus some functions are hypothesized on the basis of what occurs in the rhizosphere, that is, the root-associated surfaces of the plant. Rhizosphere food web structure and function are summarized in Hendrix *et al.* (1986), Coleman *et al.* (1992), Ingham *et al.* (1985), and Moore *et al.* (1991).

In both the rhizosphere and phyllosphere, food web structure and function are strongly influenced by (1) colonization processes (e.g., Pedgley, 1991), (2) moisture and temperature regimes, and (3) exudate production by the plant. The composition of exudates produced by leaf surfaces (Juniper, 1991) and by stems (Andrews, 1992) varies with the species of plant, plant health, and soil type. These exudates serve as selective substrates for organism growth in the phyllosphere. However, substrates are not the only selective forces operating in the phyllosphere. To reach the phyllosphere, organisms must move through the atmosphere (Pedgley, 1991), just as rhizosphere organisms must move through the soil (Paul and Clark, 1990). Movement through soil requires different adaptations than movement through the atmosphere, especially adaptations to ultraviolet (UV) radiation, humidity, and transportation, either by wind or on the surface of another organism, such as an insect, small mammal, or bird. For these reasons, the species composition of each organism group in the phyllosphere will be different from that in the rhizosphere, although different taxonomic groups may perform similar functions. In the remainder of this chapter, the process of immigration/emigration is not further considered, but is clearly of great importance in determining which organisms establish and survive on plant surfaces.

II. Organisms in the Food Web and Their Importance for Plant Growth

Organisms growing on plant surfaces can significantly influence plant productivity. Interactions between predators (e.g., protozoa and nematodes) and prey (e.g., saprophytic bacteria and fungi) influence nutrient availability to the plant, especially nitrogen availability, as water moves through the canopy and along stems and trunks (Carroll, 1981). Two important functions are controlled by predator–prey interactions: (1) retention of N in microbial biomass and secondary metabolites, that is, immobilization processes, and (2) the production of plant-available nitrogen, that is, mineralization (Hendrix *et al.*, 1986; Ingham *et al.*, 1985; Coleman *et al.*, 1992).

From the point of view of a plant, mineralization and immobilization rates must be proportionally balanced. When plants are rapidly growing, mineralization must be proportionally greater than immobilization, such that mineral N is available to the plants. But when plants are not rapidly growing, N should be retained in organic forms and not lost to ground water or erosion. This balancing between immobilization and mineralization of nutrients improves for plants as food web complexity, and therefore ecosystem productivity, increases (Moore *et al.,* 1991).

Control of ecosystem processes by detrital or plant-based food web organisms was also demonstrated by Benedict *et al.* (1991). This summary of the literature indicates that bacteria cause both quantitative and qualitative shifts in concentrations of tannins, terpene aldehydes, and monoterpenes in the air surrounding flower buds and leaves, which, in turn, alters plant secondary metabolism. Following secondary metabolite production by plant surface-dwelling organisms, and nutrient mineralization controlled by predator–prey interactions, plants can adsorb nutrients in stem flow either through above-ground surfaces, or after incorporation into the soil (Jones, 1991).

The second process involves competition by specific species of plant surface-adapted bacteria and fungi for space and nutrients, resulting in prevention of pathogen and parasite growth (Fokkema, 1991; Jones, 1991; Juniper, 1991; Krischik, 1991; Clay, 1992). Mycorrhizal fungi in the rhizosphere perform much the same functional role (Ingham and Molina, 1991). It is beyond the scope of this chapter to discuss plant–microbe interactions following wounding or pathogen attack and the reader is directed to Krischik (1991), Benedict *et al.* (1991), and Shain ([17] in this volume).

The third process involves attack and consumption of plant pathogens by predators such as predatory nematodes, microarthropods, and macrofauna that can control fungal, bacterial, and nematode pathogens or parasites (Jones, 1991; Shaw *et al.,* 1991; Andrews, 1992). Secondary metabolites can function as antiherbivore repellents, feeding deterrents, or poisons and are frequently the focus of evolutionary responses (Nicholson and Hammerschmidt, 1992). Terpenes produced by conifers are chemically metabolized and utilized by certain herbivores as predator deterrents (*Neodiprion* sawflies on conifers; Knerer and Atwood, 1973) or as mating pheromones (scolytids; Gries *et al.,* 1990). Even if not directly useful to the herbivore, such chemicals often serve as species recognition cues once an herbivore has evolved a mechanism for their detoxification. Plant secondary chemicals may even be used by the predator of a herbivore for chemical defense. Jones (1991) summarized seven possible plant–microbe–insect interactions: (1) fungal or bacterial secondary metabolites can be directly toxic or repellent to insects; (2) fungal or bacterial metabolites may function as insect attractants; (3) bacteria and fungi can be used as food by insects; (4) bacteria or fungi may facilitate utilization of nutrients by the insect by breaking down resistant plant materials before or after insect ingestion; (5) bacteria or fungi may detoxify allelochemicals; (6) bacteria and fungi may induce plant defense against insect attack; and (7) microbes may increase sex pheromone production.

Plants that encourage pathogen competitors could benefit from this interaction. If a plant exudes relatively low-cost substrates, such as simple sugars, or metabolites that result in the growth of organisms that compete with plant pathogens, then that plant is more likely to survive and reproduce than a plant that does not encourage competitors of pathogens. Plants not encouraging these pathogen competitors must spend energy and resources to combat pathogens directly, will have reduced vigor and reduced reproduction, and will most likely succumb to the pathogen.

III. Organisms in the Food Web and Their Functions

Plant-surface food webs include primary producers, saprophytes, pathogens, herbivores, and predators. Primary producers, such as lichens, algae, mosses, and cyanobacteria, use the stems and trunks of higher plants as support surfaces, which provide surfaces where these smaller producers obtain light, carbon, and other abiotic resources while escaping competing organisms or predators (Carroll, 1981). Saprophytes or decomposers live on plant exudates or on dead or sloughed plant material. These organisms include the true bacteria as well as actinomycetes and fungi, including myxomycetes (Stephenson, 1989), oomycetes, deuteromycetes, ascomycetes, and basidiomycetes (Jones, 1991; Juniper, 1991). Plant pathogens, including viruses, plant-pathogenic bacteria and fungi, parasitic nematodes, and microarthropods, use the plant as their food resource (Andrews, 1992). Unchecked, systemic growth of pathogens can kill the host plant, while sublethal infections are often met by plant resistance, affecting the structure of the wood or architecture of the plant (Nicholson and Hammerschmidt, 1992). Small herbivores, such as nematodes and microarthropods, remove plant material through a variety of mechanisms. Sap-sucking aphids, root-feeding nematodes, or leaf-consuming insects do not kill the plant, although at times they may limit reproduction and alter plant architecture by feeding on plant tips or buds (Jones, 1991; Benedict *et al.*, 1991; Wagener, 1988). Predators, such as predatory nematodes and arthropods, prey on each of the above-mentioned groups (Hendrix *et al.*, 1986; Ingham *et al.*, 1985; Coleman *et al.*, 1992), although the community compositions of these predators have not been well quantified (Campbell, 1985; Carroll, 1981; Wagener, 1988).

Plant resistance usually involves the production of structurally complex, and thus metabolically expensive, phenolic compounds, tannins, or terpenes (see Shain [17] in this volume). These compounds can change cellular composition, altering the structure of the xylem and thus affecting plant architecture (see Gartner [6] in this volume). At times, these alterations may be undesirable, but often production of defensive metabolites is a desired characteristic. For example, cedar shingles or redwood fencing boards are more resistant to fungal attack because they contain complex, antifungal products. The concentration of these products can be greatly increased by sublethal pathogen attack (Wagener, 1988; Nicholson and Hammerschmidt, 1992).

Only one bacterial species and only two fungal species are found growing in the phloem and xylem of living plants, using plant nutrients without causing harm to the continued existence of the plant (Davis, 1989; Pearce, 1989, 1991). There are two postulated benefits of these "neutral" organisms. The first benefit is to initiate an "immune response" by the plant, which stimulates the production of terpenes, tannins, and other phenolic "antibiotics" (Pearce, 1991; Nicholson and Hammerschmidt, 1992), or resin flow (Andrews, 1992). The second postulated benefit is prevention of attack on internal tissues by other organisms by altering tissue palatability (Jones, 1991; Krischik, 1991).

The immune response involves a strengthening or thickening of cell walls, an increase in membrane strength or toughness, and an increase in the concentration of tannins and secondary metabolites inhibitory to pathogens. The mechanism for this response appears to depend on release of auxin or other plant hormones (Andrews, 1992; Juniper, 1991) and directly impacts wood quality (see Gartner [6] in this volume). In fast-growing wood products, when a denser, stronger wood is desired, it may be useful to inoculate the plant with these immune response-inducing but nonpathogenic species of bacteria and fungi.

IV. Plant Surface Food Webs

Numbers and interactions of plant-surface organisms can be represented in food web models (Ingham *et al.,* 1986; Moore *et al.,* 1991). Representatives of all functional groups likely exist on all plants, but the abundance, distribution, and activity of the specific species in these communities or groups are probably markedly different. Different communities will produce markedly different metabolites, and influence plant growth in a number of different ways, depending on the organisms actually active and performing a function in each community.

A. Plant Substrate Production

The unique communities of decomposers on any surface of the plant depend on exudates produced by the plant, on materials transported into the plant surface area by atmospheric deposition, and on sloughed and dead plant litter or woody debris caught in the above-ground parts of plants (Carroll, 1981). Root exudation has been studied more extensively than above-ground exudation (Campbell, 1985; Paul and Clark, 1990) but little is known about the rates of production, types of substrates produced, and how these exudates are influenced by the presence or absence of bacteria or fungi on either above- or below-ground surfaces.

Rain and fog deposit a variety of compounds (Pedgley, 1991) on plant surfaces. These materials are utilized by saprophytic bacteria and fungi, as well as by photosynthetic algae, moss, and lichens. As water travels down a plant surface, plant exudates and atmospheric deposition provide nutrients, but bacteria, fungi, moss, lichen, and algae remove nutrients and add metabolic waste. Research suggests that the majority of nutrients in through flow from tree trunks are in the form of bacteria, fungi and protozoa, not organic debris or mineral nutrients (A. Tuininga, personal communication). Stem flow is thus the net accumulation of all the organisms, metabolites, and processes occurring on the plant. Similar processes occur in the rhizosphere, such that all plant surfaces are rich with highly diverse and constantly changing metabolites (Foster *et al.*, 1983).

B. Bacteria and Fungi

Certain species are strict decomposers or saprophytes, only utilizing plant exudates or detritus. Other species can use detrital material, but can also attack the plant as a pathogen, if access to unprotected plant tissues occurs through wounding or damage by nematode or insect feeding. Pathogens use a variety of mechanisms to gain access to plant tissues, although the plant can prevent pathogen attack by encouraging nonpathogenic bacteria and fungi to grow on their surfaces to compete with pathogens for resources and space. Some pathogens are carried into the host plant by bark beetles (see below), or can overcome competition from plant surface organisms (Krischik, 1991). Kübler (1990), for example, found that certain fungi and bacteria loosen the cambial sheath that binds bark to wood, allowing access to the underlying plant tissues.

Specific species of bacteria and fungi are plant mutualists, such as nitrogen-fixing bacteria or mycorrhizal fungi in the rhizosphere, or endophytic fungi (Clay, 1992) in the phyllosphere. No bacterial–plant phyllosphere mutualist has been found, however.

The amount of nutrients immobilized in bacterial and fungal biomass can be considerable, from several nanograms to 10 mg or even 100 mg of biomass cm^{-2} surface area, comprising a significant portion of any stable nutrient pool (Ingham *et al.*, 1986). When the bacterial or fungal component of the soil declines, nutrients are no longer sequestered in microbial or predatory biomass and can be lost to ground and surface water (Coleman *et al.*, 1992).

A grass plant with two leaves and a stem 10 cm high may have a surface area of 10 cm^2. Under optimal growing conditions, this surface may contain 10^7 bacteria, and 0.2–0.3 mm of hyphae. Given a bacterial biomass of

1 pg/bacterium, and average hyphal diameters of 2.5 μm and densities of 0.3 g cm^{-3} (Paul and Clark, 1990), bacterial biomass would be 10 μg and fungal biomass would be 2 μg on the surface of this one small plant. If all the above-ground plant surfaces were considered, the retention of any nutrient by these organisms would be considerable. The turnover rate of these nutrient pools may be even greater, because predator organisms such as protozoa, nematodes, and microarthropods consume several hundred to several thousand prey organisms per day (Ingham *et al.*, 1985). Clearly, to understand fully the significance of the phyllosphere, these interactions need to be evaluated.

C. Protozoa and Nematodes

Protozoa, including flagellates, naked and testate amoebae, and ciliates, feed mainly on bacteria, although amoebae can feed on flagellates, while ciliates feed on flagellates, and perhaps amoebae as well. Four different functional groups of nematodes can be differentiated on the basis of their mode of feeding: bacterial feeders, fungal feeders, root feeders, and nematodes that feed on other nematodes. Consumption of bacteria and fungi by nematodes or protozoa results in nutrient mineralization, making these nutrients available for plant growth, although the biomass of the soil organisms sequesters nutrients as well.

The numbers of protozoa and nematodes on surfaces of plants have not been well quantified although as many as 1000 amoebae and 5–100 nematodes have been found per square centimeter on the bark of Douglas-fir in mature stands (Cromack *et al.*, 1988). Most of the nematodes were bacterial and fungal feeders, but several ectoparasitic root-feeding nematodes occurred as well. Did these plant-feeding nematodes "hitch a ride" on a formerly soil-dwelling arthropod, or a bird, or perhaps they were carried by rain splash? How important are these interactions for plant survival or for the structure of above-ground plant tissues?

D. Fungal-Feeding and Predatory Arthropods

Arthropods characteristically associated with bark surfaces may be divided into three categories: (1) species using bark surfaces only incidentally for portions of their life history (e.g., mating, refuging, and crypsis), (2) species associated with bark for the majority of their life cycle (corticolous) but whose food source is not wood itself, and (3) species deriving nourishment directly or indirectly from the living subcortical plant cells, usually the phloem or cambium.

Corticolous fauna feed on epiphytic mosses, lichens, algae, and microfungi and are represented by a number of distinct taxonomic groups. The most numerous, on a worldwide basis, are water bears (Tardigrada), springtails (Collembola), beetle/turtle mites (Oribatida/Cryptostigmata), and bark-lice (Psocoptera). A single Douglas-fir in Oregon may have as many as 8×10^7 individuals of a single species of oribatid mite feeding on benign decomposer microfungi such as *Cladiosporium* (André and Voegtlin, 1981). These bark-associated microarthropods can occasionally assume economic importance as vectors of disease, such as filbert blight (*Anisograma*), which destroys vascular function (G. Krantz, personal communication).

Less numerous and larger arthropods are characteristic of these microhabitats, such as moss-beetles (Byrrhidae), jumping-scorpionflies (Boreidae) and bristletails (Machilida). The fecal material produced by these organisms, which they deposit on the surface of woody plants, is rich in plant-available nutrients.

Leaf destruction by herbivores generally decreases the overall rate of plant growth and reduces seed production. Woody (perennial) plants are, however, provided with a heavy shower of nutrient-rich insect feces if plants are heavily defoliated. Defoliator outbreaks of the spruce budworm (*Choristoneura fumiferana*) are known to produce alternating periods of reduced annual ring growth (outbreak) and accelerated ring growth (postoutbreak) due to nutrients recycled from the defoliator feces by soil-inhabiting microarthropods and microbes (Wickman, 1990; Schowalter *et al.*, 1991). This fundamental recurrent pattern of wood production must have considerable impacts on both the living tree and the lumber.

In the coastal Pacific Northwest conifer forests of North America, nearly one-quarter of the gross primary production, and the majority of the fixed nitrogen, may be attributable to epiphytic cryptogams, such as the lichen species *Lobularia oregana* (Nadkarni, 1985). An epiphytic moss- and lichen-feeding corticolous fauna serves as the most predictable food source for arthropod predators, for example, spiders (Araneae), ants (Formicidae), beetles (Coleoptera), hemerobiids, and raphidians (Neuroptera). These predators serve as the major population regulatory control of potential defoliating herbivores of the "host plant" (A. Moldenke, unpublished data).

1. Sap Feeders   The most numerous and widespread of the groups obtaining their nutrition directly from living plant cells are the aphids (Aphidae) and scales (Coccoidea). Although relatively unstudied, these groups occur on a wide variety of woody taxa (e.g., aphids of the genus *Cinara* on northern hemisphere conifers; Furniss and Carolin, 1977). High densities near the growing shoot have strong (localized, <1 cm) deleterious effects on subsequent wood growth because intracellular enzymatic digestion produces irregular growth responses in nonwoody tissue. Luckily, these species are seldom gregarious, and do not often occur in densities liable to affect woody growth significantly. However, uncontrolled perennial pest infestations such as oak pit scale (*Asterolecanium* spp.) can seriously deform entire trees (Pritchard and Beer, 1950; Okiwelu, 1977).

2. Burrowing Feeders The insects receiving the greatest amount of study are those that burrow within meristematic and phloem tissue. The major cause of mortality through phloem destruction or indirectly through incidental inoculation of pathogenic fungi in both wild and plantation species of trees is frequently attributed to scolytid beetles. Phloem tissue is usually the site of maximum feeding, because it contains the most nutrients. Species feeding on the bark or xylem often start out life (the earliest instars have the most rapid tissue growth) feeding on the cambium (e.g., many cerambycids and buprestids), but become primarily fungivorous on either symbiotic fungi (e.g., ambrosia beetles) or preconditioned, heavily decayed wood. Many species in this latter category possess either intestinal or intracellular microsymbionts (Crowson, 1981). Certain species of buprestid beetles attack stressed trees, but are unable to moult to adults until the tree actually dies (sometimes a prolonged period; Anderson, 1960).

Although most of these insects attack only stressed individuals, some taxa have evolved the capacity to induce stress directly, usually by partial or entire girdling. Most of the notorious wood-feeding, stem-dwelling taxa attack large woody boles or branches. If attack does not result in tree death, it is generally assumed that the wound is healed and subsequent woody growth relatively unaffected. Girdler activity seldom results in death of the whole plant, but the effect may be long-lasting and conspicuous through significant alteration of the pattern of growing stems/trunks. The overall growth form of many hardwoods might in fact be largely determined by twig girdlers.

Insects may change tree growth form (branch initiation/dominance) by means other than actual tissue death. Gall formation on a young branch or leader may result either in reduced axial growth or change in functional status (i.e., no reproduction distal to gall). This occurs in numerous herbaceous species (e.g., on the perennial stems of *Penstemon peckii*), past which all further growth and reproduction are halted, even though the stem remains photosynthetically active and a major element of the plant for several subsequent years (A. R. Moldenke, unpublished data). If this same phenomenon occurs in woody plants, it is probably generally limited to the youngest woody structures and subsequent branch compensation limits structural and economic consequences. During some years, however, 10% of the apical 0.5–1.0 m of all branches on *Quercus garryana* in Oregon may be girdled by squirrels feeding on the galls of *Bessetia ligni* (Cynipidae; J. Miller, personal communication).

In summary, arthropod damage to woody tissues is usually of limited extent and of little concern to future growth of the tree or to the structural integrity of the wood itself. Under prolonged stressful conditions, however, wood-feeding insect populations can build to sufficient densities to disable permanently or kill a woody plant. These effects are generally confined to individual plants on poor soils, exposed slopes, or sites with intense competition. Most frequently the uppermost portion of the tree is severely affected. Indeed, entire forests of old-growth Douglas-fir in the Pacific Northwest are characterized by dead tops in perhaps 10–25% of the trees (Spies and Franklin, 1991; S. Acker, personal communication).

Occasionally truly aggressive insect pests may attack and kill healthy trees. The direct effect of wood-feeding insects that girdle or gall young branches/ leaders or kill terminal buds (i.e., tip-moths, shoot-moths, terminal-weevils) will cause altered alignments of xylem growth. If altered trunk growth involves tissues only 1–3 years old, presumably no detrimental structural changes would ensue. In contrast, if a mature top is killed, structural changes would be sufficient to preclude commercial use.

3. Relation with Fungi   Most woody plants can counteract direct insect feeding damage with wound responses. Minute blemishes might preclude use of the wood from cabinetry or trim, but the more serious effect of insect wood burrowing is introduction of fungal inocula. A slow-growing fungus that persists for many years may have detrimental effects as great as those of recognized "pathogens." There is tight community coupling between many arthropod and microbial species attacking living wood (and dead wood, too). As a wood borer attains adulthood and emerges from a woody stem, it is exposed to the spores of numerous wood-feeding fungi. When it enters a new stem, the borer inoculates the stem as it burrows and oviposits, and subsequent generations continue to inoculate new stems. Because the majority of wood-feeding insects oviposit through minute holes in the bark made with their ovipositors, inoculation potential is reduced relative to an adult insect that burrows into the wood before ovipositing. If the immature insects performing the boring require the fungal exoenzymes for wood digestion, behavioral adaptations of the parent usually ensure that such inoculation occurs synchronously with egg deposition (Crowson, 1981).

Fungal growth in the phloem and sapwood results in progressive blockage with concomitant death of downstream cells and embolism in the conductive tissue. Fungi can also grow medially and ultimately result in heavily decayed heartwood, without direct death of the tree. A large percentage of many species of trees is characterized by individuals with rotted heartwood. These fungi, although certainly detrimental to lumber production, are frequently integral to the biodiversity of the community at large by providing trees for bat roosts, large mammal nests, hibernation sites for bears, and habitat for countless species of stenotopic arthropods. When such heart rot prospers high in the tree, the susceptibility to wind damage significantly increases (Furniss and Carolin, 1977).

4. Protection by Predatory Insects from Damaging Insects   Because bark and wood are recalcitrant substances and boring is a protracted process, damaging insects are exposed during burrow initiation. The bark surfaces of most woody plants are densely populated by predaceous arthropods (e.g., spiders). Dominant tree species in the Northwest (i.e., *Alnus, Acer, Pseudotsuga,* and *Thuja*) have characteristic corticolous predator fauna, whose presence is determined by bark roughness and epiphytic cryptogamic growth (A. Moldenke, personal observation). The rougher the bark and the greater the number of epiphytes, the denser and more speciose the fauna of predators (A. R. Moldenke, unpublished data).

Numerous woody plants, especially in the tropics, have evolved commensal relationships with ants that live in the pith, galls, or inside thorns (Beattie, 1985). The plants provide nourishment for the ants in order to ensure dense populations that are capable of effective predation on potential herbivores, including mammals. The nutritive substances provided by the plant often require the continued presence of the ants to stimulate food production, either by physically walking on the surface of the plant or by timely removal of the plant food tissues.

Another beneficial insect group that frequently inhabits pith includes the solitary bees (e.g., Megachilidae and Xylocopinae). Woody plants such as *Sambucus* and *Rubus* in the Pacific Northwest may harbor large populations that service their host as well as other nearby species (Moldenke, 1976).

V. Stem Attack by Wood-Boring Insects

Bark beetles (Coleoptera: Scolytidae) are found throughout the world in association with numerous types of woody plants. Their activities may be confined to dead wood (logs, snags), living wood (generally prestressed through other causes), or even living petioles (with no adverse effects on the adjacent woody structures).

A. Multiple Lines of Defense

Most bark beetles are specialized as to the identity of the woody plant that they attack (usually to the genus or species level), and most are further specialized to the preferred diameter of stem within the woody plant (Wood, 1982). In the temperate zones the majority of species are associated with dead or dying wood (Wood, 1982; Berryman, 1986); most species have complex interdependencies with wood-metabolizing fungi, which they transport to new resources in order to obtain sufficient nutrition from the wood itself. Species capable of attacking living trees may severely damage or kill the tree through the subsequent growth of their phoretic fungal partner.

B. Dead Wood: A Successional Story

All woody plants pass through stages when major limbs or even the bole itself are dead and subject to decomposition processes. This death and decay is seldom considered as integral to healthy growth, but should be. The processes affecting an arboreal dead snag are similar to log decomposition on the ground.

The great majority of arthropod wood feeders feed on a medium that has been thoroughly infiltrated with fungal hyphae, to such an extent that the distinction between fungal feeding and wood feeding becomes moot. Most taxa of arthropods that feed on dead wood are related to species attacking stressed live trees. As a general rule, insect species attacking either the living tree or the wood immediately after death show a high degree of tree species specificity.

A critical determinant of both the speed and course of the decay process is the initial stage of fungal exploitation. This process is driven by the physical penetration of the wood surface by insect taxa, either by the maternal burrower or only by her ovipositor. The most significant insects worldwide to initially penetrate wood are bark beetles (Scolytidae) and their specialized predators and parasitoids. A beetle entering the log carries with it not only an extremely diverse fungal and bacterial inoculum, but a menagerie of phoretic nematodes and mites. Once fungal growth inhibitors secreted by the adult bark beetles have dissipated, the beetle burrows fill with fungal hyphae. The hyphae obtain nutrients initially from beetle fecal material and later from the recalcitrant wood.

This fungal jungle is fed on by diverse specialized taxa of microarthropods, whose movement permits rapid dispersal and growth of bacteria and other more generalized fungi, such as yeasts and slime molds. This in turn attracts diverse populations of invertebrates, which in turn feed on this increasingly diverse resource. As channeling by other species of arthropods proceeds, more species enter the log from the surrounding soil community.

Initial stages of wood decomposition may support several dozen species of arthropods and fungi, very few of which are characteristic of the soil food web surrounding a log. After perhaps 1 year, each log may support several hundred species of insects, several thousand bacterial and fungal species, and several tens of protozoan and nematode species. However, in later stages of decay the majority of ever-increasing numbers of taxa of bacteria, fungi, protozoa, nematodes, and microarthropods will invade from the surrounding soil. The full course of the decay process for each log in the temperate zone may involve several thousand arthropod species (A. R. Moldenke, unpublished data).

Once decay has proceeded through the rapid fungal colonization stage, logs become even more thoroughly channeled by either termites or carpenter ants (*Camponotus*). Termites actually eat the wood, often with the help of intestinal mutualist bacteria and protozoa, while carpenter ants simply remove wood as sawdust and disperse it on the soil.

After 1–2 years on the ground and the disappearance of the inner bark, most wood borers respond primarily to differences between major classes of trees (e.g., conifer vs hardwood) and to different generalized successional stages of the decomposition process. Species characteristic of the early stages of decomposition have short life cycles (usually annual or less), whereas species found in later decay stages have life cycles lasting many years. Growth in the later stages is limited by the general lack of macronutrients. Fauna within these older logs have developed complex, virtually unstudied, symbiotic relationships with microbial species for both the enzymatic breakdown of complex polysaccharides and nitrogen fixation (Crowson, 1981).

VI. Conclusions

Plants have always existed with bacteria, fungi, protozoa, and nematodes on their surfaces. A small amount of information is available on the densities and diversity of organisms inhabiting plant surfaces, but little is known about how they influence plant growth. Although numbers and species composition differ in the phyllosphere as compared to the rhizosphere, similar interactions occur in both places. The following summary statements can be made.

1. The rhizosphere and phyllosphere food webs consist of communities of bacteria, fungi, protozoa, nematodes, microarthropods, and insects driven by plant exudates and detrital material.

2. Food web structure and function are strongly influenced by colonization processes, moisture and temperature regimes, and exudate production by the plant.

3. Interactions between saprophytes and their predators alter the form of nitrogen and other nutrients in stem flow. Plants can adsorb these nutrients through above-ground surfaces, or after incorporation into the soil. How important the processes of phyllosphere immobilization and mineralization may be to plant growth is unknown.

4. The food web of organisms on the surfaces of plants provides protection against pathogens and parasites. The mechanisms preventing pathogen attack include competition for nutrients and competition for space on the surface of the plant.

5. Predators on the surface of plants protect plants from pathogen attack. Once established, bark or leaf surface organisms compete with other colonizing organisms, often preventing the establishment of pathogens on the surface of the plant. Predatory arthropods and perhaps nematodes remove potential invaders from the bark surface.

6. If the phyllosphere defense and the physical barrier of the plant surface are overcome, plants typically respond to pathogen attack by producing thicker bark, structurally denser wood, or higher levels of toxic compounds in the wood, often resulting in mechanically stronger or more resistant wood products.

Management of plant-surface microbial communities could be used to improve wood quality, but use of these interactions requires a better understanding of the physiology, ecological niche, and competitive interactions of both the surface-dwelling organisms and their host plants.

References

Anderson, R. F. (1960). "Forest and Shade Tree Entomology." John Wiley & Sons, New York.

André, H. M., and Voegtlin, D. J. (1981). Some observations on the biology of *Camisia carrolli* n. sp. (Acari: Oribatida). *Acarologia* **23,** 81–89.

Andrews, J. H. (1992). Biological control in the phyllosphere. *Annu. Rev. Phytopathol.* **30,** 603–635.

Andrews, J. H. and Hirano, S. S. (eds.). (1992). "Microbial Ecology of Leaves." Springer-Verlag, New York.

Beattie, A. (1985). "The Evolutionary Ecology of Ant-Plant Mutualisms." Cambridge University Press, Cambridge.

Benedict, J. H., Chang, J. F., and Bird, L. S. (1991). Influence of plant microflora on insect-plant relationships in *Gossypium hirsutum.* *In* "Microbial Mediation of Plant-Herbivore Interactions" (P. Barbosa, V. A. Krischik, and C. G. Jones, eds.), pp. 273–304. John Wiley & Sons, New York.

Berryman, A. A. (1986). "Forest Insects: Principles and Practice of Population Management." Plenum Press, New York.

Campbell, R. (1985). "Plant Microbiology." Edward Arnold Publishers, Baltimore, Maryland.

Carroll, G. C. (1981). Microbial productivity on aerial plant surfaces. *In* "Microbial Ecology of the Phylloplane" (J. P. Blakeman, ed.), pp. 15–46. Academic Press, London.

Clay, K. (1992). Endophytes as antagonists of plant pests. *In* "Microbial Ecology of Leaves" (J. H. Andrews and S. S. Hirano, eds.), pp. 331–357. Springer-Verlag, New York.

Coleman, D. C., Odum, E. P., and Crossley, D. A., Jr. (1992). Soil biology, soil ecology and global change. *Biol. Fertil. Soils* **14,** 104–111.

Cromack, K., Fichter, B. L., Moldenke, A. R., Entry, J. A., and Ingham, E. R. (1988). Interactions between soil animals and ectomycorrhizal fungal mats. *Agric. Ecosyst. Environ.* **24,** 161–168.

Crowson, R. A. (1981). "The Biology of the Coleoptera." Academic Press, London.

Davis, M. J. (1989). Host colonization and pathogenesis in plant diseases caused by fastidious xylem-inhabiting bacteria. *In* "Vascular Wilt Diseases of Plants" (E. C. Tjamos and C. H. Beckman, eds.), pp. 33–50. Springer-Verlag, Berlin.

Fokkema, N. J. (1991). The phyllosphere as an ecologically neglected milieu: A plant pathologist's point of view. *In* "Microbial Ecology of Leaves" (J. H. Andrews and S. S. Hirano, eds.), pp. 3–20. Springer-Verlag, New York.

Foster, R. C., Rovira, A. D., and Cock, T. W. (1983). "Ultrastructure of the Root-Soil Interface." American Phytopathology Society, St. Paul, Minnesota.

Furniss, R. L. and Carolin, V. M. (1977). "Western Forest Insects." Misc. Pub. No. 1339, USDA Forest Service, Washington, DC.

Gries, G., Leufven, A., and Lafontaine, J. P. (1990). New metabolites of α-pinene produced by the mountain pine beetle, *Dendroctonus ponderosae* (Coleoptera: Scolytidae). *Insect Biochem.* **20**, 365–371.

Hendrix, P. F., Parmelee, R. W., Crossley, D. A., Jr., Coleman, D. C., Odum, E. P., and Groffman, P. M. (1986). Detritus foodwebs in conventional and no-tillage agroecosystems. *BioScience* **36**, 374–380.

Ingham, E. R. and Molina, R. (1991). Interaction among mycorrhizal fungi, rhizosphere organisms and plants. *In* "Microbial Mediation of Plant-Herbivore Interactions" (P. Barbosa, V. A. Krischik, and C. G. Jones, eds.), pp. 169–198. John Wiley & Sons, New York.

Ingham, E. R., Trofymow, J. A., Ames, R. N., Hunt, H. W., Morley, C. R., Moore, J. C., and Coleman, D. C. (1986). Trophic interactions and nitrogen cycling in a semiarid grassland soil. I. Seasonal dynamics of the soil foodweb. *J. Appl. Ecol.* **23**, 608–615.

Ingham, R. E., Trofymow, J. A., Ingham, E. R., and Coleman, D. C. (1985). Interactions of bacteria, fungi and their nematode grazers: Effects on nutrient cycling and plant growth. *Ecol. Monogr.* **55**, 119–140.

Jones, C. G. (1991). Interactions of among insects, plants and microorganisms: A net effects perspective on insect performance. *In* "Microbial Mediation of Plant-Herbivore Interactions" (P. Barbosa, V. A. Krischik, and C. G. Jones, eds.), pp. 7–36. John Wiley & Sons, New York.

Juniper, B. E. (1991). The leaf from the inside and the outside: A microbe's perspective. *In* "Microbial Ecology of Leaves" (J. H. Andrews and S. S. Hirano, eds.), pp. 21–42. Springer-Verlag, New York.

Knerer, G., and C. E. Atwood. 1973. Diprionid sawflies: Polymorphism and speciation. *Science* **179**, 1090–1099.

Krischik, V. A. (1991). Specific or generalized plant defense: Reciprocal interactions between herbivores and pathogens. *In* "Microbial Mediation of Plant-Herbivore Interactions" (P. Barbosa, V. A. Krischik, and C. G. Jones, eds.), pp. 309–340. John Wiley & Sons, New York.

Kübler, H. (1990). Natural loosening of the wood/bark bond: A review and synthesis. *For. Prod. J.* **40**, 25–31.

Moldenke, A. R. (1976). California pollination ecology and vegetation types. *Phytologia* **34**, 305–361.

Moore, J. C., Hunt, H. W., and Elliott, E. T. (1991). Ecosystem properties, soil organisms and herbivores. *In* "Microbial Mediation of Plant-Herbivore Interactions" (P. Barbosa, V. A. Krischik, and C. G. Jones, eds.), pp. 105–140. John Wiley & Sons, New York.

Nadkarni, N. M. (1985). Biomass and mineralization capacity of epiphytes in *Acer macrophyllum* communities of a temperate moist conifer forest, Olympic Peninsula, Washington State. *Can. J. Bot.* **62**, 2223–2228.

Nicholson, R. L., and Hammerschmidt, R. (1992). Phenolic compounds and their role in disease resistance. *Annu. Rev. Phytopathol.* **30**, 369–389.

Okiwelu, S. N. (1977). Studies on a pit-making scale, *Asterolecanium minus*, on *Quercus lobata*. *Ann. Entomol. Soc. Am.* **70**, 615–621.

Paul, E. A., and Clark, F. E. (1990). "Soil Microbiology and Biochemistry." Academic Press, San Diego.

Pearce, R. B. (1989). Cell wall alterations and antimicrobial defense in perennial plants. *In* "Plant Cell Wall Polymers: Biogenesis and Biodegradation" (N. G. Lewis and M. G. Paice, eds.), pp. 346–360. American Chemical Society, Washington, D.C.

Pearce, R. B. (1991). Reaction zone relics and the dynamics of fungal spread in the xylem of woody angiosperms. *Physiol. Mol. Plant Pathol.* **39**, 41–55.

Pedgley, D. E. (1991). Aerobiology: The atmosphere as a source and sink for microbes. *In* "Microbial Ecology of Leaves" (J. H. Andrews and S. S. Hirano, eds.), pp. 43–59. Springer-Verlag, New York.

Pritchard, A. E., and Beer, R. E. (1950). Biology and control of *Asterolecanium* scales on oak in California. *J. Econ. Entomol.* **43,** 494–497.

Schowalter, T. D., Sabin, S. E., Stafford, S. G., and Sexton, J. M. (1991). Phytophage effects on primary production, nutrient turnover, and litter decomposition in young Douglas-fir in western Oregon. *For. Ecol. Manage.* **42,** 229–243.

Shaw, C. H., Lundkvist, H., Moldenke, A. R., and Boyle, J. R. (1991). The relationships of soil fauna to long-term forest productivity in temperate and boreal ecosystems: Processes and research strategies. *In* "Long-Term Field Trials to Assess Environmental Impacts of Harvesting" (W. J. Dyck and C. A. Mees, eds.), pp. 39–77. FRI Bulletin No. 161. Forest Research Institute, Rotorua, New Zealand.

Spies, T. A., and Franklin, J. F. (1991). The structure of natural young, mature and old growth Douglas-fir forests in Oregon and Washington. *In* "Wildlife and Vegetation of Unmanaged Douglas-Fir Forests" (L. Ruggiero, ed.), pp. 91–110. Gen. Tech Rept. PNW-GTR-285. U.S. Department of Agriculture, Portland, Oregon.

Stephenson, S. L. (1989). Distribution and ecology of myxomycetes in temperate forests. *Mycologia* **81,** 608–621.

Wagener, M. R. (1988). Induced defenses in Ponderosa pine against defoliating insects. *In* "Mechanisms of Woody Plant Defenses against Insects" (W. J. Mattson, J. Levieux, and C. Bernard-Dagan, eds.), pp. 141–155. Springer-Verlag, New York.

Wickman, B. E. (1990). Increased growth of white fir after a Douglas-fir tussock moth outbreak. *J. For.* **78,** 31–33.

Wood, D. L. (1982). "The Bark and Ambrosia Beetles of North and Central America (Coleoptera: Scolytideae): A Taxonomic Monograph." Great Basin Naturalist, Memoirs No. 6. Brigham Young University Press, Provo, Utah.

12

Developmental Potential of Shoot Buds

Joel P. Stafstrom

I. Introduction

Plant shoots are constructed from repeating units or modules, which are products of shoot apical meristems. These modules are composed of a leaf, one or more axillary buds, and a section of stem consisting of a node and an internode. Shoot apical meristems within axillary buds have the potential to develop into branches. In turn, buds on primary branches may develop into secondary branches. This pattern of organogenesis could be repeated indefinitely. Development of all apical meristems would lead to competition between modules for limited resources and would reduce the vigor of the genetic individual (genet) and of its component modules (ramets). Successful development requires that only a few specified buds grow and that undeveloped axillary buds either become dormant or abort. The "reserve meristems" contained within dormant buds are important for future growth of the plant. The developmental potential of reserve meristems may be mobilized (1) following a period of climate-induced arrest such as winter dormancy, (2) to supplement the population of developing shoots during the growing season, or (3) to replace growing shoots that are lost due to disease, herbivory, pruning, or differentiation into determinate organs.

Developmental potential of shoot buds is addressed by examining several specific questions: what are the biochemical and cellular activities that distinguish dormant buds from growing shoots? How does the position of a bud influence its potential to develop into a branch? How is branch development influenced by environmental conditions and the genotype of a plant? What is the developmental potential or fate of individual buds and how does this potential change during ontogeny? The focus of this volume is on the structure and function of stems, with particular emphasis on trees and woody plants. Currently, many research problems are more tractable when studied using well-characterized organisms. In this chapter, work from the author's laboratory on the control of axillary bud development in the garden pea (*Pisum sativum*) is highlighted. This work is discussed in relation to research problems pertaining to bud development in other groups of plants, including crown development in woody perennials, tillering in grasses, and ecological and evolutionary aspects of ramet development in clonal plants.

II. Ontogeny and Development of Vegetative Buds

A. Apical Meristems and Modular Plant Development

Shoot apical meristems are the ultimate source of all cells in the shoot. Apical meristems initiate new modules (also called phytomers or metamers) through precise patterns of cell division, cell differentiation, and organogenesis (Sussex, 1989; Medford, 1992). Phyllotaxy describes the orderly and predictable arrangement of leaves on the stem. The position of the next incipient leaf primordium is determined by interactions between the apical meristem and one or more extant leaf primordia. These interactions probably are mediated by diffusible chemical messengers, perhaps auxin (Meicenheimer, 1981). One or more buds commonly develop in each leaf axil. Surgical manipulations that alter the position of leaves also alter the position of buds (Wardlaw, 1965). From these and other experiments, it has been concluded that leaf position is causal for bud position. Axillary buds are formed from cells in all layers of the apical meristem (exogenous origin). This ontogenetic pattern distinguishes axillary buds from adventitious buds, which develop from internal tissues (endogenous origin). Adventitious buds probably represent the last option of a plant for obtaining growing shoots. These buds can develop from parenchyma or cambial cells on virtually any plant organ (stump sprouts and root suckers) or from cultured callus (Bell, 1991; Sachs, 1991). Preformed or preventitious axillary buds can develop into growing shoots more quickly.

Axillary meristems may develop into determinate or indeterminate organs (Fig. 1). Determinate organs, such as flowers, thorns, or tendrils, will eventually senesce and die, whereas indeterminate or vegetative buds can generate additional meristems. Buds containing dormant meristems are held in reserve for future development. Ecologists refer to populations of dormant seeds and buds as seed banks and bud banks (Harper, 1977). A restrictive definition of a bud bank might include only buds associated with a variety of subterranean organs such as bulbs, bulbils, rhizomes, corms, or tubers. For example, ericaceous shrubs growing in a pine barren ecosystem regenerate following fire from previously buried rhizome buds (Matlack *et al.,* 1993). The term is used more broadly here to include all dormant buds on a plant. The energetic costs of making and maintaining a bud bank might be most apparent in plants growing in harsh environments. The fact that *Betula cordifolia* trees growing near tree line rely on bud banks for sustained growth suggests that the resources invested in these buds are small compared to their value (Maillette, 1987, 1990). Not all plants contain banks of dormant buds. For example, some palms contain only a single shoot apical meristem, which forms a monopodial vegetative axis and then a single inflorescence (architectural model of Holttum; reviewed in Bell, 1991). In *Polygonum arenastrum,* all buds develop either into indeterminate vegetative branches or determinate flowers (Geber, 1990). Ecotypes of this plant that initiate flowering early are assured of leaving offspring, even if conditions deteriorate, but overall fecundity is low. Ecotypes that delay flowering contain many more branches and flowers, and enjoy higher fecundity, but only if they survive for prolonged periods of time. Plants that employ these life history strategies, which are referred to as ruderal and competitive, respectively, can be highly successful in certain environments (Grime *et al.,* 1986). Developmental plasticity, which represents the range of possible morphologies within the genetic repertoire of an individual, is evoked by specific environmental conditions (Schlichting, 1986; Trewavas, 1986). Plasticity itself is a trait on which selection can act (Scheiner, 1993).

Individual plants (genets) may be regarded as colonies of meristem-containing modules (ramets) that are interconnected by stems and cooperate in their development and exchange of nutrients to variable degrees (White, 1979; Harper, 1985). Development of all buds on a genet would lead to competition among ramets for light and other resources, and would lead to reduced vigor of all parts. One mechanism for avoiding competition is to inhibit or delay the growth of certain modules. A second mechanism is the differential elongation of shoots. Rich, local resources can be exploited by clusters of closely spaced leaves on short shoots. In contrast, new areas that are potentially richer in resources can be explored by long shoots (cf. Hardwick, 1986). These alternative patterns of shoot elongation are exemplified by ramet development in *Ranunculus repens,* a clonal perennial (Lovett Doust, 1981): a grassland population used a short shoot or "phalanx" strategy to quickly conquer nearby resources whereas a woodland (more shaded) population used a long shoot or "guerrilla" strategy to colonize new areas.

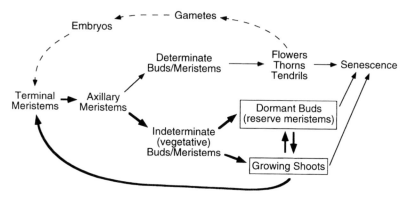

Figure 1 Developmental fates of shoot apical meristems. Axillary meristems are products of growing terminal meristems. The fate of axillary meristems is usually determined at or before the time of their formation. Determinate meristems give rise to flowers, thorns, or tendrils. Flowers can give rise to additional apical meristems through sexual reproduction (dashed line). Indeterminate or vegetative meristems can grow, at which time they may be considered new terminal meristems. The reiterative cycle of new meristem formation is indicated by a heavy solid line. Most axillary meristems are retained as "reserve meristems" within dormant buds. The growing and dormant meristem states may be interconverted repeatedly (boxed segments). Reversibility can occur between or within growing seasons for different types of dormancy.

B. Bud Dormancy

Dormancy is an adaptive mechanism that allows plants and plant organs to survive adverse conditions and resume growing when conditions improve. Dormancy is a reversible developmental state (Fig. 1). Dormancy is frequently linked to seasonal cycles, such as cold temperatures at high latitudes (Nooden and Weber, 1978; Powell, 1988) or drought in some tropical regions (Borchert, 1991). The annual growth cycle of temperate perennials includes at least three distinct types or phases of dormancy (Fuchigami and Nee, 1987; Borchert, 1991). Lang (1987) introduced a new terminology for various classes of dormancy (indicated below in italics), stressing the nature of the regulatory signal, its source, and the organ that responds to the signal. Following a flush of spring growth in temperate species, meristems made during the current or previous years stop growing. Because growth of terminal and axillary buds is regulated by physiological processes occurring throughout the plant, this type of within-season dormancy is called correlative inhibition. The best known example of correlative inhibition is regulation of axillary bud development by growing terminal buds, also called apical dominance (*apical paradormancy*). Dormant apical meristems may be reactivated and initiate one or more late-season growth flushes, for example, lammas shoots that form near Lammas Day in early August (Kozlowski, 1971). Periodic growth flushes may be linked to root development and water availability (Borchert, 1991), or to "loss" of an inhibiting meristem owing to its development into a flower. Stumps can generate an abundance of new shoots from adventitious buds. The author has observed stump sprouts of *Ulmus pumila* containing three additional orders of branches, that is, initiation of a bud, its elongation into a branch, and development of its buds, all were repeated three times within a single growing season (J. P. Stafstrom, unpublished observations).

Winter dormancy or rest in buds is a multistep process. The onset of dormancy is promoted by short photoperiods (*photoperiodic endodormancy*) (Nooden and Weber, 1978). Morphological changes necessary for cold acclimation usually include development of protective bud scales. Ensuing cold temperatures fulfill the chilling requirement of a bud (*cryogenic endodormancy*). Buds then become competent to grow and actually develop after being exposed to warm temperatures (*thermal ecodormancy*). In general, one phase of the seasonal cycle must be completed before the next can begin (Fuchigami and Nee, 1987). Thus, reversibility between dormant and growing states can occur within a season for buds arrested by correlative inhibition but only between seasons for winter dormant buds. The extent to which various types of bud dormancy may be similar in their hormonal regulation, patterns of gene expression, or biochemical control mechanisms is largely unknown and, therefore, presents a major challenge to researchers in many areas of applied and basic research.

C. Correlative Regulation of Bud Development

The establishment and maintenance of a bipolar shoot-root system in a plant require communication between its growing and dormant modules. Sachs (1991) has identified several general rules that define the types of interactions that occur within and between shoots and roots: (1) a growing organ tends to inhibit the development of similar organs; (2) developing shoots promote root development, and vice versa; and (3) growing organs tend to continue growing and dormant organs tend to remain dormant, probably owing to as yet undefined positive feedback mechanisms. Auxins and cytokinins, which are synthesized predominantly in growing shoot and root apices, respectively, are the most important mediators of these interactions (see Little and Pharis [13] in this volume). For example, each hormone inhibits growth locally and promotes growth at a distance. Relative levels of these hormones appear to be critical for initiating and maintaining each meristematic state (Skoog and Miller, 1957). Experiments testing the roles of these and other "classic" plant hormones have been reviewed several times (Tamas, 1988; Cline, 1991, 1994). Despite the central role of auxin in apical dominance, its effects are almost certainly mediated by one or more secondary inhibitors (Snow, 1937; Hillman, 1984; Stafstrom, 1993).

In other experiments, the synthesis or perception of hormones has been altered using genetic mutants and molecularly engineered transgenic plants (Klee and Estelle, 1991). For example, a transgenic *Arabidopsis* plant that overexpressed auxin was crossed with a mutant that was defective in detecting ethylene. Hybrid plants selected for both traits exhibited strong apical dominance, indicating that ethylene is not a secondary inhibitor of bud development (Romano *et al.*, 1993). Abscisic acid remains a good candidate for the job of secondary inhibitor (Gocal *et al.*, 1991). However, virtually nothing is known about the possible effects on bud development of more recently discovered growth regulators including jasmonates (Sembdner and Parthier, 1993), oligosaccharins (Ryan, 1994), salicylic acid (Raskin, 1992), brassinosteroids (Zurek and Clouse, 1994), and peptides such as systemin (McGurl *et al.*, 1991).

Roots can influence shoot development by regulating the transport of water or the breakdown products of stored starch. Periodic delivery of water from roots is closely correlated with recurrent flushes of shoot growth in certain tropical trees (Borchert, 1991). Plants that live in fire-prone areas regenerate following fire as either "resprouters" or "reseeders" (see by Gill [14] in this volume). Among closely related species, resprouters store large amounts of starch in their roots whereas reseeders do not (Bowen and Pate, 1993; see also Pate and Jeschke [8] in this volume). An understanding of how the development of plant modules may be coordinated is complicated by the fact that certain domains of shoots, roots, or both may be linked by specific vascular connections. Thus, subsections of a plant can function as "integrated physiological units" (Watson and Casper, 1984; Pitelka and Ashmun, 1985; Price *et al.*, 1992).

III. Biochemical and Cytological Changes during Bud Development

A. Dormancy Cycles and Gene Expression

Dormancy in pea axillary buds is equivalent to correlative inhibition of buds in perennial plants. Pea seedlings (*P. sativum* cv. Alaska) are excellent subjects for studying apical dominance. Early experiments using these plants implicated auxin as the primary inhibitor of axillary bud growth (Skoog and Thimann, 1934). Pea seedlings are easy to grow in large numbers and are suitable for experiments 7 days after sowing. We have analyzed the development of two buds at the second node, which are called "large" and "small." On intact plants these buds do not grow, but following decapitation of the main shoot, visible growth of both buds is evident within 8 hr. After 2 to 3 days, rapid growth of the large bud causes the small bud to cease growing and become dormant again; the small bud will resume growing if the large shoot is removed. More than one complete growth-dormancy cycle (dormancy → growth → dormancy → growth) can be completed in 6 days (Stafstrom and Sussex, 1992).

Stage-specific gene expression has been used to study interconversion of the growing and dormant states in pea buds. Accumulation of mRNA corresponding to the ribosomal protein L27 gene (*rpL27*) is tightly linked to the growing state (Stafstrom and Sussex, 1992). *In situ* hybridization experiments were used to determine which cells express *rpL27* at each stage of development. Only background levels of *rpL27* mRNA can be detected in dormant buds (Fig. 2A). Within 1 hr of decapitation increased levels of this mRNA are present in all areas of large and small buds (Fig. 2B). Therefore, regulatory signals from the plant must diffuse or be transported into the buds rapidly, and every bud cell must be competent to respond to these signals. By 6 hr after decapitation, high levels of *rpL27* mRNA are present in all areas of the buds (Fig. 2C). Recall that visible bud growth does not begin until 8 hr. There is no further change in cellular expression of *rpL27* after buds actually begin to grow (Stafstrom and Sussex, 1992).

The growth-to-dormancy transition in the small buds revealed an unanticipated feature of gene expression in developing buds. At 4 to 5 days after decapitation, these buds had ceased growing and RNA gel blots indicated that they contained only basal levels of *rpL27* mRNA (Stafstrom and Sussex, 1992). However, expression persisted at high levels in the apical meristem during this transition (Fig. 2D). Because all bud cells probably are exposed to the identical developmental signals from the plant (see above), apical meristem cells must interpret and respond to these signals differently than their neighbors.

B. Cell Cycle Regulation

Cells in a nondividing state are said to be quiescent and cells progressing through the cell cycle are said to be proliferating (Jacobs, 1992; Murray and Hunt, 1993). Certain "cell cycle genes" are expressed in a phase-specific manner. For example, high levels of histone mRNAs are found only during S phase (Mikami and Iwabuchi, 1992; Tanimoto *et al.*, 1993). In plants, cyclin B mRNA accumulates predominantly during late G_2 and mitosis (Hirt *et al.*, 1992). In frog embryos, cyclin message levels remain constant throughout the cell cycle but cyclin protein is degraded during each mitosis (Murray and Hunt, 1993). Other mRNAs, such as that of the cdc2 kinase gene, accumulate in all proliferating cells without regard to a specific phase of the cell cycle (Hemerly *et al.*, 1993).

The pea bud system was used to examine the relationship between the growth state of a whole organ (dormant versus growing) and the cell cycle state of its component cells (quiescent versus proliferating) (Stafstrom *et al.*, 1993; Devitt and Stafstrom, 1995). In small buds, accumulation of histone

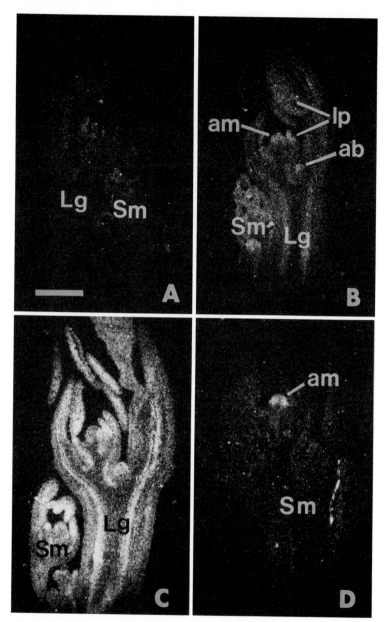

Figure 2 *In situ* expression of rpL27 mRNA in pea axillary buds. White areas in these dark-field micrographs represent mRNA distribution in large (Lg) and small (Sm) buds. (A) Dormant buds from an intact plant. (B) Early dormancy-to-growth transition (1 hr after decapitation). (C) Late dormancy-to-growth transition (6 hr after decapitation). (D) Growth-to-dormancy transition in a small bud (5 days after decapitation). ab, Secondary axillary bud; am, apical meristem; lp, leaf primordium. Bar: 0.5 mm. (From Stafstrom and Sussex, 1992. Copyright American Society of Plant Physiologists, used with permission.)

H2A and H4, cdc2, cyclin B, and mitogen-activated protein (MAP) kinase messages was tightly linked to the growing state during more than one complete growth–dormancy cycle. Expression of histone and ribosomal protein genes has been demonstrated in growing shoot apices of other species (Medford, 1992; Fleming *et al.*, 1993). Mitogen-activated protein kinase from vertebrates and yeasts is part of a phosphorylation cascade that leads to cell division and other responses (Ruderman, 1993). In these organisms, MAP kinase mRNA and protein are equally abundant in quiescent and proliferating cells. Accumulation of MAP kinase mRNA only in proliferating cells of pea buds demonstrates how evolutionarily conserved genes and proteins may have distinct functions and modes of regulation in different organisms. Nonetheless, the activity of the MAP kinase protein from plants is probably regulated by phosphorylation on the same amino acid residues as on animal and yeast MAP kinases (Duerr *et al.*, 1993).

Migration of plant cells is greatly limited by their rigid cell walls, and therefore cell division must be regulated precisely in space as well as in time. During the formation of leaf primordia at the shoot apex, the rate of cell division, the plane of cell division, and the orientation of cell elongation are altered during each plastochron (Lyndon and Cunninghame, 1986). Before mitosis begins, the preprophase band of microtubules establishes where cytokinesis will occur (Wick, 1991; Palevitz, 1993). How the plasma membrane or the cortical cytoplasm might "remember" the location of the preprophase band has been enigmatic. It was discovered recently that p34 kinase, the product of the *cdc2* gene, is associated with the preprophase band (Colasanti *et al.*, 1993). It is intriguing to think that this kinase might be involved in regulating both when and where cells divide.

C. Metabolic Activity and Gene Expression in Dormant Buds

Metabolic rates are low in overwintering floral and vegetative buds of woody plants. In dormant floral buds of cherry, the first significant increases in RNA, DNA, and protein content do not occur until the "first swell" stage in early spring (Wang *et al.*, 1985). In vegetative buds of *Populus balsamifera,* an increase in respiratory capacity first occurs in mid-March, the same time that buds show an increased capacity to develop when transferred to warm temperatures (breaking of *thermoendodormancy*). High respiratory capacity was not observed until bud-break in mid-May (Bachelard and Wightman, 1973). Dormant, growing, and transition-stage pea buds incorporate radiolabeled amino acids into proteins at similar rates (Stafstrom and Sussex, 1988). In this respect, dormant pea buds are as metabolically active as growing buds.

Despite a high rate of protein synthesis, dormant pea buds do not accumulate high levels of protein over time. It is likely that a high rate of protein synthesis is matched by a comparable rate of protein degradation. Rapid degradation of regulatory proteins is an effective means of controlling their activity. For example, the products of two auxin-induced genes are thought to mediate auxin-regulated transcription of other genes. These proteins have extremely short half-lives (about 6 to 8 min), thus their presence in a cell is closely correlated with the presence of auxin (Abel *et al.*, 1994). Similarly, a highly dynamic signaling pathway might be involved in the rapid interconversions between growing and dormant states in axillary buds.

The existence of dormancy-promoting genes and their importance to plant survival is demonstrated by a nondormant mutant of *Corylus*. Buds on these plants continue to grow through the winter; buds and plants may survive mild winters but they are killed by colder winters (Thompson *et al.*, 1985). Analysis of bud proteins from pea by two-dimensional gel electrophoresis showed that certain proteins were specifically expressed in either growing or dormant buds (Stafstrom and Sussex, 1988; Stafstrom, 1993). For example, a protein designated **B** was found only in dormant buds and protein **C** was found only in buds that had been stimulated to grow (Fig. 3A-C). Currently, the author's laboratory is isolating dormancy-specific genes from pea. We are eager to determine the identity of these genes, how they are regulated, and how their expression might cause or maintain the dormant state.

The effects of auxin and kinetin on the expression of growth- and dormancy-specific proteins in pea buds were also investigated (Stafstrom and Sussex, 1988). Direct application of kinetin to buds on intact plants promoted their growth to the same extent as decapitation. Expression of proteins **B** and **C** in these buds was identical to that in buds on decapitated plants after 6 or 24 hr (Fig. 3D and E). Application of auxin in lanolin to the stumps of decapitated plants completely inhibited axillary bud growth. It was expected that these buds would remain dormant, that is, they would express protein **B** continuously and never express protein **C**. This pattern of expression was observed 24 hr after auxin treatment (Fig. 3G). After 6 hr, however, **C** had increased and **B** had declined (Fig. 3F). This pattern was identical to that of the other 6-hr experiments (Fig. 3B and D). During this early phase, auxin may have been inactivated by indoleacetic acid (IAA) oxidase as a result of wounding, or perhaps its transport out of the lanolin did not begin immediately. Buds apparently sensed a decline in auxin transport in the stem and initiated biochemical events associated with growth. As auxin levels increased, buds again synthesized dormancy-specific proteins. Thus, transient "biochemical growth" can occur in the absence of physical growth.

It is likely that buds on trees, grasses, and other species are continually apprised of the vigor of the plant as a whole, or of the branch or the integrated physiological unit of which they are a part. As environmental conditions improve or deteriorate, these buds might grow transiently and then become

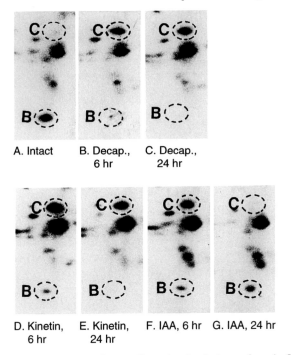

A. Intact   B. Decap.,   C. Decap.,
          6 hr   24 hr

D. Kinetin,   E. Kinetin,   F. IAA, 6 hr   G. IAA, 24 hr
   6 hr   24 hr

Figure 3 Analysis of bud proteins by two-dimensional gel electrophoresis. Small portions of two-dimensional polyacrylamide gels demonstrate the dynamic expression patterns of a dormancy-specific protein and a growth-specific protein (**B** and **C,** respectively). (A–C) Expression in buds on intact plants and following decapitation. (D and E) Expression in kinetin-treated buds on intact plants (10 μg in 10 μl of 50% ethanol and 5% Carbowax was added directly to buds). Pattern is identical to that of buds on decapitated plants at each time. (F and G) Expression in buds of auxin-treated plants (1% IAA in lanolin was added to the stumps of decapitated plants). These buds did not grow, but at 6 hr they expressed the growth-specific pattern of proteins. (Modified from Stafstrom and Sussex, 1988. Copyright Springer-Verlag, used with permission.)

dormant again. A better understanding of patterns of bud development between and within growing seasons will allow these growth–dormancy cycles to be analyzed using improved molecular and biochemical tools.

IV. Patterns of Axillary Bud Development

A. Branching and Plant Architecture

The primary functions of stems and branches are to support a canopy of photosynthetically active leaves (see Givnish [1] in this volume) and to support the development and display of flowers and fruits (see Waller and

Steingraeber [2] in this volume). The architectural form of a plant results from many developmental and stochastic processes. Differential activation and elongation of individual axillary buds are of primary importance in determining plant form. In addition, branch angle, allometric relationships between coarseness of branching and leaf size (Corner's rules; Bond and Midgley, 1988), tropic responses of individual branches, branch abscission, and other factors contribute to the form of a plant. The regulation of each process results from genetic and environmental factors (Hallé *et al.*, 1978; Tomlinson, 1983; Bell, 1991).

Genetic control of branch angle, for example, is readily apparent in the weeping variant of European beech (*Fagus sylvatica* var. Pendula) and in the narrow, columnar crown of Lombardy poplar (*Populus nigra* var. Italica). A dwarf mutant of sweetgum (*Liquidambar*) has short internodes, as expected, but in addition its shape is converted from an excurrent "tree" with a single trunk to a decurrent "shrub" with many overtopping branches (Zimmermann and Brown, 1971). The form of a plant is influenced greatly by the environment in which it grows. Tulip poplar (*Liriodendron*) is typically thought of as an excurrent tree, but it can have a decurrent crown in dry environments. Trees that grow near the tree line are commonly stunted and gnarled compared to their down-slope siblings. Individuals of the same genotype of poison oak (*Toxicodendron diversilobum*) can grow as vines or shrubs depending on whether they encounter physical support (Gartner, 1991). Such developmental plasticity makes it impossible to categorically define *the* form of any species or genotype. In this context, Wilson ([4] in this volume) discusses what may or may not be a "shrub."

One might expect that strong apical dominance—inhibition of axillary bud development by an actively growing terminal bud—would be correlated with excurrent tree form, whereas weak apical dominance would occur in decurrent species. Instead, Brown and co-workers (1967) discovered an inverse relationship between these factors: buds on first-year twigs of excurrent species tended to develop whereas those of decurrent species did not. In subsequent years, however, lateral shoots in excurrent plants grew less than terminal shoots and those in decurrent plants grew quickly and overtopped the terminal shoots. These authors have suggested that the term "apical dominance" be restricted to describing bud and shoot development within a growing season and "apical control" be used to describe the more complex interactions that occur between growing shoots and dormant buds in subsequent seasons. An appropriate level of caution is suggested by the following quote: "The disparity between the release of lateral buds on herbaceous plants following decapitation and the natural release of inhibited lateral buds on twigs after over-wintering . . . is not nearly as simple as it might first appear" (Zimmermann and Brown, 1971, p. 132).

The position of a bud on a twig influences its developmental potential.

Branches and main shoots of English oak (*Quercus petraea*) show an acrotonic pattern of development, that is, the most distal (terminal) buds are most likely to develop into branches (Harmer, 1991). This pattern is due at least in part to bud size, because terminal buds are larger than subterminal whorl buds, which are larger than interwhorl buds. The largest buds are the first to be activated in the spring and the last to be arrested at the end of the growth flush. Coppice shoots of mulberry (*Morus alba*) also show an acrotonic branching pattern (Suzuki, 1990). Decapitation of these shoots at any position promotes development of highest remaining buds. Even basal buds are competent to develop, but their potential is held in reserve as long as apical buds are available.

B. Position-Dependent Bud Development in Pea

The pea genome contains at least five loci that influence branch development (*ramosus* mutants; Murfet and Reid, 1993) and additional loci (*procumbens, ascendens*) that influence branch angle (Blixt, 1972). The author has studied branching in plants homozygous for *rms*-1 (L.5237) and *rms*-2 (L.5951), and cv. Parvus (L.1107), from which both mutants were derived (obtained from the Nordic Genebank, Alnarp, Sweden). Position-dependent branch development is regulated by both genetic and environmental factors. Plants grown in a growth chamber demonstrate the "typical" form of each genetic line (Fig. 4A–C): L.1107 had branches at upper nodes only (aerial branching); L.5237 contained well-developed branches at nearly every node (complete branching); and L.5951 had well-developed branches at basal and aerial nodes, but not at intermediary nodes (gap branching).

The same lines were grown in the greenhouse during the winter, either with or without supplemental lighting. Without supplemental lighting, branching was drastically reduced in all lines (Fig. 4D–F): branches failed to develop on L.1107; L. 5237 had basal and aerial branches; and L.5951 contained only basal branches. Twelve hours of supplemental lighting gave rise to branching patterns similar to those observed on plants grown in the growth chamber (Fig. 4G–I). In this experiment, supplemental lighting began 17 days after sowing. In a final experiment, supplemental lighting was provided beginning at the time of sowing (Fig. 4J–L). L.1107 now contained basal branches as well as aerial branches (gap phenotype), and L.5237 and L.5951 contained multiple branches at basal nodes, which had not been observed previously in L.5237. F_1 plants from all possible crosses between these lines and the Alaska cultivar were grown with supplemental lighting from the time of sowing. All of these plants had the gap phenotype (data not shown). The formation of basal branches in the Alaska crosses indicates the presence of a dominant branching gene in the other three lines. This gene is the photoperiodic gene *Sn,* which is known to influence

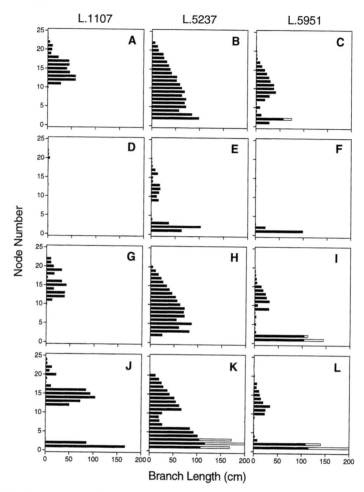

Figure 4 Genetic and environmental regulation of branch development in pea. Branch length is graphed as a function of nodal position; each white bar represents a second branch from the same node (the cotyledonary node is node 0). The pea lines studied were L.1107 (parental line) and two branching mutants, L.5237 (*rms-1*) and L.5951 (*rms-2*). (A–C) Grown in a growth chamber under a 16-hr photoperiod (fluorescent and incandescent lamps provided ca. 50 μmol m^{-2} sec^{-1} at pot top). (D–F) Grown in a greenhouse during the winter without supplemental lighting. (G–I) Conditions as for (D–F), except supplemental lighting provided beginning on day 17 (12 hr/day overlapping the natural photoperiod, from 1000-W multivapor lamps, ca. 100 μmol m^{-2} sec^{-1} at pot top). (J–L) Conditions as for (G–I), except supplemental lighting provided from the time of sowing.

branching but has been studied more extensively for its role in controlling flowering (Murfet and Reid, 1993). *Sn* also may be responsible for increased basal branching in L.5951 and L.5237 plants.

L.1107 plants contained basal branches when supplemental light was provided beginning at the time of sowing (Fig. 4J) but not when supplemental lighting began 17 days after sowing (Fig. 4G). This result suggests that there is a limited period during which basal buds are competent to develop. This hypothesis was tested by sowing plants in inductive (greenhouse, 12-hr photoperiod) or noninductive (growth chamber, 24-hr photoperiod) environments and switching them at various times. In control experiments, only plants growing in the greenhouse developed basal branches (data not shown). Switching plants to the greenhouse after 7, 10, or 14 days resulted in strong basal branch development, but basal branches were absent on plants switched after 17 or 21 days. In reciprocal experiments, plants were switched from the greenhouse to the growth chamber. Again, the critical period for induction of basal branching occurred between 14 and 17 days.

Different patterns of branch development in pea plants grown with or without supplemental lighting might suggest that light intensity is important in regulating this process. Saplings of *Castanopsis,* a tree from southern China, developed fewer basal branches and grew taller when grown under relatively "high-shade" (low-light) conditions (Cornelissen, 1993). Shading also inhibited the development of epicormic branches from suppressed trace buds (Ward, 1966). Many shade effects may be regulated by light quality rather than light intensity. For example, widely spaced, noncompeting wheat plants formed five times more branch tillers and eight times more seed than closely spaced plants. Tillering was shown to be inhibited by far-red light and promoted by red light, indicating regulation by phytochrome (Kasperbauer and Karlen, 1986). Other shade-induced growth phenomena also appear to be mediated by ratios of red and far-red light (Ballaré *et al.,* 1990; Schmitt and Wulff, 1993).

V. Plasticity of Developmental Potential

A. Alternative Patterns of Branch Development

Vegetative buds may develop into shoots and branches with a wide range of morphologies. For example, shoots may grow orthotropically or plagiotropically, that is, either vertically or at some angle away from the vertical. In many plants, this distinction is merely a reflection of the position of a branch in the canopy. In others, phyllotaxy, leaf shape, and other characters may be indicative of each type of shoot and may reflect a permanent or developmentally determined state. In *Theobroma,* the morphological characters that distinguish orthotropic and plagiotropic shoots are retained when either is removed from the parent plant and rooted (Bell, 1991). The presence of juvenile and adult shoots in some plants is another example of phenotypic plasticity. The juvenile form of ivy (*Hedera helix*) has distichous phyllotaxy and lobed leaves, forms adventitious roots but no flowers, and grows by climbing or spreading; in contrast, the adult form has spiral phyllotaxy and entire leaves, forms flowers but no roots, and grows upright or horizontally. When each type of shoot is cultured, new shoots that regenerate are of the same type, indicating that each state is determined at the cellular level (cf. Lyndon, 1990). Finally, buds may develop as long shoots or short shoots. As indicated previously, long shoots have the capacity to explore new areas for resources whereas short shoots are well suited to exploiting local resources. Because buds in a basal position frequently develop as short shoots and those in a terminal position become long shoots, this phenomenon may be regarded as a form of apical dominance. In *Liquidambar,* a monopodial perennial, the same apical meristem may form long shoots or short shoots in successive years, demonstrating that this meristem is not determined to form only one type of shoot (Zimmermann and Brown, 1971).

B. Alternative Patterns of Shoot Development in Pea

The morphology of branch shoots on Alaska pea plants was analyzed with regard to the position of the bud on the plant axis and the stage of plant development at the time of decapitation (Fig. 5; Stafstrom, 1995). The largest axillary bud at the cotyledonary node through node 2 (N0, N1, and N2L buds, respectively) plus the second largest bud at node 2 (N2S bud) were studied. These buds were stimulated to develop by decapitating the main shoot when buds were still growing (4-day plants), shortly after buds became dormant (7-day plants), or after the main shoot had flowered (postflowering plants, about 21 days after sowing). Branch shoots were scored for node of floral initiation (NFI), shoot length, and node of multiple leaflets (NML), a measure of leaf complexity. The NFI score on 4- or 7-day plants was one to two nodes greater than on postflowering plants, perhaps because a cotyledon-derived floral inhibitor had been depleted in the latter plants (Murfet and Reid, 1993). The NFI score for shoots derived from buds at all nodes on postflowering plants was about 4, indicating that the position of a bud is not important in determining NFI (Fig. 5A). Whether a bud was growing or dormant when the plant was decapitated also did not influence NFI. In contrast to these results, nodal position of a bud and its state of growth are important regulators of the transition to reproductive development in Wisconsin-38 tobacco plants (McDaniel and Hsu, 1976; McDaniel *et al.,* 1989). Shoots on 4-day plants were about 20% longer than those on 7-day plants and more than five times longer than those on postflowering plants (Fig. 5D). These differences may be due in part to the depletion of cotyledon-derived gibberellic acids during ontogeny. The NFI and NML scores for the main shoot and for axillary shoots were similar under some experimental conditions, but different under other conditions (Fig. 5C). Therefore, it is likely that different node-counting mechanisms account for each trait. These results demonstrate that the morphology of

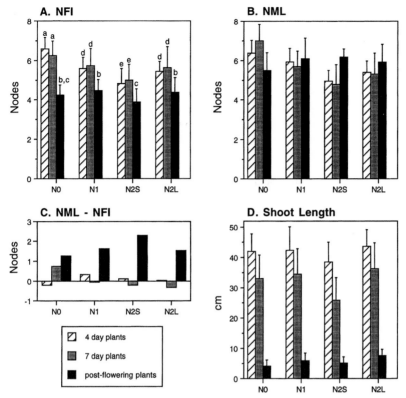

Figure 5 Branch morphology on decapitated pea plants (cultivar Alaska). Plants were grown in a growth chamber under a 16-hr photoperiod. Plants were decapitated before buds became dormant (4-day plants), shortly after buds became dormant (7-day plants), or after the main shoot had flowered (postflowering plants; about 21 days under these conditions). The largest axillary bud at the cotyledonary node, node 1 and node 2 (N0, N1, and N2L buds, respectively), plus the second largest bud at node 2 (N2S bud) were studied. Branch shoots were scored for (A) node of floral initiation (NFI); (B) node of multiple leaflets (NML), the first node to contain a leaf with more than two leaflets; (C) difference between NML and NFI; and (D) branch length to NFI. Data represent the mean ± SD; in (A), means marked with different letters were significantly different ($p<0.05$) according to Student's t test. (From Stafstrom, 1995. Copyright Annals of Botany Company, used with permission)

pea branches is influenced to a greater extent by when a bud is stimulated to grow than by where the bud is located on the plant axis.

C. How Long Do Dormant Buds Remain Competent to Develop?

The period of time over which a dormant bud remains competent to develop is an important feature of the ability of a plant to track its environment or respond to damage. Developmental competence spanning only several weeks or months, such as occurs in pea plants, will seem trivial to those who study woody perennials. However, it is common for buds to senesce soon after they are formed. The fate of buds of water hyacinth (*Eichornia crassipes*) depends on their position and stage of ontogeny (Richards, 1982). When terminal meristems become reproductive, subterminal axillary buds develop as replacement shoots and basal buds may give rise to new stolons (functionally equivalent to short shoots and long shoots, respectively). There is a limited period during which basal buds can develop. The position of a ramet within the colony and competition for light and nutrients dictate whether a particular bud will develop or senesce. Plasticity of branch development in water hyacinth also is influenced by the genotype of a plant (Geber *et al.*, 1992). It was mentioned previously that all buds on mulberry coppice shoots were competent to develop under certain conditions (Suzuki, 1990). On intact shoots, however, basal buds senesce by early summer. Buds at different positions on rose and apple shoots also differed in size, morphology, physiological responses, and in their potential to develop into branches (Zamski *et al.*, 1985; Theron *et al.*, 1987).

One might expect that the record for dormant bud longevity would occur in long-lived trees, but most buds actually develop within 1 or 2 years of being formed. Epicormic branches can develop from buds stored within the bark of trunks or branches. Careful anatomical studies are necessary to determine whether these buds are adventitious or preventitious in origin (Fink, 1983). Regardless of origin, buds must grow enough each year to keep pace with the expanding periderm. Vascular traces produced by these buds can traverse dozens of annual growth rings. Because they grow each year "trace buds" are considered to be suppressed rather than truly dormant (Kozlowski, 1971; Zimmermann and Brown, 1971). Harper writes that "a most remarkable example of vegetative dormancy comes from the regrowth of stumps of Coolibah trees (*Eucalyptus microtheca*) which remained dormant for 69 years after felling and, after a storm in 1974, 60% of the stumps produced vigorous new shoots" (Harper, 1977, p. 110). Because eucalypts have a high capacity for regenerating new shoots (Cremer, 1972), it is not clear whether the buds that formed these shoots were preventitious or adventitious, or when they were formed. Pitcher plant rhizomes can remain dormant for decades, where dormancy is defined as the absence of either flowers or highly modified pitcher leaves (Folkerts, 1990). However, rhizomes contain inconspicuous photosynthetic phyllodia that could support a minimal level of growth and metabolism, and therefore the dormancy state of these buds also is unclear.

VI. Summary: Development of Reserve Meristems

Growing shoots may be lost due to disease, herbivory, or a variety of natural disasters, and thus the maintenance of banks of dormant buds is relevant to practical problems related to agriculture, horticulture, forestry, and range science, and to a fundamental understanding of plant development and evolution. Increased branching may be beneficial to the plant or to goals of the planter. Reproductive development and agricultural yield are related to development of a photosynthetic canopy (Gifford *et al.,* 1984). Highly branched wheat plants produce severalfold more grain than plants with fewer branches. Because close spacing of plants reduces branching, yield in the field might be considerably lower (Kasperbauer and Karlen, 1986). When yield characters of a branched variety of pea and its parental line were compared in field studies over several seasons, the branched line consistently outperformed the parental line by about 3%, a small but agronomically important difference (Gelin, 1955). Vegetative reproduction following fire requires a supply of dormant, reserve meristems (Matlack *et al.,* 1993) or the ability to generate adventitious meristems (Bowen and Pate, 1993). Range grasses need a supply of dormant tiller buds to survive grazing. Tiller buds on two species of *Agropyron* are morphologically identical but, following grazing, *A. desertorum* produces up to 18 times as many tillers as *A. spicatum* (Mueller and Richards, 1986). Similarly, two rangeland shrubs, sagebrush (*Artemisia tridentata*) and bitterbrush (*Purshia tridentata*), differ in their tolerance to browsing, which reflects the different developmental potentials of their dormant buds (Bilbrough and Richards, 1993). In many instances, increased branching may be anathema to agricultural goals. Increased branching is disadvantageous to the tomato crop, because excessive "suckers" must be removed manually. In lumber production, increased branching can reduce the amount of wood in the main bole and increase the number of knots, which reduces lumber quality (Kozlowski, 1971). In all cases, however, the availability of reserve meristems is paramount to survival.

In pea, the dormant and growing developmental states can be interconverted rapidly and repeatedly. This and other features were demonstrated by the expression of stage-specific genes and proteins. Position-dependent branch development is affected by genetic background, environmental conditions, and the stage of ontogeny at which a plant is exposed to inductive conditions. Branch morphology also is influenced by when a bud is stimulated to develop. Among our current challenges is to determine how apical dominance, bud dormancy, and related developmental phenomena are regulated in other herbaceous dicots, woody plants, and grasses. In the future, available and emerging molecular technologies might be used to manipulate bud growth and dormancy, with the aim of altering plant form and agricultural yield.

Acknowledgments

I thank Dr. Carl Von Ende for many helpful discussions and Drs. D. A. Steingraeber, I. M. Sussex, and P. B. Tomlinson for comments on the manuscript. This work was supported by the Plant Molecular Biology Center (Northern Illinois University, De Kalb, IL).

References

Abel, S., Oeller, P. W., and Theologis, A. (1994). Early auxin-induced genes encode short-lived nuclear proteins. *Proc. Natl. Acad. Sci. USA* **91**, 326–330.

Bachelard, E. P., and Wightman, F. (1973). Biochemical and physiological studies on dormancy release in tree buds. I. Changes in degree of dormancy, respiratory capacity, and major cell constituents in overwintering buds of *Populus balsamifera*. *Can. J. Bot.* **51**, 2315–2326.

Ballaré, C. L., Scopel, A. L., and Sánchez, R. A. (1990). Far-red radiation reflected from adjacent leaves: An early signal of competition in plant canopies. *Science* **247**, 329–332.

Bell, A. D. (1991). "Plant Form." Oxford University Press, Oxford.

Bilbrough, C. J., and Richards, J. H. (1993). Growth of sagebrush and bitterbrush following simulated winter browsing: Mechanisms of tolerance. *Ecology* **74**, 481–492.

Blixt, S. (1972). Mutation genetics in *Pisum*. *Agric. Hortic. Genet.* **30**, 1–293.

Bond, W. J., and Midgley, J. (1988). Allometry and sexual differences in leaf size. *Am. Nat.* **131**, 901–910.

Borchert, R. (1991). Growth periodicity and dormancy. *In* "Physiology of Trees" (A. S. Raghavendra, ed.), pp. 221–245. John Wiley & Sons, New York.

Bowen, B. J., and Pate, J. S. (1993). The significance of root starch in post-fire shoot recovery of the resprouter *Stirlingia latifolia* (Proteaceae). *Ann. Bot.* **72**, 7–16.

Brown, C. L., McAlpine, R. G., and Kormanik, P. P. (1967). Apical dominance and form in woody plants: A reappraisal. *Am. J. Bot.* **54**, 153–162.

Cline, M. G. (1991). Apical dominance. *Bot. Rev.* **57**, 318–358.

Cline, M. G. (1994). The role of hormones in apical dominance. New approaches to an old problem in plant development. *Physiol. Plant.* **90**, 230–237.

Colasanti, J., Cho, S.-O., Wick, S., and Sundaresan, V. (1993). Localization of the functional p34^cdc2 homolog of maize in root tip and stomatal complex cells: Association with predicted division sites. *Plant Cell* **5**, 1101–1111.

Cornelissen, J. H. C. (1993). Above ground morphology of shade-tolerant *Castanopsis fargesii* saplings in response to light environment. *Int. J. Plant Sci.* **154**, 481–495.

Cremer, K. W. (1972). Morphology and development of primary and accessory buds of *Eucalyptus regnans*. *Aust. J. Bot.* **20**, 175–195.

Devitt, M. L., and Stafstrom, J. P. (1995). Cell cycle regulation during growth-dormancy cycles in pea axillary buds. *Plant Mol. Biol.*, in press.

Duerr, B., Gawienowski, M., Ropp, T., and Jacobs, T. (1993). MsERK1: A mitogen-activated protein kinase from a flowering plant. *Plant Cell* **5**, 87–96.

Fink, S. (1983). The occurrence of adventitious and preventitious buds within the bark of some temperate and tropical trees. *Am. J. Bot.* **70**, 532–542.

Fleming, A. J., Mandel, T., Roth, I., and Kuhlemeier, C. (1993). The patterns of gene expression in the tomato shoot apical meristem. *Plant Cell* **5**, 297–309.

Folkerts, G. W. (1990). The white-topped pitcher plant—a case of precarious abundance. *Oryx* **24**, 201–207.

Fuchigami, L. H., and Nee, C.-C. (1987). Degree growth stage model and rest-breaking mechanisms in temperate woody perennials. *Hortic. Sci.* **22**, 836–845.

Gartner, B. L. (1991). Is the climbing habit of poison oak ecotypic? *Funct. Ecol.* **5**, 696–704.

Geber, M. A. (1990). The cost of meristem limitation in *Polygonum arenastrum*: Negative genetic correlations between fecundity and growth. *Evolution* **44**, 799–819.

Geber, M. A., Watson, M. A., and Furnish, R. (1992). Genetic differences in clonal demography in *Eichornia crassipes*. *J. Ecol.* **80**, 329–341.

Gelin, O. E. V. (1955). Studies on the X-ray mutation Stral pea. *Agric. Hortique Genet.* **13**, 183–193.

Gifford, R. M., Thorne, J. H., Hitz, W. D., and Giaquinta, R. T. (1984). Crop productivity and photoassimilate partitioning. *Science* **225**, 801–808.

Gocal, G. F. W., Pharis, R. P., Yeung, E. C., and Pearce, D. (1991). Changes after decapitation of indole-3-acetic acid and abscisic acid in the larger axillary bud of *Phaseolus vulgaris* L. cv Tender Green. *Plant Physiol.* **95**, 344–350.

Grime, J. P., Crick, J. C., and Rincon, J. E. (1986). The ecological significance of plasticity. *Symp. Soc. Exp. Biol.* **40**, 5–29.

Hallé, F., Oldeman, R. A. A., and Tomlinson, P. B. (1978). "Tropical Trees and Forests. An Architectural Analysis." Springer-Verlag, New York.

Hardwick, R. C. (1986). Physiological consequences of modular growth of plants. *Philos. Trans. R. Soc. London Ser. B* **313**, 161–173.

Harmer, R. (1991). The effect of bud position on branch growth and bud abscission in *Quercus petraea* (Matt.) Liebl. *Ann. Bot.* **67**, 463–468.

Harper, J. L. (1977). "Population Biology of Plants." Academic Press, London.

Harper, J. L. (1985). Modules, branches, and the capture of resources. *In* "Population Biology and Evolution of Clonal Organisms" (J. B. C. Jackson, L. W. Buss, and R. E. Cook, eds.), pp. 1–33. Yale University Press, New Haven, Connecticut.

Hemerly, A. S., Ferreira, P., de Almeida Engler, J., Van Montagu, M., Engler, G., and Inzé, D. (1993). *cdc2a* expression in *Arabidopsis* is linked with competence for cell division. *Plant Cell* **5**, 1711–1723.

Hillman, J. R. (1984). Apical dominance. *In* "Advanced Plant Physiology" (M. B. Wilkins, ed.), pp. 127–148. Pitman, London.

Hirt, H., Mink, M., Pfosser, M., Bogre, L., Gyorgyey, J., Jonak, C., Gartner, A., Dudits, D., and Heberle-Bors, E. (1992). Alfalfa cyclins: Differential expression during the cell cycle and in plant organs. *Plant Cell* **4**, 1531–1538.

Jacobs, T. W. (1992). Control of the cell cycle. *Dev. Biol.* **153**, 1–15.

Kasperbauer, M. J., and Karlen, D. L. (1986). Light-mediated bioregulation of tillering and photosynthate partitioning in wheat. *Physiol. Plant.* **66**, 159–163.

Klee, H. J., and Estelle, M. A. (1991). Molecular genetic approaches to plant hormone biology. *Annu. Rev. Plant Physiol. Plant Mol. Biol.* **42**, 529–551.

Kozlowski, T. T. (1971). "Growth and Development of Trees," Vol. I: Seed Germination, Ontogeny, and Shoot Growth. Academic Press, New York.

Lang, G. A. (1987). Dormancy: A new universal terminology. *Hortic. Sci.* **22**, 817–820.

Lovett Doust, L. (1981). Population dynamics and local specialization in a clonal perennial (*Ranunculus repens*). I. The dynamics of ramets in contrasting habits. *J. Ecol.* **69**, 734–755.

Lyndon, R. F. (1990). "Plant Development." Unwin-Hyman, London.

Lyndon, R. F., and Cunninghame, M. E. (1986). Control of shoot apical development via cell division. *Symp. Soc. for Exp. Biol.* **40**, 233–255.

Maillette, L. (1987). Effects of bud demography and elongation patterns of *Betula cordifolia* near the tree line. *Ecology* **68**, 1251–1261.

Maillette, L. (1990). The value of meristem states, as estimated by discrete-time Markov chain. *Oikos* **59**, 235–240.

Matlack, G. R., Gibson, D. J., and Good, R. E. (1993). Regeneration of the shrub *Gaylussacia baccata* and associated species after low-intensity fire in an Atlantic coastal plain forest. *Am. J. Bot.* **80**, 119–126.

McDaniel, C. N., and Hsu, F. C. (1976). Position-dependent development of tobacco meristems. *Nature (London)* **259**, 564–565.

McDaniel, C. N., Sangery, K. A., and Singer, S. R. (1989). Node counting in axillary buds of *Nicotiana tabacum* cv. Wisconsin 38, a day-neutral plant. *Am. J. Bot.* **76**, 403–408.

McGurl, B., Pearce, G., Orozco-Cardenas, M., and Ryan, C. A. (1991). Structure, expression, and antisense inhibition of the systemin precursor gene. *Science* **255**, 1570–1573.

Medford, J. I. (1992). Vegetative apical meristems. *Plant Cell* **4**, 1029–1039.

Meicenheimer, R. D. (1981). Changes in *Epilobium* phyllotaxy induced by *N*-1-naphthylphthalamic acid and α-4-chlorophenoxyisobutyric acid. *Am. J. Bot.* **68**, 1139–1154.

Mikami, K., and Iwabuchi, M. (1992). Regulation of cell cycle-dependent gene expression. *In* "Control of Plant Gene Expression" (D. P. S. Verma, ed.), pp. 51–68. CRC Press, Boca Raton, Florida.

Mueller, R. J., and Richards, J. H. (1986). Morphological analysis of tillering in *Agropyron spicatum* and *Agropyron desertorum*. *Ann. Bot.* **58**, 911–921.

Murfet, I. C., and Reid, J. B. (1993). Developmental mutants. *In* "Peas—Genetics, Molecular Biology and Biotechnology" (D. R. Davies and R. Casey, eds.), pp. 165–216. CAB International, Wallingford, UK.

Murray, A. W., and Hunt, T. (1993). "The Cell Cycle: An Introduction." W. H. Freeman, New York.

Nooden, L. D., and Weber, J. A. (1978). Environmental and hormonal control of dormancy in terminal buds of plants. *In* "Dormancy and Developmental Arrest" (M. E. Clutter, ed.), pp. 221–268. Academic Press, New York.

Palevitz, B. A. (1993). Morphological plasticity of the mitotic apparatus in plants and its developmental consequences. *Plant Cell* **5**, 1001–1009.

Pitelka, L. F., and Ashmun, J. W. (1985). Physiology and integration of ramets in clonal plants. *In* "Population Biology and Evolution of Clonal Organisms" (J. B. C. Jackson, L. W. Buss, and R. E. Cook, eds.), pp. 399–435. Yale University Press, New Haven, Connecticut.

Powell, L. E. (1988). The hormonal control of bud and seed dormancy in woody plants. *In* "Plant Hormones and Their Role in Plant Growth and Development" (P. J. Davies, ed.), pp. 539–552. Kluwer Academic, Dordrecht, the Netherlands.

Price, E. A. C., Marshall, C., and Hutchings, M. J. (1992). Studies of growth in the clonal herb *Glechoma hederacea*. I. Patterns of physiological integration. *J. Ecol.* **80**, 25–38.

Raskin, I. (1992). Role of salicylic acid in plants. *Annu. Rev. Plant Physiol. Plant Mol. Biol.* **43**, 439–463.

Richards, J. H. (1982). Developmental potential of axillary buds of water hyacinth, *Eichhornia crassipes* Solms. (Pontederiaceae). *Am. J. Bot.* **69**, 615–622.

Romano, C. P., Cooper, M. L., and Klee, H. J. (1993). Uncoupling auxin and ethylene effects in transgenic tobacco and *Arabidopsis* plants. *Plant Cell* **5**, 181–189.

Ruderman, J. V. (1993). MAP kinase and the activation of quiescent cells. *Curr. Opin. Cell Biol.* **5**, 207–213.

Ryan, C. A. (1994). Oligosaccharide signals: From plant defense to parasite offense. *Proc. Natl. Acad. Sci. U.S.A.* **91**, 1–2.

Sachs, T. (1991). "Pattern Formation in Plant Tissues." Cambridge University Press, Cambridge.

Scheiner, S. M. (1993). Genetics and evolution of phenotypic plasticity. *Annu. Rev. Ecol. Syst.* **24**, 35–68.

Schlichting, C. D. (1986). The evolution of phenotypic plasticity in plants. *Annu. Rev. Ecol. Syst.* **17**, 667–693.

Schmitt, J., and Wulff, R. D. (1993). Light spectral quality, phytochrome and plant competition. *Trends Ecol. Evol.* **8**, 47–51.

Sembdner, G., and Parthier, B. (1993). The biochemistry and the physiological and molecular actions of jasmonates. *Annu. Rev. Plant Physiol. Plant Mol. Biol.* **44**, 569–589.

Skoog, F., and Miller, C. O. (1957). Chemical regulation of growth and organ formation in plant tissues cultured *in vitro*. *Symp. Soc. Exp. Biol.* **11**, 118–131.

Skoog, F., and Thimann, K. V. (1934). Further experiments on the inhibition of the development of lateral buds by growth hormone. *Proc. Natl. Acad. Sci. U.S.A.* **20**, 480–485.

Snow, R. (1937). On the nature of correlative inhibition. *New Phytol.* **36**, 283–300.

Stafstrom, J. P. (1993). Axillary bud development in pea: Apical dominance, growth cycles, hormonal regulation and plant architecture. *In* "Cellular Communication in Plants" (R. M. Amasino, ed.), pp. 75–86. Plenum Press, New York.

Stafstrom, J. P. (1995). Influence of bud position and plant ontogeny on the morphology of branch shoots in pea (*Pisum sativum* L. cv. Alaska). *Ann. Bot., in press.*

Stafstrom, J. P., and Sussex, I. M. (1988). Patterns of protein synthesis in dormant and growing vegetative buds of pea. *Planta* **176**, 497–505.

Stafstrom, J. P., and Sussex, I. M. (1992). Expression of a ribosomal protein gene in axillary buds of pea. *Plant Physiol.* **100**, 1494–1502.

Stafstrom, J. P., Altschuler, M., and Anderson, D. H. (1993). Molecular cloning and expression of a MAP kinase homologue from pea. *Plant Mol. Biol.* **22**, 83–90.

Sussex, I. M. (1989). Developmental programming of the shoot meristem. *Cell* **56**, 225–229.

Suzuki, T. (1990). Apical control of lateral bud development in mulberry (*Morus alba*). *Physiol. Plant.* **80**, 350–356.

Tamas, I. A. (1988). Hormonal regulation of apical dominance. *In* "Plant Hormones and Their Role in Plant Growth and Development" (P. J. Davies, ed.), pp. 393–410. Kluwer, Dordrecht, the Netherlands.

Tanimoto, E. Y., Rost, T. L., and Comai, L. (1993). DNA replication-dependent histone H2A mRNA expression in pea root tips. *Plant Physiol.* **103**, 1291–1297.

Theron, K. I., Jacobs, G., and Strydom, D. K. (1987). Correlative inhibition of axillary buds in apple nursery trees in relation to node position, defoliation, and promalin treatment. *J. Am. Soc. Hortic. Sci.* **112**, 732–734.

Thompson, M. M., Smith, D. C., and Burgess, J. E. (1985). Nondormant mutants in a temperate tree species, *Corylus avellana* L. *Theor. Appl. Genet.* **70**, 687–692.

Tomlinson, P. B. (1983). Tree architecture. *Am. Sci.* **71**, 141–149.

Trewavas, A. J. (1986). Resource allocation under poor growth conditions. A major role for growth substances in developmental plasticity. *Symp. Soc. Exp. Biol.* **40**, 31–76.

Wang, S. Y., Faust, M., and Steffens, G. L. (1985). Metabolic changes in cherry flower buds associated with breaking of dormancy in early and late blooming cultivars. *Physiol. Plant.* **65**, 89–94.

Ward, W. W. (1966). Epicormic branching of black and white oaks. *For. Sci.* **12**, 290–296.

Wardlaw, C. W. (1965). Leaves and buds: Mechanisms of local induction in plant growth. *In* "Cell Differentiation and Morphogenesis," (W. Beermann, R. J. Gautheret, P. D. Nieuwkoop, C. W. Wardlaw, V. B. Wigglesworth, E. Wolff, and J. A. O. Zeevaart, eds.), pp. 96–119. North-Holland, Amsterdam.

Watson, M. A., and Casper, B. B. (1984). Morphogenetic constraints on patterns of carbon distribution in plants. *Annu. Rev. Ecol. Syst.* **15**, 233–258.

White, J. (1979). The plant as a metapopulation. *Annu. Rev. Ecol. Syst.* **10**, 109–145.

Wick, S. (1991). Spatial aspects of cytokinesis in plant cells. *Curr. Opin. Cell Biol.* **3**, 253–260.

Zamski, E., Oshri, S., and Zieslin, N. (1985). Comparative morphology and anatomy of axillary buds along a rose shoot. *Bot. Gaz.* **146**, 208–212.

Zimmermann, M. H., and Brown, C. L. (1971). "Tree Structure and Function." Springer-Verlag, New York.

Zurek, D. M., and Clouse, S. D. (1994). Molecular cloning and characterization of a brassino-steroid-regulated gene from elongating soybean (*Glycine max* L.) epicotyls. *Plant Physiol.* **104**, 161–170.

13

Hormonal Control of Radial and Longitudinal Growth in the Tree Stem

C. H. Anthony Little and Richard P. Pharis

I. Introduction

Hormones are chemical signals that are widely believed to transduce many of the environmental cues known to affect the growth of plants. The evidence implicating the currently recognized hormone classes in the regulation of radial and longitudinal growth in the stem and shoots of woody species is briefly reviewed in this chapter. Emphasis is placed on investigations that used temperate-zone tree species as the experimental material and modern physicochemical or immunoassay techniques to identify and measure endogenous hormone levels. Understanding the roles of hormones, and the mechanisms regulating their absolute and relative levels, not only would significantly increase our basic knowledge about how trees grow and develop, but also could have practical applications, for example, in the development of methods for early screening of inherently fast growth in breeding programs, and for using genetic engineering to alter traits such as wood quantity and quality (Whetten and Sederoff, 1991) and tree form.

Longitudinal growth involves the elongation of preformed stem units [node (typically leaf plus axillary bud) plus subjacent internode] after a period of dormancy ("fixed growth") or the concurrent initiation and extension of new stem units ("free growth"), or some combination of these two processes (Lanner, 1976). It is localized to current-year shoots and is associated with the activity of the subapical meristems. The apical meristem of the current-year shoot gives rise to the procambium and primary vascular tissues associated with radial growth in the elongating part of the shoot, and produces the primordia in the developing buds. Radial growth associated with the vascular cambium, which produces secondary xylem and phloem, and the phellogen, which gives rise to the periderm, commences at the base of the current-year shoot and progresses acropetally as elongation ceases in successively more distal portions. Below the current-year shoot, radial growth typically occurs along the entire length of the stem. Both longitudinal and radial growth involve the division of meristematic cells and the differentiation of specialized cell types, and vary with such factors as genotype, age, within-tree position, site, weather and competition (e.g., Kozlowski *et al.,* 1991). The apical and cambial meristems exhibit an annual cycle of activity and dormancy, with the latter having two stages: rest and quiescence (Reinders-Gouwentak, 1965; Little and Bonga, 1974; Lang *et al.,* 1985; Powell, 1987). Rest develops at the beginning of the dormant period and is imposed by internal factors that prevent activation of the meristem under environmental conditions favorable for growth. Exposure to chilling temperatures (ca. 2–10°C) gradually changes rest into quiescence, during which stage the dormancy is caused solely by unfavorable environmental conditions, typically low temperature. The timing of the rest–quiescence transition, and the amount of chilling required to break rest, vary with genotype, age, and temperature regime.

II. Identification, Metabolism, and Movement of Hormones

All known classes of plant hormones occur in vegetative tissues of both conifers and woody angiosperms. Auxins [to date, indole-3-acetic acid (IAA) is the only one characterized in shoots of woody species; Table I], gibberellins (GAs; Table II), cytokinins (CKs; Table III), and abscisic acid

Table I   Characterization of Endogenous Indole-3-acetic Acid in Vegetative Parts of Tree Shoots

Species	Part	Ref.
Abies balsamea	Cambial region	Sundberg *et al.* (1987)
Acer pennsylvanicum	Developing xylem	Savidge (1990)
Acer saccharum	Developing xylem	Savidge (1990)
Alnus rugosa	Developing xylem	Savidge (1990)
Betula alleghaniensis	Developing xylem	Savidge (1990)
Betula papyrifera	Developing xylem	Savidge (1990)

continues

Table I   *Continued*

Species	Part	Ref.
Citrus sinesis	Shoots	Plummer *et al.* (1991)
	Leaves	Vine *et al.* (1987)
Cornus alternifolia	Developing xylem	Savidge (1990)
Corylus avellana	Shoots	Rodríguez *et al.* (1991)
Cryptomeria japonica	Cambial region	Funada *et al.* (1990)
Fagus grandifolia	Developing xylem	Savidge (1990)
Fraxinus pennsylvanica	Developing xylem	Savidge (1990)
Larix decidua	Cambial region	Savidge and Wareing (1982)
Malus domestica	Buds, leaves	Buta *et al.* (1989)
Malus malus	Developing xylem	Savidge (1990)
Malus pumila	Cambial region	Browning and Wignall (1987)
	Shoots	Alvarez *et al.* (1989); Vine *et al.* (1987)
Picea glauca	Developing xylem	Savidge (1990)
Picea rubens	Developing xylem	Savidge (1990)
Picea sitchensis	Cambial region	Little *et al.* (1978)
Pinus banksiana	Developing xylem	Savidge (1990)
Pinus contorta	Cambial region	Savidge and Wareing (1982)
	Leaves, shoots	Zhang (1990)
Pinus radiata	Shoots	Zabkiewicz and Steele (1974)
	Leaves, shoots	Zhang (1990)
Pinus resinosa	Developing xylem	Savidge (1990)
Pinus strobus	Developing xylem	Savidge (1990)
Pinus sylvestris	Seedlings	Sandberg *et al.* (1981)
	Cambial region	Stiebeling *et al.* (1985); Sundberg *et al.* (1986); Wodzicki *et al.* (1987)
Populus grandidentata	Developing xylem	Savidge (1990)
Populus tremuloides	Developing xylem	Savidge (1990)
Prunus cerasus	Shoots	Baraldi *et al.* (1988)
Prunus domestica	Shoots	Vine *et al.* (1987)
Prunus jamasakura	Hypocotyls	Saotome *et al.* (1993)
Prunus serotina	Developing xylem	Savidge (1990)
Pseudotsuga menziesii	Shoots, xylem sap	Caruso *et al.* (1978); DeYoe and Zaerr (1976); Crozier *et al.* (1980)
Pyrus communis	Shoots	Browning *et al.* (1992)
Quercus robur	Cambial region	Browning and Wignall (1987)
Quercus rubra	Developing xylem	Savidge (1990)
Rhus typhina	Developing xylem	Savidge (1990)
Salix nigra	Developing xylem	Savidge (1990)
Salix pentandra	Shoots	Jensen and Junttila (1982)
Sorbus decora	Developing xylem	Savidge (1990)
Syringa vulgaris	Developing xylem	Savidge (1990)
Thuja occidentalis	Developing xylem	Savidge (1990)
Tsuga heterophylla	Buds	Sheng *et al.* (1993)
Ulmus americana	Developing xylem	Savidge (1990)

Table II Characterization of Endogenous Gibberellins in Vegetative Parts of Tree Shoots

Species	GA number	Part	Ref.
Citrus sinensis	1, iso-3, 8, 17, 19, 20, 29	Shoots	Poling and Maier (1988)
	1, 3-epi-1, 3, iso-3, 8, 20, 29, 2-epi-29	Leaves	Turnbull (1989)
	1, 8, 17, 19, 20, 29	Shoots	Talón et al. (1990)
Dalbergia dolichopetala	1, epi-1, 3, 4, 5, 8, 20, 28	Germinated seed	Moritz and Monteiro (1994)
Eucalyptus globulus	1, 19, 20, 29	Cambial region	Hasan et al. (1994)
Eucalyptus nitens	1, 19, 20	Buds	Hasan et al. (1994)
Juglans regia	19	Xylem sap	Dathe et al. (1982)
Malus domestica	1, 9, 19, 20	Shoots	Koshioka et al. (1985)
	1, 3, 8, 19, 20, 29	Shoots	Steffens and Hedden (1992a)
Picea abies	1, 3, 9	Shoots	Odén et al. (1987)
Picea sitchensis	Iso-9	Leaves	Lorenzi et al. (1975a)
	1, 3, 4, 9	Shoots	Moritz et al. (1989b)
Pinus contorta	1, 3, 4, 7, 8, 9, 15, 20	Shoots	Zhang (1990)
	1, 3, 4, 7, 8, 9, 20	Leaves	Zhang (1990)
Pinus radiata	1, 3, 4, 7, 8, 9, 15	Shoots	Zhang (1990)
	9	Leaves	Zhang (1990)
Pinus sylvestris	1, 4, 7, 9, 20	Cambial region	Stiebeling et al. (1985)
	4, 7, 9	Cambial region	Wang et al. (1992)
Populus hybrid	1, 19, 20	Shoots	Rood et al. (1988)
Pseudotsuga menziesii	1, 3, 4, 7, 9	Shoots	Doumas et al. (1992)
	1, 3, 4, 7, 9	Buds	Doumas et al. (1993)
Salix dasyclados	1, 4, 8, 9, 19, 20, 29	Shoots	Junttila et al. (1988)
Salix pentandra	1, 8, 19, 20, 29	Shoots	Davies et al. (1985); Olsen et al. (1994)

Table III   Characterization of Endogenous Cytokinins in Vegetative Parts of Tree Shoots

Species	Cytokinin[a]	Part	Ref.
Abies balsamea	Z, [9R]Z	Cambial region	Little *et al.* (1979)
Acer pseudoplatanus	Z, [9R]Z, (diH)Z	Xylem sap	Purse *et al.* (1976)
Acer saccharum	iP, [9R]iP	Xylem sap	Waseem *et al.* (1991)
Castanea spp.	Z, [9R]Z, iP, [9R]iP	Shoots	Yokota and Takahashi (1980)
Citrus jambhiri	Z, [9R]Z	Xylem sap	Dixon *et al.* (1988)
Cryptomeria japonica	Z, [9R]Z	Cambial region	Funada *et al.* (1992)
Gymnocladus dioica	[9R]Z, [9R]iP, (diH)[9R]Z	Xylem sap	Hautala *et al.* (1986)
Litchi chinensis	Z, [9R]Z, iP, [9R]iP	Buds	Chen (1991)
Picea abies	[9R]iP	Leaves	Imbault *et al.* (1993)
Picea sitchensis	[9R]Z	Leaves	Lorenzi *et al.* (1975b)
Pinus radiata	[9R]Z	Buds	Taylor *et al.* (1984)
Pinus resinosa	[9R]Z	Shoots	Meilan *et al.* (1993)
Pinus sylvestris	[9R]Z	Cambial region	Stiebeling *et al.* (1985)
	[9R]Z, iP, [9R]iP, (diH)Z, (diH)[9R]Z	Cambial region	T. Moritz and B. Sundberg (unpublished)
Populus × *canadensis*	(oOH)BAP	Leaves	Strnad *et al.* (1992)
Populus × *robusta*	(oOH)[9R]BAP	Leaves	Horgan *et al.* (1975)
Pseudotsuga menziesii	Z, [9R]Z, [9R]iP	Buds	Morris *et al.* (1990)

[a]iP, N^6(Δ^2-isopentenyl)adenine; [9R]iP, N^6(Δ^2-isopentenyl)adenosine; Z, zeatin; [9R]Z, zeatin riboside; (diH)Z, dihydrozeatin; (diH)[9R]Z, dihydrozeatin riboside; (oOH)BAP, N^6(*o*-hydroxybenzyl)adenine; (oOH)[9R]BAP, N^6(*o*-hydroxybenzyl)adenosine.

(ABA; Table IV) have been conclusively identified, typically by combined gas chromatography-mass spectrometry (GC-MS; full-scan spectrum and/or selected ion monitoring), either in whole shoots or more specifically in buds, leaves, stem, cambial region, or xylem sap. Gas chromatography alone has been used to demonstrate that the stem or shoots of many woody species produce ethylene (Little and Savidge, 1987; Savidge, 1988; Eklund and Little, 1995a). GC-MS has also been employed to characterize brassinosteroids and jasmonates, two classes of potential plant hormones (Table V). Polyamines, another possible plant hormone class, have been detected by high-pressure liquid chromatography (HPLC) in shoots of *Citrus sinensis* (Friedman *et al.*, 1986), *Malus domestica* (Wang and Faust, 1993), *Picea abies* (Königshofer, 1991), and *Pinus sylvestris* (Sarjala and Kaunisto, 1993).

Experiments involving debudding, defoliation, girdling, exogenous application, and measurement of endogenous levels indicate that expanding buds and leaves are rich sources of IAA and ABA (Little and Savidge, 1987; Sundberg and Little, 1990; Thorsteinsson *et al.*, 1990; Rinne *et al.*, 1993, 1994a). Sandberg *et al.* (1990) showed that IAA biosynthesis and catabolism can occur in the cytosol of protoplasts obtained from *Pinus sylvestris* leaves. Roots are another likely site of ABA synthesis, particularly under environ-

Table IV   Characterization of Endogenous Abscisic Acid
in Vegetative Parts of Tree Shoots

Species	Part	Ref.
Abies alba	Leaves	Kraus and Ziegler (1993)
Abies balsamea	Buds	Little *et al.* (1972)
Acer pseudoplatanus	Leaves	Cornforth *et al.* (1965)
Acer saccharum	Xylem sap	Waseem *et al.* (1991)
Betula pubescens	Buds, leaves	Rinne *et al. (1994a)*
Citrus sinensis	Leaves, stem	Plummer *et al.* (1991)
	Leaves	Vine *et al.* (1987)
Corylus avellana	Shoots	Rodríguez *et al.* (1991)
Cryptomeria japonica	Shoots	Ogiyama *et al.* (1980)
Juglans regia	Xylem sap	Dathe *et al.* (1982)
Juglans spp.	Leaves	Shaybany and Martin (1977)
Malus domestica	Buds	Wang *et al.* (1987)
Malus pumila	Shoots	Vine *et al.* (1987)
	Cambial region	Browning and Wignall (1987)
Picea abies	Shoots	Andersson *et al.* (1978)
Picea glauca	Shoots	Roberts and Dumbroff (1986)
Picea mariana	Shoots	Roberts and Dumbroff (1986)
Picea sitchensis	Cambial region	Little *et al.* (1978)
Pinus banksiana	Shoots	Roberts and Dumbroff (1986)
Pinus contorta	Leaves, shoots	Zhang (1990)
Pinus densiflora	Cambial region	Funada *et al.* (1988)
Pinus radiata	Stems	Jenkins and Shepherd (1972)
	Leaves, shoots	Zhang (1990)
Pinus sylvestris	Shoots	Andersson *et al.* (1978);
		Hoque *et al.* (1983)
Populus hybrids	Stem	Blake and Atkinson (1986)
Prunus armeniaca	Xylem sap	Loveys *et al.* (1987)
Prunus domestica	Shoots	Vine *et al.* (1987)
Pseudotsuga menziesii	Leaves	Blake and Ferrell (1977);
		Meyer *et al.* (1986)
	Shoots	Webber *et al.* (1979);
		Kannangara *et al.* (1989)
Quercus robur	Cambial region	Browning and Wignall (1987)
Salix pentandra	Shoots	Jensen *et al.* (1986)
Salix viminalis	Buds	Barros and Neill (1986)
Tsuga heterophylla	Buds	Sheng *et al.* (1993)

mental conditions that induce water stress (Khalil and Grace, 1993; Munns
and Sharp, 1993). Two long-distant pathways of IAA transport have been
demonstrated using labeled IAA (Morris and Johnson, 1985). One is a slow,
basipetally polar movement located mainly in the cambial zone and differentiating xylem when the cambium is active and in the phloem parenchyma
during dormancy (Little, 1981; Lachaud and Bonnemain, 1984). The

Table V　Characterization of Endogenous Brassinosteroids
and Jasmonates in Vegetative Parts of Tree Shoots

Species	Compound[a]	Part	Ref.
Brassinosteroids			
Picea sitchensis	CAS, TYP	Shoot	Yokota *et al.* (1985)
Pinus sylvestris	BL, CAS	Cambial region	Kim *et al.* (1990)
Jasmonates			
Fagus sylvatica	JA	Leaves	Meyer *et al.* (1984)
Quercus robur	JA	Leaves	Meyer *et al.* (1984)

[a]BL, brassinolide; CAS, castasterone; JA, jasmonic acid; TYP, typhasterol.

other, whose physiological significance is uncertain, is a relatively rapid movement located in the sieve elements. Abscisic acid has been detected in the xylem (Table IV) and phloem (Weiler and Ziegler, 1981) saps, and likely moves in both pathways (Zeevaart and Creelman, 1988; Kelner *et al.*, 1993). Many IAA metabolites, mainly conjugates and catabolites, have been detected either as naturally occurring substances or as metabolites of labeled IAA in shoots or shoot parts of various woody species (Sundberg *et al.*, 1985, 1990; Sundberg, 1987; Wodzicki *et al.*, 1987; Pilate *et al.*, 1989; Plüss *et al.*, 1989; Sagee *et al.*, 1990; Sandberg *et al.*, 1990; Östin *et al.*, 1992a,b; Saotome *et al.*, 1993). Abscisic acid metabolites have also been found in woody shoots (Sivakumaran *et al.*, 1980; Little and Wareing, 1981; Seeley and Powell, 1981; Dathe *et al.*, 1982, 1984; Hoque *et al.*, 1983).

The occurrence of high levels of CKs in the xylem sap (Table III; Doumas and Zaerr, 1988; Tromp and Ovaa, 1990; Rinne and Saarelainen, 1994) and roots (Doumas *et al.*, 1989; Meilan *et al.*, 1993) supports the widespread belief that CKs are produced in root tips and transported in the xylem to the shoot. However, CKs also have been found in leaves, buds, and phloem sap (Table III; Taylor *et al.*, 1990; Komor *et al.*, 1993), suggesting that they are synthesized in various shoot parts as well. Direct evidence for CK synthesis in both roots and shoots is the finding that *Pisum sativum* stems, leaves, and roots, as well as cambial cells isolated from *Daucus carota* roots, converted [8-^{14}C]adenine into radioactive CKs, the root apparently being the primary site (Chen *et al.*, 1985). Naturally occurring glucosides of [9R]Z (zeatin riboside) have been detected in buds of *Pinus radiata* (Taylor *et al.*, 1984) and *Pseudotsuga menziesii* (Morris *et al.*, 1990), and Duke *et al.* (1979) demonstrated that *Populus alba* leaves could metabolize exogenous Z and [9R]Z to a complex of O-glucosides.

Of the 95 GAs thus far identified in plants and fungi (Mander, 1992; Pearce *et al.*, 1994), relatively few have been characterized in shoots of woody species (Table II). The presence of GAs in leaves and xylem

(Table II), as well as in phloem (Weiler and Ziegler, 1981; Hoad *et al.*, 1993) and roots (Olsen *et al.*, 1994), suggests that they are readily transported throughout the tree. The occurrence of GA biosynthesis in shoots is indicated by the several demonstrations of labeled-GA metabolism in this organ: (1) GA_4 to GA_2 and GA_{34} in *Pseudotsuga menziesii* (Wample *et al.*, 1975) and *Picea abies* (Dunberg *et al.*, 1983), (2) GA_4 to GA_1 (Junttila, 1993a) and GA_9 to GA_{20}, GA_1, and GA_{29} (Junttila *et al.*, 1992) in *Salix pentandra*, (3) GA_{20} to GA_1, GA_4 to GA_1, and GA_5 to GA_3 in *Dalbergia dolichopetala* (Moritz and Monteiro, 1994), (4) GA_9 to GA_4 in *Picea abies* (Moritz and Odén, 1990), and (5) GA_9 to GA_4, GA_{34} and GA_1, and GA_4 to GA_{34} and GA_1 in *Picea sitchensis* (Moritz *et al.*, 1989a). Evidence for GA conjugates, mainly glucosides, has been obtained in experiments with shoots of *Malus* × *domestica* (Richards *et al.*, 1986), *Picea abies* (Moritz and Odén, 1990), *Pseudotsuga menziesii* (Doumas *et al.*, 1992), *Picea sitchensis* (Moritz, 1992), and *Dalbergia dolichopetala* (Moritz and Monteiro, 1994).

Considerable evidence indicates that shoots of woody species contain 1-aminocyclopropane-1-carboxylic acid (ACC) and can convert it to ethylene (Savidge *et al.*, 1983; Yamamoto *et al.*, 1987b; Yamamoto and Kozlowski, 1987b–e; Savidge, 1988; Ingemarsson, 1994). Both ACC (Yamamoto *et al.*, 1987b; Yamamoto and Kozlowski, 1987b–e) and ethylene (Eklund, 1993a) are transported in the xylem. The conjugation of ACC has been detected in *Picea abies* hypocotyls (Ingemarsson, 1994).

Radial movement between the xylem and phloem, presumably via the rays, has been demonstrated with labeled IAA, kinetin (K), GA_3, and ABA (Little and Savidge, 1987; Kelner *et al.*, 1993).

III. Hormonal Control of Radial Growth

A. Vascular Cambium

1. Auxins An essential role for IAA in the initiation and growth of the vascular cambium is evident from experiments involving exogenous IAA. Leaf excision and IAA application studies have demonstrated that procambium development and primary xylem and phloem differentiation depend on a continuous supply of basipetally transported IAA (Jacobs and Morrow, 1957; Bruck and Paolillo, 1984; DeGroote and Larson, 1984). Similarly, exogenous IAA was shown to be required for cambium initiation and growth in isolated *Raphanus sativus* roots (Torrey and Loomis, 1967). The application of IAA also promoted cambium differentiation in the callus that develops on the wound surface after a *Betula pubescens* stem has been bark-girdled and protected from dessicating (Cui *et al.*, 1995). It is well documented that the growth of the vascular cambium is inhibited when the supply of endogenous IAA to the cambial region is decreased by debudding, defoliation, girdling, or by applying an inhibitor of basipetal IAA transport such as *N*-1-naphthylphthalamic acid (NPA), and is promoted by applying IAA to the apical cut surface of debudded shoots (Little and Savidge, 1987; Little *et al.,* 1990; Sundberg and Little, 1990). In experiments with *Pinus sylvestris* cuttings, Sundberg and Little (1990) showed that the IAA level in the cambial region at a distance below the shoot apex in debudded shoots treated apically with IAA was similar to that in intact shoots with expanding buds. This indicates that exogenous IAA can induce a physiologically relevant internal IAA level basipetally. This conclusion is further supported by the finding that the pattern of protein synthesis revealed by *in vivo* labeling with [^{35}S]methionine in cambial region cells of *Pinus sylvestris* was the same in debudded shoots treated apically with IAA as in budded shoots (Sitbon *et al.,* 1993). Sundberg and Little (1990) also observed that the cambial region IAA level in IAA-treated debudded shoots was positively related to cambial growth, as measured by tracheid production. A positive relationship between exogenous IAA concentration and the production and size of tracheary elements has been observed in many conifers and woody angiosperms (Little and Savidge, 1987; Zakrzewski, 1991; Mellerowicz *et al.,* 1992a). A stimulatory effect of IAA on primary-wall cell enlargement is well documented, particularly in herbaceous species (Terry *et al.,* 1982; Lorences and Zarra, 1987; Kutschera, 1994). In contrast, Aloni and Zimmermann (1983) hypothesized that tracheary element size is negatively related to the auxin concentration, as they observed that vessel radial diameter increased basipetally in decapitated *Phaseolus vulgaris* shoots treated apically with auxin (see also Aloni, 1988). It is likely, however, that vessel diameter was reduced near the auxin application point in their experiments because the IAA level was physiologically supraoptimal in that region (Warren Wilson and Warren Wilson, 1991). A high dose of applied IAA induces compression wood formation near the application site in conifers, whereas exogenous IAA suppresses tension wood formation in woody angiosperms (Little and Savidge, 1987). Other experiments with exogenous IAA suggest that auxin induces the formation of vertical resin ducts (Fahn and Zamski, 1970; Fahn *et al.,* 1979), prevents fusiform cambial cells from differentiating into axial parenchyma (Savidge, 1983; Cui *et al.,* 1992), and directs the movement of ^{14}C-labeled photosynthate (Little *et al.,* 1990) and the orientation of cambial zone cells and tracheary elements (Little and Savidge, 1987; Harris, 1989; Kurczyńska and Hejnowicz, 1991). Considerable evidence indicates that IAA is required for tracheary element differentiation (Ramsden and Northcote, 1987; Eklund, 1991a; Fukuda, 1994), but additional regulatory substances may also be involved (Savidge, 1994).

Except for the consistent demonstration that a significant amount is present throughout the year, measurements of endogenous IAA levels in the cambial region in relation to cambial growth have yielded conflicting results. The possibility that the level of IAA controls the rate and seasonal periodicity of cambial activity is supported by the finding of an increased IAA content during the growing season, compared to the dormant period, in *Picea sitchensis* (Little and Wareing, 1981), *Pinus contorta* (Savidge and Wareing, 1984), *Pinus sylvestris* (Sandberg and Ericsson, 1987), *Abies balsamea* (Sundberg *et al.,* 1987), and *Larix laricina* (Savidge, 1991). However, no such relationship was observed in *Quercus robur* (Wignall and Browning, 1988) or *Pyrus serotina* (Yang *et al.,* 1992), or in other studies with *Pinus sylvestris* (Sundberg *et al.,* 1990, 1991, 1993). Nor was IAA concentration related to annual ring width in *Pinus sylvestris,* measured during the cambial growing period both at the top and bottom of individual trees and in trees growing at different rates (Sundberg *et al.,* 1993). Similarly, the decrease in tracheary element radial width that is associated with the earlywood– latewood transition was reported to be temporally related to a reduced IAA level in some investigations (Savidge and Wareing, 1984; Sundberg *et al.,* 1987; Wignall and Browning, 1988), but not in others (Little and Wareing, 1981; Sundberg *et al.,* 1990, 1993). Inconsistent results have also been obtained in studies investigating the relationship between the level of endogenous IAA and the formation of reaction wood. An elevated IAA concentration on the side of compression wood formation was observed in inclined stems of *Cryptomeria japonica* (Funada *et al.,* 1990), but not in reoriented branches of *Pseudotsuga menziesii* (Wilson *et al.,* 1989) or bent stems of *Pinus sylvestris* (B. Sundberg and C. H. A. Little, unpublished). Moreover, the induction of compression wood formation above an NPA application point was not accompanied by an increase in the concentration, conjugation, or catabolism of IAA (Sundberg *et al.,* 1994).

The failure to find a consistent relationship between the level of endogenous IAA in the cambial region and a particular aspect of cambial growth has a number of possible explanations, several of which probably can be invoked concomitantly, and in the case of other hormones as well. First, the accuracy of the IAA measurement may be confounded by the crudeness of the sampling procedure. Indole-3-acetic acid currently is measured in a bulk cambial region sample comprised of varying proportions of different cell types (Sundberg *et al.,* 1991), each presumably containing characteristic amounts of IAA in particular parts of the cell at different times of the year. Ideally, however, the measurement should be localized to the subcellular compartment(s) of each cell type in the cambial region where IAA actually acts. Second, although GC-MS and stable isotope-labeled standards typically are used at present to quantify IAA, differences in the procedures used to harvest and store the samples, and to extract the IAA, may affect the IAA estimate. Third, changes in the level of IAA may be less important than fluctuations in (1) the level of additional substances that may regulate cambial growth, such as the other hormones covered in this chapter, polyamines (Königshofer, 1991), and oxygen (Eklund, 1990, 1993b), (2) the character of the IAA waves that may be generated during IAA transport (Wodzicki *et al.*, 1987; Wodzicki and Zajączkowski, 1989), (3) the rate of IAA turnover, and (4) the "sensitivity" (Trewavas, 1991) of cambial region cells to IAA. If sensitivity is indeed a factor, it is speculated to reflect receptor number or availability (Napier and Venis, 1990). Cambial IAA sensitivity, measured as the ability of the cambium to produce xylem and phloem in response to exogenous IAA, has been shown to decrease with increasing cambial age and to vary markedly during the year (Little and Savidge, 1987; Sundberg *et al.*, 1987; Little *et al.*, 1990; Little and Sundberg, 1991; Mellerowicz *et al.*, 1992a; Savidge, 1993). Under environmental conditions favorable for growth, applied IAA induces vigorous cambial activity when the cambium is active or quiescent, but not when it is in rest. Whether the decreased responsiveness of the cambium to IAA during rest is due to receptor deficiency (Riding and Little, 1984; Lachaud, 1989) is not known. Cambial rest was overcome in detached *Fraxinus ornus* shoots by exposure to ethylene chlorohydrin vapor (Reinders-Gouwentak, 1965), but not in *Abies balsamea* cuttings treated basally with ethephon (2-chloroethylphosphonic acid, another ethylene generator) or apically with GA_3 or K (Little and Bonga, 1974; Eklund and Little, 1995a). Cambial rest was not associated with inhibited IAA transport in *Abies balsamea* (Little, 1981) and *Pinus densiflora* (Odani, 1985) or with increased ABA content in the cambial region (see Section A, 4, below). However, numerous ultrastructural and biochemical changes in cambial zone cells have been detected during the activity–dormancy cycle, particularly in *Abies balsamea*, including oscillations in plasma membrane infolding, radial wall thickening, nucleolar activity, nuclear genome size, relative ribosomal RNA gene content, and cytoplasmic RNA, protein, lipid, and carbohydrate staining (Riding and Little, 1984, 1986; Mellerowicz *et al.*, 1989, 1990, 1992b, 1993; Catesson, 1990, 1994; Zhong *et al.*, 1995; Lloyd *et al.*, 1994).

2. Gibberellins Several GAs have been identified in the cambial region (Table II), and accumulating evidence suggests that this class of hormones is involved in the control of cambial growth. Although GA levels have yet to be measured in the cambial region during the annual cycle of activity and dormancy, stem diameter and, in particular, stem dry weight and volume, were positively related to the needle content of GA_9 in seedlings of *Pinus radiata* families (Zhang, 1990). Similarly, a positive relationship was observed between needle or stem levels of GA_9, or GA_9 combined with GA_4, GA_7, and GA_{20}, and family rank for stem dry weight in *Pinus contorta* seedlings (Zhang, 1990). For both species, family GA_9 levels were positively correlated with family performance in field progeny trials (Zhang, 1990; Pharis *et al.*, 1992, 1993). Applying GA_3 to intact or debudded shoots has been observed to enhance the stimulatory effect of IAA on cambial cell division and tracheary element differentiation in many conifers and woody angiosperms, although not without exceptions (Little and Savidge, 1987). In *Populus robusta*, high and low IAA-to-GA$_3$ ratios favored the production of xylem and phloem, respectively, and GA$_3$ in the presence of IAA increased xylem fiber length (Digby and Wareing, 1966). Similarly, the relative concentrations of exogenous GA$_3$ and IAA were observed to affect the size of primary phloem fibers, and the formation of lignin in these fibers and in secondary xylem, in *Coleus blumei* stems (Aloni *et al.*, 1990). It has also been reported that GA$_3$ alone stimulated cambial activity without inducing vessel differentiation in debudded shoots of several woody angiosperms (Digby and Wareing, 1966; Zakrzewski, 1983), and promoted sieve cell differentiation in *Pinus strobus* stem explants (DeMaggio, 1966), phloem production in *Pinus brutia* needles (Ewers and Aloni, 1985), and lignification in *Prunus spachiana* hypocotyls (Nakamura *et al.*, 1994) and dwarf *Pisum sativum* stems (Cheng and Marsh, 1968). In decapitated *Cupressus arizonica* seedlings, exogenous GA$_3$ enhanced branch hyponasty by promoting compression wood formation (Blake *et al.*, 1980), an event that could be counteracted by applying growth retardants known to inhibit GA biosynthesis (Pharis *et al.*, 1965, 1967). Soil-applied GA$_3$ also stimulated hyponasty in the stem of *Tsuga heterophylla* seedlings (Pharis and Ross, 1976). In application experiments with other GAs, GA$_1$ synergized tracheary element differentiation in *Lactuca sativa* cultures treated with optimal IAA plus K (Pearce *et al.*, 1987), and GA$_4$ alone or together with ABA increased tracheid radial width in *Pinus radiata* seedlings (Pharis *et al.*, 1981). Considerable evidence suggests that GAs regulate the arrangement of cortical microtubules, hence the polarity of cell enlargement (Baluška *et al.*, 1993).

Additional evidence for a causal role of GA in cambial growth is the finding that applying GA$_3$ or GA$_{4/7}$ as a stem injection, topical application, or soil drench to seedlings of both conifers and woody angiosperms variously increased stem radial increment, longitudinal growth, dry weight, or volume (Pharis, 1976; Pharis and Ross, 1976; Pharis and Kuo, 1977; Webber *et al.*, 1985; Little and Savidge, 1987; Pharis *et al.*, 1987, 1991; Wang *et al.*, 1992), although typically at the expense of branch and root growth (Ross *et al.*, 1983; Little and Savidge, 1987; Teng and Timmer, 1993). Richards *et al.* (1986) fed [^{3}H]GA$_4$ to the xylem below dwarfing or nondwarfing interstocks grafted into *Malus domestica* trees, and found that the total amount of free [^{3}H]GA$_4$ and its acidic metabolites was higher, and the proportion of putative [^{3}H]GA glucosyl conjugates lower, in the dwarfing interstocks, in which radial growth is also greater. An increase in tracheid production and stem elongation induced by a soil drench of GA$_{4/7}$ in *Pinus sylvestris* seedlings was associated with elevated cambial region contents of GA$_4$, GA$_7$,

GA_9, and, most importantly, IAA in the terminal shoot (Wang *et al.*, 1992). Additional research is required to determine not only if GAs enhance cambial growth either directly or indirectly through raising the IAA content, but also which is the active GA(s) per se.

3. Cytokinins Several lines of evidence suggest that CKs play a role in the regulation of cambial growth, but much additional research is required to establish their role(s) unequivocally. Bioactive forms are present in the cambial region (Table III), and seasonal changes in levels have been detected by combined HPLC-mass spectrometry in the cambial region of *Pinus sylvestris* (T. Moritz and B. Sundberg, unpublished), as well as by immunoassay after HPLC purification of the cambial region microdialysate of *Picea abies* (Eklund, 1991b) and the xylem sap of *Pseudotsuga menziesii* (Doumas and Zaerr, 1988), *Malus domestica* (Tromp and Ovaa, 1990), and *Betula pubescens* (Rinne and Saarelainen, 1994). However, the relationships between the levels of endogenous CKs and the seasonal periodicity and rate of cambial growth are obscure. Exogenous Z, [9R]Z, K, and N^6-benzyladenine (BA), alone or together with auxin or auxin plus GA_3, have been observed to promote cambial growth and ray formation in the stem of several conifers and woody angiosperms, although not in all cases (Little and Savidge, 1987). Similarly, K stimulated secondary xylem fiber differentiation in *Helianthus annuus* hypocotyls (Saks *et al.*, 1984) and secondary xylem development in *Pisum sativum* epicotyls (Sorokin *et al.*, 1962), the latter stimulation being mediated through activation of the fascicular and interfascicular cambia. Torrey and Loomis (1967) demonstrated an absolute requirement for CK in the initiation and growth of the cambium in isolated *Raphanus sativus* roots. Cytokinin is also essential for tracheary element differentiation in cell suspension cultures (Ramsden and Northcote, 1987; Fukuda, 1994).

4. Abscisic Acid Although ABA is present in many parts of the tree, including the cambial region (Table IV), its involvement in the control of cambial growth is uncertain. An inhibitory role is suggested by the finding that applying ABA to stems with an active cambium decreased the production and radial width of tracheids in *Abies balsamea* and *Picea glauca* (Little and Eidt, 1968, 1970; Little, 1975) and *Pinus radiata* (Jenkins, 1974). However, Pharis *et al.* (1981) subsequently reported that the effect of exogenous ABA on tracheid radial width in *Pinus radiata* varied during the growing season, being inhibitory in midsummer but ineffective or even somewhat stimulatory at other times. The reputation of ABA as a growth inhibitor has prompted several investigations concerning its cambial region level in relation to the transition between earlywood and latewood, the cessation of cambial activity, and the imposition of cambial rest. Despite bioassay data to the contrary, the endogenous ABA content did not increase during the earlywood–latewood and activity–rest transitions in either conifers (Webber *et al.*, 1979; Little and Wareing, 1981; Savidge and Wareing, 1984) or woody angiosperms (Wignall and Browning, 1988; Plummer *et al.*, 1991). Similarly, an increased ABA level was not detected during the development of cambial dormancy induced by short day length in stems of *Picea sitchensis* (Little and Wareing, 1981). Whether exogenous ABA actually can induce the cessation of cambial activity and/or the development of cambial rest needs to be investigated.

The possibility that changes in ABA levels induce the false-ring formation associated with drought imposition and relief has also been examined. It is well established that drought elevates the endogenous ABA level throughout the tree (Blake and Ferrell, 1977; Sivakumaran *et al.*, 1980; Little and Wareing, 1981; Hoque *et al.*, 1983; Roberts and Dumbroff, 1986; Khalil and Grace, 1993), and there is evidence that exogenous ABA and water stress similarly inhibit tracheid production and reduce tracheid radial width in *Pinus radiata* (Jenkins, 1974) and *Abies balsamea* (Little, 1975). Little and Wareing (1981) demonstrated that drought-induced false-ring formation in *Picea sitchensis* seedlings was temporally associated with a transient increase in ABA concentration in the cambial region. However, the IAA level was transiently reduced at the same time, which by itself could explain the formation of the false ring.

5. Ethylene   There is evidence for and against ethylene playing a direct role in the control of the duration and rate of cambial growth. The evolution of endogenous ethylene, measured in the cambial region of *Picea abies* (Eklund, 1991b), excised phloem plus cambium tissues of *Chamaecyparis obtusa* (Yamanaka, 1985), the outer sapwood of *Picea abies*, *Pinus sylvestris*, *Acer platanoides*, and *Quercus robur* (Eklund, 1990, 1993b; Ingemarsson *et al.*, 1991b; Eklund *et al.*, 1992), and 1-year-old *Abies balsamea* cuttings (Eklund and Little, 1995a), was higher when the cambium was active than during cambial dormancy. The diameter of *Pinus taeda* stems was positively correlated with ethylene production per square centimeter of vascular cambium in seedlings subjected to mechanical shaking, and negatively correlated with ethylene production per gram fresh weight of stem tissue in control seedlings (Telewski, 1990). In contrast, no relationship was found between ethylene evolution and IAA-induced tracheid production in *Abies balsamea* cuttings treated basally with ethephon (Eklund and Little, 1995a). These investigators also observed that applying ethephon apically to debudded shoots or basally to cuttings treated apically with IAA did not promote tracheid production, although ethylene evolution was increased. However, ringing a stem with ethephon increases the production of xylem, cortex, and ray parenchyma at the application point in many conifers and woody angiosperms, as well as resin canals in *Pinus* spp. (Little and Savidge, 1987; Yamamoto *et al.*, 1987a; Yamamoto and Kozlowski, 1987a,b,e; Telewski, 1990; Eklund and Little, 1995a,b). Eklund and Little (1995b) showed that ringing *Abies balsamea* seedlings with ethephon increased both the evolution of ethylene and the cambial region IAA level at the ethephon application point. They attributed this ethephon-induced promotion of radial growth to the increase in IAA content, which they proposed was caused by the ethephon raising the ethylene level to the point that basipetal IAA transport was inhibited (Abeles *et al.*, 1992). Other research indicates that ethylene is involved in the control of tracheary element differentiation, and that it acts both by inducing the activity of lignification enzymes, particularly peroxidase (Miller *et al.*, 1984, 1985; Hennion *et al.*, 1992), and by influencing carbohydrate deposition (Eklund, 1991a; Ingemarsson *et al.*, 1991a) and cortical microtubule orientation (Shibaoka, 1994).

A role for ethylene in the induction of reaction wood formation has been suspected since the first demonstration that bending a shoot increases its ethylene production (Robitaille and Leopold, 1974). Such a role is supported by the detection of ACC in the cambial region only on the lower side of *Pinus contorta* branches where compression wood was forming (Savidge *et al.*, 1983). Moreover, ethylene evolution was greater from the lower side than from the upper side in *Cupressus arizonica* branches producing compression wood on the lower side (Blake *et al.*, 1980) and vice versa in inclined *Eucalyptus gamphocephala* seedlings forming tension wood on the upper side (Nelson and Hillis, 1978). In contrast, ethylene production by the upper and lower sides was the same in inclined *Pinus densiflora* seedlings (Yamamoto and Kozlowski, 1987b), and the same or greater by the lower side in bent shoots of *Acer platanoides* (Yamamoto and Kozlowski, 1987e) and *Betula* spp. (Rinne, 1990). Furthermore, lateral ethephon application not only failed to induce the production of typical compression wood in vertical stems of *Pinus halepensis* (Yamamoto and Kozlowski, 1987a) and *Pinus densiflora* (Yamamoto and Kozlowski, 1987b), but also suppressed compression wood formation in inclined *Pinus densiflora* seedlings (Yamamoto and Kozlowski, 1987b). Similarly, treating *Acer platanoides* stems with ethephon did not induce tension wood formation in vertical seedlings and blocked it in bent seedlings (Yamamoto and Kozlowski, 1987e).

B. Phellogen

There has been little research aimed at elucidating the role of hormones in the regulation of phellogen initiation and activity. The meager evidence available suggests that periderm formation is inhibited by auxin and promoted by ethylene (Lev-Yadun and Aloni, 1990; Cui *et al.*, 1995). Endogenous IAA has been detected in the outermost layers of crushed secondary phloem, where the periderm forms (Sundberg *et al.,* 1990).

IV. Hormonal Control of Longitudinal Growth

A. Auxins

Considerable research with nonwoody species (e.g., Yang *et al.,* 1993) indicates that IAA is a causal factor in longitudinal growth. The evidence for woody species is relatively sparse. Exogenous IAA promoted the elongation of intact hypocotyls and hypocotyl sections in *Prunus jamasakura* (Saotome *et al.,* 1993; Nakamura *et al.,* 1994) and *Pinus* spp. (Zakrzewski, 1975; Carpita and Tarmann, 1982; Terry *et al.,* 1982). Seedling height growth was increased by applying potassium naphthenate to *Pseudotsuga menziesii* (Wort, 1975) and a low but not a high concentration of IAA to *Pinus caribaea* (Bhatnagar and Talwar, 1978). Indirect evidence of a role for IAA in stem elongation is the finding that triiodobenzoic acid, an inhibitor of polar auxin transport, reduced shoot elongation in *Pinus strobus* (Little, 1970), *Tsuga heterophylla* (Cheung, 1975), and *Pseudotsuga menziesii* (Ross *et al.,* 1983).

In an unusual situation with *Pinus radiata* in New Zealand, where 3-year-old field-grown seedlings exhibited a "retarded leader" syndrome, Pharis (1976) found that IAA applied together with $GA_{4/7}$ to the terminal shoot further inhibited its longitudinal growth relative to the "normal" control, the retarded leader control, and a retarded leader plus $GA_{4/7}$ treatment. However, for those trees in which IAA inhibited elongation of the already "retarded" terminal shoot, longitudinal growth of the lateral shoots in the uppermost whorl was enhanced. Pharis (1976) speculated that endogenous IAA levels were already at inhibitory levels in the terminal shoot of seedlings exhibiting the retarded leader syndrome, but were still suboptimal for elongation of the lateral shoots. However, the possibility of "compensatory growth" by the laterals when the longitudinal growth of the terminal was further reduced by applied IAA should not be overlooked. It is also possible that the $GA_{4/7}$ diffused into the lateral shoots and induced an increase in endogenous IAA (Wang *et al.,* 1992). That supraoptimal levels of IAA can inhibit shoot elongation is suggested by the finding that applying IAA to the 1-year-old internode of intact *Pinus sylvestris* branches reduced the elongation of the distal current-year terminal shoot (Sundberg and Little, 1990), the supposition being that an inhibitory amount of exogenous IAA moved into the elongating shoot.

In conifers, high endogenous IAA levels have been correlated with both rapid and diminished shoot elongation. The IAA content in *Picea abies* shoots was highest during the period of maximum longitudinal growth, dropping quickly after elongation ceased (Dunberg, 1976). Sandberg and Ericsson (1987) noted that the IAA level in the terminal shoot of *Pinus sylvestris* rose during the period of rapid elongation, but was maximal after extension ended. In phytotron-grown seedlings of *Pinus radiata*, Zhang (1990) found that the IAA level in the terminal shoot tip was higher in slow-growing families than in fast-growing families, which suggests that the IAA content was supraoptimal in the slow growers. A transient increase in IAA content was observed in *Pseudotsuga menziesii* buds during the transition between quiescence and activity (Pilate *et al.*, 1989).

High levels of endogenous IAA have often, but not always, been positively correlated with shoot elongation in woody angiosperms. In *Carya illinoensis*, the IAA content in buds increased at bud-break (Wood, 1983). Rodríguez *et al.* (1991) reported that IAA levels in *Corylus avellana* shoots were maximal when the rate of shoot elongation was fastest. However, the IAA content in *Pyrus serotina* shoots peaked prior to the period of most rapid extension growth (Yang *et al.*, 1992). Indole-3-acetic acid levels in *Malus domestica* leaves were higher in a vigorously growing cultivar than in a dwarf cultivar both early and late in the elongation period, however, the converse was true for the buds (Buta *et al.*, 1989). In two *Betula* species, coppice shoots elongated more than seedlings, but there was no consistent difference in IAA level (Rinne *et al.*, 1993). The application of paclobutrazol, an inhibitor of GA biosynthesis, decreased longitudinal growth in *Pyrus communis* shoots without affecting the IAA level (Browning *et al.*, 1992).

B. Gibberellins

Of all the hormone classes, the case is clearest for GAs being causal factors in the control of shoot elongation in both woody angiosperms and conifers. Early evidence, mostly based on the use of applied GAs, which promote longitudinal growth, and/or plant growth retardants known to inhibit GA biosynthesis, which decrease shoot elongation, is cited in Pharis (1976), Pharis and Kuo (1977), Ross *et al.* (1983), and Junttila (1991).

For most woody angiosperms, GA_1 is likely to be the endogenous "effector" of shoot elongation (Junttila, 1991; Junttila *et al.*, 1992). However, GA_3 is also native to shoots of these species (Table II) and would be active per se whenever present. Additionally, the possibility that GA_4 is active per se should not be ruled out. Thus, shoot elongation in woody angiosperm is probably caused by the same "effector" GAs that control longitudinal growth in herbaceous monocots and dicots (Phinney and Spray, 1990; Reid, 1990). Strong evidence that GAs do influence shoot elongation in woody angiosperms has been obtained by Junttila and co-workers, who used the reduced elongation of *Salix* spp. under short day length as a tool to examine (1) the effect on longitudinal growth of applying different GAs, (2) the metabolism of ²H- and ³H-labeled GAs, and (3) the changes in levels of endogenous GAs (Junttila and Jensen, 1988; Junttila *et al.*, 1992). When shoot longitudinal growth was retarded with prohexadione, a known inhibitor of the GA_{20}-to-GA_1 hydroxylation step, only applied GAs with a C-3β hydroxyl could restore normal elongation in *Salix pentandra* (Junttila *et al.*, 1991) and *Betula pubescens* and *Alnus glutinosa* (Junttila, 1993b). Furthermore, Hasan (1993) found that *Eucalyptus* shoots whose elongation was retarded by root collar application of paclobutrazol had reduced levels of GA_1. Steffens and Hedden (1992b) measured similar levels of GA_1 and GA_3 in standard and thermosensitive dwarf cultivars of *Malus domestica* during shoot elongation, although shoots of standard trees contained more GA_{20} and GA_{19} (immediate precursors of GA_1). During the high temperatures of summer, however, the GA_{19} levels were higher in the dwarf lines, implying a reduced conversion of GA_{19} to GA_{20}. A positive correlation was found between the content of GA-like substances, later identified as GA_{19} and GA_1, and height growth and shoot dry weight in *Populus* crosses exhibiting hybrid vigor (Bate *et al.*, 1988). Finally, it has been demonstrated with many woody angiosperms that GA_3 application can replace the chilling requirement of vegetative buds in rest (Larson, 1960; Saunders and Barros, 1987; Luna *et al.*, 1991; Frisby and Seeley, 1993).

In conifers, the question of which endogenous GAs may be the "effectors" of shoot elongation is more complex than in woody angiosperms. The major GAs found in shoots of Cupressaceae, Pinaceae, and Taxodiaceae species are GA_1, GA_3, GA_4, GA_7, and GA_9 (Table II). Generally, the level of GA_9 is highest (Moritz *et al.*, 1990). The occurrence of GA_3 and GA_7 is sporadic; however, when present, the content of GA_7, especially, can be high (Zhang, 1990; Doumas *et al.*, 1993; R. P. Pharis, R. Zhang, G. Thompson, K. Ogiyama, C. H. A. Little, unpublished). Height growth in seedlings of eight half-sib *Pinus contorta* families was correlated with needle GA_9 levels (Zhang, 1990). Pharis *et al.* (1992) reported a similar correlation between needle GA_9 levels and family ranking in stem elongation for full-sib *Pinus radiata* seedlings. In *Pseudotsuga menziesii*, GA_3 application overcame the inhibition of bud-break caused by cold (5°C) soil temperatures (Lavender *et al.*, 1973). Shoot elongation in *Cupressus arizonica* and *Sequoia sempervirens* was retarded by several growth retardants known to inhibit GA biosynthesis, and applied GA_3 restored longitudinal growth to near normal levels (Pharis and Kuo, 1977). In *Cupressus arizonica*, the content of endogenous GA_3 and other GA-like substances was positively correlated with height growth (Pharis, 1976). A result consistent with the thesis that GA_4 per se may be an "effector" of longitudinal growth in conifers is the finding that $[^3H]GA_4$ metabolism in *Pseudotsuga menziesii* shoots was slower when elongation was rapid than during bud-break or bud-set (Wample *et al.*, 1975). In contrast, Moritz *et al.* (1990) observed that the GA_4 content in *Picea sitchensis* shoots was highest early in the shoot elongation period, with the levels of GA_1, GA_3, and GA_9 peaking later. As the content of GA_4 was much lower than that of either GA_1 or GA_3, the latter GAs would seem to be the logical "effectors" of elongation in this species.

Single-gene dwarf mutants of conifers do not appear to have been characterized, and variants with dwarf habits have not been extensively studied with regard to their response to applied GAs. However, Pharis *et al.* (1991) showed that height increment in nine full-sib *Picea mariana* families treated with $GA_{4/7}$ was related to inherent growth capability, that is, $GA_{4/7}$-induced longitudinal growth of the slow-growing families was disproportionately greater than that of the fast growers. Even more striking was the response of two selfed families, both of which exhibited a dwarf phenotype. The two selfs had the greatest height growth promotion, and their stem dry weight was increased 1.5- to twofold.

The results of GA application experiments tend to separate species in the Cupressaceae and Taxodiaceae from those in the Pinaceae. Both young and old trees of many species within the Cupressaceae and Taxodiaceae, which generally have indeterminate growth, elongate in response to exogenous GA_1, GA_3, GA_4, and GA_7, with GA_3 tending to be more effective than $GA_{4/7}$ (Pharis, 1976; Ross *et al.*, 1983). Pinaceae species are often relatively nonresponsive to exogenous GA_1 or GA_3, but generally can be promoted by applying $GA_{4/7}$, especially to seedlings in the free growth phase. For Pinaceae trees older than 1 year, GA_3 is in general a poor promoter of shoot elongation, whereas $GA_{4/7}$ remains effective (Ross *et al.*, 1983; Webber *et al.*, 1985; Pharis *et al.*, 1987). There is also a need to time the $GA_{4/7}$ application carefully, relative to the stage of shoot elongation. For example, $GA_{4/7}$ promoted current-year longitudinal growth in *Pseudotsuga menziesii* only when applied prior to bud-break, later applications being ineffective (Pharis *et al.*, 1987). Applying $GA_{4/7}$ when *Picea sitchensis* shoots were 65–85% extended increased leader length the year after treatment, but not in the current year (Philipson, 1983). A similar promotion of shoot elongation the year after treatment by applied $GA_{4/7}$ was noted for *Pinus contorta* (Longman, 1982). Ross *et al.* (1983) cited a personal communication from G. B. Sweet, where $GA_{4/7}$ applied to *Pinus radiata* saplings undergoing recurrent longitudinal growth flushes had no effect on internodes that were currently elongating, but rather promoted growth of the embryonic shoot within the bud at the time of hormone application. Both GA_3 and $GA_{4/7}$ increased the dry weight of developing long-shoot primordia in *Pinus radiata* buds, but only $GA_{4/7}$ enhanced the differentiation into female cone buds (Ross *et al.*, 1984). Shoot elongation in several Cupressaceae, Pinaceae, and Taxodiaceae species was reduced by applying inhibitors of GA biosynthesis (Weston *et al.*, 1980; Ross *et al.*, 1983).

C. Cytokinins

Accumulating evidence implicates CKs in the control of longitudinal growth in both conifers and woody angiosperms. The application of CKs such as [9R]Z and BA, and the CK mimic thidiazuron, has been shown to reduce the chilling requirement for bud-break and to promote the initiation and outgrowth of axillary buds on current-year shoots and the opening of quiescent buds (e.g., Little, 1985; Saunders and Barros, 1987; Wang *et al.*, 1987; Steffens and Stutte, 1989; Qamaruddin *et al.*, 1990). Height growth in *Pinus palustris* seedlings in the grass stage, when stem elongation normally is inhibited, was stimulated by BA, particularly when combined with GA_3 or certain salts (Kossuth, 1981; Hare, 1984). However, longitudinal growth was inhibited by BA in *Pseudotsuga menziesii* seedlings (Ross *et al.*, 1983) and by K in *Pinus sylvestris* hypocotyl sections (Zakrzewski, 1975).

Early work with woody angiosperms indicated that endogenous CK levels in buds and/or xylem sap increased in late winter and peaked about bud-break (Hewett and Wareing, 1973; Taylor and Dumbroff, 1975; Alvim *et al.*, 1976; Purse *et al.*, 1976; Wood, 1983). In the xylem sap of *Malus domestica* shoots, Z and [9R]Z were the major CKs present, with Z predominating except in the spring (Tromp and Ovaa, 1990). The content of total CKs increased rapidly near the start of bud-break, then declined to a minimum about the time that extension growth ceased. Young (1987) observed that maximum bud-break in *Malus domestica* required root chilling, which could be substituted for by BA. Subsequently, Young (1989) found that the endogenous CK content of xylem sap in partially chilled, dormant *Malus domestica* trees placed under environmental conditions favorable for growth increased whether the trees were additionally chilled or not, although the post-bud-break decline in CK levels was most pronounced in the chilled trees, in which bud-burst was also greater. Treating *Malus domestica* shoots in early autumn with "rest-breaking" chemicals promoted bud-break and induced a rapid rise in xylem sap CK levels that peaked about bud-break, confirming that chilling per se does not cause the CK increase in this species (Cutting *et al.*, 1991). Finally, in coppicing experiments, Taylor *et al.* (1982) observed that CK-like activity increased in the stump of *Eucalyptus* spp. within 1 week of decapitation, while Rinne and Saarelainen (1994) found that the export of CKs in bleeding sap was correlated positively with the initiation and elongation rate of coppice shoots in *Betula pubescens*.

The occurrence of high endogenous CK levels about the time of bud-break has also been observed in experiments with conifers. Qamaruddin *et al.* (1990) found that $N^6(\Delta^2$-isopentenyl)adenosine ([9R]iP) and [9R]Z levels were low in needles and buds of dormant *Pinus sylvestris* seedlings but increased in response to chilling, attaining a maximum in the buds approximately when they began to elongate. Similarly, the start of shoot longitudinal growth was associated with a peak in CK content in the xylem sap of *Pseudotsuga menziesii* (Doumas and Zaerr, 1988) and the buds and needles of *Picea sitchensis* (Lorenzi *et al.*, 1975b). Working with terminal buds of dormant clonal cuttings of *Pseudotsuga menziesii,* Pilate *et al.* (1989) found that chilling decreased the content of Z and [9R]Z while increasing that of [9R]iP, whereas after transfer to environmental conditions favorable for bud elongation, the [9R]iP level declined rapidly and the Z and [9R]Z levels increased.

D. Abscisic Acid

There is a copious literature on the possible causal involvement of ABA in shoot elongation and, in particular, bud dormancy. Some of the early work (summarized in Ross *et al.,* 1983) showed that applied ABA can inhibit, have no effect, or even promote longitudinal growth, and that correlations of endogenous ABA levels with shoot elongation and bud dormancy were generally equivocal.

More recent literature also provides conflicting evidence concerning the role of ABA in the control of longitudinal growth and bud dormancy. High doses of exogenous ABA inhibited shoot elongation under long day length in *Picea abies* (Heide, 1986) and *Salix pentandra* (Johansen *et al.,* 1986), but normal winter buds were not induced. However, applied ABA accelerated bud-set under dormancy-inducing conditions (short day length, cold temperatures) in *Pseudotsuga menziesii* and *Picea engelmannii* (Blake *et al.,* 1990), as well as in several woody angiosperms (see Seeley and Powell, 1981). An increase in endogenous ABA content at bud-break and/or during the shoot elongation period has been observed in the buds, leaves, or shoots of *Malus domestica* (Singha and Powell, 1978; Seeley and Powell, 1981), *Salix viminalis* (Barros and Neill, 1986, 1987), *Pseudotsuga menziesii* (Pilate *et al.,* 1989), *Citrus sinensis* (Plummer *et al.,* 1991), *Corylus avellana* (Rodríguez *et al.,* 1991), and *Betula pubescens* (Rinne *et al.,* 1994b). However, the cessation of shoot elongation and the formation of winter buds were not temporally associated with high ABA levels (see also Kelner *et al.,* 1993). Qamaruddin *et al.* (1993) observed that needle ABA levels were higher in the faster elongating of two *Picea abies* populations. Similarly, in full-sib *Pinus radiata* and half-sib *Pinus contorta* seedlings, needle ABA levels tended to be positively related to more rapid height growth, both between families and within a family, although the ABA content in the stem tip showed no such trend (Zhang, 1990). However, needle ABA content was not related to postplanting vigor in *Pseudotsuga menziesii* seedlings subjected to various lifting dates and cold storage treatments (Puttonen, 1987). The cessation of shoot elongation induced by short day length was not associated with an increased level of endogenous ABA in *Picea sitchensis* (Little and Wareing, 1981), *Salix pentandra* (Johansen *et al.,* 1986), and *Salix viminalis* (Barros and Neill, 1987), but was so in *Pinus sylvestris* (Odén and Dunberg, 1984), *Betula pubescens* (Rinne *et al.,* 1994a), and a southern population of *Picea abies,* although not a northern one (Qamaruddin *et al.*, 1993). Bud or shoot ABA content declined during the autumn and winter to a minimum, which occurred prior to bud-break in *Malus domestica* (Seeley and Powell, 1981), *Carya illinoensis* (Wood, 1983), *Salix viminalis* (Barros and Neill, 1986, 1987), *Corylus avellana* (Rodríguez *et al.*, 1991), and *Betula pubescens* (Rinne *et al.*, 1994b). However, this decline was not specifically related to the rest–quiescence transition induced by chilling. Similarly, artificial chilling did not affect the endogenous ABA content in buds of *Salix viminalis* (Barros and Neill, 1986), *Pseudotsuga menziesii* (Pilate *et al.*, 1989), and *Betula pubescens* (Rinne *et al.*, 1994a), although it increased the needle ABA level in a northern but not a southern population of *Picea abies* (Qamaruddin *et al.*, 1993). Exogenous ABA has been observed to inhibit springtime bud-break in many woody species (e.g., Little and Eidt, 1968; Haissig and King, 1970; Suzuki and Kitano, 1989; Rinne *et al.*, 1994a), and this inhibition was antagonized by the application of GA_3 in *Morus alba* (Suzuki and Kitano, 1989) and BA in *Malus domestica* (Sterrett and Hipkins, 1980). Similarly, Barros and Neill (1987) observed that the exogenous ABA-induced inhibition of longitudinal growth in *Salix viminalis* was relieved by applying GA_3 to rooted cuttings and GA_9 plus [9R]Z to cultured shoot tips. Barros and Neill (1986) demonstrated a marked seasonal variation in the ability of isolated *Salix viminalis* buds in culture to respond to applied ABA, with ABA preventing bud-break only when the buds were entering or in rest. Finally, when bud-break in *Malus domestica* was stimulated with thidiazuron, subsequent application of ABA further promoted bud growth, and the thidiazuron treatment actually increased the ABA content of the buds (Wang *et al.*, 1987). Similarly, exogenous IAA raised the ABA levels in the stem of *Populus tremula* (Eliasson, 1975) and *Picea sitchensis* (Little and Wareing, 1981).

E. Ethylene

Ethylene has been causally implicated in the inhibition of shoot elongation in many herbaceous species (Abeles *et al.*, 1992), and there is evidence that it has a similar role in woody species. Mechanical perturbation or wind, which promote endogenous ethylene production (Telewski, 1990), inhibited stem elongation in *Liquidamber styraciflua* (Neel and Harris, 1971), *Malus domestica* (Robitaille and Leopold, 1974), *Abies fraseri* (Telewski and Jaffe, 1986a), and *Pinus taeda* (Telewski and Jaffe, 1986b). Rinne (1990) noted that a variety of stress treatments that reduced height growth in two *Betula* species also increased stem ethylene evolution. The inhibition of shoot elongation and the increase in ethylene evolution induced by stress treatment were both greater in *Betula pendula* than in *Betula pubescens*. Ethylene gassing inhibited terminal shoot elongation in *Cupressus arizonica;* however, interpretation of this result is complicated by the concomitant increase in elongation of the lateral branches, presumably reflecting the loss of apical control (Blake *et al.*, 1980). Ethephon application inhibited shoot elongation in *Malus domestica* (Robitaille and Leopold, 1974), *Pinus radiata* (Barker, 1979), *Pinus contorta* and *Picea glauca* (Weston *et al.*, 1980), and *Pinus taeda* (Telewski and Jaffe, 1986c), although not in *Pinus halepensis* (Yamamoto and Kozlowski, 1987a), *Pinus densiflora* (Yamamoto and Kozlowski, 1987b), and *Abies balsamea* (Eklund and Little, 1995b). Weaver and Pool (1969) showed early on that ethephon reduced longitudinal growth in *Vitis vinifera,* and shoot tip applications of ethephon are now used in vineyards in New Zealand, at least, to reduce subsequent cane growth without appreciable decreases in fruit set (D. I. Jackson, personal communication). In contrast, ethylene application promoted stem elongation in rice, *Ranunculus,* and other water plants (Abeles *et al.*, 1992), as well as in *Pinus elliottii* and *Pinus taeda* (Gagnon and Johnson, 1988). Ethephon also has been observed to promote, inhibit, and have no effect on bud-break (Paiva and Robitaille, 1978; Gagnon and Johnson, 1988; Eklund and Little, 1995b).

The mechanism for the inhibition of longitudinal growth by ethylene may involve GAs, because ethylene-induced inhibition is so readily reversed by applying GA_3 (Abeles *et al.*, 1992). Additional support for this conclusion is provided by the finding that the endogenous level of GA_1 in sunflower seedlings was reduced by ethylene, as was the conversion of $[^2H_2]GA_{20}$ to $[^2H_2]GA_1$ (Pearce *et al.*, 1991). Moreover, gibberellin application usually reverses the inhibition of shoot elongation induced by mechanical perturbation (Biddington, 1986). In contrast, the mechanism for the promotion of longitudinal growth by ethylene in species such as deep-water rice apparently involves an elevated GA_1 content, together with a reduction in ABA (Hoffmann-Benning and Kende, 1992). Speculatively, in this system ethylene could be inhibiting a catabolic GA hydroxylation step, for example, the conversion of GA_1 to GA_8. Alternatively, ethylene may affect longitudinal growth by altering the IAA level, as there is evidence that ethylene inhibits basipetal IAA transport and increases IAA catabolism and conjugation (Sagee *et al.*, 1990; Abeles *et al.*, 1992).

V. Conclusions and Future Directions

Representatives of all the major classes of plant hormones have been identified unequivocally, and in some cases quantified, in shoots or individual shoot parts of both conifers and woody angiosperms. The source of each hormone has not been established rigorously, but the leaves, cambial region, and rapidly growing shoot and root tissues are likely sites of synthesis. Shoots can also catabolize and conjugate hormones. However, it is not known in which cells biosynthesis, catabolism and conjugation actually occur.

The significance of hormones in the regulation of cambial and longitudinal growth in woody shoots is still unknown, although at least some of them likely play key roles. The evidence obtained to date is derived primarily from the results of treatment with exogenous hormones or inhibitors of hormone biosynthesis and action, together with the measurement of endogenous hormone levels in whole shoots or shoot parts in relation to varying growth rates and physiological conditions. The use of genotypes with different growth capacity and crown form is increasing and should help in defining the role of each hormone.

Although unequivocal proof has not yet been obtained, it seems likely that IAA is required for the initiation of the cambium, that IAA and GAs are essential for the division of cambial cells and the differentiation of their derivatives, and that CKs are necessary for bud expansion, with GAs and optimal levels of IAA being required for rapid shoot elongation. More information is needed to assess the importance of CKs, ABA, and ethylene for cambial growth, ABA and ethylene for shoot elongation, and all hormone classes for phellogen initiation and activity. Additional investigation is also required to determine the roles of brassinosteroids, polyamines, and jasmonates in radial and longitudinal growth.

Understanding the roles played by hormones in the control of the rate and seasonal periodicity of radial and longitudinal growth in shoots of woody species will depend ultimately on knowing the mechanism and mode of action of every bioactive hormone for each of the component processes involved in the division and differentiation of cells associated with the cambial and apical meristems. To this end many questions need to be answered, including the following: (1) What are the bioactive hormones in each growth and differentiation process, and in which cells and subcellular compartments are they synthesized, transported, conjugated and catabolized? (2) How are hormone levels and the "sensitivity" of dividing and differentiating cells to hormones controlled in time and space? (3) To what extent do the various hormones interact and how is this manifested? (4) Where are the receptor(s) and signal transduction pathway(s) located and how do they function? (5) What is the impact of physiological conditions such as age and water stress, and of environmental factors such as temperature and light intensity, duration and quality, on the levels of hormones and the sensitivity of cells to hormones?

There has been rapid progress in characterizing genes that respond to applied hormones or are responsible for specific steps in hormone biosynthesis. Moreover, it is now possible to transform plants, including several tree species, with such genes and work is in progress to obtain DNA sequences enabling the expression of genes in a time- and tissue-specific manner. The interfacing of hormone physiology and biochemistry with molecular biology offers exciting opportunities for clarifying the roles of hormones in the mechanisms controlling radial and longitudinal growth in the tree stem.

Acknowledgments

We thank Drs. D. M. Reid and P. C. Odén for reviewing the manuscript.

References

Abeles, F. B., Morgan, P. W., and Saltveit, M. E. (1992). "Ethylene in Plant Biology." Academic Press, San Diego, California.

Aloni, R. (1988). Vascular differentiation within the plant. *In* "Vascular Differentiation and Plant Growth Regulators" (L. W. Roberts, P. B. Gahan, and R. Aloni, eds.), pp. 39–62. Springer-Verlag, New York.

Aloni, R., and Zimmermann, M. H. (1983). The control of vessel size and density along the plant axis—a new hypothesis. *Differentiation* **24**, 203–208.

Aloni, R., Tollier, M. T., and Monties, B. (1990). The role of auxin and gibberellin in controlling lignin formation in primary phloem fibers and in xylem of *Coleus blumei* stems. *Plant Physiol.* **94**, 1743–1747.

Alvarez, R., Nissen, S. J., and Sutter, E. G. (1989). Relationship between indole-3-acetic acid levels in apple (*Malus pumila* Mill) rootstocks cultured *in vitro* and adventitious root formation in the presence of indole-3-butyric acid. *Plant Physiol.* **89**, 439–443.

Alvim, R., Hewett, E. W., and Saunders, P. F. (1976). Seasonal variation in the hormone content of willow. I. Changes in abscisic acid content and cytokinin activity in the xylem sap. *Plant Physiol.* **57**, 474–476.

Andersson, B., Häggström, N., and Andersson, K. (1978). Identification of abscisic acid in shoots of *Picea abies* and *Pinus sylvestris* by combined gas chromatography-mass spectrometry. *J. Chromatogr.* **157**, 303–310.

Baluška, F., Parker, J. S., and Barlow, P. W. (1993). A role for gibberellic acid in orienting microtubules and regulating cell growth polarity in the maize root cortex. *Planta* **191**, 149–157.

Baraldi, R., Chen, K.-H., and Cohen, J. D. (1988). Microscale isolation technique for quantitative gas chromatography-mass spectrometry analysis of indole-3-acetic acid from cherry (*Prunus cerasus* L.). *J. Chromatogr.* **442**, 301–306.

Barker, J. E. (1979). Growth and wood properties of *Pinus radiata* in relation to applied ethylene. *N.Z. J. For. Sci.* **9**, 15–19.

Barros, R. S., and Neill, S. J. (1986). Periodicity of response to abscisic acid in lateral buds of willow (*Salix viminalis* L.). *Planta* **168**, 530–535.

Barros, R. S., and Neill, S. J. (1987). Shoot growth in willow (*Salix viminalis*) in relation to abscisic acid, plant water status and photoperiod. *Physiol. Plant.* **70**, 708–712.

Bate, N. J., Rood, S. B., and Blake, T. J. (1988). Gibberellins and heterosis in poplar. *Can. J. Bot.* **66**, 1148–1152.

Bhatnagar, H. P., and Talwar, K. K. (1978). Studies on the effect of growth regulators on growth and tracheid characters of *Pinus caribaea* seedlings. *Indian For.* **104**, 333–354.

Biddington, N. L. (1986). The effects of mechanically-induced stress in plants—a review. *Plant Growth Regul.* **4,** 103–123.

Blake, T. J., and Atkinson, S. M. (1986). The physiological role of abscisic acid in the rooting of poplar and aspen stump sprouts. *Physiol. Plant.* **67,** 638–643.

Blake, J., and Ferrell, W. K. (1977). The association between soil and xylem water potential, leaf resistance, and abscisic acid content in droughted seedlings of Douglas-fir (*Pseudotsuga menziesii*). *Physiol. Plant.* **39,** 106–109.

Blake, T. J., Pharis, R. P., and Reid, D. M. (1980). Ethylene, gibberellins, auxin and the apical control of branch angle in a conifer, *Cupressus arizonica. Planta* **148,** 64–68.

Blake, T. J., Bevilacqua, E., Hunt, G. A., and Abrams, S. R. (1990). Effects of abscisic acid and its acetylenic alcohol on dormancy, root development and transpiration in three conifer species. *Physiol. Plant.* **80,** 371–378.

Browning, G., and Wignall, T. A. (1987). Identification and quantitation of indole-3-acetic and abscisic acids in the cambial region of *Quercus robur* by combined gas chromatography-mass spectrometry. *Tree Physiol.* **3,** 235–246.

Browning, G., Singh, Z., Kuden, A., and Blake, P. (1992). Effect of (*2RS, 3RS*)-paclobutrazol on endogenous indole-3-acetic acid in shoot apices of pear cv. Doyenne du Comice. *J. Hortic. Sci.* **67,** 129–135.

Bruck, D. K., and Paolillo, D. J. (1984). Replacement of leaf promodia with IAA in the induction of vascular differentiation in the stem of *Coleus. New Phytol.* **96,** 353–370.

Buta, J. G., Reed, A. N., and Murti, G. S. R. (1989). Levels of indole-3-acetic acid in vigorous and genetic dwarf apple trees. *J. Plant Growth Regul.* **8,** 249–253.

Carpita, N. C., and Tarmann, K. M. (1982). Promotion of hypocotyl elongation in loblolly pine (*Pinus taeda* L.) by indole-3-acetic acid. *Physiol. Plant.* **55,** 149–154.

Caruso, J. L., Smith, R. G., Smith, L. M., Cheng, T.-Y., and Daves, G. D. (1978). Determination of indole-3-acetic acid in Douglas fir using a deuterated analog and selected ion monitoring. Comparison of microquantities in seedlings and adult trees. *Plant Physiol.* **62,** 841–845.

Catesson, A.-M. (1990). Cambial cytology and biochemistry. *In* "The Vascular Cambium" (M. Iqbal, ed.), pp. 63–112. Research Studies Press, Ltd., Taunton, England.

Catesson, A.-M. (1994). Cambial ultrastructure and biochemistry: Changes in relation to vascular tissue differentiation and the seasonal cycle. *Int. J. Plant Sci.* **155,** 251–261.

Chen, C.-M., Ertl, J. R., Leisner, S. M., and Chang, C.-C. (1985). Localization of cytokinin biosynthetic sites in pea plants and carrot roots. *Plant Physiol.* **78,** 510–513.

Chen, W.-S. (1991). Changes in cytokinins before and during early flower bud differentiation in lychee (*Litchi chinensis* Sonn.). *Plant Physiol.* **96,** 1203–1206.

Cheng, C. K.-C., and Marsh, H. V. (1968). Gibberellic acid-promoted lignification and phenylalanine ammonia-lyase activity in a dwarf pea (*Pisum sativum*). *Plant Physiol.* **43,** 1755–1759.

Cheung, K. (1975). Induction of dormancy in container-grown western hemlock: Effects of growth retardants and inhibitors. *B.C. For. Serv. Res. Note* No. 73.

Cornforth, J. W., Milborrow, B. W., Ryback, G., and Wareing, P. F. (1965). Identity of sycamore "dormin" with abscisin II. *Nature (London)* **205,** 1269–1270.

Crozier, A., Loferski, K., Zaerr, J. B., and Morris, R. O. (1980). Analysis of picogram quantities of indole-3-acetic acid by high performance liquid chromatography-fluorescence procedures. *Planta* **150,** 366–370.

Cui, K., Little, C. H. A., and Sundberg, B. (1992). Cambial activity and the effects of exogenous IAA in the stem of *Pinus sylvestris* L. *Acta Bot. Sin.* **34,** 515–522.

Cui, K., Wu, S., Wei, L., and Little, C. H. A. (1995). Effect of exogenous IAA on the regeneration of vascular tissues and periderm in girdled *Betula pubescens* stems. *Chinese J. Bot.* (in press).

Cutting, J. G. M., Strydom, D. K., Jacobs, G., Bellstedt, D. U., Merwe, K. J. V. D., and Weiler, E. W. (1991). Changes in xylem constituents in response to rest-breaking agents applied to apple before budbreak. *J. Am. Soc. Hortic. Sci.* **116,** 680–683.

Dathe, W., Sembdner, G., Yamaguchi, I., and Takahashi, N. (1982). Gibberellins and growth inhibitors in spring bleeding sap, roots and branches of *Juglans regia* L. *Plant Cell Physiol.* **23**, 115–123.

Dathe, W., Schneider, G., and Sembdner, G. (1984). Gradient of abscisic acid and its β-D-glucopyranosyl ester in wood and bark of dormant branches of birch (*Betula pubescens* Ehrh.). *Biochem. Physiol. Pflanzen* **179**, 109–114.

Davies, J. K., Jensen, E., Junttila, O., Rivier, L., and Crozier, A. (1985). Identification of endogenous gibberellins from *Salix pentandra*. *Plant Physiol.* **78**, 473–476.

DeGroote, D. K., and Larson, P. R. (1984). Correlations between net auxin and secondary xylem development in young *Populus deltoides*. *Physiol. Plant.* **60**, 459–466.

DeMaggio, A. E. (1966). Phloem differentiation: Induced stimulation by gibberellic acid. *Science* **152**, 370–372.

DeYoe, D. R., and Zaerr, J. B. (1976). Indole-3-acetic acid in Douglas fir. Analysis by gas-liquid chromatography and mass spectrometry. *Plant Physiol.* **58**, 299–303.

Digby, J., and Wareing, P. F. (1966). The effect of applied growth hormones on cambial division and the differentiation of the cambial derivatives. *Ann. Bot.* **30**, 539–548.

Dixon, R. K., Garrett, H. E., and Cox, G. S. (1988). Cytokinins in the root pressure exudate of *Citrus jambhiri* Lush. colonized by vesicular-arbuscular mycorrhizae. *Tree Physiol.* **4**, 9–18.

Doumas, P., and Zaerr, J. B. (1988). Seasonal changes in levels of cytokinin-like compounds from Douglas-fir xylem extrudate. *Tree Physiol.* **4**, 1–8.

Doumas, P., Bonnet-Masimbert, M., and Zaerr, J. B. (1989). Evidence of cytokinin bases, ribosides and glucosides in roots of Douglas-fir, *Pseudotsuga menziesii. Tree Physiol.* **5**, 63–72.

Doumas, P., Imbault, N., Moritz, T., and Odén, P. C. (1992). Detection and identification of gibberellins in Douglas fir (*Pseudotsuga menziesii*) shoots. *Physiol. Plant.* **85**, 489–494.

Doumas, P., Ross, S. D., Webber, J. E., Owens, J. N., Bonnet-Masimbert, M., and Pharis, R. P. (1993). Endogenous gibberellins in primordia and shoots of Douglas-fir during floral differentiation. IUFRO Symposium on the Biology and Control of Reproductive Processes in Forest Trees. University of Victoria, Victoria, Canada. [Abstract]

Duke, C. C., Letham, D. S., Parker, C. W., MacLeod, J. K., and Summons, R. E. (1979). The complex of O-glucosylation derivatives formed in *Populus* species. *Phytochemistry* **18**, 819–824.

Dunberg, A. (1976). Changes in gibberellin-like substances and indole-3-acetic acid in *Picea abies* during the period of shoot elongation. *Physiol. Plant.* **38**, 186–190.

Dunberg, A., Malmberg, G., Sassa, T., and Pharis, R. P. (1983). Metabolism of tritiated gibberellins A_4 and A_9 in Norway spruce, *Picea abies* (L.) Karst. *Plant Physiol.* **71**, 257–262.

Eklund, L. (1990). Endogenous levels of oxygen, carbon dioxide and ethylene in stems of Norway spruce trees during one growing season. *Trees* **4**, 150–154.

Eklund, L. (1991a). Relations between indoleacetic acid, calcium ions and ethylene in the regulation of growth and cell wall composition in *Picea abies. J. Exp. Bot.* **42**, 785–789.

Eklund, L. (1991b). Hormone levels in the cambial region of intact *Picea abies* during the onset of cambial activity. *Physiol. Plant.* **82**, 385–388.

Eklund, L. (1993a). Movement and possible metabolism of ethylene in dormant *Picea abies. Plant Growth Regul.* **12**, 37–41.

Eklund, L. (1993b). Seasonal variations of O_2, CO_2, and ethylene in oak and maple stems. *Can. J. For. Res.* **23**, 2608–2610.

Eklund, L., and Little, C. H. A. (1995a). Interaction between indole-3-acetic acid and ethylene in the control of tracheid production in detached shoots of *Abies balsamea. Tree Physiol.* **15**, 27–34.

Eklund, L., and Little, C. H. A. (1995b). Laterally applied Ethrel locally increases radial growth and indole-3-acetic acid content in *Abies balsamea* shoots. *Tree Physiol.* (submitted).

Eklund, L., Cienciala, E., and Hällgren, J.-E. (1992). No relation between drought stress and ethylene production in Norway spruce. *Physiol. Plant.* **86**, 297–300.

Eliasson, L. (1975). Effect of indoleacetic acid on the abscisic acid level in stem tissue. *Physiol. Plant.* **34**, 117–120.

Ewers, F. W., and Aloni, R. (1985). Effects of applied auxin and gibberellin on phloem and xylem production in needle leaves of *Pinus. Bot. Gaz.* **146**, 466–471.

Fahn, A., and Zamski, E. (1970). The influence of pressure, wind, wounding and growth substances on the rate of resin duct formation in *Pinus halepensis* wood. *Isr. J. Bot.* **19**, 429–446.

Fahn, A., Werker, E., and Ben-Tzur, P. (1979). Seasonal effects of wounding and growth substances on development of traumatic resin ducts in *Cedrus libani. New Phytol.* **82**, 537–544.

Friedman, R., Levin, N., and Altman, A. (1986). Presence and identification of polyamines in xylem and phloem exudates of plants. *Plant Physiol.* **82**, 1154–1157.

Frisby, J. W., and Seeley, S. D. (1993). Chilling of endodormant peach propagules. IV. Terminal shoot growth of cuttings, including gibberellic acid treatments. *J. Am. Soc. Hortic. Sci.* **118**, 263–268.

Fukuda, H. (1994). Redifferentiation of single mesophyll cells into tracheary elements. *Int. J. Plant Sci.* **155**, 262–271.

Funada, R., Sugiyama, T., Kubo, T., and Fushitana, M. (1988). Determination of abscisic acid in *Pinus densiflora* by selected ion monitoring. *Plant Physiol.* **88**, 525–527.

Funada, R., Mizukami, E., Kubo, T., Fushitani, M., and Sugiyama, T. (1990). Distribution of indole-3-acetic acid and compression wood formation in the stems of inclined *Cryptomeria japonica. Holzforschung* **44**, 331–334.

Funada, R., Sugiyama, T., Kubo, T., and Fushitani, M. (1992). Identification of endogenous cytokinins in the cambial region of *Cryptomeria japonica* stem. *Mokuzai Gakkaishi* **38**, 317–320.

Gagnon, K. G., and Johnson, J. D. (1988). Bud development and dormancy in slash and loblolly pine. II. Effects of ethephon applications. *New For.* **2**, 269–274.

Haissig, B. E., and King, J. P. (1970). Influence of (*RS*)-abscisic acid on budbreak in white spruce seedlings. *For. Sci.* **16**, 210–211.

Hare, R. (1984). Stimulation of early height growth in longleaf pine with growth regulators. *Can. J. For. Res.* **14**, 459–462.

Harris, J. M. (1989). "Spiral Grain and Wave Phenomena in Wood Formation." Springer-Verlag, New York.

Hasan, O. (1993). The effect of paclobutrazol on flowering activity and gibberellin levels in *Eucalyptus nitens* and *Eucalyptus globulus*. Ph.D. thesis. University of Tasmania, Hobart, Australia.

Hasan, O., Ridoutt, B. G., Ross, J. J., Davies, N. W., and Reid, J. B. (1994). Identification and quantification of endogenous gibberellins in apical buds and the cambial region of *Eucalyptus. Physiol. Plant.* **90**, 475–480.

Hautala, E., Stafford, A., Corse, J., and Barker, P. A. (1986). Cytokinin variation in the sap of male and female *Gymnocladus dioica. J Chromatogr.* **351**, 560–565.

Heide, O. M. (1986). Effects of ABA application on cessation of shoot elongation in long-day grown Norway spruce seedlings. *Tree Physiol.* **1**, 79–83.

Hennion, S., Little, C. H. A., and Hartmann, C. (1992). Activities of enzymes involved in lignification during the postharvest storage of etiolated asparagus spears. *Physiol. Plant.* **86**, 474–478.

Hewett, E. W., and Wareing, P. F. (1973). Cytokinins in *Populus* × *robusta:* Changes during chilling and budburst. *Physiol. Plant.* **28**, 393–399.

Hoad, G. V., Retamales, J. A., Whiteside, R. J., and Lewis, M. J. (1993). Phloem translocation of gibberellins in three species of higher plants. *Plant Growth Regul.* **13**, 85–88.

Hoffmann-Benning, S., and Kende, H. (1992). On the role of abscisic acid and gibberellin in the regulation of growth in rice. *Plant Physiol.* **99**, 1156–1161.

Hoque, E., Dathe, W., Tesche, M., and Sembdner, G. (1983). Abscisic acid and its β-D-glucopyranosyl ester in saplings of Scots pine (*Pinus sylvestris* L.) in relation to water stress. *Biochem. Physiol. Pflanzen* **178**, 287–295.

Horgan, R., Hewett, E. W., Horgan, J. M., Purse, J., and Wareing, P. F. (1975). A new cytokinin from *Populus* × *robusta*. *Phytochemistry* **14**, 1005–1008.

Imbault, N., Moritz, T., Nilsson, O., Chen, H.-J., Bollmark, M., and Sandberg, G. (1993). Separation and identification of cytokinins using combined capillary liquid chromatography/mass spectrometry. *Biol. Mass Spectrom.* **22**, 201–210.

Ingemarsson, B. S. M. (1994). Ethylene in conifers: Involvement in wood formation and stress. Ph.D. thesis. Stockholm University, Stockholm, Sweden.

Ingemarsson, B. S. M., Eklund, L., and Eliasson, L. (1991a). Ethylene effects on cambial activity and cell wall formation in hypocotyls of *Picea abies* seedlings. *Physiol. Plant.* **82**, 219–224.

Ingemarsson, B. S. M., Lundqvist, E., and Eliasson, L. (1991b). Seasonal variation in ethylene concentration in the wood of *Pinus sylvestris* L. *Tree Physiol.* **8**, 273–279.

Jacobs, W. P., and Morrow, I. B. (1957). A quantitative study of xylem development in the vegetative shoot apex of *Coleus*. *Am. J. Bot.* **44**, 823–842.

Jenkins, P. A. (1974). Influence of applied indoleacetic acid and abscisic acid on xylem cell dimensions in *Pinus radiata* D. Don. *Bull. R. Soc. N.Z.* **12**, 737–742.

Jenkins, P. A., and Shepherd, K. R. (1972). Identification of abscisic acid in young stems of *Pinus radiata* D. Don. *New Phytol.* **71**, 501–511.

Jensen, E., and Junttila, O. (1982). Indolyl-3-acetic acid from shoots of *Salix pentandra*. *Physiol. Plant.* **56**, 241–244.

Jensen, E., Rivier, L., Junttila, O., and Crozier, A. (1986). Identification of abscisic acid from shoots of *Salix pentandra*. *Physiol. Plant.* **66**, 406–408.

Johansen, L. G., Odén, P. C., and Junttila, O. (1986). Abscisic acid and cessation of apical growth in *Salix pentandra*. *Physiol. Plant.* **66**, 409–412.

Junttila, O. (1991). Gibberellins and the regulation of shoot elongation in woody plants. *In* "Gibberellins" (N. Takahashi, B. O. Phinney, and J. MacMillan, eds.), pp. 199–210. Springer-Verlag, New York.

Junttila, O. (1993a). Exogenously applied GA_4 is converted to GA_1 in seedlings of *Salix*. *J. Plant Growth Regul.* **12**, 35–39.

Junttila, O. (1993b). Interaction of growth retardants, daylength, and gibberellins A_{19}, A_{20}, and A_1 on shoot elongation in birch and alder. *J. Plant Growth Regul.* **12**, 123–127.

Junttila, O., and Jensen, E. (1988). Gibberellins and photoperiodic control of shoot elongation in *Salix*. *Physiol. Plant.* **74**, 371–376.

Junttila, O., Abe, H., and Pharis, R. P. (1988). Endogenous gibberellins in elongating shoots of clones of *Salix dasyclados* and *Salix viminalis*. *Plant Physiol.* **87**, 781–784.

Junttila, O., Jensen, E., and Ernstsen, A. (1991). Effects of prohexadione (BX-112) and gibberellins on shoot growth in seedlings of *Salix pentandra*. *Physiol. Plant.* **83**, 17–21.

Junttila, O., Jensen, E., Pearce, D. W., and Pharis, R. P. (1992). Stimulation of shoot elongation in *Salix pentandra* by gibberellin A_9; activity appears to be dependent upon hydroxylation to GA_1 via GA_{20}. *Physiol. Plant.* **84**, 113–120.

Kannangara, T., Wieczorek, A., and Lavender, D. P. (1989). Immunoaffinity columns for isolation of abscisic acid in conifer seedlings. *Physiol. Plant.* **75**, 369–373.

Kelner, J.-J., Lachaud, S., and Bonnemain, J.-L. (1993). Seasonal variations of the tissue distribution of [³H]ABA and [³H]nutrients in apical buds of beech. *Plant Physiol. Biochem.* **31**, 531–539.

Khalil, A. A. M., and Grace, J. (1993). Does xylem sap ABA control the stomatal behaviour of water-stressed sycamore (*Acer pseudoplatanus* L.) seedlings? *J. Exp. Bot.* **44**, 1127–1134.

Kim, S.-K., Abe, H., Little, C. H. A., and Pharis, R. P. (1990). Identification of two brassinosteroids from the cambial region of Scots pine (*Pinus sylvestris*) by gas chromatography-mass spectrometry, after detection using a dwarf rice lamina inclination bioassay. *Plant Physiol.* **94**, 1709–1713.

Komor, E., Liegl, I., and Schobert, C. (1993). Loading and translocation of various cytokinins in phloem and xylem of the seedlings of *Ricinus communis* L. *Planta* **191**, 252–255.

Königshofer, H. (1991). Distribution and seasonal variation of polyamines in shoot-axes of spruce (*Picea abies* (L.) Karst.). *J. Plant Physiol.* **137**, 607–612.

Koshioka, M., Taylor, J. S., Edwards, G. R., Looney, N. E., and Pharis, R. P. (1985). Identification of gibberellins A_{19} and A_{20} in vegetative tissue of apple. *Agric. Biol. Chem.* **49**, 1223–1226.

Kossuth, S. V. (1981). Shortening the grass stage of longleaf pine with plant growth regulators. *For. Sci.* **27**, 400–404.

Kozlowski, T. T., Kramer, P. J., and Pallardy, S. G. (1991). "The Physiological Ecology of Woody Plants." Academic Press, San Diego, California.

Kraus, M., and Ziegler, H. (1993). Quantitative analysis of abscisic acid in needles of *Abies alba* Mill. by electron capture gas chromatography. *Trees* **7**, 175–181.

Kurczyńska, E. U., and Hejnowicz, Z. (1991). Differentiation of circular vessels in isolated segments of *Fraxinus excelsior*. *Physiol. Plant.* **83**, 275–280.

Kutschera, U. (1994). The current status of the acid-growth hypothesis. *New Phytol.* **126**, 549–569.

Lachaud, S. (1989). Participation of auxin and abscisic acid in the regulation of seasonal variations in cambial activity and xylogenesis. *Trees* **3**, 125–137.

Lachaud, S., and Bonnemain, J. L. (1984). Seasonal variations in the polar transport pathways and retention sites of [^{3}H]indole-3-acetic acid in young branches of *Fagus sylvatica* L. *Planta* **161**, 207–215.

Lang, G. A., Early, J. D., Arroyave, N. J., Darnell, R. L., Martin, G. C., and Stutte, G. W. (1985). Dormancy: Toward a reduced, universal terminology. *HortScience* **20**, 809–812.

Lanner, R. M. (1976). Patterns of shoot development in *Pinus* and their relationship to growth potential. *In* "Tree Physiology and Yield Improvement" (M. G. R. Cannell and F. T. Last, eds.), pp. 223–243. Academic Press, London.

Larson, P. R. (1960). Gibberellic acid-induced growth of dormant hardwood cuttings. *For. Sci.* **6**, 232–239.

Lavender, D. P., Sweet, G. B., Zaerr, J. B., and Hermann, R. K. (1973). Spring shoot growth in Douglas-fir may be initiated by gibberellins exported from the roots. *Science* **182**, 838–839.

Lev-Yadun, S., and Aloni, R. (1990). Polar patterns of periderm ontogeny, their relationship to leaves and buds, and the control of cork formation. *IAWA Bull. n.s.* **11**, 289–300.

Little, C. H. A. (1970). Apical dominance in long shoots of white pine (*Pinus strobus*). *Can. J. Bot.* **48**, 239–253.

Little, C. H. A. (1975). Inhibition of cambial activity in *Abies balsamea* by internal water stress: Role of abscisic acid. *Can. J. Bot.* **53**, 3041–3050.

Little, C. H. A. (1981). Effect of cambial dormancy state on the transport of [1-^{14}C]indol-3-ylacetic acid in *Abies balsamea* shoots. *Can. J. Bot.* **59**, 342–348.

Little, C. H. A. (1985). Increasing lateral shoot production in balsam fir Christmas trees with cytokinin application. *HortScience* **20**, 713–714.

Little, C. H. A., and Bonga, J. M. (1974). Rest in the cambium of *Abies balsamea*. *Can. J. Bot.* **52**, 1723–1730.

Little, C. H. A., and Eidt, D. C. (1968). Effect of abscisic acid on budbreak and transpiration in woody species. *Nature (London)* **220**, 498–499.

Little, C. H. A., and Eidt, D. C. (1970). Relationship between transpiration and cambial activity in *Abies balsamea*. *Can. J. Bot.* **48**, 1027–1028.

Little, C. H. A., and Savidge, R. A. (1987). The role of plant growth regulators in forest tree cambial growth. *Plant Growth Regul.* **6**, 137–169.

Little, C. H. A., and Sundberg, B. (1991). Tracheid production in response to indole-3-acetic acid varies with internode age in *Pinus sylvestris* stems. *Trees* **5**, 101–106.

Little, C. H. A., and Wareing, P. F. (1981). Control of cambial activity and dormancy in *Picea sitchensis* by indol-3-ylacetic and abscisic acids. *Can. J. Bot.* **59**, 1480–1493.

Little, C. H. A., Strunz, G. M., France, R. L., and Bonga, J. M. (1972). Identification of abscisic acid in *Abies balsamea*. *Phytochemistry* **11**, 3535–3536.

Little, C. H. A., Heald, J. K., and Browning, G. (1978). Identification and measurement of indoleacetic and abscisic acids in the cambial region of *Picea sitchensis* (Bong.) Carr. by combined gas chromatography-mass spectrometry. *Planta* **139**, 133–138.

Little, C. H. A., Andrew, D. M., Silk, P. J., and Strunz, G. M. (1979). Identification of cytokinins zeatin and zeatin riboside in *Abies balsamea. Phytochemistry* **18**, 1219–1220.

Little, C. H. A., Sundberg, B., and Ericsson, A. (1990). Induction of acropetal ^{14}C-photosynthate transport and radial growth by indole-3-acetic acid in *Pinus sylvestris* shoots. *Tree Physiol.* **6**, 177–189.

Lloyd, A. D., Mellerowicz, E. J., Chow, C. H., Riding, R. T., and Little, C. H. A. (1994). Fluctuations in ribosomal RNA gene content and nucleolar activity in the cambial region of *Abies balsamea* (Pinaceae) shoots during reactivation. *Am. J. Bot.* **81**, 1384–1389.

Longman, K. A. (1982). Effects of gibberellin, clone and environment on cone initiation, shoot growth and branching in *Pinus contorta. Ann. Bot.* **50**, 247–257.

Lorences, E. P., and Zarra, I. (1987). Auxin-induced growth in hypocotyl segments of *Pinus pinaster* Aiton. Changes in molecular weight distribution of hemicellulosic polysaccharides. *J. Exp. Bot.* **38**, 960–967.

Lorenzi, R., Horgan, R., and Heald, J. K. (1975a). Gibberellins in *Picea sitchensis* Carriere: Seasonal variation and partial characterization. *Planta* **126**, 75–82.

Lorenzi, R., Horgan, R., and Wareing, P. F. (1975b). Cytokinins in *Picea sitchensis* Carriere: Identification and relation to growth. *Biochem. Physiol. Pflanz.* **168**, 333–339.

Loveys, B. R., Robinson, S. P., and Downton, W. J. S. (1987). Seasonal and diurnal changes in abscisic acid and water relations of apricot leaves (*Prunus armeniaca* L.). *New Phytol.* **107**, 15–27.

Luna, V., Reinoso, H., Lorenzo, E., Bottini, R., and Abdala, G. (1991). Dormancy in peach (*Prunus persica* L.) flower buds. II. Comparative morphology and phenology in floral and vegetative buds, and the effect of chilling and gibberellin A_3. *Trees* **5**, 244–246.

Mander, L. N. (1992). The chemistry of gibberellins: An overview. *Chem. Rev.* **92**, 573–612.

Meilan, R., Horgan, R., Heald, J. K., LaMotte, C. E., and Schultz, R. C. (1993). Identification of the cytokinins in red pine seedlings. *Plant Growth Regul.* **13**, 169–178.

Mellerowicz, E. J., Riding, R. T., and Little, C. H. A. (1989). Genomic variability in the vascular cambium of *Abies balsamea. Can. J. Bot.* **67**, 990–996.

Mellerowicz, E. J., Riding, R. T., and Little, C. H. A. (1990). Nuclear size and shape changes in fusiform cambial cells of *Abies balsamea* during the annual cycle of activity and dormancy. *Can. J. Bot.* **68**, 1857–1863.

Mellerowicz, E. J., Coleman, W. K., Riding, R. T., and Little, C. H. A. (1992a). Periodicity of cambial activity in *Abies balsamea*. I. Effects of temperature and photoperiod on cambial dormancy and frost hardiness. *Physiol. Plant.* **85**, 515–525.

Mellerowicz, E. J., Riding, R. T., and Little, C. H. A. (1992b). Periodicity of cambial activity in *Abies balsamea*. II. Effects of temperature and photoperiod on the size of the nuclear genome in fusiform cambial cells. *Physiol. Plant.* **85**, 526–530.

Mellerowicz, E. J., Riding, R. T., and Little, C. H. A. (1993). Nucleolar activity in the fusiform cambial cells of *Abies balsamea* (Pinaceae): Effect of season and age. *Am. J. Bot.* **80**, 1168–1174.

Meyer, A., Miersch, O., Büttner, C., Dathe, W., and Sembdner, G. (1984). Occurrence of the plant growth regulator jasmonic acid in plants. *J. Plant Growth Regul.* **3**, 1–8.

Meyer, A., Schneider, G., and Sembdner, G. (1986). Endogenous gibberellins and inhibitors in the Douglas-fir. *Biol. Plant.* **28**, 52–56.

Miller, A. R., Pengelly, W. L., and Roberts, L. W. (1984). Introduction of xylem differentiation in *Lactuca* by ethylene. *Plant Physiol.* **75**, 1165–1166.

Miller, A. R., Crawford, D. L., and Roberts, L. W. (1985). Lignification and xylogenesis in *Lactuca* pith explants cultured *in vitro* in the presence of auxin and cytokinin: A role for endogenous ethylene. *J. Exp. Bot.* **36**, 110–118.

Moritz, T. (1992). The use of combined capillary liquid chromatography/mass spectrometry for the identification of a gibberellin glucosyl conjugate. *Phytochem. Anal.* **3**, 32–37.

Moritz, T., and Monteiro, A. M. (1994). Analysis of endogenous gibberellins and gibberellin metabolites from *Dalbergia dolichopetala* by gas chromatography-mass spectrometry and high-performance liquid chromatography-mass spectrometry. *Planta* **193**, 1–8.

Moritz, T., and Odén, P. C. (1990). Metabolism of tritiated and deuterated gibberellin A_9 in Norway spruce (*Picea abies*) shoots during the period of cone-bud differentiation. *Physiol. Plant.* **79**, 242–249.

Moritz, T., Philipson, J. J., and Odén, P. C. (1989a). Metabolism of tritiated and deuterated gibberellins A_1, A_4 and A_9 in Sitka spruce (*Picea sitchensis*) shoots during the period of cone-bud differentiation. *Physiol. Plant.* **77**, 39–45.

Moritz, T., Philipson, J. J., and Odén, P. C. (1989b). Detection and identification of gibberellins in Sitka spruce (*Picea sitchensis*) of different ages and coning ability by bioassay, radioimmunoassay and gas chromatography-mass spectrometry. *Physiol. Plant.* **75**, 325–332.

Moritz, T., Philipson, J. J., and Odén, P. C. (1990). Quantitation of gibberellins A_1, A_3, A_4, A_9, and a putative A_9-conjugate in grafts of Sitka spruce (*Picea sitchensis*) during the period of shoot elongation. *Plant Physiol.* **93**, 1476–1481.

Morris, D. A., and Johnson, C. F. (1985). Characteristics and mechanisms of long-distance auxin transport in intact plants. *Acta Univ. Agric. (Brno, Czech.) Fac. Agron.* **33**, 377–383.

Morris, J. W., Doumas, P., Morris, R. O., and Zaerr, J. B. (1990). Cytokinins in vegetative and reproductive buds of *Pseudotsuga menziesii*. *Plant Physiol.* **93**, 67–71.

Munns, R., and Sharp, R. E. (1993). Involvement of abscisic acid in controlling plant growth in soils of low water potential. *Aust. J. Plant Physiol.* **20**, 425–437.

Nakamura, T., Saotome, M., Ishiguro, Y., Itoh, R., Higurashi, S., Hosono, M., and Ishii, Y. (1994). The effects of GA_3 on weeping of growing shoots of the Japanese cherry, *Prunus spachiana*. *Plant Cell Physiol.* **35**, 523–527.

Napier, R. M., and Venis, M. A. (1990). Receptors for plant growth regulators: Recent advances. *J. Plant Growth Regul.* **9**, 113–126.

Neel, P. L., and Harris, R. W. (1971). Motion-induced inhibition of elongation and induction of dormancy in *Liquidambar*. *Science* **173**, 58–59.

Nelson, N. D., and Hillis, W. E. (1978). Ethylene and tension wood formation in *Eucalyptus gomphocephala*. *Wood Sci. Technol.* **12**, 309–315.

Odani, K. (1985). Indole-3-acetic acid transport in pine shoots under the stage of true dormancy. *J. Jpn. For. Soc.* **67**, 332–334.

Odén, P. C., and Dunberg, A. (1984). Abscisic acid in shoots and roots of Scots pine (*Pinus sylvestris* L.) seedlings grown in controlled long-day and short-day environments. *Planta* **161**, 148–155.

Odén, P. C., Schwenen, L., and Graebe, J. E. (1987). Identification of gibberellins in Norway spruce (*Picea abies* [L.] Karst.) by combined gas chromatography-mass spectrometry. *Plant Physiol.* **84**, 516–519.

Ogiyama, K., Yasue, M., and Pharis, R. P. (1980). Endogenous plant growth regulating substances in the foliage of *Cryptomeria japonica* D. Don. *J. Jpn. Wood Res. Soc.* **26**, 823–827.

Olsen, J. E., Moritz, T., Jensen, E., and Junttila, O. (1994). Comparison of endogenous gibberellins in roots and shoots of elongating *Salix pentandra* seedlings. *Physiol. Plant.* **90**, 378–381.

Östin, A., Moritz, T., and Sandberg, G. (1992a). Liquid chromatography/mass spectrometry of conjugates and oxidative metabolites of indole-3-acetic acid. *Biol. Mass Spectrom.* **21**, 292–298.

Östin, A., Monteiro, A. M., Crozier, A., Jensen, E., and Sandberg, G. (1992b). Analysis of indole-3-acetic acid metabolites from *Dalbergia dolichopetala* by high performance liquid chromatography-mass spectrometry. *Plant Physiol.* **100**, 63–68.

Paiva, E., and Robitaille, H. A. (1978). Breaking bud rest on detached apple shoots: effects of wounding and ethylene. *J. Am. Soc. Hortic. Sci.* **103**, 101–104.

Pearce, D., Miller, A. R., Roberts, L. W., and Pharis, R. P. (1987). Gibberellin-mediated synergism of xylogenesis in lettuce pith cultures. *Plant Physiol.* **84,** 1121–1125.

Pearce, D. W., Reid, D. M., and Pharis, R. P. (1991). Ethylene-mediated regulation of gibberellin content and growth in *Helianthus annuus* L. *Plant Physiol.* **95,** 1197–1202.

Pearce, D. W., Koshioka, M., and Pharis, R. P. (1994). Chromatography of gibberellins. *J. Chromatogr. A* **658,** 91–122.

Pharis, R. P. (1976). Probable roles of plant hormones in regulating shoot elongation, diameter growth and crown form of coniferous trees. *In* "Tree Physiology and Yield Improvement" (M. G. R. Cannell and F. T. Last, eds.), pp. 291–306. Academic Press, London.

Pharis, R. P., and Kuo, C. G. (1977). Physiology of gibberellins in conifers. *Can. J. For. Res.* **7,** 299–325.

Pharis, R. P., and Ross, S. D. (1976). Gibberellins: Their potential uses in forestry. *Outlook Agric.* **9,** 82–87.

Pharis, R. P., Ruddat, M., Phillips, C. C., and Heftmann, E. (1965). Gibberellin, growth retardants, and apical dominance in Arizona cypress. *Naturwissenschaften* **52,** 88–89.

Pharis, R. P., Ruddat, M., Phillips, C., and Heftmann, E. (1967). Response of conifers to growth retardants. *Bot. Gaz.* **128,** 105–109.

Pharis, R. P., Jenkins, P. A., Aoki, H., and Sassa, T. (1981). Hormonal physiology of wood growth in *Pinus radiata* D. Don: Effects of gibberellin A₄ and the influence of abscisic acid upon [³H]gibberellin A₄ metabolism. *Aust. J. Plant Physiol.* **8,** 559–570.

Pharis, R. P., Webber, J. E., and Ross, S. D. (1987). The promotion of flowering in forest trees by gibberellin A₄/₇ and cultural treatments: A review of the possible mechanisms. *For. Ecol. Manage.* **19,** 65–84.

Pharis, R. P., Yeh, F. C., and Dancik, B. P. (1991). Superior growth potential in trees: What is its basis, and can it be tested for at an early age? *Can. J. For. Res.* **21,** 368–374.

Pharis, R. P., Zhang, R., Jiang, I. B.-J., Dancik, B. P., and Yeh, F. C. (1992). Differential efficacy of gibberellins in flowering and vegetative shoot growth, including heterosis and inherently rapid growth. *In* "Progress in Plant Growth Regulation" (C. M. Karssen, L. C. Van Loon, and D. Vreugdenhil, eds.), pp. 13–27. Kluwer Academic Publishers, Dordrecht, the Netherlands.

Pharis, R. P., Zhang, R., Wu, H. X., Yeh, F. C., and Dancik, B. P. (1993). Early evaluation of inherently superior growth in forest trees and its physiological basis. 24th Meeting Can. Tree Improv. Assoc. Ottawa.

Philipson, J. J. (1983). The role of gibberellin A₄/₇, heat and drought in the induction of flowering in Sitka spruce. *J. Exp. Bot.* **34,** 291–302.

Phinney, B. O., and Spray, C. R. (1990). Dwarf mutants of maize—research tools for analysis of growth. *In* "Plant Growth Substances 1988" (R. P. Pharis, and S. B. Rood, eds.), pp. 64–73. Springer-Verlag, New York.

Pilate, G., Sotta, B., Maldiney, R., Jacques, M., Sossountzov, L., and Miginiac, E. (1989). Abscisic acid, indole-3-acetic acid and cytokinin changes in buds of *Pseudotsuga menziesii* during bud quiescence release. *Physiol. Plant.* **76,** 100–106.

Plummer, J. A., Mullins, M. G., and Vine, J. H. (1991). Seasonal changes in endogenous ABA and IAA and the influence of applied ABA and auxin in relation to shoot growth and abscission in Valencia orange (*Citrus sinensis* (L.) Osbeck). *Plant Growth Regul.* **10,** 139–151.

Plüss, R., Jenny, T., and Meier, H. (1989). IAA-induced adventitious root formation in greenwood cuttings of *Populus tremula* and formation of 2-indolone-3-acetylaspartic acid, a new metabolite of exogeneously applied indole-3-acetic acid. *Physiol. Plant.* **75,** 89–96.

Poling, S. M., and Maier, V. P. (1988). Identification of endogenous gibberellins in navel orange shoots. *Plant Physiol.* **88,** 639–642.

Powell, L. E. (1987). Hormonal aspects of bud and seed dormancy in temperate-zone woody plants. *HortScience* **22,** 845–850.

Purse, J. G., Horgan, R., Horgan, J. M., and Wareing, P. F. (1976). Cytokinins of sycamore spring sap. *Planta* **132,** 1–8.

Puttonen, P. (1987). Abscisic acid concentration in Douglas-fir needles in relation to lifting date, cold storage, and postplanting vigor of seedlings. *Can. J. For. Res.* **17**, 383–387.

Qamaruddin, M., Dormling, I., and Eliasson, L. (1990). Increases in cytokinin levels in Scots pine in relation to chilling and budburst. *Physiol. Plant.* **79**, 236–241.

Qamaruddin, M., Dormling, I., Ekberg, I., Eriksson, G., and Tillberg, E. (1993). Abscisic acid content at defined levels of bud dormancy and frost tolerance in two contrasting populations of *Picea abies* grown in a phytotron. *Physiol. Plant.* **87**, 203–210.

Ramsden, L., and Northcote, D. H. (1987). Tracheid formation in cultures of pine (*Pinus sylvestris*). *J. Cell Sci.* **88**, 467–474.

Reid, J. B. (1990). Gibberellin synthesis and sensitivity mutants in *Pisum*. In "Plant Growth Substances 1988" (R. P. Pharis and S. B. Rood, eds.), pp. 74–83. Springer-Verlag, New York.

Reinders-Gouwentak, C. A. (1965). Physiology of the cambium and other secondary meristems of the shoot. *Encyclopedia Plant Physiol.* **15(1)**, 1077–1105.

Richards, D., Thompson, W. K., and Pharis, R. P. (1986). The influence of dwarfing interstocks on the distribution and metabolism of xylem-applied [^{3}H]gibberellin A$_4$ in apple. *Plant Physiol.* **82**, 1090–1095.

Riding, R. T., and Little, C. H. A. (1984). Anatomy and histochemistry of *Abies balsamea* cambial zone cells during the onset and breaking of dormancy. *Can. J. Bot.* **62**, 2570–2579.

Riding, R. T., and Little, C. H. A. (1986). Histochemistry of the dormant vascular cambium of *Abies balsamea:* Changes associated with tree age and crown position. *Can. J. Bot.* **64**, 2082–2087.

Rinne, P. (1990). Effects of various stress treatments on growth and ethylene evolution in seedlings and sprouts of *Betula pendula* Roth and *B. pubescens* Ehrh. *Scand. J. For. Res.* **5**, 155–167.

Rinne, P., and Saarelainen, A. (1994). Root produced DHZR-, ZR- and iPA-like cytokinins in xylem sap in relation to coppice shoot initiation and growth in cloned trees of *Betula pubescens*. *Tree Physiol.* **14**, 1149–1161.

Rinne, P., Tuominen, H., and Sundberg, B. (1993). Growth patterns and endogenous indole-3-acetic acid concentrations in current-year coppice shoots and seedlings of two *Betula* species. *Physiol. Plant.* **88**, 403–412.

Rinne, P., Saarelainen, A., and Junttila, O. (1994a). Growth cessation and bud dormancy in relation to ABA level in seedlings and coppice shoots of *Betula pubescens* as affected by a short photoperiod, water stress and chilling. *Physiol. Plant.* **90**, 451–458.

Rinne, P., Tuominen, H., and Junttila, O. (1994b). Seasonal changes in bud dormancy in relation to bud morphology, water and starch content, and abscisic acid concentration in adult trees of *Betula pubescens*. *Tree Physiol.* **14**, 549–561.

Roberts, D. R., and Dumbroff, E. B. (1986). Relationships among drought resistance, transpiration rates, and abscisic acid levels in three northern conifers. *Tree Physiol.* **1**, 161–167.

Robitaille, H. A., and Leopold, A. C. (1974). Ethylene and the regulation of apple stem growth under stress. *Physiol. Plant.* **32**, 301–304.

Rodríguez, A., Canal, M. J., and Tames, R. S. (1991). Seasonal changes of growth regulators in *Corylus. J. Plant Physiol.* **138**, 29–32.

Rood, S. B., Bate, N. J., Mander, L. N., and Pharis, R. P. (1988). Identification of gibberellins A$_1$ and A$_{19}$ from *Populus balsamifera* × *P. deltoides*. *Phytochemistry* **27**, 11–14.

Ross, S. D., Pharis, R. P., and Binder, W. D. (1983). Growth regulators and conifers: their physiology and potential uses in forestry. In "Plant Growth Regulating Chemicals" (L. G. Nickell, ed.) pp. 35–78. CRC Press, Boca Raton, Florida.

Ross, S. D., Bollmann, M. P., Pharis, R. P., and Sweet, G. B. (1984). Gibberellin A$_{4/7}$ and the promotion of flowering in *Pinus radiata*. Effects on partitioning of photoassimilate within the bud during primordia differentiation. *Plant Physiol.* **76**, 326–330.

Sagee, O., Riov, J., and Goren, R. (1990). Ethylene-enhanced catabolism of [^{14}C]indole-3-acetic acid to indole-3-carboxylic acid in citrus leaf tissues. *Plant Physiol.* **92**, 54–60.

Saks, Y., Feigenbaum, P., and Aloni, R. (1984). Regulatory effect of cytokinin on secondary xylem fiber formation in an *in vivo* system. *Plant Physiol.* **76**, 638–642.

Sandberg, G., and Ericsson, A. (1987). Indole-3-acetic acid concentration in the leading shoot and living stem bark of Scots pine: Seasonal variation and effects of pruning. *Tree Physiol.* **3**, 173–183.

Sandberg, G., Andersson, B., and Dunberg, A. (1981). Identification of 3-indoleacectic acid in *Pinus sylvestris* L. by gas chromatography-mass spectrometry, and quantitative analysis by ion-pair reversed-phase liquid chromatography with spectrofluorimetric detection. *J Chromatogr.* **205**, 125–137.

Sandberg, G., Gardeström, P., Sitbon, F., and Olsson, O. (1990). Presence of indole-3-acetic acid in chloroplasts of *Nicotiana tabacum* and *Pinus sylvestris*. *Planta* **180**, 562–568.

Saotome, M., Shirahata, K., Nishimura, R., Yahaba, M., Kawaguchi, M., Syôno, K., Kitsuwa, T., Ishii, Y., and Nakamura, T. (1993). The identification of indole-3-acetic acid and indole-3-acetamide in the hypocotyls of Japanese cherry. *Plant Cell Physiol.* **34**, 157–159.

Sarjala, T., and Kaunisto, S. (1993). Needle polyamine concentrations and potassium nutrition in Scots pine. *Tree Physiol.* **13**, 87–96.

Saunders, P. F., and Barros, R. S. (1987). Periodicity of bud bursting in willow (*Salix viminalis*) as affected by growth regulators. *Physiol. Plant.* **69**, 535–540.

Savidge, R. A. (1983). The role of plant hormones in higher plant cellular differentation. II. Experiments with the vascular cambium, and sclereid and tracheid differentiation in the pine, *Pinus contorta*. *Histochem. J.* **15**, 447–466.

Savidge, R. A. (1988). Auxin and ethylene regulation of diameter growth in trees. *Tree Physiol.* **4**, 401–414.

Savidge, R. A. (1990). Characterization of indol-3-ylacetic acid in developing secondary xylem of 26 Canadian species by combined gas chromatography—mass spectrometry. *Can. J. Bot.* **68**, 521–523.

Savidge, R. A. (1991). Seasonal cambial activity in *Larix laricina* saplings in relation to endogenous indol-3-ylacetic acid, sucrose, and coniferin. *For. Sci.* **37**, 953–958.

Savidge, R. A. (1993). In vitro wood formation in "chips" from merchantable stem regions of *Larix laricina*. *IAWA J.* **14**, 3–11.

Savidge, R. A. (1994). The tracheid-differentiation factor of conifer needles. *Int. J. Plant Sci.* **155**, 272–290.

Savidge, R. A., and Wareing, P. F. (1982). Apparent auxin production and transport during winter in the nongrowing pine tree. *Can. J. Bot.* **60**, 681–691.

Savidge, R. A., and Wareing, P. F. (1984). Seasonal cambial activity and xylem development in *Pinus contorta* in relation to endogenous indol-3-yl-acetic and (*S*)-abscisic acid levels. *Can. J. For. Res.* **14**, 676–682.

Savidge, R. A., Mutumba, G. M. C., Heald, J. K., and Wareing, P. F. (1983). Gas chromatography-mass spectroscopy identification of 1-aminocyclopropane-1-carboxylic acid in compression-wood vascular cambium of *Pinus contorta* Dougl. *Plant Physiol.* **71**, 434–436.

Seeley, S. D., and Powell, L. E. (1981). Seasonal changes of free and hydrolyzable abscisic acid in vegetative apple buds. *J. Am. Soc. Hortic. Sci.* **106**, 405–409.

Shaybany, B., and Martin, G. C. (1977). Abscisic acid identification and its quantitation in leaves of *Juglans* seedlings during waterlogging. *J. Am. Soc. Hortic. Sci.* **102**, 300–302.

Sheng, C., Pharis, R. P., and Ross, S. D. (1993). Effect of sex-modification treatments on flowering and endogenous ABA and IAA in newly-formed conebuds of western hemlock ramets. IUFRO Symp. on the Biology and Control of Reproductive Processes in Forest Trees. University of Victoria, Victoria, Canada. [Abstract]

Shibaoka, H. (1994). Plant hormone-induced changes in the orientation of cortical microtubules: Alterations in the cross-linking between microtubules and the plasma membrane. *Annu. Rev. Plant Physiol. Plant Mol. Biol.* **45**, 527–544.

Singha, S., and Powell, L. E. (1978). Response of apple buds cultured *in vitro* to abscisic acid. *J. Am. Soc. Hortic. Sci.* **103**, 620–622.

Sitbon, F., Eklöf, S., Riding, R. T., Sandberg, G., Olsson, O., and Little, C. H. A. (1993). Patterns of protein synthesis in the cambial region of Scots pine shoots during reactivation. *Physiol. Plant.* **87**, 601–608.

Sivakumaran, S., Horgan, R., Heald, J., and Hall, M. A. (1980). Effect of water stress on metabolism of abscisic acid in *Populus robusta* × schnied and *Euphorbia lathyrus* L. *Plant Cell Environ.* **3**, 163–173.

Sorokin, H. P., Mathur, S. N., and Thimann, K. V. (1962). The effects of auxins and kinetin on xylem differentiation in the pea epicotyl. *Am. J. Bot.* **49**, 444–454.

Steffens, G. L., and Hedden, P. (1992a). Effect of temperature regimes on gibberellin levels in thermosensitive dwarf apple trees. *Physiol. Plant.* **86**, 539–543.

Steffens, G. L., and Hedden, P. (1992b). Comparison of growth and gibberellin concentrations in shoots from orchard-grown standard and thermosensitive dwarf apple trees. *Physiol. Plant.* **86**, 544–550.

Steffens, G. L., and Stutte, G. W. (1989). Thidiazuron substitution for chilling requirement in three apple cultivars. *J. Plant Growth Regul.* **8**, 301–307.

Sterrett, J. P., and Hipkins, P. L. (1980). Response of apple buds to pressure injection of abscisic acid and cytokinin. *J. Am. Soc. Hortic. Sci.* **105**, 917–920.

Stiebeling, B., Pharis, R. P., Taylor, J. S., Wodzicki, T., Abe, H., and Little, C. H. A. (1985). An analysis of hormones from the cambial region of Scots pine. 12th Intl. Conf. on Plant Growth Substances, Heidelberg, Germany. [Abstract.]

Strnad, M., Peters, W., Beck, E., and Kaminek, M. (1992). Immunodetection and identification of N^6-(o-hydroxybenzylamino)purine as a naturally occurring cytokinin in *Populus* × *canadensis* Moench cv *Robusta* leaves. *Plant Physiol.* **99**, 74–80.

Sundberg, B. (1987). Quantitative and metabolic studies of indole-3-acetic acid in conifers, with special reference to tracheid production. Ph.D. thesis. Swedish University of Agricultural Sciences, Umeå, Sweden.

Sundberg, B., and Little, C. H. A. (1990). Tracheid production in response to changes in the internal level of indole-3-acetic acid in 1-year-old shoots of Scots pine. *Plant Physiol.* **94**, 1721–1727.

Sundberg, B., Sandberg, G., and Jensen, E. (1985). Catabolism of indole-3-acetic acid to indole-3-methanol in a crude enzyme extract and in protoplasts from Scots Pine (*Pinus sylvestris*). *Physiol. Plant.* **64**, 438–444.

Sundberg, B., Sandberg, G., and Crozier, A. (1986). Purification of indole-3-acetic acid in plant extracts by immunoaffinity chromatography. *Phytochemistry* **25**, 295–298.

Sundberg, B., Little, C. H. A., Riding, R. T., and Sandberg, G. (1987). Levels of endogenous indole-3-acetic acid in the vascular cambium region of *Abies balsamea* trees during the activity-rest-quiescence transition. *Physiol. Plant.* **71**, 163–170.

Sundberg, B., Little, C. H. A., and Cui, K. (1990). Distribution of indole-3-acetic acid and the occurrence of its alkali-labile conjugates in the extraxylary region of *Pinus sylvestris* stems. *Plant Physiol.* **93**, 1295–1302.

Sundberg, B., Little, C. H. A., Cui, K., and Sandberg, G. (1991). Level of endogenous indole-3-acetic acid in the stem of *Pinus sylvestris* in relation to the seasonal variation of cambial activity. *Plant Cell Environ.* **14**, 241–246.

Sundberg, B., Ericsson, A., Little, C. H. A., Näsholm, T., and Gref, R. (1993). The relationship between crown size and ring width in *Pinus sylvestris* L. stems: Dependence on indole-3-acetic acid, carbohydrates and nitrogen in the cambial region. *Tree Physiol.* **12**, 347–362.

Sundberg, B., Tuominen, H., and Little, C. H. A. (1994). Effects of the indole-3-acetic acid (IAA) transport inhibitors N-1-naphthylphthalamic acid and morphactin on endogenous IAA dynamics in relation to compression wood formation in 1-year-old *Pinus sylvestris* (L.) shoots. *Plant Physiol.* **106**, 469–476.

Suzuki, T., and Kitano, M. (1989). Dormancy and spring development of lateral buds in mulberry (*Morus alba*). *Physiol. Plant.* **75**, 188–194.

Talón, M., Hedden, P., and Primo-Millo, E. (1990). Gibberellins in *Citrus sinensis:* A comparison between seeded and seedless varieties. *J. Plant Growth Regul.* **9**, 201–206.

Taylor, J. S., and Dumbroff, E. B. (1975). Bud, root, and growth-regulator activity in *Acer saccharum* during the dormant season. *Can. J. Bot.* **53**, 321–331.

Taylor, J. S., Blake, T. J., and Pharis, R. P. (1982). The role of plant hormones and carbohydrates in the growth and survival of coppiced *Eucalyptus* seedlings. *Physiol. Plant.* **55**, 421–430.

Taylor, J. S., Koshioka, M., Pharis, R. P., and Sweet, G. B. (1984). Changes in cytokinins and gibberellin-like substances in *Pinus radiata* buds during lateral shoot initiation and the characterization of ribosyl zeatin and a novel ribosyl zeatin glycoside. *Plant Physiol.* **74**, 626–631.

Taylor, J. S., Thompson, B., Pate, J. S., Atkins, C. A., and Pharis, R. P. (1990). Cytokinins in the phloem sap of white lupin (*Lupinus albus* L.). *Plant Physiol.* **94**, 1714–1720.

Telewski, F. W. (1990). Growth, wood density, and ethylene production in response to mechanical perturbation in *Pinus taeda. Can. J. For. Res.* **20**, 1277–1282.

Telewski, F. W., and Jaffe, M. J. (1986a). Thigmomorphogenesis: Field and laboratory studies of *Abies fraseri* in response to wind or mechanical perturbation. *Physiol. Plant.* **66**, 211–218.

Telewski, F. W., and Jaffe, M. J. (1986b). Thigmomorphogenesis: Anatomical, morphological and mechanical analysis of genetically different sibs of *Pinus taeda* in response to mechanical perturbation. *Physiol. Plant.* **66**, 219–226.

Telewski, F. W., and Jaffe, M. J. (1986c). Thigmomorphogenesis: The role of ethylene in the response of *Pinus taeda* and *Abies fraseri* to mechanical perturbation. *Physiol. Plant.* **66**, 227–233.

Teng, Y., and Timmer, V. R. (1993). Growth and nutrition of hybrid poplar in response to phosphorus, zinc, and gibberellic acid treatments. *For. Sci.* **39**, 252–259.

Terry, M. E., McGraw, D., and Jones, R. L. (1982). Effect of IAA on growth and soluble cell wall polysaccharides centrifuged from pine hypocotyl sections. *Plant Physiol.* **69**, 323–326.

Thorsteinsson, B., Tillberg, E., and Ericsson, T. (1990). Levels of IAA, ABA and carbohydrates in source and sink leaves of *Betula pendula* Roth. *Scand. J. For. Res.* **5**, 347–354.

Torrey, J. G., and Loomis, R. S. (1967). Auxin-cytokinin control of secondary vascular tissue formation in isolated roots of *Raphanus. Am. J. Bot.* **54**, 1098–1106.

Trewavas, A. (1991). How do plant growth substances work? II. *Plant Cell Environ.* **14**, 1–12.

Tromp, J., and Ovaa, J. C. (1990). Seasonal changes in the cytokinin composition of xylem sap of apple. *J. Plant Physiol.* **136**, 606–610.

Turnbull, C. G. N. (1989). Identification and quantitative analysis of gibberellins in *Citrus. J. Plant Growth Regul.* **8**, 273–282.

Vine, J. H., Noiton, D., Plummer, J. A., Baleriola-Lucas, C., and Mullins, M. G. (1987). Simultaneous quantitation of indole 3-acetic acid and abscisic acid in small samples of plant tissue by gas chromatography/mass spectrometry/selected ion monitoring. *Plant Physiol.* **85**, 419–422.

Wample, R. L., Durley, R. C., and Pharis, R. P. (1975). Metabolism of gibberellin A_4 by vegetative shoots of Douglas fir at three stages of ontogeny. *Physiol. Plant.* **35**, 273–278.

Wang, Q., Little, C. H. A., Sheng, C., Odén, P. C., and Pharis, R. P. (1992). Effect of exogenous gibberellin $A_{4/7}$ on tracheid production, longitudinal growth and the levels of indole-3-acetic acid and gibberellins A_4, A_7 and A_9 in the terminal shoot of *Pinus sylvestris* seedlings. *Physiol. Plant.* **86**, 202–208.

Wang, S. Y., and Faust, M. (1993). Comparison of seasonal growth and polyamine content in shoots of orchard-grown standard and genetic dwarf apple trees. *Physiol. Plant.* **89**, 376–380.

Wang, S. Y., Ji, Z. L., and Faust, M. (1987). Effect of thidiazuron on abscisic acid content in apple bud relative to dormancy. *Physiol. Plant.* **71**, 105–109.

Warren Wilson, J., and Warren Wilson, P. M. (1991). Effects of auxin concentration on the dimensions and patterns of tracheary elements differentiating in pith explants. *Ann. Bot.* **68,** 463–467.

Waseem, M., Phipps, J., Carbonneau, R., and Simmonds, J. (1991). Plant growth substances in sugar maple (*Acer saccharum* Marsh) spring sap. Identification of cytokinins, abscisic acid and an indolic compound. *J. Plant Physiol.* **138,** 489–493.

Weaver, R. J., and Pool, R. M. (1969). Effect of ethrel, abscisic acid, and a morphactin on flower and berry abscission and shoot growth in *Vitis vinifera. J. Am. Soc. Hortic. Sci.* **94,** 474–478.

Webber, J. E., Laver, M. L., Zaerr, J. B., and Lavender, D. P. (1979). Seasonal variation of abscisic acid in the dormant shoots of Douglas-fir. *Can. J. Bot.* **57,** 534–538.

Webber, J. E., Ross, S. D., Pharis, R. P., and Owens, J. N. (1985). Interaction between gibberellin $A_{4/7}$ and root-pruning on the reproductive and vegetative process in Douglas-fir. II. Effects on shoot elongation and its relationship to flowering. *Can. J. For. Res.* **15,** 348–353.

Weiler, E. W., and Ziegler, H. (1981). Determination of phytohormones in phloem exudate from tree species by radioimmunoassay. *Planta* **152,** 168–170.

Weston, G. D., Carlson, L. W., and Wambold, E. C. (1980). The effect of growth retardants and inhibitors on container-grown *Pinus contorta* and *Picea glauca. Can. J. For. Res.* **10,** 510–516.

Whetten, R., and Sederoff, R. (1991). Genetic engineering of wood. *For. Ecol. Manage.* **43,** 301–316.

Wignall, T. A., and Browning, G. (1988). Epicormic bud development in *Quercus robur* L. Studies of endogenous IAA, ABA, IAA polar transport and water potential in cambial tissues and effects of exogenous hormones on bud outgrowth from stem explants. *J. Exp. Bot.* **39,** 1667–1678.

Wilson, B. F., Chien, C.-T., and Zaerr, J. B. (1989). Distribution of endogenous indole-3-acetic acid and compression wood formation in reoriented branches of Douglas-fir. *Plant Physiol.* **91,** 338–344.

Wodzicki, T. J., and Zajączkowski, S. (1989). Auxin waves in cambium and morphogenetic information in plants. *In* "Signals in Plant Development" (J. Krekule and F. Seidlová, eds.), pp. 45–64. SPB Academic Publishing, The Hague, the Netherlands.

Wodzicki, T. J., Abe, H., Wodzicki, A. B., Pharis, R. P., and Cohen, J. D. (1987). Investigations on the nature of the auxin-wave in the cambial region of pine stems. *Plant Physiol.* **84,** 135–143.

Wood, B. W. (1983). Changes in indoleacetic acid, abscisic acid, gibberellins, and cytokinins during budbreak in pecan. *J. Am. Soc. Hortic. Sci.* **108,** 333–338.

Wort, D. J. (1975). Mechanism of plant growth stimulation by naphthenates: Some effects on photosynthesis and respiration. *Proc. Ann. Mtg. Can. Soc. Plant Physiol.* [Abstract]

Yamamoto, F., and Kozlowski, T. T. (1987a). Effect of ethrel on growth and stem anatomy of *Pinus halepensis* seedlings. *IAWA Bull. h. s.* **8,** 11–19.

Yamamoto, F., and Kozlowski, T. T. (1987b). Effects of flooding, tilting of stems, and ethrel application on growth, stem anatomy and ethylene production of *Pinus densiflora* seedlings. *J. Exp. Bot.* **38,** 293–310.

Yamamoto, F., and Kozlowski, T. T. (1987c). Effects of flooding of soil on growth, stem anatomy, and ethylene production of *Thuja orientalis* seedlings. *IAWA Bull. n. s.* **8,** 21–29.

Yamamoto, F., and Kozlowski, T. T. (1987d). Effect of flooding of soil on growth, stem anatomy, and ethylene production of *Cryptomeria japonica* seedlings. *Scand. J. For. Res.* **2,** 45–58.

Yamamoto, F., and Kozlowski, T. T. (1987e). Effects of flooding, tilting of stems, and ethrel application on growth, stem anatomy, and ethylene production of *Acer platanoides* seedlings. *Scand. J. For. Res.* **2,** 141–156.

Yamamoto, F., Angeles, G., and Kozlowski, T. T. (1987a). Effect of ethrel on stem anatomy of *Ulmus americana* seedlings. *IAWA Bull. n. s.* **8,** 3–9.

Yamamoto, F., Kozlowski, T. T., and Wolter, K. E. (1987b). Effect of flooding on growth, stem anatomy, and ethylene production of *Pinus halepensis* seedlings. *Can. J. For. Res.* **17,** 69–79.

Yamanaka, K. (1985). Ethylene production in *Chamaecyparis obtusa* phloem and xylem tissues in response to wounding. *Mokuzai Gakkaishi* **31,** 703–710.

Yang, H. M., Ozaki, T., Ichii, T., Nakanishi, T., and Kawai, Y. (1992). Diffusible and extractable auxins in young Japanese pear trees. *Sci. Hortic.* **51,** 97–106.

Yang, T., Law, D. M., and Davies, P. J. (1993). Magnitude and kinetics of stem elongation induced by exogenous indole-3-acetic acid in intact light-grown pea seedlings. *Plant Physiol.* **102,** 717–724.

Yokota, T., and Takahashi, N. (1980). Cytokinins in shoots of the chestnut tree. *Phytochemistry* **19,** 2367–2369.

Yokota, T., Arima, M., Takahashi, N., and Crozier, A. (1985). Steroidal plant growth regulators, castasterone and typhasterol (2-deoxycastasterone) from the shoots of Sitka spruce (*Picea sitchensis*). *Phytochemistry* **24,** 1333–1335.

Young, E. (1987). Effects of 6-BA, GA$_{4+7}$, and IBA on growth resumption of chilled apple roots and shoots. *HortScience* **22,** 212–213.

Young, E. (1989). Cytokinin and soluble carbohydrate concentrations in xylem sap of apple during dormancy and budbreak. *J. Am. Soc. Hortic. Sci.* **114,** 297–300.

Zabkiewicz, J. A., and Steele, K. D. (1974). Root-promoting activity of *P. radiata* bud extracts. *Bull. R. Soc. N.Z.* **12,** 687–692.

Zakrzewski, J. (1975). Response of pine hypocotyl sections to growth regulators and related substances. *Acta Soc. Bot. Polan.* **43,** 123–132.

Zakrzewski, J. (1983). Hormonal control of cambial activity and vessel differentiation in *Quercus robur*. *Physiol. Plant.* **57,** 537–542.

Zakrzewski, J. (1991). Effect of indole-3-acetic acid (IAA) and sucrose on vessel size and density in isolated stem segments of oak (*Quercus robur*). *Physiol. Plant.* **81,** 234–238.

Zeevaart, J. A. D., and Creelman, R. A. (1988). Metabolism and physiology of abscisic acid. *Annu. Rev. Plant Physiol. Plant Mol. Biol.* **39,** 439–473.

Zhang, R. (1990). Investigations of the Possible Hormonal Basis for Genetically Superior Growth Capacity in Two Conifers, *Pinus radiata* and *Pinus contorta*. M.Sc. thesis. University of Calgary, Calgary, Alberta, Canada.

Zhong, Y., Mellerowicz, E. J., Lloyd, A. D., Leinhos, V., Riding, R. T., and Little, C. H. A. (1995). Seasonal variation in the nuclear genome size of ray cells in the vascular cambium of *Fraxinus americana* (L.). *Physiol. Plant.* **93,** 305–311.

IV

Roles of Stems in Preventing or Reacting to Plant Injury

14

Stems and Fires

A. Malcolm Gill

I. Introduction

Stems and fires, and the environments in which they occur, show enormous diversity. Consider cacti and conifers, palms and parasitic plants, bracken and bamboo. Each of these forms may be exposed to fires. Consider the contrasts between crown fires in tall forests, peat fires smoldering away under heath, and the short flickering flames of a low-intensity fire trickling through a deciduous woodland. Stems exposed to fires occur in a variety of contrasting environments. Consider deserts with succulents, wet–dry tropics with rain forests and woodlands, and subalpine regions with heaths and herblands. In brief, the way stems respond to fires depends on their intrinsic properties, the environments in which they occur, and the nature of the fires to which they are exposed. The possible circumstances concerning interactions between stems, fires, and environments in nature are legion, and therefore attention in this chapter is directed to principles governing these interactions. Despite the variety of form and circumstance, some generalizations are possible.

The responses of stems to fires can be considered in terms of injuries sustained, chances of death, and the occurrence of recovery processes. Susceptibility to injury or death can be considered at several levels of organization such as cellular and plant levels. At the first of these levels, susceptibility of the cell to injury or death can be related to the temperatures required for cell injury or death and the temperatures attained in the fire.

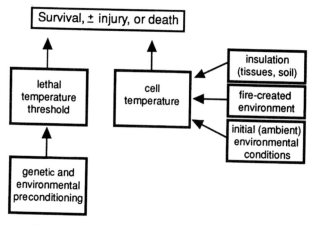

Figure 1   The main factors influencing cell response to elevated temperature.

At the second level, the susceptibility of the plant to injury or death depends on the nature and distribution of critical tissues, the nature and extent of its insulating material, and the distribution and value of external temperatures in fires.

At the cellular level, temperatures attained in the fire depend on temperatures just prior to the time of fire arrival (ambient conditions), the fire-created thermal environment, and the extent and type of tissue insulation (Fig. 1). The conditions for death of cells depends on both genetic and environmental effects. Research on cell death and ambient temperatures of plants has focused on leaves. How the results from such studies have been applied to other tissues, such as those in seeds and stems, is discussed. The effects of various types of fires (above ground and peat fires) on tissue temperatures are considered together with an evaluation of the role that insulation of critical tissues (as affected by soil covering and plant vasculature) plays in plant survival.

At the whole-plant level, susceptibility to injury or death also depends on a number of ecological and organismal factors identified in Fig. 2. In turn, these factors are influenced or controlled by others. Thus, the distributions of buds, critical to the survival of plants after injury by fires, are controlled by genetic and ontogenetic factors. Furthermore, the types and thicknesses of insulating materials (such as peat, mineral soil, and bark) over critical tissues and organs—moderating their fates during fires—may depend on location of critical tissues within the plant, the species of plant, and the fire history of the site. Finally, the important environmental context of the plant, typified by the temporal and spatial distributions of fire-created temperatures, depends on the type of fire and its "intensity."

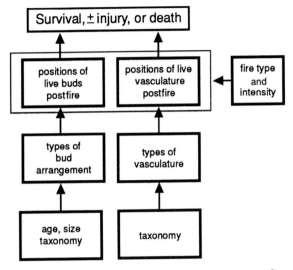

Figure 2   The main factors influencing plant response to fire.

Plant stature, affecting the exposure of tissues to above-ground fires in particular and therefore important in survival vs death, is discussed in another context by Givnish ([1] in this volume). Stafstrom ([13] in this volume) discusses the distribution of buds and meristems, another key element in the responses of plants after fires.

II. Cell-Level Injury and Recovery

A. Temperatures of Cell Death

Critical temperatures for cell death vary considerably among organisms. Even among "higher" plants, which are the main concern here, there is no single temperature to typify cell death because the temperatures of cell death are affected by their temperature histories, osmotic status, exposure to drought and genetic factors (Levitt, 1980), as well as the time course of exposure to elevated temperatures during the course of the fire.

Exposure of cells to high temperatures can cause death, initiate repair processes, and/or promote adaptation (Alexandrov, 1977). Death or adaptation only are considered here but the potential for subcellular repair within damaged cells should not be forgotten. The extensive, mostly Russian, research reported by Alexandrov (1977) provides a useful reference point for our discussion because of the number of investigations cited and the relative uniformity of methods. The method of evaluation of response, in particular, can have a quantitative effect on the result. Therefore, declaring that "death" occurred at a particular temperature or series of exposures to various temperatures should be qualified according to the method of determination of death. In Alexandrov's monograph, many of the examples related to cells that were exposed for 5 min and in which death was assumed when protoplasmic streaming ceased. From comparisons among six species belonging to three genera (p. 32 in Alexandrov, 1977), apparently without heat hardening, a range of 6°C in temperature for thermoresistance was observed. Heat hardening can occur with even short exposures, however [e.g., 1 hr at 40°C (p. 40 in Alexandrov, 1977)]. Heat hardening after a 3-hr exposure (in this case using chloroplast phototaxis as an indicator) may increase tolerance by as much as 5°C (p. 44 in Alexandrov, 1977).

The extent of physiological adjustment in thermal properties is variable among species. Helmuth (1971) exposed shoots to various elevated temperatures for 30 min minutes and watched for signs of tissue damage in six perennial species from the arid zone of Australia; Helmuth found that the critical temperature for heat resistance varied by up to 7°C among species and rose by 3 to 7°C in the hotter, drier part of the year compared with the cooler, wetter winter period. Using conspecific plants from contrasting "cool" and "hot" environments, Bjorkman et al. (1980) reported that the upper temperature limits for photosynthesis showed negligible change or increased by up to about 10°C when plants were grown in a "hot" environment rather than a "cool" one (p. 241 of Bjorkman et al., their Fig. 15.6).

A number of authors have demonstrated that there is an exponential relationship between the time of exposure to high temperature and the temperature for cell death (Helgerson, 1990). Alexandrov (1977, p. 9), using a particularly wide range of temperatures, showed that there were two phases involved in the persistence (or cessation) of protoplasmic streaming, a measure of cell health. The first phase, below 42°C, involved exposure times from 10 min to 10 hr, a time of exposure that may be relevant to tissues near "ground" ("peat") fires (see Section II,D below). The second phase, above 42°C, is more relevant to potential death of cells in "surface" fires (see Section II,D below) because times of exposure were less than 10 min.

Although among investigations the exposures to high temperature vary, the methods vary, and the indicators used for determining that death has occurred in tissues also vary, it is of interest to know what various authors have determined as the critical temperatures for cell death in different tissues. Nelson (1952) considered that death of pine needles was instantaneous at 64°C; Helgerson (1990) found that stem bases of seedlings became injured when soil surface temperatures were between 52 and 66°C; and Carmichael (1958) found that seeds may survive exposures over 100°C, the lethality of the temperature depending on the humidity. Succulent species have high temperature tolerances that allow survival of tissues that attain relatively high ambient temperatures during daytime because stomata are then normally closed and transpirational cooling is absent (Levitt, 1980, p. 401).

Critical tissue temperatures for cell death have been related to habitat by Smillie and Nott (1979) who found a gradient from an average of about 48°C for alpine plants to an average of about 53°C for tropical plants. Table 12.2 in Levitt (1980; after Lange, 1959) indicated "killing temperatures" for rain forest species between 44 and 52°C and for desert species between 49 and 58°C.

To what extent the range of intrinsic variation in heat resistance overlaps the extent of possible heat hardening in hydrated tissues is unknown. However, a difference of at least 10°C in heat resistance may be expected from various causes.

B. Ambient Tissue Temperatures

The prefire tissue temperature has an important bearing on the potential for death or injury of tissues. The amount of heat required to kill a leaf is related (although not necessarily linearly) to the difference in temperature between that required for cell death and actual tissue temperature. Actual tissue temperatures may vary substantially from ambient.

As modeled by Van Gardingen and Grace (1991), temperature differences between leaf and air were more sensitive in large leaves (characteristic dimension of 100 mm) than tiny leaves (characteristic dimension of 1 mm) to changes in net radiation flux ($+450$ to -50 W m^{-2}) and wind speed (up to 5 m sec). Their model assumed, for convenience, that stomatal conductance was constant. Modeled tissue temperatures were up to about 9°C above or below ambient.

Table 1 shows a range of measurements of temperature differences between air and the surfaces of leaves, barks, and soils. The values in Table I are extremes for the studies quoted. Temperature differences may vary within canopies because of differences in insolation and wind (Smith, 1978; Van Gardingen and Grace, 1991) and temperatures may vary on different sides of trees (Greaves, 1965), both of which may affect tissue survival during fires. If air temperature is equated with tissue temperature in fire-effects models, errors are likely under some circumstances.

The substantial differences in leaf and ambient temperature (Table I) could affect the height above ground to which leaf damage and death occur in fires. High tissue temperatures relative to air temperatures are likely when stomata are shut—during drought or periods of high evaporative demand, for example. On the other hand, relatively low tissue temperatures are likely when soil water is readily available, wind is flowing over the leaves, and insolation is high (Van Gardingen and Grace, 1991). The depth within canopies at which these relative temperature changes occur will vary with

Table I   Extremes of Temperature Difference Noted between Bark, Leaf, and Soil Surfaces (T_s) and Air (T_a)

Location	$T_s - T_a$ (°C)	Ref.
Snowy Mountains, southeast Australia	+7 in tree leaves	Korner and Cochrane (1983)
	+13 in shrub leaves	Korner and Cochrane (1983)
	+21 in dwarf shrub leaves	Korner and Cochrane (1983)
Sonoran Desert, U.S.	+20 in cactus	Smith (1978)
	−17 in large leaves	Smith (1978)
	+2.4 in small leaves	Smith (1978)
North Coast, New South Wales, Australia	+18 on bark surface	Greaves (1965)
Marburg, Germany	+30 on bark surface	Nicolai (1986)
	+20 at cambium	Nicolai (1986)
Snowy Mountains, southeast Australia	+47 at soil surface	Korner and Cochrane (1983)

time of day, leaf angle, and leaf density. Light penetration and wind velocity drop off rapidly within dense canopies and radiation load varies with the geometry of leaf angle and sun angle as well as time of day. Maximum scorch heights (the maximum heights of leaf death) in forests are likely when trees are open-crowned and have large leaves, when ambient temperatures are high, and when the insolation on leaves is at it peak and soil moisture is depleted. At these times, heat hardening is also likely to have occurred, so that the impact of the environmental conditions is moderated. Potential scorch height can probably exceed the height of the tallest trees known.

While large temperature differences between ambient and tissue temperatures have been predicted and measured, their actual importance to cell death during fires has not been evaluated. The circumstances are complex because smoke, arising at a distance, may blot out or reduce solar radiation on plant surfaces, thereby changing ambient conditions even before the arrival of the fire at the site.

C. Cell Insulation by Soil, Bark, and Wood

Insulation of live plant cells is common and takes the form of other cells (dead or alive) and soil. There are many variations on the theme. Insulating tissues can be wood (for some seeds), soil (for some stems, seeds, and roots), and dead or live leaf bases as in some tree ferns and the endemic *Xanthorrhoea* spp. of Australia, for example. The ability of a material to in-

Table II Values Reported for Thermal Diffusivity
of Soil, Bark, and Wood

Material	Diffusivity (m² sec⁻¹)	Ref.
Wood	$0.87 \cdot 10^{-7}$	Costa *et al.* (1991)
	$1.1–1.9 \cdot 10^{-7}$	Kollman and Côté (1968)
Bark	$0.65 \cdot 10^{-7}$	Costa *et al.* (1991)
	$1.3 \cdot 10^{-7}$	Martin (1963)
	$0.7–0.9 \cdot 10^{-7}$	Reifsnyder *et al.* (1967)
Dry sand	$1.4 \cdot 10^{-3}$	Priestley (1959)
Wet sand	10^{-2}	Priestley (1959)
Stirred water	100	Priestley (1959)

sulate is described by its thermal diffusivity. Thickness of the insulation, and its flammability, also influence the effectiveness of the material.

Thermal diffusivities reflect the ability of the material to propagate a temperature wave. Thermal diffusivity is equal to the thermal conductivity divided by volumetric heat capacity: the lower the diffusivity, the better the insulation. Organic tissues and soils are good insulators (Table II). The insulating ability of tissues and soils in fires can be shown by the sharp drops in temperature that occur below their surfaces (e.g., Costa *et al.*, 1991, for plants and Aston and Gill, 1976, for soils). As the depth within the insulator increases, the amplitude of the temperature wave decreases (Priestley, 1959).

Thicknesses of soil over regenerative tissues range from centimeters to decimeters. The penetration of temperature waves into soils is generally small (centimeters) but is enhanced if the soil is organic and it burns, or if there is a substantial quantity of fuel, such as logging slash, at the surface. Frandsen (1987) has defined the ignition limits of organic soil in relation to moisture and mineral matter while Tunstall *et al.* (1976a) have measured the substantial temperatures reached in a soil volume (maximum of 800°C at the surface and 100°C at a depth of 0.4 m) when fuel loadings were artificially large (0.5 t of air-dry billets m⁻²) and the fuels and soils were dry. In general, the drier and finer the soil, the greater the fire-induced soil temperature (Aston and Gill, 1976). Temperature increases in moist soil are limited to 100°C (thermal arrest) by latent heat of vaporization. Thus, at depth, temperatures reached in dry soils may be greater than those in wet soils despite the higher thermal diffusivity of wet soil (Table II).

Just as the flammability of organic soil is important to survival of tissues therein, the flammability of dry barks and woody hollows in the tree can affect stem survival by thinning tissues and decreasing the effectiveness of insulation. Barks vary widely in flammability. *Eucalyptus* spp. with dry, stringy barks are very flammable whereas the smooth, live and moist barks of related species are more difficult to ignite (A. M. Gill, personal observation).

Bark thicknesses and diffusivities are most important to the survival of stem tissues during surface fires. Variations in bark diffusivity have been found to be relatively unimportant in affecting tissue temperatures beneath them, compared with variations in bark thickness, because thermal diffusivities of bark are somewhat insensitive to variations in structure and moisture content (Reifsnyder *et al.*, 1967; Vines, 1968). Bark thicknesses are affected by species, position within the plant, and fire history. The bark of tall *Sequoia gigantea* may be decimeters thick on the bole (Fritz, 1931) while thin on twigs. Even short plants of some species have thick bark. The South American rosette shrub *Neblinaria celiae* has bark averaging a maximum of 2.2 cm thick on a stem of only 8.5-cm maximum diameter (Givnish *et al.*, 1986). On the other hand, the barks of some species of trees may be limited even when boles are large. Bark thickness may increase linearly (see Ryan, 1982; Peterson *et al.*, 1991) or curvilinearly with girth (e.g., Gill and Ashton, 1968; Harmon, 1984). Bark tends to thin with height independently of girth (Gill and Ashton, 1968; A. M. Gill, personal observation). Healthy vigorous trees have thicker bark than unhealthy trees; bark area in some eucalypts is related to leaf area and sapwood cross-sectional area (Brack *et al.*, 1985). For species without bark, tissue insulation may be through substantial thicknesses of persistent, dead, tightly packed leaf bases such as those in suffrutescent monocotyledonous *Xanthorrhoea* spp. (Gill and Ingwersen, 1976).

D. Fire-Created Environments

For convenience, fires may be classified into two main types: ground fires (burning in peat or deep duff); and surface fires (burning above the soil surface whether or not that surface is a mineral one). Ground fires seldom occur without surface fires (which are their source of ignition). These two fire types are defined because of their vastly different properties and because of the different ways in which they affect ecosystems, let alone stems. Because ground fires persist in one place for perhaps hours rather than minutes or seconds and smolder rather than flame, they can be distinguished in time and mode of propagation if not by place. Fires burning in shallow duff layers may be difficult to classify as one type or the other. Surface fires may be subdivided according to the predominant type of fuel they consume—litter, grass, and shrub and tree canopies. Crown fires potentially involve all these fuel categories. Further subdivision into fires burning with or against the wind may be necessary because they may have different temperature–time characteristics; of course, fires may burn in any direction relative to the wind within any fire perimeter. Note that usage of "fire" often implies a portion of a fire perimeter, a sometimes desirable distinc-

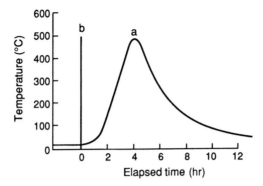

Figure 3 Duration of temperatures for surface fires compared to ground fires. The surface fire (b) (A. M. Gill and P. H. R. Moore, unpublished data) elicited an elevated temperature trace that, at the scale shown, appears instantaneous. The duff fire temperature trace (a; after Ryan and Frandsen, 1991), by way of contrast, shows elevated temperatures lasting for hours rather than minutes, although reaching a similar maximum.

tion because of the wide variation in properties found around a wind-blown surface fire at any one time (Catchpole *et al.*, 1992).

Fires, in the past, have been studied largely in relation to their rates of spread. However, rates of spread may be irrelevant to the response of a stem in the path of a fire. Rather, the persistence of the fire or, better still, the temperature–time curve (see Sections II,E and III,B, below) is more appropriate.

Temperatures vary widely around stems during fires according to the type of fire, the rates of combustion, and the location of interest. While relatively little attention has been given to the measurement of ground fires, Ryan and Frandsen (1991), examining smoldering fires in the duff around the bases of conifers, quantified the expected long persistence of high temperatures there. They found temperatures over 100°C to persist for hours, rather than the seconds or minutes during which they occur in surface fires (Fig. 3).

E. Models of Tissue Injury

In this section, models predicting death or survival of tissues in leaves, stems, and seeds are briefly reviewed.

Scorch height (the height to which leaf death as shown by the browning or "scorching" of leaves occurs) has particular relevance to forestry, as the proportion of crown death can have a marked effect on wood production of individual tree stems (Peterson *et al.*, 1991). Two approaches to the prediction of scorch height have been used. In one, the flame height has been the independent variable (McArthur, 1962) whereas in the other, Byram's intensity (the mathematical product of heat of combustion, fuel loading, and fire rate of spread; Byram, 1959) has been used (Van Wagner, 1973). Van Wagner (1973) based his model of scorch height on plume theory, developing equations from this theory that include declarations of the lethal temperatures of leaves (set at 60°C in his case) and leaf temperature (set at ambient temperature). Wind may affect the plume angle and leaf cooling and this has also been included in one equation. Accurately assessing the values for lethal and prefire tissue temperatures is difficult in the practical application of the models.

Because seeds in woody fruits and cambia under bark have significant insulation, unlike leaves, models for injury and death of these tissues take temperature–time curves, or their surrogates, into account. In trees of *Eucalyptus*, Gill *et al.* (1986) used depth of fire-killed bark as their indicator of potential injury to cambia. They found that by using the presumed flame residence time for the fuel as the time temperatures persisted over 100°C that depth of bark killed was estimated by the error function solution to the heat flow equation; however, the authors noted that the result could have been somewhat fortuitous given the accuracy of their inputs. Other authors have developed more elaborate models involving inputs of the whole temperature–time curve (Costa *et al.*, 1991). Mercer *et al.* (1994), concerned with the survival of seeds, examined the effect of simplifying the temperature–time curve by arresting temperature rise at 100°C (in accordance with the effects of latent heat of vaporization). They found that such a simplification gave a reasonable result. If this simplification has general application, then the time during which the temperature at the surface of the tissue exceeds 100°C may be a suitable input more readily measured than the whole temperature–time curve. The various assumptions made by different authors about the thermal diffusivity of bark (cf. Reifsnyder *et al.*, 1967) affect the prediction of tissue response (Mercer *et al.*, 1994).

Soil temperature (e.g., Aston and Gill, 1976; Pafford *et al.*, 1991) and water movement in soil (Aston and Gill, 1976) have been modeled for the courses of surface fires. The results are relevant to the survival and germination of soil seed and to the tissues of buried stems and roots. Unless the site has artificially enhanced fuel loadings, or tissues are close to the surface, damage to buried tissues by surface fires is usually negligible.

Patterns of tissue damage around stems can be complicated by the production of vortices that hold flames on the lee side of the tree and cause fire scars to form. Gill (1974) used scale models of trees and fires to demonstrate the processes of vortex formation, while Tunstall *et al.* (1976b) measured the three-dimensional variations in temperature experienced by stemlike cylinders in fires in the field. Under certain circumstances, the asymmetrical distribution of heat through lee-side vortices could improve the chances of stem survival (Tunstall *et al.*, 1976b).

In ground fires, spread is extremely slow; thus the times of elevated temperature are long. These conditions may cause other variables, such as cooling by mass transport of fluids through xylem and phloem, to be considered in the prediction of tissue damage (Ryan and Frandsen, 1991). Girdling may occur as a result of smoldering fires, the death of the stem being delayed for perhaps a year after fire occurrence.

III. Plant Level

A. Distributions of Tissues and Organs Essential for Plant Survival

Different species vary in their ability to recover after fire. Given the same extent and locations of injury, much of this variation in recovery may be explained by the distribution of buds. We can distinguish, albeit tentatively, a number of bud distribution types according to the presence or absence of buds in nonfoliated aerial stems and in roots and rhizomes (Table III). In type A plants, buds are absent from the nonfoliated aerial stems; they may, however, be present in the foliated zones of stems either as terminal buds only (e.g., in the single-stemmed palm, *Livistona australis,* or in the much-branched conifer, *Pinus strobus*) or found in axillary positions as well, as in the small Australian tree, *Acacia longifolia.* In type B plants buds are also absent from aerial nonfoliated stems but present in underground tissues. This pattern is unstudied; its incidence is unknown but inferred from Rackham's (1976) observation that some trees in Britain cannot be pollarded but do sucker. Type C and D distributions, both having buds in nonfoliated aerial stems but differentiated on the basis of the presence (type C) or absence (type D) of buds in subterranean tissues, are common in woody plants. An example of a type C plant is *Eucalyptus regnans,* the world's tallest hardwood species, whereas a well-studied example of a root-suckering species, probably type D, is *Populus tremuloides* (Schier, 1978).

Table III   Key to Simple Classification
of Bud Distribution Types in Woody Plants

Description	Type
Buds present in foliated parts of stems, absent in nonfoliated parts of aerial stems:	
Buds absent in roots or rhizomes	A
Buds present in roots or rhizomes	B
Buds present in both foliated parts of stems and in aerial stems generally:	
Buds absent in roots or rhizomes	C
Buds present in roots, rhizomes, or buried stem bases	D

Bud distribution types may change with age (and the correlate, size) of the plant. An apparently common pattern with increasing stem age is to change from a whole aerial stem distribution to one in which the base of the stem ceases to have viable buds. This change in pattern may explain the observation that older plants may be more vulnerable to shoot damage than younger plants (e.g., Mooney and Hobbs, 1986).

Species whose mature members are killed even by low-intensity fires are often called "seeders," whereas those species including mature plants that usually survive the same intensity of surface fire are called "sprouters" (see Gill and Bradstock, 1992). The nomenclature has little value when considering species responses to ground fires (see Section III,C). Seeders would be expected to have a type A or type C pattern of bud distribution. Sprouters would be expected to have a type B or type D bud pattern, although there may be some overlap with type C patterns.

Critical tissues for the survival of the stem tissues of many trees and shrubs, such as most dicotyledons and gymnosperms, are their cambia. However, many plants, such as monocotyledons (including palms, pandans, and bamboos), cycads, and ferns, have xylem–phloem strands dispersed throughout the stem (Tomlinson and Zimmermann, 1969). In the barked stems, insulation is provided by a strongly insulative material (Table II) but one in which the thickness of the material is important to the survival of tissues beneath (Gill and Ashton, 1968; Vines, 1968). Little is known about the fire resistance of plants with dispersed vascular bundles, but we may assume that most of the phloem in a cross-section of the stem needs to be disrupted before the stem will cease to function; if this is so, the insulative quality of the stem may be proportional to the diameter of the stem. In these species, stem diameter is largely determined at an early stage and it remains more or less constant during the life of the plant, although some monocotyledons with this type of vasculature do have secondary thickening (Tomlinson and Zimmermann, 1969). Using palms and bamboos as examples, it is apparent from the wide range of stem radii that their species also exhibit a wide range of resistance to fires. Often, stem radii of species with dispersed vasculature are substantial relative to the usual thicknesses of bark involved in the protection of cambia.

Other types of vascular patterns exist for dicotyledons but their resistance to fires has not been investigated. Examples are the "anomalous" secondary thickenings of many vines (e.g., Haberlandt, 1928) and divided stems (e.g., Jones and Lord, 1982). However, it may be predicted that the depth of the innermost cambium will indicate the resistance of the stem.

Seeds in woody fruits can be the sole source of regeneration for seeder species after fire (e.g., Gill, 1981), and therefore the impact of fire on fruits and seeds is a critical factor in determining the local persistence or extinction of seeder species. Woody fruits may be found in many species and genera (Gill, 1975), not all of them seeders. Woody fruits may be found close to the ground in the canopies of shrubs, or tens of meters above ground in tall trees; they may have woody walls that are thin (usually in taller plants) or thick (up to 7 cm thick in shrubs of *Hakea* spp.; Pate and Hopper, 1993). Mercer *et al.* (1994) have modeled the survival of seeds in woody fruits, using a variety of laboratory and field-determined temperature–time inputs (with and without thermal arrest) and thermal diffusivities.

B. Distribution of Temperatures in Fires

In surface fires, temperature–time curves usually show a rapid rise followed by a slower, exponential decline, the length of time of elevated temperature being measured in minutes (Weber *et al.*, 1994a). The time to rise from ambient to peak temperature approximates the time that the flame persists at the point of measurement (Rothermel and Deeming, 1980). However, the entire temperature–time curve, not just the initial rise, may be significant in determining the impact of the fire. Difficulties in measuring temperatures aside, maximum temperatures in fires are around 1000°C; they vary with the rate of heat release. Maximum temperatures are highest near the ground and decline with height (Van Wagner, 1975; Tunstall *et al.*, 1976b; Williamson and Black, 1981; Weber *et al.*, 1994b). A generalized curve of maximum temperature with height shows three zones (Weber *et al.*, 1994b): the lowest is a zone of more-or-less constant maximum temperature with height; next is a transition zone; the third is a zone with a rapid decline in height (the "plume" zone). A division of the first zone into two parts may be warranted as more data become available on the significance and extent of the cooler zone sometimes measured close to the soil surface (Tunstall *et al.*, 1976a; Trabaud, 1979). Sometimes the first zone is absent, so that the change in maximum temperature with height can be hyperbolic (Van Wagner, 1975). Temperatures over 100°C may persist for up to several minutes in the zone of maximum temperature. Because flames can reach even the tops of tall trees, high temperatures can span the range of stem heights. Measurements of temperatures during fires have been at heights up to only 9 m so far. These curves emphasize the importance of plant stature, and the locations of plant parasites or saprophytes within trees, to fire injury.

C. Patterns of Injury and Death

Plants with different characteristics respond to fires of varying severity and type with numerous patterns of injury and causes of death. In this section, a few of those patterns are highlighted for trees subject to ground or surface fires (see Section II,D). "Injury" here means that all cells in the tissues concerned have been killed; live tissue remains, and thus the plant is not dead at the time the injury is sustained. For surface fires, two associated severities of injury are distinguished: canopy death and aerial shoot death. Note that the characteristics of surface fires that actually achieve these levels of injury may vary for plants of different sizes. An herbaceous plant or small shrub may have its aerial shoot system completely consumed in a fire of even moderate intensity, whereas higher intensities may be necessary to kill the shoot systems of the trees illustrated in Figure 4. For ground fires, two associated levels of severity are also defined: basal stem girdling and complete subterranean tissue death. The first of these two levels of injury can occur with the smoldering combustion of several centimeters of peat over mineral soil (or over deeper, sodden layers of peat) around the base of a thin-barked tree (e.g., *Pinus contorta*) while the second can

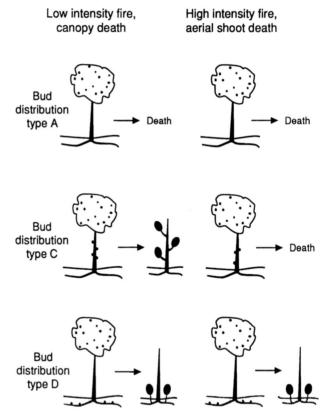

Figure 4 Plant survival or death as a result of surface fires with two levels of severity defined in terms of comparable levels of injury and bud distribution (from Table III). The impact of these fires on plants with three types of bud distribution is indicated. Plants affected by fires of relatively low intensity (on the left) have only their canopies killed; those affected by fires of relatively high intensity (on the right) have their aerial shoots killed. The silhouettes to the right of the arrows represent the patterns of recovery of the plants that survive. The dots on stems and roots represent buds.

occur when the trees are rooted entirely in peat (e.g., some spruce) and the peat profile is consumed. Such injuries caused by ground fires can take place independently of any surface fire effects. Given these types of fires and levels of injury, the responses of trees with three different bud distribution types (Table III) is considered (Figs. 4 and 5).

The more moderate level of injury from surface fire may be sufficient to kill plants with type A buds but not those with the other bud distribution types (Fig. 4), whereas the more severe injury will kill plants with type C bud

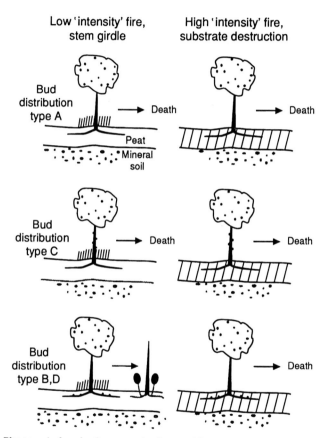

Figure 5 Plant survival or death as a result of ground fires with two levels of severity defined in terms of comparable levels of injury and bud distribution (from Table III). The impact of these fires on plants with various types of bud distribution is indicated. Plants affected by fires of relatively low intensity (on the left) have their aerial shoot systems killed by ringbarking; those affected by fires of relatively high intensity (on the right) have their root systems consumed by the burning of the peat substrate in which they are embedded. The silhouettes to the right of the arrows represent the patterns of recovery of the plants that survive. The dots on stems and roots represent buds.

distributions as well. A different picture emerges when injuries from ground fires are considered (Fig. 5). At the lower level of injury, plants with types A and C bud distributions are killed (Fig. 5) whereas all plants are killed with the more severe level of injury regardless of their bud type.

D. Plant Recovery from Injury

Individuals that survive fire often recover from it completely as assessed by attainment of prefire levels of height, leaf area, reproductive capacity, bark thickness, and so on. Thus, declaring when a plant has recovered will depend on the item of measurement, the intrinsic properties of the species, and the nature of the postfire environment. Height recovery of stems may take a few to many years according to the extent of stem death. Gill (1978) showed that leaf weight (and probably leaf area) and canopy architecture were restored independently of the level of height reduction by fire in small trees of *Eucalyptus dives*. Reproductive capacity depends to a great extent on canopy architecture (see Waller and Steingraeber [2] in this volume). It can be enhanced by fire injury in some species (e.g., *Xanthorrhoea australis;* Gill and Ingwersen, 1976) while in other species reproductive capacity is greatly curtailed by fire injury for many years.

There is little information on the recovery of stems from injury. Stems may recover from fire if vascular tissues, cambia, and buds remain intact in suitable positions. For example, ecologists commonly show that trees hundreds of years old may have been subject to, and survived, numerous fires (e.g., Kilgore and Taylor, 1979). Buds may grow out and restore foliage and canopy architecture. Restoration rate of height and canopy characteristics may depend on the extent of the perturbation of the shoot-to-root ratio, which tends to be fixed for a set of given conditions. In the same way, there appears to be a bark-to-xylem ratio in some trees, at least, which if perturbed by local bark thinning tends to be restored by preferential growth of the bark (Gill, 1980). Bark recovery rate depends on the rate of crown recovery and the extent of bark injury (Gill *et al.*, 1995). Rates of recovery may be expected to vary with postfire weather. In stems with dispersed vasculature, damage may be permanent unless it is slight and can be reversed by secondary thickening.

IV. Fire Injury and Invasions by Invertebrates and Fungi

Tree stem survival in fires is common in many species but the fires may leave a legacy of injury, such as fire scars, which can lead to invasion of the tree by various organisms. Perry *et al.* (1985), for example, found in Australia that fungi invaded fire scars on trees and paved the way for the entry of termites. Similarly, Gara *et al.* (1985) found that fungal invasion of trees through fire scars in *Pinus contorta* in North America was followed by invasion of mountain pine beetles, *Dendroctonus ponderosae*, which eventually killed the host trees. The bark beetles then invaded uninfected trees, causing them to die and provide fuel for further fires. The effect of further interactions of multiple perturbations on stem death is discussed by Bryant and Shain ([16] and [17], respectively, in this volume).

V. Conclusions

The responses of stems to fires need to be considered on at least two levels. At the cellular level the effects of elevated temperatures on hardening, repair, and survival can be considered; at the plant level, stem responses to fires can be considered in relation to the arrangements of critical tissues such as buds and cambia with respect to the fire-created environment. There are many topics requiring further study if we are to fully understand stem responses to fires. In particular, more needs to be known about the distributions of ambient temperatures of tissues at times of fire and the effect of smoke on them; the fire-created temperature environment around plants in both surface and ground fires; quantitative patterns of bud distributions in relation to life stage and environment; plant recovery rates after fires of different intensities; the relationships between bark, sapwood, and leaf dimensions; and the fire tolerances of species with dispersed vasculature.

Acknowledgments

I thank Drs. Bill De Groot, Tom Givnish, Ross Wein, and Jann Williams for their comments on the draft manuscript.

References

Alexandrov, V. Y. (1977). Cells, molecules and temperatures. *In* "Ecological Studies," Vol. 21. Springer-Verlag, Berlin.

Aston, A. R., and Gill, A. M. (1976). Coupled soil moisture, heat and water vapor transfers under simulated fire conditions. *Aust. J. Soil Res.* **14,** 55–66.

Bjorkman, O., Badger, M. R., and Armond, P. A. (1980). Response and adaptation of photosynthesis to high temperatures. *In* "Adaptations of Plants to Water and High Temperature Stress" (N. C. Turner and P. J. Kramer, eds.), pp. 233–249. John Wiley & Sons, New York.

Brack, C. L., Dawson, M. P., and Gill, A. M. (1985). Bark, leaf and sapwood dimensions in *Eucalyptus. Aust. For. Res.* **15,** 1–7.

Byram, G. (1959). Combustion of forest fuels. *In* "Forest Fire: Control and Use" (K. P. Davis, ed.), pp. 61–89. McGraw-Hill, New York.

Carmichael, A. J. (1958). Determination of maximum temperature tolerated by red pine, jack pine, white spruce and black spruce seeds at low relative humidities. *For. Chron.* **34**, 387–392.

Catchpole, E. A., Alexander, M. E., and Gill, A. M. (1992). Elliptical fire perimeter and area intensity distributions. *Can. J. For. Res.* **22**, 968–972.

Costa, J. J., Oliveira, L. A., Viegas, D. X., and Neto, L. P. (1991). On the temperature distribution inside a tree under fire conditions. *Int. J. Wildl. Fire* **1**, 87–96.

Frandsen, W. H. (1987). The influence of moisture and mineral soil on the combustion limits of smoldering forest duff. *Can. J. For. Res.* **17**, 1540–1544.

Fritz, E. (1931). The role of fire in the redwood region. *J. For.* **29**, 939–950.

Gara, R. I., Littke, W. R., Agee, J. K., Geiszler, D. R., Stuart, J. D., and Driver, C. H. (1985). Influence of fires, fungi and mountain pine beetles on development of a lodgepole pine forest in south-central Oregon. *In* "Lodgepole Pine: The Species and Its Management" (D. M. Baumgartner, R. G. Krebill, J. T. Arnott, and G. F. Weetman, eds.), pp.153–162. Washington State University, Pullman, Washington.

Gill, A. M. (1974). Toward an understanding of fire-scar formation: Field observation and laboratory simulation. *For. Sci.* **20**, 198–205.

Gill, A. M. (1975). Fire and the Australian flora: A review. *Aust. For.* **38**, 4–25 .

Gill, A. M. (1978). Crown recovery of *Eucalyptus dives* following wildfire. *Aust. For.* **41**, 207–214.

Gill, A. M. (1980). Restoration of bark thickness after fire and mechanical injury in a smooth-barked eucalypt. *Aust. For. Res.* **10**, 311–319.

Gill, A. M. (1981). Coping with fire. *In* "The Biology of Australian Plants" (J. S. Pate and A. J. McComb, eds.), pp. 65–87. University of Western Australia Press, Nedlands, Western Australia.

Gill, A. M., and Ashton, D. H. (1968). Role of bark type in relative tolerance to fire of three central Victorian eucalypts. *Aust. J. Bot.* **16**, 491–498.

Gill, A. M., and Bradstock, R. A. (1992). A national register for the fire responses of plant species. *Cunninghamia* **2**, 653–660.

Gill, A. M., and Ingwersen, F. (1976). Growth of *Xanthorrhoea australis* R. Br. in relation to fire. *J. Appl. Ecol.* **13**, 195–203.

Gill, A. M., Cheney, N. P., Walker, J., and Tunstall, B. R. (1986). Bark losses from two eucalypt species following fires of different intensities. *Aust. For. Res.* **16**, 1–7.

Gill, A. M., Moore, P. H. R., and Pook, E. W. (1995). In preparation.

Givnish, T. J., McDiarmid, R. W., and Buck, W. R. (1986). Fire adaptation in *Neblinaria celiae* (Theaceae), a high elevation rosette shrub endemic to a wet equatorial tepui. *Oecologia* **70**, 481–485.

Greaves, T. (1965). The buffering effect of trees against fluctuating air temperature. *Aust. For.* **29**, 175–180.

Haberlandt, G. (1928). "Physiological Plant Anatomy." Mcmillan, London.

Harmon, M. E. (1984). Survival of trees after low-intensity surface fires in Great Smoky Mountains National Park. *Ecology* **65**, 796–802.

Helgerson, O. T. (1990). Heat damage in tree seedlings and its prevention. *New For.* **3**, 333–358.

Helmuth, E. O. (1971). Eco-physiological studies on plants in arid and semi-arid regions of western Australia. V. Heat resistance limits of photosynthetic organs of different seasons, their relation to water deficit and cell sap properties and the regeneration ability. *J. Ecol.* **59**, 365–374.

Jones, C. S., and Lord, E. M. (1982). The development of split axes in *Ambrosia dumosa* (Gray) Payne (Asteraceae). *Bot. Gaz.* **143**, 446–453.

Kilgore, B. M., and Taylor, D. (1979). Fire history of a sequoia-mixed conifer forest. *Ecology* **60**, 129–142.

Kollman, F. F. P., and Côté, W. A. (1968). "Principles of Wood Science and Technology," Vol I: Solid Wood, p. 251. Springer-Verlag, Berlin.

Korner, C., and Cochrane, P. (1983). Influence of plant physiognomy on leaf temperature on clear midsummer days in the Snowy Mountains, south-eastern Australia. *Acta Oecologica/ Oecol. Plant.* **4,** 117–124.

Lange, O. L. (1959). Untersuchungen über Warmeshaushalt und Hitzeresistenz mauretanischer Wusten-und Savannenpflanzen. *Flora (Jena)* **147,** 595–651.

Levitt, J. (1980). "Responses of Plants to Environmental Stresses," 2nd Ed. Academic Press, New York.

Martin, R. E. (1963). A basic approach to fire injury in tree stems. Proc. 2nd Annu. Tall Timbers Fire Ecol. Conf., pp. 151–162. Tall Timbers Research Station, Tallahassee, Florida.

McArthur, A. G. (1962). Control burning in eucalypt forests. Commonwealth of Australia, Forest and Timber Bureau Leaflet No. 80.

Mercer, G. N., Gill, A. M., and Weber, R. O. (1994). A time dependent model of fire impact on seeds in woody fruits. *Aust. J. Bot.* **42,** 71–81.

Mooney, H. A., and Hobbs, R. J. (1986). Resilience at the individual plant level. *Tasks Veg. Sci.* **16,** 65–82.

Nelson, R. M. (1952). Observations on heat tolerance of southern pine needles. *USDA For. Serv. Southeastern For. Exp. Stat. Pap.* **14,** 6.

Nicolai, V. (1986). The bark of trees: Thermal properties, microclimate and fauna. *Oecologia* **69,** 148–160.

Pafford, D., Dhir, V. K., Anderson, E., and Cohen, J. (1991). Analysis of experimental simulation of ground surface heating during a prescribed burn. *Int. J. Wildl. Fire* **1,** 125–146.

Pate, J. S., and Hopper, S. D. (1993). Rare and common plants in ecosystems with special reference to the south-west Australian flora. *Ecol Stud.* **99,** 293–325.

Perry, D. H., Lenz, M., and Watson, J. A. L. (1985). Relationships between fire, fungal rots and termite damage in Australian forest trees. *Aust. For.* **48,** 46–53.

Petersen, D. L., Arbaugh, M. J., Pollock, G. H., and Robinson, L. J. (1991). Post-fire growth of *Pseudotsuga menziesii* and *Pinus contorta* in the northern Rocky Mountains, USA. *Int. J. Wildl. Fire* **1,** 63–71.

Priestley, C. H. B. (1959). Heat conduction and temperature profiles in air and soil. *J. Aust. Inst. Agric. Sci.* June, 94–107.

Rackham, O. (1976). "Trees and Woodland in the British Landscape." J. M. Dent and Sons, London.

Reifsnyder, W. E., Herrington, L. P., and Spalt, K. W. (1967). Thermophysical properties of bark of shortleaf, longleaf and red pine. Yale University School of Forestry Bull. No. 70. Yale University Press, New Haven, Connecticut.

Rothermel, R. C., and Deeming, J. E. (1980). Measuring and interpreting fire behavior for correlation with fire effects. *USDA For. Serv. Gen. Tech. Rep.* INT-93.

Ryan, K. C. (1982). Evaluating potential tree mortality from prescribed burning. *In* "Site Preparation and Fuels Management on Steep Slopes" (D. M. Baumgartner, ed.), pp. 167–174. Symposium Proceedings. Washington State University Press, Pullman, Washington.

Ryan, K. C., and Frandsen, W. H. (1991). Basal injury from smoldering fires in mature *Pinus ponderosa* Laws. *Int. J. Wildl. Fire* **1,** 107–118.

Schier, G. A. (1978). Variation in suckering capacity among and within lateral roots of an aspen clone. *USDA For. Serv. Res. Note* INT-241.

Smillie, R. M., and Nott, R. (1979). Heat injury in leaves of alpine, temperate and tropical plants. *Aust. J. Plant Physiol.* **6,** 135–141.

Smith, W. K. (1978). Temperatures of desert plants: Another perspective on the adaptability of leaf size. *Science* **201,** 614–616.

Tomlinson, P. B., and Zimmermann, M. H. (1969). Vascular anatomy of monocotyledons with secondary growth—an introduction. *J. Arnold Arboretum* **50,** 160–179.

Trabaud, L. (1979). Etude du comportement du feu dans la garrique de chene kermes a partir des temperatures et des vitesses de propagation. *Ann. Sci. For.* **36,** 13–38.

Tunstall, B. R., Martin, T., Walker, J., Gill, A. M., and Aston, A. (1976a). Soil temperatures induced by an experimental logpile fire: Preliminary data analysis. CSIRO Land-Use Research Tech. Memo. 76/20, p. 40.

Tunstall, B. R., Walker, J., and Gill, A.M. (1976b). Temperature distribution around synthetic trees during grass fires. *For. Sci.* **22**, 269–76.

Van Gardingen, P., and Grace, J. (1991). Plants and wind. *Adv. Bot. Res.* **18**, 189–253.

Van Wagner, C. E. (1973). Height of crown scorch in forest fires. *Can. J. For. Res.* **3**, 373–378.

Van Wagner, C. E. (1975). Convection temperatures above low intensity forest fires. *Can. For. Serv. Bi-mon. Res. Notes* **31**, 21.

Vines, R. G. (1968). Heat transfer through bark, and the resistance of trees to fire. *Aust. J. Bot.* **16**, 499–514.

Weber, R. O., Gill, A. M., Lyons, P. R. A., and Mercer, G. N. (1994a). Time dependence of temperature above wildland fires. *CALM Sci.* (in press).

Weber, R. O., Gill, A. M., Lyons, P. R. A., Moore, P. H. R., Bradstock, R. A., and Mercer, G. N. (1994b). Modelling wildland fire temperatures. *CALM Sci.* (in press).

Williamson, G. B., and Black, E. M. (1981). High temperature of forest fires under pines as a selective advantage over oaks. *Nature (London)* **293**, 643–644.

15

Response of Stem Growth and Function to Air Pollution

James A. Weber and N. E. Grulke

I. Introduction

Exposure to air pollutants can result in reduced stem growth, changes in wood density, and/or deposition of pollutants in the stem. Several reviews summarize the known effects of air pollutants on plant growth and function (Wellburn, 1988; Unsworth and Ormrod, 1982; Darrall, 1989; Alscher and Wellburn, 1994; Weber *et al.*, 1994), including trees (Pye, 1988). Air pollutants may also change the defensive capacities of stems (Cobb *et al.*, 1968; also see Bryant and Raffa [16] in this volume) through alteration in chemical constituents (Pathak *et al.*, 1986; Patel and Devi, 1986).

In this chapter we review the literature on the effects of several major types of air pollutants on stem growth and function, with the goals of better defining our knowledge in these areas and of suggesting areas in need of further investigation.

II. Types of Air Pollutants and Their Effects

In the last century, air pollution was recognized as a major problem in areas with heavy industries (e.g., metal refining). Trees in forests around such facilities were often severely damaged or killed by the emissions of SO_2 and heavy metals (Thomas and Hendricks, 1956; Thomas, 1960; Weber *et al.*, 1994). With the development of technologies to reduce and/or disperse emissions, acute damage has been reduced; however, lower levels of some pollutants are now found over larger areas [Environmental Protection Agency (EPA), 1982a,b, 1986)]. In addition, secondary pollutants (e.g., ozone) have become more prominent. This shift in the type and concentration of pollutants has resulted in much larger areas being chronically exposed to low levels of air pollutants. The primary air pollutants of concern currently are ozone, acid deposition, and elevated CO_2. Heavy metals are primarily of concern near emission sources.

The effect of air pollutants on plants depends on the pollutant, the exposure pattern, and the site of absorption. A conceptual model (Fig. 1) of the effects of air pollutants on stem growth would include effects on net photosynthesis (including photosynthetic capacity and leaf longevity), allocation of resources (particularly carbohydrates), and stem growth (including deposition of pollutants in wood, modification of chemical constituents, and changes in structure). Most air pollutants are absorbed through the stomates on the leaves and result in reduced net carbon gain and/or leaf longevity (Weber *et al.*, 1994). The importance of direct uptake by stems (e.g., through lenticles) is in need of further study. Heavy metals,

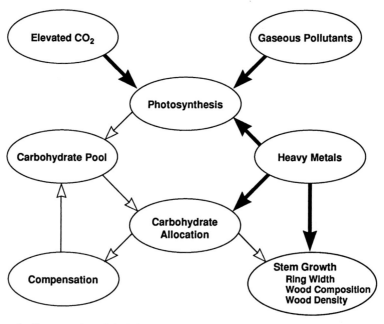

Figure 1 Conceptual model of the effects of air pollutants on stem growth and function. Primary effects are indicated by solid, boldface arrows; secondary effects by open arrows. Compensation is any adjustment the plant makes to reduce the effect of the pollutants, for example, replacement of damaged foliage.

sulfate, and nitrate could be absorbed through the leaf cuticle or bark, or could be deposited on the soil and taken up by the roots. The relative importance of indirect effects (e.g., reduced carbohydrate content) and direct effects (disruption of stem metabolism) are not known.

Acid precipitation, which is produced by the interaction of NO_x and SO_2 with water in the atmosphere, has been of concern in the last few decades, particularly with the apparent decline of spruce/fir forests in the eastern United States (Hornbeck and Smith, 1985; Hornbeck *et al.*, 1986; McLaughlin *et al.*, 1987). However, effects of acid deposition on forest productivity were difficult to quantify (Barnard *et al.*, 1991). In the cell both SO_2 and NO_x will form acids and can thereby change the cellular pH balance; SO_2 can also react with cellular constituents to produce other phytotoxic compounds (Bytnerowicz and Grulke, 1992). Because both sulfur and nitrogen are important mineral nutrients, under conditions of sulfur or nitrogen limitation uptake of NO_x and SO_2 may reduce effects of the limitation for the plant. For example, in the Sierra Nevada of California, an area with nitrogen–deficient soils, deposition of NO_x could enhance growth in some species (Peterson, 1994).

Ozone is a product of a complex of reactions between NO_x and volatile organic carbons in the presence of sunlight and can be transported long distances (EPA, 1986). In recent decades, ozone has become a widespread problem in agricultural and forested areas (Fig. 2; Weber *et al.*, 1994). Studies in the mountains around Los Angeles, California have shown that ozone can have a major impact on tree growth (Miller *et al.*, 1982, 1991). Similar results have been found around Mexico City (de Bauer *et al.*, 1985). In general, crop species are more susceptible than conifers to ozone damage (Darrall, 1989). This difference in sensitivity among plant species may in large part be the result of differences in stomatal conductance (Reich, 1987), although biochemical processes (e.g., detoxification) may also play a role (Weber *et al.*, 1994).

Unlike either SO_2 or NO_x, ozone provides no known physiological benefit to a plant. The biochemical mode of action within the cell is not well known because of the essentially nonspecific nature of the reactions and because of the lack of a tracer (Wellburn, 1988; Heath, 1994). However, it has been shown that after ozone fumigation the primary carboxylating enzyme [ribulose-bisphosphate (RuBP) carboxylase, EC 4.1.1.39] becomes more oxidized, leading to reduced activity (Dann and Pell, 1989; Pell *et al.*, 1994).

In Europe, decline of conifers has stimulated much research into the effects of air pollution on trees (Schulze *et al.*, 1989). Stands of *Picea abies* (Norway spruce) with obvious decline (reduced crown density and yellow needles) produced only 65% of the wood of healthy stands (Oren *et al.*, 1988). The cause of this decline has not been identified as yet, but several

Estimated 3 Month SUMO6 Exposures (1988)

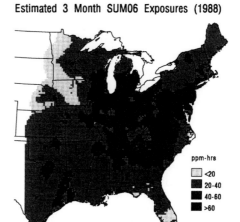

Estimated 3 Month SUMO6 Exposures (1989)

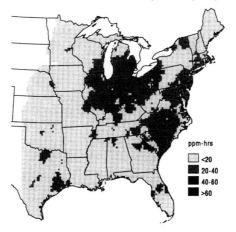

Figure 2 Maps showing the extent of ozone exposure (calculated as the sum of all hourly average ozone concentrations equal to or greater than 0.06 ppm) for a high-ozone year (1988) and a low-ozone year (1989) in the eastern United States. (See Lee *et al.*, 1991, 1994 for details on data and calculations.)

possibilities, including acid deposition and ozone, are being investigated (Schulze *et al.*, 1989).

Large stems probably do not respond directly to uptake of air pollutants because of the large resistance to uptake in the bark; however, research on this topic is lacking. Most likely air pollutants have an indirect effect on stem growth through reduction in resources (especially carbohydrates) available for growth, although heavy metals may be transported from the site of uptake to the stem, where they may affect stem growth directly. Phloem structure and function in petioles and small stems has been reported to be affected by ozone exposure (Matyssek *et al.*, 1992; Spence *et al.*, 1990). Most of the experimental data available on stem growth response to ozone has been gathered using seedlings and young trees for only one or a few growing seasons. However, for those studies carried out over two or three seasons, a pattern has developed that shows root growth is reduced more than other parts of the plant (e.g., Hogsett *et al.*, 1985). Growth (increase in dry weight, basal diameter, and/or height) of the stem is frequently also reduced with increasing ozone exposure.

The effects of heavy metals are complex and depend on the site of uptake, path of transport, ionic form, and metabolism of the tissue. Heavy metals can be transported in the xylem and/or phloem, and have the potential to affect the growth of the stem directly. Lamoreaux and Chaney (1977) found that cadmium decreased the conductivity of xylem in silver maple (*Acer saccharinum*) through decreased proportion of xylem available for conduction, decreased vessel diameter, and increased blockage of vessel elements. Several studies have shown that heavy metals can decrease photosynthesis (Lamoreaux and Chaney, 1978; Schlegel *et al.*, 1987) and shoot growth (Kelly *et al.*, 1979; Denny and Wilkins, 1987; Carlson and Bazzaz, 1977). From these data it is clear that heavy metals can affect stem growth in at least two ways: (1) reduction in the amount of photosynthate available for growth, and (2) reduction in xylem production and conductance.

Finally, human activity has led to a major increase in atmospheric CO_2 concentration, which is predicted to lead to changes in the global climate (Lashoff, 1989). While increasing CO_2 concentration in itself is not likely to damage plant growth, even at concentrations two to three times current levels, shifts in biomass allocation resulting from elevated CO_2 and climate change are likely to lead to changes in forest productivity and in the species composition of those forests. However, climate change will likely affect the distribution of rain and/or temperature and have greater effects on tree growth than the elevated CO_2 itself (Solomon, 1986; Solomon and Bartlein, 1992; Davis and Zabinski, 1992).

III. Evidence from Studies of Tree Rings

Air pollution may affect annual growth rings through changes in ring width, element composition, or organic composition. We examine three types of data that have been collected using tree rings: ring width/basal area increment, isotopic composition, and density and chemical composition (Table 1).

Table I   Studies Relating Width of Tree Rings, Biomass, and Elemental Composition
to Various Pollutants

Species	Pollutant	Measurement	Response	Ref.
		Gaseous Pollutants		
Abies concolor	Ozone[a]	Ring width	Decrease	Ohmart and Williams (1979)
Pinus jeffreyi	Ozone	Ring width	Decrease	Peterson *et al.* (1987)
Pinus ponderosa	Ozone	Ring width	Decrease	Ohmart and Williams (1979)
	Ozone	Ring width	No change	Peterson *et al.* (1989)
	Ozone	Ring width	No change	Peterson and Arbaugh (1988)
	Ozone	Ring width	Decrease	Peterson *et al.* (1991)
	Ozone	Ring width	No change	Peterson *et al.* (1993)
Pinus strobus	Ozone	Ring width	Decrease	Benoit *et al.* (1982)
	Ozone	Ring width	Decrease	McLaughlin *et al.* (1982)
	Ozone	δ-^{13}C	Increase	Martin *et al.* (1988)
	Ozone	Lignin and "extractives"	Increase	Pathak *et al.* (1986)
Pinus taeda	Ozone	Basal area increment	Decrease	Sheffield and Cost (1987)
	Ozone	Ring width	Decrease	Zahner *et al.* (1989)
Picea abies	Ozone	Density	No change	Sachsse and Hapla (1986)
Picea rubens	Ozone	Ring width	Decrease	Hornbeck and Smith (1985)
	Ozone	Ring width	Decrease	McLaughlin *et al.* (1987)
Populus deltoides × *trichocarpa*	Ozone	Biomass	Decrease	Reich and Lassoie (1985)
Pseudostuga menziesii	Ozone	δ-^{13}C	Increase	Martin *et al.* (1988)
	Cu smelter	δ-^{13}C	Increase	Martin and Sutherland (1990)
Quercus alba	Ozone	Basal area increment	Decrease	Phipps and Whiton (1988)
Mixed species[b]	Mixture[c]	δ-^{13}C	Increase	Freyer (1979)
Mixed species[d]	Mixture[e]	Lipid content	Increase	Patel and Devi (1986)
		Elemental Content		
Betula alleghaniensis	Cd	Growth	Decrease	Kelly *et al.* (1979)
Fagus sylvatica	Cd, Pb, Zn	Elemental content	No pattern	Hagemeyer *et al.* (1992)
	Fe, Al	Elemental content	Increase	Meisch *et al.* (1986)
	Ca, Mg, Mn, Zn		Decrease	
Liriodendron tulipifera	Cd	Growth	Decrease	Kelly *et al.* (1979)
Pinus echinata	S	Elemental content	Increase	Ray and Winstead (1991)
	Fe, Ti	Elemental content	Increase	Baes and McLaughlin (1984)
Pinus strobus	Cd	Growth	Decrease	Kelly *et al.* (1979)
Pinus sylvestris	Cd, Cu, Pb, Zn	Elemental content	Increase	Symeonides (1979)
	Cu, Pb	Growth	Decrease	

continues

Table I   *Continued*

pecies	Pollutant	Measurement	Response	Ref.
Pinus taeda	Cd, Pb, Zn	Growth	Decrease	Jordan *et al.* (1990)
	Cd	Growth	Decrease	Kelly *et al.* (1979)
Prunus virginiana	Cd	Growth	Decrease	Kelly *et al.* (1979)
Quercus petraea,				
Q. robur	Cd, Pb	Elemental content	Increase	Queirolo *et al.* (1990)
Mixed species	S, N	Elemental content	Increase	Ohmann and Grigal (1990)
Mixed species	N, P, K, S, Fe, Cu, Al, Ca, Mg, Mn, B, Zn	Elemental content	For use in monitoring	Riitters *et al.* (1991)

a Ozone refers here to field exposures to naturally occurring ozone and not to controlled exposures.
b Quercus robur, Aeschulus hippocastaneum, Fraxinus excelsior, and *Pinus sylvestris.*
c Emissions from a coal-fired foundry (SO$_2$, CO$_2$, particulates).
d Mangifera indica, Syzygium cumini, and *Tamarindus indica.*
e Emissions of a fertilizer plant (NH$_3$, As, NO$_2$, SO$_2$, hydrocarbons, P, HF, particulates, and traces of O$_3$).

A. Tree Ring Width and Basal Area Increment

Many studies have compared tree ring width with variations in air pollutants (see Fig. 3 for an example). Given the high ozone concentrations and long exposures found in the mountains around the Los Angeles basin in California, one might expect to find a clear decline in tree ring growth or basal area increment in the trees there. Ohmart and Williams (1979) found that basal area increment was lower in *Pinus ponderosa* (ponderosa pine) and *Abies concolor* (white fir), with visible foliar damage (needle retention, length, and condition, and branch mortality) compared to those with no signs of damage. Developing clear patterns of tree rings for *P. ponderosa* and *Pinus jeffreyi* (closely related species) was hindered because of incomplete and missing rings (Cemmill *et al.,* 1982). Ring width decreased with increasing ozone exposure in *P. jeffreyi* in the Sierra Nevada (Peterson *et al.,* 1987); however, no clear pattern was found in *P. ponderosa* (Peterson and Arbaugh, 1988; Peterson *et al.,* 1989). Peterson *et al.* (1991) found evidence for a reduction in growth in this species at sites with high ozone exposure, but not for a general decline throughout the area. No clear effect was found for this species in the Colorado Rockies (Peterson *et al.,* 1993).

In the eastern United States *Picea rubens* (red spruce) was studied because of interest in the decline observed in parts of its range (McLaughlin *et al.,* 1987). Hornbeck and Smith (1985) found a decline in basal area increment in *P. rubens* starting about 1960, possibly caused by normal aging, budworm, climate change, and/or acid deposition/air pollution. In further analyses

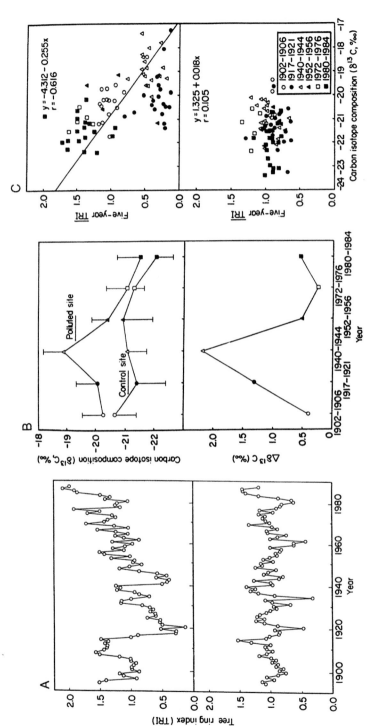

Figure 3 Effect of pollution from a copper smelter on ring width and $\delta^{13}C$ in *Pseudotsuga menziesii*. (A) Tree ring index for polluted (top) and control (bottom) sites. (B) $\delta^{13}C$ of cellulose of polluted and control sites (top); difference in $\delta^{13}C$ between polluted and clean sites (bottom). (C) Relation between tree ring index and $\delta^{13}C$ for polluted (top) and clean (bottom) sites. [Reprinted from Martin and Sutherland (1990). Used with permission of Blackwell Scientific Publishing, Ltd.]

involving both *P. rubens* and *Abies balsamea* (balsam fir), Hornbeck *et al.* (1986) and Federer and Hornbeck (1987) concluded that much of the decline in growth could be assigned to aging of stands, although the coincident increase in air pollution complicates the analysis. McLaughlin *et al.* (1987), in a study of over 1000 cores of *P. rubens* from 48 sites in the eastern United States, found several periods of reduced ring width across a range of tree sizes that in general coincided with drought and insect infestation. However, a decrease in ring width, beginning in the 1950s and 1960s and still evident about 1980, appeared "unique in magnitude and duration within the available tree-ring record of surviving trees over the past 200 years" (McLaughlin *et al.*, 1987, pp. 499–500). Changes in climate, competition, or disease did not appear to explain these results adequately.

While correlations such as these (Table I) do not provide definite proof of the effect of air pollution on growth, they do provide some support for an effect of air pollution on stem growth. It should also be recognized that identification of a particular causal pollutant is in many cases difficult if not impossible. As noted by Innes and Cook (1989, p. 186):

> Although tree-ring analysis can help to pinpoint some of the cause–effect relationship in the pollution debate, it is unsuitable for establishing dose–response relationships, as information on doses are rarely available for the sites under investigation. In addition, it is important to remember that the ring width is the sum of a whole suite of processes acting on a tree. Pollution may be one of these, but tree-ring analysis is unlikely to be able to determine precisely the contribution that pollution is making to any observed decline.

B. Variation in δ-^{13}C

Changes in the ^{13}C content [measured as the deviation (δ-^{13}C) of ^{13}C content of the sample from that of a reference, in parts per mil] of tissues have been used as a means for monitoring the response of plants to changes in the environment. The primary mechanism affecting δ-^{13}C is the discrimination against ^{13}CO$_2$ by RuBP carboxylase (O'Leary, 1981). For C$_3$ plants, this discrimination changes the content of δ-^{13}C by about -25 to $-30‰$ compared to the standard. Drought has been shown to increase δ-^{13}C (Farquhar *et al.*, 1989; Rundel *et al.*, 1988), probably through decreased conductance to CO$_2$. Matyssek *et al.* (1992), using cuttings of birch (*Betula pendula*) exposed to ozone, found that δ-^{13}C increased with ozone exposure; however, stomatal conductance did not decrease. Thus, some process that controls movement of CO$_2$ to the site of fixation, other than stomatal conductance, must have been affected by ozone exposure.

Only a few studies have investigated the relationship of δ-^{13}C content of wood and pollution exposure. Freyer (1979) found that δ-^{13}C was increased by $1-2‰$ in polluted compared to nonpolluted sites during periods in which the polluted site experienced pollution, but δ^{13}C was the same when the source of pollution, a coal-fired foundry, was shut down. When the foundry was in operation, the polluted site experienced increased air pollution, especially SO_2, and slightly elevated CO_2. Martin *et al.* (1988) found that the δ-^{13}C values of wood of *Pinus ponderosa* and *Pseudotsuga menziesii* (Douglas fir) increased during a period when the trees were exposed to air pollution (O_3 and SO_2) and decreased when pollution was reduced. Martin and Sutherland (1990) found similar results when they analyzed the δ-p3^{13}C of cores from *Pseudotsuga menziesii* trees exposed to pollution from a copper smelter. These authors found that changes in ring width and δ-^{13}C correlated well (Fig. 3) with periods when the smelter was operating.

C. Variation in Wood Density and Chemical Composition

Little information is available on the density and composition of wood as a function of air pollution. Lewark (1986), reviewing literature on X-ray densitometry, found evidence of decreases in density of latewood in several species in a German forest. However, Sachsse and Hapla (1986), using microscopic techniques, found no evidence of change in tracheid packing density (gm/cm^3) in *Picea abies* exposed to air pollution in a German forest. Other studies show that air pollution can affect the secondary chemical composition of wood to some degree. Pathak *et al.* (1986) found that "extractives" and lignin content of *Pinus strobus* (eastern white pine) were different between sites with different levels of air pollution (NO_3^- and SO_4^{2-}). Patel and Devi (1986) found that lipid content of the stem increased in some species of trees exposed to a mixture of air pollutants from a fertilizer plant in India. While these data suggest that air pollution can affect the biochemical composition of woody tissue, our current state of knowledge in this area is fragmentary.

Exposure to various pollutants, especially heavy metals, can lead to their deposition in the wood (Table I). To some extent this phenomenon can be used as a historical record of air pollution. For the most part these studies assessed pollutant exposure over time and showed that heavy metals, sulfur, and nitrogen accumulated in wood during periods of pollution. As shown in Table I, exposure to heavy metals has been associated with reduced stem growth.

IV. Effect of CO_2 Enrichment on Stem Growth in Trees

The response of forest trees to elevated CO_2 exposure has been reviewed by Mousseau and Saugier (1992), but the role of CO_2 in stem growth is far from clear. Eamus and Jarvis (1989) suggest from experimental work that an increasing CO_2 concentration should increase total tree productivity, including stems. Oechel and Strain (1985) suggest that CO_2 enrichment will result in greater allocation of resources to structural tissue compared to other tissues. The effect of elevated CO_2 on tree growth has been studied in seedlings and saplings of several species (Table II). In general, biomass (including stem biomass) increases with elevated CO_2. However, the length of the experiment, growth conditions (particularly water and nutrient stress), species, and seed source can have major effects on the results. For example, in a 24-week experiment with *Liriodendron tulipifera* (tulip-poplar) the shoots grew more in elevated CO_2 than ambient (O'Neill *et al.*, 1987); however, when grown for 3 years stem growth was not affected (Norby *et al.*, 1992). One possible reason for the lack of an effect in the second study is the reduction in leaf biomass under elevated CO_2. One problem not fully appreciated in earlier studies was the effect of restriction of root growth by small pots on plant response (Thomas and Strain, 1991). Allocation patterns and sink strengths are likely to have major impacts on whether the stem responds to elevated CO_2.

Even with the same experimental design, different seed stocks from the same geographic area may have differing responses to CO_2 enrichment. Stem height in two full-sibling crosses of *P. ponderosa* (one slow and one fast-growing stock) was decreased by elevated CO_2 in a 4-month, CO_2-enrichment experiment with fertilization (Grulke *et al.*, 1993). For a nearly identical experiment with two half-sibling crosses of *P. ponderosa* (again, one slow and one fast-growing stock), the percentage biomass allocation to stems at 6 weeks was significantly greater for the slower growing family cross and lower with CO_2 enrichment for the faster growing family cross. However, biomass sampling 1 month later showed no significant differences between family crosses or CO_2 levels (N. E. Grulke, S. Sparks, J. Johnson, A. Bytnerowicz, and D. Crowley, unpublished data).

Nutrient levels can affect plant response to elevated CO_2. Two half-sibling families of *Pinus radiata* were exposed to ambient and CO_2-enriched air with a combination of two levels of phosphate (Conroy *et al.*, 1990). One of the families had a significantly greater ratio of stem to foliage dry weight with CO_2 enrichment, independent of phosphate levels, and the second family showed only an increase in structural tissue with an increase in phosphate.

Tree ring analysis provides our only view of the long-term effects of CO_2 enrichment on stem growth of mature trees. The first research that ascribed growth enhancement to atmospheric CO_2 enrichment was that of La-Marche *et al.* (1984), who showed an increase in ring width in *Pinus aristata* (bristlecone pine). Similar results have been reported for *Picea abies* (Kienast and Luxmoore, 1988), silver fir in France (Becker, 1989), European conifers (Britta, 1992), *Pinus palustris* (longleaf pine) (West *et al.*, 1993), and subalpine conifers in the United States (Peterson, 1994). However, Graumlich (1991) did not find increased growth in three species from the east slope of the Sierra Nevada.

Table II Effect of Elevated CO_2 on Stem Growth and Allocation

Species	Exposure	Component	Response	Ref.
Acer saccharinum	300, 600, 1200 ppm CO_2; 35 days; fertilized	Total biomass	Increase in all components	Carlson and Bazzaz (1980)
Castanea sativa	350, 700 ppm CO_2; 5 months	Stem	No change	El Kohen *et al.* (1992, 1993)
		Roots	Increase	
Fagus grandifolia	400, 700 ppm CO_2; 60–100 days	Root/shoot	Increase	Bazzaz *et al.* (1990)
		Stem height and diameter	Increase	
		Leaf area	Increase	
Fagus sativa	350, 700 ppm CO_2; 5 months	Stem, roots	Increase	El Kohen *et al.* (1993)
Liriodendron tulipifera	367, 692 ppm CO_2; 24 weeks; nutrient limited	Roots	Increase	O'Neill *et al.* (1987)
		Shoot	Increase	
		Shoot height and diameter	Increase	
		Stem density	Decrease	
	354, 503, 656 ppm CO_2; 3 years; nutrient limited	Stem	No change	Norby *et al.* (1992)
		Fine roots	Increase	
		Leaves	Decrease	
Pinus ponderosa	350, 700 ppm CO_2; 4 months	Stem height	Decrease	Grulke *et al.* (1993)

Species	Treatment	Response	Effect	Reference
Pinus radiata	340, 600 ppm CO_2; 2 years	Stem	Increase (family differences)	Conroy *et al.* (1990)
		Roots	Increase (family differences)	
		Wood density	Decrease	
Platanus occidentalis	300, 600, 1200 ppm CO_2; 35 days; fertilized	Total biomass	Increase	Carlson and Bazzaz (1980)
Populus deltoides	300, 600, 1200 ppm CO_2; 35 days; fertilized	Biomass	Increase in all components	Carlson and Bazzaz (1980)
Pseudotsuga menziesii	+/− fertilized	Stem diameter	Increased with fertilizer	Gillham *et al.* (1994)
Quercus alba	362, 690 ppm CO_2; 40 weeks	Biomass	Increase; roots > shoot	Norby *et al.* (1986)
Acer saccharum	400, 700 ppm CO_2; 60–100 days	Root/shoot	No significant change	Bazzaz *et al.* (1990)
A. rubrum		Stem height	No significant change	
Betula papyrifera		Stem diameter	No significant change	
Pinus strobus		Leaf area	No significant change	
Prunus serotina				
Tsuga canadensis				

Isolating atmospheric CO_2 enrichment from the other associated global warming components, such as increased spring temperatures and modified precipitation pattern, is difficult at best. The magnitude and direction of the signal from global CO_2 enrichment will depend on the sites studied and the co-occurring stresses, as well as on the species. A clear, widespread signal in long-term dendrochronologies of many species in the temperate forest would provide strong evidence of climate change.

V. Model of Air Pollutant Effects on Stem Growth

Mechanistic models are not well developed for stem growth. Given the complexity of the processes and the massive amount of integration that occurs in plant growth and response to the environment, the lack of a mechanistic model for plant growth is not surprising. However, some models have been developed that are instructive. The series of models developed by Luxmoore and co-workers (Dixon *et al.*, 1978a,b; Luxmoore *et al.*, 1978) provide some insights into how heavy metals might be taken up, translocated, and deposited in a tree and how trees might respond to uptake of heavy metals. More recently, models of the response of trees to ozone exposure have been developed (Weinstein and Beloin, 1990; Weinstein *et al.*, 1991; Chen and Gomez, 1990). In the program TREGRO (Weinstein and Beloin, 1990; Weinstein *et al.*, 1991) ozone has its effect through reduction in carbohydrates available for growth, which is controlled by variation in the timing and strengths of canopy carbohydrate production and of various sinks for carbohydrate. Simulations with this model, parameterized for *P. ponderosa*, showed that reduction in carbohydrate availability reduced simulated growth of stems, with much of the reduction occurring at relatively low ozone exposures (Fig. 4).

VI. Conclusions

The effects of air pollution on stem growth are for the most part subtle and indirect. There is ample evidence from chamber exposure studies that stem growth in young trees can be reduced by ozone and other pollutants. The mechanisms through which pollutants affect stem growth are likely to be as diverse as the pollutants. Those pollutants that affect resource acquisition either through the leaves (carbon fixation) or through the roots (water and mineral nutrients) will affect the potential for stem growth indirectly. Those pollutants that are transported in the xylem and/or phloem (e.g., heavy metals) or that are directly absorbed by stems have the potential to affect function of the stem tissue directly. The effect of elevated CO_2 on

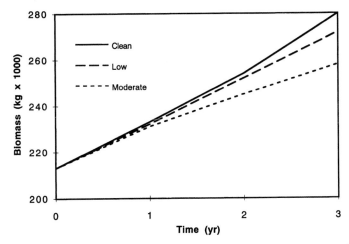

Figure 4 Simulation of the effect of increasing ozone exposure on stem growth, using TREGRO (Weinstein and Beloin, 1990; Weinstein *et al.*, 1991. version 2.2.15). Clean (—): SUM06 = 0, 20 ppm–hr total ozone exposure; low (– – –): SUM06 = 15, 70 ppm–hr; moderate (---): SUM06 = 78, 120 ppm–hr. Total ozone exposure calculated as the sum of all average hourly ozone concentrations.

stem growth is as yet unclear, with some studies showing increased stem growth and others showing none.

Several important questions that need to be addressed concern the response of stems to air pollution: to what extent do stems respond directly to pollutants? How are indirect effects of air pollution (e.g., reduced carbohydrate availability) controlled? What are the pathways and mechanisms through which the stem responds to air pollutants? What changes occur in biochemical constituents as a result of pollutant exposure? With the development of new techniques (e.g., ^{13}C measurement) these questions, among others, can be addressed.

Acknowledgments

We gratefully acknowledge the reviews of Michael Arbaugh, Jeff Lee, and Michael Unsworth. The preparation of this document has been funded by the U.S. Environmental Protection Agency. It has been subjected to agency review and approved for publication.

References

Alscher, R. G., and Wellburn, A. R., eds. (1994). "Plant Responses to the Gaseous Environment: Molecular, Metabolic and Physiological Aspects." Chapman & Hall, London.

Baes, C. F., III, and McLaughlin, S. B. (1984). Trace elements in tree rings: Evidence of recent and historical air pollution. *Science* **224**, 494–496.

Barnard, J. E., Lucier, A. A., Johnson, A. H., Brooks, R. T., Karnosky, D. F., and Dunn, P. H. (1991). "Changes in Forest Health and Productivity in the United States and Canada. Acidic Deposition: State of Science and Technology." National Acid Precipitation Assessment Program, Washington, D.C.

Bazzaz, F. A., Coleman, J. S., and Morse, S. R. (1990). Growth response of seven major co-occurring tree species of the northeastern United States to elevated CO_2. *Can. J. For. Res.* **20**, 1479–1484.

Becker, M. (1989). The role of climate on present and past vitality of silver fir forests in the Vosges mountains of northeastern France. *Can. J. For. Res.* **19**, 1110–1117.

Benoit, L. F., Skelly, J. M., Moore, L. D., and Dochinger, L. S. (1982). Radial growth reduction of *Pinus strobus* correlated with foliar ozone sensitivity as an indicator of ozone induced losses in eastern forests. *Can. J. For. Res.* **12**, 673–678.

Britta, K. R. (1992). Increasing productivity of "natural growth" conifers in Europe over the last century. *In* "Tree Rings and Environment. LUNDQUA Rep. 34. Proceedings of International Dendrological Symposium" (T. S. Bartholin, B. E. Berghard, and D. E. Eskstein, eds.) pp. 64–71. University of Lund, Lund, Sweden.

Bytnerowicz, A., and Grulke, N. (1992). Physiological effects of air pollutants on western trees. *In* "The Response of Western Forests to Air Pollution" (R. K. Olson, D. Binkley, and M. Bohm, eds.), pp. 183–233. Springer-Verlag, New York.

Carlson, R. W., and Bazzaz, F. A. (1977). Growth reduction in American sycamore (*Plantanus occidentalis* L.) caused by Pb-Cd interaction. *Environ. Pollut.* **12**, 243–253.

Carlson, R. W., and Bazzaz, F. A. (1980). The effects of elevated CO_2 concentrations on growth, photosynthesis, transpiration, and water use efficiency of plants. *In* "Environmental and Climatic Impact of Coal Utilization" (J. J. Singh and A. Deepak, eds.), pp. 609–623. Academic Press, New York.

Cemmill, B., McBride, J. R., and Laven, R. D. (1982). Development of tree-ring chronologies in an ozone air pollution-stressed forest in southern California. *Tree-Ring Bull.* **42**, 23–31.

Chen, C., and Gomez, L. E. (1990). Modeling tree responses to interacting stresses. *In* "Process Modeling of Forest Growth Responses to Environmental Stress" (R. K. Dixon, R. S. Meldahl, G. A. Ruark, and W. G. Warren, eds.), pp. 338–350. Timber Press, Portland, Oregon.

Cobb, F. W., Jr., Wood, D. L., Stark, R. W., and Parmeter, J. R., Jr. (1968). Theory on the relationships between oxidant injury and bark beetle infestation. *Hilgardia* **39**, 141.

Conroy, J. P., Milham, P. J., Mazur, M., and Barlow, E. W. R. (1990). Growth, dry weight partitioning and wood properties of *Pinus radiata* D. Don. after 2 years of CO_2 enrichment. *Plant Cell Environ.* **13**, 329–338.

Dann, M. S., and Pell, E. J. (1989). Decline of activity and quantity of ribulose bisphosphate carboxylase/oxygenase and net photosynthesis in ozone-treated potato foliage. *Plant Physiol.* **91**, 427–432.

Darrall, N. M. (1989). The effect of air pollutants on physiological processes in plants. *Plant Cell Environ.* **12**, 1–30.

Davis, M. B., and Zabinski, C. (1992). Changes in geographical range resulting from greenhouse warming: Effects on biodiversity in forests. *In* "Global Warming and Biological Diversity" (R. L. Peters and T. E. Lovejoy, eds.), pp. 297–308. Yale University Press, New Haven, Connecticut.

de Bauer, M. L., Tegeda, T. H., and Manning, W. J. (1985). Ozone causes needle injury and tree decline in *Pinus hartwegii* at high altitudes in the mountains around Mexico City. *J. Air Pollut. Control Assoc.* **35**, 838.

Denny, H. J., and Wilkins, D. A. (1987). Zinc tolerance in *Betula* spp. I. Effect of external concentration of zinc on growth and uptake. *New Phytol.* **106**, 517–524.

Dixon, K. R., Luxmoore, R. J., and Begovitch, C. L. (1978a). CERES—a model of forest stand biomass dynamics for predicting trace contaminant, nutrient, and water effects. I. Model description. *Ecol. Modelling* **5**, 17–38.

Dixon, K. R., Luxmoore, R. J., and Begovitch, C. L. (1978b). CERES—a model of forest stand biomass dynamics for predicting trace contaminant, nutrient, and water effects. II. Model application. *Ecol. Modelling* **5**, 93–114.

Eamus, D., and Jarvis, P. G. (1989). The direct effects of increases in the global atmospheric CO_2 concentration on natural and commercial temperate trees and forests. *Adv. Ecol. Res.* **19**, 1–49.

El Kohen, A., Rouhier, H., and Mousseau, M. (1992). Changes in dry weight and nitrogen partitioning induced by elevated CO_2 depends on soil nutrient availability in sweet chestnut (*Castanea sativa* Mill.). *Ann. Sci. For.* **48**, 307–319.

El Kohen, A., Venet, L., and Mousseau, M. (1993). Growth and photosynthesis of two deciduous forest species at elevated carbon dioxide. *Funct. Ecol.* **7**, 480–486.

Environmental Protection Agency (EPA) (1982a). "Air Quality Criteria for Particulate Matter and Sulfur Oxides." EPA-600/8-82-029. Environmental Criteria and Assessment Office, Research Triangle Park, North Carolina.

EPA (1982b). "Air Quality Criteria for Oxides of Nitrogen," EPA-600/8-82-026. Environmental Criteria and Assessment Office, Research Triangle Park, North Carolina.

EPA (1986). "Air Quality Criteria for Ozone and Other Photochemical Oxidants." EPA-600/8-84-020. Environmental Criteria and Assessment Office, Research Triangle Park, North Carolina.

Farquhar, G. D., Ehleringer, J. R., and Hubick, K. T. (1989). Carbon isotope discrimination and photosynthesis. *Annu. Rev. Plant Physiol. Mol. Biol.* **40**, 503–537.

Federer, C. A., and Hornbeck, J. W. (1987). Expected decreases in diameter growth of even-aged red spruce. *Can. J. For. Res.* **17**, 266–269.

Freyer, H. D. (1979). On the delta-13-C record in tree rings. II. Registration of microenvironmental CO_2 and anomalous pollution effects. *Tellus* **31**, 308–312.

Gillham, M. L., Perry, D. A., Grulke, N. E., and Winner, W. E. (1994). Growth and allocation of Douglas-fir seedlings in response to CO_2, temperature, and nitrogen. *Bull. Ecol. Soc. Am.* **75**, 76.

Graumlich, L. T. (1991). Subalpine tree growth, climate, and increasing CO_2: An assessment of recent growth trends. *Ecology* **72**, 1–11.

Grulke, N. E., Hom, J. L., and Roberts, S.W. (1993). Physiological adjustment of two full-sib families of ponderosa pine to elevated CO_2. *Tree Physiol.* **12**, 391–401.

Hagemeyer, J., Lulfsmann, A., Perk, M., and Breckle, S. W. (1992). Are there seasonal variations of trace element concentrations (Cd, Pb, Zn) in wood of *Fagus* trees in Germany? *Vegetatio* **101**, 55–63.

Heath, R. L. (1994). Alterations of plant metabolism by ozone exposure. *In* "Plant Responses to the Gaseous Environment" (R. G. Alscher and A. R. Wellburn, eds.), pp. 121–145. Chapman & Hall, London.

Hogsett, W. E., Plocher, M., Wildman, V., Tingey, D. T., and Bennett, J. P. (1985). Growth response to two varieties of slash pine seedlings to chronic ozone exposures. *Can. J. Bot.* **63**, 2369–2376.

Hornbeck, J. W., and Smith, R. B. (1985). Documentation of red spruce growth decline. *Can. J. For. Res.* **15**, 1199–1201.

Hornbeck, J. W., Smith, R. B., and Federer, C. A. (1986). Growth decline in red spruce and balsam fir relative to natural processes. *Water Air Soil Pollut.* **31**, 425–530.

Innes, J. L., and Cook, E. R. (1989). Tree-ring analysis as an aid to evaluating the effects of pollution on tree growth. *Can. J. For. Res.* **19**, 1174–1189.

Jordan, D. N., Wright, L. M., and Lockaby, B. G. (1990). Relationship between xylem trace metals and radial growth of loblolly pine in rural Alabama. *J. Environ. Qual.* **19**, 504–508.

Kelly, J. M., Parker, G. R., and McFee, W. W. (1979). Heavy metal accumulation and growth of seedlings of five forest species as influenced by soil cadmium level. *J. Environ. Qual.* **8**, 361–364.

Kienast, F., and Luxmoore, R. L. (1988). Tree-ring analysis and conifer growth response to increased atmospheric CO_2 levels. *Oecologia* **76**, 487–495.

LaMarche, V. C., Graybill, D. A., Fritts, H. C., and Rose, M. R. (1984). Increasing atmospheric carbon dioxide: Tree-ring evidence for growth enhancement in natural vegetation. *Science* **223**, 1019–1021.

Lamoreaux, R. J., and Chaney, W. R. (1977). Growth and water movement in silver maple seedlings affected by cadmium. *J. Environ. Qual.* **6**, 201–205.

Lamoreaux, R. J., and Chaney, W. R. (1978). The effect of cadmium on net photosynthesis, transpiration, and dark respiration of excised silver maple leaves. *Physiol. Plant.* **43**, 231.

Lashoff, D. A. (1989). Thermodynamic greenhouse: Feedback processes that may influence future concentrations of greenhouse gases and climate change. *Climate Change* **14**, 213–242.

Lee, E. H., Tingey, D. T., and Hogsett, W. E. (1991). Adjusting ambient ozone air quality indicators for missing values. *In* "1991 Proceedings of the Business and Economic Section, American Statistical Association," pp. 198–203. American Statistical Association, Alexandria, Virginia.

Lee, E. H., Hogsett, W. E., and Tingey, D. T. (1994). Attainment and effects issues regarding the secondary ozone air quality standard. *J. Environ. Qual.* **23**, 1129–1140.

Lewark, S. (1986). The method of X-ray densitometry of wood and its use in studies of effects of air pollution. *Forstarchiv* **57**, 105–107.

Luxmoore, R. J., Begovich, C. L., and Dixon, K. R. (1978). Modelling solute uptake and incorporation into vegetation and litter. *Ecol. Modelling* **5**, 137–171.

Martin, B., and Sutherland, E. K. (1990). Air pollution in the past recorded in width and stable carbon isotope composition of annual growth rings of Douglas-fir. *Plant Cell Environ.* **13**, 839–844.

Martin, B., Bytnerowicz, A., and Thorstenson, Y. R. (1988). Effects of air pollutants on the composition of stable carbon isotopes, $\delta^{13}C$, of leaves and wood, and on leaf injury. *Plant Physiol.* **88**, 218–223.

Matyssek, R., Gunthardt-Goerg, M. S., Saurer, M., and Keller, T. (1992). Seasonal growth, $\delta^{13}C$ in leaves and stem, and phloem structure of birch (*Betula pendula*) under low ozone concentrations. *Trees* **6**, 69–76.

McLaughlin, S. B., McConathy, R. K., Duvick, D., and Mann, L. K. (1982). Effects of chronic air pollution stress on photosynthesis, carbon allocation, and growth of white pine trees. *For. Sci.* **28**, 60–70.

McLaughlin, S. B., Downing, D. J., Blasing, T. J., Cook, E. R., and Adams, H. S. (1987). An analysis of climate and competition as contributors to decline of red spruce in high elevation Appalachian forests of the eastern United States. *Oecologia* **72**, 487–501.

Meisch, H. U., Kessler, M., Reinle, W., and Wagner, A. (1986). Distribution of metals in annual rings of the beech (*Fagus sylvatica*) as an expression of environmental changes. *Experientia* **42**, 537.

Miller, P. R., Taylor, O. C., and Wilhour, R. G. (1982). "Oxidant Air Pollution Effects on a Western Coniferous Forest Ecosystem.", Research Triangle Park, NC. Environmental Research Brief EPA-600/D-82-276. Environmental Protection Agency.

Miller, P. R., McBride, J. R., and Schilling, S. L. (1991). Chronic ozone injury and associated stresses affect relative competitive capacity of species comprising the California mixed conifer forest type. *In* "Memorias del Primer Simposio Nacional. Agricultura Sostenible: Una Opción para el Desarrollo sin Deterioro Ambiental," pp. 161–172. Comisión de Estudios Ambientales C.P. y M.O.A. International, Montecillo, Mexico.

Mousseau, M., and Saugier, B. (1992). The direct effect of increased CO_2 on gas exchange and growth of forest tree species. *J. Exp. Bot.* **43**, 1121–1130.

Norby, R. J., O'Neill, E. G., and Luxmoore, R. J. (1986). Effects of atmospheric CO_2 enrichment on the growth and mineral nutrition of *Quercus alba* seedlings in nutrient-poor soil. *Plant Physiol.* **82,** 83–89.

Norby, R. J., Gunderson, C. A., Wullschleger, S. D., O'Neill, E. G., and McCracken, M. K. (1992). Productivity and compensatory responses of yellow-poplar trees in elevated CO_2. *Nature (London)* **357,** 322–324.

Oechel, W., and Strain, B. R. (1985). Native species responses to increased carbon dioxide concentration. *In* "Direct Effects of Increasing Carbon Dioxide on Vegetation," pp. 117–154. U.S. DOE National Technical Information Service, Springfield, Virginia.

Ohmann, L. F., and Grigal, D. F. (1990). Spatial and temporal patterns of sulfur and nitrogen in wood of trees across the north central United States. *Can. J. For. Res.* **20,** 508–513.

Ohmart, C. P., and Williams, C. B., Jr. (1979). The effects of photochemical oxidants on radial growth increment for five species of conifers in the San Bernardino National Forest. *Plant Dis. Rep.* **63,** 1038–1042.

O'Leary, M. H. (1981). Carbon isotope fractionation in plants. *Phytochemistry* **20,** 553–567.

O'Neill, E. G., Luxmoore, R. J., and Norby, R. J. (1987). Elevated atmospheric CO_2 effects on seedling growth, nutrient uptake, and rhizosphere bacterial populations of *Liriodendron tulipifera*. *Plant Soil* **104,** 3–11.

Oren, R., Schulze, E.-D., Werk, K. S., Meyer, J., Schneider, B. U., and Heilmeier, H. (1988). Performance of two *Picea abies* (L.) Karst. stands at different stages of decline. I. Carbon relations and stand growth. *Oecologia* **75,** 25–37.

Patel, J. D., and Devi, G. S. (1986). Variations of starch, IP and lipid contents in bark and wood of trees growing under air pollution stress of a fertilizer complex. *Phytomorphology* **36,** 73–77.

Pathak, S. N., Love, D. V., and Roy, D. N. (1986). Determination of a chemical basis of air-pollution stress in wood of mature white pine trees in the susceptive forest ecosystems. *Water Air Soil Pollut.* **31,** 385–392.

Pell, E. J., Landry, L. G., Eckardt, N. A., and Glick, R. E. (1994). Air pollution and RubisCO: Effects and implications. *In* "Plant Responses to the Gaseous Environment: Molecular, Metabolic and Physiological Aspects" (R. G. Alscher and A. R. Wellburn, eds.), pp. 239–253. Chapman & Hall, London.

Peterson, D. L. (1994). Recent changes in the growth and establishment of subalpine conifers in western North America. *In* "Mountain Environments in Changing Climates" (M. Bernstan, ed.), pp. 234–243. Routledge, London.

Peterson, D. L., and Arbaugh, M. J. (1988). An evaluation of the effects of ozone injury on radial growth of ponderosa pine (*Pinus ponderosa*) in the southern Sierra Nevada. *J. Air Pollut. Control Assoc.* **38,** 921–927.

Peterson, D. L., Arbaugh, M. J., Wakefield, V. A., and Miller, P. R. (1987). Evidence of growth reduction in ozone-injured Jeffrey pine (*Pinus jeffreyi* Grev. and Balf.) in Sequoia and Kings Canyon National Parks. *J. Air Pollut. Control Assoc.* **37,** 906–912.

Peterson, D. L., Arbaugh, M. J., and Robinson, L. J. (1989). Ozone injury and growth trends of ponderosa pine in the Sierra Nevada. *In* "Effects of Air Pollution on Western Forests" (R. K. Olson and A. S. Lefohn, eds.), APCA Transactions Series 16, pp. 293–307. Air and Waste Management Association, Pittsburgh, PA.

Peterson, D. L., Arbaugh, M. J., and Robinson, L. J. (1991). Regional growth changes in ozone-stressed ponderosa pine (*Pinus ponderosa*) in the Sierra Nevada, California, USA. *Holocene* **1,** 50–61.

Peterson, D. L., Arbaugh, M. J., and Robinson, L. J. (1993). Effects of ozone and climate on ponderosa pine (*Pinus ponderosa*) growth in the Colorado Rocky Mountains. *Can. J. For. Res.* **23,** 1750–1759.

Phipps, R. L., and Whiton, J. C. (1988). Decline in long-term growth trends of white oak. *Can. J. For. Res.* **18,** 24–32.

Pye, J. M. (1988). Impact of ozone on the growth and yield of trees: a review. *J. Environ. Qual.* **17,** 347–360.

Queirolo, F., Valenta, P., Stegen, S., and Breckle, S. W. (1990). Heavy metal concentrations in oak wood growth rings from the Taunus (Federal Republic of Germany) and the Valdivia (Chile) regions. *Trees* **4,** 81–87.

Ray, D. L., and Winstead, J. E. (1991). Increased sulfur deposition in wood of shortleaf pine from the Cumberland Plateau of Kentucky, 1962–1986. *Trans. Kentucky Acad. Sci.* **52,** 97–100.

Reich, P. B. (1987). Quantifying plant response to ozone: a unifying theory. *Tree Physiol.* **3,** 63–91.

Reich, P. B., and Lassoie, J. P. (1985). Influence of low concentrations of ozone on growth, biomass partitioning and leaf senescence in young hybrid poplar. *Environ. Pollut.* **39,** 39–51.

Riitters, K. H., Ohmann, L. F., and Grigal, D. F. (1991). Woody tissue analysis using an element ratio technique (DRIS). *Can. J. For. Res.* **21,** 1270–1277.

Rundel, P. W., Ehleringer, J. R., and Nagy, K. A. (1988). "Stable Isotopes in Ecological Research." Springer-Verlag, New York.

Sachsse, V. H., and Hapla, F. (1986). Changes in the cell wall structure of wood in Norway spruce trees exposed to air pollution. *Forstarchiv* **57,** 12–14.

Schlegel, H., Godbold, D. L., and Huttermann, A. (1987). Whole plant aspects of heavy metal induced changes in CO_2 uptake and water relations of spruce (*Picea abies*) seedlings. *Physiol. Plant.* **69,** 265–270.

Schulze, E.-D., Oren, R., and Lange, O. L. (1989). Processes leading to forest decline: A synthesis. *In* "Ecological Studies" (E.-D. Schulze, O. L. Lange, and R. Oren, eds.), pp. 459–468. Springer-Verlag, Berlin.

Sheffield, R. M., and Cost, N. D. (1987). Behind the decline. *J. For.* **85,** 29–35.

Solomon, A. M. (1986). Transient response of forest to CO_2-induced climate change: Simulation modeling experiments in eastern North America. *Oecologia* **68,** 567–579.

Solomon, A. M., and Bartlein, P. J. (1992). Past and future climate change: Response by mixed deciduous-coniferous forest ecosystems in northern Michigan. *Can. J. For. Res.* **22,** 1727–1738.

Spence, D. R., Rykiel, E. J., Sharpe, J. R., and Sharpe, P. J. H. (1990). Ozone alters carbon allocation in loblolly pine: Assessment with carbon-11 labeling. *Environ. Pollut.* **64,** 93–106.

Symeonides, C. (1979). Tree-ring analysis for tracing the history of pollution: Application to a study in northern Sweden. *J. Environ. Qual.* **8,** 482–486.

Thomas, M. D. (1960). "Air Pollution." Columbia University Press, New York.

Thomas, M. D., and Hendricks, R. H. (1956). Effect of air pollution on plants. In: "Air Pollution Handbook" (P. L. Magill, F. R. Holden, and C. Ackley, eds.). McGraw-Hill, New York.

Thomas, R. B., and Strain, B. R. (1991). Root restriction as a factor in photosynthetic acclimation of cotton seedlings grown in elevated carbon dioxide. *Plant Physiol.* **96,** 627–634.

Unsworth, M. H., and Ormrod, D. P. (1982). "Effects of Gaseous Air Pollution in Agriculture and Horticulture." Butterworth Scientific, London.

Weber, J. A., Tingey, D. T., and Andersen, C. P. (1994). Plant response to air pollution. *In* "Plant-Environment Interactions" (R. E. Wilkinson, ed.), pp. 357–389. Marcel Dekker, New York.

Weinstein, D. A., Beloin, R. M., and Yanai, R. D. (1991). Modeling changes in red spruce carbon balance and allocation in response to interacting ozone and nutrient stresses. *Tree Physiol.* **9,** 127–146.

Weinstein, D. A., and Beloin, R. (1990). Evaluating effects of pollutants on integrated tree processes: A model of carbon, water, and nutrient balances. *In* "Process Modeling of Forest Growth Responses to Environmental Stress" (R. K. Dixon, R. S. Meldahl, G. A. Ruark, and W. G. Warren, eds.), pp. 313–323. Timber Press, Portland Oregon.

Wellburn, A. (1988). "Air Pollution and Acid Rain." Longman Scientific & Technical, Essex, England.

West, D. C., Toyle, T. W., Tharp, M. L., Beauchamp, J. J., Platt, W. J., and Downing, D. J. (1993). Recent growth increases in old growth longleaf pine. *Can. J. For. Res.* **23,** 846–853.

Zahner, R., Saucier, J. R., and Myers, R. K. (1989). Tree-ring model interprets growth decline in natural stands of loblolly pine in the southeastern United States. *Can. J. For. Res.* **19,** 612–621.

16

Chemical Antiherbivore Defense

John P. Bryant and Kenneth F. Raffa

I. Introduction

The normal functioning and survival of woody plants depend on the successful defense of stems against attack by herbivores and pathogens. In this chapter we discuss chemical defense against herbivores.

The stem-eating herbivore guild is taxonomically and functionally diverse. It includes vertebrate herbivores and invertebrate herbivores that range in feeding habit from specialists to obligate generalists. In a brief review such as this it would be impossible to discuss how stems are chemically defended against all of these herbivores. Thus, we have focused on mammals and aggressive bark beetles, because these two groups span the range of herbivore specialization. Moreover, mammals and bark beetles are particularly severe threats to stems, and therefore the chemical defense against them has been well studied in comparison to the chemical defense against other stem-eating herbivores.

II. Mammals

Browsing mammals are obligate generalist herbivores (Freeland and Janzen, 1974; McArthur *et al.*, 1991). In a single day an individual browser usually forages in habitats ranging from dystrophic to eutrophic, and in each habitat chooses to feed or not to feed on woody stems of a variety of species and ecotypes in different stages of ontogenetic development. Furthermore, mammals usually live for at least 1 year; thus the same individual will feed on stems in all stages of phenological development. Each of these foraging decisions will be strongly influenced (if not determined) by stem chemical defenses (Palo and Robbins, 1991; Bryant *et al.*, 1992). Thus, understanding chemically mediated interactions between browsing mammals and woody stems requires knowledge of causes of variation in stem chemical defense, and obtaining this knowledge requires answering three questions: (1) Why have stems of some species and ecotypes evolved better chemical defenses than stems of other species and ecotypes? (2) How does variation in the physical environment and biotic environment in which a woody plant grows affect phenotypic expression of stem chemical defense? (3) What sorts of allelochemicals defend stems against browsing?

A. Evolution of Stem Chemical Defense

At least three factors have influenced the evolution of stem chemical defense; (1) adaptation to resource (mineral nutrients, light, and water) limitation (Bryant *et al.*, 1983; Coley *et al.*, 1985), (2) the plant's stage of ontogenetic development (Bryant *et al.*, 1983, 1992), and (3) historical risk of herbivory (Bryant *et al.*, 1989, 1992, 1994). In the following three sections we briefly discuss each factor.

1. Adaptation to Resource Limitation Woody species characteristic of resource-deficient habitats generally cannot acquire sufficient resources to support rapid growth. The evolutionary response of plants to resource limitation of growth appears to have been a low maximum potential growth rate (Grime, 1977; Chapin, 1980). Low resource-adapted plants also have a limited capacity to acquire resources (Grime, 1977): trees and shrubs characteristic of resource-limited environments generally have low nutrient absorption capacity (Chapin, 1980) and a low photosynthetic rate (Pearcy *et al.*, 1987) in comparison to trees and shrubs typical of productive habitats.

Inherently slow growth and a limited ability to acquire resources restrict the ability of the plant to replace tissues eaten by herbivores (Archer and Tieszen, 1986; Bryant and Chapin, 1986; Whitham *et al.*, 1991). These limitations appear to have favored evolution of defenses that deter herbivory (Bryant *et al.*, 1983; Coley *et al.*, 1985). Moreover, productive habitats are often recently disturbed habitats, because destruction of above-ground biomass by events such as wildfire and insect outbreak opens the canopy and results in release of nutrients previously locked in living plant biomass. Early successional woody species adapted to regrow above-ground parts destroyed by disturbance and capitalize on this pulse of resources resulting from disturbance are preadapted to tolerate browsing. This preadaptation appears to have reduced selection for chemical defense (Bryant *et al.*, 1983). Thus, chemical defense of stems against browsing is expected to increase as the supply of resources declines and disturbance declines (Bryant and Kuropat, 1980; Bryant *et al.*, 1983; Coley *et al.*, 1985).

Studies of foraging by browsing mammals generally support this prediction (Palo and Robbins, 1991; Bryant *et al.*, 1992). From the arctic to the tropics, wild browsing mammals and domestic browsing mammals feed preferentially on stems of rapidly growing species characteristic of productive habitats and avoid eating stems of slowly growing species characteristic of unproductive habitats (Table I). The primary reason slow-growing spe-

Table I   Food Preferences of Browsing Mammals [a]

Ecosystem	High-resource fast grower	Low-resource slow grower	Source
Shrub tundra	(*Salix–Betula* versus *Ledum–Empetrum–Cassiope*)		
Collared lemming	8	2	Batzli and Jung (1980)
Brown lemming	10	0	Batzli and Jung (1980)
Tundra vole	9	Trace	Batzli and Jung (1980)
Ground squirrel	9	1	Batzli and Jung (1980)
Muskoxen	10	0	Robus (1981)
Caribou	10	0	Kuropat (1984)
Reindeer	9	1	Trudell and White (1981)
Willow ptarmigan	10	0	Williams *et al.* (1984)
Rock ptarmigan	10	0	Weeden (1969)
White-tailed ptarmigan	10	0	Weeden (1969)
Boreal forest	(*Salix–Populus–Betula* versus *Ledum–Picea*)		
Snowshoe hare	9	Trace	Bryant (unpublished)
Mountain hare	8	2	Pulliainen (1972)
Moose	10	0	Miquelle (1983)
Tropical rainforest	(pioneer species versus	persistent species)	
Black colobus monkey	8	2	McKey *et al.* (1981)
Red colobus monkey	3	7	Struhsaker (1968)
Subtropical savanna	(fertile soil versus infertile soil)		
Kudu	9	1	Cooper and Owen-Smith (1985)
Impala	9	1	Cooper and Owen-Smith (1985)
Boer goat	7	3	Cooper and Owen-Smith (1985)
Caatinga	(fire-adapted versus shade-tolerant)		
Goat	High preference	Low preference	Pfister (1983)
Sheep	High preference	Low preference	Pfister (1983)

[a]Preference indices comparing high resource-adapted, fast-growing plants and low resource-adapted, slow-growing plants were computed from results of cafeteria feeding trials and field measurements of preference (use/availability ratios) and range from 0 (never eaten) to 10 (always preferred). Plant groups compared are indicated for each biome.

cies are avoided by browsing mammals is their highly effective chemical defense (Palo and Robbins, 1991; Bryant *et al.,* 1991a,b, 1992).

2. Age-Specific Selection for Defense   Throughout the world's forests, woodlands, shrublands, and savannas, browsing by mammals on stems of seedlings and saplings reduces recruitment of woody plants. Examples of mammals that frequently cause significant mortality of tree and shrub recruitment are microtine rodents (Hannson and Zejda, 1977), hares (Aldous and Aldous, 1944; Sullivan and Sullivan, 1982; Bergeron and Tardiff, 1988), beaver (Johnson and Naiman, 1990), deer (Beals *et al.,* 1960), moose (Bergerud and Manuel, 1968; Bedard *et al.,* 1978; McInnes *et al.,* 1992), and African elephant (Laws *et al.,* 1975). This browsing-caused mortality occurs in pristine ecosystems, and therefore browsing by mammals has likely been a threat to survival of juvenile woody plants throughout their evolution (Bryant *et al.,* 1992).

Juvenile woody plants appear to have responded evolutionarily to browsing by increased physical and chemical defense of stems. Stems of thorny or spinescent woody plants are usually most thorny or most spinescent in the juvenile stage of development (Kozlowski, 1971), and thorns and spines defend woody stems against browsing by mammals (Cooper and Owen-Smith, 1986). Similarly, stems of the juvenile stage are often more defended chemically against browsing than are stems of the conspecific mature stage (Bryant *et al.,* 1983, 1991a,c, 1992).

An excellent example of enhanced chemical defense of juvenile-stage stems against browsing is provided by hares in boreal forests. In every case that has been studied chemically, stems of the juvenile stage have been found to be less palatable to hares than stems of the conspecific mature stage, because epidermis and bark of the juvenile stage contain higher concentrations of feeding deterrent allelochemicals than does bark of the conspecific mature stage (Table II). For example, the stem of juvenile Alaska paper birch (*Betula resinifera*) is defended against winter browsing by snowshoe hares by terpenes, such as papyriferic acid (Reichardt, 1981), that are not even found in stems of mature Alaska paper birch (Reichardt *et al.,* 1984).

3. Browsing History   Biogeographical studies have demonstrated that stem chemical defenses of juvenile woody plants vary along latitudinal and longitudinal gradients (Bryant *et al.,* 1989, 1994; Rousi *et al.,* 1991; Swihart *et al.,* 1994). Although the evolutionary basis for this biogeographic variation in stem defense is relatively unexplored, it appears to relate to browsing by mammals. Stems of juvenile woody plants from regions with a history of intense browsing by mammals have more effective chemical defenses against browsing by mammals than do stems of juvenile woody plants from

Table II Comparative Palatabilities to the Snowshoe hare of the Juvenile Phase and Mature Phase of Boreal Trees in Winter and Identified Chemical Defenses[a] of the Juvenile Phase[b]

Species	Comparative palatability	Defense[a]	Palatability Ref.
Betulaceae			
Alnus crispa	4	PSI, PME	Clausen *et al.* (1986)
Betula pendula	15	PA	Bryant *et al.* (1989)
B. resinifera	18	PA	Reichardt *et al.* (1984)
Pinaceae			
Picea glauca	6	CA	Sinclair *et al.* (1988)
P. mariana	2	TR	Bryant (unpublished data)
Salicaceae			
Populus balsamifera	50	SA, 6-HCH	Reichardt *et al.* (1990a)
P. balsamifera	75	2,4,6-THDC	Jogia *et al.* (1989)
Salix caprea	5	PG	Tahvanainen *et al.* (1985)
S. nigricans	8	PG	Tahvanainen *et al.* (1985)
S. pentandra	9	PG	Tahvanainen *et al.* (1985)
S. phyllicifolia	5	PG	Tahvanainen *et al.* (1985)

[a]Chemical defenses: PSI, pinosylvin; PME, pinosylvin methyl ether; PA, papyriferic acid; GA, greenic acid; CA, camphor; SA, salicaldehyde; 6-HCH, 6-hydroxycyclohexenone; 2,4,6-THDC, 2,4,6-trihydroxydihydrochalcone; PG, phenolic glycosides; TR, terpene resin.

[b]Comparative palatabilities are the ratio of mature-stage biomass eaten/juvenile-stage biomass eaten.

regions with a history of less intense browsing (Bryant *et al.*, 1989, 1992, 1994; Swihart *et al.*, 1994).

B. Phenotypic Expression of Defense against Mammals

1. Effects of Resource Limitation   Chapin (1991) has suggested that all plants adjust physiologically to low resource supply in basically the same way: through a decline in growth rate and by adjusting their rate of resource acquisition. This stress response is hormonally regulated but also involves integrated changes in plant carbon–nutrient balance (CNB), and changes in this balance affect allocation of resources by plants to secondary metabolism (Bryant *et al.*, 1983; Waterman and Mole, 1989). When growth is more nutrient than carbon limited, carbohydrate often accumulates in excess of growth demands (Chapin, 1980), with the result that synthesis of secondary metabolites such as phenolics that contain no nitrogen is facilitated. By contrast, when growth is carbon limited, as occurs in deep shade, carbohydrate concentrations decline, and synthesis of secondary metabolites that contain no nitrogen becomes substrate limited. In a survey of the literature Reichardt *et al.* (1991) found the CNB hypothesis correctly predicted the responses of woody plant secondary metabolism to nitrogen supply and shade about 80% of the time.

2. Effects of Growth and Differentiation   Growth per se results in competition for resources between chemical defense and other plant functions (Lorio and Sommers, 1986; Herms and Mattson, 1992), and this competition affects stem chemical defense throughout the life cycle of a woody plant. For example, stems of seedlings of species that reproduce by small seeds are often less defended against browsing than are stems of saplings, because shortly after germination growth demands for carbon are exceptionally high (Bryant and Julkunen-Tiitto, 1994). As woody plants increase in size and architectural complexity their growth becomes more nutrient than carbon limited (Moorby and Waring, 1963). As a result, defense of stems by substances such as phenolics and terpenes is less costly, and therefore production of these substances often increases (Bryant *et al.*, 1991c). However, with the onset of flowering, defense often declines as a result of the resource demands of flowering (Bazzaz *et al.*, 1987).

Stem chemical defense also changes during the annual cycle of growth, with low levels of defense coinciding with periods of rapid growth. Presumably this seasonal decrease in defense is caused by increased competition for resources between growth and defense in periods of rapid growth (Lorio and Sommers, 1986; Herms and Mattson, 1992). An example of this phenological variation in defense of stems against browsing is provided by balsam poplar (*Populus balsamifera*) saplings (Reichardt *et al.*, 1990b). Two secondary metabolites, salicaldehyde and 6-hydroxycyclohexenone (6-HCH), defend stems of juvenile balsam poplar against browsing by mammals. Concentrations of these substances are lower in the growing season than in the dormant season.

3. Responses to Herbivory   Herbivory per se can affect the phenotypic expression of chemical defense (Tallamy and Raup, 1991). In the case of woody stems and mammals, severe browsing of a mature plant causes a reversion to the juvenile stage (Bryant, 1981; Bryant *et al.*, 1983, 1991c). From the perspective of browsing mammals, a juvenile reversion results in an increased defense of stems in the next year. However, this increase is not the result of an "inducible defense" *sensu* Haukioja (1980). It is the result of the constitutive defenses of the juvenile stage being more effective than constitutive defenses of the mature stage (Bryant *et al.*, 1983, 1991c).

By contrast, severe browsing of juvenile woody plant results in a carbon stress that reduces the constitutive defense (Bryant *et al.*, 1983; Chapin *et al.*, 1985). Thus, when browsing overwhelms the constitutive chemical defenses of the juvenile stage, it can initiate a feedback that results in progressively more severe browsing, which in turn results in death of the plant (Bryant *et al.*, 1983).

C. Chemistry of Stem Defense against Browsing

Until about a decade ago, knowledge of chemical defenses against browsing was generally limited to an understanding that concentrations of general classes of secondary metabolites (e.g., terpenes, phenolics, and alkaloids) were often inversely correlated with the use of woody plants by browsing mammals (Bryant and Kuropat, 1980; Van Soest, 1982; Robbins, 1983). During the past decade this view has changed because growing evidence indicates that individual allelochemicals mediate plant–mammal interactions (Bryant *et al.*, 1991a,b, 1992).

An example of the chemical specificity characteristic of interactions between secondary metabolites and woody stems is provided by woody plants and snowshoe hares (*Lepus americanus*) in boreal forests. Individual monoterpenes (Sinclair *et al.*, 1988; Reichardt *et al.*, 1990b), triterpenes (Reichardt, 1981; Reichardt *et al.*, 1984), phenols (Clausen *et al.*, 1986; Jogia *et al.*, 1989), and substances with obscure biosynthetic origins (Reichardt *et al.*, 1990a) deter feeding by snowshoe hares. Moreover, phytochemicals belonging to similar biosynthetic classes do not necessarily have similar effects on hares. For example, pinosylvin is a strong feeding deterrent, pinosylvin methyl ether is effective but less potent, and pinosylvin dimethyl ether is virtually inactive (Clausen *et al.*, 1986).

Chemical defenses against mammals have been classified as being based on either toxins or generalized digestion inhibitors, although overlap between the categories has been recognized (Feeny, 1976; Rhoades and Cates, 1976). Although digestion inhibition has been traditionally considered the most important mode of chemical defense against mammals (Van Soest, 1982; Robbins, 1983), this view is changing (Provenza *et al.*, 1990; Meyer and Karazov, 1991; Palo and Robbins, 1991; Bryant *et al.*, 1991b) because studies of wild mammals and domestic mammals fed unpalatable woody browse normally available to them, or extracts of this browse, suggest toxicity is closely associated with feeding deterrence. For example, snowshoe hares (Reichardt *et al.*, 1984), bushy tailed woodrats (Neotoma lepida) (Meyer and Karazov, 1989, 1991), microtine rodents (Batzli, 1983), mule deer (Odecoileus hemionus) (Schwartz *et al.*, 1980a,b), and moose (Alces alces) (Schwartz *et al.*, 1981) all voluntarily reduce food intake to well below maintenance levels when fed woody browse containing high concentrations of feeding-deterrent allelochemicals, or artificial diets treated with these substances. Reduced voluntary intake by a mammalian herbivore indicates toxicity rather than digestion inhibition (McArthur *et al.*, 1991).

III. Bark Beetles

Aggressive bark beetles capable of killing living hosts are comparatively specialized herbivores, having few hosts within a single genus (Raffa *et al.*, 1993). Furthermore, aggressive beetle species are intimately associated with pathogenic fungi that aid the beetle in overcoming the defenses of the host (Raffa and Klepzig, 1992; Harrington, 1993). Thus, the challenge of understanding how woody stems are defended chemically against specialist herbivores such as bark beetles lies in understanding how constitutive chemical defenses and inducible chemical defenses of an individual plant interact to prevent successful colonization by the beetle and pathogens it vectors (Raffa, 1991).

A. Constitutive Defense

Constitutive chemical defenses located in the bark and phloem are the first line of defense of the host tree against attack by aggressive bark beetles (Nebeker *et al.*, 1992). Aggressive beetle species use visual and possibly chemical clues to land on potential hosts (Rhoades, 1990) and determine host suitability on close inspection. On landing, chemical signals perceived either by olfaction, physical contact, or biting are used to determine whether to enter the tree (Elkinton and Wood, 1981). Most beetles are deterred at this stage (Wood, 1982) by chemically unidentified feeding repellents in the bark. However, if beetles continue their attack, an interaction among at least three sets of phytochemicals located in the phloem determines whether they excavate deeply into phloem: one set incites feeding, one set stimulates sustained feeding, and one set deters feeding. If the host is vigorous, the repellent fraction deters deep penetration into the phloem (Raffa and Berryman, 1982a).

Several species of pine (Pinus) use a further and particularly effective constitutive defense to deter pioneering beetles: oleoresin. During excavation of the phloem, beetles sever resin ducts. If the host is vigorous, resin flows rapidly into the wounds, physically impeding further excavation by most beetles. Equally importantly, resin accumulation can limit the pheromonal communication pioneering beetles use to incite a mass attack on the tree, and delay the progress of pioneer beetles until induced defenses are activated (Raffa and Berryman, 1983a). Duct resins also contain monoterpenes toxic to a wide variety of insects and microorganisms (Brattsten, 1983). These chemicals are also toxic to bark beetles and their fungal associates, but not at concentrations usually found in constitutive resins of healthy hosts (Smith, 1963, 1965).

B. Induced Defense

Although constitutive defenses effectively terminate many beetle attacks, induced defenses are an essential component of stem defense against bark beetles, because these defenses can kill both pioneering beetles and the pathogenic fungi beetles vector (Raffa, 1991).

Chemicals produced by symbiotic fungi vectored by beetles are suspected to be the primary elicitors of the induced response (Shrimpton, 1973a,b; Raffa and Berryman, 1982b, 1983b; Cook and Hain, 1986; Paine and Stephen, 1987). These elicitors include fungal cell wall fragments and products of active fungal metabolism such as proteinase inhibitor inducing factors (Miller *et al.*, 1986; Lieutier and Berryman, 1988) that initiate a cascade of histological and chemical changes in tissues being excavated by beetles.

The first stage of the response is an almost immediate increase in monoterpene cyclase activity, particularly among genera such as Abies and Picea with low constitutive defenses against bark beetles (Lewinsohn *et al.*, 1991). Subsequently, an elliptical necrotic lesion forms in advance of the insect–fungal complex (Reid *et al.*, 1967). Resin then floods the beetle gallery, confining the beetle–fungi complex within the reaction zone, with the result that the attack is usually contained. After containment, wound periderm forms. This tissue protects adjacent healthy tissue from damage by defensive substances (Lieutier and Berryman, 1988). Then the wound area completely heals as new tissue is laid down over the next several years.

Chemicals that accumulate during defensive reactions are largely responsible for the failure of beetles and associated fungi to become established. No one group of secondary metabolites dominates induced defenses. Terpenoids such as mono- and sesquiterpenes, oxygenated terpenes, resin acids, and phenolics are involved (Shrimpton, 1973a,b; Raffa and Berryman, 1982b).

The best understood group of allelochemicals involved in the induced response is the monoterpenes (Raffa, 1991). Total monoterpene content within the reaction zone increases exponentially in the early stages of the response (Raffa and Berryman, 1982b; Cook and Hain, 1986; Paine *et al.*, 1987; Raffa, 1991). Additionally, qualitative changes in the monoterpene composition of resin occur (Shrimpton, 1973a,b). An example of this response is provided by grand fir (Abies grandis) (Table III; Raffa and Berryman, 1982b). The constitutive defense of *A. grandis* is primarily composed of two monoterepenes, α-pinene and β-pinene. Elicitation of the induced response results the total quantity of defensive resin exponentially increasing to about four times the total quantity found before induction. Moreover, after induction, resin contains large amounts of several new monoterpenes such as myrcene, sabinene, *d*-3-carene, and limonene that are

Table III Compositional Changes of Volatiles from Grand Fir (*Abies grandis*) Wound Reactions 14 Days after Inoculation with *Trichosporium symbioticum* or Mechanical Injury [a]

Volatile	Uninjured phloem	Days after: Inoculated [b]	Days after: Mechanical wound [b]
Tricyclene	1.39	1.00	0.76
α-Pinene	48.14	26.68***	45.00
Camphene	1.22	0.32***	1.48
Unknown 1	0	0	0.02
β-Pinene	42.01	23.73***	33.88
Myrcene	4.45	22.54***	9.27
Sabinene	2.20	7.62**	2.96
3-Carene	0.30	8.82***	3.14*
Unknown 5	0	1.82*	0.56
Limonene	0.23	2.99**	1.06
β-Phellandrene	0.01	1.66**	0.56
Terpinolene	0.17	1.46**	0.60

[a]Values in percentage of total monoterpenes. Levels of significance indicate difference from uninjured phloem. (Data from Raffa and Berryman, 1982b.)

[b]*$p < 0.05$; **$p < 0.01$; ***$p < 0.001$.

particularly toxic to the beetle and its fungal symbionts. Thus, if the tree is healthy, induced chemical defenses usually kill both beetles and the pathogenic fungi beetles vector to the tree. However, under conditions stressful for the host, beetles can colonize and kill otherwise healthy hosts.

C. Mass Attack and Host Stress

Successful colonization of a healthy host depends on pioneering beetles eliciting a mass attack that overwhelms the constitutive and inducible defenses of the host (Raffa and Berryman, 1983a). Mass attacks are elicited by pheromones produced by either direct bioconversion of an acquired host compound or from precursors with structurally dissimilar carbon skeletons (Byers, 1981; Wood, 1982; Borden *et al.,* 1986). Microbial associates of beetles also produce beetle pheromones, but their significance under natural conditions is unclear. Irrespective of the source of the aggregation pheromones, the success of a mass attack depends on a rapid response by a sufficient number of beetles to allow the beetle–fungi complex to overwhelm the defenses of the host.

The success of a mass attack also depends on the vigor of the host, because pioneering beetles rarely survive the defenses of a healthy host long enough to initiate a mass attack (Safranyik *et al.,* 1975). Thus, stresses that reduce host vigor play a central role in successful beetle attacks. These stresses include physical stresses such as drought and mechanical damage, biotic stresses such as disease and insect defoliation, and competition with other plants (Lorio and Hodges, 1968; Wright *et al.*, 1979, 1984; Raffa and Berryman, 1982c; Waring and Pitman, 1983; Miller *et al.*, 1986; Paine and Stephen, 1987; Dunn and Lorio, 1992; Nebeker *et al.*, 1993). The common denominator of reduced host vigor appears to be carbon stress (Waring and Pitman, 1983). Breakdown of defenses under conditions of carbon stress is not surprising given the high carbon cost of producing chemical defenses such as the terpenes (Gershenzon, 1994) that characterize both constitutive and inducible defenses against aggressive beetle species (Raffa, 1991).

The importance of this proposed relationship among carbon stress, the cost of defense, and the density of attacking beetles is that it indicates that a threshold of resistance is central to the beetle reproductive rate that leads to beetle outbreaks (Berryman, 1982). Below this threshold, the host constitutive and inducible defenses repel attack, thereby keeping beetle populations in check. Above this numerical threshold, colonizing beetles can reproduce, and subsequent generations have the higher densities needed to mount the mass attacks against healthy trees that initiate an outbreak.

IV. Conclusions

Woody plant stems are challenged by a diversity of herbivores that range from generalists such as browsing mammals to comparative specialists such as bark beetles. Chemical defenses stems employ against these broad classes of herbivores differ in certain respects, and share certain similarities. Perhaps the most significant difference is the importance of constitutive defense versus inducible defense. In the case of mammals, inducible defense *sensu* Haukioja (1980) appears to be uncommon. By contrast, in the case of bark beetles, inducible defense is critically important.

The most important similarity in chemical defense against mammals and bark beetles is the impact carbon stress has on the effectiveness of chemical defense. In both the case of the constitutive defenses employed against mammals and the inducible defenses used against bark beetles, carbon stress reduces defense. Thus, we suggest that research leading to a better understanding of the physiological regulation of carbon allocation among chemical defense and competing plant functions under conditions of stress will be rewarding and of practical value.

References

Aldous, C. M., and Aldous, S. E. (1944). The snowshoe hare—a serious enemy of forest plantations. *J. For.* **42,** 88–94.

Archer, S. R., and Tieszen, L. L. (1986). Plant responses to defoliation: Hierarchical considera-tions. *In* "Grazing Research at Northern Latitudes" (B. Gudmundson, ed.), pp. 45–59. Ple-num Press, New York.

Batzli, G. O. (1983). Responses of arctic rodent populations to nutritional factors. *Oikos* **40,** 396–406.

Batzli, G. O., and Jung, H. G. (1980). Nutritional ecology of microtine rodents: Resource utili-zation near Atkasook, Alaska. *Arc. Alp. Res.* **12,** 483–499.

Bazzaz, F. A., Chiariello, N. R., Coley, P. D., and Pitelka, L. F. (1987). Allocating resources to reproduction and defense. *BioScience* **37,** 58–67.

Beals, E. W., Cottam, G. W., and Vogal, R. J. (1960). Influence of deer on vegetation of the Apostle Islands, Wisconsin. *J. Wildl. Manage.* **24,** 68–79.

Bedard, J., Crete, M., and Audy, E. (1978). Short-term influence of moose upon woody plants of an early searal wintering site in Gaspe Peninsula, Quebec. *Can. J. For. Res.* **8,** 407–415.

Bergeron, J. M., and Tardiff, J. (1988). Winter browsing preferences of snowshoe hares for coniferous seedlings and its implication in large-scale reforestation programs. *Can. J. For. Res.* **18,** 280–282.

Bergerud, A. T., and Manuel, F. (1968). Moose damage to balsam fir-white birch forests in central Newfoundland. *J. Wildl. Manage.* **32,** 729–46.

Berryman, A. A. (1982). Population dynamics of bark beetles. In "Bark Beetles in North Ameri-can Conifers" (J. B. Mitton and K. B. Stugen, eds.), pp. 264–314. University of Texas Press, Austin, Texas.

Borden, J. H., Hunt, D. W. A., Miller, D. R., and Slessor, K. N. (1986). Orientation in forest Coleoptera: An uncertain outcome to responses by individual beetles to variable stimuli. *In* "Mechanisms in Insect Olefaction" (T. L. Payne, M. C. Birch, and C. E. J. Kennedy, eds.), pp. 97–109. Oxford University Press, Oxford.

Brattsten, L. B. (1983). Cytochrome P-450 involvement in the interactions between plant ter-penes and insect herbivores. *In* "Plant Resistance to Insects" (P. A. Hedin, ed.), pp. 173–198. American Chemical Society, Washington, D.C.

Bryant, J. P. (1981). Phytochemical deterrence of snowshoe hare browsing by adventitious shoots of four Alaskan trees. *Science* **313,** 889–890.

Bryant, J. P., and Chapin, F. S., III (1986). Browsing-woody plant interactions during boreal forest succession. *In* "Ecosystems in the Alaskan Taiga" (K. VanCleve, F. S. Chapin, III, P. W. Flanagan, L. A. Viereck, and C. T. Dryness, eds.), pp. 2143–2225, Springer-Verlag, New York.

Bryant, J. P., and Julkunen-Tiitto, R. (1995). Ontogeny of plant defense systems. *J. Chem. Ecol.* (in press).

Bryant, J. P., and Kuropat, P. J. (1980). Selection of winter forage by subarctic browsing verte-brates: The role of plant chemistry. *Annu. Rev. Ecol. Syst.* **11,** 261–285.

Bryant, J. P., Chapin, F. S., III, and Klein, D. R. (1983). Carbon/nutrient balance of boreal plants in relation to vertebrate herbivory. *Oikos* **40,** 357–368.

Bryant, J. P., Tahvanainen, J., Sulkinoja, M., Julkunen-Tiitto, R., Reichardt, P. B., and Green, T. (1989). Biogeographic evidence for the evolution of chemical defense by boreal birch and willow against mammalian browsing. *Am. Nat.* **134,** 20–34.

Bryant, J. P., Kuropat, P. J., Reichardt, P. B., and Clausen, T. P. (1991a). Controls over allocation of resources by woody plants to chemical antiherbivore defense. *In* "Plant Defenses against Mammalian Herbivory" (R. T. Palo and C. T. Robbins, eds.), pp. 83–102. CRC Press, Boca Raton, Florida.

Bryant, J. P., Provenza, F. D., Pastor, J., Reichardt, P. B., Clausen, T. P., and du Toit, J. T. (1991b). Interactions between woody plants and browsing mammals mediated by secondary metabo-lites. *Annu. Rev. Ecol. Syst.* **22,** 431–446.

Bryant, J. P., Danell, K., Provenza, F., Reichardt, P. B., Clausen, T. P., and Werner, R. A. (1991c). Effects of mammal browsing on the chemistry of deciduous woody plants. *In* "Phytochemical Induction by Herbivores" (D. W. Tallamy and M. J. Raup, eds.), pp. 135–154. John Wiley & Sons, New York.

Bryant, J. P., Reichardt, P. B., Clausen, T. P., Provenza, F. D., and Kuropat, P. J. (1992). Woody plant-mammal interactions. *In* "Herbivores: Their Interactions with Secondary Plant Metabolites" (G. A. Rosenthal and M. R. Berenbaum, eds.), Vol. II, 2nd Ed., pp. 343–370. Academic Press, New York.

Bryant, J. P., Swihart, R. K., Reichardt, P. B., and Newton, L. (1994). Biogeography of woody plant chemical defense against snowshoe hare browsing: Comparison of Alaska and eastern North America. *Oikos* **70**, 385–395.

Byers, J. A. (1981). Pheromone biosynthesis in the bark beetle *Ips paraconfusus* during exposure to vapors of host plant precursors. *Insect Biochem.* **11**, 563–569.

Chapin, F. S., III (1980). The mineral nutrition of wild plants. *Annu. Rev. Ecol. Syst.* **11**, 233–260.

Chapin, F. S., III (1991). Integrated responses of plants to stress: A centralized system of physiological responses. *BioScience* **41**, 29–36.

Chapin, F. S., III, Bryant, J. P., and Fox, J. F. (1985). Lack of induced chemical defense in juvenile Alaskan woody plants in response to simulated browsing. *Oecologia (Berlin)* **67**, 457–459.

Clausen, T. P., Bryant, J. P., and Reichardt, P. B. (1986). Defense of winter-dormant green alder against snowshoe hares. *J. Chem. Ecol.* **12**, 2117–2131.

Coley, P. D., Bryant, J. P., and Chapin, F. S., III (1985). Resource availability and plant antiherbivore defense. *Science* **230**, 895–899.

Cook, S. P., and Hain, F. P. (1986). Defensive mechanisms of loblolly and shortleaf pine against attack by southern pine beetle, *Dendroctonus frontalis* Zimmermann (Coleoptera: Scolytidae) and its fungal associate, *Ceratocystis minor* (Hedgecock) Hunt. *J. Chem. Ecol.* **12**, 1397–1406.

Cooper, S. M., and Owen-Smith, N. (1985). Condensed tannins deter feeding by browsing ruminants in a South African savanna. *Oecologia (Berlin)* **67**, 142–146.

Cooper, S. M., and Owen-Smith, N. (1986). Effects of spinescence on large mammalian herbivores. *Oecologia (Berlin)* **68**, 446–445.

Dunn, J. P., and Lorio, P. L. (1992). Effects of bark girdling on carbohydrate supply and resistance of loblolly pine to southern pine beetle (*Dendroctonous frontalis* Zimm.) attack. *For. Ecol. Manage.* **50**, 317–330.

Elkinton, J. W., and Wood, D. L. (1981). Feeding and boring behavior of the bark beetle, *Ips paraconfusus,* in extracts of ponderosa pine phloem. *J. Chem. Ecol.* **7**, 209–220.

Feeny, P. (1976). Plant apparency and chemical defense. *In* "Biochemical Interactions between Plants and Insects" (J. W. Wallace and R. L. Mansell, eds.), pp. 168–123. Plenum Press, New York.

Freeland, W. J., and Janzen, D. H. (1974). Strategies in herbivory by mammals: The role of plant secondary compounds. *Am. Nat.* **108**, 269–289.

Gershenzon, J. (1994). Metabolic costs of terpenoid accumulation in higher plants. *J. Chem. Ecol.* **20**, 1281–1238.

Grime, J. P. (1977). Evidence for the existence of three primary strategies in plants and its relevance to ecological and evolutionary theory. *Am. Nat.* **111**, 169–1194.

Hannson, L., and Zejda, J. (1977). Plant damage by bank voles (*Clethrionomys glareolus* (Schreber)) and related species in Europe. *Bull. Org. Eur. Mediterr. Prot. Plant.* **7**, 233–242.

Harrington, T. T. C. (1993). Biology and taxonomy of fungi associated with bark beetles. *In* "Beetle-Pathogen Interactions in Conifer Forests" (T. D. Schowalter and G. M. Filip, eds.), pp. 37–58. Academic Press. New York.

Haukioja, E. (1980). On the role of plant defenses in the fluctuations of herbivore populations. *Oikos* **35**, 202–213.

Herms, D. A., and Mattson, W. J. (1992). The dilemma of plants: To grow or defend. *Q. Rev. Biol.* **7**, 283–334.

Jogia, M. K., Sinclair, A. R. E., and Anderson, R. J. (1989). An antifeedent in balsam poplar inhibits browsing by snowshoe hares. *Oecologia (Berlin)* **79**, 189–192.

Johnson, C. A., and Naiman, R. J. (1990). Browse selection by beaver: Effects of riparian forest composition. *Can. J. For. Res.* **20**, 1036–1043.

Kozlowski, T. T. (1971). "Growth and Development of Trees," Vol. 1. Academic Press, New York.

Kuropat, P. J. (1984). Foraging Behavior of Caribou on a Calving ground in Northwestern Alaska. MSc. thesis, University of Alaska, Fairbanks, Alaska.

Laws, R. M., Parker, I. S., and Johnstone, R. C. B. (1975). "Elephants and Their Habits." Clarendon Press, Oxford.

Lewinsohn, E. M., Gitzen, M., and Croteau, R. (1991). Defense mechanisms of conifers. *Physiol. Plant. Pathol.* **96**, 38—43.

Lieutier, F., and Berryman, A. A. (1988). Elicitation and defensive reactions in conifers. *In* "Mechanisms of Woody Plant Defenses against Insects" (W. J. Mattson, J. Levieux, and C. Bernard-Dagen, eds.), pp. 313–320. Springer-Verlag, New York.

Lorio, P. L., and Hodges, J. D. (1968). Microsite effects on oleoresin pressure of large loblolly pines. *Ecology* **49**, 1207–1210.

Lorio, P. L., Jr., and Sommers, R. A. (1986). Evidence for competition for photosynthates between growth processes and oleoresion synthesis in *Pinus taeda* L. *Tree Physiol.* **2**, 301–306.

McArthur, C., Hagerman, A., and Robbins, C. T. (1991). Physiological strategies of mammalian herbivores against plant defenses. *In* "Plant Defenses against Mammalian Herbivory" (R. T. Palo and C. T. Robbins, eds.), pp. 103–114. CRC Press, Boca Raton, Florida.

McInnes, P. F., Naiman, R. J., Pastor, J., and Cohen, Y. (1992). Effects of moose browsing on vegetation and litterfall of the boreal forests of Isle Royale, Michigan, U.S.A. *Ecology* **73**, 2059–2075.

McKey, D. B., Gartlan, J. S., Waterman, P. G., and Choo, G. M. (1981). Food selection by black colobus monkeys (*Colobus satanus*) in relation to plant chemistry. *Biol. J. Linn. Soc.* **16**, 115–146.

Meyer, M., and Karasov, W. H. (1989). Antiherbivore chemistry of *Larrea tridentata:* Effects on woodrat (*Neotoma lepida*) feeding and nutrition. *Ecology* **70**, 953–961.

Meyer, M., and Karasov, W. H. (1991). Chemical aspects of herbivory in arid and semiarid habitats. *In* "Plant Defenses against Mammalian Herbivory" (R. T. Palo and C. T. Robbins, eds.), pp. 167–188. CRC Press, Boca Raton, Florida.

Miller, R. A., Berryman, A. A., and Ryan, C. A. (1986). Biotic elicitors of defense reactions in lodgepole pine. *Phytochemistry* **25**, 611–612.

Miquelle, D. G. (1983). Browse regrowth and consumption following summer defoliation by moose. *J. Wildl. Manage.* **47**, 17–24.

Moorby, J., and Waring, P. F. (1963). Aging in woody plants. *Ann. Bot. (N.S.)* **106**, 291–309.

Nebeker, T. E., Hodges, J. D., Blanche, C. A., Honea, C. R., and Tisdale, R. A. (1992). Variation in the constitutive defensive system of loblolly pine in relation to bark beetle attack. *For. Sci.* **38**, 457–466.

Nebeker, T. E., Hodges, J. D., and Blanche, C. A. (1993). Host response to bark beetle and pathogen colonization. *In* "Beetle-Pathogen Interactions" (T. D. Schowalter and G. M. Filip, eds.), pp 157–178. Academic Press, New York.

Paine, T. D., and Stephen, F. M. (1987). Influence of tree stresses and site quality on the induced defensive system of loblolly pine. *Can. J. For. Res.* **17**, 569–571.

Paine, T. D., Blanche, C. A., Nebeker, T. E., and Stephen, F. M. (1987). Composition of loblolly pine resin defenses: Comparison of monoterepenes from induced defensive system of loblolly pine. *Can. J. For. Res.* **17**, 1202–1206.

Palo, R. T., and Robbins, C. T. (1991). "Plant Defenses against Mammalian Herbivory." CRC Press, Boca Raton, Florida.

Pearcy, R. W., Bjorkman, O., Caldwell, M. M., Keeley, J. E., Monson, R. K., and Strain, B. R. (1987). Carbon gain by plants in natural environments. *BioScience* **37**, 21–29.

Pfister, J. A. (1983). Nutrition and feeding behavior of goats and sheep grazing deciduous shrub-woodland in northeastern Brazil. Ph.D. dissertation. Utah State University, Logan, Utah.

Provenza, F. D., Burrit, E. A., Clausen, T. P., Bryant, J. P., Reichardt, P. B., and Distel, R. A. (1990). Conditioned flavor aversion: A mechanism for goats to avoid condensed tannins in blackbrush. *Am. Nat.* **136**, 810–838.

Pulliainen, E. (1972). Nutrition of mountain hare (*Lepus timidus*) in northeastern Lapland. *Ann. Zool. Fenn.* **9**, 17–22.

Raffa, K. F. (1991). Induced defensive reactions in conifer-bark beetle systems. *In* "Phytochemical Induction by Herbivores" (D. W. Tallamy and M. J. Raup, eds.), pp. 245–276. John Wiley & Sons, New York.

Raffa, K. F., and Berryman, A. A. (1982a). Gustatory cues in the orientation of *Dendroctonus ponderosae* (Coleoptera: Scolytidae) to host trees. *Can. Entomol.* **114**, 97–103.

Raffa, K. F., and Berryman, A. A. (1982b). Accumulation of monoterpenes and associated volatiles following fungal inoculation of grand fir with a fungus transmitted by the fir engraver *Scolytus ventralis* (Coleoptera: Scolytidae). *Can. Entomol.* **114**, 797–810.

Raffa, K. F., and Berryman, A. A. (1982c). Physiological differences between lodgepole pines resistant and susceptible to the mountain pine beetle and associated microorganisms. *Environ. Entomol.* **11**, 486–492.

Raffa, K. F., and Berryman, A. A. (1983a). The role of host plant resistance in the colonization behavior and ecology of bark beetles. *Ecol. Monogr.* **53**, 27–49.

Raffa, K. F., and Berryman, A. A. (1983b). Physiological aspects of lodgepole pine wound responses to a fungal symbiont of the mountain pine beetle. *Can. Entomol.* **115**, 723–724.

Raffa, K. F., and Klepzig, K. D. (1992). Tree defense mechanisms against fungi associated with insects. *In* "Defense Mechanisms of Woody Plants against Fungi" (R. A. Blanchette and A. R. Biggs, eds.), pp. 354–389. Springer-Verlag, New York.

Raffa, K. F., Philips, T. W., and Salom, S. M. (1993). Strategies and mechanisms of host colonization by bark beetles. *In* "Beetle-Pathogen Interactions in Conifer Forests," pp. 103–128. Academic Press, New York.

Reichardt, P. B. (1981). Papyriferic acid: A triterpenoid from Alaskan paper birch. *J. Org. Chem.* **46**, 1576–1578.

Reichardt, P. B., Bryant, J. P., Clausen, T. P., and Wieland, G. (1984). Defense of winter-dormant Alaska paper birch against Snowshoe hare. *Oecologia (Berlin)* **65**, 58–59.

Reichardt, P. B., Bryant, J. P., Anderson, B. J., and Clausen, T. P. (1990a). Germacrone defends Labrador tea from browsing by snowshoe hares. *J. Chem. Ecol.* **16**, 1961–1970.

Reichardt, P. B., Bryant, J. P., Mattes, B. R., Clausen, T. P., and Myer, M. (1990b). The winter chemical defense of balsam poplar against snowshoe hares. *J. Chem. Ecol.* **16**, 1941–1960.

Reichardt, P. B., Chapin, F. S., III, Bryant, J. P., Mattes, B. R., and Clausen, T. P. (1991). Carbon/nutrient balance does not fully explain patterns of plant defense in Alaskan balsam poplar. *Oecologia (Berlin)* **16**, 1941–1959.

Reid, R. W., Whitney, H. S., and Watson, J. A. (1967). Reactions of lodgepole pine to attack by *Dendroctonus ponderosae* Hopkins and blue stain fungi. *Can. J. Bot.* **49**, 349–351.

Rhoades, D. F. (1990). Analysis of monoterpenes emitted and absorbed by undamaged boles of lodgepole pine trees, *Pinus contorta murrayana*. *Phytochemistry* **29**, 1463–1465.

Rhoades, D. F., and Cates, R. G. (1976). Toward a general theory of plant antiherbivore chemistry. *In* "Biochemical Interactions between Plants and Insects" (J. W. Wallace and R. L. Mansell, eds.), pp. 168–213. Plenum Press, New York.

Robbins, C. T. (1983). "Wildlife Nutrition." Academic Press, New York.

Robus, M. (1981). Foraging Behavior of Muskoxen in Arctic Alaska. M.S. thesis. University of Alaska, Fairbanks, Alaska.

Rousi, M., Tahvanainen, J., and Uotila, I. (1991). Mechanism of resistance to hare browsing in winter-dormant European white birch *Betula pendula. Am. Nat.* **137,** 64–82.

Safranyik, L., Shrimpton, D. M., and Whitney, H. S. (1975). An interpretation of the interaction between lodgepole pine, the mountain pine beetle and its associated blue stain fungi in western Canada. *In* "Management of Lodgepole Pine Ecosystems" (D. M. Baumgartner, ed.), pp. 406–428. Washington State Univ. Press, Pullman, WA.

Schwartz, C. C., Reglin, W. L., and Nagy, J. G. (1980a). Deer preference for juniper forage and volatile oil treated foods. *J. Wildl. Manage.* **44,** 114–120.

Schwartz, C. C., Reglin, W. L., and Nagy, J. G. (1980b). Juniper oil yield, terpenoid concentration, and antimicrobial effects on deer. *J. Wildl. Manage.* **44,** 107–113.

Schwartz, C. C., Franzmann, A. W., and Johnson, D. C. (1981). "Moose Research Center Report," Vol. XII. Project progress report federal aid in wildlife restoration project. W-21-2, Job 1.28R, pp. 16–17. Alaska Dept. of Fish and Game.

Shrimpton, D. M. (1973a). Extractives associated with the wound response of lodgepole pine to inoculation with *Europhium clavigerum. Can. J. Bot.* **51,** 527–534.

Shrimpton, D. M. (1973b). Age- and size-related response of lodgepole pine to inoculation with *Europhium clavigerum. Can. J. Bot.* **51,** 1155–1160.

Shrimpton, D. M. (1978). Resistance of lodgepole pine to mountain pine beetle infestation. *In* "Theory and Practice of Mountain Pine Beetle Management in Lodgepole Pine Forests" (A. A. Berryman, G. D. Amman, R. W. Stark, and D. L. Kibbee, eds.), pp. 64–76. Moscow, College of Forest Resources, University of Idaho, Moscow, Idaho.

Sinclair, A. R. E., Jogia, M. K., and Anderson, R. J. (1988). Camphor from juvenile white spruce as an antifeedent for snowshoe hares. *J. Chem. Ecol.* **14,** 1505–1514.

Smith, R. H. (1963). Toxicity of pine resin vapors to three species of *Dendroctonus* bark beetles. *J. Econ. Entomol.* **56,** 823–831.

Smith, R. H. (1965). Effects of monoterpene vapors on the western pine beetle. *J. Econ. Entomol.* **58,** 509–510.

Struhsaker, T. T. (1968). Interrelationships of red colobus monkeys and rainforest trees in the Kibale Forest, Uganda. *In* "The Ecology of Arboreal Foliavores" (G. G. Montgomery, ed.), pp. 397–437. Smithsonian Inst. Press, Washington, D.C.

Sullivan, T. P., and Sullivan, D. S. (1982). Influence of fertilization on feeding attacks to lodgepole pine by snowshoe hares and red squirrels. *For. Chron.* **58,** 263–266.

Swihart, R. K., Bryant, J. P., and Newton, L. (1994). Latitudinal patterns in consumption of woody plants by snowshoe hares in the eastern United States. *Oikos* **70,** 427–434.

Tahvanainen, J., Helle, E., Julkunen-Tiitto, R., and Lavola, A. (1985). Phenolic compounds of willow bark as deterrents against feeding by mountain hare. *Oecologia (Berlin)* **65,** 319–323.

Tallamy, D. W., and Raup, M. J. (1991). "Phytochemical Induction by Herbivores." John Wiley & Sons, New York.

Trudell, J., and White, R. G. (1981). The effect of forage structure and availability on food intake, biting rate, bite size and daily eating time of reindeer. *J. Appl. Ecol.* **18,** 63–81.

Van Soest, P. (1982). "Nutritional Ecology of the Ruminant." O & B. Books, Corvallis, Oregon.

Waring, R. H., and Pitman, G. B. (1983). Physiological stress in lodgepole pine as a precursor to mountain pine beetle attack. *Z. Angew. Entomol.* **96,** 265–270.

Waterman, P. G., and Mole, S. (1989). Extrinsic factors influencing production of secondary metabolites in plants. *In* "Insect-Plant Interactions" (E. A. Bernays, ed.), Vol. 1, pp. 107–134. CRC Press, Boca Raton, Florida.

Weeden, R. B. (1969). Foods of rock and willow ptarmigan in central Alaska with comments on interspecific competition. *Auk* **86,** 271–281.

Whitham, T. G., Maschinski, F., Larsen, K. C., and Paige, K. N. (1991). Plant responses to herbivory: The continuum from negative to positive and underlying physiological mechanisms. *In* "Plant-Animal Interactions: Evolutionary Ecology in Tropical and Temperate Regions" (P. W. Price, T. M. Lewinsohn, G. W. Fernandes, and W. W. Benson, eds.), pp. 227–256. John Wiley & Sons, New York.

Williams, J. B., Best, D., and Warford, C. (1984). Foraging ecology of ptarmigan at Meade River, Alaska. *Wilson Bull.* **92,** 341–351.

Wood, D. L. (1982). The role of pheromones, kariomones, and allomones in the host selection behavior of bark beetles. *Annu. Rev. Entomol.* **27,** 411–446.

Wright, L. E., Berryman, A. A., and Gurusiddiah, S. (1979). Host resistance to the fir engraver beetle, *Scolytus ventralis* (Coleoptera:Scolytidae): Effect of defoliation on wound monoterpenes and inner bark carbohydrate concentrations. *Can. Entomol.* **111,** 1255–1261.

Wright, L. E., Berryman, A. A., and Wickman, B. E. (1984). Abundance of the fir engraver, *Scolytus ventralis,* and the Douglas-fir beetle, *Dendroctonus pseudotsugae,* following tree defoliation by the Douglas-fir tussock moth, *Orgyria pseudotsugata. Can. Entomol.* **116,** 293–305.

17

Stem Defense against Pathogens

Louis Shain

I. Introduction

The pathogens most associated with diseases of tree stems are fungi. These plant-pathogenic fungi have a variety of means to gain entrance and colonize host tissue, including production of lytic enzymes and toxic substances and the ability to detoxify antifungal host substances. Trees, to a greater or lesser degree, have the means to protect themselves against the action of these pathogens. Were this not so, they would have ceased to exist. It follows, therefore, that the form and function of tree stems were conditioned during their evolution for protection against stress factors including pathogens. A dynamic interaction exists between pathogen and host, the outcome depending on the virulence of the pathogen, the ability of the host to defend, and environmental factors that may predispose the pathogen or this perennial host to greater or lesser virulence or resistance, respectively.

The focus of this chapter is on how trees, particularly tree stems, defend themselves against fungal pathogens. A treatise on the defense of trees as a whole against fungi may be found in Blanchette and Biggs (1992). Information regarding the defense of stems against herbivores is provided by Bryant and Raffa ([16] in this volume). Many of the mechanisms described are largely nonspecific and could be invoked for other injurious biotic and abiotic agents. Numerous mechanisms have been proposed for host defense. Others, undoubtedly, are yet to be identified. Defense mechanisms are described as passive if they occur prior to infection or active if they are induced during the infection process. Passive and active mechanisms are further subdivided into anatomical or physical barriers and chemical barriers.

II. Defense of Bark

A. Passive Mechanisms of Bark Defense

1. Passive Anatomical Barriers in Bark Defense The outer bark, or rhytidome, is composed of sequent layers of nonliving periderm (Esau, 1965). The cork layer, or phellum, is the outermost layer of each periderm. It is composed of cells whose walls frequently contain suberin, a polyester linked to a phenolic matrix (Kolattukudy, 1981), and wax lamellae. Few pathogens that attack stems are capable of breaching this hydrophobic suberized layer. Trees, therefore, may remain uninfected for decades if this protective barrier is not breached by a wounding event.

2. Passive Chemical Barriers in Bark
  a. Constitutive Nonproteinaceous Bark Extracts Tannins, both hydrolyzable and condensed, are likely candidates for passive defense and have been so implicated (Scalbert, 1991). The inner bark of some species contains considerable amounts of these polyphenolic compounds, for example, up to 16% in *Quercus prinus* (Rowe and Conner, 1979). These compounds tan leather by binding to and thereby denaturing protein. Defense might be expected if these tannins similarly denatured the proteinaceous enzymes secreted by microorganisms during pathogenesis. A previous report that the hydrolyzable tannins from inner bark conferred resistance of Chinese chestnut (*Castanea mollissima*) to blight (Nienstaedt, 1953), however, has been refuted (Anagnostakis, 1992) as tannin extracts of this species were not inhibitory to the chestnut blight fungus, *Cryphonectria* (*Endothia*) *parasitica*. Bark tannin from Chinese chestnut, furthermore, was catabolized as a carbon source by *C. parasitica* within 4–10 days (Elkins *et al.*, 1982).

  While tannins may serve as markers for host resistance (Griffin, 1986), there is little evidence to support their direct role in the defense of bark against fungal pathogens. It is interesting to speculate, however, that specific bark tannins may influence the host range of bark pathogens. For example, gallic acid and quercetin, frequent phenolic moieties of hydrolyzable and condensed tannins, respectively (Rowe and Conner, 1979), were inhibitory to some pathogens that cause wood decay (Hintikka, 1971; Kuć and Shain, 1977).

  Simple phenols that reside constitutively in inner bark have been implicated in its defense. As examples, five phenols isolated from Norway spruce (*Picea abies*) inhibited the growth of the root and stem decay pathogen *Het-*

erobasidion annosum in vitro. These were the flavonoids quercitin, taxifolin, and D-catechin, and glucosides of the stilbenes piceatannol and isorhapontigenin. Drought stress decreased the concentration of these antifungal compounds (Alcubilla *et al.,* 1971). The stilbene glucosides astringin and rhaponticin and the aglycone of the latter, isorhapontigenin, were identified as the major antifungal compounds in Sitka spruce (*Picea sitchensis*) inner bark (Woodward and Pearce, 1988).

Antifungal phenols also have been identified in the bark of angiosperms. As an example, *Hypoxylon mammatum,* an important canker and sapwood pathogen of quaking aspen (*Populus tremuloides*), was totally inhibited *in vitro* by pyrocatechol (Hubbes, 1962) and the aglycones salicylic acid at $5 \times 10^{-3} M$ and benzoic acid at $4 \times 10^{-3} M$. Media containing both aglycones each at $2 \times 10^{-3} M$ also totally inhibited this pathogen, indicating synergism between the two phenolic acids (Hubbes, 1969). The pathogen was inhibited on live bark and autoclaved bark meal but not on live sapwood or autoclaved sapwood meal. The fungus, furthermore, was isolated from necrotic sapwood underlying healthy bark beyond the limits of cankers. These results provided the basis for the hypothesis that the pathogen first invades the nonhostile sapwood and then kills the cambium and bark by a toxic metabolite. The pathogen then invades necrotic bark (Hubbes, 1964) on the presumed detoxification of the antifungal phenols.

b. Constitutive Bark Proteins Preformed macromolecules have been implicated in the protection of bark. Wargo (1975) reported that chitinase and β-1,3-glucanase occurred constitutively in healthy bark of sugar maple (*Acer saccharum* and three species of oak (*Quercus rubra, Q. velutina,* and *Q. alba*). These enzymes could play a role in defense in that they hydrolyze the major components of fungal cell walls, that is, chitin and β-1,3-glucan. Evidence was presented that stem and root extracts containing these enzymes degraded the cell walls of the decay fungus *Armillaria mellea.* These enzymes also are induced and are discussed more fully in Section II,B,2,b.

A proteinaceous inhibitor of the polygalacturonase (PG) produced by the chestnut blight fungus was extracted from chestnut barks. Polygalacturonase hydrolyzes pectin, the intercellular substance that binds plant cells together. Inhibition of PG by this extract from resistant Chinese chestnut was more than twice that from equal amounts of extract from susceptible American chestnut bark (McCarroll and Thor, 1985).

c. Bark Exudates Various exudates occur in bark and sapwood of different trees (Hillis, 1987). These exudates (and their major constituents) include oleoresin (terpenoids) in *Pinaceae,* gum (polysaccharides) in *Prunus* and *Acacia,* kino (proanthocyanidins) in *Eucalyptus,* and latex (polyisoprenes) in *Hevea.* It is tempting to speculate that these exudates have a protective role, for example, as moisture barriers to seal wounds or as antifungal agents. The latex of the rubber tree (*Hevea brasiliensis*) contains a small antifungal protein that has a chitin-binding domain (Van Parijs *et al.*, 1991). Most research on putative protective roles of exudates, however, has been conducted on oleoresin, which may be constitutive or induced. Oleoresin occurs mainly in sapwood and, therefore, is considered in Section III,B,2,a.

B. Active Mechanisms of Bark Defense

Living tissues, including those of the inner bark, are capable of responding actively to defend themselves against injury and infection. Defense responses may be induced by mechanical wounding (Biggs, 1985) or by a variety of the pathogen metabolites that cause host cell damage, such as enzymes (Bateman and Millar, 1966) and toxins (Mitchell, 1984). The activity of these injurious agents leads to the production of elicitors that sometimes are the breakdown products of host cell walls (endogenous elicitors, Nothnagel *et al.*, 1983) or fungal cell walls (exogenous elicitors, Miller *et al.*, 1986). It is thought that the binding of these elicitors to receptors initiates a cascade of metabolic events that results in the activation and expression of defense genes and their products.

1. Active Anatomical Responses in Bark   Lignification was the first histologically detectable event in the process of wound periderm formation (Hebard *et al.*, 1984; Biggs, 1985). This was followed, usually at about 10 days postwounding, by the formation of a boundary zone characterized by the deposition of suberin lamellae to form a lignin–suberin complex in the lumens of cells present at the time of wounding (Biggs, 1985). Boundary zones were originally reported to be nonsuberized (Mullick, 1977). This tissue was designated as impervious tissue (IT) owing to its inability to conduct water (Mullick, 1977) and thus seal off the necrotic area. Cells adjacent and internal to the boundary zone redifferentiate to form a new phellogen that subdivides to form the wound or necrophylactic periderm (NP). The latter term was coined (Mullick, 1977) to distinguish those periderms that separate living from dead tissues, and presumably protect the former from the cause of the latter, from first and sequent external or exophylactic periderms (EP) (Fig. 1). Lignin and suberin are deposited in cell walls of both boundary zone and newly formed phellum. In the temperate-zone trees studied, IT formation occurred more quickly during the growing than the dormant season (Mullick and Jensen, 1976), and at 17.5°C than at 12.5°C

Figure 1   Micrograph of canker in peach bark (*Prunus persica* cv. Sunhaven) induced by *Leucostoma cincta*. Residual autofluorescence of suberin in external, preformed exophylactic periderm (EP) and in internal, induced necrophylactic periderm (NP). Bar: 20 μm. [Figure reprinted, with permission, from Biggs (1986).]

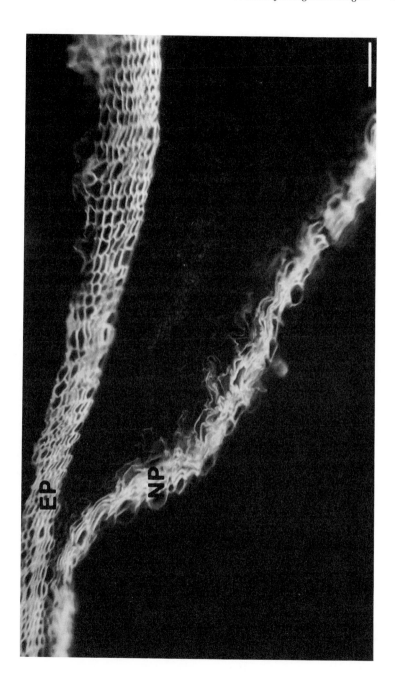

(Biggs and Northover, 1985). Necrophylactic periderm development was reduced when trees were under moisture stress (see Section II,B,3).

2. Active Chemical Responses in Bark

a. Induced Nonproteinaceous Defense Compounds   A rapid increase in ethylene production is one of the first measurable events to occur in response to wounding or challenge by a pathogen or its metabolites (Shain and Wheeler, 1975). The conversion of 1-aminocyclopropane-1-carboxylic acid to ethylene is mediated by superoxide (Drolet *et al.*, 1986), which is generated during an oxidative burst associated with the early induction of some mechanisms of host defense (Sutherland, 1991). In addition to its activity as a plant stress hormone, ethylene is also involved in other plant processes including growth, development, and senescence (Abeles *et al.*, 1992; see also Little and Pharis [13] in this volume). Ethylene has been implicated in the regulation of several defense genes, including some required for the synthesis of certain phenolic compounds, hydroxyproline-rich glycoproteins (Ecker and Davis, 1987), and the pathogenesis-related proteins chitinase and β-1,3-glucanase (Mauch and Staehelin, 1989). While ethylene greatly increases the mRNAs of plant defense genes (Ecker and Davis, 1987), the molecular mechanism for its action(s) is not known.

Antimicrobial compounds induced during infection are termed phytoalexins. Many of these are phenolic (Kuć and Shain, 1977). Reports of phytoalexins in bark are few, probably because they have been the subject of so few investigations. Flores and Hubbes (1980) reported the induction of a water-soluble compound, probably a phenolic glycoside, in the inner bark of *P. tremuloides* that inhibited germination of *H. mammatum* ascospores.

The synthesis of phenols is mediated by some of the same enzymes that mediate lignin synthesis. The final step in lignin biosynthesis is the oxidation of cinnamyl alcohols, which is mediated by peroxidase and hydrogen peroxide. The resulting free radicals couple randomly with themselves and with their phenolic precursors to form this complex biopolymer that is resistant to most microorganisms. Ethylene-mediated increases in peroxidase production (Gahagan *et al.*, 1968) and concomitant lignification were related to disease resistance in several herbaceous plant systems (Vance *et al.*, 1980). Lignification was preceded by ethylene production by disks of chestnut bark in response to inoculation with *C. parasitica* or exposure to its metabolites (Hebard and Shain, 1988).

b. Induced Defense Proteins   While chitinase and β-1,3-glucanase were reported to be expressed constitutively in oak and maple bark (Wargo, 1975), their induction by a variety of abiotic and biotic agents in a variety of plant species has attracted the attention of numerous plant scientists. These enzymes, therefore, appear to be a part of the nonspecific but coordinated (Vögeli *et al.*, 1988) cascade of plant responses induced on injury or infection. A model outlining the putative roles of these enzymes in plant defense was proposed by Mauch and Staehelin (1989). Their most obvious role is the hydrolysis of the major constituents of the fungal cell wall, leading to the lysis of hyphal tips. In addition, the oligomers released during hydrolysis of fungal (Keen and Yoshikawa, 1983) and host cell walls (Nothnagel *et al.*, 1983) serve as exogenous and endogenous elicitors, respectively, for the induction of phytoalexins. Tests *in vitro* suggest that these enzymes usually react synergistically with regard to antifungal activity (Mauch *et al.*, 1988). Transgenic tobacco plants constitutively coexpressing a chitinase gene from rice and a β-1,3-glucanase gene from alfalfa were substantially more resistant to the fungal pathogen *Cercospora nicotianae* than those plants expressing genes for either or none of these antifungal hydrolases (Zhu *et al.*, 1994).

Despite this level of research activity in herbaceous plants, reports of the induction of these hydrolases in bark of tree stems are almost nonexistent. They were detected, however, in the bark of American and Chinese chestnut, which were inoculated with *C. parasitica* or incubated in ethylene (Shain *et al.*, 1994). Isoforms of chitinase and β-1,3-glucanase induced in American chestnut differed from those in Chinese chestnut. Native proteins from ethylene-treated bark of both species, but not from untreated bark or boiled extract from treated bark, lysed the hyphae of *C. parasitica*. In preliminary results, protein extracts from Chinese chestnut bark were more antifungal than those from equal amounts of American chestnut bark. Further research is needed to assess the role of these hydrolases in woody stem protection.

Hydroxyproline-rich glycoproteins are structural proteins that occur in plant cell walls. Increased production of these proteins in response to infection has been related to disease resistance in some herbaceous plants (Ecker and Davis, 1987), but reports of their occurrence in woody species appear to be lacking. Proteinase inhibitors (Ryan, 1990) have received far more attention from entomologists than phytopathologists. While it seems logical to suppose that inhibition of pathogen proteinases would contribute to host defense, more research is required to establish such a role.

c. Induced Local vs Induced Systemic Defense   Host defense responses may be local, affecting only the injured and neighboring cells, and they also may be systemic, affecting tissues far removed from the site of infection. The rapid, or hypersensitive, death of infected cells is sometimes considered an effective means of limiting the pathogen to further ingress (Müller, 1959). This is particularly true if the pathogen is a biotroph, for example, rust fungus, which requires living host tissue for its nutrition. Hypersensitivity also may delimit nonbiotrophic pathogens owing to the induction of phytoalexins during host necrosis.

The induction of resistance in plant parts distant from the site of infection, termed systemic acquired resistance (SAR), infers movement of a signal, that is, signal transduction, from infected to noninfected plant parts. Genes that encode proteinase inhibitors (*Pin*) were systemically induced by wounding a distant leaf (Green and Ryan, 1972). A search for the proteinase inhibitor inducing factor (PIIF) has included several chemical candidates including salicylic acid (Gaffney *et al.*, 1993), jasmonic acid (Farmer and Ryan, 1992), and the polypeptide systemin (Pearce *et al.*, 1991). In contrast, Wildon *et al.*, (1992) reported that *Pin* was induced electrically.

Little has been published on SAR in trees. Helton and Braun (1971) reported that prior inoculation of *Prunus domestica* with the canker pathogen *Cytospora cincta* protected branches from later infection as far as 120 cm away. More recently two genes, with high similarity to those that encode chitinase in several herbaceous plants, were isolated from unwounded hybrid poplar leaves from a stem whose lower leaves were mechanically wounded. These genes were not detectable in leaves from plants that were not similarly wounded (Parsons *et al.*, 1989). The significance of SAR in the defense of tree stems awaits further investigation.

3. Bark Moisture and Its Relation to Bark Defense   High bark turgidity has been related to the resistance of trees to some canker diseases. Bier (1964) concluded that cankers develop after bark relative turgidity falls below the critical threshold of 80%. Schoeneweiss (1981) similarly reported a predispositional threshold of xylem water potential at -1.2 to -1.3 MPa for infection of a variety of woody hosts by the canker pathogen *Botryosphaeria dothidea*. Bark moisture stress appears to have a greater effect on host susceptibility than on pathogen virulence because the growth of pathogens was also reduced as the water potential of growth media was reduced (Hunter *et al.*, 1976). The reason for increased susceptibility to bark pathogens during moisture stress is unclear. Hyphal tips of *B. dothidea* were swollen and lysed significantly more frequently in unstressed as compared to drought-stressed seedlings of *Betula alba*. Hyphae of this canker pathogen were thin and confined to within 5 mm of the inoculation site in unstressed seedlings, whereas they were thick and ramified extensively in drought-stressed seedlings. Chitinase and β-1,3-glucanase were mentioned as possible causes of fungal lysis but tests for these enzymes were not conducted (McPartland and Schoeneweiss, 1984).

Griffin *et al.* (1986) correlated increases in proline, alanine, and glutamine with increased moisture stress and infection of aspen by *H. mammatum*. Because these amino acids stimulated growth of the pathogen *in vitro*, it was suggested that they may also account for the increased susceptibility of aspen to this pathogen during drought stress. Protein degradation was enhanced during moisture stress (Dungey and Davies, 1982).

Aspects of wound or necrophylactic periderm (NP) formation also were adversely affected by moisture stress. Puritch and Mullick (1975) reported that the induction of an early stage of this process, which they referred to as nonsuberized impervious tissue, was delayed substantially at −1.5 MPa in *Abies grandis*. Biggs and Cline (1986), on the other hand, found differences in the later stages of NP formation: fewer suberized phellum cells were produced around wounds of nonirrigated as compared to irrigated peach (*Prunus persica* cv. Candor) trees.

As mentioned above, drought stress was associated with a decrease in preformed antifungal phenols in the bark of *P. abies* (Alcubilla *et al.*, 1971).

III. Defense of Sapwood

A. Passive Mechanisms of Defense

Nonliving sapwood, whether in trees (Fig. 2) or forest products, usually will be consumed readily by wood decay fungi when exposed to conditions that favor decay (Scheffer and Cowling, 1966). This implies that preformed

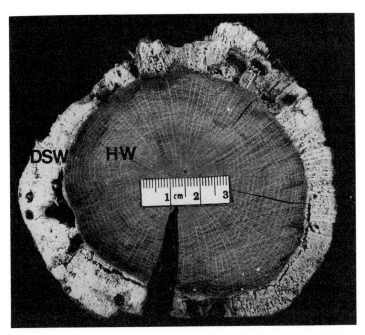

Figure 2   Cross-section of oak (*Quercus*) showing highly decayed sapwood (DSW) contiguous with sound heartwood (HW).

antifungal compounds usually are not present in sufficient amounts to protect sapwood from the pathogenic fungi most associated with xylem decay, the hymenomycetes. These fungi include some of the few microorganisms capable of metabolizing the components of the highly lignified woody cell wall.

There are, however, few reports of the occurrence of antifungal compounds in sapwood (e.g., Shortle *et al.,* 1971; Dumas and Hubbes, 1979). Gallic acid was detected in the clear sapwood of *Acer rubrum* and *A. saccharum* at a concentration of about 1%. It was not detected in wood decayed by *Oxyporus populinus* (*Fomes connatus*) or in the discolored wood that separates decayed and clear wood. *Phialophora melinii,* a nonhymenomycete that frequently inhabits this discolored zone, was capable of growing *in vitro* on medium containing gallic acid. *Oxyporus populinus,* however, was incapable of growing on this medium until it was first altered by *P. melinii.* These results suggest that sapwood invasion by *O. populinus* is facilitated by the removal of an inhibitory phenol by *P. melinii* (Shortle *et al.,* 1971). In this manner the decay process may proceed by a succession of microorganisms each of which is best adapted to a particular stage in the catabolism of the woody substrate (Shigo, 1967).

Oleoresin is produced constitutively in the sapwood of several genera of the Pinaceae, including *Pinus, Picea, Larix,* and *Pseudotsuga* (Brown *et al.,* 1949). Because it accumulates on wounding and infection in these genera and in other genera (e.g., *Abies, Sequoia,* and *Tsuga*) on the induction of traumatic resin canals, it is considered under active mechanisms of defense (Section III,B,2,a).

It has been proposed that sapwood defense can be explained solely by its high moisture content and concomitant reduced aeration (Boddy and Rayner, 1983). Infected tissue, however, frequently is separated from functional sapwood by reaction and transition zones described below (Fig. 4). The moisture contents of these tissues, particularly that of transition zones, are well below saturation. It can be argued, therefore, that decay fungi are localized by the contents of these tissues rather than the wetter functional sapwood, which these fungi would not have encountered. Fungi that decay tree interiors, furthermore, are tolerant of low aeration (Gunderson, 1961; Scheffer, 1986). Finally, data indicate that nearly 50% of the moisture in some tree stems may be replaced by gas during the growing season (Clark and Gibbs, 1957). Inoculation and wounding studies indicate that trees compartmentalize infection best during the growing season (Shain, 1967; Shain and Miller, 1988) when sapwood moisture contents tend to be diminished rather than elevated, but when trees are most active physiologically.

B. Active Mechanisms of Sapwood Defense

In contrast to dead sapwood, which readily decays, live sapwood may remain relatively free of infection for many years even when neighboring sap-

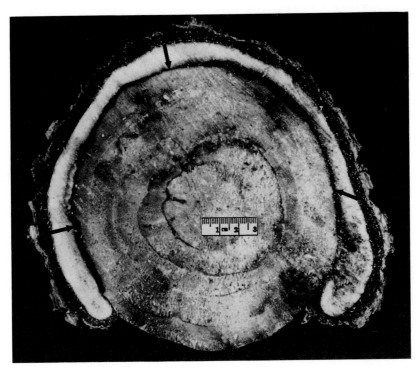

Figure 3   Cross-section of eastern cottonwood (*Populus deltoides*) with barrier zone (arrows) separating xylem present at the time of wounding, which subsequently decayed, from xylem produced after wounding, which is not decayed.

wood or heartwood is extensively decayed (see Figs. 3 and 4). A number of active mechanisms have been proposed to explain sapwood defense.

1. Anatomical Defense

   a. Callus   Wound healing is initiated by parenchyma of the xylem and phloem by the production of large cells that divide successively to produce callus. A new cambium differentiates in callus from points where callus is in contact with the uninjured vascular cambium. Wound healing is completed when the new cambium produces xylem and phloem in continuity with that of uninjured tissue to close the wound (Esau, 1965). Ethylene (Stoutemyer and Britt, 1970) and other phytohormones have been implicated in the regulation of those processes (Bloch, 1952).

   Factors reported to affect the rate of wound closure include wound size and tree growth rate (e.g., Neely, 1983) as well as season when wound occurred and tree genetics (e.g., Shain and Miller, 1988). In a seasonal wounding study of clonal eastern cottonwood (*Populus deltoides*), wound closure was greatest during the 3-month period from May to August although

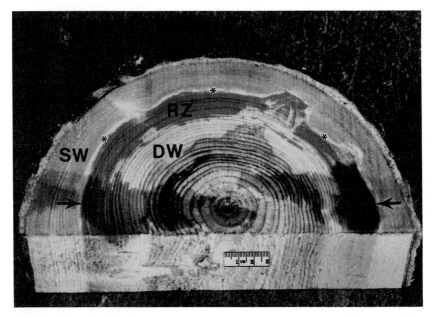

Figure 4 Cross-section of Norway spruce (*Picea abies*) infected by *Heterobasidion annosum*. Decayed wood (DW) is separated from sound sapwood (SW) by a necrotic reaction zone (RZ) and a dry, metabolically active, transition zone (*). Additional darkening (arrows) of RZ is due to reaction with chlorophenol red (left) or phenol red (right) and indicates elevated pH (ca. 8.0) of this tissue.

the rate of closure differed significantly among clones. These clones also differed significantly in their capacity to compartmentalize decay and discoloration. Rapid closure, however, was not predictive of good compartmentalization (Shain and Miller, 1988). These results support the hypothesis that wound closure and compartmentalization are under separate genetic control (Garrett *et al.*, 1979).

b. Barrier Zones Barrier zones result from an anatomical response of the cambium to injury. Their effect is to limit decay and discoloration to the xylem present when the injury occurred, thus protecting the xylem formed subsequent to injury (Fig. 3). This induced tissue is analogous to wall 4 of the CODIT "compartmentalization of decay in trees" model (Shigo, 1984).

Barrier zones form largely by the production of axial parenchyma by the cambium that survived the wound. Their production may be discontinuous as in sweetgum (*Liquidambar styraciflua*), in which it extended ≤60 cm longitudinally above and below wounds and <50% of the circumference of the tree (Moore, 1978), or continuous as in shoots of *Prunus pensylvanica* and *Populus balsamifera* following inoculation with the Dutch elm fungus, *Ophios-*

toma ulmi, which is not considered a pathogen of these species (Rioux and Ouellette, 1991a). Barrier zones were observed 22 days after inoculation in *Ulmus americana,* a host of this pathogen, but on average only 7 days after inoculation in the nonhost species. Fibers were the major component of barrier zones of *P. balsamifera.* Traumatic gum canals (Moore, 1978; Rioux and Ouellette, 1991b) and resin canals (Tippett and Shigo, 1981) were produced in these tissues in some angiosperms and gymnosperms, respectively.

Barrier zones frequently are suberized (Pearce and Rutherford, 1981; Pearce, 1990; Rioux and Ouellette, 1991a,b) and contain antifungal compounds (Moore, 1978, Pearce and Rutherford, 1981). The suberized parenchyma of a barrier zone from *Quercus robur* did not decay as did adjoining unsuberized sapwood when incubated with the decay fungus *Stereum gausapatum.* Only after saponification and consequent breakdown of the suberin did these cells decay (Pearce and Rutherford, 1981). Ultrastructural studies (Rioux and Ouelette, 1991b) indicate that these suberized cells become necrotic shortly after their formation and bear similarity to the phellum cells of necrophylactic periderm described earlier.

Trees tend to compartmentalize decay and discoloration to the cone of xylem present at the time of wounding, even when the anatomical defenses described above are not evident, (see, e.g., Moore, 1978). The mechanisms of signal transduction and protection of xylem produced years after wounding by a nondescript barrier are challenging questions for the investigator.

2. Active Chemical Defense Responses in Differentiated Sapwood   Active chemical defenses in differentiated sapwood frequently are organized in tissues described as reaction zones (RZs). This term was first applied to a necrotic tissue enriched with oleoresin and antifungal stilbenes (pinosylvins) in the sapwood of loblolly pine (*Pinus taeda*), which was induced in advance of *H. annosum* infection (Shain, 1967). The formation of similar tissues in other conifer and angiosperm sapwoods in response to a variety of injurious stimuli has been described (Shain, 1971; Biggs, 1987; Pearce, 1990) (Fig. 4). Reaction zones therefore appear to be a general nonspecific response to such stimuli. Other terms that have been used to describe similar tissues include protection wood (Jorgensen, 1961), discolored wood (Shigo, 1965), and walls 1, 2, and 3 of the CODIT model proposed by Shigo (1984).

Reaction zones frequently are surrounded by dry, metabolically active zones called transition zones (TZs). The moisture contents of TZs and sound sapwood of *P. abies* attacked by *H. annosum* were about 40 and 120% (dry weight basis), respectively (Alcubilla *et al.,* 1974). The rapid formation of dried zones in response to external injury of sapwood whose water columns are in hydrostatic tension may be explained by the introduction of gas emboli (see more discussion on cavitation in Sperry [5] in this volume). The mechanism for replacing water with gas to form dry zones in tissues not in direct contact with the atmosphere, that is, TZs that surround RZs in tree interiors, is more difficult to explain. Some possible mechanisms have been proposed (Shain, 1979).

The metabolic activity of TZs includes increased synthesis of ethylene, phenols, respiratory dehydrogenases, and catabolism of starch (Shain, 1979). Lesions in sapwood of Monterey pine (*Pinus radiata*) caused by a wood wasp (*Sirex noctilio*) and its associated decay fungus *Amylostereum areolatum* produced a 17-fold increase in ethylene as compared to unaffected sapwood (Shain and Hillis, 1972). Negligible amounts of ethylene, however, were produced by lesions when their TZs were removed, demonstrating that the locus of ethylene production was the TZ. Pinosylvin, an antifungal stilbene (see Section III,B,2,b), was detected in TZs in *P. radiata* sapwood 2 days after inoculation with *Sirex-Amylostereum* (Shain, 1979) and 2 days after incubation of sapwood in 5 ppm ethylene (Shain and Hillis, 1973). Chitinase and β-1,3-glucanase were induced in the sapwood of Chinese and American chestnuts after incubation in ethylene (L. Shain and R. J. Spalding, unpublished). This appears to be the first report of these antifungal hydrolases in tree xylem.

As the parenchyma in TZs die in a hypersensitive response, RZs form with the accumulation of protective substances. Those identified include oleoresin, phytoalexins, suberin, and minerals. Reports of defense-related proteins in RZs are almost nil, probably because they have not yet been sought. Reaction zones are viewed as dynamic rather than static barriers. As fungi slowly penetrate this tissue and metabolize its contents (Shain, 1967; Hart, 1981), hosts continue to respond with the conversion of additional sapwood to TZs and TZs to RZs. The major components of some RZs follow.

a. Oleoresin   The oleoresin produced by genera of the Pinaceae is a hydrophobic mixture composed largely of resin and fatty acids in a volatile oil. Mono- and sesquiterpenes and a few alkanes are the major components of the volatile oil. Resin acids, which comprise the major portion of the nonvolatile fraction of oleoresin, are diterpenes (Mutton, 1962).

Oleoresin is produced and maintained under pressure in resin canals by epithelial parenchyma. Oleoresin exudation and soaking of tissues occurs when resin canals are severed or when the epithelial parenchyma is killed. In *Pinus*, which has a well-developed resin canal system, accumulation seems to occur primarily by the mobilization of preformed oleoresin to the wound site, as indicated by little change in monoterpene cyclase between wounded and unwounded saplings. Monoterpene cyclase activity, however, increased significantly in wounded as compared to unwounded *Abies grandis, Picea pungens,* and *Thuja plicata,* indicating that *de novo* synthesis of oleoresin occurs in some species whose resin canal systems are not as well developed as that in *Pinus* (Lewinsohn *et al.,* 1991).

The accumulation of oleoresin near wounds and infections may protect trees from pathogens by serving as a mechanical barrier, a water-deficient barrier, or a chemical barrier (Kuć and Shain, 1977). The bulk of evidence strongly indicates that some of the volatile oil, resin acid, and fatty acid components of oleoresin are antifungal at concentrations that occur *in vivo*. As examples, a saturated atmosphere of *n*-heptane completely inhibited the mycelial growth of *H. annosum in vivo* whereas inhibition by myrcene and limonene was 72% (Cobb *et al.*, 1968). Hintikka (1970) reported that limonene at 0.005% (v/v) completely inhibited the growth of 8 of 16 hymenomycetes that degrade conifers and 22 of 22 that degrade hardwoods. This author suggested that atmospheres of wound sites in *Pinus* and *Picea* are monoterpene saturated and that these compounds could play roles in resistance as well as host selectivity among decay fungi. Wood blocks impregnated to contain about 15% of their dry weight in dehydroabietic acid or a mixture of resin acids (35% dehyroabietic, 35% abietic, and smaller amounts of other resin acids and oxidized materials) were decayed less by two decay fungi than were unimpregnated blocks (Hart *et al.*, 1975). A branched-chain fatty acid, 14-methylhexadecanate, found in *Picea abies* sapwood, totally inhibited *H. annosum* at 0.1% (w/w) (Henriks *et al.*, 1979).

b. Phytoalexins Phytoalexins are low molecular weight antimicrobial compounds induced nonspecifically in response to injurious agents. According to phytoalexin theory (Müller and Börger, 1940), their production occurs in resistant and susceptible hosts but they are induced more quickly in the former. In trees, this term was first applied to antifungal compounds that accumulate in RZs induced by *H. annosum* in the sapwood of *P. taeda* (Shain, 1967). The stilbenes pinosylvin and pinosylvin monomethyl ether were among the antifungal constituents in this RZ as well as in those of other *Pinus* spp. in response to the same (Prior, 1976) or other pathogens (Shain and Hillis, 1972). Other phytoalexins have been reported in similar tissues in other conifers, for example, the lignan liovil (Popoff *et al.*, 1975) in *Picea abies* and norlignans, especially hinokiresinol (Yamada *et al.*, 1988), in *Cryptomeria japonica*. Examples of photoalexins in angiosperms are the sesquiterpene mansonones in *Ulmus* spp. (Burden and Kemp, 1984) and 7-hydroxycalamenene (Burden and Kemp, 1983) in *Tilia europea*. In several instances RZ components were antifungal but their identity was not determined (e.g., Pearce and Woodward, 1986). Additional information about antifungal compounds in trees may be found in reviews by Gottstein and Gross (1992), Kemp and Burden (1986), and Kuć, and Shain (1977).

Phytoalexins in trees frequently are phenolic and usually are also found in the heartwood of their respective species. It is likely, therefore, that antifungal compounds identified in heartwood (e.g., Scheffer and Cowling, 1966) will also be induced in sapwood, although in different ratios (Shain, 1967; Shain and Hillis, 1971; Yamada *et al.*, 1988). In some cases, however, compounds not produced in heartwood are induced in sapwood in response to infection (Hillis and Swain, 1959). The list of xylem phytoalexins has considerable potential for growth as additional research is undertaken.

c. Suberin   Already mentioned in the protection of bark (Sections II,A,1 and II,B,1), suberin has also been detected in RZs. Biggs (1987) wounded 2- to 5-year-old branches of 15 angiosperms and 2 gymnosperms during the growing season. Within 21 days, RZs in all species were suberized primarily in parenchyma but less frequently in their conductive elements. Suberized cells formed a continuous boundary in the RZs of most of the species studied. This was viewed as *de novo* synthesis, although in some species suberin was observed in unwounded sapwood. Pearce (1990) examined the RZs of species that were infected naturally with decay fungi. Of these, suberin was detected in the parenchyma, vessel linings, or tyloses of 22 of 31 species. Therefore suberization, while frequent, was not universally present in RZs. It tended to be more limited in gymnosperms than in angiosperms probably owing to the less frequent xylem parenchyma in the former.

d. Minerals   The mineral content and pH of RZs is elevated in some angiosperms [e.g., sugar maple (*A. saccharum;* Good *et al.,* 1955) and gymnosperms (e.g., *P. abies;* Shain, 1971)] as compared to that in sound sapwood. Of the minerals assayed, potassium and calcium were highest in concentration. The pH of these RZs was ca. 8.0 (Fig. 4). Tests with the spruce RZ indicated that basic organic compounds were not the cause of elevated pH. The RZs of both species, however, effervesced on application of dilute acid, indicating that the elevated pH was due to the accumulation of inorganic carbonates. While the mechanism for their accumulation has not been elucidated, minerals associated with elevated pH probably contribute to sapwood defense in that growth of decay fungi is inhibited under alkaline conditions (Rennerfelt and Paris, 1953).

e. Proteins   Reaction zones frequently darken when cut surfaces are exposed to the air (Shain, 1971; Pearce and Woodward, 1986). Phenoloxidase was identified in the RZ of *P. abies* (Shain, 1971) and probably occurs in the RZ of other trees. Evidence suggested that this enzyme was of host rather than microbial origin. Phenol oxidases catalyze the oxidation of phenols to more antifungal quinones in the presence of air. Quinones, however, may autopolymerize quickly to form less toxic colored products (Lyr, 1965). Other proteins and, of particular interest, those related to host defense apparently have not yet been sought in this necrotic tissue.

IV. Defense of Heartwood

Heartwood is the dead central core of trees. It is formed as a result of senescence of inner sapwood parenchyma. As these cells die, frequently in a dry transition zone that separates heartwood from live sapwood, reserves (e.g., starch) are utilized and secondary metabolites characteristic of the species are synthesized. Some of these metabolites, or heartwood extractives, are antifungal as determined by *in vitro* bioassays and by decay tests of wood with or without them. Antifungal heartwood extractives therefore contribute to the decay resistance of the heartwoods in which they occur (Scheffer and Cowling, 1966) (Fig. 2), particularly when these heartwoods are converted to forest products. The heart rot fungi that attack living trees, however, may be highly adapted to exploit this niche. Incense cedar (*Libocedrus decurrens*), for example, contains several antifungal tropolones and terpenoids in its heartwood (Anderson *et al.*, 1963), which is durable as a forest product; nevertheless, heart rot has claimed more than 36% of the volume of this species in California (Wagener and Bega, 1958). Bioassays indicated that *Polyporus amarus*, the heart rot fungus largely responsible for these losses, was more tolerant of the heartwood extractives of *L. decurrens* than were two fungi that decay conifer wood products (Wilcox, 1970). Similarly, the heartwood of black locust (*Robinia pseudoacacia*) is durable in service but is decayed substantially and selectively by *Fomes rimosus*. This fungus was more tolerant to dihydrorobinetin, a major antifungal constituent of black locust heartwood, than was a fungus that decays angiosperm wood products (Shain, 1976). The effect of these adaptations is that few fungi are capable of decaying the heartwood of some trees but the amount of decay they cause is substantial. In the absence of these antifungal heartwood extractives, however, the decay rate would be expected to be far greater.

Shigo and Shortle (1979) reported that heartwood of red oak (*Q. rubra*) was capable of compartmentalizing wounds and thereby concluded that heartwood was not dead. In the absence of cytological evidence for vitality, it seems more likely that the reactions they observed were not the products of live heartwood parenchyma. All enzymes, for example, do not cease to function at the heartwood boundary. Phenol oxidases, but not respiratory dehydrogenases, were active within the heartwood of *P. radiata* (Shain and Mackay, 1973). The decrease in decay resistance of aging heartwood has been related to the oxidation of antifungal phenols (Anderson *et al.*, 1963).

V. Conclusions

Trees may survive for centuries despite an array of biotic and abiotic agents that can cause them considerable harm. Implicit in their longevity is that they have developed means to protect themselves. Some putative mechanisms have been described at the elemental, compound, cellular, tissue, and whole-plant levels.

Trees, therefore may have multiple mechanisms for defense, each being a part of a resistance mechanism system. Each putative mechanism may be controlled by genes at one or several loci and it may function qualitatively or quantitatively by either stopping or slowing disease progress, respectively. Pathogens may or may not have the ability to fully or partially circumvent each resistance mechanism. The ability of a pathogen to circumvent a resistance mechanism may be controlled at one or more loci (Carson and Carson, 1989). Resistance mechanisms, therefore, may vary in their relative protective roles against different pathogenic taxa.

Evidence supporting the role(s) of proposed resistance mechanisms in defense is largely circumstantial but in some cases compelling. There can be little doubt of the protection afforded by unwounded periderm, and particularly the thickened rhytidome, in maintaining vascular function and preventing ingress of most pathogens. The significance of other putative passive or active mechanisms is less certain. Some may be the result rather than the cause of resistance, as has been suggested for the hypersensitive reaction (Király *et al.*, 1972).

The era of molecular biology, which we have entered, promises to provide more definitive answers with regard to the significance of some mechanisms already proposed, and some yet to be proposed, for host defense. As in the past, far more workers will utilize herbaceous plants rather than trees for such studies for reasons of resource allocation and convenience. We must learn from our colleagues who use tobacco, *Arabidopsis,* or other herbaceous model systems. Considering that trees are the predecessors of their herbaceous relatives, research findings from the latter frequently may be applicable to the former. Some of the present difficulty in transforming trees for subsequent testing of differentiated tissue for the expression of a putative resistance factor may be avoided by looking first to the pathogen. For example, to answer if a polygalacturonase (PG) inhibitor in bark is an important mechanism of resistance, it would be far more efficient to delete the PG gene(s) from the pathogen than to delete the PG inhibitor gene(s) from the resistant host or transfer it to a susceptible host. If the pathogenicity of the PG^- transformant is similar to that of the PG^+ wild type, then the PG inhibitor would not be an effective defense against this test pathogen because the enzyme it inhibits was not required for pathogenicity. An understanding of the molecular basis of host resistance, through gene disruption and gene transfer studies, may offer the opportunity to engineer hosts that are resistant to their major pests (Lamb *et al.*, 1992; Kamoun, 1993).

Acknowledgments

Some of the research reported herein was supported by USDA Grant No. 85-FSTY-9-0138. Manuscript review by J. P. Bryant is gratefully acknowledged. This is published as contribution No. 94-11-138 of the University of Kentucky Agricultural Experiment Station.

References

Abeles, F. B., Bosshart, R. P., Forrence, L. E., and Habig, W. H. (1971). Preparation and purification of glucanase and chitinase from bean leaves. *Plant Physiol.* **47**, 129–134.

Abeles, F. B., Morgan, P. W., and Saltveit, M. E., Jr. (1992). "Ethylene in Plant Biology," 2nd Ed. Academic Press, New York.

Alcubilla, M., Diaz-Palacio, M. P., Kreutzer, K., Laatsch, W., Rehfuess, K. E., and Wenzel, G. (1971). Beziehungen zwischen dem Ernährungszustand der Fichte (*Picea abies* Karst.), ihrem Kernfaulebefall und der Pilzhemmwirkung ihres Basts. *Eur. J. For. Pathol.* **1**, 100–114.

Alcubilla, M., Aufsess, H. V., Cerny, G., and Rehfuess, K. E. (1974). Untersuchungen über die Pilzhemmwirkung des Fichtenholzes (*Picea abies* Karst.). *In* "Proc. 4th Int. Conf. *Fomes annosus*" (E. G. Kuhlman, ed.), pp. 139–162. USDA Forest Service Asheville, North Carolina.

Anagnostakis, S. L. (1992). Chestnut bark tannin assays and growth of chestnut blight fungus on extracted tannin. *J. Chem. Ecol.* **18**, 1365–1373.

Anderson, A. B., Scheffer, T. C., and Duncan, C. G. (1963). The chemistry of decay resistance and its decrease with heartwood aging in incense cedar (*Libocedrus decurrens* Torrey). *Holzforschung* **17**, 1–5.

Bateman, D. F., and Millar, R. L. (1966). Pectic enzymes in tissue degradation. *Annu. Rev. Phytopathol.* **4**, 119–146.

Biggs, A. R. (1985). Suberized boundary zones and the chronology of wound response in tree bark. *Phytopathology* **75**, 1191–1195.

Biggs, A. R. (1986). Comparative anatomy and host response of two peach cultivars inoculated with *Leucostoma cincta* and *L. persoonii*. *Phytopathology* **76**, 905–912.

Biggs, A. R. (1987). Occurrence and location of suberin in wound reaction zones in xylem of 17 tree species. *Phytopathology* **77**, 718–725.

Biggs, A. R., and Northover, J. (1985). Formation of the primary protective layer and phellogen following leaf abscission in peach. *Can. J. Bot.* **63**, 1547–1550.

Biggs, A. R., and Cline, R. A. (1986). Influence of irrigation on wound response in peach bark. *Can. J. Plant Pathol.* **8**, 405–408.

Bier, J. E. (1964). The relation of some bark factors to canker susceptibility. *Phytopathology* **54**, 250–253.

Blanchette, R. A., and Biggs, A. R., eds. (1992). "Defense Mechanisms of Woody Plants against Fungi." Springer-Verlag, New York.

Bloch, R. (1952). Wound healing in higher plants. II. *Bot. Rev.* **18**, 655–679.

Boddy, L., and Rayner, A. D. M. (1983). Origins of decay in living deciduous trees: The role of moisture content and a re-appraisal of the expanded concept of tree decay. *New Phytol.* **94**, 623–641.

Brown, H. P., Panshin, A. J., and Forsaith, C. C. (1949). "Textbook of Wood Technology," Vol. 1. McGraw-Hill, New York.

Burden, R. S., and Kemp, M. S. (1983). 7-Hydroxycalamenene, a phytoalexin from *Tilia europea*. *Phytochemistry* **22**, 1039–1040.

Carson, S. D., and Carson, M. J. (1989). Breeding for resistance in forest trees—a quantitative genetic approach. *Annu. Rev. Phytopathol.* **27**, 373–395.

Clark, J., and Gibbs, R. D. (1957). Studies in tree physiology. IV. Further investigations of seasonal changes in moisture content of certain forest trees. *Can. J. Bot.* **35**, 219–253.

Cobb, F. W., Jr., Krstic, M., Zavarin, E., and Barker, H. W, Jr. (1968). Inhibitory effects of volatile oleoresin components on *Fomes annosus* and four *Ceratocystis* species. *Phytopathology* **58**, 1327–1335.

Drolet, G., Dumbroff, E. B., Legge, R. L., and Thompson, J. E. (1986). Radical scavenging properties of polyamines. *Phytochemistry* **25**, 367–371.

Dumas, M. T., and Hubbes, M. (1979). Resistance of *Pinus densiflora* and *Pinus rigida* × *radiata* to *Fomes annosus*. *Eur. J. For. Pathol.* **9**, 229–238.

Dungey, N. O., and Davies, D. D. (1982). Protein turnover in isolated barley leaf segments and the effects on stress. *J. Exp. Bot.* **33**, 12–20.

Ecker, J. R., and Davis, R. W. (1987). Plant defense genes are regulated by ethylene. *Proc. Natl. Acad. Sci. U.S.A.* **84**, 5202–5206.

Elkins, J. R., Lawhorn, Z., and Weyand, E. (1982). Utilization of chestnut tannins by *Endothia parasitica*. *In* "Proceedings of the U.S. Forest Service, American Chestnut Cooperative Meeting" (H. C. Smith and W. L. MacDonald, eds.), pp. 141–144. West Virginia University Press, Morgantown, West Virginia.

Esau, K. (1965). "Plant Anatomy," 2nd Ed. John Wiley & Sons, New York.

Farmer, E. E., and Ryan, C. A. (1992). Octadecanoid-derived signals in plants. *Trends Cell Biol.* **2**, 236–241.

Flores, G., and Hubbes, M. (1980). The nature and role of phytoalexin produced by aspen (*Populus tremuloides* Mich.). *Eur. J. For. Pathol.* **10**, 95–103.

Gaffney, T., Friedrich, L., Vernooij, B., Negrotto, D., Nye, G., Uknes, S., Ward, E., Kessman, H., and Ryals, J. (1993). Requirement of salicylic acid for the induction of systemic acquired resistance. *Science* **261**, 754–756.

Gahagan, H. E., Holm, R. E., and Abeles, F. B. (1968). Effect of ethylene on peroxidase activity. *Physiol. Plant.* **21**, 1270–1279.

Garrett, P. W., Randall, W. K., Shigo, A. L., and Shortle, W. C. (1979). Inheritance of compartmentalization of wounds in sweetgum (*Liquidambar styraciflua* L. and eastern cottonwood (*Populus deltoides* Bartr.). USDA Forest Service Research Paper NE-443.

Good, H. M., Murray, P. M., and Dale, H. M. (1955). Studies on heartwood formation and staining in sugar maple, *Acer saccharum* Marsh. *Can. J. Bot.* **33**, 31–41.

Gottstein, D., and Gross, D. (1992). Phytoalexins of woody plants. *Trees Struct. Funct.* **6**, 55–68.

Green, T. R., and Ryan, C. A. (1972). Wound induced proteinase inhibitors in plant leaves: A possible defense mechanism against insects. *Science* **175**, 776–777.

Griffin, D. H., Quinn, K., and McMillen, B. (1986). Regulation of hyphal growth rate of *Hypoxylon mammatum* by amino acids: stimulation by proline. *Exp. Mycol.* **10**, 307–314.

Griffin, G. J. (1986). Chestnut blight and its control. *Hortic. Rev.* **8**, 291–336.

Gunderson, K. (1961). Growth of *Fomes annosus* under reduced oxygen pressure and the effect of carbon dioxide. *Nature (London)* **190**, 649–650.

Hart, J. H. (1981). Role of phytostilbenes in decay and disease resistance. *Annu. Rev. Phytopathol.* **19**, 437–458.

Hart, J. H., Wardell, J. F., and Hemingway, R. W. (1975). Formation of oleoresin and lignans in sapwood of white spruce in response to wounding. *Phytopathology* **65**, 412–417.

Hebard, F. V., Griffin, G. J., and Elkins, J. R. (1984). Developmental histopathology of cankers incited by hypovirulent and virulent isolates of *Endothia parasitica* on susceptible and resistant chestnut trees. *Phytopathology* **74**, 140–149.

Hebard, F. V., and Shain, L. (1988). Effects of virulent and hypovirulent *Endothia parasitica* and their metabolites on ethylene production by bark of American and Chinese chestnut and scarlet oak. *Phytopathology* **78**, 841–845.

Helton, A. W., and Braun, J. W. (1971). Induced resistance to *Cytospora* in bearing trees of *Prunus domestica*. *Phytopathology* **61**, 721–723.

Henriks, M.-L., Ekman, R., and von Weissenberg, K. (1979). Bioassay of some resin and fatty acids with *Fomes annosus*. *Acta Acad. Aboen. Ser. B* **39**, 1–7.

Hillis, W. E. (1987). "Heartwood and Tree Exudates." Springer-Verlag, Berlin.

Hillis, W. E., and Swain, T. (1959). Phenolic constituents of *Prunus domestica*. III. Identification of the major constituents in the tissues of victoria plum. *J. Sci. Food Agric.* **10**, 533–537.

Hintikka, V. (1970). Selective effect of terpenes on wood-decomposing hymenomycetes. *Karstenia* **11**, 28–32.

Hintikka, V. (1971). Tolerance of some wood-decomposing basidiomycetes to aromatic compounds related to lignin degradation. *Karstenia* **12**, 46–52.

Hubbes, M. (1962). Inhibition of *Hypoxylon pruinatum* by pyrocatechol isolated from bark of aspen. *Science* **136**, 156.

Hubbes, M. (1964). New facts on host-parasite relationships in the *Hypoxylon* canker of aspen. *Can. J. Bot.* **42**, 1489–1494.

Hubbes, M. (1969). Benzoic and salicylic acids isolated from a glycoside of aspen bark and their effect on *Hypoxylon pruinatum*. *Can. J. Bot.* **47**, 1295–1301.

Hunter, P. P., Griffin, G. J., and Stipes, R. J. (1976). The influence of osmotic water potential on the linear growth of *Endothia* species. *Phytopathology* **66**, 1418–1421.

Jorgensen, E. (1961). The formation of pinosylvin and its monomethyl ether in the sapwood of *Pinus resinosa* Ait. *Can. J. Bot.* **39**, 1765–1772.

Kamoun, S., and Kado, C. I. (1993). Genetic engineering for plant disease resistance. *In* "Advanced Engineered Pesticides" (L. Kim, ed.), pp. 165–198. Marcel Dekker, New York.

Keen, N. T., and Yoshikawa, M. (1983). β-1,3-Endoglucanase from soybean releases elicitor-active carbohydrates from fungus cell walls. *Plant Physiol.* **71**, 460–465.

Kemp, M. S., and Burden, R. S. (1986). Phytoalexins and stress metabolites in the sapwood of trees. *Phytochemistry* **25**, 1261–1269.

Király, Z., Barna, B., and Érsek, T. (1972). Hypersensitivity as a consequence, not the cause, of plant resistance to infection. *Nature (London)* **239**, 456–458.

Kolattukudy, P. E. (1981). Structure, biosynthesis and biodegradation of cutin and suberin. *Annu. Rev. Plant Physiol.* **32**, 539–567.

Kuć, J., and Shain, L. (1977). Antifungal compounds associated with disease resistance in plants. *In* "Antifungal Compounds" (H. D. Sisler and M. R. Siegel, eds.), Vol. 2, pp. 497–595. Marcel Dekker, New York.

Lamb, C. J., Ryals, J. A., Ward, E. R., and Dixon, R. A. (1992). Emerging strategies for enhancing crop resistance to microbial pathogens. *Biotechnology* **10**, 1436–1445.

Lewinsohn, E., Gijzen, M., and Croteau, R. (1991). Defense mechanisms of conifers. 1. Differences in constitutive and wound-induced monoterpene biosynthesis among species. *Plant Physiol.* **96**, 44–49.

Lyr, H. (1965). On the toxicity of oxidized polyphenols. *Phytopathol. Z.* **52**, 229–240.

Mauch, F., and Staehelin, L. A. (1989). Functional implications of the subcellular localization of ethylene-induced chitinase and β-1,3-glucanase in bean leaves. *Plant Cell* **1**, 447–457.

Mauch, F., Mauch-Mani, B., and Boller, T. (1988). Antifungal hydrolases in pea tissue. II. Inhibition of fungal growth by combinations of chitinase and β-1,3-glucanase. *Plant Physiol.* **88**, 936–942.

McCarroll, D. R., and Thor, E. (1985). Pectolytic, cellulytic and proteolytic activities expressed by cultures of *Endothia parasitica* and inhibition of these activities by components extracted from Chinese and American chestnut inner bark. *Physiol. Plant Pathol.* **26**, 367–378.

McPartland, J. M., and Schoeneweiss, D. F. (1984). Hyphal morphology of *Botryosphaeria dothidea* in vessels of unstressed and drought-stressed stems of *Betula alba*. *Phytopathology* **74**, 358–362.

Miller, R. H., Berryman, A. A., and Ryan, C. A. (1986). Biotic elicitors of defense reactions in lodgepole pine. *Phytochemistry* **25**, 611–612.

Mitchell, R. E. (1984). The relevance of non-host-specific toxins in the expression of virulence by pathogens. *Annu. Rev. Phytopathol.* **22**, 215–245.

Moore, K. E. (1978). Barrier-zone formation in wounded stems of sweetgum. *Can. J. For. Res.* **8**, 389–397.

Müller, K. O. (1959). Hypersensitivity. *In* "Plant Pathology, an Advanced Treatise" (C. J. G. Horsfall and A. E. Diamond, eds.), Vol. 1, pp. 469–519. Academic Press, New York.

Müller, K. O., and Börger, H. (1940). Experimentelle Untersuchungen über die *Phytophthora* Resistenz der Kartoffel. *Arb. Biol. Reichsanst. Land-, Forstwirtsch. Berlin-Dahlem* **23**, 189–231.

Mullick, D. B. (1977). The non-specific nature of defense in bark and wood during wounding, insect and pathogen attack. *In* "Recent Advances in Phytochemistry" (F. A. Loweus and V. C. Runeckles, eds.), Vol. 11, p. 395–441. Plenum, New York.

Mullick, D. B., and Jensen, G. D. (1976). Rates of non-suberized impervious tissue development after wounding at different times of the year in three conifer species. *Can. J. Bot.* **54**, 881–892.

Mutton, D. B. (1962). Wood resin. *In* "Wood Extractives" (W. E. Hillis, ed.), pp. 331–363. Academic Press, New York.

Neely, D. (1983). Tree trunk growth and wound closure. *HortScience* **18**, 99–100.

Nienstaedt, H. (1953). Tannin as a factor in the resistance of chestnut, *Castanea* spp., to the chestnut blight fungus, *Endothia parasitica* (Murr) A. and A. *Phytopathology* **43**, 32–38.

Nothnagel, E. A., McNeil, M., and Albersheim, P. (1983). Host-pathogen interactions: XXII. A galacturonic acid oligosaccharide from plant cell walls elicits phytoalexins. *Plant Physiol.* **71**, 916–926.

Parsons, T. J., Bradshaw, H. D., Jr., and Gordon, M. P. (1989). Systemic accumulation of specific mRNAs in response to wounding in poplar trees. *Proc. Natl. Acad. Sci. U.S.A.* **86**, 7895–7899.

Pearce, R. B. (1990). Occurrence of decay-associated xylem suberization in a range of woody species. *Eur. J. Forest Pathol.* **20**, 275–289.

Pearce, R. B., and Rutherford, J. (1981). A wound-associated suberized barrier to the spread of decay in the sapwood of oak (*Quercus robur* L.). *Physiol. Plant Pathol.* **19**, 359–369.

Pearce, R. B., and Woodward, S. (1986). Compartmentalization and reaction zones barriers at the margin of decayed sapwood in *Acer saccharinum* L. *Physiol. Mol. Plant Pathol.* **29**, 197–216.

Pearce, G., Strydom, D., Johnson, S., and Ryan, C. A. (1991). A polypeptide from tobacco leaves induces the synthesis of wound inducible proteinase inhibitor proteins. *Science* **253**, 895–898.

Popoff, T., Theander, O., and Johansson, M. (1975). Changes in sapwood of roots of Norway spruce attacked by *Fomes annosus*. II. Organic chemical constituents and their biological effects. *Physiol. Plant.* **34**, 347–356.

Prior, C. (1976). Resistance by Corsican pine to attack by *Heterobasidion annosum*. *Ann. Bot.* **40**, 261–279.

Puritch, G. S., and Mullick, D. B. (1975). Studies of periderm. VIII. Effect of water stress on the rate of non-suberized impervious tissue (NIT) formation following wounding in *Abies grandis*. *J. Exp. Bot.* **26**, 903–910.

Rennerfelt, E., and Paris, S. K. (1953). Some physiological and ecological experiments with *Polyporus annosus* Fr. *Oikos* **4**, 58–76.

Rioux, D., and Ouellette, G. B. (1991a). Barrier zone formation in host and nonhost trees inoculated with *Ophiostoma ulmi*. I. Anatomy and histochemistry. *Can. J. Bot.* **69**, 2055–2073.

Rioux, D., and Ouellette, G. B. (1991b). Barrier zone formation in host and nonhost trees inoculated with *Ophiostoma ulmi*. II. Ultrastructure. *Can. J. Bot.* **69**, 2074–2083.

Rowe, J. W., and Conner, A. H. (1979). Extractives in eastern hardwoods. Gen. Tech. Rep. FPL 18, Forest Products Laboratory, Forest Service, USDA, Madison, Wisconsin.

Ryan, C. (1990). Proteinase inhibitors in plants: Genes for improving defenses against insects and pathogens. *Annu. Rev. Phytopathol.* **28**, 425–449.

Scalbert, A. (1991). Antimicrobial properties of tannins. *Phytochemistry* **30**, 3875–3883.

Scheffer, T. C. (1986). O_2 requirements for growth and survival of wood-decaying and sapwood-staining fungi. *Can. J. Bot.* **64**, 1957–1963.

Scheffer, T. C., and Cowling, E. B. (1966). Natural resistance of wood to microbial deterioration. *Annu. Rev. Phytopathol.* **4**, 147–170.

Schoeneweiss, D. F. (1981). The role of environmental stress in diseases of woody plants. *Plant Dis.* **65**, 308–314.

Shain, L. (1967). Resistance of sapwood in stems of loblolly pine to infection by *Fomes annosus*. *Phytopathology* **57**, 1034–1045.

Shain, L. (1971). The response of sapwood of Norway spruce to infection by *Fomes annosus*. *Phytopathology* **61**, 301–307.

Shain, L. (1976). The effects of extractives from black locust heartwood on *Fomes rimosus* and other decay fungi. *Proc. Am. Phytopath. Soc.* **3**, 216. [Abstract]

Shain, L. (1979). Dynamic responses of differentiated sapwood to injury and infection. *Phytopathology* **69**, 1143–1147.

Shain, L., and Hillis, W. E. (1971). Phenolic extractives in Norway spruce and their effects on *Fomes annosus*. *Phytopathology* **61**, 841–845.

Shain, L., and Hillis, W. E. (1972). Ethylene production in *Pinus radiata* in response to *Sirex-Amylostereum* attack. *Phytopathology* **62**, 1407–1409.

Shain, L., and Hillis, W. E. (1973). Ethylene production in xylem of *Pinus radiata* in relation to heartwood formation. *Can. J. Bot.* **51**, 1331–1335.

Shain, L., and MacKay, J. F. G. (1973). Phenol-oxidizing enzymes in the heartwood of *Pinus radiata*. *Forest Sci.* **19**, 153–155.

Shain, L., and Miller, J. B. (1988). Ethylene production by excised sapwood of clonal eastern cottonwood and the compartmentalization and closure of seasonal wounds. *Phytopathology* **78**, 1261–1265.

Shain, L., Miller, J. B., and Spalding, R. J. (1994). Responses of American and Chinese chestnut to *Cryphonectria parasitica* and ethylene. In "Proceedings of the International Chestnut Conference" (M. L. Double and W. L. MacDonald, eds.), pp. 97–101. West Virginia University Press, Morgantown, West Virginia.

Shain, L., and Wheeler, H. (1975). Production of ethylene by oats resistant and susceptible to victorin. *Phytopathology* **65**, 88–89.

Shigo, A. L. (1965). Decay and discolorization in red maple. *Phytopathology* **55**, 957–962.

Shigo, A. L. (1967). Successions of organisms in discoloration and decay of wood. In "International Review of Forest Research" (J. A. Romberger and P. Mikola, eds.), Vol. II, pp. 237–239. Academic Press, New York.

Shigo, A. L. (1984). Compartmentalization: A conceptual framework for understanding how trees grow and defend themselves. *Annu. Rev. Phytopathol.* **22**, 189–214.

Shigo, A. L., and Shortle, W. C. (1979). Compartmentalization of discolored wood in heartwood of red oak. *Phytopathology* **69**, 710–711.

Shortle, W. C., Tattar, T. A., and Rich, A. E. (1971). Effects of some phenolic compounds on the growth of *Phialophora melinii* and *Fomes connatus*. *Phytopathology* **61**, 552–555.

Stoutemyer, V. T., and Britt, O. K. (1970). Ethrel and plant tissue cultures. *Bioscience* **20**, 914.

Sutherland, M. W. (1991). The generation of oxygen radicals during host plant responses to infection. *Physiol. Mol. PlantPathol.* **39**, 79–93.

Tippett, J. T., and Shigo, A. L. (1981). Barriers to decay in conifer roots. *Eur. J. For. Pathol.* **11**, 51–59.

Vance, C. P., and Kirk, T. K., and Sherwood, R. T. (1980). Lignification as a mechanism of disease resistance. *Annu. Rev. Phytopathol.* **18**, 259–288.

Van Parijs, J., Brockaert, W. F., Goldstein, I. J., and Peumans, W. J. (1991). Hevein: An antifungal protein from rubber-tree (*Hevea brasiliensis*) latex. *Planta* **183**, 258–264.

Verrall, A. F. (1938). The probable mechanism of the protective action of resin in fire wounds on red pine. *J. For.* **36**, 1231–1233.

Vögeli, U., Meins, F., and Boller, T. (1988). Co-ordinated regulation of chitinase and β-1,3-glucanase in bean leaves. *Planta* **174**, 364–372.

Wagener, W. W., and Bega, R. V. (1958). Heartrots of incense cedar. USDA Forest Service, Forest Pest Leaflet 30, p. 7.

Wargo, P. M. (1975). Lysis of the cell wall of *Armillaria mellea* by enzymes from forest trees. *Physiol Plant Pathol.* **5**, 99–105.

Wilcox, W. W. (1970). Tolerance of *Polyporus amarus* to extractives from incense cedar heartwood. *Phytopathology* **60**, 919–923.

Wildon, D. C., Thain, J. F., Minchin, P. E. H., Gubb, I. R., Reilly, A. J., Skipper, Y. D., Doherty, H. M., O'Donnell, P. J., and Bowels, D. J. (1992). Electrical signalling and systemic protein-ase inhibitor induction in the wounded plant. *Nature (London)* **360,** 62–65.

Woodward, S., and Pearce, R. B. (1988). The role of stilbenes in the resistance of sitka spruce (*Picea sitchensis* (Bong) Carr.) to the entry of decay fungi. *Physiol. Mol. Plant Pathol.* **33,** 127–149.

Yamada, T., Tamura, H., and Mineo, K. (1988). The response of sugi (*Cryptomeria japonica* D. Don) sapwood to fungal invasion following attack by the sugi bark borer. *Physiol. Mol. Plant Pathol.* **33,** 429–442.

Zhu, Q., Maher, E. A., Masoud, S., Dixon, R. A., and Lamb, C. J. (1994). Enhanced protection against fungal attack by constitutive coexpression of chitinase and glucanase genes in trans-genic tobacco. *Bio/Technology* **12,** 807–812.

V

Synthesis

18

Stems in the Biology of the Tissue, Organism, Stand, and Ecosystem

Thomas M. Hinckley and Paul J. Schulte

Stems come in many forms, have a wide range of longevities, and serve a number of different functions. Almost all stems have served humans as sources of fuel, fiber, and building materials for thousands of years. From the dugout canoes of the indigenous people of the Amazon to the western redcedar bark baskets of the coastal tribes of the Pacific Northwest region of North America to the extraction of the cancer-suppressing chemical taxol from the bark of *Taxus,* the role of the stem and its parts in human culture and history is impressive. For these sociological and economic reasons, a book on the basic biology of stems has merit. However, there are even more compelling reasons for such a book. The control of carbon allocation to the stem is important to individuals in production ecology and silviculture programs. The control of carbon utilization in the stem is important to individuals in a variety of end-product fields including those in pulp and paper, wood products, and construction. Although less visually dramatic, stems play a critical role in agriculture and horticulture: included are issues associated with crop density, foliar display, cutting longevity, harvesting technology and biofuel production. Carbon acquisition and storage, the movement of materials and energy in biological systems, canopy structure and spatial heterogeneity, snags, and coarse woody debris all involve stems, their historical and present function, their physical size and structure, and their chemical nature. Much of the discussion of stems in this book focuses on evolutionarily advanced woody plants; however, most of the functions discussed also existed in early vascular plants such as *Psilo-*

tum, in which stems are the primary support, storage, and photosynthetic structures.

For the organism of which they are part, stems have been traditionally recognized to serve three primary functions: support, transport, and storage. The preceding chapters serve to remind us that stems are involved in other functions and processes in addition to those traditionally recognized. Although it is obvious that stems link the water- and nutrient-absorbing surfaces with the carbon-capturing surfaces, how this linkage is structurally and functionally regulated is currently one of the most intense research areas in biology (Hinckley and Ceulemans, 1989; Chapin, 1991; Meinzer and Grantz, 1991; Jackson, 1993; Tardieu and Davies, 1993; Sperry and Saliendra, 1994; Fuchs and Livingston, 1995). In addition to new insights into the mechanisms behind these functions and associated structures, additional functions are recognized and described in this book. Our role in this final chapter is to synthesize and highlight information developed within the book. Key in our approach will be to examine themes that emerged either in the individual chapters or in the workshop itself.

I. The Nature of Stems

Stems occupy a unique position and have many unique characteristics as components of plants. They are arguably the least disposable part of a plant and yet they are frequently exposed to the greatest stresses. A stem may fail physiologically (i.e., cavitation) or mechanically (i.e., some loading stress exceeds its capacity) or it may be induced to failure by herbivory, disease, fire, or gravity. Stems may be mechanically abraded by soil, ice particles, animals, or even other stems. Given the trade-offs associated with carbon allocation in a resource-limited environment, stems are frequently cited as having the lowest or one of the lowest priorities for carbon allocation within a plant. Because the stem is vulnerable to both abiotic and biotic stresses and because of its low priority for carbon allocation, two developmental features appear to be very important: the ability to compartmentalize wounds and the presence of structural and functional redundancy.

Stems, which undergo secondary development, compartmentalize injury rather than heal it. How this tendency to compartmentalize affects stem–branch junctions and, therefore, disease, developmental, and transport interactions has been discussed widely (e.g., Zimmermann, 1983; Shigo, 1985; Julin *et al.*, 1993). Compartmentalization involves a series of biochemical, morphological, and developmental responses following injury. Locations where twigs join branches or branches join the main stem frequently serve as infection courts when the twig or branch dies. This junction of branches with the stem is a region with a high occurrence of xylem vessel endings.

Possibly there are no continuous vessels extending through stem–branch junctions. Therefore, the lack of a continuous, direct vascular connection between the secondary xylem of the stem and that of the branch appears to enable the stem to compartmentalize the dead branch stub and isolate it from the living tissue of the stem. However, this isolation may have consequences for water and nutrient movement from the stem to the branch. In contrast to the lack of continuous linkage of secondary xylem vessels, the vessels in the primary xylem of young branches do extend into the stem (e.g., Zimmermann, 1983; Dickson and Isebrands, 1991). However, this direct linkage is of short duration as the primary tissue is quickly supplanted by secondary tissue. In many long-lived conifers, older, foliage-bearing, elongating branches do not produce a new ring at the base of the branch every year—further illustrating the lack of a direct linkage between the vascular system of branches and stems (Roberts, 1994).

Redundancy is manifested in a number of ways. Root growth capacity, refoliation potential, epicormic meristems, adventitious meristems, multiple stems, vast expanses of parallel water-conducting (i.e., xylem) and food-conducting (i.e., phloem) conduits, storage capacity, and buffering capacity are all expressions of this redundancy. The stem appears to have as many redundant elements as any other major part of the plant. One important aspect of redundancy is the presence of multiple, repetitive units of growth and function (e.g., White, 1979; Watson and Casper, 1984; Watkinson and White, 1985; Hardwick, 1986; Watson, 1986; Barlow, 1989; Kelly, 1992). These units have been termed modules, metamers, or physiologically independent units. A module is defined as the leaf, the stem to which it is attached, and the subtending axillary bud. For the plant, modular growth is made possible by localizing cell division to meristematic areas, although this limits the potential growth rate of the plant (in contrast with algae or bacteria). Modular growth enables small regions of a plant to attain autonomy with respect to carbon resources while, through repetition of parts (modules), reaching a large final size. With modular growth, opportunities to allocate limited resources and the flexibility to respond to changes in resource availability become possibilities while the proportion of the organism that is vulnerable (developing) at any given time is limited. For example, the development and growth of most modules are suppressed through the inhibition of lateral meristems and will be expressed only under special conditions (Senn and Haukioja, 1994; Honkanen *et al.*, 1994). Even when resources are plentiful, the number of modules actually growing versus the potential number that could be growing is low.

In efforts to scale or integrate physiological processes studied at the organ level to the whole organism or to subsample the entire organism, a scale between the organ and organism has been sought. Frequently, the branch is cited as such an intermediate scale (e.g., Ford *et al.*, 1990; Houpis *et al.,* 1991; Sprugel *et al.,* 1991; Teskey *et al.,* 1991; Barton *et al.,* 1993; Dufrene *et al.,* 1993). Critical in the definition of a module is its absolute carbon autonomy; that is, once developed, a module no longer imports carbon (Sprugel *et al.,* 1991). Developmentally and physiologically, it is clear that the only truly autonomous unit is the module as defined above. However, many investigators have chosen to lump extensive numbers of modules together in the form of a branch and consider this new unit as the autonomous unit. Although Sprugel *et al.* (1991) found considerable justification for this broader definition, especially from a carbon consideration, they cautioned that a number of natural and experimental conditions violated the definition of autonomy or functional independence. Thus, the rules of autonomy may be obeyed when a branch serves merely as an unaltered study unit whereas manipulating the branch may result in a breakdown of autonomous behavior.

Allometric relations are pervasive in the growth and development and, therefore, the management and research of trees. Such relations are due to "correlated growth patterns" and are also indicative of structural–functional relationships (Sinnott, 1963). Every forest manager depends on simple measures of stem diameter at 1.37 m (breast height) to yield information about height, volume, and market value. Scientists use measures of stem dimensions for information about fine root production (Vogt *et al.,* 1985), foliage quantity (Huber, 1924; Shinozaki *et al.,* 1964; Grier and Waring, 1974), and whole-organism productivity (Gholz, 1982). At a fine scale, conducting capacity of vascular tissue has been correlated with the maximum tree height possible for a given site quality (Pothier *et al.,* 1989; Yoder *et al.,* 1994) and with the maximum potential rate of gas exchange (Mishio, 1992; Shumway *et al.,* 1993). Unfortunately, many allometric considerations, whether at the macro- or microscale, are plagued by the chicken-and-the-egg syndrome; that is, does stem capacity determine foliage capacity or is foliage capacity set by a limiting resource (e.g., light or nutrients) that then sets stomatal, stem hydraulic, and stem growth capacities (Meinzer and Grantz, 1991; Meinzer *et al.,* 1992; Hinckley *et al.,* 1994)?

As illustrated in Fig. 1, stems can be viewed from a number of different scales of biological organization. Because many current topics in physiological ecology and developmental biology are focused on issues of scale, it is worth using Fig. 1 to illustrate how these scales might affect our perception of critical issues and how certain processes and structures, which assume importance at one scale, may be largely unimportant at others. The tree line situation depicted in Fig. 1 (top) suggests issues of climate change, population biology, and environmental gradients. The small group of trees seen in the distance in Fig. 1 (top) and close up in Fig. 1 (middle) evoke other issues—competition, protection, and microrelief. The individual branch circled in Fig. 1 (middle) and shown in cross-section in Fig. 1 (bot-

Figure 1   A consideration of stems or parts of stems from three different perspectives. (A) Landscape perspective illustrating trees near timberline in the Colorado Rockies. (B) Stand perspective showing trees in one part of the landscape perspective. (C) Branch to tissue level perspective of a branch located on the leeward side of the stand or clump shown in (B). (Modified after Katz *et al.*, 1989.)

tom) indicates a completely different set of issues—conducting ability, storage capacity, ring width growth, and so on. As scientists, we may isolate ourselves in one issue, but that issue is not isolated within the system we are studying. For example, ring width growth and hydraulic conductivity of the stem section shown in Fig. 1 (bottom) cannot be effectively studied unless we know something about where the branch came from and the general environment in which the branch/tree are growing.

First, at the ecosystem or community level, stems are important as they (1) provide vertical and horizontal structure, (2) influence microclimate, (3) directly and indirectly influence soil-building processes, (4) affect hydrological processes, (5) provide structure in the form of both fine and coarse woody debris to their own system as well as to other systems (e.g., streams), (6) are the major form of above-ground carbon storage, and (7) are an important component of ecosystem legacy. Because of disturbance, ecosystems are disrupted and, as a consequence, large stems may provide a means by which the former ecosystem links structurally and functionally with the new, developing ecosystem. Second, at the stand or individual organism level, a number of other issues regarding stems arise. These include root–foliage linkages, the influence of genetic variation of productivity or reproductive success, the importance of sexual or asexual reproduction, the nature of the phenological patterns and their control, the response of stems to environmental factors such as wind and snow, and the nature of competitive interactions between individual plants. Last, at the organ or tissue level, issues are considered such as cell production, the response of different tissue types to environmental cues and stresses, the nature and control of growth, the role of tissues in particular functions such as transport, strength, and defense, the induction and release of living tissues from dormancy, the patterns of carbon and nutrient allocation, and the integration of function by various cell types in various configurations.

These issues, features, and concepts, as well as others, have been the general focus of the preceding chapters. From these chapters and our own considerations, a number of themes/questions have emerged and we treat these individually.

II. Constraints on Capabilities and Functions of Stems

Stems must be functional for the present and yet must be the foundation for the future. As a consequence, stems must be "tough" and must have an ability to buffer abiotic/biotic pressures. Successful buffering frequently results in longevity and an accumulation of size, structure, biomass, and "history." Because of their size and longevity, stem tissues cannot be costly to build and, most importantly, to maintain. The presence of heartwood and the small percentage of tissue that is actually alive in the sapwood are reflections of these constraints. Limits on growth, as set by the rules of modularity and seasonality, and limits on unidirectional tissue expansion, as set by meristematic geometry and resource availability, are all manifestations of the constraints placed on stems.

Stems are largely manifestations of the long-term investment of carbon; their form and position within a community are mostly the result of the interaction between their long life span and abiotic and biotic pressures. Although we appreciate this, we do not fully understand how genetic background (as it provides architectural, physiological, and developmental constraints and opportunities), prior history, and the current abiotic and biotic environment interact to affect present patterns of response, growth, and allocation. Key present and future research topics are the following: how do trade-offs play out in different environments, and how are resources allocated to affect these trade-offs.

The long-lived nature of stems means that a number of safety issues are important in their continued function. These issues include mechanical support, hydraulic conducting ability, developmental responses to abiotic and biotic pressures, protective mechanisms against physical and biotic injury, and the ability to replace, repair, or compartmentalize injuries. The stem must be capable of responding to breakdown in each of the important functions it serves. A number of mechanical support/safety issues are highlighted in this book, including the need for developmental responses to changing loads and to physical cracks in the stem. Loss of conducting ability in the xylem must be localized to minimize spread and lost conducting elements must be either refilled or replaced through renewed cambial activity. Likewise, sapwood pathogens must be compartmentalized to prevent their spread into uninvaded sapwood and new, developing xylem. Plants faced with frequent disturbances, such as fire and avalanche, must have life history strategies associated with their ability to withstand or recover from disturbance.

III. Throwaway Concept

Another theme in many of the chapters and workshop discussions involves a concept of plant structures that are replaceable or only functional for short periods. A rachis, with its attached leaflets, can be considered throwaway in comparison to twigs or short shoots. Multiple stems in shrubs may represent throwaway units and this growth form may be particularly suited to harsh, risky environments such as extremes of hot, dry, or cold, where this form tends to dominate. The earlywood vessels of ring-porous species, which in a sense are optimal for conduction when the soil is wet and xylem tensions are low, become dysfunctional either later in the growing season or during the winter. Bark also follows a throw-away strategy in many woody plant species. Even the entire above-ground structures may be throwaway in some fire-tolerant species with stored reserves underground or near the base of the stem. Following a fire and the destruction of the canopy, a new canopy emerges from the base and provides carbohydrates for whole-plant growth and production of the next canopy.

As discussed previously, the crown of a tree may be regarded as a series of structurally linked, semiautonomous units. Such a developmental plan means that many of the units are repetitious and, therefore, throwaway. An additional consequence of this modularity is that only a few of the potential modules are actually growing while the rest are dormant. Branches in trees may thus represent throwaway structures in a sense similar to the stems of shrubs. As the local environment changes, such as through increased shading among lower branches as a tree grows, these structures may be shed. An interesting extension of this is found with short shoots of *Populus trichocarpa*, a species native to the Pacific Northwest of North America. Short shoots, when dropped either because of drought or mechanical stresses, can root and form new ramets of the parent tree.

IV. Stem Development

The morphology of a woody plant can be viewed in terms of (1) a developmental perspective, in which the apical meristem itself can be separated into organogenesis (plastochronal activity) and extension activity (growth), and (2) a structural or architectural perspective (Champagnat, 1989). The shoot system is made up of individual shoots of different branching orders. As discussed earlier, shoots are composed of repetitive units called modules or metamers. For roots, the module is less clearly defined but parallels to shoot modules exist; for example, the developmental pattern for lateral roots is analogous to sylleptic shoots of the shoot system (Barlow, 1989). Similar to the shoot system, the root system can be broken down easily into different branching orders and these orders may have different morphogenetic characteristics (Coutts, 1989). However, our understanding of the below-ground crown is far weaker than that of the above-ground crown.

An important and emerging theme in plant biology concerns the nature of the response of the plant to stimuli, that is, how the stimulus (light, gravity, wind, cold, etc.) elicits a response and how this response is transmitted to other parts of the plant (e.g., hormonally, hydraulically, chemically, mechanically, electrically, etc.). For example, at the membrane level, mechanosensors may be involved, translating mechanical movement or changes in mechanical stress to gradients in calcium, responses in calmodulin, and changes in electropotential between cells (Pickard, 1984; Telewski, 1995). A mechanistic foundation at many different levels of biological organization is clearly important in our efforts to understand how wind, gravity, and biomechanical stresses are translated into changes in vascular structure and branch and stem form. Models will be one means by which these foundations are linked across scales (e.g., Fisher, 1992; Ford, 1992; Chen *et al.*, 1994). Most reviews of the interaction of plant growth substances with growth and development present the reader with a thorough and critical view of where we are with regard to each plant growth substance or hormone, but not a developmentally, spatially, and temporally integrated focus. In addition, questions regarding the intellectual framework, the measurement technique, appropriate experimental design and protocol, and other features cloud our understanding of the role and function of these substances (e.g., Trewavas, 1986; Jackson, 1993; Sachs *et al.*, 1993). Given what is known about autonomous development and the presence of semiautonomous units, it seems unwise to use an animal analog for understanding these substances or how the perception of a stimulus elicits a response. An example of the kind of careful work necessary to tease apart the role of growth substances in plant development is provided by Sharp *et al.* (1994). Woody plants will remain largely a frontier in this arena for many years.

As in other areas, unanswered questions come to mind from the material in the previous chapters concerned with stem development. What controls structure and function, their interaction and feedback, and how is this interaction regulated? What regulates or controls cell number, expansion, size, and cell wall form and content?

V. The Stem as a Research Subject: Experimental Limitations

Plants with large woody stems such as trees present a number of experimental limitations or difficulties. They may be difficult to access, to sample, or to manipulate because of their size. Because they are very long-lived, the influence of a single point-in-time external abiotic or biotic factor may have no effect (i.e., its impact is buffered), a very long-term influence or its effect may lag by several years (e.g., Woodward *et al.*, 1994). In addition, the long life span means that trees are in a sense an integration of their entire past history—this history then partially or largely shapes their present response to abiotic and biotic factors. Pragmatically, working with these plants often means studying nonmodel species for which little fundamental physiological or anatomical information exists. Other difficulties that arise from the nature of the stem involve issues of scaling. It is not a trivial exercise to reconstruct a large object (like an entire tree) from an understanding of its parts at a microscopic scale when the behavior of large objects can become more than a simple sum of processes in their parts.

Another limitation of studying the stem is the intermediate location of the stem between organs at either end. Manipulating the organs in order to study their responses is frequently done; however, rarely is the stem manipulated independently of the root and foliage organs in order to study it. Its intermediate position creates both a structural and an intellectual barrier to an experimental approach (as compared to descriptive studies). Other difficulties associated with the stem occur because it links above- and below-ground processes, both in a linear, direct (e.g., hydraulic) way and in far more complex ways (e.g., nutrient translocation), and it may have simple to complex interactions with other organisms. The linkage between the stem and below-ground processes is also difficult to study because of the size of these organisms and the relative inaccessibility of the below-ground components.

In a positive light, many stems chronicle the past in the form of the growth ring or in the nature of the stable isotopes stored in the wood (Cook and Kairiukstis, 1990; Telewski and Lynch, 1991; Livingston and Spittlehouse, 1993). Dendrochronology, growth analysis (e.g., Duff and Nolan, 1953), and analysis of the stable isotopes of carbon and oxygen all provide interesting and sometimes sensitive insights into the past. One important area of future research involves the linkage of physiological mechanism and developmental biology to the formation and character of a tree ring. A considerable intellectual foundation already exists; however, a full understanding has not been achieved.

Additional positive features of large stems are their experimental importance in understanding water flow and its control, and water potential gradients and their development (Zimmermann, 1983; Pallardy *et al.*, 1995). Conceptual advances in our understanding of cavitation, embolism, and hydraulic architecture have arisen largely because of research focused on large woody stems. One interesting development has been the challenge to the cohesion theory (Zimmermann *et al.* 1993; 1994a,b; Sperry and Saliendra, 1994). Ultimately, experiments involving large woody plants, linked with good theory and sound experimentation, will lead to the resolution of this conflict.

VI. Function and Process Interactions

The functions and processes occurring in stems often interact, although such interactions do not always represent trade-offs (see Section VII). The presence of terminal flowers on stems strongly affects branching patterns as the shoot develops. Stems of trees versus shrubs with horizontal stems have different mechanical support needs. Transport processes in the xylem interact with leaf processes that control water loss rates. Plants may operate in terms of leaf and stem water potential near the point of runaway xylem breakdown due to cavitation and embolism. Thus stomatal behavior is coupled to the conductance of the stem. A number of other interactions are involved with xylem structure. For hydraulic functions, conduit diameter and variation in diameter over a growth ring interact with the seasonality of embolisms to determine conducting ability. Cell diameter is also related to mechanical support abilities. Aside from transport in the xylem, the nature of the phloem tissue regarding the shunting of solutes in and out of the phloem may determine the temporal separation of root and cambial growth. Ray parenchyma, a rather minor tissue in terms of percentage stem volume occupied, plays a myriad of roles including storage, defense, mechanical padding, repair, and lateral transport.

Other processes, such as the assimilation of metabolites in stems, interact with gas exchange to determine the O_2 concentration present at the cambium. The structural needs of the stem for support have led to an organ with a low surface area-to-volume ratio and hence difficulty in O_2 diffusion. These characteristics may lead to hypoxic conditions in metabolically active regions such as the cambium.

In any discussion of function, process, and structure interactions, issues of scale rapidly assume a role of major concern. Following an examination of the role of photosynthesis in the distribution of rain forest plants, Field (1988) stated that "photosynthetic characteristics are several steps removed from ecological success." Even more strongly worded are the conclusions of Küppers (1994) that investigators "reduce (their) attention to unnecessary details of leaf physiology, morphology, and partitioning that do not have significance at higher levels of integration." Küppers arrived at this conclusion following a study of photosynthetic performance of two Australian *Eucalyptus* species and how such a comparison yielded little insight into the life history strategies of these two species. Leaves of *Eucalyptus pauciflora* (snow gum) have almost twice the photosynthetic capacity of leaves of *Eucalyptus delegatensis* (alpine ash); however, differences in leaf longevity and leaf area index per plant result in similar total carbon balances. Where it might be hypothesized that height growth should be the highest priority in potential competitive situations, the snow gum is much shorter than the alpine ash. However, the greater allocation of carbon into a lignotuber and thick bark by the snow gum results in a greater survival in both fire and frost situations. A combination of frost pockets and fire borders appears to explain the local separation of these two species. This research by Küppers illustrates how carbon allocation to the stem differs depending on environmental pressures and on how an examination of the properties of the leaf alone would not have resulted in an understanding of the physical separation of these two species.

VII. Trade-offs

In the preceding chapters of this book we have seen many illustrated cases of trade-offs between the various functions and processes of stems. These stand out separately from the previously described interactions because the interacting processes or functions may negatively influence one another. Even within a particular stem function, trade-offs can be apparent.

The tissues making up stems are largely nonphotosynthetic and hence nonproductive for carbon gain, and yet this organ is essential for overtopping adjacent plants. Some stems are photosynthetic, however, and are capable of positive rates of net assimilation. Stem photosynthesizers will have poor insulation against thermal injury from fire and perhaps even from high radiation loads—species of *Arbutus* (e.g., *A. menziesii, A. unedo,* and *A. andranae*) have green stems in the spring, orange stems in the summer, and then the orange-brown layer peels off either in the fall or spring to reveal a green stem. Stems also support populations of epiphytes and some species of epiphytes are able to fix nitrogen; however, changes in the population of an epiphyte on a photosynthetic stem can alter its ability to fix carbon.

The stem is important in displaying and orienting structures carried by the shoot. An optimum leaf display for photosynthesis, such as horizontal shoots, can have a high mechanical support cost. Placement of leaves at the top of a canopy may be optimum for photosynthesis, but has high support and transport costs. An optimal floral display from the pollination and seed dispersal perspective (flowers and fruits at ends of branches) may also have a high mechanical support cost.

The water transport functions of stems display several trade-offs. Wide xylem conduits have lower flow resistance, but may be more susceptible to blockage (particularly from freezing-induced embolisms) or to the movement of disease organisms. Some species operate with small safety margins (water potential close to that leading to runaway cavitation of the xylem), and these species exert a tight control over leaf water potential or foliar abscission and do not display significant osmotic adjustment in response to water stress. In contrast, other species have a large safety margin (conductance loss due to cavitation occurs gradually as water potential declines) and they utilize osmotic adjustment to tolerate low leaf water potentials. Storage tissue can buffer the leaves against changes in water potential, but may influence mechanical stability of the plant (e.g., Andean rosette). Water storage in the stem is best located near leaf surfaces; however, it should not be too available. Although water storage in the stem serves a positive function, the tissues associated with storage have a high construction and maintenance cost. The importance in controlling water loss from the stem affects the diffusion of gases in and out of the stem. Stems may have specialized structures when this trade-off becomes important (e.g., lenticels).

As stem size increases, trade-offs between a number of features appear to change. For example, response times become longer and investments in preservation must increase. Storage capacity increases, but maintenance costs increase, although perhaps not proportionately to the increase in size. Last, the ability to acclimate or adjust decreases, while the ability to influence, or dominate, the community increases.

As in other areas, unanswered questions come to mind from the material in the previous chapters concerned with trade-offs. Can optimization be used to understand trade-offs (see below)? The entire role of ray and longitudinal parenchyma is not fully understood; their maintenance clearly represents a carbon cost, but their presence may be an important element in stem redundancy, in the ability to take up compounds actively from the xylem, in lateral transfer of material, and in the ability of the stem of the plant to compartmentalize injury. What are their patterns with evolutionary origin, within the same genus, with evergreen vs deciduous species, root sprouters vs seeders, or with easy vs difficult cavitators?

VIII. The Optimization Issue

Many topics discussed at the workshop and in the preceding chapters raise the issue of the optimization of specific functions versus an optimization response that covers multiple functions. Stems have some particular set of characteristics, including a set of mechanical–structural properties, a set of hydraulic properties, and perhaps others as well. These properties, in part, determine the ability of the stem to carry out certain functions such as support and transport. In relating structural characteristics and function (like Little Red Riding Hood biology: "Grandma, what big eyes you have!" "The better to see you with . . .") we sometimes tend to wonder how well particular structures are tuned for one or more of the stem functions. For example, it is easy in studying water transport to view the stem as a conducting organ and to restrict the evolutionary perspective to the development of tissues and cell types toward some combination of low resistance and safe conduits. Even here we see potential trade-offs.

It would seem that in any case in which there are organs with multiple functions or there are potential trade-offs in structures fulfilling even a single function, there exists the likelihood of interactions between structural solutions to the various problems in each function. It is also likely that

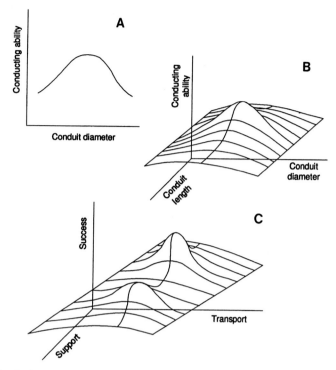

Figure 2 Optimization of characteristics and functions is complicated by the interactions between tissue or cell characteristics and particular functions. Although an optimum characteristic may exist when related to a single function (A), considerations of the same function with respect to multiple characteristics may or may not lead to a single optimum solution (B). Multiple solutions may exist for combinations of various stem functions leading to successful overall stem function (C).

multiple solutions exist that provide local optima in a solution space. An example of these possibilities is illustrated in Fig. 2. Here, if a single variable such as vascular conduit diameter is considered as affecting conducting ability, perhaps there might be some optimum diameter combining the effects of diameter on flow resistance and conduit vulnerability as affected by freeze-induced embolism (Fig. 2A). If another structural characteristic is included, such as conducting cell length, we now have a two-dimensional surface relating conducting ability to these two structural variables. It is possible that a unique combination of the two variables exists that maximizes conducting ability (Fig. 2B). However, the surface may have multiple peaks, each representing different solutions to the problem (Wright, 1988). A similar approach may be used to relate stem functions as independent variables and organism survival or evolutionary success as the dependent variable. Here again, there may be many solutions (or, graphically, local peaks) to the problem of how stems are able to function (Fig. 2C). Therefore we should be careful in thinking about optimization so that we are not focusing too narrowly on a particular function when the associated structures may have evolved in a broader context (Parker and Maynard Smith, 1990). In addition, much of what we see in an organism, particularly a long-lived one, was determined or influenced by history. The particular set of circumstances determining stem shape, for example, may no longer be present; therefore, the use of present conditions to assess issues of optimization may be fraught with error.

IX. Conclusions

In *Exploitation of Environmental Heterogeneity by Plants* (Caldwell and Pearcy, 1994), both the authors and the editors emphasize the significance of the pattern and scale of temporal and spatial heterogeneity in resources and how, at the level of the individual organism, carbon allocation, architectural plasticity, physiological plasticity, and linked developmental and physiological plasticity may be involved in the response of the plant to this heterogeneity. A considerable body of literature exists on the mechanisms of acquisition and response to broad differences in resource availability and, as a consequence, the allocation of biomass to capture these resources (Gulmon and Chu, 1981; Huston and Smith, 1987; Tilman, 1988; Borchert, 1991; Chapin, 1991; Grime, 1994; Stitt and Schulze, 1994). Superimposed on this relatively gross scale of heterogeneity are smaller and smaller scales of heterogeneity, from the seasonal to the millisecond changes in resources and from one position to another in the foliar and in the root canopy. Many current topics in physiological ecology and developmental biology are largely focused on these issues of resource capture and utilization by plants in a patchy world.

In such discussion, the stem clearly represents not only the critical link between roots and leaves, but it also assumes a major role in the exploitation of above-ground resources. As we have learned in this book, the stem, its form, its durability, its role in storage, transport and support, protection and defense, is a critical albeit underacknowledged component of the plant. Only in production forestry does the stem assume a dominant role in the literature and usually for its economic role. On the basis of what we have learned in this book, several general messages can be presented.

At the scale of the tissue or organ, the following points appear to be important.

- Stems are composed of modules.
- Stems compartmentalize wounds; stems also compartmentalize function.
- Stems of different species have a highly variable mix of cell types and configurations, all of which yield successful physiological and mechanical organs.
- Stems serve transport, storage, and support roles. They are physiologically and mechanically important. In many cases they exert active control over which parts of the shoot receive resources.
- The stem is vulnerable; this includes vulnerability to both abiotic and biotic stresses. A stem may fail physiologically or mechanically or it may be induced to fail by other agents.
- Some stems or parts of stems are throwaway. However, primary stems are rarely as disposable as leaves, fine roots, or branches.

At the scale of the whole organism, the following points are important.

- Stems are architecturally and functionally important in that they are involved in the display of both foliage and reproductive structures.
- Stems may be extremely durable and long-lived; however, there is considerable variation, from the stem of a desert annual to the stem of a *Pinus longaeva* tree.
- Stems require surprisingly little carbon and nutrients to maintain themselves once constructed.
- Often embedded in the annual rings and branch scars of many stems is the history of the whole organism and how it interacted with the climate and its neighbors.

At the stand or community level, the following points are made.

- Stems create their own microenvironment, which changes as the stand develops.
- Stems contain surprisingly little living biomass when they are alive, but may contain more living biomass, in the form of other organisms, when they are dead.

Finally, at the ecosystem level, stems are important for a number of reasons.

- Stems channel water and nutrients in two directions: from the soil to the atmosphere and from the canopy to the ground (as stem flow).
- Stems provide vertical and horizontal structure.
- Stems provide structure to other systems such as riparian zones.
- Stems are the major form of stored carbon and standing biomass in many of the ecosystems of the world.
- Stems form an important component of ecosystem legacy.

Although important and revealing issues emerge at each scale, it is critical to retain the perspective of Allen and Hoekstra (1992): "For any level of aggregation, it is necessary to look both to larger scales to understand the context and to smaller scales to understand mechanism; anything else would be incomplete." This book provides the reader with an appreciation of the stem from a wide diversity of perspectives while giving the reader the conceptual and experimental foundation to apply the perspective of Allen and Hoekstra. As biologists we tend to study our small piece of the stem, but if we are to understand it as an entire structure, we need to take this broader view.

References

Allen, T. F. H., and Hoekstra, W. T. (1992). "Toward a Unified Ecosystem." Columbia University Press, New York.

Barlow, P. W. (1989). Meristems, metamers and modules and the development of shoot and root systems. *Bot. J. Linn. Soc.* **100**, 255–279.

Barton, C. V. M., Lee, H.S.J., and Jarvis, P.G. (1993). A branch bag and CO_2 control system for long-term CO_2 enrichment of mature Sitka spruce. *Plant Cell Environ.* **16**, 1139–1148.

Borchert, R. (1991). Growth periodicity and dormancy. *In* "Physiology of Trees" (A. S. Raghavendra, ed.), pp. 221–245. John Wiley & Sons, New York.

Caldwell, M. M., and Pearcy, R. W. (eds.) (1994). "Exploitation of Environmental Heterogeneity by Plants." Academic Press, San Diego, California.

Champagnat, P. (1989). Rest and activity in vegetative buds of trees. *Ann. Sci. For.* **46**, 9s–26s.

Chapin, F. S., III (1991). Integrated responses of plants to stress. *BioScience* **41**, 29–36.

Chen, S. G., Ceulemans, R., and Impens, I. (1994). A fractal-based *Populus* canopy structure model for the calculation of light interception. *For. Ecol. Manage.* **69**, 97–110.

Cook, E. R., and Kairiukstis, L. A. (1990). "Methods of Dendrochronology: Applications in the Environmental Sciences." Kluwer Academic Publishers, Norwell, Massachusetts.

Coutts, M.P. (1989). Factors affecting the direction of growth of tree roots. *Ann. Sci. For.* **46**, 277s–287s.

Dickson, R. E., and Isebrands, J. G. (1991). Leaves as regulators of stress response. *In* "Response of Plants to Multiple Stresses" (H. A. Mooney, W. E. Winner, and E. J. Pell, eds.), pp. 3–34, Academic Press, San Diego, California.

Duff, G. H., and Nolan, N. J. (1953). Growth and morphogenesis in the Canadian forest species. I. The controls of cambial and apical activity in *Pinus resinosa* Ait. *Can. J. Bot.* **31**, 471–513.

Dufrene, E., Pontailler, J.-Y., and Saugier, B. (1993). A branch bag technique for simultaneous CO_2 enrichment and assimilation measurements on beech. *Plant Cell Environ.* **16**, 1131–1138.

Field, C. B. (1988). On the role of photosynthetic responses in constraining the habitat distribution of rainforest plants. *Aust. J. Plant Physiol.* **15**, 343–358.

Fisher, J. B. (1992). How predictive are computer simulations of tree architecture? *Int. J. Plant Sci.* **153**, S137–S146.

Ford, E. D. (1992). The control of tree structure and productivity through the interaction of morphological development and physiological processes. *Int. J. Plant Sci.* **153**, S147–S162.

Ford, E. D., Avery, A., and Ford, R. (1990). Simulation of branch growth in the Pinaceae: Interactions of morphology, phenology, foliage productivity, and the requirement for structural support, on the export of carbon. *J. Theor. Biol.* **146**, 13–36.

Fuchs, E. E., and Livingston, N. J. (1995). Hydraulic control of stomatal conductance in two tree species. *Plant Physiol.* (in press).

Gholz, H. (1982). Environmental limits on aboveground net primary production, leaf area, and biomass in vegetation zones of the Pacific Northwest. *Ecology* **63**, 469–481.

Grier, C. C., and Waring, R. H. (1974). Estimating Douglas-fir and noble fir foliage mass from sapwood area. *For. Sci.* **20**, 205–206.

Grime, J. P. (1994). The role of plasticity in exploiting environmental heterogeneity. *In* "Exploitation of Environmental Heterogeneity by Plants" (M. M. Caldwell and R. W. Pearcy, eds.), pp. 1–19. Academic Press, San Diego, California.

Gulmon, S. L., and Chu, C. C. (1981). The effects of light and nitrogen on photosynthesis, leaf characteristics, and dry matter allocation in the chaparral shrub, *Diplacus aurantiacus*. *Oecologia* **49**, 207–212.

Hardwick, R. C. (1986). Physiological consequences of modular growth in plants. *Philos. Trans. R. Soc. London Ser. B* **313**, 161–173.

Hinckley, T. M., and Ceulemans, R. (1989). Current focuses in woody plant water relations and drought resistance. *Ann. Sci. For.* **46**(Suppl.), 317–324.

Hinckley, T. M., Brooks, J. R., Cermák, J., Ceulemans, R, Kucera, J., Meinzer, F. C., and Roberts, D. A. (1994). Water flux in a hybrid poplar stand. *Tree Physiol.* **14**, 1005–1018.

Honkanen, T., Haukioja, E., and Suomela, J. (1994). Effects of simulated defoliation and debudding on needle and shoot growth in Scots pine (*Pinus sylvestris*): Implications of plant source/sink relationships for plant-herbivore studies. *Funct. Ecol.* **8**, 631–639.

Houpis, J. L. J, Costella, M. P., and Cowles, S. (1991). A branch exposure chamber for fumigating Ponderosa pine to atmospheric pollution. *J. Environ. Qual.* **20**, 467–474.

Huber, B. (1924). Die Beurteilung des Wasserhaushaltes der Pflanze. Ein Beitrag zur vergleichenden Physiologie. *Jahr. Wiss. Bot.* **64**, 1–120.

Huston, M. A., and Smith, T. M. (1987). Plant succession: Life history and competition. *Am. Nat.* **130**, 168–198.

Jackson, M.B. (1993). Are plant hormones involved in root to shoot communication? *Adv. Bot. Res.* **10**, 104–138.

Julin, K. R., Shaw, C. G., III, Farr, W. A., and Hinckley, T.M. (1993). The fluted western hemlock of Alaska. II. Stand observations and synthesis. *For. Ecol. Manage.* **60**, 133–141.

Katz, C., Oren, R, Schulze, E.-D., and Milburn, J. A. (1989). Uptake of water and solutes through twigs of *Picea abies* (L.) Karst. *Trees* **3**, 33–37.

Kelly, C. K. (1992). Resource choice in *Cuscuta europaea*. *Proc. Natl. Acad. Sci. U.S.A.* **89**, 12194–12197.

Küppers, M. (1994). Canopy gaps: Competitive light interception and economic space filling—a matter of whole-plant allocation. *In* "Exploitation of Environmental Heterogeneity by Plants" (M. M. Caldwell and R. W. Pearcy, eds.), pp. 111–144. Academic Press, San Diego, California.

Livingston, N. J., and Spittlehouse, D. L. (1993). Carbon isotope fractionation in tree rings in relation to growing season water balance. *In* "Perspectives of Plant Carbon and Water Relations from Stable Isotopes" (J. H. Ehleringer, J. Hall, and G. D. Farquhar, eds.), pp. 141–153, Academic Press, San Diego, California.

Meinzer, F. C., and Grantz, D. A. (1991). Coordination of stomatal, hydraulic, and canopy boundary layer properties: Do stomata balance conductances by measuring transpiration? *Physiol. Plant.* **83**, 324–329.

Meinzer, F. C., Goldstein, G., Neufeld, H. S., Grantz, D. A., and Crisosto, G. M. (1992). Hydraulic architecture of sugarcane in relation to patterns of water use during plant development. *Plant Cell Environ.* **15**, 471–477.

Mishio, M. (1992). Adaptations to drought in five woody species co-occurring on shallow-soil ridges. *Aust. J. Plant Physiol.* **19**, 539–553.

Pallardy, S. G., Cermák, J., Ewers, F. W., Kaufmann, M. R., Parker, W. C., and Sperry, J. S. (1995). Water transport dynamics in trees and stands. *In* "Resource Physiology of Conifers" (W. K. Smith and T. M. Hinckley, eds.), pp. 301–389. Academic Press, San Diego, California.

Parker, G. A., and Maynard Smith, J. (1990). Optimality theory in evolutionary biology. *Nature (London)* **348**, 27–33.

Pickard, B. L. (1984). Voltage transients elicited by sudden step-up of auxin. *Plant Cell Environ.* **7**, 171–178.

Pothier, D., Margolis, H. A., and Waring, R. H. (1989). Patterns of change of saturated sapwood permeability and sapwood conductance with stand development. *Can. J. For. Res.* **19**, 432–439.

Roberts, S. D. (1994). The occurrence of non-ring producing branches in *Abies lasiocarpa*. *Trees* **8**, 263–267.

Sachs, T., Novoplansky, A., and Cohen, D. (1993). Plants as competing populations of redundant organs. *Plant Cell Environ.* **16**, 765–770.

Senn, J., and Haukioja, E. (1994). Reactions of the mountain birch to bud removal: Effects of severity and timing, and implications for herbivores. *Funct. Ecol.* **8**, 494–501.

Sharp, R. E., Wu, Y., Voetberg, G. S., Saab, I. N., and LeNoble, M. E. (1994). Confirmation that abscisic acid accumulation is required for maize primary root elongation at low water potentials. *J. Exp. Bot.* **45**, 1743–1751.

Shigo, A. L. (1985). How tree branches are attached to trunks. *Can. J. Bot.* **63**, 1391–1401.

Shinozaki, K., Yoda, K., Hozumi, K., and Kira, T. (1964). A quantitative analysis of plant form—the pipe model theory. I. Basic analyses. *Jpn. J. Ecol.* **14**, 97–105.

Shumway, D. L., Steiner, K. C., and Kolb, T. E. (1993). Variation in seedling hydraulic architecture as a function of species and environment. *Tree Physiol.* **12**, 41–54.

Sinnott, E. W. (1963). "The Problem of Organic Form." Yale University Press, New Haven, Connecticut.

Sperry, J. S., and Saliendra, N. Z. (1994). Intra- and inter-plant variation in xylem cavitation in *Betula occidentalis*. *Plant Cell Environ.* **17**, 1233–1241.

Sprugel, D. G., Hinckley, T. M., and Schaap, W. (1991). The theory and practice of branch autonomy. *Annu. Rev. Ecol. Syst.* **22**, 309–334.

Stitt, M., and Schulze, E.-D. (1994). Plant growth, storage, and resource allocation: From flux control in a metabolic chain to the whole-plant level. *In* "Flux Control in Biological Systems" (E.-D. Schulze, ed.), pp. 57–118. Academic Press, San Diego, California.

Tardieu, T., and Davies, W. J. (1993). Integration of hydraulic and chemical signaling in the control of stomatal conductance and water status of droughted plants. *Plant Cell Environ.* **16**, 341–349.

Telewski, F. W. (1995). Wind induced physiological and developmental responses in trees. *In* "Wind and Wind-Related Damage to Trees" (M. Coutts and J. Grace, eds.). Cambridge University Press, Cambridge (in press).

Telewski, F. W., and Lynch, A. M. (1991). Measuring growth and development of stems. *In* "Techniques and Approaches in Forest Tree Ecophysiology" (J. P. Lassoie and T. M. Hinckley, eds.), pp. 503–555. CRC Press, Boca Raton, Florida.

Teskey, R. O., Dougherty, P. M., and Wieslogel, A. E. (1991). Design and performance of branch chambers suitable for long term ozone fumigation of foliage in large trees. *J. Environ. Qual.* **20**, 591–596.

Tilman, D. (1988). "Plant Strategies and the Structure and Dynamics of Plant Communities." Princeton University Press, Princeton, New Jersey.

Trewavas, A. (1986). Resource allocation under poor growth conditions: A major role for growth substances in developmental plasticity. *In* "Plasticity in Plants" (D. H. Jennings and A. Trewavas, eds.), pp. 31–76, Cambridge University Press, Cambridge.

Vogt, K. A., Vogt, D. J., Moore, E. E., Littke, W., Grier, C. C., and Leney, L. (1985). Estimating Douglas-fir fine root biomass and production from living bark and starch. *Can. J. For. Res.* **15**, 177–179.

Watkinson, A. R., and White, J. (1985). Some life-history consequences of modular construction in plants. *Philos. Trans. R. Soc. London Ser. B* **313**, 31–51.

Watson, M. A., and Casper, B. B. (1984). Morphogenetic constraints on patterns of carbon distribution in plants. *Annu. Rev. Ecol. Syst.* **15,** 233–258.

Watson, M. A. (1986). Integrated physiological units in plants. *Trends Ecol. Evol.* **1,** 119–123.

White, J. (1979). The plant as a metapopulation. *Annu. Rev. Ecol. Syst.* **10,** 109–145.

Woodward, A., Silsbee, D. G., Schreiner, E. G., and Means, J. E. (1994). Influence of climate on radial growth and cone production in subalpine fir (*Abies lasiocarpa*) and mountain hemlock (*Tsuga mertensiana*). *Can. J. For. Res.* **24,** 1133–1143.

Wright, S. (1988). Surfaces of selective value revisited. *Am. Nat.* **131,** 115–123.

Yoder, B. J., Ryan, M. G., Waring, R. H., Schoettle A. W., and Kaufmann, M. R. (1994). Evidence of reduced photosynthetic rates in old trees. *For. Sci.* **40,** 513–527.

Zimmermann, M. H. (1983). "Xylem Structure and the Ascent of Sap." Springer-Verlag, Berlin.

Zimmermann, U., Haase, A., Langbein, D., and Meinzer, F. (1993). Mechanisms of long-distance water transport in plants: A re-examination of some paradigms in the light of new evidence. *Philos. Trans. R. Soc. London Ser. B* **341,** 19–31.

Zimmermann, U., Meinzer, F. C., Benkert, R., Zhu, J. J., Schneider, H., Goldstein, G., Kuchenbrod, E., and Haase, A. (1994a). Xylem water transport: Is the available evidence consistent with the cohesion theory. *Plant Cell Environ.* **17,** 1169–1181.

Zimmermann, U., Zhu, J. J., Meinzer, F., Goldstein, G., Schneider, H., Zimmermann, G., Benkert, R., Thürmer, F., Melcher, P., Webb, D., and Haase, A. (1994b). High molecular weight organic compounds in the xylem sap of mangroves: Implications for long-distance water transport. *Bot. Acta* **107,** 218–279.

Index

Physiological Ecology
A Series of Monographs, Texts, and Treatises

Continued from page ii

F. S. CHAPIN III, R. L. JEFFERIES, J. F. REYNOLDS, G. R. SHAVER, and J. SVOBODA (Eds.). Arctic Ecosystems in a Changing Climate: An Ecophysiological Perspective, 1991

T. D. SHARKEY, E. A. HOLLAND, and H. A. MOONEY (Eds.). Trace Gas Emissions by Plants, 1991

U. SEELIGER (Ed.). Coastal Plant Communities of Latin America, 1992.

JAMES R. EHLERINGER and CHRISTOPHER B. FIELD (Eds.). Scaling Physiological Processes: Leaf to Globe, 1993

JAMES R. EHLERINGER, ANTHONY E. HALL, and GRAHAM D. FARQUHAR (Eds.). Stable Isotopes and Plant Carbon–Water Relations, 1993

E.-D. SCHULZE (Ed.). Flux Control in Biological Systems, 1993

MARTYN M. CALDWELL and ROBERT W. PEARCY (Eds.). Exploitation of Environmental Heterogeneity by Plants: Ecophysiological Processes Above- and Belowground, 1994

WILLIAM K. SMITH and THOMAS M. HINCKLEY (Eds.). Resource Physiology of Conifers: Acquisition, Allocation, and Utilization, 1995

WILLIAM K. SMITH AND THOMAS M. HINCKLEY (Eds.). Ecophysiology of Coniferous Forests, 1995

MARGARET D. LOWMAN and NALINI M. NADKARNI (Eds.). Forest Canopies, 1995

BARBARA L. GARTNER (Ed.). Plant Stems: Physiology and Functional Morphology, 1995